THREADS OF CONCEIT

THE CORE TRILOGY
BOOKS 1-3

BY

MAQUEL A. JACOB

Copyright © 2016

Cover Art by Dar Albert
http://www.wickedsmartdesigns.com

ISBN: 978-0-9979564-2-9

Published by MAJart Works
2001 NW Aloclek Dr Suite 211
Hillsboro Oregon 97124

http://www.majartworks.com

ACKNOWLEDGEMENTS

This is the end of our heroes and villains journey, for now, and I hope you enjoyed the Core Trilogy

I would like to thank NaNoWriMo for having a platform that push- es writers to find out what they're really made of by making us kick out a novel in 30 days. Core of Confliction was born from the 2013 madness of National Novel Writing Month which happens every November. I also met my awesome author buddy Dr. Laurel Standley who writes Eco-Thrillers so please check out her books.

To all my fellow authors at NIWA, I give you great big hugs. I learned so much about the business end of writing and publishing from you.

A big thanks to my mom, Camille, who patiently listened as I read book one to her and she pointed out a lot of weird mistakes. To her husband, Chris Downing, who actually came up with the title Core of Confliction, you come in handy sometimes.

Last but not least, all my friends, family and beta readers I send you my love and gratitude. Stay tuned for my next endeavor.

CORE CONTAINER

PART ONE: CORE OF CONFLICTION

PART TWO: SEEDS OF CONVICTION

PART THREE: BONDS OF CONTRITION

PART ONE:
CORE OF CONFLICTION

ONE:

What on Earth

Charles hated strip malls; the socially tainted badlands of suburban America that spread like a virus through small towns and barren areas in need of construction. They were like a ghost town during working hours but somehow maintained business with the help of weekend warriors. It was a mystery how those infestations came about but it had something to do with revenue. Every one of them developed out of the machine, in cookie cutter fashion, tailored to the demographics of its proposed district.

This particular one set the bar a little lower. Indigenous trees, held upright by two sticks and a chain hidden from view by their foliage, were planted strategically around the perimeter with wooden benches nearby. A designated eating area, littered with ugly round umbrella topped tables, was right smack in the middle with long picnic style benches to sit at on either side of them. Cigarette butts were scattered on the ground and there was no telling what lay directly under the table tops.

His own justification for being there; it was the only place within close proximity of his territory that had offerings of sustenance resembling something edible.

His team consisted of two other men and one woman. They sat at one of the eatery benches with him waiting for their order of cheap pizzas. He used a coupon to get the buy three get one free special, so everyone could have their own. They were taking a break from their daily drug runs and as long as his team met their dealer quota for the boss, nothing else mattered. Right now, it was not worth the wait.

Glancing up at the sky he watched the sun struggling to peek out from behind the clouds. Even without direct sunlight the heat lingered, prompting Sara to let out a heavy sigh. It irritated him whenever she disturbed his reverie and caused the others to turn towards her with looks of disdain. This was an ongoing thing and today there was no reason to state the obvious. Charles felt like he was being steam ironed with his clothes on. They were all tired, hot, and hungry.

He watched Sara try to tame her unruly more- dirty - than - blonde curly hair, frizzing from the heat, with an old tattered hair tie. She looked sloppy and miserable as usual, sitting next to her dealing partner, Klein, who kept repeatedly pulling on his shirt to force some sort of breeze down into it. His thick brown mop of hair was retaining the heat and sweat dampened the sides of his face. He wished for death or air conditioning earlier. Charles was ready to give him the latter.

It didn't help matters that they were all dressed in their organization's so-called uniform of dark slacks and a grey polo shirt sporting its logo on the left sleeve. Not a summer outfit by any means. All it needed to be complete was a baseball cap and they would look like workers ready to do an armored truck heist. Having the organization's logo in plain sight helped society identify them as criminals. It was run by a new crime boss who came on the scene unknown and eliminated most of the competition.

Many from the old guard now operated under the organization's umbrella. There were factions of Yakuza, Russian Mafia and Triad members. The boss had no qualms of broadcasting his activities. On one hand, it made illegal deals a little difficult in heavily policed areas, and with competitors rolling through territories to shoot them on sight. The upside, not many people messed with them. Their employer seemed to not take anything lightly, even the occasional legitimate arrest, care of local law enforcement. Bodies of innocent bystanders, federal agents and snitches were found in various forms of dismemberment within the city. So much for discretion.

An older lady came out of the pizzeria and walked toward the courtyard. Her silver curly hair was tucked neatly under a baseball cap with an image of a pizza slice embroidered on the front. Her white shirt had the same design on the sleeves. She scooted merrily along, her posture perfect as she carried the large pizza in the palm of one hand. Although one could tell she was older, there was not a wrinkle on her face and her eyes had an unnatural spark in them.

To the group's disappointment, she made a beeline for the only other people in the area and delivered their order. As she turned to head back into the pizzeria, she acknowledged Charles with a wink and went through the glass doors of Rooter's Pizza Parlor.

Another sigh from Sara was rewarded with yet another look of utter exasperation by the men. The youngest of the three men, Jared, reached down and petted his German Shepard, who lounged by his feet. His short dark hair and pale skin with androgynous facial features gave him an exotic, almost feminine, appeal. Being underweight for his five foot eleven frame did not make it any better. When Charles had first met him, he thought 'what a scrawny woman'. The dog yawned and settled further down on the ground. He too appeared to be tired, hot, and possibly hungry.

Charles turned his right wrist over to check his watch as he ran the other hand through his hair. It was short in the back but longer in the front, so it flopped forward, his gel-sculpting technique completely unraveled. He could tell, by the greasy feel on his fingers, the heat had evaporated any hair products that might have existed in it. There really was no point in grooming it in the summertime, but his vanity always kicked him at the last minute each morning. He understood it was not a popular trait, but it got him by. A stomach was heard growling and he looked around to see whose it was. No one gave the impression they were the culprit.

They glanced at the dog.

The silver haired lady came back out with a stack of pizza boxes, heading their way. All of them came to attention in anticipation. Finally, sustenance had arrived and not a moment too soon. Any longer and they would be drooling shamelessly. She smiled wide, setting the load down on the edge of the table. Charles gave her a tip of ten dollars and thanked her graciously.

"You are a life saver. Thank you so much."

"Not a problem, dearie." Her voice sounded younger than her looks. She had barely left the bench when hands attacked the boxes, dragging them to each hungry team member.

While they ate in silence, he saw Klein notice some weird items laying on the ground near their bench. There was a knobby ball, some dice, some other small items he couldn't decipher and a wide tooth comb. None of these things were around the bench before the pizza came so it dawned on all of them, simultaneously, that the older woman must have dropped them there, which seemed odd, raising suspicion and heightened paranoia. Their organization had a running supply of enemies.

There was enough garbage laying around where they sat and less was better. Klein eyed her as she headed back to the pizzeria, but it seemed she had no intention of coming back. Instead of getting up to ask her if the items belong to her he leaned down to the left of him, scooped the items up in one hand and tossed them away towards the nearby trees. He nodded to himself in justification. Charles raise an eyebrow at him.

While the items were still in midair, the German Shepard leapt up and with one swipe of his paw, knocked them back to the ground. As he landed, all the items, except for the wide toothed comb secured in his mouth, lay scattered around him. He trotted back and to the group's amazement, climbed up onto the bench and sat down as if he were a person. Extending his left paw to remove the comb from his mouth he enclosed the comb in a fist.

No one else was around save the old lady who stopped halfway to the pizzeria to watch, and the other customers sitting under one of the umbrella topped tables farthest from the store front. Charles's group leaned back in unison away from the dog as it combed its mane, each stroke further transforming it into a different creature. The nose moved upward as the eyes set wider apart. Its limbs lengthened and grew meatier to compensate for the torso elongating. The fur became less dense, almost fine covering a beast now twice its original size. Strips of cloth whirled around it assembling into a garment of sorts.

Jared was seated next to the creature and his eyes started to glaze over while Sara and Klein sat dumbfounded across from him. The dog was now a six foot four-inch-tall wolf like creature wearing a Japanese style monks robe. Its mane was dark brown, cascading down its back with the top like a lion's, adding another three inches to its height.

"I always wear my hair like this," the wolf like creature spoke.

Silence.

Not a word, a bird, or wind could be heard. Charles had not moved but as soon as he blinked, all hell broke loose as Sara and Klein abandoned their pizzas to attack the creature.

Sara went low with a punch. it dodged her attempt just as Klein hopped onto the top of the bench to deliver a flying kick. That too was a miss. They were not assassin quality fighters but did learn a few things from various members of the organization. The two advanced, each trying to land a hit, the creature's reflexes just too fast for any to connect.

When the creature morphed again into a more human, less hairy, form its arms bulged with muscles and the mouth now resembled that of a lion. The massive frame grew wider yet its reflexes sped up. Sara and Klein were able to get a quick nod to each other before going into a defense stance. For a brief moment, there was no movement.

Both parties launched at each other and a melee ensued. Sara was bobbing and weaving like a boxer to avoid getting hit to no avail. The creature's claws had got her a few times but she was trying to match its speed, so they only grazed her. She never knew she could move that fast. In her peripheral view to the left she could see Klein using some of the martial arts techniques he learned from a triad member. He too moved faster than she had ever seen and not doing so well either. She came back to attention in time to see the claws swipe in front of her eyes as she leaned back almost in a back bend. Jumping back, she slid to a stop and launched herself back into the fight. Klein needed back up, fast.

Charles watched the combat with no expression on his face. They were moving so fast a normal person would only see blurred lines of color. He had seen such lightning fast fighting techniques from the organization's high-level enforcers so his eyes were able to track each motion.

Enforcers were a strange breed of unarmed soldiers commanded by the top generals. Many of them did not quite resemble humans and their strength was unparalleled. When those enforcers were sent out, you were in trouble. Their fighting skills seemed other worldly with movements rivaling the speed of light and blows capable of caving in the side of buildings. The bear like creature moved just like them, Sara and Klein somehow keeping up. His mind calculated every movement.

Jared now sat in shock and great danger of getting hit by any one of the bodies moving at incredible speed around him, and he was oblivious to it all. The, now human like, creature saw his body sway and switched maneuvers in order to protect Jared from the chaos. He slowed down the speed of his attacks while still holding Sara and Klein at bay.

The older woman ran back to the area and stopped near the bench. She picked up the ball, which tuned into a glowing orb, and extended her hands out in front of her. It became a blackish blue vortex forming between them and as it grew, floated upwards then back to position itself behind her. Its gaping mouth gave view to the twinkling darkness of a universe swirling at dizzying speed. Strong wind shot from it, making a weird sucking sound as it started to pull the man beast, Jared, and the older woman in.

The man beast wrapped his arms around Jared, securing him tightly as they were sucked in, while the older lady dug her heels in the dry dirt to keep the vortex steady.

In a soft deep voice, the man beast tried to reassure a comatose Jared.

"Everything will be okay now, I promise. I will protect you always."

The vortex snapped shut like a vice once the older woman stepped inside it, leaving no trace of its existence or the people it consumed. In the blink of an eye, everything screeched to a halt. Sara and Klein stood poised for attack, breathing heavily, frozen in place. The center of the strip mall bore witness to scattered debris, two wild eyed men and a deranged looking female. Across the way, the other customers sat mid consumption of their pizza. Slices had fallen onto the table and the ground from their hands, now empty.

"What the fuck!" Sara screamed, breaking the silence.

That snapped them out of their shock. Grabbing their things, the other customers abandoned the pizza and ran to the parking lot.

Noticing he had tried not to breathe in quite a while, Charles took a few breaths then shook his head to clear it as he replayed the scene. He concluded, based on the fighting skills of the former German Shepard and the teleportation used by the older woman, they were a possible enemy of the organization and whatever that black hole was did not belong on Earth. He wondered how they knew his team was going to be there at this hour. It smacked of a set up leaving a bad taste in his mouth.

"You guys go on ahead and make a report. I am going to find out some more info since it's obvious we were targeted. There's a contact not far from here so, don't call me. I'll come talk to you guys later."

With that, he stood and left the two, still exhausted from the fight, to handle the rest. Both shook their heads in disbelief of what just happened, their group leader unfettered by it. That always disturbed them; how calmly he dealt with things. Sara and Klein looked at each other seeing the blood and bruises all over their bodies through ripped clothing and let out little laughs. It had been a long time since they were in a fight and this was more intense than any they'd ever been in. Picking up their gear, and whatever pizza wasn't ruined in the fight, they returned to head- quarters. Not another soul could be found in the strip mall.

Traveling through the vortex, the manbeast visualized the safe house they had to reach once the vortex reopened at the exit. He made a mental picture of a room with the bare minimum of furniture, such as a bed, a table, a chair, and a small window. As they came out of the vortex, their bodies were spewed out. The landing was hard but the manbeast softened it for Jared by sheltering his body as they rolled to a stop. Still in shock, he laid on the floor staring at the ceiling. The manbeast picked him up gently then set him on the bed. His form was now mostly human, and he stood at six feet seven inches tall, his dark mane swept back from his face, with eyes the color of molten steel. Setting himself down in the chair across from the bed, he watched over Jared.

Charles

Inside the city, everything moved at a fast pace, meaning Charles had to act quickly. Contacts didn't stay put in one place for too long and his employer had ties with criminals of all sorts. One such place run by the organization's faction of the Yakuza was nearby.

Five young Japanese boys, all taller than their native country's average, lounged in front of the restaurant, sheathed Katanas in plain sight. Their conversation came to a halt when they saw Charles approach. Even seeing the organization's insignia on his sleeve, they were going to give him a hard time. He knew better than to show up there without permission and there was no information of any errands being run for their site today. The tallest of the five stood to his full height of six feet two inches and pushed his palm into Charles' chest.

"Uh-uh." The Yakuza boy waved his finger at him. "You not welcomed here."

"I just need some information."

Charles had a main contact but there were channels to maneuver before he could meet her. She was the boss' undersecretary and his sometimes lover.

"Gomen'na sai." He bowed slightly.

The young man turned to his cohorts and nodded. Two grabbed him by the arms while the others went ahead to the back where their boss was. They shoved him into the office where he landed on both knees. He looked around with just his eyes, not making any sudden head movements. Slight rays of sunlight seeped through the tiny window near the ceiling of the back office making it dimly lit. The boys snickered amongst themselves hoping for a show when their boss arrived.

Yakuza bosses are very stylish, Charles thought as the owner came out from behind a beaded curtain.

His hair slicked back, secured in a tight ponytail, showed off his porcelain skin and distinct Asian features. The suit was an Armani, something Charles had a thing for and could identify on the spot. He felt a twinge of jealously.

"How much did that outfit set you back? I'm thinking of getting one next pay." Charles gave a crooked smile as he asked.

Two of the young boys hit him from each side in the ribs. It took the air out of him and he slumped over, his forehead touching the filthy car-pet. Addressing the boss directly was stupid but he never did have a filter when it came to authority. He found it amusing, their sense of superiority.

"What did you come here for, trash?"

The owner was just as tall as his errand boys, towering over Charles and looking down on him with disgust.

"I just need to get a report to the Undersecretary but, you know…"

Charles sat up and shrugged in defeat.

"No," the owner cracked his knuckles, "I don't."

Charles realized his plan of gaining an audience with the owner of the restaurant to locate his source was more complicated than anticipated. Too many questions were not looked upon nicely. He pre- pared to receive his information with a bloody nose and a couple of bruised ribs. It was an expected outcome, so he brushed it off and braced himself just as the owner plowed a fist into the side of his face. The owner asked him again.

"Why are you here?"

Charles gave a revised recount of the incident in the strip mall, leaving out transforming dogs and vortexes.

"My crew was ambushed in a strip mall by my territory. They got away and took one of my men. I sent the others to give a report."

"Is that so?" The boss sniffed then resumed hitting him.

After giving Charles a brief reprieve from getting beaten, the owner nodded to his right-hand man standing near the curtain. He disappeared for about two minutes which made Charles a little nervous about his chances of escaping. When the thug came back, he whispered into the owner's ear.

"It seems you DO need to make a report, quickly." He nodded to the man who scribbled something on a piece of paper and threw it down by Charles' feet. "Get him out of here." He turned and went back through the curtain, his thug in tow. Charles left by air as two of the younger boys stood at the entrance and tossed him out onto the sidewalk.

✳✳☼✳✳

Leaving the lively part of the city for the inner, he made his way to the rendezvous point. It was an old heap of a shed that sat unattached to the closed business next to it. He managed convincing one of the Yazuka boys to relay a message to the undersecretary about the location. At the en-trance of the rundown shack sitting on the outskirts he peered through the rusted metal door to see if anyone was inside. Making sure the coast was clear, he entered and waited for her to arrive. He didn't have to wait long.

"What in god's name are you doing?"

She stormed in and came right up to him. The metal door wheezed in protest before banging shut. She wore a dark slate grey skirt suit with a two-button jacket and navy pumps. Her straight dark hair lay loose past her shoulder blades, the ends cut perfectly across as if a line had been drawn to separate her lower body from the upper. Her cupid shaped lips were pursed into two ruby slits. She was angry.

"Good to see you too."

He pushed his hands into the front pockets of his slacks.

"This is not funny!" She pointed a manicured ruby nail at him.

"Did my guys report to the boss about what happened?"

"Yes, we heard, and you need to leave this alone and let us handle this."

"One of my guys was taken. And that thing that was our dog…"

"Look," she moved so close to him that they exchanged air, "I know this is all a bit crazy but if you just calm down."

"I am calm, I'm just angry."

She searched his face for some evidence of that and as usual found none. Charles did not show emotion. It unnerved her whenever she saw a dull uninterested look on his face, like the boss.

"Come with me and lay low for a while, okay."

Her voice was soothing.

They touched foreheads and after a few moments, he nodded. She could tell he needed some release after all the crazy shit going on so far. As she led the way to her car parked around back, she made eye contact with the two enforcers standing off to the side across the street. They nodded to her as she got into the driver's seat and knew they were going to report to the boss' liaison. No one could be allowed to run around knowing about what happened at a strip mall in the suburbs of their city.

Jared

"Where am I? What happened?"

Jared sat up slowly from his position on the stiff bed. He was asking himself more than anything and was not prepared for an answer.

"Somewhere safe, for now."

The manbeast stood up and went to his side. His robes made a soft swishing sound as the bottom dragged across the wood floor.

Jared reared back further on the bed against the wall. He was too tired and too scared to fight but he wasn't so far gone as to submit to whatever came next.

"I would never hurt you, Jared."

"How do you know my name?" Just as he asked it, he felt stupid. Of course, it would know his name. The thing had been his pet German Shepard for a long time. "What are you going to do with me? I mean, what the hell is going on?"

"If I said we were going to our home world soon, how would you feel about that?"

"Who are you? What are you?"

Jared was getting sleepy again, his words slurring with the slump of his body back to a lying position on the bed. It was all too much for his mind to bear.

"I am Modas and I am yours. We will explain when you feel better."

"We?" Jared fell asleep.

His body relented to gravity and fell sideways on the bed.

Modas reached out his hand to move strands of hair from Jared's face but stopped himself. Not being able to convey how he was feeling at that moment tortured him. He sat back down in the chair and waited for the older woman to show up. From there everything would be set back right.

Small tingling sensations ran through his body as it settled into its original form, grateful to not be a pet dog anymore. It had been a de- meaning existence for him because being a warrior meant more than anything, except for being a father and mate. These thoughts went through his head as he too fell asleep dreaming of times past and what was to come.

✱✱☼✱✱

Muted sunlight shone down on the fields of flowers while children ran through them laughing in merriment. Even with a weakened sun high in the hazy ochre colored sky, some slight warmth could be felt. Near the temple on the hill a bright orb appeared, shaking the ground. Workers and children stopped with bated breath at the entry.

Out stepped the old woman with the silver curly hair. She nodded to the guard standing at the console that controlled the transport gate without slowing her stride towards the temple. The children resumed playing in the fields and the workers returned to their duties. She smiled at them, knowing what everyone was thinking when the alternate gate opened.

In the temple, she quickly changed clothes then headed for the garden on the side of the structure. Many of her people toiled endlessly to keep the garden flush with energy to maintain the life held in suspense there. It was not a garden of plants. All the small buds of light were soul cores rescued after the disintegration of their home world. So much life had been lost but once vessels were found for the cores, they would start a new cycle to rebuild their race.

The first step was to find the ones whose bodies were intact but missing their original cores. They were scattered across different worlds and dimensions. Who the race really needed was their leader and the old woman had found him on Earth with three of his cabinet members. She had also found the monster who had destroyed their world. Bending down to stroke one of the glowing cores, her gaze fell across the garden. Soon, everything would be right. She got up and headed back to the gate for her travel to the safe house where Modas and Jared hid.

Bright light jolted Modas out of his slumber and the chair he was sleeping in. It careened across the room into a wall as his body automatically crouched into a defense stance. Seeing it was the old woman, he relaxed. The vortex closed, and he sighed with relief.

"You frightened me."

"Who else would it have been? You are too on guard. No one knows about this place except us." She looked upon Jared. "How is he doing? I see he is still asleep."

"In shock still. Which there will be more of when we get his core back into him."

"You miss her greatly."

Modas kept silent. It needed no reply. He too, strolled through the garden from time to time checking on some of the cores that remained. He knew which ones were his family. Ganna motioned to Jared and Modas picked him up, cradling Jared in his arms.

"Let's hurry."

"What about our leader? Chardon could be in danger."

"I know, but my cover is compromised, as is yours, so we must be careful. I am sure you don't want to be a pet dog again."

"No." Modas shifted Jared's weight towards him. "I'm ready, let's go."

☀

The undersecretary slid out from underneath the covers and out of bed. Her movements were like a cat as she padded naked in silence to the living room. Finding her purse, she reached in, pulled out her mobile vid-com and dialed. A face appeared on the tiny screen revealing one of the boss' henchman. She leaned in closer to the screen and whispered angrily.

"What does he want me to do about Charles? He's asking a lot of questions in the wrong parts of town. I can't keep him locked down."

"Do nothing. Tell him you have a meeting with the boss and he is to stay put. We will come get him."

The smile on the henchman's face was crooked.

"Fine, I'll do that, but he's not stupid. If he senses something is wrong, he will run."

"Not your concern. We can handle this. Do as you're told."

The screen went dark.

Placing the device back into her purse, she went to wake up Charles. He could at least have a decent breakfast before the enforcers came for him. At the bedroom doorway, she stopped for a moment to stare at his sleeping body under the sheets. She went over to the side of the bed and started kicking it lightly.

"Wake up, you. I'm hungry. What are you going to fix me?"

After the tenth kick, Charles stirred, turning his head to face her. She was beautiful with a well-proportioned athletic body but knew she did nothing for him emotionally. She was just a warm body to alleviate his tension when needed. Their relationship was against the rules but he never cared about that. He sat up on his knees, letting the sheet fall back behind him and wiped his face with his bare hands.

"I thought you were going to cook for me."

"Alright, how about we do it together?"

"Sounds like fun"

"It has to be fast though. I have to meet the boss. He seems to want to talk to me."

"Good. Ask him about that creature I saw."

He climbed out of bed to search for his pants. She raised an eyebrow at his nakedness debating on a second round and saw him tense up.

Not today.

Near the end of breakfast, she let out a deep sigh and turned to him.

"I need you to stay here until I get back."

"Why?" He set his spoon down in the half-eaten bowl of oatmeal.

"Because it's not safe, Charles. There are strange things running around and you talked to a few people who don't like being asked questions. So, stay put." Her finger extended at his nose.

They finished up and went back to the bedroom to get dressed and make the bed. He had not answered her, and she kept glancing at him until he did.

"Fine."

He pushed off the edge of the bed, finishing the corners of the sheets by tucking them under. Relieved, she let him follow her to the front door.

"I'll call you when I am on my way back, okay." She gave him a quick kiss and left.

Outside she could see in the corner of her vision four of the organization's enforcers waiting across the street for her to get in her vehicle and leave before moving in.

It was his own fault, she thought as she got in and pulled off.

Charles sat down on a stool at the black marbled island in the kitchen. He always wondered why her place was all black and stainless steel. It reminded him of an underground bunker. His thoughts went over the scene from the strip mall, finding it hard to believe less than forty-eight hours had past.

Midway through his mind drifting, it snapped back into reality as he noticed the silence. She lived on a pretty lively inner city block and there was usually a lot of noise. But, no traffic or people could be heard and right about now he could probably hear a pin drop. Cursing under his breath, he made his way to the door and laid in wait for his attackers. If they were coming in hot, he had to be ready for a world of harm. It was not a long wait.

A New World

The weak sunlight still made Jared squint as he woke up in another bare room. He sat up and looked around surveying the area. So many questions were going through his head. He figured they would tell him what's what soon enough. Modas had stepped out of the vortex onto solid ground, setting him down right before the exit and he felt a little funny about it. Was he really so out of it? He must have been because he remembered fainting not long after that.

One thing was certain before he lost consciousness; this was not Earth. The air smelled different and the sky had a weird orange color, not blue. Even the grassy knolls were not quite green. What had made him pass out was the sighting of a strange little field creature that scurried across not far away.

Testing his footing on the floor, he went to the door and it opened to a hallway. He left the solitary room and headed down until reaching an archway outside. The grass was tall along the pathway and he brushed his hands against it as he walked. Near a clearing, he saw children laughing and playing in the fields. To the right of him was another path leading to a rocky area with a creek. He followed it, amazed at how bold he was going off on his own.

On a huge rock in the middle of the creek sat Modas in front of the waterfall. His mane of hair was swept away from his face and cascaded down his back to his waist. He wore a sleeveless thin bluish grey robe over a rough woven brown long sleeved one making him look like a monk. Modas meditated sitting akimbo and he was beautiful. Jared felt himself blush.

Modas must have felt his presence because he opened his eyes and turned towards him but didn't get up.

"Are you feeling better?" Modas asked.

"I guess, if you consider I am on a different planet or something, sure." His own sarcasm felt wrong and he wondered why.

Ganna had apparently followed him out of the room and now came over to them. Her silver curls bounced freely around her shoulders. How could I not have seen or heard her? A feeling of uneasiness washed over him. Something about her, he didn't like.

"With you awake, we can begin. Shall we?"

Waving an arm in the direction of the temple was her way of requesting they both follow her. She led the way, walking briskly.

He began thinking in his head, *"No way that woman is old. Grandma has too much pep in her step"*.

A rundown temple came into view and they went in, heading towards the back, then turning to end up on the side of the structure. He saw the garden of glowing buds and inhaled with wonder. So enchanted, he went to touch them. Modas grabbed his wrist to stop him.

"Not yet. Please, wait."

Jared looked up at Modas with a confused face. Ganna sighed heavily, stepping next to Jared.

"My name is Ganna. I am one of the cabinet members here at the temple. Since the destruction of our world, what was left of the governing structure convened under the care of the few temple servants who had survived. We conduct meetings here for convenience," she paused, chuckling, "and divine counsel. What you see before you in this garden are the souls of our fallen people, their cores. We were only able to save this many. Some of them need new vessels whereas for others, we need to find their vessels."

"Their vessels?"

"Their physical bodies," Modas interjected.

"Our consciousness, or soul, resides in our physical bodies. They can be removed if the body is too damaged to sustain it. Souls manifest as orbs of energy, as you see here, and can be reinstated in a new or re- paired vessel. When our world was attacked, a vortex had been opened. Through that opening, many of our kind were thrown into other planes, other planets and other worlds which ripped their cores out of their bodies, leaving behind one or the other."

"So, you're searching all over the place. But, their, um, vessels could take a long time, right?"

"Time was not of importance until now. We have found at least some of the cabinet members and our leader, so there is hope."

"Why is time not important now?"

Jared felt like a broken record but Ganna was taking too long explaining for him.

"The one who destroyed our world knows we have survived. He is on that planet called Earth running some kind of crime ring, as they call it."

"Wait," Jared held up one hand having a thought. "Am I a hostage, like your ticket to get close to my boss?"

Modas looked pained while Ganna grimaced. Jared was confused.

He could not figure out what they wanted from him. Modas stepped into the garden, went about one hundred feet and picked up one of the glowing buds of energy. He came back and placed it in Jared's hands. Almost instantly, Jared's entire body jolted, and memories flooded into him. Tears spilled down his face with every heart wrenching moment crashing against him making his grip tighten on the core until it made contact with his abdomen, forcing the core to slowly disappear into him.

Jared went down hard to the ground, his eyes rolled up in their sockets and he started to convulse. Modas held him down with all his strength because Jared had become incredibly strong. Ganna ran into the temple to find a healer. She grabbed one and ordered them to bring a sedative to administer. As the drug was injected into him and began to work, Jared ceased to move. Modas touched his face gently.

Jared's body slowly shifted back into its original form. His short dark hair turned light brown and grew to his shoulders, his features softened, and his skin went a shade darker. Breasts and hips swelled beneath the constricting human clothes, creating tears in the fabric. This form was female, and her name was Jaron.

Sara and Klein were escorted by three enforcers into the great hall of the mansion where they now stood. The entire room was stark white from floor to ceiling and smack in the middle against the far wall sat a giant white marbled throne. It seemed unreal, and a bit silly, to imagine their boss actually sitting on it dictating orders from above. Klein smirked, and Sara elbowed him in the ribs. A low grunt left his mouth. The side door had opened and out came the man himself.

The boss was tall and slender with straight pitch-black hair hanging to his waist. His sinister eyes were an odd color of dirty forest green. This man had killed, possibly murdered, many in his lifetime. Klein gulped. The boss walked slowly up to his throne and sat, throwing a leg over one side, his elbow resting on the other to hold his head as he cocked it sideways.

"So," he drawled, "I hear you had an encounter with some sort of manbeast. Tell me, what did it look like again?" An eerie hush fell on the room.

The two looked at each other and nodded.

"Well," Sara started, "at first it was our pet dog but then it changed into this bear like thing, but it changed again and had a lot of long hair and claws but a human face."

"Slow down," Klein whispered to her. She was talking a mile a minute.

"You know, when I destroyed that putrid world of yours, I expected the two of you to go with it. But low and behold, here you are as my ignorant employees."

Klein's face wrinkled.

"What are you talking about?" He snapped.

He heard Sara gasp and immediately became surprised at his own boldness.

The boss threw back his head and let out a loud fit of laughter. No one else in the room joined in. Afterwards, he brought his head back and his eyes bore into theirs. It was clear he was not amused in any way.

"Do you know why your planet was destroyed? Because the two of you betrayed your own kind and opened the gate for me. You have no memories of it because your cores were ripped out. You're just soulless empty vessels doing my bidding. Shameful really."

They both stood stunned like two deer in headlights. None of what their boss was saying made any sense, but to insinuate they betrayed someone causing the destruction of a planet was too much.

"You're lying! That's a lie!" Sara began to cry. Her body moved towards him but Klein stopped her. "We would never do something like that!" She clamped her hands over her mouth in fear.

"No?" The boss slid his leg off the side of the throne, sitting upright, then leaned forward. Dark tresses of hair fell across his shoulders covering the white shirt he wore. "Such deceit the two of you had in you. And now your kind has scrounged up what is left of it to come and rescue its lost vessels. Should I let them take you? Have your souls returned to you? So they can all know the truth about their demise?"

Klein shook with rage and confusion, grabbing Sara's hand. The boss sat back and waved his hand toward them.

"Get back to work, you haven't met your quota for the week."

"What about Charles and Jared?" Klein was scared but some assertive streak had taken hold of him.

"Your fearless leader and his cabinet member? I am taking care of that. By the way, that creature, formerly your pet dog, is really one of the great beast warriors of your kind." He laughed again.

****☼****

Jaron opened her eyes and focused on yet another bare room with sparse furniture and no windows. Turning her head to one side she saw Modas curled up in a chair next to the bed. His sleeping face caused a twinge in her chest. As much as she loved him, she was never able to show her affection. It pained her still, but she did not disturb him.

Lost in her thoughts, she did not notice him awaken and their eyes locked. Having her core back was a curse and a joy. She remembered her time on Earth, also the carnage left by the attack that destroyed her world. The heartache was much worse as she remembered the death of their children. She knew Modas could see it all on her face.

"Don't think of that. I can't bear to see you crumble anymore." He pleaded softly.

"How many?" She barely whispered, fearing the answer.

"Jaron." Modas reached up to touch her face.

"How many?" She screamed, slapping his hand away.

"Three." Her face blanched. "Their cores are in the garden."

"Out of seven of our children, only three." Jaron sank down onto the bed and covered her face with both hands. "Only three." She felt Modas move from the chair and climbed on top of her, his body heat too warm. "Please, don't try to comfort me."

"I won't let you go."

He lowered himself onto her and rested his head in her bosom while she cried silently. His hands tightening into fists as he gripped the blanket beneath her.

The Big Boss

Undersecretary Janice paced around the anteroom chewing on her thumbnail. Seeing the boss had that effect on her from the day they met. Something about him was not quite right, like he didn't belong in this world. She had seen him do impossibly horrid things to people and swore to herself that none of it was real. Still, there were the nightmares.

"He is ready to see you now."

A grotesque looking enforcer had come to escort her. His features were off as if he was wearing human skin not fitted correctly.

"Thank you."

She turned around with an air of authority and hurried out to the throne room.

There he was, Halfar, lounging on his throne as usual with his left leg tossed over the side. He seemed bored and agitated at the same time, which would be impossible for a normal human being.

"I can smell him on you. Soap and water does not wash away a stench so powerful. How is Charles?"

He never even looked at her when he asked it, unnerving her to the point where she became scared. She wondered how he knew what Charles smelled like causing her insides to churn uneasily; making her nauseous.

"I would assume angry since your enforcers waited outside my place to pick him up."

She heard her own voice quiver.

His gaze turned on her and she froze with fear. Those were the eyes of a monster.

"Are you questioning my methods?"

"Not at all, sir."

She gulped to clear the lump in her throat. He heard it.

"It would seem we underestimated Charles because he is not here. And neither are my enforcers. What do you think happened?"

"I..."

No words came to mind. It never occurred to her that Charles could defend himself against enforcers.

"I'm not sure, sir. I left him there as instructed."

She tried to conjure up an image of Charles taking on enforcers and failed. It was not feasible.

"Yes, it is." He replied, having somehow read her mind. She felt the color drain from her face. "I know Charles better than anyone. I was not consulted about his little quest therefore I lost enforcers. Not even Charles knows how good he really is."

"I don't understand." She licked her lips. It was clear she had been left in the dark on something very important.

"Nor will you. You won't see him again. I am assigning you to another district effective immediately." She was about to protest, and he raised his hand. "Now."

As the undersecretary was escorted out, one of the boss' generals came into the throne room. He was not very tall at six feet two inches compared to the rest of the boss' entourage, but his body was all lean muscle. His wavy hair had a dark oily look and his eyes were an odd shade of amber. Tearing apart flesh was a specialty of his. It was rumored that his very presence made the other men's skin crawl. The boss sat correctly, and a smile crossed his lips.

"What do you think, Rass? Shall we prepare for war?"

"Not likely." General Rass stood next to the throne and motioned for the room to be cleared. The long robe he wore laid open in the front and was secured around his waist with a thin sash, exposing his tight tunic and animal hide leggings. "That race is in shambles and it would be years before they can muster up the courage, let alone the numbers, to come at you with an army."

"I do not want to let Charles go."

"Hmm, well it may be beneficial if you do. He is easy to control because his core is missing, but that's not what you want. You want him whole again."

"Whole again, yes, but still under my thumb." The boss wagged his index finger at Rass.

"Who you need to worry about are those two imbeciles who betrayed their own kind. If they are capable of such treachery, then there is no doubt they will do the same to you."

The boss' right arm morphed into a giant reddish black claw with pincers that glistened as if dripping with blood and he snapped them once, the sound echoing within the room.

"Then I guess they will have to be sliced in half, hmm? Find Charles."

Rass gave a hideous smile. He went back through the door from which he came. Time to go hunting for insubordinates and bring them back for his own brand of sentencing, which he doled out with great pleasure.

"Charles." The boss closed his eyes remembering the last time they talked. "Chardon."

****☼****

The sky was cloudy, signaling rain which would be good for the crops. He watched Chardon breathe in the fresh air then open his eyes to stare into Halfar's. As the ruler of his home world he traveled a lot, but had come to see Chardon for a personal agenda.

"You will not accept my proposal?" Halfar was tense.

"No. I will not submit to your terms just so you can enslave my race."

"It is not slavery, just safe keeping from harm of other more powerful forces."

"That is not what you are doing!" Chardon turned away from him but glanced back.

"I can destroy you!" Halfar could feel himself shake with anger, regretting what he said.

"And, that is why you will never win."

"Listen to me! This will not end well. You know how she is!"

Chardon balled his hands into fist and whirled on him.

"I know better than anyone." He hissed.

"No, you don't." Halfar turned and walked out of the room.

Not long after that Halfar sent a planet destroyer through the portal gate Sara and Klein had given him access to. He opened his eyes, still burning with even more regret, and surveyed the empty throne room. It should not have happened. He truly wanted to protect them except, his ego was hurt so he reacted like a spoiled child, annihilating Chardon's entire world.

To the right of the throne, double doors opened and his other General, Kur, entered. His flowing locks of deep green hair bounced slightly around him as he strolled slowly towards Halfar, frowning at the expression on his lord's face.

"That is not the face of our cunning ruler. What could possibly make you look this way?"

"I haven't killed anyone in over three months." Halfar made sure his face conveyed boredom. It was good to keep up appearances.

"Ahh, so I was mistaken, it being a lovelorn look. Surely, Rass is not slacking?"

His question dripped with sarcasm. Kur fancied himself having more flare than the crude and messy Rass.

"We must keep it down to a minimum or we lose allies."

"Allies! These disgusting, fragile humans? You must be joking! They are a means to an end for our race to take over and enslave them."

"True but they have a saying here I have grown fond of. You catch more bees with honey."

"What does that even mean?"

Kur did not like being confused or taunted.

"How I understand it is we give them what they want, make them feel safe and when everything is in place, we take it all away. WE have to get them on board first."

"Sounds lovely. It does have a nice ring to it." Crude knotty wings a darker shade than his hair tore out of Kur's back and he knelt in a launching position. "I shall return with something good for you to play with."

His body shot straight upwards towards the skylight, causing a funnel of wind to spiral after him. As he got close to the ceiling, it split in two opening to let him through.

Halfar rose from his throne and went to the double doors on the left leading to his personal chamber. As ruler of his race, he knew what they expected of him. He was getting weary of being so ruthless and cunning. He wanted peace. He wanted … love.

Extraction

Charles was cold, hurting and angry. A lot of his energy was used to take those enforcers down and he had a few deep lacerations as a memento. Those wounds would heal after some time. Knowing that Janice had set him up was a whole other matter. One would think there was some level of trust when two people were intimate, but it seemed not the case. An ambush in broad daylight meant the organization didn't care about the laws of the land anymore.

As usual, the people in the neighborhood had hid themselves, leaving Charles to fend for himself. The only reason he got away moderately injured was the low level of the enforcers sent. He realized halfway into the fight how fast he was moving and how easy it felt. Still, those buggers fought him hard before going down. It was usually anything for the boss' glory but Charles was fighting for himself now.

Tearing more fabric off his shirt to tend yet another wound, he rose and peeked cautiously around the corner. The alleyway hid him well enough but not if enforcers were lurking. Those monsters could see through walls and Charles had not figured out how yet. Pulling the piece of cloth tight around his forearm with his teeth, he winced from the pain. At least the bleeding had stopped. It was clear to him that the boss wanted to speak with him, preferably alive but not necessarily undamaged.

"Shit, Charles, you need a plan," he said to himself as he crouched back down to think. His eyes went blank again, his face expressionless.

✳✳☼✳✳

Ganna tapped the side of Modas' and Jaron's chamber door frame. She had left them alone for a few days after Jaron's full awakening. According to her patients who had gone through the process, getting back your soul was exhausting and the memories flooding in all at once took a toll. That was the consensus. She had never lost her core.

"How are you feeling, Jaron?"

She found her up and about fixing the bed covers.

"A bit weary but more than anything, I'm angry."

Jaron leaned over the bed to straighten up the pillows as the sleeves of her robe dragged across them. She was wearing the white and blue cabinet member robes.

"To know that I was working for our enemy! He must have been full of smug joy ordering us around."

"Yes, well the dire matter at hand is getting Chardon and the rest out of there and back to this world so we can reinstate their cores."

"That should be easy since they are not in any danger."

"We are not certain of that. Since you were brought back and all of you did see Modas, it is safe to assume they reported the incident to their boss' henchmen. That means, Halfar knows we exist and may take drastic measures to keep them."

"Then we have no time. Do you have a plan in mind?"

"Besides going in blazing? Not really, but I do have a way of pinpointing Chardon's whereabouts. Retrieving him comes first."

"When do we go?" Jaron stood upright ready to walk out with her.

"YOU do not. A small team will go through the gate and get him." Ganna wagged her finger.

"Why not?" Jaron yelled.

"How are your powers?"

Jaron stopped advancing towards her and frowned. She lifted her right hand and a small orb of light blue energy formed.

"Damn it!" It shrunk, disappearing in the air.

"Give it time. For now, just rest and try to be nice to your mate. I never understood how he could love someone like you who always ignores him or treats him badly."

Jaron looked away and went to hide her face against a nearby wall. Ganna knew she didn't need to tell her that. It was a work in progress, especially now.

"Maybe he sees something in you that the rest of us do not." Ganna turned to leave. "At any rate, some bonding time is much needed. I won't need to report, we will all know when Chardon has arrived."

With that, she left realizing she had overstepped her boundaries. Jaron probably wanted to burn her to cinders, but Ganna couldn't care less.

Out of the corner of her eye, Jaron saw Modas get up from the chair and head towards her. She stiffened for no reason and spun around to face him. He stopped, hesitant to continue, then followed through, grabbing her by the back of the neck to draw her close to him. He kissed her hard. She pushed him away, sending him across the room back near the chair he had just vacated.

"What are you doing? There's no time for that!"

The moment she pushed and yelled at him her heart felt great pain.

Why did I do that?

Watching Modas get up with no ill intent towards her made it worse. He just stared at her, not saying a word.

"I need to assess the level of my power. Show me a vacant area on this world."

Jaron hurried out the door, Modas not far behind.

****☼****

A street vendor dropped his tongs in the hotdog water, his mouth gaped open at the sight of a black hole appearing on the road right in front of him. Warping inward like liquid it enlarged to a size big enough that four figures emerged from. Once they were securely on the ground, the vortex vanished. There was really nothing strange about them except their entry. The vendor packed up and left the area without saying a word, pushing his cart down the street as fast as he could. In that part of town, crime was rampant. No one bothered to notice since anything or anyone that might look bad was avoided. Nothing had been seen or heard if anyone asked.

The team nodded to each other acknowledging the situation was better than perfect. If a fight broke out between them and enforcers it would be a no holds barred brawl. It was best to avoid casualties and witnesses. A small ball of light formed in the leader's hand. They all looked at it to see how far Chardon was from their location. Finding him, they headed in that direction.

"I'm just having a really bad day, aren't I?" Charles backed up from the group of enforcers forming a semi-circle around him. "Come on, guys, it doesn't take this many of you for little old me." They were a good foot taller or more than him. Advanced group.

They all morphed at once and Charles saw what the enforcers really were. Their arms turned into various claw like appendages and their faces distorted into monstrous creatures. He looked around and noticed everyone on the streets had vanished. So much for someone calling for help. He was in deep trouble. As the enforcers bounded towards him, a bright light engulfed the area.

The team saw the enforcers a block beforehand and took offensive positions. A surprise attack was the only way to win this fight and get Chardon back safely. A brutal fight ensued as the team went toe to toe with enforcers, tearing off limbs and tossing them haphazardly into the street. Their movements were a blur of colors and Charles had a repeat show of the strip mall fight. He noticed their technique was creating a clear path straight for him. Arriving at his side the team swooped in and grabbed him forcefully while collectively creating a vortex.

Charles had no time to think as his body was pulled through. He saw the carnage left behind and two enforcers still intact take pursuit. Whoever his saviors were, he was grateful and more confused than ever. All this from one little incident in a strip mall.

He hated strip malls.

****☼****

Charles kept his mouth shut witnessing the gate open. It seemed almost comical. There was no reason for him to laugh in his situation. In reality it was not funny in the least. All the same he wanted to burst out loud. Monsters, vortexes, strange powers and what not. He felt his body slow down as they approached the exit and he could see fields of strange tall plant life swaying in the wind behind a male figure standing at what looked like a console. As his feet hit solid ground, the vortex closed, and the male figure bowed down on one knee to him.

"Now I know something is not right." He turned to his saviors and saw they too had gone on bended knees. "Please, get up. This is embarrassing."

"It is only fitting that we should bow to our leader." Ganna stepped out from the shadows. "Welcome home, Chardon." She bowed down low.

"Leader my ass! What the hell is going?" He felt a twinge of anger.

Being kept out of the loop irritated him.

"Forgive me, I will explain immediately."

"You bet your ass, you will! And my name is not Chardon!" Though it seemed to fit him as he heard himself say it.

"But, it is. Tell me, do you have any memories from before you worked for your organization?"

"What? Of course I…!"

Charles stopped, his eyes wide.

He didn't. It never occurred to him.

"Come, walk with me."

Ganna held out her arm and Charles took it, letting her lead the way.

"This is some crazy shit."

Looking around at the environment, he shook his head. The tall grass was a strange orange color with tiny off-white flowers at the base. Looking up, he saw the murky sky with its weak sun. Something that reminded him of a guinea pig, except with spiraled horns and a long alligator like tail, scooted across their path. This was definitely not Earth.

People all around him stopped what they were doing and bowed low to him. He was getting annoyed. As they made their way to what looked like a temple, he noticed the scenery did not match. There were newly constructed buildings right alongside clearly dilapidated ones. Once they entered the temple, Ganna led him to the garden.

She began to tell the story of Lassa's destruction, giving the short version as he made it clear he had no patience for details. He remained silent throughout the explanation of how the original planet had been destroyed. His brow furrowed with each word. Afterwards, she moved into the garden of cores.

He stood on the edge of the core garden letting the vast knowledge of what those glowing buds of energy were. To see the embodiment of souls clustered in one place left him shocked and saddened. His feet moved on their own, steering his body into the garden towards the center where he stopped in front of a core pulsing brighter than all the others with a rainbow of energy.

With trembling hands, he picked it up and held it to his body, slowly letting it meld into him. His head snapped back, causing him to fall to his knees in the dirt. All his memories came to him in a rush, mingling with his experiences on Earth, making him whole again. An urge to fall uncon-scious swept over him and he fought through it, eventually able to stand. His vision changed, with clearer focus.

Energy swirled around him like wisps of smoke, lighting up the fields. Workers and children stopped to witness the event while Ganna steadily backed away from the buzzing air. A giant orb of light formed outward from his body to engulf a thousand feet radius, tiny sparks shimmering around the edges. He could see everyone staring, mesmerized by the display. When all the energy and lights subsided, Chardon took a deep breath and slowly exhaled.

"Most usually lose consciousness when they are re-established with their core." Ganna kept her distance as she spoke.

"I am not most." Chardon turned to face her. "I feel better already, but mostly I am angry."

"Jaron said the same thing. She wanted to be the one to come and extract you from that world."

"Is that so? Why didn't she?"

"I seem to have not regained my full power." Jaron came up to the garden's edge.

"It will come back soon enough. Are you treating Modas well?" He watched the struggle play on Jaron's face. "I guess there is a learning curve when it comes to love."

"We need to get Sara and Klein, too. I'm sure Halfar is going to have them on a short leash now that he knows we survived."

Chardon nodded in agreement, contemplating how to get his other cabinet members out of the demon's stronghold. Halfar was not to be underestimated. There was no way he would turn them over without a fight and Chardon was not yet ready for another. His wounds had healed instantly when his core was returned yet he could still feel them. Enforcers were nasty creatures who obeyed Rass and Kur more so than Halfar. He speculated it was because Halfar didn't like getting his hands dirty these days.

"For now, they are safe. Halfar would not jeopardize a potential meeting with me by harming one of my kind. No, he sees this as a second chance."

Sara and Klein

Sara and Klein walked accompanied yet again by guards to the throne room. That room had such a horrible feeling to it despite the pure white interior, throne included. White symbolized purity in most cultures but Klein knew the boss had somehow bastardized it. As they entered the room, Rass greeted them with a slow bow and a sheepish grin. To the left of the room, were two men, on their knees wearing disheveled clothes, looking scared shitless.

"Good morning, my little traitors. I thought you would appreciate some entertainment before breakfast." The boss lounged on his throne as usual. "Rass, what have we got today?"

"Two dealers who were not only insubordinate but, tried to make a profit off the merchandise in the tune of a quarter million."

"Is that so? Hmm."

The boss tapped his index finger to his temple for a moment.

Klein had a bad feeling about what was about to happen. He always wondered how the room stayed so white. Someone had to clean it on a daily basis, but why? The answer became clear.

"Sara, close your eyes," he whispered urgently.

The boss had heard him.

"No! You will both witness my judgment." Leaning further back into his throne, he declared, "Skin them," with no emotion or fanfare.

Rass' hands grew into talons two feet long and just as the first man started to scream, one of the talons pierced his chest running down it like a scalpel. The other man screamed and cried, begging for mercy as blood from his partner splattered on him in waves. The skinning was done slowly and when the screaming had gone on too long for everyone's taste, the boss' arm became a huge claw reaching across the room to snap the dying man's head clean off. His partner stopped screaming out of sheer terror, defecating himself. Rass continued the skinning of the now decapitated dealer with utter delight.

Sara vomited on her own feet, slumping to the floor as she slipped in it. Klein could not move to help her back up. His mind had unhinged looking at the boss, who watched with an expression of disinterest on his face. Klein's eyes burned with such hatred, he felt ill.

Halfar stepped down from the throne, stood in front of the traumatized dealer and punched through his rib cage with the claw. He snapped the claw shut as it tilted up, cutting the dealer in half from sternum to head. Only the lower body remained. Halfar returned his hands to human form and sat back down on his throne dripping blood down the armrest.

"You see, I do have some sense of mercy. Don't you think?"

A smile crept on his face.

"Monster," was all Klein could utter.

"Humph. Go, you will be late for morning roll call, and breakfast."

Two enforcers picked Sara up from the floor, her body limp in their arms. The other two yanked Klein away to the exit. The left side of the throne room lay covered in red. He felt sorry for whoever had to clean that macabre scene.

"Bring in the horde." Rass instructed the guards.

There was no need for Klein's pity. The double doors to the right opened to reveal a cluster of hideous monsters salivating from the smell of blood. Upon seeing the carnage, they rushed for it, slopping up blood and pieces of flesh. The sounds were horrifying to the human ears and Halfar again showed mercy by letting the human guards leave the room. A handful of enforcers stayed to join the festivities. Klein conjured up every grain of his sanity so he could remember this day.

Halfar stayed until the end, hating every moment of it. It was a barbaric ritual at best and it did nothing to entertain him anymore. This was a lashing out on his part for losing Chardon. He should have known a team would be dispatched to get him and now Halfar was down eight enforcers in one fell swoop. Deep in thought, he did not notice Kur enter the throne room. When he did, Kur was staring at him, questioning. If there was one who didn't need to know what Halfar was thinking it was Kur. He averted his eyes in a weary sort of way to signal that he was bored and nothing more.

Kur was not convinced. He felt something was amiss with his ruler since the destruction of that backwards world he favored. Keeping the only known survivors was not Kur's choice, preferring the entire race be extinct. Not knowing why Halfar wanted to embrace them, he had a hunch the key was Chardon. Kur left the room, also bored of the bloody scene whose screams had lured him to investigate. There was no finesse at all in Rass' punishment.

****☼****

"We have to get out of here," Sara hissed her words like a snake. She paced the length of her tiny room the organization supplied to low level runners and dealers. "He's going to kill us!"

Her face, still pale from vomiting, was now clean and she had changed her shirt.

"I don't think so." Klein stood legs wide apart, his right hand cradling the side of his face.

"How can you think that? Did you see?"

"Of course I did!" Her tone irritated him.

"Do you remember what he said about us?" Sara stopped pacing and stared at him in confusion. He sighed. She was not too bright to begin with so probably wasn't listening to the boss. "If what he says is true then that means Charles and Jared are going to try and rescue us. We can be free of him."

"That was just some bullshit he was spouting to scare us."

"Umm, did you not see Jared's pet dog turn into a huge creature and some old lady make a vortex they all disappeared in?" His eyebrows raised.

"But, we caused our world to be destroyed? He said that, didn't he?"

So, she was listening to some degree.

Klein shook his head to clear out the numbness in his head created by her absentmindedness.

"They don't know we are the reason. We're traitors, right?"

"So," Sara walked closer to him, "we can get to our world, get our cores back and then high tail it out of there before anyone finds out what we really did."

"You are assuming we would know how to create one of those black holes. And go where exactly?"

"Oh." She looked like a deer in headlights, her mouth slightly open in the shape of her word.

Klein now saw how their supposed plan had failed and an entire race nearly wiped from the universe. This was his partner in crime? Holy Toledo. He decided to make amends, if possible. There had to be a reason why the two of them had sided with the boss, betraying their own kind. To figure it out, they needed their original cores. It would be easy to play dumb for now because they really just had the boss' word regarding their treachery, and he took that with a grain of salt.

"Don't say a word." His mind made up.

"About what?" Sara's head cocked to one side.

Klein rolled his eyes.

"To Charles or Jared, do not say anything about what we may or may not have done in our original lives."

"Oh." Again, that deer in headlights look or had her expression not changed from before?

"We have chow, let's go."

"I am NOT eating!"

"We still have to go, genius." He pulled her along out the door.

****☼****

Chardon was not happy to see the core count for the garden. So many of his people died on a tyrant's whim. Entire families were wiped out, the planet scorched black. He could see it in his memories as the last thing known. A creak from behind alerted him to another presence in the room and he turned to find Modas silently entering. For such a massive beast, he was quite stealthy, and dangerous.

"Is Jaron being unreasonable again?"

"She's just frustrated she has to work so hard to regain her power."

"Did she really think it would be that easy?"

"And there is the loss of our children."

Chardon looked away. He had heard about what remained of their litter. How heart breaking it must have been to learn that. His wife, Sestis, was also among the dead, her core destroyed with the planet. Luckily, he had no children to mourn.

"I believe this is a perfect time to start over until most of the vessels are found. We can create new ones for the cores left without one. If you play your cards right, she may be willing."

"It's not about if she is willing or not. That will happen regardless. It's that she's full of vengeance, her actions seem desperate."

"You can't blame her for that." Chardon faced him. "I also want justice for all this and knowing I was a tool, a play thing, for Halfar on Earth makes me angry." Modas nodded in agreement. "I have never known you to speak this much, Modas."

"Only when it's necessary."

The manbeast left the room just as silently as he came in.

Chardon turned his attention to the sky. The weak sun spoke volumes to the condition of their new home. Chardon knew his race needed to adapt for a century or two before they found a new world to inhabit. A not so great planet trumped a dead one. He still didn't understand how the planet destroyer got through the gate. It bothered him as he checked his memories seeing how the blast came rushing across the land, disintegrating everything in its path, spreading like fire.

How did the gate get opened from the outside? Did Halfar figure out how from his last visit to their world?

For now, Chardon had one mission: to get Sara and Klein off Earth and back to this world. They had to be a little frightened by now since he and Jaron had not reappeared. This time he would go with a team of six knowing Halfar would not be naïve to send just a handful of enforcers again.

⁎⁎☼⁎⁎

"Any luck?" Ganna had crept up behind Jaron who was practicing making orbs of energy in her hands.

"As a matter of fact, yes."

Showing proof, she expanded a ball of light and sent it outwards, letting it go wide. It splintered a tree off in the distance.

"Did you really have to destroy that tree? It meant you no ill will."
Jaron laughed.

"I will have another one planted and matured."

"It may take more time on this planet with its weak sun."

"I had forgotten." Jaron felt a twinge of regret over the former tree. This was not their home world. She glanced up at the sky noticing how it did not harm her eyes. "We can't stay here."

"It will do for now. Come, we're ready for a meeting on how to get Sara and Klein back."

"Excellent! I want to try my hand at eliminating some enforcers.

She went around Ganna and together they headed for Chardon's chamber.

The Return of the Traitors

Halfar sensed the vortex opening almost instantly and summoned Rass to handle the situation. His henchmen were in the process of locating Sara and Klein who had skipped out on an errand and were currently on the run. Chardon's team would get to them first, but it didn't bother him in the least. Those two had to face a very angry council of their people. Halfar smiled a little at that. Would Chardon forgive them?

'Of course, he would because he is merciful', Halfar thought to himself.

It was a trait he himself had learned about some time ago. Ten enforcers were dispatched with Rass. He had a feeling only half would come back intact.

****☼****

Like a scene from a sci-fi horror movie, the now vacant inner city streets were showered in colored lights blazing across the sky along with bloody pieces of unknown origin. Some of it rained down on a few pedestrians still in the process of taking cover. No screaming was heard, only the sickly wet sounds of a massacre. Large cavities were blown out from nearby buildings, sidewalks sunk in towards the middle of the street and blood splattered everywhere.

Chardon came prepared for a fight but not like this. Jaron was keeping enforcers at bay on the opposite side of him and the other four team members were fighting for their lives. They had located Sara and Klein easy enough and were ready to move out when enforcers showed up. Sara was crouched on the ground with her hands covering her ears while Klein's eyes darted about, possibly looking for a pathway into the middle where he and Jaron were.

For the second time, Chardon realized he was near a rundown strip mall. How ironic, he grimaced. The fighting was going in their favor until he saw Rass coming at him from the mall's direction. Summoning his energy to form a barrier, he barely made it in time as Rass slammed into it, trying to break through. Chardon pushed the field forward and Rass flew backwards away from him, landing on his praying mantis like legs with hatred in his eyes.

"Come to take your traitors back?" Rass yelled, blowing strands of black oily hair from his eyes.

Chardon, Jaron and the rest of the team were able to quickly glance at each other as they continued fighting. He saw Klein wincing with his hands clasped together in prayer.

"Oh, yessss," Rass hissed, "didn't you know it was them?"

He launched himself back into the melee targeting Jaron this time, landing a blow. She was knocked into the side of a building, some of the bricks crumbling from the impact.

"Is that what Halfar told you?" Chardon asked as he went to shield Jaron, only to be attacked from behind. He felt the talons of an enforcer slice through his back.

"Of course, they have no memory of it since their cores are gone." Rass laughed as Chardon saw two other team members get raked across their bodies by four enforcers, two on each side.

"Then it's his word against theirs?"

"Halfar doesn't lie." Rass spat.

Which was true, and Chardon knew that. He may never speak what's on his mind but if you asked him, he would tell you.

"No matter, I am going to slice all of you to pieces and serve you to him on a platter!" He again launched himself towards them.

A vortex opened and out of its gaping mouth sprung Modas meeting Rass midair to strike him down into the pavement, which caved in as they landed. Standing up, Modas spun around, grabbed Jaron and threw her into the vortex. In two steps, he had Sara and Klein, doing the same. Nearing Chardon, he nodded to the team and they all leapt into the vortex. They were able to hear Rass screaming in angry dissatisfaction before the closed vortex silenced it.

Halfar conjured up energy in the palm of his hand to create a viewing orb and watched the battle as it ensued. Out of ten enforcers, six were intact. He was glad but didn't like that Chardon himself had come. If he had known, Halfar would have gone to retrieve him instead. Seeing Rass go into a fit of rage over defeat almost made him laugh.

"How childish and uncouth," Kur said as he entered without Halfar knowing yet again. He stood watching the scene as well. "He really has no flair for getting the most out of a battle."

"He has his own way of doing things. We can't all be as pristine as you, Kur."

"You would think he had learned something from me by now."

Halfar dissolved the energy orb and the scene faded. Back in a lounging position on his throne, he watched, out of the corner of his eye, Kur trying to decipher what bothered him about his illustrious ruler. Halfar would tell him if asked. That would take the fun out of it.

"What will you do now that the remaining survivors have reunited to wage war against us?" Kur asked.

"Nothing. Do you really think a small group of a nearly extinct race can win against an army such as ours?"

"Stranger things have been known to happen."

"Not that." Halfar slid off his throne and headed for the double doors leading to his chamber. "Please make sure to congratulate Rass on his magnificent defeat."

Kur grunted as he turned and left through the main door at the center. He would do just that by challenging him to a duel out of spite. It was going to be a productive evening for his generals.

****☼****

Sara and Klein hit the ground hard as they landed from their toss through the vortex. It was apparent that Modas had such violent force when it came to battle. Klein hit his head on the stone console in front of him as he tried to get up. Sara was in tears from sustaining scrapes and cuts from her fall. Behind them, Ganna was tending to Jaron just as Modas, Chardon and the team stepped out of the vortex onto solid ground.

A group of people in brown robes came rushing out to meet them, taking great care of Jaron and Chardon. Two of them came upon Sara but in her madness, she started screaming repeatedly, "Don't touch me!" Klein frowned and turning, punched her so hard, she fell back to the ground unconscious. The two in brown robes stared at him in awe, eyes wide, then picked her up and carried her away.

"That was a bit uncalled for, Klein." Chardon seemed angry, but not necessarily at him.

"Yeah, well, would you have done better?" Klein shot back as he rocked onto his feet.

"You do know I want the truth from both of you?"

"I don't see how, our cores were destroyed, right?" For the first time, he realized how different Chardon looked from before, and the extent of the man's battle wounds. "Right?"

Chardon turned to Ganna. "Find their cores and return them to me."

"Of course." She bowed low and headed for the garden.

Klein sat back on his haunches in a daze. He wasn't sure if it was a blessing or a curse but now he had a chance to make amends or be persecuted. He wondered what his original self was like and if Sara was just as irritating as she was now. Looking up at the sky into the weak sun he made his resolution.

****☼****

Sara woke up flinging herself out of the bed she lay on, gasping for air. The left side of her head was in pain and she held fast to it rocking back and forth hoping to ease the burning sensation. In a flash, she remembered Klein had socked her there and with a rage not felt before she went into a fit, arms flailing about her, as she screamed at the top of her lungs. Abruptly, she stopped, realizing someone else was in the room with her.

Modas sat across the room watching her with no emotion on his face. He stared into her eyes and she saw what real fury looked like. Not the passionate burning kind, but the cold unfeeling kind. He could murder me right now, she thought. He didn't say a word but his eyes concurred as if

35 | THREADS OF CONCEIT

he had heard her thoughts. Seeing him close up, she noticed how large and formidable he was. *Where is Klein?* Now would be a good time for him to come to her rescue. She scanned the room, hopeful.

"Klein is with Chardon."

Modas continued to stare at her, his eyes never wavering.

She almost said, oh. Knowing how much that irritated Klein she knew it would probably do the same for Modas. Her lips were parched so she licked them with her nearly dry tongue. It hurt.

"Will he be back soon?"

"That depends on Chardon."

"You know, the boss may have been lying about us being traitors, you know? I mean, we don't have any memories or anything because of our cores or whatever," she rambled out.

"Fascinating." Modas rose from the chair in disgust.

"What?" Sara felt like she had been slapped in the face and insulted at the same time.

"Even without your core, you are still just as arrogant and selfish, as a woman."

Sara sat up straight and turned her nose up at him trying to appear unafraid. She was about to make a snide remark when what he said at the end rung in her ear.

"Huh?" She hiccupped.

Three medical sages tended to Chardon, bandaging his rib cage and treating the wounds on his back. From what Klein had heard, they would be healed by tomorrow. The treatment was merely a precautious. The enforcers who injured him before were low level and did not cause much damage. In the last battle, they were henchmen of Rass and deadlier. Chardon winced as one of the medics pulled the bandage tight. Klein listened to him vow payback in the worst way for Rass and his band of enforcers. He was glad Halfar himself did not show up, or Kur for that matter.

Klein sat on his knees silent as the murky dawn. Chardon seemed angry about the treachery but was more upset about the fact that Klein had taken Halfar's word without argument.

"So, despite not having any memories of who you really are, let alone traitors to your race, you believed every word Halfar told you?"

Feeling ashamed, Klein nodded with his eyes squeezed shut.

How stupid.

It never crossed his mind that the boss might be lying, but, something inside him knew it was true.

"Please, no matter what happens, I want to make amends. I really do."

"And how are you going to do that?" Chardon's eyes went wide. "Our world is dead!"

Klein flinched back and hung his head lower. He knew there was probably no redemption for him but doing nothing was not an option. He sucked in his chest, raised his head and said, "Give me back my core and I will prove myself to you. I will be able to tell you everything."

Chardon waved off the medics, standing over Klein as he rose.

"I have an idea of what happened and yes you will tell me why. First we will go get your lover and head to the garden."

"My lover?" Klein was confused for a moment, then his face paled. "You don't mean Sara?" He heard Chardon sigh. "What's in the garden?"

"Klein, get up."

Everyone headed for the door, Klein picking up the rear.

At the garden, Sara was like a kid at a petting zoo. A lot of "Ooh's" and "Ah's" escaped her lips as she stood on the edge staring at the glowing buds. Klein was not so enamored because he understood what those things were. It pained him to see so many yet so little left of their race and he didn't even have his core back yet. He turned to Sara.

"Stop that!" He was seething with anger. "Do you even know what you're looking at?"

"Why are you yelling at me? And why are you so angry?" She yelled back.

"Tell her!" He directed Ganna.

"Cores." Was all she said, and that snapped Sara out of her stupor.

"All those?" She whispered, tears forming in the corners of her eyes.

A worker came up to Klein with a core in his hands giving it to him. Klein cradled it in his arms like a newborn and let it sink into him, disappearing. The jolt to his body was so severe even Sara jumped back in fear. He fell to the ground face down convulsing. Tears poured out of him as both memories intertwined. He could do nothing but lie there and take the brunt of it all. Medics rushed to him and used light energy to ease his suffering before taking him away.

Sara started shaking her head back and forth.

"No, no, no. No!"

Another worker was coming towards her and she knew it had to be her core. This is not what she wanted. She wanted to go back to Earth where it was relatively safe aside from the part where Halfar's organization was taking over the whole damn United States. She tried to back up but Ganna was behind her and held her still while the worker touched her abdomen with the core.

As it entered her, she understood what Modas meant. Memories of a young man laughing with Klein, talking with Klein, kissing Klein flooded in and her body began to shift into that man. It did not take long. The pain was excruciating as bone and muscle reconfigured.

Their body thrashed about in convulsions, gurgled shrieks emitting from their mouth. With the transformation complete, he sprung forward into a sitting position and let out a scream so loud the nearby trees vibrated. Then he passed out. Two more medics came for him.

Chardon and Ganna glanced sideways at each other and she giggled.

"How dramatic," Ganna quipped. "Talas always made things more entertaining than necessary."

"Humph. I think it will be interesting to know how Talas felt about being a female Earthling."

"I find it interesting that they were not lovers on Earth as they were here."

"That is curious. Klein seemed to barely tolerate her instead of having any affection."

"Well, tomorrow we will get answers. Modas and Jaron should be kept at bay."

"No, they need to be there to hear what these two have to say. I will stop them if they try to kill them."

"Good to know."

TWO:

Homeward

The throne was awash with black blood as Halfar entered. He cocked his head to one side to ask why as he made eye contact with Kur standing covered in his own green blood mingled with the thick purple of another, turning it black. Hence, the mess. Near the double doors on the left where Halfar had just come through lay Rass in a crouched position breathing heavily covered in the same mixture.

"We were having a slight disagreement on strategy, my lord."

Kur bowed in jest.

"I will not be made a mockery of!" Rass was ready to launch.

With one swish of his arm, Halfar knocked Rass into the wall near the main entrance and headed towards Kur. He was not going to tolerate such nonsense without approval.

"I was just congratulating him on his defeat as you instructed."

Kur's voice was cut short by Halfar's claw clamping around his neck, lifting him off the floor. He knew the look in his eyes let Kur know that he had overstepped his boundaries.

"My apologies," Kur gasped and Halfar let him go.

"Clean this mess before I get back."

"Where are you going?"

"Since I am unable to use my throne room, I will have to settle for a stroll into the city."

Kur and Rass' eyes went wide with fear. That was never a good idea in any circumstance.

"You can't be serious!" They both exclaimed in unison.

Halfar turned to them.

"I need to blow off some steam, don't you think?" With that, he left.

Rass ordered some of his guards to clean the mess, as did Kur, and they both hurried after him in an attempt to stop him, leaving a bloody trail down the hall. The last time Halfar went into the city he ended up destroying a five-block radius because a taco vendor mouthed off to him for not buying before eating. Trying to explain that to the authorities was not something to be desired. Yes, they were not of this planet and could annihilate it on a whim, but that was not on the agenda for a few years yet.

"Please, my lord, we are deeply sorry. Come and relax for a moment." Rass talked fast.

"Where would that be?"

"The garden is in full bloom, don't you want to see how our native flowers are doing in this wretched planet's soil?" Kur also talked as fast as he could.

Halfar stopped walking.

"They were planted?"

They halted a few feet away from him.

"Of course, my lord."

"When?"

"Nearly three months ago," Kur squinted as he thought, guessing.

"Then let us go see how they are faring before I go out."

"This way, please."

Rass bowed deep and waited for Halfar to pass before following, shooting Kur a dirty look as they both closed in behind him. Halfar knew they were relieved that some mass destruction had been averted so far.

Kelin lay resting on a bed weary and deep in thought. It was funny that Halfar had given him the human name Klein, seeing the similarities. If it were not for the ruckus going on in the room nearby, he would have rested for a few more hours. He could imagine one person having such a fit and it was none other than Talas.

Sitting up with the weight of his upper body supported by his elbows he let his head flop backwards. Every muscle in his body felt strained and he just wanted to stay in bed. That was now impossible with Talas thrashing about next door, so Kelin flung the covers off and marched over.

"For the love of Lassa, shut up!"

There were at least seven people in the room, him included and he felt like an imbecile. Everyone stood in place staring at him. Talas, still shaking with fury, advanced on him.

"Talas," he warned him. Too late. Kelin fended him off by putting him in a choke hold before he could get any closer. They wrestled to the floor and as Kelin held him steady he said, "It's alright. There's no need to fight." He felt Talas relax then start sobbing quietly.

"I would ask if this was a good time for your confessions, but it seems that is not the case."

Chardon had entered the room followed by Jaron, Ganna, Modas and three other cabinet members. Jaron could hardly contain her rage. It poured out of her entire body.

"There is no good time for it so now is better than never." Talas lifted himself from Kelin, wiping away tears, to confront them head on. "I know what we did was unforgiveable, and it cannot be fixed. All I can do is pledge my loyalty to my kind, never to waver under promises and false hopes. So, I beg you," Talas went down on his knees and bowed low, his forehead nearly touching he floor, "please, forgive me."

Kelin, still down on the floor, sat in awe of Talas. Especially when Jaron stepped forward to look down on him and slammed her fist into

Talas' face as he looked up at her. Everyone else in the room flinched.

"Do you feel better now?" Chardon asked Jaron.

"No! Not in the least." Jaron ran out of the room, Modas in tow.

"Shall we begin?"

Chardon motioned for everyone to take a seat within the chamber, instructing Talas with a finger to wipe the blood from his mouth. He looked toward Kelin and nodded.

The Agenda

Lassa Fifty years ago

Halfar and his entourage had come visiting yet again to negotiate with Chardon some form of submission to his Armada. The cabinet members were angry but kept their tongues, all but one: Talas. Due to his outbursts, Chardon had ordered him out of the council chamber and the meeting adjourned for a little while. Sestis, Chardon's mate, found Talas pacing in a full rage near the grain field.

"You know this will end badly." She said sweetly.

Talas halted his pacing and regarded her with contempt. How dare that monster speak to me! He did not move an inch as she came closer. As revered as she may be, Talas knew she was capable of awful things. He just didn't have any proof.

"Our leader is going to get the entire race killed and all of you are going to let him."

"Better dead than slaves for that monster," Talas spat.

Sestis laughed. "It doesn't have to be that way. I have a proposal." "What is it, then?" Being in her presence alone agitated him.

"I believe we can coexist. I propose there be a delegate to oversee our kind to ensure it continues."

"We have a leader."

"One who does not see reason and humiliates one of his own cabinet members in front of the enemy?" She shook her head looking mournful. Talas' eyes went downcast and he clenched his fists at his sides. "That was uncalled for to say the least." She moved closer to Talas. "I believe you can make him aware of his short comings."

"How?"

Talas seemed uneasy. This was Chardon's mate but did she really have their race's best interest at heart?

"When Halfar invades this world, I shall negotiate to appoint you and one other to rule over our race. Chardon will be at Halfar's palace and no longer leader. That would put him in his place, don't you think?"

"You would do this?"

"Of course. But, only if the invasion is a success." Sestis walked off into the distance towards her entourage of handmaids, who were just released from the council chamber to fetch her and smiled.

Talas stood in the same spot for a long time, delusions of grandeur dancing in his head. There was only one person who was meant to rule with him and that was Kelin. He needed to convince him that Sestis was right about making the invasion go smoothly to avoid loss of lives. It took only a few months to do so.

"You will not accept my proposal?" Halfar was livid.

"No. I will not submit to your terms just so you can enslave my race."

"It is not slavery, just safe keeping from harm of other more powerful forces."

"That is not what you are doing!" Chardon turned away from him. He was not amused.

"I can destroy you!" Halfar shook with anger.

"And, that is why you will never win!"

"You will regret this."

Halfar hurried off with his entourage to the gate escorted by Modas' personal army. As they waited for the guardian to open a vortex, he saw Talas and Kelin nearby motioning him away from the not so watchful eye of the guardians towards them.

"I take it didn't go too well." Kelin was not surprised.

"It can still be accomplished." Halfar had a monstrous idea in his head but did not reveal it. "If you can open the gate in three days, I can send my Armada through with directions to help you with transition."

"Transition for what?" Talas anxious.

"For the cohabitation, of course," He replied sweetly, "and the naming of their new rulers." Making sure to stare at them until they got the point.

"Three days?"

"Three days." Halfar saw the gate had been opened. His entourage, and he, marched through.

Once he arrived back on his own world, Halfar turned to his two generals, Rass and Kur, eyes burning with rage. They were surprised since he seemed to like that pathetic world.

"Prepare a world ender. I want it sent through the moment that gate to their world opens."

Kur raised an eyebrow. "Is there a radius you wish to declare?"

"NO! Scorch it all, the entire world."

"As you wish, my lord." He headed for the arsenal to inform their scientists to prepare the bomb.

"Are you sure?" Rass stopped not four feet from him to whispered it.

"Get it done!" Halfar nearly ran to his chamber doors, flinging them open with such force, a gust of wind blew Rass back.

"Are you sure this is what we want?" Kelin stood over the guardian he had knocked unconscious as Talas worked the console.

"This is the best way to ensure our survival and plus, we will be able to rule over our race however we see fit. Chardon won't have a say anymore."

"Let's just hurry and get this done."

A vortex began to form at the center of the gate and they braced themselves for the armada that was sure to come in full force.

With a jolt of fear and regret, Halfar sat up from his bed and gasped. "No, no, no!" He hurried out into the corridor and screamed, "Wait!"

"What is it, my lord?" Rass came briskly to him.

"Chardon! You need to get Chardon!"

"I am sorry, my lord, but the planet destroyer is already traveling through the vortex."

Halfar grabbed Rass by the neck, lifting him off the ground.

"You will do this."

He let Rass go and returned to his bed chamber.

Rass stood for a moment trying to figure out why his ruler would request such a thing then gave up and went to see what he could do. There was a way, but he was sure Halfar would still be grateful, regardless of the outcome.

Children played in the fields, warriors were in the middle of their daily training, the high council was in a meeting and the sun shone down on them all unaware that Kelin and Talas were opening the gates of Hell. Both stood proud ready to greet their new allies. Chardon had skipped the council meeting to tend a fruit patch when he felt the vortex.

The gate opened.

Heat shot forth past Kelin and Talas, scorching the ground and air behind them. Screams were short lived as many were incinerated on contact. Ganna knew instantly that their race was about to be extinct so she coordinated with other council members to rescue as many as they could while she opened alternate gates with random destinations. Anywhere was better than what would now be a dead planet.

Chardon rushed to the console to try and close it but it was too late. He felt his core ripped out of him as his body was sucked into the vortex. Jaron tried to reach for him but the same happened to her along with Talas and Kelin. The last thing they saw before their souls died was the bomb going off in the distance, scorching the entire planet black.

Truth Sets You Free

Chardon thought hearing the truth would make him more objective, he was wrong. His heart raced with emotions of hate, despair, and shame all rolled into one. But, he knew there was one responsible for it all and that was his mate, Sestis. Talas and Kelin were just pawns.

"How stupid can you be?" Jaron had come back to hear the confession. "You thought the two of you could RULE over us?" She moved to strike, but Modas stopped her, shaking his head. It was not worth it anymore.

"I..," Kelin began to say.

"Don't." Chardon raised one hand up. "Loving someone doesn't mean following them blindly. You should have had the common sense to deter Talas from such deceit."

"I understand."

"Do you, Kelin? No matter, what's done is done." He got up from his sitting position on the floor and made eye contact with everyone in the room. "None of this leaves here! The last thing we need is our people hearing that Sestis had a hand in this." He left as did the rest of the cabinet members, leaving Talas and Kelin alone to think about what they wanted to do next. Atonement was not going to be easy.

Chardon paced the length of his chamber, doubt welling up about how to deal with the two. Somewhere deep in his core, he knew that he was in some degree to blame for their actions. His race would have been enslaved, probably, and the death toll, although intolerable would have been minimal. Most of their race would be alive instead of nearly extinct. He had been unwilling to submit to Halfar un- der any circumstance and this was the result.

Back then, Sestis acted like a tyrant when she visited other worlds to establish their place among the galaxy, spouting her own agenda without asking anyone's opinion. His passive aggressive, power hungry mate never turned away from new ideals because it kept her in high standing with the other councils. It should have been obvious what kind of manipulative female she was, but he was blinded by some sense of accomplishment. It fell apart when he met Halfar at one of the interplanetary conferences.

How could he have let all this happen?

He looked out the window when it came into view as he slowed his pacing to a stop. Children played as if nothing was wrong. Workers tended

the fields in silence with small smiles on their faces. That weak, dull sunlight muted the planet's colors. Some of the people's eyes were beginning
to change in compensation for it. This was not how it should be.

He laid his palms flat against the walls on either side of the window
shifting his weight to them. So much damage had been done. Even if Talas
and Kelin had not betrayed their race, he believed the outcome would be
no different. Chardon was not willing to condemn the pawns for the sake
of the leader's reputation.

Eyes a dull bluish grey, the color of a dark, cold, churning sea reflected
back at him through the window pane. On Earth, his eyes were a dark blue
and even then, they seemed cold. He let out a deep sigh, hanging his head
for a moment before pushing off the wall to stand straight. This time he
would make better choices and right now, he needed to find a way to fix this
planet for longevity. They would no longer run from their enemies.

Modas silently stood behind Chardon who jumped with fright as he
turned to leave, nearly running into him. Such stealth in someone so massive
still seemed to amaze him.

"Modas, please refrain from entering my chamber without permission."

"My apologies. I felt it would be better to come unannounced to clarify what you intend to do about those two."

"Absolutely nothing."

"Not even an apology?"

Chardon begin to shake a little.

"I can't do that."

"Why not?"

"Because then they would ask me why!" Tears started to form in his
eyes but he refused to let even one drop. "I will make it right in my own
way."

"You can't make it right, Chardon, and you can't keep secrets forever."

Modas stepped aside so Chardon could flee out of the room before
him. He was the only other one who knew the reason for what happened
thus far and would keep it to himself as long as Chardon wished. There
was no need to cause more chaos and distrust among their race. He headed
back to Talas' temporary chamber to break the good news that all was
forgiven.

Unlike Chardon, he held the two of them responsible for the simple
fact that they opened the gate. Chardon may have wounded Halfar's ego,
the outcome possibly the same, but there was no way that planet bomb
would have succeeded without a doorway to go through. For Modas,
Chardon's conscience was clean, Talas and Kelin's were not. He knew
Jaron felt the same way.

✳✶☼✶✳

Talas jumped up from the bed with an expression of joy.

"Really? We are forgiven?"

"According to Chardon, yes. You can both regain your status as cabinet members."

"But not by you." Kelin could see it in his eyes.

"No." Modas left the room.

Talas was left standing with an awkward half opened smile on his face. He closed his mouth and sat back down. It occurred to him that would be the case. Their race needed them but Jaron and Modas could care less. Most of their children were dead: no cores or vessels remained.

"Kelin."

"There is nothing we can say or do to make this right. We need to come up with a plan to get this planet right for our race and find a way to defeat Halfar because he will not stop at Earth for conquest. He knows we have a new home and if he is still angry, he will come after us out of spite."

"I'm not so sure." Talas leaned toward Kelin. "Did it seem odd to you that Halfar was not too interested in the bloody mess going on in that throne room?" Kelin thought back on it. "I think he wants to get the whole conquest over with, leave it to his generals and abdicate."

Jaron returned after cooling off, followed by Ganna, Modas and the other council members.

"We could use that to our advantages."

Kelin had ideas swirling in his head.

"That 'we' better mean the entire council and not the two of you doing something stupid on your own, resulting again in the destruction of our race." Jaron came into the room slamming the door open with such force the bang echoed throughout the compound, making them both jump back in fear.

"Of course not," Talas mumbled under his breath.

"What could be at our advantage?"

Kelin explained the killing ritual they witness in the throne room. They all listened, their stomachs made ill. He left nothing out because he wanted them to know just how frightful a creature Halfar really was.

"Disgusting. That is their idea of entertainment?" One of the council men shivered.

"If he is so detached then it may be possible to actually negotiate with that monster." Jaron rested one elbow in the hand of his other arm and tapped his fingers to his lips. "We first need to know what it is he seeks."

"Chardon," Modas blurted out at the same time the man himself entered the room. No one realized his blunder except Chardon and his eyes narrowed at him.

"Yes, I am here."

Chardon used the opportunity to shy them away from it.

"I wish there was a way to sneak onto Earth and take them all out quietly but he can sense a vortex opening anywhere in close proximity." "The problem is those enforcers are kept partially evolved therefore they have no real mind of their own. Whatever their leader orders they obey."

Chardon could still feel the wounds that were no longer there. "To stop the enforcers, we must first stop Rass and Kur."

That was an unpleasant thought for everyone in the room. Hideous creatures, the both of them, in their true forms and deadly. Maybe more so than Modas in close combat. Nothing, short of tearing them apart, would suffice as victory.

"No way do we get to Halfar without doing that. How many warriors can we have within the next two to three Earth years?" Talas knew it was a short timeline.

"With our dwindled population, possibly two hundred." Another female council member calculated.

"That's plenty."

Kelin was shocked by the number. He was expecting somewhere around Fifty.

Chardon looked up at the ceiling contemplating something. All eyes were on him. When he looked back down at them he made a proposal. "We send only fifty to Earth and the rest will stay to defend this planet if necessary. The fifty will be split into four squadrons surrounding Halfar's palace from all sides."

"That's an odd number for a four-corner enclosure."

"No, it's not. Ten for each squadron and we will go into the main entrance to confront Halfar."

"We?" Jaron tilted her head.

"You, Modas, seven warriors and I."

"Do you think that wise?" Ganna interjected.

"It was started with Halfar and I, so it must end that way as well."

And the four squad leaders?"

Kelin was curious but could feel it in his gut.

"Jaron, Talas, Ganna, and you."

The rest of the council's heads bobbed collectively in agreement. Better this way than the recruitment of council members with no combat experience. They would stay on the planet and oversee everyday expectations. Bloodshed was not their forte.

"We must go through the vessels that were saved and see how many match the cores in the garden. All the ones that do not have one or the other should be made compatible to ensure every core and vessel is consumed. From there, we can have a more accurate population count."

Ganna did not like that last suggestion. Forcing a core into a vessel not naturally its own could be dangerous. At the same time, having empty vessels and homeless cores was not an option either. "I will oversee that myself until it is time for deployment to Earth. Come," she gestured to the other council members.

"Modas." The tone of Chardon's voice was a warning and a beckon.

Modas went to his side.

Kelin and Talas sat back watching Modas and Chardon whisper to each other while Jaron, still elbow in hand, paced staring unwavering at them. Kelin saw the cold rage in her eyes as her gaze fell on Kelin and deepened as she caught Talas'. She had every right to wish them dead so he did not flinch this time and neither did Talas. It was clear that if she had the means to murder them without the wrath of Chardon coming down on her, she would do it.

"Jaron, let's go." Modas was done talking with Chardon and they both waited for her to leave with them. She hesitated at first. "We have work to do." Modas insisted.

As the room cleared once again, Talas let out a deep breath releasing tension. Kelin seemed perplexed. They were both silent for a long time, Talas broke it.

"What are you thinking about, my love?"

Kelin glanced sideways at him. The "my love" sounded condescending at best. He chewed his lower lip for a moment. Something was amiss.

"What do you think Chardon and Modas were discussing earlier?"

"Who knows," Talas shrugged, laying his head on Kelin's shoulder.

"I think it had something to do with Halfar."

"Mmm." Talas was falling asleep.

Kelin remembered what Chardon said about all of this starting with him and Halfar. It hit him as he also remembered Modas saying Chardon's name when no one knew he had entered the room yet. Could it really be that Halfar wants Chardon? Why? What were the terms of the negotiations that the council was not privy to? All these questions were going to get answered one way or another, he counted on it.

Talas was asleep on his shoulder and for the first time since they were made whole again by their cores, he stared at his sleeping face. Talas was never beautiful as Sara, but now he was a stunning sight to behold. How he must have hated being unintelligent and weak minded as a female earthling. Kelin put his arms around him, pulling him closer. He could smell Talas' natural scent and breathed it in.

Halfar usually liked conquering worlds. He just found conquering Earth to be banal. Humans were so easily manipulated by power and greed they forgot to assume their enemies end game. For now, Halfar gave them power to attain status and money but, that would all be for naught once his armada moved in. The ones who defied him were smart to rebel. He smiled a little before frowning. Kur had, yet again, crept into the throne room unannounced to catch him in some un-ruler like mood which started to get annoying.

"Does that smile preclude good news on our timeline?" Kur asked.

"It does. In another two years, we will be able to lock down this continent and move into the next. I look forward to getting off this world and on to more challenging ones."

"Granted, there are no unforeseen complications with this invasion."

"What could possibly go wrong?" Halfar raised his eyebrows.

"I believe there is a race that is not too happy to be nearly extinct because of you."

"They do not have enough warriors or destructive power to challenge us."

"Many battles have been won by sheer determination against foes bigger than us. Be careful, my lord, not to let your guard down."

"That is what my generals are for." Halfar glared at him.

Kur let out a smirk. He knew all too well what his role was in Halfar's armada. Leaving, he strode past Rass as he entered the throne room. He watched them give each other hateful smiles of acknowledgment. Soon, he would appoint one of them to be in control of his Armada. It was just a matter of who and how.

✳✳☼✳✳

Modas slid onto the bed, hovering over Jaron as she slept on her side. He listened to the even breathing escaping her partially opened lips. How beautiful she was laying there unsuspecting of his intentions at this very moment. He pulled the covers off her in one stroke, startling her out of sleep. Jaron curled upwards glaring at him in distaste for waking her in such a manner. He didn't care about that. Grabbing her by an ankle, he pulled her flat below him.

"Stop it, you beast! Let me go!" Jaron tried sitting up to strike him but missed as her center of gravity was off and she landed flat on her back again.

"No."

Was all Modas replied as he used one hand to remove her robe and the other held both ankles down. It usually happened this way: Jaron protesting half-heartedly and Modas being passive aggressive. He moved closer towards her so that the weight of his lower body held hers in place and removed his robes. For one brief instant, Jaron stopped fighting to gaze at his massive muscular body. She was tempted to reach out and touch him but restrained herself. It was too late, he saw the look in her eyes and with one movement pulled her legs through his and spread them around his waist.

"Stop!" Jaron swung at him, her wrist caught in midair to be repositioned above her head.

He entered her roughly, his weight bearing down, forcing her legs open wider. They were now eye to eye and he did not disconnect his gaze even as she turned her head to the side trying to bear the pain and ecstasy without him knowing. To be this close and connected to her was almost too much for him but he could not and would not stop until he had his fill of her. He grabbed her by the back of her neck and turned her to him, kissing her hard. She finally submitted to him and buried her fingers deep into his thick mane, returning his kiss. The sun had not yet set.

Ganna had followed Modas in an attempt to discuss battle plans but stopped outside of the bed chamber door when she realized he hadn't noticed her. He had another agenda on his mind. She heard sounds of mating from inside and lingered a bit before leaving. It did not surprise her that they would produce a litter so soon after returning. Ganna smiled.

If it were up to Chardon, he would create new vessels and start over but knew that option was a last resort. For now, the matching of core to vessel would take precedence to ensure a pure race. The process would take nearly a year to complete and, after that, preparations for the attack on Halfar would begin. Just seeing the garden made him feel helpless and guilty.

A small gust of wind blew his ever growing hair, now almost to the middle of his back, with slight waves, into his face. He remembered it being as long before their world was destroyed.

Running his fingers through his hair he saw an image flash before him from long ago. Halfar in full regalia standing in front of him with his hand tangled in Chardon's hair against the backdrop of an aqua green sky.

Chardon knelt down next to a row of cores, staring into the soil, mesmerized. It should not have happened this way. He could still see the look of longing on Halfar's face, his strange murky green eyes narrowed in frustration. Not wanting to recall those moments, Chardon shook his head in defiance. This was not the time for that. He stood and sensed Ganna getting closer to his location.

"Taking a short reprieve from the council?"

Ganna side stepped a garden slug under her feet.

"It has gotten cooler. The air feels nice."

"Hmm, you seemed far away a moment ago."

"Just, thinking about the past. Did you get to talk with Modas?"

Ganna's cheeks flushed and Chardon raised his eyebrows questioning.

"He is preoccupied with mating right now."

"Oh." Chardon was a bit taken aback. He had not expected them to do that so soon. "I guess it can't be help. Even though they were always together on Earth, it is much different now."

"I am surprised he waited as long as he did. How frustrated he must have felt."

"I almost feel bad for Jaron, forcing herself to try and resist his advances all the while enjoying every minute of it."

"She is so dishonest with herself. Why does she torment him so?"

A worker came up to them and bowed.

"I double checked all the vessels and the recorded cores and, I apologize, your mate's core and vessel were one of the ones destroyed."

Chardon looked away, his eyes downcast with no feelings in them. He had known that was the case and never asked for anyone to find her. It was for the best anyway. He didn't love her to begin with; she was just a means to an end for companionship.

"Thank you, there is no need to apologize. Go, finish your work."

As the worker left, Ganna watched Chardon shuffle his feet in the dirt.

"You couldn't care less about her being destroyed." She said so unceremoniously.

"I did care for her but, love her, no. If only you knew what kind of creature she really was."

"I do know. That is why I do not mourn her unlike our people."

Longing

Rass could see that Halfar was in no mood for entertainment this evening. His lord's facial expression was of someone far away in another land. He had an idea where, and who, he was thinking of. It was a bond not easily broken, apparently. He motioned his enforcers to drag away the carnage into an adjacent room to finish up and stepped closer to the throne in ear shot of Halfar.

"Does the sun not shine on your precious planet?"

Without noticing who was asking, Halfar answered.

"It shines no more since the planet is now dead."

He blinked hearing his own voice and seeing Rass so close to him.

"As I thought, you still want Chardon back. What is it about that inferior species you can't seem to break from?"

"You would not understand if I explained it."

"Explain what, my lord?"

Kur slowly waltzed into the room, his long sword swinging in its holster behind him causing his cape to flow out. He might have passed for beautiful if his smile was not so menacing, and sent people running in terror because they knew what it communicated.

"Good of you to check in, General Kur."

Rass was taunting him into a fight to steer from the conversation. For Kur to know any more than he already did, which was plenty, would not be in Halfar's best interest.

Kur was not fooled but decided to play the game.

"I always make sure our ruler is up to date on my success. Tell me, how many sectors have you claimed this week?" He smiled.

Two grunt workers came in to report an uprising in one of Rass' sec- tors, making him curse and hurry out of the room. Kur watched him go, a look of pleasure that his little prank had come to fruition, then turned to Halfar. That faraway look had returned and Kur did not like it.

"So, my lord, what is it that needs explaining? Does it pertain to our campaign?"

"No, it docs not. You need not know."

Halfar rose from his throne and exited to his private chamber. Kur's curiosity rattled him. He needed some time to think.

In his bed chamber, Halfar laid down closing his eyes. He drifted off to a memory long ago when Chardon traveled to different worlds gathering information as he had. They were collecting data on new technologies and other resources that could benefit their race. Some of the other rulers tried getting what they needed through manipulation. Halfar was ruthless and blunt where Chardon tried the honest approach, although he was constantly undermined by Sestis. She has just as ma- nipulative as the others, only with a superficial sweet nature. On those off days where no trade negotiations commenced, Chardon and Halfar talked.

✱✱☼✱✱

"This world reeks."

Chardon covered his face with a sleeve in an effort to ward off the stench. He eyed the large metal structures spewing pollutants into the air only a few miles away. The landscape reminded him of some poor species' guts thrown onto it then coated with liquid metal. That was just about the right description of the smell Chardon tried to not breathe in.

"It is an industrial planet." Halfar laughed. "Many different chemicals are produced here to make other products for distribution."

"It still reeks."

"How childish of you."

Halfar removed Chardon's hand from his face, lacing his fingers into his hair as he did so. A slight breeze came across the balcony where they stood. Their eyes locked on each other for a brief moment. The Aqua colored sky yielded to the sun tinting it with green, accenting his strange murky green eyes.

"Don't." Chardon whispered, his eyes never leaving Halfar's.

"I want you to rule with me."

"Please."

Halfar's eyes narrowed. He had been rejected before by others but from Chardon it was unbearable. He didn't know why, but there was no one in the universe he wanted more than Chardon. As if their life forces drew off each other.

"I won't give up." He slid his hand out of Chardon's hair.

"I know, but, the answer is still no. I have a mate."

"Who you despise."

"I do not despise her, just her way of doing things."

"You don't love her."

Chardon severed the gaze.

"It doesn't matter. Our people adore her."

"How?" Halfar jolted back. That was incredulous to him.

"She is not like this on our world. Only when we are on other planets does she show this side of herself."

"All the more reason."

A soldier from his armada came up and whispered into his ear. Annoyance spread on his face.

"I must go. Will I see you at the evening eating party?"

"Yes, my mate and I will be there."

"I didn't ask about her."

Halfar turned and left Chardon alone on the balcony.

Halfar could still remember how soft and smooth Chardon's hair felt. He wondered why he thought of that day in particular and knew the instant after thinking it. Their minds were linked meaning Chardon had remenbered as well not too long ago. Laying his hand on his chest he took a few deep breaths. Thinking of Chardon made his blood race.

Pregnancy made Jaron moodier than usual so everyone, except Modas, steered clear of her. She had a tendency to hiss at anyone who came near her. Modas was not affected in any way by this. He still stole kisses from her and climbed atop her in the middle of the night, with her protesting at every turn.

Jaron could not fathom why she did all this. She loved her mate more than life and cared deeply for her race but her emotions were all over the place. It didn't help that she felt heavy from carrying Modas' litter inside of her. There would be four, possibly five, little ones with either Modas' traits or hers. The thought made her smile a little. She felt the presence of some children nearby and turned to give them an icy cold stare. They stopped dead in their tracks, eyes wide, then ran from her. That also made her smile but in a mischievous way.

"You need more nourishment than that."

Ganna stood beside her, pointing to the small bowl of raw fruits and vegetables on the ground by her feet.

"Yes, yes, I know that. This is just to hold me over until sunset meal." Jaron grabbed a fruit and took a big bite out of it, chewing noisily. "It's a good thing they are tiny little creatures because I could not haul them around like this feeding them constantly."

"You make it sound so unbearable." Ganna clucked at her. "Really, Jaron."

Swallowing a chewed up chunk of fruit, Jaron replied, "I know."

A look of sorrow replaced the frustration on her face.

Why do I act this way and say things I don't mean?

From the other side of her, a plate of steaming meat simmering in its juices was laid next to the bowl of produce by Modas. He stepped away and sat down on the grass nearby, waiting for her to eat it. There would be no argument about it. Jaron used her fingers to tear apart a piece of meat and put it in her mouth.

"Well, I will let you enjoy that wonderful offering of nutrients from your beloved mate."

As Ganna walked away, Jaron slid a glare at Modas. He didn't register it. She sighed and continued to eat the meat along with the fruits and vegetables. Both sat in silence, neither moving from their positions.

"Why do you even put up with me?"

Jaron asked with a mouth full of food.

"You mean everything to me."

Modas came forward and kissed her deeply. At the last moment, she turned, pulling away from him. Immediately, she hated doing that. He could probably tell by the way she tried to act like nothing happened and continued to eat.

"See you at home."

Jaron gave birth to five little ones. Three were tiny balls of fur not yet ready to uncurl and open their eyes, and two were smooth skinned crying infants. She kept them close to her body for warmth, shooing Modas away whenever he came to try picking any of them up. Some days her level of territorialism was high, other times she would wave Modas away with them as if they were a bother.

As the little balls of fur uncurled, she could see their tiny noses, tightly shut eyelids and partial mouths. They resembled baby hedgehogs she had seen on Earth. Their fur ran from the top of their heads to their feet. Once they start growing, the fur would recede up to the middle of their spines.

Jaron wanted them to open their eyes so she could see what color they were. Usually, the entire litter had the same eye color but it's never a guarantee. She hoped they had Modas' eyes.

Chardon watched the workers carefully move the three vessels into the cryochamber and place the cores inside. Depending on how well the vessels could regenerate determined how long it would take for them to fully awaken. Two were badly mutilated and the other was partially scorched. It would take some time but he knew their cores were strong. Those three were necessary to revive in the first wave because he needed them as warriors.

Swiping his hand gently across the chambers, he whispered, "Your arrival will be a much-celebrated event, young ones."

With that, Chardon left the medical bay for sunset meal.

THREE:

Tribulations

Government sectors fell instantly in the North American region. Kur's enforcers laid waste to entire districts as a warning to officials who dared defy Halfar. An invisible barrier had been erected that enclosed strategic areas of the continent for easy targeting. It was safe to assume that the next country would not fare well against Halfar's armada and yet he drug out the assault for the sake of entertaining his generals with new missions to conquer. But, even they began to tire of them.

"Maybe we should just leave this place and send a planet destroyer," Rass stated. He appeared to be up to the task.

"How tasteless." Kur shook his head in disgust. "That would not be dignified."

"Your aesthetics towards bloodshed are getting tiresome."

Both drew weapons with one hand and morphed the other arm into pincers. As the clashing of hard shells rang through the halls, Halfar ended it.

"Enough!" He was irritable at best and had no tolerance for their foolish taunting. "What are the reports from the inner city?"

Rass sheathed his weapon and bowed to him, his arm reverting to normal.

"The people outside of the district are unaware of the chaos. Dealers are still making a profit, they just have no idea where the merchandise is coming from."

"Good. Let's keep it that way for the next few months."

"Are we not moving the timetable up?" Kur seemed baffled.

"There is no rush."

Halfar assumed his usual lounging position on his throne. Kur glance at Rass who shrugged and they went to dispatch more enforcers to a region three states over, per his previous instructions. At least they were being kept busy for now.

✲

Modas reached into the sandbox and picked up the rowdy fur ball by its midsection. It curled around his hand trying to make itself into a ball again. He carried it over to the climbing rock: a black monolith that reached towards the heavens and planted it on the surface. Tiny claws came out to grab onto the rock.

"Now, use up that energy of yours with this." He watched the little one sniff at the rock and readjust its claws. "Go on." It inched upwards a bit, making a trill coo sound, then went a little more. "I will call you Trinon." His son turned towards him and cooed again in approval. Modas smiled. They were so much fun when that tiny.

"What are you doing?" Jaron came screaming towards him.

"He was terrorizing his siblings."

"So you stick him on that giant monolith so he can get hurt?"

"He's not hurt." Trinon lost his grip and fell onto the ground with a high-pitched yelp. "Oh."

Modas saw blood on his tiny claws as Trinon mewed in pain, rolling around back and forth.

Jaron glared at him as she picked up her tiny son and held him close to her breast.

"Monster."

"Hmm." Modas checked the claws. "He will learn how to do it without falling."

"When he's older!"

"He's fine."

Trinon was already struggling to get out of his mother's grasp.

"Did you name him?"

"Trinon."

She picked him up and held him high while he still squirmed. He could see her emotions going haywire again but knew she understood that Trinon would be protected like his siblings. The little one was feisty to say the least. She reluctantly handed him over and went back to tend to the others. Modas raised him in the air the same way she had done. Trinon liked it even less.

Modas brought all of the little ones to the fields so they could roll around as they pleased while he and Jaron kept watch. The weak sun was at its brightest time of day. The sound of them cooing made them both happy and they stared in awe. Sensing someone coming near their spot and they both looked out to see who it was.

And sat stunned.

A young manbeast in workers robes walked slowly towards the fields. He was nearly six feet seven inches tall with dark brown hair parted in the middle at the top and cascaded down his back. His full lips he inherited from his mother and his eyes, a deep shade of metallic silver, from his father.

As he got closer, seeing the shock on their faces, he realized Chardon had not informed them of his arrival.

"Well, I see you have replaced me with a new litter already." He laughed. Jaron and Modas did not. "I'm joking." Tears welled up in Jaron's eyes. "Please, don't do that."

Trinon rolled into his foot so he stooped down to pick him up by his midsection. He held him up high and grinned at the squinty eyed rebellious face.

"Mota." Was all Jaron could say.

"At least you remember my name." He set Trinon back down.

"That's not funny."

"Sorry." He went to her and hugged her tight. "I didn't think I would ever see you again."

"Nor I." Jaron cried into his chest.

Her face showed hope that it wasn't a dream, glad it was not.

Modas stood with his hands clinched tight into fists. He did not know what to do or say. One of their children, known to be dead, was standing here in front of them. It was too much to bear. Mota looked over and grinned. Mota always had that face even in bad times. He took things in stride and not too seriously. When Jaron finally disengaged, Modas hugged him.

"My apologies for not telling you sooner." Chardon said loudly as he came up the hill to stand next to them and bowed humbly.

"You conniving…" Modas stopped Jaron from advancing towards him, arm raised.

"I thought you would be happy."

"That's not the point!"

"Isn't it?" Chardon stepped closer to her. Jaron lowered her arm. "Even you cannot be so heartless as to suggest he is not wanted."

"There is more. You need to tell them, Chardon," Mota said while taunting Trinon in the sandbox.

"Stop that!" Jaron commanded him. She turned to Chardon. "What else is there?"

"We were able to find two other vessels of your children. They are still regenerating. Mota seemed to recover faster than we hoped."

"Of course he did," Modas said matter of fact.

"I was a bit of a mess, though. My last memory was not pleasant."

"Speaking of which, I need to get you up to speed. Can you swear to no retaliation on your part?" Chardon was being serious now.

"Retaliate? Against who?" Mota snorted.

"Let's just say, your mother and father do not agree with my decision."

Mota glanced from mother to father, questioning them silently. Modas was aware how apparent their anger was regarding it.

"I can't say that, but I will hear what you have to say."

"Good, follow me."

Mota flicked Trinon's tiny nose hard and laughed when he mewed in pain. Toying with the little ones was a fun past time of his. The others rolled away or crawled from him but Trinon was not backing down and Modas felt he would suffer for it.

"Mota!" Jaron went to soothe Trinon.
"Sorry." He left the room with Chardon.
"Will he be just as angry as we are?" Jaron asked.
"Probably not." Modas knew his son well.
"I am trying to forgive them, but I will never forget."
"As it should be."
He circled her waist from behind and kissed the back of her neck.

Mirrors fascinated Halfar. Humans were so vain to care about such things as clothing and appearances. There was only one rule for his race and many others: be presentable and wash when needed. In battle there was no time for primping to impress the enemy.

He stood in front of the huge embellished oval mirror across from his bed and stared at his reflection. It occurred to him that his skin had darkened due to the intense sunlight on this planet and his hair had gotten longer with lighter streaks in it. All in all, he was more than presentable, even strikingly handsome as he heard some females say.

One who needed no help to look perfect was Chardon. Halfar thought of him more than usual lately. Perhaps due to the fact that he knew Chardon would come personally to stop his conquest of Earth. He looked forward to seeing him again as his true self, not Charles. The image of him on the balcony was replaced by a different memory.

****☼****

He could hear water swishing in the chamber ahead and knew it was Chardon's. Nearing the door, he noticed it was ajar and entered without announcement. Chardon stood in female form, naked, dripping wet from the bath. Her hair flowed down the middle of her back, stuck to the skin. The slight curves of her body were silhouetted by the sunlight entering the solitary window on the left of the chamber.

Chardon's body went stiff and she turned her head around to see him standing there with lust in his eyes. She quickly went behind the changing curtain.

"What are you doing in here? Why are you not escorted?"

She threw on a dressing robe and came from behind the curtain; the thin robe clung in certain spots where her body was still wet.

"Your guards are lacking. It was quiet, so I came to find you."

He moved further into the room until they stood inches from each other face to face. His hands ran across her breast then down. She slapped his hand away and he laughed.

"But, you like that."

"I never said such a thing."

"You didn't have to."

Halfar extended a dark red talon that curved to widen in diameter. Sunlight made it glossy in appearance and it was quite smooth. Chardon did not move as he slid the talon underneath the drape and slowly inserted it into her. He watched her shudder.

"Submit to me."

Her stare glazed over and he removed his talon, glistened with her juices, from inside. He watched her gaze shift to the wetness between her thighs and attempt to wipe it away, her hand stopping short.

"Don't." She pleaded.

He grabbed her face with both hands and kissed her passionately. She tried to push him away, fearful someone might come through the door he left ajar. Then she returned his advances in kind. They exchanged breaths for what seemed like an eternity until they heard movement down the hallway. She wrenched from him, a tiny tendril of saliva briefly connecting them.

"You need to go." Chardon went further into her chamber to change back into male form and dress in council robes.

Ganna and four manbeasts came into the chamber, surrounding him. He felt a smile form on his lips as one of the manbeasts gestured for him to vacate the room. Ganna seemed annoyed by his expression. As Halfar was escorted out, he turned to see Chardon come out to follow them, as if nothing had happened. Still somewhat damp but always beautiful, Halfar thought to himself.

He averted his gaze from the mirror, turning around to sit on the mantle below, letting his weight settle against it.

"Come quickly, I don't how much more I can endure."

"Is something so dire that it needs to be endured?"

Kur's voice broke his thoughts.

He was standing in the doorway of Halfar's chamber and this disturbed Halfar greatly. Kur had never done such a thing without expressed permission.

"Why have you come through my hall and now stand at my chamber door?" His hostility was duly noticed.

"You were not in the throne room, so I felt concerned for your well- being."

"Do not condescend me!"

Halfar pushed himself off the mantle blocking the doorway.

"I get the feeling you are not taking this conquest seriously, my lord."

The last part was spat out.

"Are you questioning my strategy?"

"I am merely trying to figure out what it is that you hope to accomplish by stalling this." Kur stepped back into the hall. "What are you waiting for?"

"A resolution." Halfar closed the double doors, not before seeing Kur's narrowed stare.

Severing the bond between Halfar and himself would have been ideal, if he knew how, but at the same time, Chardon didn't want to break it. Currently, the shared memories had become a nuisance, creeping up on them even though they were worlds apart. Halfar catching him off guard in his chamber was not something he wanted to think about right now while he sat with the council discussing battle strategies.

"Are you not satisfied with the plan, Chardon?" A council member was staring at him in concern.

"Yes, it sounds fine. We just need to fine tune it so that the number of casualties is kept to a minimum. I would prefer none, if possible."

"There is no guarantee of that when it comes to battle, Chardon."

"I know. Find a way, regardless."

As the meeting adjourned he caught Modas' sight locked on him. He sighed heavily and tried to avoid any probing questions from the manbeast.

"Yes, I was thinking about Halfar. How many warriors will you have by the next moon?"

Modas noticed the quick change in topic and decided to wait to have his questions answered.

"It seems to be around twenty, give or take."

"Will Mota have his own to command?"

"That is the reason you revived him."

"That is not the only reason, Modas." Chardon was angry. To know that is what Modas and Jaron thought of his actions pained him. "I understand your hurt and wanted to alleviate it, even just a little."

"I know. I am sorry."

"If only things had been done differently."

"Do you think our race would have been saved if you had submitted to Halfar?"

"The way he was then, no. But, we would have had a fighting chance to turn the tables. We would have had a choice."

Mota sat on a tree stump lost in thought, not hearing or noticing his mother coming his way. She stopped a few feet away. He could feel the question coming from her body language. It was not that he wanted justice, or anything like it, he wanted peace. Causing such conflicts with their own race never made sense. On the battlefield was different.

"I understand why you are so angry, mother, but it does not change what has occurred. We must move forward." He turned to make eye contact with her. "Please. Let it be."

His mother's hands balled into fists and she bit down on her lower lip, fighting back tears. He sensed her rage for his refusal to agree with her on the matter. Even though he was asking as her son to forgive he acknowledged that she could not do that, it was not justice in her mind.

"I am still here." Mota could read her body language. "Yes, only three of us survived. Are we not good enough?" Jaron's head snapped back, and her gaze went wide. "You know what I mean, mother."

Tears streamed down her face as she stood frozen. He regretted saying it and went to her, pulling her close to him. She did not return the gesture as he knew she wouldn't. He always wondered why she did not like showing affection, physical or otherwise.

✳✳☼✳✳

Kelin slowly eased up out of bed so not to disturb Talas who was still sleeping. Cold air hit his naked body, making him shudder. The window had been left open all night and even though the morning sun shined, the room was cold. He was tempted to crawl back into bed and steal Talas' body heat for a few more moments. They were both exhausted from mating during the night, possibly overdoing it since their last time together. He leaned over towards Talas and kissed his cheek.

A knock on the chamber door made him realize that they had missed the council meeting.

"Stay a moment!" He called out as he grabbed his robes, dressing quickly. Opening the door revealed Ganna looking moody.

"My apologies, Ganna. I overslept."

"Both of you?" She was a little testy indeed.

From the bed, Talas rose to sit on his knees, his back to them.

"What time is it?"

His speech was slurred from sleep. His pale, bare skin flushed with heat from being under the covers and his hair a tangled mess.

Ganna grimaced at the sight. She did not have the same admiration for their mating as she did Modas and Jaron. He resented the fact that something about the two of them copulating made her skin crawl. Even when Talas was in female form, which was rare, it seemed to irk Ganna. Talas was stunningly pretty but had an air about him that did reek of dishonesty.

"Chardon would like you both to come to his chamber for a briefing since the council was not important enough for the two of you to attend."

"Mmm." Talas's back arched letting his hair brush across the bed covers behind him. He turned his head sideways towards her. "Is that a hint of sarcasm?"

"If you would please make it there at your earliest convenience."

"I feel good." He shook his hair out, sighing. "Thank you, my love."

Kelin blushed with embarrassment as he saw Ganna get angry and storm out of the room.

"Why do you torment her like that?" He went over to the bed and stroked his spine. Talas leaned further back and kissed him. "You really are such a menace."

"But you love me all the same." Talas stretched forward like a cat and moaned looking over his shoulder. "We should go before lord Chardon finds us uncooperative."

"Don't do that. We are indebted to him for letting us stay on this planet with what is left of our race. You know, the one we betrayed for nonexistent glory."

"Yes, yes. I am eternally grateful." Kelin raised an eyebrow. "Truly."

"Get dressed. I'll wait for you."

"No bath first?" Talas pouted.

"No time." He pulled Talas off the bed and dragged him behind the changing curtain.

Chardon had his arms folded in front of him, a gesture he learned while on Earth to make him look more important, or so he thought. Talas and Kelin poured over the plans with such intensity that Chardon was almost impressed. Thinking about why their race had to go through this in the first place because of them, squashed that sentiment.

"So, you want us to be separate from each other during this little insurgence."

Talas looked up from the hologram plans on the table. Chardon did not fully trust them yet and his strategy said as much.

"You each have unique talents that would be beneficial on different fronts as opposed to in one sector. This is not punishment as you think."

"Halfar will be waiting," Kelin stated. "The throne room is such an open space. There's nowhere to hide if a fight breaks out. Are you sure going straight in is a good idea?"

"He may be waiting but his minions would never suspect it."

"How bold, and almost insane, of you, Chardon." Talas was not in agreement.

"I will not cower in fear of him."

"Yes, but marching in for a fight is not very delicate."

"You sound like Kur." Kelin said incredulous.

"Well, we do have certain aesthetics in common. I will acknowledge that."

"I'll have Mota back you up near the side of the palace," Chardon announced.

"Charming," Talas rolled his eyes.

"Talas!" Kelin winced as he yelled it.

Chardon undid his arms and watched them argue for a bit. They did work like a well-oiled machine together but there lay the problem; they influenced the other's judgment too easily. Keeping them separate during the battle was Ganna's intuition and Chardon had to concur.

"Enough." He didn't yell and was just as effective. "I will trust you as much as you trust in me."

Chardon got up to leave.

"What if we don't?" Talas was just being hypothetical, but he still didn't like it.

"Then we have a problem, don't we?"

"We do trust you, Chardon. Talas is just being, well, Talas." Kelin shrugged.

"It's not funny." Chardon left.

Kelin shook his head at Talas.

"Again, why?"

There was no reason for it, the way he antagonized Chardon by throwing distrust around.

"I wanted to see how far he would let it go. Relax, he knows I was kidding." Kelin's face said he wasn't so sure. "That frontal assault still bothers me. We know that throne room and even with Modas with him, it will get more than a little hairy." Kelin raised an eyebrow again. "No pun intended."

"You were on Earth too long. A pun, really?" Kelin settled back down to scan the hologram again. "You're right though. It is a bold maneuver. So bold that it makes me wonder if Chardon has an ulterior motive."

"Your theory again?"

"Something about the negotiations did not sit well with me after the fact. To destroy an entire world and its race on a whim because its leader would not submit is extreme. Chardon is hiding something and Modas knows what it is."

Jaron could not believe that another one her children lay in a cryochamber almost completely regenerated. Her daughter, Mara, whose body had been scorched black on the entire right side, was asleep with new skin. She watched her bare bosom move up and down, wishing she could reach into the chamber and feel the warmth of her body. Her daughter's light brown hair was splayed around her head like a giant fan, her long body lean with muscle. She was nearly as tall as Mota minus two inches. The air from her partially opened pink lips fogged the glass.

On the opposite side was her eldest son's vessel also in a cryochamber but, she could not bear to watch his regeneration. His body had been blown apart, so the medics arranged the pieces as best they could to resemble a full body. The regeneration was nearly complete with only a few body parts needing to reattach themselves. As his mother it especially hurt to see.

Mota strode in with Trinon wrapped around an arm, the little one's tiny teeth embedded in his forearm. It was obviously in retaliation for whatever torture Mota had subjected him to.

"Is my sister not ready to grace us with her presence?"

He reached over his mother and rapped the glass. Trinon disengaged for a moment to view his older sister then resumed trying to inflict pain on Mota who just laughed at him.

"What have you done to him?" She pulled Trinon off Mota's arm. "And don't hit the chamber!"

"I'm sure she doesn't mind." He glanced over at Trinon. "He's just sensitive. I didn't do anything that I haven't done already."

"That's the problem."

"He's getting bigger, you know. You can't treat him like a baby beast much longer."

Jaron held Trinon to her and he immediately found his way into her robes and latched on a breast to feed, his tiny claws just barely sinking into her flesh.

"He's a little greedy, too," Mota laughed.

Jaron rolled her eyes at him.

"So were you." She saw even Trinon gave him a woeful look between suckling. "Why just him?"

Mota stood up straight still staring down at his sister.

"Because, he's stronger than you think."

He walked off and yelled over his shoulder, "Tell the lazy one to wake up already."

Jaron sighed and tickled Trinon behind his ear. He did have a strong grip, maybe too strong. In another year he will be walking and trying to climb that behemoth of a mountainside. She was amazed that it had also been transported from their home world.

Looking down on Trinon, she knew he would need training to curb that urge to outdo everyone. She remembered assisting with her daughter's training and how the poor girl tried too hard by conjuring up energy to impress the elders.

The smell of sea water and beast invaded her senses. Modas had been meditating by the waterfall earlier and must have just finished. He was damp from misty spray that made the outline of his body shimmer in the sunlight. Jaron felt the pull of lust but refrained from showing it even a little by glowering at him. As usual, Modas was not convinced.

"Finally came to see how your children are doing?"

"We have more than three now," was all he said.

"If it were up to you, we would have four or five litters running around."

"We'll have another soon enough."

"What makes you think I would have another litter with you?"

Jaron tried to sound angry but it came out in a quivering voice. She cursed herself. Modas did not answer.

Instead, he went over to the other side to check on their eldest still regenerating. It didn't bother him at all to see his son like that. Jakar was just as strong as his father so she assumed that's why Modas had no worries. A small chunk of flesh merged into a body part near the ribcage and healed the skin, leaving no marks. It was only a matter of time before he awakened.

Trinon's soft mewing could be heard throughout the room and Modas swung around in his seat just in time to see Trinon falling asleep in Jaron's arms. In those few moments, Jaron became filled with love and affection. Of the five, he was the fussiest, angriest, most sensitive and the strongest. Jaron knew Modas was playing favorites, but he also had great plans for this one. Unlike, Mota, who was just tormenting the little one, he was going to train him properly.

Feeling her mate's stare, she tensed up. She had let her guard down. It was so easy to do when she was nursing one of their young. With not much fanfare, she wiped the excess milk off the breast Trinon had been suckling as if disgusted and covered herself back up. Looking up, she saw a wall of fabric as Modas leaned down to kiss the top of her head softly.

She did not even hear him move from across the room.

"You should rest."

He could somehow always tell when she was tired.

"I will." Jaron began to stand but faltered from fatigue. "I guess I need a little help."

She did not fight him.

He picked her up while she still held the sleeping Trinon and carried her to their chamber.

Regrets

So many, Chardon spoke in his head as he combed the memorial site for the dead.

Whole families had been annihilated with no one to remember them, making the count inaccurate. Out of the corner of his vision he spotted Modas carrying Jaron to their housing. The one thing Chardon regretted most was that someone knew his secrets. He wished they had been buried in the memorial with all the other lost souls.

"I'm so sorry," he whispered to the dead.

"Why should you be sorry?" Kelin startled him. "There was nothing you could have done to prevent such a tragedy."

"True, but I like to think that I could have in some way."

Chardon's expression changed, and he realized too late it was a mistake to let Kelin notice. By the way Kelin stared at him he was probably thinking yes, maybe it could have been prevented regardless of their foolish stunt opening the gate.

"Whatever Halfar promised was all lies. You were right not to submit to his demands. We would all be slaves right now."

"Maybe."

Chardon turned and walked away from the memorial grounds.

☼

Rass was already walking faster than normal to keep up with Halfar who nearly sped down the hall to the battle room where Kur was waiting for him. The large entourage also struggled with Halfar's pace. He could tell just how angry his lordship was by the exposed, half formed, exoskeleton sections protruding from his skin. He had to do something, quickly.

"My lord!"

"I will not be made a mockery of by my own subordinates!"

"My lord!" Halfar was about to turn the corner that led to the battle room's hallway. "Stop!"

Everyone in the entourage halted; the enforcers stunned, Halfar incredulous. He turned slowly and walked back to where Rass stood in the middle of the hall.

"Did you just command me to stop?" Halfar had one arm formed into a claw.

"Please, my lord, come walk with me." Something in the way he said it made Halfar pause. "I need you to listen to me right now before you go in there."

"Everyone stand and wait," he ordered and walked with Rass.

"I know how frustrated you are with Kur and his solo antics, but that is what he wants. The more riled up you get the better his case to eliminate you. I know why you are stalling and I wish you success."

"Do you?" Halfar stopped walking and face him. "My success would mean leaving the Armada behind to live on whatever world she is in."

"Conquering Earth was not your idea, it was Kur's and now not even he wants to be on this wretched rock. The invasion will grind to a halt and then we leave."

"So, if I were to storm into the battle room in a rage."

"Kur would have his enforcers cut you down without so much as a witness to his treachery. It would be…glorious. His words, not mine."

"Then what would you have me do?"

"I can handle Kur. You just need to focus on your agenda."

Halfar relented and slapped a hand on Rass' shoulder.

"Even if I give you the reigns of the armada, he would fight you to the death for it."

"And I will make sure that I win so you can return our race to its true calling."

"You loved him once."

"But, he loves himself more than he ever loved me."

"Now what?"

Halfar removed his hand and there they stood alone with no guards while Kur waited for a fight to come to him.

"You go to your chamber and I will inform Kur of your displeasure."

"Can you really defeat him?"

"You, more than anyone, know the power I keep hidden."

"That is not what I mean, Rass."

He probed his face for acknowledgement.

"I know. Yes, I can, if it is the only way to stop him from pitching our race into ruin." He headed towards the battle room. "Go, my lord." He bowed deeply mid stride and continued on.

Halfar began to realize just how deadly the situation had become. Kur was now the enemy and there was no letting his guard down for a second. It always bothered him that Kur was near whenever he didn't want him to be. There was a way to avoid him and that meant going out into the streets incognito. He knew Rass would help him with the logistics of it.

"Well, Kur, let's see how well you fare against me."

A small troop arrived to escort him to his chamber hall. As they marched onward, Halfar had a vicious plan in store for Kur when the time came. No one defied him and got away with it. He slowed his walk as he thought about it and how that logic applied to Chardon. No, that was entirely different. His bond with Chardon was eternal, his connection to Kur was based on military might.

In his chamber, he stripped off his battle gear and robes to stand naked in the middle of the room. The cool air engulfed his body and he stretched upward. Crawling onto the bed, his thoughts drifted to Chardon on a faraway world he had yet to find.

⚙

Somewhere off in the distant fields, Kelin attempted to clear his mind by hunting small game with an archaic handmade projectile weapon likened to a crossbow. Although the creatures on their new home were a bit strange, the meat was somewhat similar in taste to what he was used to. Keeping his thoughts away from the topic of battle plans and Chardon was his goal for the day.

He saw something scurry on his right and swung the weapon towards the sound, releasing the metal rod. A soft squeal and a thump came right after. It was the fourth one today which was enough for Talas and himself. Each chamber had to fend for themselves food wise twice a moon cycle. Evening meal captured, Kelin headed back home.

Talas was waiting for him as he entered the chamber. His long dirty blonde hair was slightly wavy from being damp after bathing without Kelin. He sat cross legged on the bed with a hologram of the revised battle plans in front of him. The look on Talas' face made Kelin want to turn around and go back into the fields.

"This is not looking like an easy exit for our little groups," Talas blurted.

"Please. I just want a quiet evening with you and not talk about any of this or Chardon for that matter." He plopped their supper on the cut- ting block in the kitchenette.

"Why are you bringing up Chardon?" Then he remembered. "Ahh, your theory."

"A bit more than a theory. I think Chardon feels far more responsible for what happened than we do. I just can't seem to figure it out and there is no way Modas will ever tell me what he knows."

"Modas," Talas climbed off the bed to stand by him, "will never tell you anything, let alone speak to you unless it was necessary."

"I know."

"Then let it run its course. You will find out what's really going on, soon enough."

"Yet, I get the feeling you already know what's going on. Why are you feigning ignorance?"

"Because there is no point. And I know you would rather find out on your own as opposed to me just laying it out for you."

"True, but I still think you could at least give me a hint."

Talas eyed Kelin's bundle of dead meat and smirked.

"And what are we having with that?"

"That is your duty, I hunted them."

"I don't think hunt is the word for such tiny creatures."

Kelin washed his hands in the basin behind the changing curtain then flopped down on the bed exhausted. The topper molded around his body and he started to drift off into sleep when Talas whacked him on the thigh.

"You're filthy! Go bathe at least!"

He forcibly pushed Kelin out of the bed. They both laughed.

A loud screech filled the chamber forcing Jaron and Modas to wake from their midday slumber and run to the sandbox that housed the little ones. One of the male baby beasts, Und, had Trinon by the face with his tiny claws and a look of frustration. The screech had come from him as a battle cry. Trinon had Und by the mane, refusing to let go until his opponent yielded.

"Stop that!"

Jaron could not believe the scene before her. The others just laid there in the sandbox watching with disinterest like this was an everyday ordeal, and it was to some degree. Modas had stopped at the edge of the sandbox and kneeled. He too had the same look. She reached in and tried to disengage them.

"Let go this instant!"

Mota came from behind her, flicked both of them hard on the head and drew Trinon out. The little ones wailed loudly, tears and blood on their faces. It was clear who the aggressor had been. Trinon wiggled all over the place in an effort to get out of Mota's clutches without success. When Mota turned him over, Trinon bit into the meat of his bicep. It didn't hurt him in the least.

"Why is this happening?" Jaron demanded of Mota, knowing he was to blame. "And why are you doing nothing?" This was directed at Modas who just glanced up at her.

"Have you forgotten what it was like when I was a baby beast?" Mota smiled.

"That is not the issue!"

Modas picked up Und by the back of his mane and turned him so they were nose to nose. Und stopped crying and mewed at him.

"Good." He set his son back down in the sandbox with his other siblings. "He's a fighter."

Jaron was on the verge of imploding with rage. She leaned over towards Modas and slapped him in the back of his head then turned on Mota, doing the same. They both were stunned into submission as she stormed out of the chamber.

"Father, I believe we must start training them sooner than later. Mother is not about to tolerate much more disobedience." Modas nodded in agreement, holding the back of his neck.

Halfar was not lounging lazily on his throne today as Kur had antici-pated. The great ruler seemed to avoid him at all costs, always sending Rass to do his bidding. Kur made a grunting sound of disgust. Ever since he had rejected Rass' affections, his counterpart had become one of Halfar's lapdogs, confirming his initial thoughts about him. Wiping that out of his mind he focused on Halfar seated on his throne looking as menacing as he once was, tapping a clawed finger on the arm rest.

"Are your enforcers in place?"

Kur nearly stepped backwards at the onslaught of the question.

"Almost, my lord." Halfar was not in the mood for games. "We are positioning a small team on their blind side to ensure coverage."

"That's good to hear. And?"

"My lord?" Kur was confused.

"Why have you come here? Surely it was not to report that you are in fact not ready? What other reason did you have to see me at this time of day?"

Kur had in fact come to irritate him for the pleasure of it but now that he had been called out on it, he was not too confident in doing so.

"I was worried since you had not been to the battle room in some time and sending Rass with your instructions."

"Is not Rass a General such as yourself?"

"Of course. I was not questioning your motives." He bowed low. "I shall take my leave to finish the preparations." As he left cursing under his breath, he made a detour to the battle room.

"Well, that went smoothly."

Rass came out from behind the double doors of Halfar's hallway.

"I wanted to rip one of his limbs off."

"As you said, he is one of your Generals."

"Why is he, suddenly, so insubordinate? I don't understand."

"Simple. He is just as bored as you are and wants to engage in a real fight."

"A real fight means going against an unknown foe leading to casualties we cannot afford."

"Yes, that last battle saw our armada nearly cut in half. Luckily no one knows this, not even Kur." Rass' lip twitched into an almost sheepish smile.

"There is no reason for Kur to return to our home world and find out either. What is the status of our soldiers?"

"There are currently two thousand in the birthing tanks. This is the second batch and the third will be ready in under ten years." Halfar nodded. "It seems as you destroyed one world, our fate was sealed with the near destruction of your own."

Halfar stepped down from his throne to floor level.

"Which is why I want to make things right again. I wish you would stay with me when I find what world Chardon is on."

"I could not live with that race." Rass laughed.

"Why not?"

"I like things a bit messy."

"Hmm. You're right, it's not a good idea. The moment they open a vortex, trace it before closes. I need to be able to get there shortly after."

"As you command, my lord."

With a low bow Rass was gone. His boots echoed in the hall.

✱✱☼✱✱

Mota carried Trinon by the mane swinging him lightly like a small sack as he strolled towards the giant rock monolith covered in claw marks from generations of manbeasts scaling it. As he neared it, he swung upwards towards the rock and released Trinon who went smack into it, his claws scrambling to grab a hold.

There were strange whimpering sounds along with the scraping of claws on stone then heavy breathing from tiny nostrils. Trinon had managed to secure himself on the monolith. Mota threw his head back and laughed so loud that some of the workers in the distance popped their heads up looking around for where it came from.

"That's not very nice, brother."

His sister, Mara, walked slowly down the hill. A tiny grin spread on her face. She was wearing a sleeveless grey robe over a long sleeved white one that flowed to the ground causing small whirlwinds.

"But look at him! It's amusing to see him struggle."

"You know, just because you were tormented as a baby beast does not give you license to do the same with our little siblings."

"What do you know? You were not born a manbeast." He wagged his finger at her.

"That did not stop any of you from trying even though I am older than you."

"But not older than Jakar."

Mara frowned. Their older brother was not yet ready to be awakened. She had peeked into the cryochamber and nearly gasped in horror.

"He's almost complete, you know," she whispered.

"Why is everyone so sad? He's much stronger than any of us so let's not fool ourselves into thinking he will need some sort of pampering."

Mota watched Trinon inch his way up.

"That's not what I meant! Mota, you exasperate me." She moved a lock of hair that the breeze had whipped into her eyes. "I would have said the same if it was you in there."

"I WAS in there, sister." He turned to her with softened eyes. "This was not supposed to be this way. I understand how you feel, I really do."

They hugged each other for a brief moment, disengaging when they heard a yelp followed by a thud. Trinon had fallen.

"He is adorable." She knelt next to him. "Look at that face!"

"I know, right?" Mota stood by her and they both watched Trinon wiggle to and fro on the ground until he came up on all fours. His eyes burned with anger and he shook his whole body to get rid of dirt imbedded in his fur. "I can't wait until he starts walking."

Modas stood nearby watching them torment Trinon and did nothing to alleviate him from their idea of entertainment. He couldn't wait either. Many plans went through Modas' head regarding the training he would have his children endure. He nodded his head and sighed.

Ganna couldn't stand to see anymore of Talas' amazing fighting skills. It irked her to no end that he was so good at battle, yet his personality reeked like a long dead animal carcass. What made it worse was that he smiled whenever he defeated an opponent.

"Narcissistic pig." She muttered under her breath the phrase she had learned during her stay on Earth.

"What was that, my sweet?"

Talas had not quite heard her, but he knew it was directed at him.

"I am not your sweet."

"No," Talas moved towards her, "you certainly are not."

"Stay away from me, you…"

Talas grinned. "Betrayer? Coward? Tell me what you think I am, Ganna." He swung his long sword with ease letting it stop short of her chest. She refused to play his game and left.

She heard his older sparring partner chastise him.

"You know, that behavior is not gaining you any points. We all wonder if you are capable of turning against us again."

"Let me make this clear, I will NEVER betray my kind again. That lesson has been learned in the harshest way." Talas returned to him. "Let's continue. I have a battle coming up in a years' time."

Ganna frowned. *I hope you get gutted like an animal*, she cursed him.

Secrets

Her body arched high above the bed as her hands dug deeper into herself. A sharp intake of breath was the result of her fingers finding that one spot inside, making her juices flow out to drip onto the bed coverings below her. Beads of sweat covered her entire body. She thrashed about for a split moment letting out a high-pitched noise. In her mind she was being so brutally violated yet could not stop herself from the ecstasy it gave her. She could feel his large member penetrating her without mercy.

"Chardon?" A female voice called from the doorway, muffled by the closed entry.

Her body froze, hands still deep between her thighs. She eased back down flat onto the bed.

"Are you awake? The council has called a meeting. I am here to escort you."

"Yes," Chardon managed to breathe out loudly. "Please stay a moment."

She flung the covers away and went behind the changing curtain to wipe herself down with water. There was no time for a bath. Taking a deep breath, she forced her body to shift back into male form.

Once complete, Chardon yanked on his council robes and stepped out into the room. He looked around to make sure there was no evidence and saw the bed drenched in sweat and other fluids he did not want to name. Throwing the covers back onto the bed to cover the mess, he headed out the door where his escort waited for him. He felt exhausted. Thinking of Halfar did that to him.

****☼****

Halfar jolted from sleep, sitting up in a fog of images as he tried to slow down his heavy breathing. What he experienced, in what he thought was a dream, took most of the energy out of him. He remembered the last time he mated with Chardon and it was nothing so intense as that. It wasn't the fact that he could feel, but also see what Chardon was doing while she remembered.

His bed was drenched, he could feel it and he knew Chardon's was even more so. If he knew what world Chardon was on right now, he would go there and drag her by that soft hair of hers back to his palace to have his way with her for eternity. The entire ordeal was maddening, and he knew there was no way he could think straight today; let alone command an army.

"Chardon, what are you trying to do to me?"

Wiping his wet hair from his face, he got up.

****☼****

The cryochamber on the other end of the medical facility glowed softly as energy pulsed through it. Inside, Jakar slept soundly while his core integrated with his now fully regenerated body. Above him, Modas waited patiently for him to wake up. It had been so long since he talked to his eldest son and there was so much to tell.

A beep sounded, the cryochamber's locking mechanisms sprung and the canopy slid back filling the area with icy mist. As it cleared, Modas was able to see Jakar in his entirety. The muscles began to move and slowly, his eyes opened revealing the steely blues inherited from his father.

"How was your nap?"

Jakar glanced over at him and licked his lips. They were severely cracked, and his dry tongue did nothing to cure them. Modas dipped a finger into the water basin next to him and lifted it over Jakar's mouth to let the moisture drip down. After a few drops, his son replied.

"I'm sure I was dead, so a nap is not correct." Jakar strained his muscles, forcing his upper body to sit upright. His long dark brown mane came up with him, the ends curving as they fell onto the chamber bed. "A robe would be nice." Modas grabbed the spare garments from the edge of the cryochamber and laid them on Jakar's lap. "Thank you, father."

Jakar swung his legs over the chamber's edge and stood. At six feet seven inches, he was only an inch shorter than Modas with just as much muscle only slightly leaner. He dressed in silence, making sure his hair did not get caught in the fabric of the outer robe.

"So, now you can tell me what happened."

"What do you remember?"

"Playing with Hon near the sandbox and then being blown to pieces. I do believe I watched one of my arms and a leg veer into separate directions before someone snatched my core out of me."

Modas' eyes darkened.

"Sit." He told Jakar about Talas and Kelin and the planet they were on now. Jakar listened without speaking a word or asking any questions. When Modas was done, he got up and walked out into the weak sunlight.

Mara came rushing into the medical room only to find her father sitting alone.

"Where is he?" She asked.

"Walking."

"Why?"

"I explained everything to him."

Mara lowered her eyes. "That would make sense." She dragged a seat over to where he was and sat down next to him. "Was he angry?" Modas turned to her. "Of course he is, he just doesn't show it." She laid her head on her father's shoulder.

✳✳☼✳✳

As great a fighter Talas was, he could never compare to a manbeast of Modas' descent. He watched a figure coming towards the sparring ring where he was showing off with some of the other warriors. As the figure came closer he hissed in fear, recognizing Jakar. There was no expression on the manbeast's face which meant the same as when Modas looked that way: he was angry.

Jakar was still a good two hundred meters away as Talas tried to get around one of the men to make a break for it. It was too late as he witnessed Jakar move with lightning speed towards him, knocking his body backward twenty yards from where he had stood. Jakar now stood in the previous spot Talas had occupied on the sparring platform. He jumped down from it and walked slowly to Talas who had a hard time getting up. Talas raised his good arm from underneath him, the other its shoulder dislocated from the hit. Talking his way out of it was not going to work, he knew this but still wanted to try and reason with the overpowering Jakar whose claws extended.

"Please, I know that I can never atone for my mistakes! Don't…"

Jakar's talons went through his dislocated shoulder and part of his chest like liquid but the pain was nothing so smooth. Talas let out half a scream before he thought better of it and clenched his teeth shut so hard, blood trickled from his mouth.

Jakar leaned in close to his face and whispered. "I won't kill you." He retracted the claws and stood, towering over Talas, malicious intent still in his eyes. "A reminder from me."

He walked away just as workers came running with medics. Talas watched Jakar head off into the fields. His vision started to blur as the manbeast got further away into the distance.

Kelin must have heard the ruckus going on near the sparring ring as did Ganna because both came rushing over to see the aftermath of Jakar's wrath. Kelin hurried to comfort him while Ganna examined the wound out of curiosity, nodding in approval of the mess. There was blood everywhere.

"Nicely done. The wound should heal perfectly but it will leave a scar."

Ganna had a smirk on her face that neither liked, but Talas was awe struck when Kelin backhanded her with rage.

"You filthy..!" Kelin was about to stand when a hand clamped down on his shoulder.

"No need for more violence." Chardon had arrived as well.

"I demand that he be locked in a room of solace!" Ganna shrieked, holding the side of her face. Her expression crumbled as Chardon's gaze bore down on her in disgust. Talas had never seen such a look from Chardon.

"Kelin," he redirected his eyes towards him, "go and make sure everything goes well with the medics."

As everyone dispersed, Chardon swung around to face Modas coming up the hill, in no hurry to explain, with Mara in tow. He watched their eyes follow the entourage of medics and soldiers helping Talas.

"Was my decree not clear?" He also glanced back at Ganna still on the ground.

"My apologies."

"That is not acceptable, Modas!"

Even Mara flinched from the hostility in Chardon's voice. Ganna crept further away from him.

Modas and Chardon stood face to face a few inches apart and a silent battle raged. Jaron, Mota and three council members stared at the six feet eight inches tall manbeast and their leader, who was just above six feet three, square off. Chardon's power was just as deadly as Modas' fighting skills.

"If my apology is not to your liking, we can accommodate." Modas dead panned.

"Will your children mourn you when I flay your corpse?" Chardon's eyes did not waver.

Just as they stepped back into fighting stances, Jaron and Mara threw up an energy barrier between the two. The look of fright and horror on their faces made Modas and Chardon stop. Everywhere around them, people had halted their activities ready to run if necessary. Both men felt ashamed at their display.

"I am sorry, your apology is more than enough. I know Jakar does not forgive easily." Chardon stood tall.

"Understood."

Modas retracted his claws, also straightening his stance.

Jakar came back after some thought and realized his error, witnessing the near showdown with his father and Chardon. His eyes widened with fear, then relaxed as his mother and sister put an end to it. All of this happened because he could not contain his temper. He saw Chardon, fist clenched in obvious frustration, leave the area and head towards the commons.

"My apologies, I didn't mean to cause such a mess." He bowed to his father.

"No, it's fine."

"But…"

"You did what I wanted but could not." Jaron went to him. "Because of Chardon's decree to accept them back into our good graces, we are not allowed to touch them, but you did not now this."

Jakar turned to his father. "So, I was not told everything?" Modas did not reply. "It was intentionally omitted in your recital."

"Father!" Mara spun on him. "That's irresponsible!"

"But," Mota slapped his older brother on the shoulder, "it was so worth it!" he laughed heartily.

Jakar felt a pull at the corners of his mouth.

"It did feel liberating. It was the first time I was able to use my claws since waking up."

They all laughed loudly for a moment then stopped, noticing Ganna was still there. She picked herself up feeling distraught. Seeing them, she understood her anger and meddling was petty compared to what they had gone through.

"Excuse me. I have to go check on Talas to make sure he is comfortable before surgery." Her steps were a bit unsteady, so she corrected her center of balance.

She could feel Jaron watch her with disdain. She knew the woman only tolerated her for her medical expertise but nothing more. After seeing and hearing what she had done, Jaron probably thought it served her right when Kelin knocked her around. There was no love lost between them. Ganna had lost no one important because she had always been alone. She liked it that way; sometimes.

A final backwards glance revealed Jaron stepping closer to her eldest son and craning her neck to look up at him. "This can never happen again."

Like his father, all Jakar said was, "Understood."

Feeling lower than she had ever felt in her life, Ganna made her way through the crowd surrounding Talas in the medical chamber. She shooed everyone out except two medical assistants, even forcing Kelin to leave. She set herself next to the surgeon's table Talas had been placed on.

He was pale and shaking uncontrollably but did not reflect pain in his half-closed eyelids. She knew how excruciating that wound must be but said nothing. He turned to her, his hair drenched in sweat, plastered against his cheeks. She gulped.

"Come to finish me off, my dear." His voice cracked a bit. He licked his lips, tasting his own blood.

"No, Talas. I am first and foremost a surgeon."

"Really? You seemed to be entertained by my injuries." His body shuddered.

Ganna placed a hand on the bloodied arm bent against his side.

"I apologize for that. It was wrong of me and I am ashamed. Now," she motioned an assistant to hand her the sealing tool. "This may hurt a bit since we are going to be forcing the wound closed. Are you ready?"

"Hah!" Talas took a deep breath. "You're going to have to do better than that to threaten me."

"Close the doors." She instructed the assistants.

Talas may be strong, but she guaranteed he would scream through this. A wound from a manbeast was no easy fix. Even with the doors sealed Kelin, and the others, would still hear the muffled sounds of Talas screaming. Ganna forced herself to ignore it as it rang in her ears. She continued with the operation. It would definitely leave a scar.

****☼****

Scanning the area, Halfar noticed with disdain the nearby strip mall. It never failed to make him question humans' logic when constructing those things. The concept of currency was mind boggling as well. What need was there for such a thing when you could just take what was needed.

He heard it explained before and still didn't understand why people spent it at some random smorgasbord cluster of shops in the middle of nowhere. They called it convenience. Halfar had another less tasteful name for it. Chardon would agree.

Rass came out of what looked like an abandoned building but was in fact a safe house for local dealers whenever law enforcement decided to do a crackdown. It made Halfar laugh. He marched up to Halfar and came as close as possible so he could whisper.

"Some government officials have sent spies into our territory and we caught them a few days ago. One of the spies was able to get a message out about the barrier but he was dispatched immediately after. Needless to say, our time table has been moved up unexpectedly."

"How long before they can get someone to test the rumor?"

"I say in the next 48 hours. They can't just send reinforcements, there is a protocol to go through and this just happened about five hours ago."

"Drop the barrier for seventy-two hours, starting now, just in case."

"As you command." Rass made a bow and left.

It had been awhile since he had been outside among the humans and he remembered why he stayed in his throne room. The air on Earth reeked. He could never figure out where it came from being all over, in every country. Maybe a planet destroyer would do it some good and cleanse the whole ball of wretchedness.

On his left he saw a drunk couple stagger out of a bowling alley and into the clothing store next to it and an ice cream parlor. It was two in the afternoon. Halfar shook his head in disbelief along with the human patrons who bore witness. He officially hated strip malls.

✻

Down on the ground with his weight on the balls of his feet, Chardon planted his hands deep into the soil and retched until vomit spewed from his mouth. Being so enraged had formed knots in his stomach causing nausea. Spitting the last of it out, he let his hearing focus on distance and could hear the muffled laughter of manbeasts along with Jaron and Mara. He felt played for a fool. His fists slammed into the dirt and he was ready to weep silently.

"It was bound to happen." Kelin stood a few feet from him looking haggard, his sudden appearance cutting Chardon's self-pity short.

"Was I wrong to grant the two of you lenience?"

Chardon rose, brushing dirt off his robes then wiping left over vomit and spittle from his mouth. His eyes were bloodshot, so he didn't turn around. No one needed to see their leader in such a state.

"We are grateful for it. I fear the people may not have agreed with your decision."

"How is Talas?"

"Screaming his heart out while Ganna seals his wounds."

"I am sorry."

He frowned, hearing it sounded like he was apologizing for more than just Talas. As if picking up on it, Kelin stepped closer.

"What exactly were the negotiations for back then?"

"Just like we had discussed." Chardon's eyes narrowed at the off-topic question, not liking the direct approach.

"But, you seem a little more than distraught about what happened. More so than Talas and I."

Chardon unclenched his fists and let out a heavy sigh. Keeping secrets was going to become more difficult as time went on but he was going to hold fast until there was no other alternative. Turning to face him, he moved a few steps away from Kelin to gain some distance and laid a hand on his shoulder.

"I am because as our race's leader, their lives were my responsibility, I failed everyone."

"You made a decision that you thought was right."

"And I was wrong. Possibly this time as well. But I stand by it."

"I need to go check on Talas."

Kelin went off to the medical chamber, leaving Chardon standing alone looking confused. He could tell Kelin knew he was dodging the question and it would confirm his suspicions even more.

****☼****

As the battle date grew closer, everyone did their part to make sure all preparations were underway. The population was on the verge of tripling in such a short time and the workers had found a way for the planet's soil to yield more produce. All the willing volunteers of warrior age were being trained daily and they had improved considerably. Mota watched with arms across his chest as Trinon, now a good four feet tall, clawed his way up the monolith determined to reach the top, which he was unable to do yet. The look a sheer will on his little face made Mota grin. He was a bit disappointed that Trinon was no longer small enough to be tossed against the wall anymore, but he had found other ways to torment him. Their mother had another litter so new victims were imminent for next season. He could hear their little mews even from this distance.

Back to watching Trinon, he noticed his progress had taken him halfway up. That was too far up for him. If he fell all his bones would be broken, so Mota jumped from where he stood and landed a few inches above Trinon on the wall and snatched him off. He landed on the ground below in a soft thud with Trinon tucked under one arm screeching up an angry storm.

"Not so fast, little snotter." There was literally snot coming out of his nose. Calling him that only made him yell more. "Now, what would you have done if you fell from there?"

"I can land!"

"No, you can't. I have seen the way you 'land' and it is not a pretty sight."

"Why don't you go pick on Und? He's almost a quarter of the way up!"

"Und may not be able to climb as high as you yet but he knows how to land."

Trinon pouted and tried wiggling his way out of Mota's arms. He was flicked hard in the forehead, making him yelp and bring tears to his eyes. Und stopped climbing to look their way, a dead expression on his face. He hung securely from the wall almost lazily. This apparently made Trinon jealous and angrier. He had yet to master digging his claws in deep enough to hold on like that even though he could get up quite high faster.

His thoughts were so transparent that Mota flicked him again and carried his crying bundle to the washing chamber for the little ones. Trinon was filthy, covered in gravel and sweat. He also stunk which kept Mota from bringing him forward for Jaron to see. Their mother had a sensitive nose these days. Once they entered the washing room, Mota fought trying to undress him.

The wailing between flicks and rough housing brought their mother into the chamber looking annoyed at the noise. She bent down and came nose to nose with Trinon.

"Stop it!" she hissed. Her direct stare made him stop in mid tantrum. She turned to Mota. "You better make sure he is clean, understood?" Mota also went speechless, so nodded his head. Jaron left the room.

"That was scary, huh?"

Trinon gulped and nodded. There was no more fighting while Mota washed him up except when it came to cleaning behind the ears. There was some protest.

Und came in and observed the scene from the doorway. It amused him to see the dynamic between his two brothers. He was more like their father, quiet yet fierce and that's why Mota didn't spot him on the wall much. If anyone came to check on his progress it was Jakar.

Und could see why everyone focused on Trinon. If he could master his climb and landing, he would be just as great a warrior as their father. His temper needed some work though. For such a small manbeast, Und prided himself on being more intelligent than his siblings. He sat on the dirt floor at the entrance and waited for the two of them to finish so he could take his bath alone.

Without knocking or announcing his entrance, Modas entered Chardon's chamber to find their leader soaking in the large circular basin built into the floor. It protruded up at least two feet making it four feet deep. A ledge ran the perimeter on the inside of it.

Chardon was in female form with her head thrown back and eyes closed. Her skin had an almost golden sheen to it blending with the incoming sunlight. He noticed because she was flushed with ecstasy. It made his skin crawl knowing who she thought of at that moment.

He spoke, jolting her out of her reverie.

"The council wants a meeting."

Water swished out of the basin onto the floor as Chardon abruptly sat up in surprise. Her eyes burned with anger when she turned her head to acknowledge his presence. Modas stood motionless. She eased forward out of the water, exposing her full nakedness, then leaned over to grab her covering robe on the opposite wall. Chardon never bothered to dry off and most days wringing water out of her hair was good enough.

"I really don't appreciate you coming in unannounced."

"My apologies."

"It's disrespectful and obviously intentional."

"That is not my…"

"Did you not all have a good laugh at my expense that day?"

Chardon turned around to face him from across the basin. He was back in male form.

Modas narrowed his eyes. "I did not find it amusing."

"But your family did."

He came around to the changing curtain and dressed in his council robes on top of the covering robe. He apparently had no inclination to stay with the council any longer than necessary and return to his chamber after the meeting.

"Let's go." He didn't wait for Modas to answer him.

"You trimmed your hair." Modas noticed it as Chardon came towards him to leave.

"Yes, well it would have been a nuisance during battle." With that he left the chamber.

Modas glanced at the basin. It was made by Chardon's request but had been suggested by Halfar long ago. This was the first time Modas had seen it, let alone being used.

Walking after Chardon he could tell his leader was struggling with demons of his own. Secrets were something that could tear a planet apart and he knew why he had to keep this one.

Chardon's mate was not who she had seemed. Modas wanted to kill her many times over but her reach was long in the galaxy, she made sure of that. It was all in the guise of being a loving mate to Chardon who she despised for his diplomacy. Falling in love with Halfar was probably inevitable.

Their race could not know just how horrid their beloved Sestis was and their leader being a shifter in love with the enemy who nearly destroyed them. They reached the council room and Modas took his place by the doorway to stand guard. He remembered when he had first learned of Halfar and Chardon's secret rendezvous.

****☼****

It was a late afternoon with everyone involved in the negotiations taking a much-needed rest. Modas had just finished escorting Halfar and his entourage back to the gate. The council wanted to have another session to discuss the proposals Halfar suggested and he could not find Chardon.

On a whim, he had gone to Chardon's personal chamber to see if he was in there. And Chardon was there; in female form. The fact that she was naked didn't bother him; it was the smell coming off of her, permeating the room. She seemed to have been in the process of trying to clean herself off but had passed out. Candles flickered even though it was not yet sunset.

"What have you done?"

Modas covered his nose with the sleeve of his robe. He fought the urge to gag, feeling his throat contract from nausea.

Chardon turned her glazed eyes towards him, her body still flushed with sweat from mating. She tried to sit up, her body not listening. One arm flung out from the under the bed covering to dangle on the side of the bed. Modas braved the stench to get closer to her so he could hear her speak. Her lips were moving.

"You can't..." Was what he heard.

"Something is wrong with you." He turned to leave in search of help and Chardon's iron grip held him by the wrist.

"You can't."

Her eyes pleaded with him even as he saw them go off far away and her body arched slightly on the bed. A breath sounding like a moan escaped her lips and she thrashed about for a split second from an orgasm. Mota wanted to wrench away from her, her actions tossing up more of the vile smell.

"You reek of something unnatural. You need to clean yourself off, now!"

"I'm trying."

"The council is reconvening by sunset to discuss Halfar's proposal." Modas hissed at her.

"Help me up." He yanked her out of bed and into the washing station next to the changing curtain. "I'm sorry." She whispered. "Thank you." Her eyes glanced back at him. "I'm still beautiful, am I not, Modas?" A mischievous smile crept on her lips.

"I'll wait outside." He stopped. "We have to eliminate that stench."

He knew she was not listening since now her focus was on getting clean and shifting back into her male form, his failure to answer her question forgotten. From the window he saw the field of herbs nearby and dashed out to grab a hand full.

Back in Chardon's chamber, he burned the herbs and waved them throughout every corner of the room. A small amount he didn't burn went into the wash basin Chardon was using. There was a bowl of powdered ice near the bed, so he picked it up and dumped some of it on her. Chardon stood erect from the shock and back handed Modas with such unexpected strength that he flew backwards into the wall on the opposite side of the room. The bowl and remaining ice landed on each side of him.

Chardon's body shook from the chill and rage but immediately vanished as she came to her senses. He could see the clarity return to her eyes. She finished cleaning herself off and dressed in council robes at the same time reverting into male form. It was a seamless transformation.

"You will tell no one!" He said it soft enough for Modas to hear but with an edge of anger.

"Understood." Modas wiped a trickle of blood from the corner of his mouth.

"After you," Chardon motioned towards the doorway.

His body trembled slightly.

Modas closed the door after them and helped Chardon whenever he faltered. It would have been better if he could rest until the end of the day, but the council waited.

****☼****

Pale skin ran the lines of the now closed wounds where new skin had begun to form. Talas studied every section and decided it wasn't so bad. The patterns left from the scars made them look like imprints in his skin. His admiration was witnessed by Kelin standing near the changing curtain.

"Does it make you proud to have survived the wrath of the manbeast?"

"He is right, it is a reminder but not the way he wanted. It gives me resolve." Talas twisted his naked body to get a better view in the harshly made mirror. The surface was not as clear as the ones on Earth. They made due with the resources their new planet had to offer. "Not to your liking, my beloved?"

Kelin walked over and traced the white scars with his index finger. He went around from back to front until they were face to face.

"Nothing can ever take away your beauty." He replied softly.

"How wonderful to hear." Talas encircled him in his arms and they touched foreheads.

"By the way, I was right."

"About what?"

"My theory, about Chardon."

Talas leaned back. "How do you figure?"

"He basically avoided answering my question. He is just as guilty as we are."

"You asked him outright?"

"It was a window of opportunity."

"Hmmm. I think you should have waited a bit longer."

"What secret could be so dire that even Modas has to keep it?"

Talas pulled away from him and dressing in a covering robe sat on the bed.

"Did it not seem odd to you that Chardon has not mourned the death of his beloved mate? It's as if he couldn't care less."

Kelin's eyes opened wider than normal. The idea of someone not mourning their mate seemed extreme. No matter how much you may disagree, that person was still your mate and Sestis was beloved by their people. Her core and vessel had been destroyed yet at the memorial ceremony, her name was never mentioned by Chardon or anyone else from the council.

"I think you need to figure out what is really going on. You'd think we would have had a separate mourning for Sestis by now, but we didn't. No one has brought it up yet so we all just continue forgetting about her." He saw Kelin's temple wrinkle deep in thought.

"Was it something that Chardon did or was it something Sestis did?" Kelin paced.

"Maybe both." Talas shrugged.

"But she was harmless. Her soft nature could do no wrong."

"Just so you know, she was not all that soft."

Kelin whipped around in shock. "What do you mean?"

"I saw her grab a little one and shake him until he went limp, all for running into her while playing with some friends. They were chasing each other, and he was on the tail end. No one saw it happen but me, I guess."

"That's…" Kelin advanced on him with such speed, Talas fell backwards on the bed. Kelin was on top of him eyes boring into him. "Why would you not say anything to anyone?" He yelled.

"No one would ever believe me. I was not well liked to begin with, remember?"

"So, our beloved Sestis was some sort of monster? But what does that have to do with Chardon's guilt over our world being destroyed because of our stupidity?"

"If Halfar saw my displeasure in Chardon's decision making, don't you think he would have gone to Sestis as well? She felt Chardon was being too steadfast with the negotiations. He was not going to budge."

"We were just pawns in a big scheme?" Kelin frowned then a new expression replaced it.

Talas almost laughed at how adorable Kelin looked all confused and awe struck when he asked it.

"Afraid so, my beloved. But," Talas sat up, his lips so close to Kelin's, "you must not confront anyone with this. If they think you know more than they think you do, it could get messy. I need you to stay safe."

He kissed him softly, teasingly until Kelin settled down on top of him. They both knew there was no point in arguing at this junction since mating was far more important.

Impatience

He could feel it, the agitation of knowing Chardon was coming for him soon. Halfar paced his bed chamber slowly, making sure to plant one foot in front of the other with every step. This had to be done since the last time he paced around thinking of Chardon he nearly injured himself running into the edge of the bed and he was far from clumsy. Chewing on his lower lip became an annoying habit he could not seem to break over the past few years, never letting anyone else see him do it.

There was movement outside his chamber in the hall forcing him to instantly cease his inner deliberations. He stood at the doors and waited for what he assumed was a troop of Kur's enforcers escorting their commander to him, and he was right. The doors flung open and Kur nearly knocked Halfar down, except he came face to face with him and halted, a look of despair washing over his face. It was obviously meant to be an ambush.

As they both stood in that moment eye to eye, Halfar tilted his head to one side, not disengaging the stare. He saw the enforcers in the hall ready to strike and from Kur's back, his talons protruded out. Kur had a look of disbelief as he looked down at his chest and saw Halfar had indeed run him through.

"You seem to have come unannounced, yet again, despite my orders to not do so ever again."

"My lord," Kur managed to get out.

"Now, I am willing to forget this matter if you are ready to obey me." Kur was having trouble breathing but replied, "Of course, my lord."

The enforcers were confused.

Halfar withdrew his claw and Kur collapsed in a heap unconscious in the doorway.

"Take him away." He barked at the enforcers.

Four of them hurriedly grabbed their commander and dragged him down the hall as they headed towards the healers. A thick trail of dark purple blood streaked the white floors. The rest turned in unison and marched back down the hall from whence they came.

"Rass!" Halfar summoned in his booming voice.

"My lord?"

Rass was at the end of the hall watching the retreat and carrying of Kur. "That was entertaining." He came forth.

"Make sure he is well guarded and well maintained."

"You wish to keep him on as a General?"

"For now, yes." Glancing at him, "Why did you not stop him?"

"I was certain you would handle the situation quickly."

"Why would he do something so detrimental to his wellbeing?"

Rass stepped past Halfar and sat on the edge of his bed. "When you shut down the barrier, Kur was in position to take control of a nearby city in one of his regions. The barrier revealed them almost instantly, so he probably assumed you had done it on purpose to dispatch him."

"Paranoia."

"Understandable when you are trying to overthrow your ruler without anyone suspecting."

"But that was how long ago?"

"Kur does like to hold a grudge."

"I thought that was against his aesthetics?"

"Hardly." Rass removed himself from the bed and headed down the hallway. "I will go attend to him and make sure he lives."

"Do not antagonize him." Rass made a face. "I mean it, Rass."

A wave of his general's hand was his reply.

****☼****

Kelin was not one to sit around and wait for the inevitable so he went straight into Chardon's battle room and demanded an answer. He didn't care if it was premature, a battle was nearing, and he needed to know what exactly he was fighting for.

"Tell me, Chardon, what kind of tragedy did Sestis bring upon us? I now know for a fact that she was not the sweet natured regent everyone thinks!" Chardon's shocked expression was enough for him to continue. "Don't you think we deserve to know?"

Chardon cut him off right there. "To know what? That she was a monster? That our world became a target because of her actions? Are you going to tell our people, who loved her more than they loved or trusted me, their leader?"

Slacked jawed, Kelin moved away from the table he had slammed his fists on to get Chardon's attention. It never occurred to him the ramifications of that information and Talas had warned him time was a sensitive matter. The people may not believe anything he or Chardon said but the other side of the coin was they would hate her. Hate was a strong emotion needing no fuel since their world was destroyed and what was left of their race now resides on a planet with a weak sun.

"But, I…" Kelin was now lost for words.

"It has come up to grant her a memorial. I tried to avoid it by averting everyone from her memory but with a new harvest the workers wanted an offering since she loved the field workers."

"No she didn't!"

Kelin spat out, remembering the story Talas told him.

"No, but that doesn't change the fact they think so."

"How did her actions end up having our world targeted? And for what?"

Taking a seat closer to Kelin he explained.

"When we went on diplomatic visits to other worlds, Sestis would use her charm to manipulate, blackmail and connive her way into getting whatever she wanted. Sometimes it was to get resources that should have gone to a needy plan- et rerouted to ours so we would have a monopoly on certain ones. She did all of this in my name and our race, boasting of our unique powers. Over time, animosity brewed and when they threatened our world she did not back down. In fact, she welcomed their wrath."

"That's insane! Wait," Kelin shook his head. "How does Halfar come into this?"

"Halfar saw what she was doing and didn't like it. If our world was going to be conquered, better he do it to ensure our race than a hostile one hell bent on vengeance to wipe us out."

"But he was the one who ended up nearly wiping our race out of existence."

"Negotiations did not go well."

"Because of Sestis?" *Incredible,* Kelin thought to himself.

"Yes," Chardon sighed heavily.

Kelin saw that was all he was going to tell him. There was no reason to say any more. He was suddenly exhausted. Kelin saw it on Chardon's face as well.

"I'm sorry you feel this way, Chardon, but the people have to know eventually."

He walked out of the battle room in turmoil over what he had discovered. It never came across as this bad when he ran the scenarios of what the secret could be. Knowing this, he hoped Chardon could postpone the memorial for as long as he could.

Back with Talas in their chamber, he relayed everything that was told to him and watched Talas start to pace. At first, he was angry at his mate for pushing the subject, then listened more intently.

"Such insanity!" Talas was flabbergasted among other things. "Who else knows this, again?"

"Chardon, Modas and now us."

"You mean, Jaron and Ganna have no clue?"

"I'm not sure but I think they are the last two who need to know."

"No, our people are the last who need to know because it would be chaos."

"The workers want a memorial offering ceremony for Sestis."

Talas' eyes became saucers. "Over my scorched corpse!"

"Chardon is trying to postpone it for as long as he can but they will not accept rejection without an explanation."

"Then he has to do that."

"What?"

"Explain!"

"Talas, there has never been a rebellion in the history of our race. This could damage us all."

"It doesn't matter. Either way, our race has to face the truth and reestablish ourselves without a false benevolent regent to hold on to."

Modas leaned against the wall of Chardon's chamber."

"You told him?"

"Not everything, but yes, I told him about Sestis' interplanetary frolics."

"A memorial would be a disaster."

"We will have one and tell them much of the truth before the offerings."

"That's madness."

"Your warriors will be there to handle any outbreaks."

"I will not harm my own people."

Chardon sighed. It was getting harder to talk to anyone let alone command them.

"Please. It will be sorrowful enough as it is."

☀

The time to implement their battle plans finally arrived and Ganna was all over the place making sure everything was set to simultaneously open five vortices. She would open the one for the main gate while the others were going to be created by revived workers a bit rusty on the uptake. They had been practicing on a smaller scale for nearly three years but not all the kinks were ironed out. It would have to do for now. As long as their warriors ended up in the correct sectors, it should be okay.

Talas was in full battle gear wearing a tan brown sleeveless robe over a skin-tight tunic. There were two long swords crisscrossed on his back held by leather straps. His dirty blond hair was still damp and hung stringy across his shoulders, down his back. Kelin was in similar gear except his attire was all black minus weapons because he was an energy user. They stared at each other in silence as their assignments required them to be apart for the duration of the battle.

Modas kept an audience of twenty warriors as he relayed their tasks. Mota and Jakar listened diligently while sharpening their claws on pieces of stone. Those were the only deadly items a manbeast needed. On the other side of the field, Jaron and Mara led a group of energy users in a last-minute practice run. Everyone seemed ready.

Chardon was alone in the council room head in his hands as he sat on a bench near the window. His body was shaking, and he didn't know why. He was confused yet resolved at the same time. Tears stung his eyes and he fought them back. With everything that had happened over the course of a year, he should not be surprised.

It took a lot of coaxing to stop people from desecrating Sestis' memorial when the truth became known, Chardon glad the rest of what she had done remained secret. He took a sharp intake of air that forced him to look up and he saw the muted sunlight trying to illuminate the room. He stared at it for a long time.

****☼****

"Multiple vortex openings have been identified." Rass reported.

The throne room was eerily quiet without Kur's enforcers running around and Halfar liked it that way. It gave him time to think. He glanced over at Rass, still bowed low on one knee.

"How many?"

"They have not been pinpointed yet."

Halfar tapped his index finger to his lips.

"Focus on any signature close to the palace."

"Then what?"

"Nothing. It would be the one Chardon appears from."

"With a troop of warriors, one possibly being that manbeast."

"No, when you intercept the signatures, you are going to do a bit of rearranging."

"You mean, as soon as all parties are outside of the vortex, we transport them. Random?"

"No." Halfar half turned to him. "Make sure the four of them are back together, without Modas."

"Ahh." Rass had an inkling of what Halfar had in mind. "They should be given an explanation after all that has transpired."

"I only need ten enforcers and you in the throne room to ensure no one does anything," he paused for the right word, "foolish."

"What about the other vortex signatures?"

"I'm sure the enforcers, along with Kur, will keep them busy."

As Rass left to do his bidding, he thought of how Kur would fare with the manbeast. He had no doubt of Kur's capabilities but a manbeast was something else entirely. Kur might actually enjoy the battle and forget about the incident where he tried to kill his ruler.

The vortex on the east side of the palace ripped open to produce Talas and his army. They were ten strong and ready for a fight. Talas set foot in front of the east wall and was attacked with his men not getting any better treatment. He drew one of his long swords and headed straight into the middle to gain leverage. After taking out three enforcers, a burst of light engulfed him, and he vanished. His army, surprised, was caught off guard and vulnerable as enforcers clambered down the walls towards them.

On the north Kelin suffered the same fate while going head to head with some of Halfar's more formidable human servants. A few enforcers were mixed in and he was able to take down two of them before being taken and replaced by Mota. Their well-structured plans turned into chaos.

Kur sent his enforcers to intercept the intruders from all sides. All along the palaces' perimeter a battle ensued causing destruction to its walls and the area surrounding it. Kur made his way down to the West side and had to bend backwards to avoid a wide angled swipe of talons. Stepping back, he caught a glimpse of Jakar before the manbeast came at him relentlessly. Kur was pleased to finally let off some steam and fight the way he wanted. He was having fun.

At the main entrance to Halfar's palace, the vortex opened with Chardon, Jaron and Modas along with seven warriors that included Mara. In an instant, they were ambushed by Rass and his enforcers. Modas took a group of four on his side while Mara used her energy to create a shield for Chardon. Midair about to strike a fatal blow to an enforcer, the manbeast and Mara were swept up, vanishing in thin air to be replaced by Talas and Kelin. Once again, all four were together under the Earth sky.

"What's going on?" Kelin hollered in fear.

He was still in an attack stance, enforcer blood spotting his robes.

This was not supposed to happen.

Modas was transported to Talas' regiment right in the middle of an attack. He had no time to regroup so used his might to drive the enforcers back. In the recesses of his mind he cursed whoever did this to leave Chardon vulnerable. He was sworn to protect his leader with his life if necessary despite their differences. Slicing an enforcer in half, black blood splattering over him, he advanced into the horde to find a way out and back to the main doors.

Mota fared no different as he appeared where Kelin had been only to find himself surrounded by a large number of enforcers and human servants. Some had sharp thin long swords which made them part of the Asian crime syndicates Talas and Kelin had referenced. He extended his claws and dropped down into attack position. These men did not look like the type who scared easily.

Chardon turned abruptly to all sides looking for the culprit but found no one. Seeing who was now in his party, it made sense. This was Halfar's will. All the enforcers present backed off, which meant he wanted them to get inside without incident. He motioned to Kelin and Talas.

"Lead the way. You know where the throne room is, correct?"

Regaining their composure, both men assumed defense stances, Kelin covering the front, Talas the rear. No way were they taking any chances on Halfar just letting them waltz in. All around them there was silence and it disturbed Chardon. As they moved into the palace itself, soft sounds of awe echoed through the halls. It was a magnificent building. At the entrance to the hallway leading to the throne room everyone stopped.

Rass stood blocking their path with ten enforcers. His smile was somewhat wicked as he bowed and moved to the side motioning them in. The enforcers closed rank after Chardon, Jaron, Talas and Kelin passed Rass. Footsteps clacked against white marble floors making the silence more prominent. The throne room doors were flung open to reveal Halfar lazily sprawled on the throne, his battle gear gone.

Even Rass raised an eyebrow at that.

"You're probably wondering how this has happened." He swung his legs forward and sat with his legs spread wide apart. "You see, I didn't want that manbeast to come in here and tear things up." He leaned further towards them. "And I think I should explain. I wanted the four of you here to understand how you ended up on this planet without your cores."

"This was your doing?" Jaron seethed. "How?"

"I wanted to extract you before the bomb hit but did not know how. Rass came up with a way in short time but I didn't know it would grab just your body and leave the core."

"Why would you extract us?"

"He didn't do it on purpose." Kelin replied.

"He only wanted Chardon." Talas completed the thought.

"That is correct. But, I am glad more of you were captured in the transport. I can't imagine the devastation Chardon would endure if your race had become extinct."

Jaron was confused. "Why? Why just Chardon?"

Halfar caught Chardon's gaze and understood the whole truth had not been told. He wasn't sure if it was a benefit or hindrance. That look in Chardon's eyes said 'don't'.

"Let's finish our negotiations, shall we?"

Halfar stepped down and the sound of weapons being drawn filled the room. He looked around and Chardon saw his warriors ready to defend against the enforcers who reacted to the hostile act. Rass extended a transformed limb protruding deadly spikes and held it at Jaron, Talas and Kelin's throats.

"Now, now. We should be more cooperative. I'm sure my lord means yours no harm."

"So true." Halfar extended his hand to Chardon. "Come."

Chardon slowly walked to him, looking back once at his entourage held hostage by Rass and the enforcers. For the first time he felt a slight twinge of fear for his friends.

"No need to worry. No one is leaving this room until the two of you return." Rass promised.

The double doors to the hallway leading to Halfar's chamber were opened by two enforcers and they entered, the doors booming shut behind them. As they walked, they talked.

"Why are you doing this?" Chardon hissed softly.

Halfar leaned towards him and whispered into his ear.

"I wanted to see you."

"What exactly are we negotiating? You destroyed our world." Halfar opened his chamber room and secured the doors once they were inside.

"I never wanted that to happen. I regret it more than you know." Chardon turned his back to him. "When I realized what I had set in motion, all I could think of was saving you over anyone else." Chardon swung around and backhanded him. The force tilted his head sideways. "I deserve more than that." Chardon made sure his eyes conveyed his fury and Halfar understood. "I played right into her hands but she still didn't win."

"No one won anything!"

Waiting no longer, Halfar grabbed Chardon's face and kissed him fervently, forcing Chardon to eventually submit. Chardon's body went limp as he shifted into female form. Halfar held her up with his arms kissing her neck, her breasts, all while she tried to feebly push him away. He hoisted her higher, tossing her onto the bed and yanked her robes off in one move. The tunic underneath he ripped to shreds with a lone talon he had extended. Sitting above her he removed his over shirt and leggings.

"You can't." Chardon pleaded softly.

Wrapping his hand around one of her ankles he dragged her towards him raising her leg to his shoulder. His gaze never leaving hers, his tongue spilled out and hung down nearly to the bed. She watched as its pointed end flicked between her thighs then entered her. Gasping, her fingers took hold of the bed cover balling them in her fists. His tongue left her center and traveled up her body as he leaned forward to hover over her then back into his mouth. Their eyes stayed locked.

"No more visions." He hissed as a talon slid deep into her.

Her fists tighten again on the bed cover, her back arched and eyes squeezed shut.

"Look at me." He commanded. With difficulty, she took deep breaths and opened her eyes. "I missed you."

He withdrew the talon replacing it with what she really wanted: him. One hand flew from the bed and slammed into his chest, her nails digging into his flesh as he entered crudely. Her mouth gaped open in shock and he sealed it with his. She knew he was going to have every bit of her until he was satisfied.

The throne room maintained an eerie silence as all occupants dared not move. Rass had the entire perimeter surrounded with enforcers. One wrong movement would start an all-out battle Chardon's team knew they would not win.

"Why have they been gone so long?" Jaron was getting worried.

"Delicate negotiations should not be rushed." Rass explained.

"It has been over an hour!"

Talas almost reached for his long sword again.

"Until they return, you will behave. Thirsty?" Rass turned to a human servant outside the main doors. "Bring some refreshments, please."

"Something is not right." Kelin kept looking around for clues.

"Whatever they wish to discuss is not of our concern."

Rass leaned against a wall, arms crossed.

"This is unacceptable!" Jaron collected threads of energy.

"You will wait!" Rass bellowed, silencing all. A cart arrived at that moment with drinks. "Now, let's have a nice chat together."

He was also puzzled by the long wait until he realized what might be occurring in his lord's bed chamber. It had been awhile since they were together. Knowing that, he sat down for the long haul. Halfar was not going to waste one moment, so Rass figured it would be at least another two hours before they emerged from that hallway. He grinned.

No one could hear Chardon's screams of pain and pleasure except Halfar. It fed his hunger for her and he touched every inch of her body with his own. They had never been able to experience mating of such magnitude because they had always needed to hold back in fear of being caught. With utter abandon, Chardon let Halfar do whatever he wanted to her, even acts of sexual depravity she never knew could be done. Their body fluids mingled, coating every inch of the bed.

Exhaustion took them instantly as they reached the final throws of orgasm together for the third time. Their bodies shuddered from over-exertion. Side by side, they tried to breathe normally and not choke on their own spittle. Halfar laid his hand on her exposed thigh and caressed it. Chardon pushed it away not bothering to turn her head to see what he was thinking. Her chest hurt, it was on fire inside. She hiccupped and cried.

"Shh."

Halfar rolled onto his side to wipe drenched hair from her face. Not being able to help himself, his left hand clutched one of her breasts and softly squeezed though not enough to hurt. He kissed her shoulder blade while his hand moved slowly down to rest between her thighs. She cried out in surprise and gasped sharply for air. Her hand instinctively went to stop him going further.

"If I had the energy to devour you, I would."

"Let me go."

"I will, soon. First we need to calm you."

He reached into the cabinet on her side of the bed and produced a tiny vial.

"No," she breathed, "don't do this."

She clasped his hand and the vial with hers.

"Are you going to reunite with your group like this? You will need this to shift back."

"No."

"Why"

"I can't." Chardon was scared. "My body won't…"

Halfar sat up and looked around the chamber. He had an idea. Taking the dropper out of the vial, he tipped it down to her mouth. She tried to turn away as he held her head steady until half of it was consumed. Her body immediately relax, her breathing slowed to normal. On the floor were the remnants of her tunic so he used them to wrap her breasts down tight until she appeared nearly flat chested. Luckily the fabric was unforgiving, albeit causing discomfort.

"It hurts."

"I know."

He helped her back into her robes noticing her eyes starting to glaze over. She was going to fall unconscious if he didn't get her back home soon. Redressing and making sure Chardon could stand, he opened the doors and led her back to the throne room. He had not planned on their negotiations to turn out this way but once he had her alone, there was no turning back until he had fulfilled his ultimate agenda.

The double doors opened.

Rass stood and bowed while Chardon's entourage retook their defensive positions with weapons drawn and energy spheres formed ready to strike. Seeing this, Rass motioned with just his head and his small army encircled them. Glancing over he could tell Chardon was not well.

"What have you done to him?" Jaron demanded raising one hand with a spinning ball of energy.

Halfar smirked. "Your leader is just fine."

Chardon moved away from him to his group.

"We must leave."

"Chardon!" Kelin made ready to strike.

"Now!" Chardon continued moving forward, his group surrounding him as he went, keeping an eye on Rass and his enforcers who also watched them retreat. "There's no time to regroup."

Outside of the palace Jaron created a vortex as fast as she could and closed the opening right as the last man stepped into it. She would send a signal for Ganna to open vortexes to retrieve the others.

Gears of Change

Back on their planet's surface, Jaron tried to get Chardon to speak to her. She could tell something was not right. Her pleas to go to the medical chamber were ignored. Talas and Kelin were no help. Both kept giving each other strange looks and watched Chardon go directly to the housing commons.

Chardon barely made it to her chamber and didn't have the mind to secure the main door before getting into bed. Under the covers, she removed her robes and the constricting fabric, tossing them on the floor. The vibrations that started coursing through her body earlier intensified. She fought hard to stop it before falling into deep sleep, not hearing anything that transgressed outside before the darkness of night as the council scrambled to get their battle squads back. No one disturbed her.

****☼****

"Did you get it?"

Halfar sat upright on his throne as Rass entered. He was tense again. A few hours with Chardon was not nearly enough to satisfy him. Finding the planet was of great importance now.

"Of course." Rass bowed. "I will relay the coordinates to you."

"Good." Halfar relaxed a bit. "Thank you for holding them at bay."

"I was certain you did not want to be intruded upon." Rass leaned closer and whispered. "So?"

"It's done."

"Ahead of schedule don't you think?"

"It couldn't be helped."

"Hmm? I didn't know you lacked such restraint." Rass stood. "Now what?"

"We wait. I will not have her life jeopardized."

"By the way, Kur is not happy that the festivities were so short lived."

"This is just the beginning. Earth is about to become a battle field."

"But we are only taking over this region, correct?"

Halfar's eyes turned into slits of hate.

"It seems, Kur has made a plea to the council and MY advisors on our home world are sending MY armada to enslave Earth. We have not conquered a world in some time and this, apparently, is a better time than any."

99 | THREADS OF CONCEIT

Rass' expression showed disagreement. He did not want to be assigned as warden to this awful rock. Halfar confirmed what had to be done just by looking at him.

"Don't worry, Kur can have it." Halfar tilted his head. "If, we capture this planet."

"Are you thinking sabotage?"

"I will not stand for my armada to be used without my consent."

"Your will is mine." Rass beamed at the thought of deceiving Kur one last time.

****☼****

The hallway was dark and quiet, made more so by the stealth of Modas moving down it towards Chardon's chamber. He entered smoothly and immediately noticed the smell. It was the stench of mating with something foul. Sitting on the side of the bed listening to the ragged breathing, Modas knew what kind of sleep she was in and would not awaken for at least a few days.

Keeping this secret was no longer an option. The medical workers, along with Ganna, would have to be informed. He stroked her sweat matted hair as if she were a little one and sighed with regret. This too should not have happened on his watch.

So many people were crammed in Chardon's chamber that Ganna demanded only those needed stay and the rest leave immediately. She did not want Chardon's sleep to be disturbed. That would be harmful to her and the unborn child. At the end of the ruckus, Jaron, Modas, their elder children, Talas, Kelin and Ganna remained in the chamber. Still too many for her taste.

"What's wrong with Chardon?" Jaron chewed her lower lip as she stared at the bed. She showed signs of deep worry.

"Well, how shall I put this?" Ganna paused.

"Halfar did something to him. He didn't look right when he came back." Kelin interjected.

Talas had crept over to the side of the bed to get a closer look and was leaning over Chardon. Ganna yanked him back away from the bed.

"She's incubating! You cannot touch her!"

There was silence, then sharp intakes of air. Talas turned to Modas knowing what the secret was he held. Jaron, still speechless, sat down on a pillow chair near the window.

Kelin had an epiphany about the so-called negotiations before their world was destroyed.

"Halfar is in love with Chardon." He blurted out for all to hear.

"More importantly," Talas raised a finger and pointed at the bed, "Chardon is a shifter."

"A shifter!" Jaron finally cried out. "Chardon is a shifter?" Finally catching on to what Ganna meant by incubating. Her head snapped around towards Modas.

"But, Sestis…" Jaron began.

"Knew." Was all Modas had to say.

Jaron's face had turned a few shades of dark pink. It was clear how furious she was to know her mate had kept this from her, let alone Chardon.

"She seems to be in pain." Talas had moved closer again.

"She's exhausted. Now, all of you, out! Jaron, help me get her into a more comfortable position."

The men left so the two women could tend to their leader. Jaron tried to lift Chardon's legs to turn them and was shocked at how heavy they were. She met Ganna's gaze.

"She's like dead weight. Ganna, is she really okay?"

"I can't know for sure until she wakes up. Until then we have to keep a constant watch."

They were able to get her on her back with her head propped up on pillows. Jaron found her covering robe to dress her in and got it on with Ganna's assistance.

Outside, Kelin sat with his head in his hands shaking it back and forth while Talas walked around in a circle next to him. So many thoughts were going through both their minds as they processed all that had happened.

"My theory was right." Kelin spoke first.

"Of course it was, beloved. But I know you could've never guessed this."

"Not in all of eternity." He looked up from his reverie. "What does this mean?"

"That there are more secrets."

"What else could there possibly be?"

"Think, beloved. Sestis, Modas and Halfar knew that Chardon was a shifter. They also knew what kind of a monster Sestis was. The next part is easy."

A light bulb lit up in Kelin's head. "Sestis had something to do with the negotiations going south and Halfar deciding to destroy us all."

"Bingo!" It was an Earth term he had picked up and thought appropriate for the occasion.

"Yes, but what was it and how? How could we have been so blind as to not see her for what she was?"

"That and more," Talas replied. "You know what I think?" Talas bent down to him and their eyes met. "You look exhausted. You should go to bed."

"Ahh, and will you be joining me?"

"Why, of course my beloved. Come, too much thinking is going on and not enough mating."

"I think Chardon and Halfar did enough of that for all of us." Kelin muttered.

Talas wagged his finger as he led Kelin back to their chamber.

"No, no. We must all do our own fair share in our own way. Yes?"

Kelin stopped talking the rest of the way.

****☼****

"I want to fight too!"

Trinon had both arms straight down on his sides, his little head tilted as far back as it could go in order to stare up into Mota's face.

Mota laughed loudly, throwing his head back. "Of course you do!" He leaned forward until he was at a ninety-degree angle, his nose nearly touching Trinon's. "You are not ready." Trinon lunged at him, and an arm appeared grabbing him up so that he dangled sideways.

"Until you can land properly and climb, it is as he says," their father bellowed.

Modas brought his son's body up until they were eye to eye. Trinon relented without struggle and his father put him down.

"This battle will not rage long, and you shall never see it. There will be more, and you must be ready." He glanced back at Mota as he walked away. They nodded to each other.

"Up you go," Mota said and without warning, grabbed Trinon and tossed him into the air towards the wall.

He may not be as small as he used to be but Mota was twice his size. Trinon hit the wall hard and, as he scrambled to grasp hold, caught sight of Und with his back against the wall holding on with the claws of his fingers and toes.

Mota shook his head seeing the jealousy in Trinon's expression.

"Focus on yourself, little one."

"I am not little!" He caught a piece of wall and secured himself on it, his face red with anger.

✱✱☼✱✱

The Americas, parts of Asia and Europe were in turmoil as enforcers took over territories with little effort. The human's military might was nothing compared to Halfar's. Government science divisions had detected the giant mother ship outside of Earth's orbit and speculations flew. Only a select few in his fold knew what it was and who it belonged to.

Halfar's armada had arrived much to his disgust. It had been three months since Chardon had been on Earth and Halfar made sure the gate was blocked so no one from her planet could come through. But, he could open the gate from his end when he needed to check up on her. Kur was becoming unmanageable again and he had to decide soon. He couldn't let his general know about his plans just yet.

✱✱☼✱✱

Ganna ran to the gate console filled with fear as the guards and she watched the vortex open, dark figures marching forward through the gate. It reminded her of when their planet had been destroyed before they knew what had really happened. She was confident in knowing who the first figure would be and she was right.

Halfar emerged from the gate with an entourage of eight bodyguards following him. The smugness in his appearance made Ganna twitch with disgust. In human form he still managed to get that result from off-worlders.

He smiled at her as a greeting and bypassed her, moving onward to the housing commons.

"I don't need an escort to Chardon's chamber," he stated. "I can smell her even from this distance."

Workers who remembered him stared in confusion and fear as he strode into the building. In the hallway, Modas was guarding the doorway. Ganna smirked as he gauged the manbeast up close and saw the realization of just how formidable he was. The look on Modas' face suggested they would not be on friendly terms. Halfar stepped back from him a bit.

"I need to see her."

Modas sneered at him but opened the door and moved to the side, allowing him access. From the doorway they could see the rise and fall of her ribcage as she breathed softly. Behind the sheer fabric surrounding her bed, she lay still in deep slumber with pain and exhaustion etched in her facial expression.

"What's wrong? Why is she still incubating?" He directed his question to the medical worker. Upon further observation of the room, Chardon's usual group was found spread around the chamber. Instead Jaron answered.

"You tell us, you monster. This is your doing!"

"Impregnating her is one thing, I am speaking of why she is this way," he snapped.

Ganna came into the chamber and went directly to check Chardon's forehead.

"She had a fever for a few weeks and did wake up on one or two occasions. I think it is because her body has not yet fully regained itself as female. It is quite possible Chardon did not shift often to female form to keep it acclimated."

"No, she wouldn't. All for the sake of your race, and HER."

They all knew who he meant. He went around to the other side of the bed and sat next to Chardon's sleeping body. He brushed strands of hair from her face and stared down at her. Everyone in the room watched, feeling awkward, an audience to his show of affection for Chardon.

"I need to tell you something," Halfar began. "It is more like a proposal."

That got Ganna's and everyone else's attention. Even Modas came into the room from out of the hallway with a bang of the door swinging open. Last time Halfar made one it meant doom for their race. Another one was not a welcome invitation. He saw the looks on their faces and held up a hand.

"Shall I explain my dilemma?" They all froze. "My armada has been sent, without my approval, to Earth."

"How can it be without your approval?"

Kelin was not buying it any more than Ganna was.

"I have not yet explained." Halfar casted a glare at him. "May I continue?"

"My apologies," Kelin muttered noticing everyone staring at him, irritated.

"Conquering Earth was not my intention. One of my Generals, Kur, had found the planet and thought it was a great race to enslave. He initiated the conquest, so I came to investigate and assist."

"Thinking nothing of destroying yet another world." Ganna piped in to their dismay.

"For the love of Lassa!" Mara balled her hands into a fist.

Halfar continued. "That is true, I thought nothing of it. I also saw it as a way to flee from my advisors and the battles. I had your vessels which my other General, Rass, helped keep hidden from prying eyes. If anyone knew what I had done, extracting all of you, my reign as ruler would be put in question and I needed to stay in control. It is now clear that Kur has relayed this information to the royal advisors."

Jaron and Talas glanced at each other and Talas was the one to speak.

"You don't want to conquer Earth? Then why not tell them to withdraw?"

"Kur has engaged in a campaign to overthrow me and claim my armada for himself. He knows in his gut I would choose Rass over him."

"Pre-emptive strike." Talas deduced.

"Correct. I want to lose this battle, get rid of Kur and return my armada to its home base."

"So, what is your proposal?"

Halfar stood from his seat by the bed and turned to face them.

"I need you to attack my forces on all fronts before my armada deploys. Take out as many of Kur's enforcers as you can. Stopping his advance is key."

"You want us to murder your own kind so you can run away?" Ganna spat.

"No." Halfar sighed in exasperation. "Kur's enforcers are replicated organisms unsanctioned by our people. I did not know about it until after the fact and by then, he had over a thousand created. Those abominations must be destroyed!" He took a deep breath and let it out slowly. "I want to stay here with Chardon and resume our interplanetary meetings. We have to try and correct the damage done by Sestis."

Ganna glanced over at Jaron who a puzzled expression regarding the logistics of the whole battle plan but not making any headway. She saw Talas obviously thinking in the same context and he went over to tap Jaron. His expression told her he had a plan.

"There is one stark problem." Kelin interjected. "You sent a planet destroyer to our world and we have this," he spread his arms towards outside, "to try and live on. Have you seen the sun?"

"I never wanted that to happen. It was childish of me and it cost you greatly. I have no way of atoning for that. I can make this planet thrive for you, though."

"How?" Kelin opened his arms wide.

"When there is a way to destroy, there is a way to create. There is a 'bomb' for that as well."

"And what? You're going to use one of those for this planet?"

"In a way, yes."

"Uh-uh, I don't trust you." Kelin pointed a finger at him.

"You say you want to get off Earth and stay here. You do realize that would leave Earth in shambles? Your forces have not been kind," Talas continued where Kelin left off.

"If there is one thing I learned about humans is that they are resilient. Nothing keeps them down for long. They can rebuild." Halfar sat back down on the bed. "If it were not for Sestis…"

Modas' head snapped towards the others in the room and he made a quick decision. "I think you all should leave for a while." They turned to stare at him confused. "Chardon needs quiet."

"What about him?" An insulted Kelin barked.

"He is not disturbing her. We can discuss the rest of this matter later." He motioned for them all to exit and Ganna felt suspicious.

What are you up to manbeast? She asked in silence as she was the last to be forcibly pushed out the chamber.

Halfar raised his eyebrows at Modas when it was just the two of them and a sleeping Chardon.

"I have my reasons," Modas said.

"I was going to finish my explanation."

"I know."

"Do you not also want to know why I did it?"

"I already know."

"Then why?"

"They do not need to know any more about Sestis and her actions." Modas recalled the memorial that had turned into a disaster. The people were so distraught and angry it nearly became a mob. "She was like poison that no one knew was already in their veins."

"Keeping it from them won't change much."

"I disagree." Modas went to the door and as he closed it shut, "When you are ready to leave, I will be outside to escort you."

"I was not escorted in."

"No, but you should have been."

With that Modas closed the door and continued to stand guard in the hallway.

Chardon stirred when Halfar climbed into the bed with her, leaning over to stroke her hair. Her eyes fluttered open and there was a brief moment of recognition before he shook his head and coaxed her back to sleep. He laid a hand on the swell of her belly feeling the life inside move around.

Their two races had never procreated together, and he wondered, no worried, about the outcome. The thought of their offspring clawing its way out her, killing her in the process, made the color drain out of him. He had to come back and have a long talk with Ganna. The sun was setting and he knew it was time to go. Kissing Chardon on the forehead, he got up and went to meet Modas outside to be escorted back to the gate. He found it curious no one had asked how he opened the gate from the outside.

On a hill not far from the commune, Talas and Jaron sat on a boulder together. They felt odd being in such close proximity alone since the two were not friendly towards each other just yet. A sort of truce had been formed to get things done.

Talas walked a few inches from the boulder and poised himself on the edge of the hill, one leg bent at the knee from resting on a large stone near the edge. In reddish brown hide leather, his long sword hanging off one side, and his dirty blonde hair getting swirled around by the breeze he looked like the warrior he was. It did nothing for Jaron.

"Is it just me, or is your mate hiding more secrets for our leader?" He started.

"He is surely hiding something. The fact that he knew all of this makes me angry."

"What do you think about Halfar's proposal?"

"There is no way we can trust him!"

"Ahh," Talas used a finger to move away some fly away hair, "but we can." He turned to her. "He loves Chardon more than anything in this universe and has for a long time. He kept all of us because if our world were dead, Chardon would at least have some of his race with him. I think, getting him off Earth would benefit us."

Jaron thought it over for a bit and nodded her head.

"The planning is the problem. How do we drive Kur off that rock without a scratch on our troops?"

"We will not come out of this one unscathed, my dear Jaron."

"I am not your dear!"

Talas let out a little laugh. "So touchy. I have no interest in you, trust me." He saw the offended look on her face. "Not everyone finds you so beautiful. The same as Ganna detests me."

Returning to his gaze across the fields, he sighed and let the breeze wash over him. He crossed his arms and leaned forward, head tilted towards the sky.

"Stop that!" She snapped, and Talas peeked at her with one eye. "Why does everything you do have to be damn erotic?"

"I'm just standing here, dearie, on a hill." Jaron's eyes narrowed at him. "Fine." Talas went back to the boulder and sat down next to her. "Not unscathed, but no casualties. I can guarantee that."

"Why is Kelin being so forceful these days?" Jaron changed the subject. It had been bothering her since they regained their cores how the lovers' dynamic had changed. "He always followed you."

"Not on Earth, he didn't." Talas cocked his head to one side. "I wonder. He's not a strategist like I am but on Earth, he was more knowledge-able." His forehead creased. "Of course, I was some sort of imbecile on that planet." It infuriated him just thinking about it. Jaron found it quite hilarious and started laughing heartily. "That's not very nice of you, dear."

"Sorry." Jaron wiped her eyes. "I just remember all of us wanting to smack you around for the sheer joy of it. We knew it would be wrong to bully you but, you made it so easy and I didn't feel the least bit guilty."

"How hateful."

"Without your core, you really were just an empty-headed shell of a being." Jaron slapped her knee and laughed again her head thrown back.

****☼****

Restraining Chardon ended up being more of a hardship than Ganna, or the workers, had anticipated as they forgot how strong she was. Her hair had gotten long again and snagged on the bed covers every time Ganna was able to get her back down only to have her push back up more furious than before.

"Let go of me!"

"Chardon, you need to listen to me and calm down!"

"I need to find him!"

"You need to let me examine your unborn child and make sure it does not mean your demise as it enters this world."

Chardon stopped fighting for a moment staring at her in confusion.

"What do you mean?"

"Our two races have never mated before and if you haven't forgotten, Halfar's true form comes with claws."

"So do manbeasts!"

"Not like this!"

Chardon thought about it again and confirmed in her mind Ganna was correct. She could feel her unborn child moving around and the tiny claws, not yet sharp enough to rip open flesh, graze across the inside of womb. Breathing deep and letting it out slowly, she let her arms slip from Ganna's grip.

"I still need to see him."

"I am already here." Halfar stepped out of the shadows near the door with Modas in tow. "You really should stay in bed resting. Ganna and I have some details to go over."

"I…" Halfar leaned in and kissed her softly on the lips making her shiver. "You're coming back?"

"Of course." He turned to Ganna. "Let's proceed."

Ganna brought over the examination tablet and held it above Chardon's belly to get a good view of the fetus. Once the image was recorded along with vital signs for both mother and child, she left the room, with Halfar in tow, to the medical research chamber.

Halfar was silent the entire time and Ganna felt she may have misjudged the tyrant. It nagged her about why their planet had been destroyed on a whim and she had an awful suspicion that Sestis, yet again, was the cause.

She silently scrutinized the image in her research lab then made a suggestion.

"We can extract him when it is time."

"How?" Halfar tensed at the sound of it.

"Cut her open." The medical workers gasped in horror and Halfar rose from his seat. "Or," she reeled back; not liking what was about to occur, "we can carefully insert a membrane around the fetus to prevent him from clawing his way out of her."

"Will you sedate her?"

"Do you think she would let me?" Ganna swirled around in her seat facing Halfar.

"No." He resumed his seat and tapped his lower lip. "I do have a way to ease her down."

An eyebrow shot up on Ganna's brow. "Please, explain."

"I had an elixir made that forces the biological system to slow down. Only a tiny bit is needed."

"You've used this elixir before then? On Chardon?"

"How did you think she was able to get back here without collapsing?"

"She did collapse! She barely made it to her chamber!"

"Don't be so dramatic! I knew the timeline and made sure there was enough in her to get her home. I am not a monster!"

"And that is what troubles me." It was Halfar's turn to seem confused. "Since you are not a monster, it makes me wonder why you sent that planet bomb."

"That was not my most glorious moment and I will regret it always." He hung his head defeated.

"Enough of that." Ganna waved her hand. "We have a new species to bring into our new world."

****☼****

Und could see from his vantage point on the other end of the wall it was going to be bad. Trinon was angry and determined to prove everyone wrong by climbing the wall today when no one was watching. They didn't mind Und and his sister, Una, because they had a somewhat responsible nature. Trinon was another matter. The fighting had begun earlier that day.

"You are to stay put!" Mota had ordered Trinon as he left for a council meeting.

"Why can't I go practice with the others?"

"You want to know why?" Mota leaned down to face him. "You are not good enough or ready to climb on your own." He straightened. "That's why. Now go sit in the sandbox and play with the little ones or something." Mota then strolled off, leaving a fuming Trinon to stand alone in the fields.

Und watched Trinon go to the sandbox while he went to the wall to practice. The look on his brother's face was nothing nice. So, it was no surprise that later in the day, Und saw him come up to the wall on the far end and stare up at it with mad fury. He attacked the wall with such speed even Und stopped climbing in a state of awe. It turned to dread as he saw how far up Trinon was. A fall would be catastrophic.

The climb was going well and Trinon had a big grin on his face despite the sweat running down his back from the exertion. His claws clinked upward, and he was three quarters of the way up when one of his claws did not find a grip. He reached with the other hand and the claws also missed causing him to slide downward.

His body gained momentum. He was going to fall if he didn't do something fast. In a panic he tried desperately to find a grip as he continued down. Some of his claws on both hands snapped off as he went further down, the pain causing him to scream. Blood streaked down the wall and Und descended as fast as he could to try and reach him. It was no use, Trinon would have to try and land no matter how bad it would be. He turned his body and ended up sideways, his torn-up hands causing his form to be unbalanced.

Mota and Modas heard the screaming first and reacted before anyone else. As they neared the wall, Und was just touching down on the ground and headed towards Trinon still in free fall. He would not make it.

Mota took off at full speed with his father behind him and barely missed Trinon as he hit the bottom. By getting somewhat under him, he softened the fall. That was the least of their concerns. Trinon lay in his arms bloody and shaking from shock. The damage to his claws was alarming. Mota kept him close to his body to minimize the tremors and turned to their father.

The horror on Modas' face was nothing compared to the screams of Jaron as she rushed forward to them. All the blood everywhere is what caused her to scream, surely fearing her little one was dead. He stopped her midway and didn't let go as she fought to be released. Und stood wide eyed with grief.

"Get Ganna." Modas commanded Mota.

"I am here!" Ganna ran up out of breath. She too must have heard the screams. "Hurry, give him to me!" Mota did not move. He was also in shock. Ganna kneeled to reason with him. "You have to give him to me! I need to treat him now!"

She laid a hand on his shoulder and felt the tension ease a bit. She motioned the medical workers who had followed her to hold him while she took Trinon out of his arms. They ran back to the medical chamber.

Jaron slid to the ground crying uncontrollably. Modas still held one of her hands in an iron grip without realizing it. His vision blurred, and he swayed. This had never happened before. Mota slowly stood up staring at his empty hands. Everyone was still until Modas let out a growl of such rage that the field workers nearby fled in fear of him going into a rampage. Und blinked for the first time since getting to the scene.

"I'm sorry." Mota whispered to Trinon. His hands trembled.

"It's not your fault, you know." Und said softly. "He just has a bad temper." Tears filled his eyes.

"Yes, it is."

Mota lifted his head to sky and saw the streaks of blood going down the face of the wall. A small cry caught in his throat and he couldn't stop tears from sliding down his face. Jakar came up behind him and rested his giant hands on his shoulders. After a moment, he went to pick Und up from where he stood frozen.

Pulling herself together, Jaron stood up and headed for the medical chamber. She stopped midway and turned to see if Modas was coming. A few seconds passed before he followed. They walked in silence as they made their way through the fields and down the slope that led to Ganna's operating room.

Inside, Ganna and the medics worked quickly to clean and close up the wounds. Trinon lay on the table his eyes still open from the shock. Not a tear could be found. He had not cried through the whole ordeal his hands literally declawed. The look of defeat and resolve on Trinon's face told Modas what he already knew. Trinon would not give up, even now.

"He's doing so well, it kind of scares me." Ganna was finishing up with the bandages. On many wounds they were fine being closed. With manbeasts and their claws it was a lot more complicated. "I want to keep him sedated for a few days."

"Fine." Modas touched Trinon's brow and traced their shape.

"Do not let him out of your sight! That boy is stubborn, and you know it."

"He won't be going anywhere."

Jaron kissed the top of his head. Modas left the room and she followed, neither saying a word. There would be no sleep tonight.

Jaron and Modas' children sat in the recreation room attached to their commune. The silence was deafening until a sniffle was heard. Una sat with her knees drawn in, head down on top. Und sat next to her, his legs stretched straight out and arms laid flat on either side of him. Mara paced while chewing her nails. Jakar was trying to get Mota to snap out of whatever state he was now in. He would not speak, just sat on the floor staring into emptiness.

"I cannot understand what you are going through if you don't tell me." Mota's eyes rotated to Jakar's voice. "No one forced him up there. He needs to learn more discipline. This happens to be a horrible way for him to learn it."

"His claws may not grow back properly." Mara said between teeth and nail.

"He's stronger than he looks. Do not underestimate him. They will come back just as strong."

Mota finally moved by leaning forward and taking a shuddering breath.

"I pushed him too hard. It seemed like fun at the time but…"

"He's hard headed and easily provoked. Reminds me of our departed brother."

"Yes, he is just like Hon," Mara piped up and laughed a little.

"Go see him." Jakar didn't yell but Mota heard it as a command. He got up and left.

****☼****

Going over scenarios on the tabletop holoscreen in the battle chamber, Rass heard footsteps echo through the hallway, leaving him little time to prepare himself for Kur's intrusion. *So, it's not just Halfar he ambushes,* he thought to himself. He turned his attention to the double doors and found Kur was already so close to him they shared the same breath. His eyes bore into Rass' like hot coals. Rass smiled at him sweetly.

"What may I…"

"Where is he?" Spittle flew into Rass' face and he calmly wiped it off. "You will tell me!"

"He is tending to some important business that doesn't pertain to you."

"I have searched this palace and this planet, and he is not here!"

"Surely, you are mistaken. Why don't you…"

"I will not be made a fool of!"

"Step away." Rass extended a razor-sharp talon at Kur's neck. This was tiring and irritating.

"Are you threatening me?"

Rass sighed and tilted his head to one side. Before Kur could react, he swung his arm and knocked him across the room into the wall.

"I told you to step away. Breathing the same air is not ideal for me." Using the same words Kur had said to him so long ago, he turned back to checking on Halfar's armada from his holoscreen. He heard the dragging of hard shell on marble floor. "Don't." He pulled out a plasma ray gun and aimed it at Kur without even looking at him. The dragging stopped.

"You will regret this." He heard Kur seethe before the doors slammed shut and Rass was alone again.

When he felt Kur had gone far enough away from the battle room, Rass headed for the other side of the palace. In the hallway leading to Halfar's private chamber, Rass glanced at the indicator on his wrist telling him the secret gate he created was opening. He had to get there to close it right as Halfar stepped out before Kur could sense the vortex.

In conjunction with keeping a constant look out for movement around him he had to make sure none of Kur's enforcers, or the man himself, were following.

As he neared the hall, a gust of air blew in making a large sucking sound. Halfar stepped out of the vortex onto the palace floor and Rass typed in commands on his wrist band to close it. They stood face to face for a moment then Halfar turned.

"Walk with me," his ruler commanded.

"Kur has been scouring the planet and the palace for you. He even tried to attack me."

"Where is he now?"

"No idea." Halfar stopped short. "He did not follow me," Rass reassured him.

They continued their fast-paced walk to the throne room, bursting in to find Kur waiting for them. He smiled and bowed at Halfar.

"My lord, you were sorely missed today."

"I did not know I was expected to be in anyone's presence."

"You have been in the palace all this time?" He asked, his tone dripping honey.

Halfar's face twitched as he settled into his throne. "Where else would I be, Kur?"

"I am only concerned for your well-being in these tumultuous times. We are at war with the humans, as dull as that may be."

"There's an uprising off the coast of Spain. If you wish, I can dispatch my enforcers to regain the region." Rass interrupted. "I believe my army is better equipped to handle them."

Kur was not to be ignored. "In that case, I will go with MY enforcers. The last thing we need is the ocean turning red with unnecessary bloodshed. Your enforcers are nothing but barbarians!"

Rass feinted hostility as Halfar commanded he do so in these situations. Kur gave a smirk and strolled pass him in triumph. Rass sighed with relief and shut the double doors to the throne room.

"Now that he is gone, how fares your pregnant mate?"

Chardon ate like a manbeast after battle just to keep her appetite at bay. She was not happy with the amount of food but knew it was necessary. Her time was near, she was due to deliver soon. Jaron had been around earlier to help with preparations. For some reason she did not feel strange or uneasy as everyone said she would be. Then, again, Chardon was not like the others of her race. That's why she was leader. Her strength and power were unmatched; it was her emotional state that made her weak at times.

"Feeling better, I see."

She noticed Ganna going over to the bed to straighten out the covers. The scientist had not left Chardon alone all day. She kept coming in unannounced to check on her.

"I've been eating." Chardon shoved another piece of grilled meat in her mouth.

"That's good, you will need all the energy you can muster."

"Really? I was under the impression my being conscious was not necessary since you plan to cut him out of me."

Ganna paused mid cleaning and didn't dare look over her shoulder at Chardon. It was an option she had floated around only to receive instant resistance from Halfar and the medical workers, but she would still do it if she could get away with it. The scientist in her called for it.

"It would have been an evasive procedure that you would not have gotten away with." Ganna flinched, satisfying Chardon with her reaction.

Halfar barely made it back in time to see the bloody slimy mess of child birth occurring in Chardon's chamber with at least five other witnesses packed in. Coming around to the foot of the bed, he saw Ganna gently pulling out a gelatinous membrane encased around a tiny life with equally tiny black talons. The sounds of it coming out reminded him of the last time he accidently stepped on fresh entrails during a battle.

The membrane was set in a large bowl at the foot of the bed and Ganna carefully sliced it open to reveal the child. Laying the filleted membrane open faced, she dug into his mouth and nostrils with her fingers and extracted the protective tissue simultaneously.

A high-pitched wail filled the room and he swiped at her, his tiny razor-sharp talons grazing her cheek leaving three thin lines of blood. She picked him up and went to the wash basin to clean him off. One of the medical workers handed her a small blanket to wrap him in.

"Here he is."

Ganna gave the little monster to Chardon then went to the mirror to examine her face.

Chardon reached into a basket near the head of her bed and palmed a handful of bandage cloth.

"Help me." She motioned to Halfar.

Together they loosely bound up his tiny claws so no one else would get sliced open. After that was done, she hoisted him up high by his under arms for inspection. The tiny slits of his eyes opened, and he stared at her with the same strange green as his father. His hair was black as pitch with honey brown streaks the color of Chardon's. She handed their child over to him and he was frightened to hold him.

"What shall we name him?" He asked her as his eyes laid transfixed on his son, mewing and clicking sounds bubbly from his tiny lips.

Lending a finger, he watched the little one take hold and open his mouth. A row of sharp tiny teeth was exposed and before Halfar could snatch his finger back, the little one chomped down. Droplets of blood formed around it.

Seeing that, Chardon decided. "His name will be Farin."

"That's quite appropriate." Jaron snorted. "It means feral fangs in our culture."

Halfar smiled at that. He liked how it fit him perfectly. Farin let go of the finger, yawned, then shivered.

"He's cold."

Chardon tossed the blanket to him and Halfar wrapped him back in it. Farin warmed up after only a few minutes and fell asleep.

"How sweet he is for such a creature." Ganna mused to herself.

Her face froze realizing she had said it out loud. She winced when silence filled the room.

Halfar knew how she felt about manbeasts, or similar species, and frowned. Jaron seemed to feel the same as he did and also not amused by Ganna's remark. Just because a child is born with talons does not make them a monster. She went over to take a look at the sleeping Farin being held in Halfar's arms.

"He's quite cute like a baby manbeast without the fur," she said glaring over at Ganna.

A small blue light flashed on the back of Halfar's hand, signaling his time was up for now. He struggled with his emotions of wanting to stay at Chardon's side or go back to deal with Earth once and for all.

Standing, he handed the sleeping bundle to Chardon, kissing them both on the forehead before grabbing his cloak and heading out the door. Rass would cover for him always but it was getting harder to go back and forth while Kur lurked in the shadows waiting for an opportunity to finish them both off. Ahead, he saw Modas opening the gate for his return.

"This won't be necessary for much longer," he told the manbeast as he stepped onto the platform. "We can go over strategy soon."

Modas' fingers worked the console as he replied.

"We will help get you off Earth but," he looked up from his work, "you have to deal with Kur on your own."

"You're right." Halfar entered the vortex and disappeared.

FOUR:

Rass moved the remains of his meal around on the plate in front of him, not having much of an appetite anymore. The great dining hall table had a capacity to seat fifty. Today only his lord and he were present. It too was pure white from floor to ceiling. Two servants stood in wait on opposite sides of the room to serve them. Halfar sat across from him, twenty feet away, on the other end of the table after just informing him of what needed to be done about Kur. Something about it pained him and he didn't like the way he was feeling.

"Can you do it?" Halfar asked urgently.

Rass was surprised he had been ignoring Halfar. He had not heard anything his ruler said after the instructions.

"You have asked me that even before this and the answer is still yes."

"Then why are you not enthused about it?"

"As you've said, I was in love with him once."

"Are you still? Do you think he will miraculously change?"

Rass tossed the fork down onto the plate and sat back in the chair sideways.

"I am not a fool, no." He squinted in aggravation at the thought of Kur. "He has made it clear I am not ideal."

"You really should find a mate soon. I worry about you."

"Hmm? This, coming from our ruthless ruler who decided to fall in love after centuries of conquests? I'll have you know, battles are what drive me, not love. Besides," he put his feet up on the edge of the table, "How can I be an objective General, all lovelorn and what not?"

More servants came in to clear away the table and Halfar noticed the half-eaten food on Rass' plate.

"Not hungry this evening?"

"Earth food is disgusting."

"You do get quite the variety."

Kur burst into the dining hall with all the flair of an entertainer.

"How fares my lord and his minion?"

He did a quick bow, smirking as he came up to the edge of the table. His sing song introduction grated on both their sensibilities.

"Did you come for dinner?" Rass motioned to the spread of food being taken away. "We are finished but there is plenty left for you."

Kur crinkled his nose. "Disgusting." He came further into the room and made his report. "I have secured the Asian border, so they will not be a problem for our forces." The emphasis on 'I' was noticed. "By the way, when is the Armada coming down to raze the surface?"

"Once we are all in position for a unified attack. I believe we are at forty percent?"

"Oh," was all Kur could muster as an answer.

Rass could see him thinking about it. It did make sense and he would just had to wait a little longer for his plan to ambush Halfar during the attacks.

"Yes, that is correct. Rest assured, we will be ready on schedule."

He bowed and exited.

Halfar drummed his fingers on the arm rests. He knew exactly what Kur was thinking and it gave him all the more reason to unleash Rass on him when the time came. Locking eyes with Rass on the other end, he nodded. Rass stood and bowed out as well to make his own battle plans. Alone in the dining hall, Halfar leaned back and thought of his new born son. A smile crept on his face. Farin being his first child, he couldn't figure out why it had taken him so long to understand the meaning of procreation. A century of frolicking produced none because he made sure it did not. Child rearing was the last thing on his agenda.

Until now.

✺*

Farin could be vicious when provoked. That didn't stop Ganna from trying to take him for some extra testing of his biological system. While the guardians at the sandbox were preoccupied, Ganna snuck in and snatched the sleeping infant without disturbing the other baby beasts.

She paid for it dearly when he woke up as they entered the lab and bit into her arm, the swiping motion of his head opening a nasty gash in her flesh. That is how Chardon found her in the search for her son; Ganna bleeding profusely cursing the infant as she tossed him aside against a nearby table to tend her wounds.

"You little monster! I'd dissect you if I thought no one would miss you." She had the sealing tool in her hands when she turned and saw Mara, with Chardon, standing in the doorway. Immersed in her own treatment, she had not seen them enter the medical chamber. There was a simmering of malice in both their eyes that left Ganna cold inside. She smiled sweetly.

"Chardon! I was going to find you later. I needed to do a check up on your little one, so I brought him here." Their expressions did not change.

Mara went around Chardon and retrieved Farin. With him safely in her arms, she left the chamber. Whatever was about to happen, she wanted no part of. Ganna felt she may have gone too far this time.

"I would like to think you were blinded by some sick sense of scientific discovery. Knowing how you really feel about manbeasts and my child, who is similar, I believe you have an intense hatred for them." Chardon stepped closer to her. "You made an error. That child you are so intent on dissecting is MY child."

She grabbed Ganna by the neck with lightning speed and picked her up from the floor. Ganna gagged dropping the sealing tool. Blood dripped onto the floor below creating a small pool. With the other hand, Chardon was in the process of forming an energy ball.

"Stop!"

Jaron flew into the room and knocked Ganna out of Chardon's grip. Her body landed against an operating table and she slid down, touching her neck.

"She is not worth it!" Jaron pulled Chardon away, leaving Ganna to herself. "Come away!"

As they left the chamber, not bothering to shut the door, and into the clearing, Chardon whirled on Jaron who was ready to defend herself.

"Why did you stop me?" she seethed calmly.

"Because, we don't need to explain the death of our lead medical healer. Whether you like it or not, we still need her."

"She is no better than Sestis."

Jaron's head snapped upward. "What do you mean?" Chardon turned away from her and headed for the sandbox. "She couldn't have! Chardon!" She went after her almost running.

Ganna crawled over to the sealing tool and used it to close her wound. Hearing the way Jaron yelled in surprise, she figured Chardon would have to tell her about Sestis.

Can't keep all your secrets hidden much longer, leader.

Jakar always had his little siblings to play with. When Mara came in, Farin in tow, he couldn't help taking him up for inspection. The tiny hands bandaged up made him frown.

Was that really necessary?

They stared at each other silently for a long time making it a peculiar sight when Jaron and Chardon walked in. It was probably endearing, if he could say so himself.

"Bonding with your new cousin?" Chardon asked.

His mother shook her head in warning as she went to check on Trinon asleep in the sandbox.

"He is quite vicious so be careful." Jakar frown at that and glance at her with doubt. "Just ask Ganna. She's probably in the process of sealing that wound he gave her."

He looked back at Farin with admiration.

"You didn't do anything drastic, right?" Mara asked Chardon.

"Your mother stopped me."

"I am relieved. I never knew she was capable of something like that. Does she feel that way towards manbeasts too?"

"Yes, she does." Jaron replied. "She hides it well enough for most. I knew long ago what she really thought and of me, who mated with one."

Bringing Farin back down, Jakar handed him over to Chardon.

"He does smell of blood."

Mara leaned over him to check again to make sure she had not missed any.

"I rinsed his mouth out with some of the spring's water. He ended up swallowing some of it though."

Seeing Trinon was indeed comfortable, His mother left, probably to find his father. He could tell by her expression that she must have found out more about Sestis and her disturbing deeds.

Was everything their race had endured really all leading up to her actions?

As angry as he was with Talas and Kelin, it was clear they were merely gears in a giant machine.

Modas was meditating by the waterfall near the mountains so Jaron approached him quietly in vain. He opened his eyes and glanced over at her. The look on her face told him whatever she wanted was serious enough to need his undivided attention.

He didn't stand up, just motioned for her to sit in front of him.

"Ganna decided in her infinite wisdom to snatch Farin from the sandbox and do some experimenting. Chardon went to the medical lab and was about to murder the conniving scientist. I had to stop her."

Modas shifted uneasily on the slab of rock. He too knew about Ganna's obsession with dissecting manbeast like creatures for her scientific research.

"Chardon had hinted about Sestis' role in torture. I have some theories on what they could have entailed. You know something, don't you? Why won't you tell me?"

"Would it matter?"

"Stop keeping secrets from me! You and Chardon always have something only the two of you know. Why is that? Tell me!"

He sighed and cleared his throat.

"She had a thing for learning how other species functioned. Her and Ganna devised ways to 'procure' specimens. It came to a head when Sestis learned of Chardon and Halfar's affair. She threatened to expose them. I decided to protect them from her and she turned on me."

"What?" Jaron reared back.

✻✻❂✻✻

Lassa: Over 100 Years Ago

Modas watched from the chamber door cracked slightly open as Sestis admired herself in the seven-foot viewing glass she had brought back from one of her interplanetary meetings. She was quite beautiful with chestnut colored curls kept piled high on her head and deep blue eyes. Her pale skin had a sheen to it, giving the illusion she glowed. At a little over six feet tall, she was statuesque.

The door made a loud creaking sound as Modas entered her private chamber, causing her to look towards it. She turned, moving the bottom of her golden embroidered robe out of the way. No one on their planet dressed as such so it made her stand out. She had said it made her feel regal whenever she wore it. Some seedy merchant on one of her many well solicited planet excursions had it made for her in exchange for company.

"Come for a mid-evening tryst with your leader?"

Her smile was wide and sinister.

"You are not my leader."

"Really? Because I am the one who rules this world, not Chardon."

"Our world has no ruler. This is not a dictatorship."

"I beg to differ, you monster!" She leaned on the banister attached to the viewing glass. "Because of me our reach spans across the galaxy."

"That is not what we wished for. We want to be left alone. If the people knew…"

"What? That their leader is a changeling mating with some disgusting off world creature? I could expose that truth!"

"No. I will tell them about you."

"You will do no such thing, manbeast!" She hissed then laughed. "If you so much as attempt to speak one word I will have you torn apart by a Razznian, your body parts tossed into the meat pile for processing. How would your mate like the taste of her beloved manbeast roasted with herbs?"

Modas moved towards her. She was quicker and rammed him into the wall, pinning him there. Tendrils of energy writhed around his neck from her fingertips.

"You are not special, monster. Chardon will be obedient and so shall you. Are we in agreement?"

"Understood."

She released him and waved her hand, signaling him to leave. He left to check on Chardon who no doubt had a similar run in with her.

Jaron was more upset by this revelation than she thought she would be from the outcome of his explanation. If Sestis were alive today, she would kill her herself. The manipulation she had engaged in was counter-productive to their race. *Their race!* Jaron recalled what Halfar said about trying to repair the damage caused by her with the interplanetary councils.

"What has she done? We don't want interference from other races. Are we now considered some galactic power?"

"Not anymore because as far as the councils know, our race was destroyed. We no longer exist."

Thinking of the implications of that, Jaron put her hands to her face and gasped. No one knew of their settlement on this planet. There was obviously no help coming and why their resources were so low. She stared at her mate and they both silently agreed once and for all to help Halfar instead of double crossing him as planned.

"We need to find out how to open the gate to the other worlds." Jaron suggested.

"Halfar knows how to access them."

"Can we really fix what she has done?"

"All we can do is try."

Chardon sat in her chamber breast feeding Farin, his tiny claws latched into her flesh. This was the only time she unwrapped his hands. Because her skin healed fast, it was of no concern. He gurgled and kept on drinking.

She was amazed he never cried and stared at everyone with such conviction, as if analyzing them. Chardon did not want to be overly protective after the incident with Ganna. She had to consider a guardian for him. Maybe Mara or Und would be willing to take on the task.

The gate opened at the far edge of the fields and Halfar hurried through the vortex and onto the planet's soil. He nodded at the guardian and walked hastily towards the housing commons to see his son. His stride slowed as he reached the entrance. Entering Chardon's chamber seeing mother and child silently sitting on the bed, Farin asleep with his claws still hooked into his mother's breast, made his chest tighten.

"I never thought you could be any more beautiful than before, yet you are."

"Don't start with that. I'm trying to keep him from waking up."

Halfar raised an eyebrow at what she was implying. Mating would be a great release for the anxiety he had pent up inside.

"That is not what I came for." He sat down next to her and kissed her shoulder, careful not to jostle Farin. "Maybe another time. He's sweet." Halfar blurted out. "It must be from your race."

"He's also vile when he attacks." Halfar leaned away, curious. "Ganna snatched him while he was asleep, so he bit a chunk out of her. All for her research, I suppose."

"Shall I give her what she wants and dissect her instead?" He was furious, deciding to remain calm. "I had a feeling she was up to something sinister when she suggested slicing you open to retrieve Farin."

"I wanted to murder her right then and there. Jaron stopped me."

"Your cousin is more level headed than you think, because she was correct."

Chardon turned to him. "How did you know we were cousins?"

"Because, I asked long ago why your names were so similar. Modas speaks when he wants to."

"Ahh. Well our parents were not very original when it came to that."

Halfar tucked his hands gently under Farin and pulled him off her, cradling him in his arms. He didn't stir as his father laid back on the bed with him.

"I want to stay."

"Then stay." Chardon crawled onto the bed to lay next to him.

"I can't, not yet. Not until this is done."

"Then get it done, quickly."

****☼****

"Don't treat me like baby!" Trinon snapped at Mota.

Some of the warriors still in the battle arena hurriedly grabbed their gear and exited into the surrounding fields. Domestic quarreling between manbeasts could get ugly.

"You need to let your hands heal!"

Mota flicked him in the forehead. He had found his little brother at the training site for combat maneuvers learning to use his legs and feet in a fight. Trying to keep Trinon in one place for more than an hour was proving to be a challenge. At the same time, he knew getting back on schedule was a good thing for him. On instinct, Trinon punched him in the stomach with both fists and regretted it. The pain made him suck in too much air and he swooned. Mota caught him and let him struggle.

"Please, just rest for the day." He felt Trinon slump and little hands wrapped around him.

Not far from them, Modas and Jakar stood watching the two brothers bond. They were unclear if Mota would be a hindrance or an asset to the coming mission. His demeanor suggested a mind too soft for combat except they both knew he could snap out of it at any moment and be just as deadly as any other warrior.

"If you need me to deal with Kur, let me know." Jakar offered.

"No need. Halfar will take care of that."

"Then I can focus on the enforcers stationed near North America."

"Just be careful. Those enforcers are not normal, as Halfar explained."

"Not to worry," Mara came up behind them, "I will back up the old one." Jakar made a face. "Yes, I am referring to you, and not our father." She flung an arm over each of their shoulders and focused on what they were observing. "Ahh, that makes me wish I were still a little one. You were so nice to me then."

"I still am."

Jakar grabbed her arm off his shoulder and flipped her over, even though she had not let go of their father. He came tumbling down as well to one knee. Jakar made no apologies to either as he stepped away from them.

"Father, sister." With that, he walked off.

"See? Even you get sucked into his ill manners." Mara brushed dirt off her robes.

Modas, still on bended knee started to smile a little then a chuckle came out of him. Mara's eyes went wide with disbelief. She saw her mother in the distance and beckoned her.

"Come quickly! Look!" Jaron tripped as she neared them seeing the silent giant, Modas, having a brief laugh at his children's expense. "He's actually laughing!"

He stopped and made a serious face as he stood to tower over his mate.

"That was not a laugh."

"Oh, it was." Jaron grinned. She jabbed him in the rib. "You should do it more often."

⁎⁎☼⁎⁎

Halfar watched the holoscreen floating in front of him while he marched towards the center of the palace with his personal army in tow. Arriving, he made sure his entourage was securely positioned in the circle carved on the floor. The entire outer ring rotated around making the center ascend to the ceiling opening above. Wind swirled down through it like a tornado as it gaped wider to let the platform through. He took his attention from the holoscreen to look up. It was about to begin.

From information leaked purposely by Rass, the military Earth forces created a unified front to engage the enemy. Makeshift underground bunkers ere made to evacuate as many civilians as possible while military guarded encampments popped up in regions farthest from the warzones for those refusing to go under and face their fate head on. He found that part rather asinine on the humans' part. There was an eerie silence around the world.

Rass relayed orders to his troops via commlink as well as to Halfar. He sent the one recruited by Kur in his plan to kill Halfar to a hostile region heavily armed by Earth forces. It would be a slaughter. Another troop he positioned to lay in wait for Kur's third wave on the Asian border.

Once Jakar arrived through the vortex, they would rendezvous and work with Earth's military forces to destroy Kur's modified enforcers. Rass would command the remaining troop himself to Kur's location off the southern coastline of North America. This time, he won't hold back his power. Kur deserved nothing less.

Since Halfar was never unguarded on a battlefield, Kur had to make sure he separated him from the main force midway in the melee and make it seem like an accident. He was not to be positioned anywhere near Halfar's troops, except his plan demanded it. A lowly enforcer was no match for their ruler. His main army would be elsewhere while four enforcers and himself blended into Halfar's army.

He smiled at the brilliance of his plan. Soon, the cherished almighty Armada would be his to command. His smile faded remembering Rass, also a General in line to take the reins. The smile returned. He would get rid of that one too. Checking the number of modified enforcers under his command, he was satisfied he could win.

"Come, my warriors! Let us strip this planet to its core and see what lies beneath!"

⚹✷✷⚹

Mota used his teeth to tighten the leather strips around his wrists, flexing his fingers to make sure they had ample movement. Trinon watched him from a seat directly below him. The sandbox was empty due to Chardon implementing a state of isolation. It was a precaution just in case the enemy somehow got through one of the gates. Sighing, Mota looked down at him.

"Well, I guess I'm off to rid Earth of some nasty enforcers."

"You'll be right back?" Trinon asked in barely a whisper.

"Of course I am!" Mota threw his head back and laughed loudly, suddenly stopping short as he noticed Trinon was not amused. The little one just sat with a downward stare. "Look at me." Trinon obeyed. "There is nothing that would stop me from coming back."

"Except death."

"I am not dying on that miserable rock and neither is anyone else. Understood?" Trinon nodded. "Good!" He bent down and ran his fingers through Trinon's mane. "No training until I get back."

Jakar startled them out of their moment. He waited for Mota to join him at the edge of the field and they left together.

"It's time."

Battle Cries

At the gate console, a small army of energy users and manbeasts were lined up in groups ready to deploy. There were nine groups in all, the main one being the largest, which included Chardon and Modas. Back in male form, Chardon was ready for battle. Jaron, Jakar, Talas, Kelin and four other warriors led a group for the assault on Kur's enforcers. The army was small enough to maneuver the landscape unnoticed yet deadly enough to cause major damage to the enforcers without any casualties of their own. Talas planned to keep his promise.

Chardon went over the rendezvous points for each group via holoscreen while Ganna input coordinates on the gate console. A virtual map of Earth's entire planet surface was floating in midair on display. The whole operation was going to be tricky since Earth defense forces had no idea they were getting assistance from them. He shut down the holoscreen in front of him with a wave of his hand and turned to Modas.

"I don't have to stress that we get in, get out and sever the entrance to that planet forever."

"No." Modas flexed his fingers.

He was itching for another fight with the enforcers.

"Do we really have to close it for good?" Ganna addressed them. "We could do some business with them. Maybe even help them with repairs in exchange for…"

Chardon did not let her finish.

"We will no longer interfere with that planet and its people. They are not ready and won't be for at least another century."

"I think gauging their readiness is premature…" Ganna started. "Someone else had the same theory and look where it got us."

There was deafening silence as all knew who he meant. Ganna frowned and returned to her duties of opening multiple vortexes. Chardon did not trust her. He motioned to Jaron signaling her to hurry with Talas' backup plan. There was no need. He noticed Talas had seen the look on Ganna's face and already started moving up the timetable in his head.

The first vortex opened for Kelin's group to arrive on the European front. He bowed to Talas then led the way through. Next was Jakar and Mota to the Asian border. Every group went in sequence as planned with Chardon's being the last to arrive in the North American region.

They would rendezvous with Halfar's troops hoping he had a plan to defeat Kur. He was the last person they wanted to deal with on the battlefield.

From the command deck on the armada's mother ship, Halfar watched cities burn across the planet called Earth. He wished it had not been so but it was too late now. This was something Kur put into motion and had to be seen to the end.

The council members, who had backed Kur on his little plan to send his armada, were executed when found on the ship. They apparently wanted front row viewing of the massacre and proof of Halfar's demise. This is why he hated politics of any kind. Not once, did his now former council think to poll the inhabitants of their world to see if they were dissatisfied with Halfar as ruler, which he knew that was not the case.

Punching in coordinates, he saw something peculiar. Kur's signa- ture was not with his forces off the southern coast. Instead, it showed he was near the rear of Halfar's army on the Northern border near Canada. Kur would not have noticed Halfar missing at the front due to it being heavily guarded as if he were. Although it disturbed him how far his gen- eral was taking this, he grinned and relayed a message to Rass.

"How clever of you," he spoke to the blinking red dot representing Kur on the screen.

Newly devised and barely tested weaponry was being rolled out against the alien enforcers and seemed fairly effective at holding them back. Jaron was almost proud of the human race but knew those same weapons would be turned on each other sometime after this battle died down. Humans were a double edged mystery to her.

As both sides retreated from the other, she made small explosions with her energy spheres to coax the enforcers into an isolated area away from the Earth forces' view. Once there, her group went into a full assault.

The Asian front was a lesson in brutality and strict methods as Jakar witnessed the streamlined attacks from their defense forces. Had he known humans were capable of this, he would have brought fewer warriors. Nonetheless, he needed Mota to draw the enemy away from the Earth people and into their combat zone. To do that, an immediate threat had to be present. He was able to lure the enforcers to an opening in the Asian forces and waited for them to retreat. It worked. Jakar's group came up from the behind the enforcers and started to take them down from there.

Chardon was having a hard time trying to keep the Earth defense forces in his region from assisting. His group had been noticed and after the human in command decided they were friend not foe attempted to ne- gotiate. He explained to the commanding officer who he was and why his race was helping but the man insisted his forces defend their own planet. He was right but Chardon knew they were no match for the enforcers Kur dispatched. It was also dangerous because when Chardon unleashed a ball of energy, it decimated a large chunk of the area. Friend and foe were not discriminated against in its path.

It was no better with Modas carving gashes into the air as he sliced up nearby enforcers. There were too many and that seemed odd. He landed from one of his high jump assaults next to Chardon and they stood back to back. Even the humans could see there was a huge disproportionate amount of enforcers for this area. Something was amiss. Chardon realized it almost in an instant.

"Kur is keeping us busy for a reason."

"He is not here, but his army is."

"Halfar." Chardon had a feeling this might happen. "Let's get this cleaned up." He turned to the commanding officer. "Are you ready?" He scanned over the dead and wounded spread across the battle grounds but the commander nodded. "Good. Here we go."

Halfar had seen enough from the view station of the mother ship's command center. Setting up such an unbalanced battle for the sole purpose of mass slaughter was a bit much for his taste. He liked being on equal ground in a fight. If it was a battle Kur wanted, then that is what he will get.

Rounding up a few more soldiers, he headed to the transport room. No matter what the consequences, he wanted to keep Chardon from harm. He had no faith in the manbeast's abilities to do so.

A bright red beam the color of blood shot down from the sky and hit the planet surface near the advancing forces in the Northern region of the Americas. On impact, a two mile radius of infrastructure and anything else in the vicinity was destroyed. The beam waned in appearance until it was gone and in its place stood Halfar and his personal guards. They marched to intercede with his forces ahead, paying no attention to the debris left in their wake.

The front guards opened up to allow Halfar and his entourage into the fold and reclosed ranks, strengthening their formation. As it moved forward, they were moved further back into the lines until Halfar and his guards were in the middle, protected on all sides. This did not go unnoticed by the rear guards some three miles away.

Kur could not believe what he had just witnessed. It never occurred to him Halfar was not commanding his own army. His rage hit a whole new level and he thought of tearing his ruler's body apart instead of just the quick death blow he had planned. The battle still in the beginning stages, he felt it was the perfect time to be rid of him. Signaling his small group of enforcers who had infiltrated Halfar's army with him to step out of ranks they headed into position.

Up ahead, a vortex opened in front of Halfar's army letting Rass and a handful of his enforcers through. He wasted no time in rushing towards the middle to grab hold of Halfar and pull him out. On his side view he could see Kur advancing from the rear.

"What are you doing?" Halfar was about to break free.

"Did you not command me to deal with Kur myself?"

Rass was des- perate and angry.

Halfar jolted still and raised his head to Rass who made sure to convey his frustration and rage in his stare. It seemed in his rush to deal with Kur his ruler had forgotten that part of the plan. Chardon and Modas were capable of defeating the army of enforcers against them. Halfar had let his emotions get the better of him.

"Then do it!"

Rass did the unthinkable in front of his ruler's army. He threw Halfar behind him and into the vortex leading to Chardon's location. It closed shut right when Kur came through the middle of the formation, cutting down enforcers as he advanced. At the clearing he nearly ran into Rass standing there waiting for him.

"Disappointed?" Rass cocked his head to one side. When Kur sneered, he went into an attack stance. Kur laughed.

"Are you going to stop me? You can't defeat me."

A vortex opened behind him and more altered enforcers spewed out unleashing death on the unsuspecting army near the middle. Rass called out an order to have the remaining forces regroup away from the vortex as it closed. Kur smiled.

"My victory is secure and when I am through with you I will go after Halfar and kill him as well!" He jumped backwards five hundred feet to let his enforcers charge Rass.

Rass was quite calm and didn't move an inch until the first wave of enforcers were in his perimeter. His whole body lit up with a red glow and with one swipe of his arm, a giant arc of red haze from his long- sword sliced through them. Black blood flew in all directions sizzling as it landed on the ground.

The second wave stopped advancing. Kur stood in shock behind them while Rass repositioned himself back into his attack mode, his long sword back behind him.

Pieces of his enforcers rained down around Kur as he stared at Rass. This was not the same easily unhinged, ragtag soldier he had been provok- ing and manipulating the past few decades. No, this was something far more dangerous. It occurred to him that Rass had been holding back his true power all this time. That angered him even more but solidified his resolve.

"There is no need for me to hold back then?" He questioned Rass. The other did not answer or move. "Very well." He drew his claws to their full length. "I'll make this quick."

It unnerved him when Rass did not have any clever jokes or got angry, making him unsure in his ability to defeat him in one blow. He leapt towards him.

A flash of light signaled the impact of their claws ramming into each other. Rass used the back of his legs to push upward into Kur's body and sent him flying with a small gash in his torso. As Kur landed, some of his enforcers moved to defend.

"No! Do not interfere!"

He looked to Rass. That same blank expression remained. Had he been wrong all this time? Could he have mated with him to produce powerful warriors?

"Why won't you say anything?" he demanded.

"There's no need."

Rass was by his side with lightning speed and it took all of Kur's strength to torque his body out of range avoiding a fatal blow. He could see Rass was dying inside but he had no choice. He could not let any emotions get in the way of defeat. Just as Kur cleared himself, Rass at- tacked him again from behind. One of his claws ripped through the back of his shoulder blade and exited out his chest in the front. He was going to go deeper and severe the entire arm but Kur spun around and pushed off of him.

Bleeding and breathing heavily, Kur held his arm together and forced the wound to congeal shut, stopping the blood flow. Even from this distance he could see the hurt in Rass' eyes. It went away as they stared at each other, the blankness returned.

"Don't you see? Halfar is making you suffer by doing this because he's a coward who refuses to face me."

Rass tried not to frown, the struggle showing on his face. He was not going to be manipulated this way and Kur understood that the moment Rass let his guard down, Kur would strike and that would be his end. Rass raised his claws and resumed his attack stance. One death blow was all he needed to land and Kur would be no more. He watched Rass' claws start to shake.

At that moment, Kur realized that he could not win this battle. The council had coerced him into this plan and were probably laughing at how foolish he was; here about to die at the hands of someone who once loved him, on a battlefield of his own doing.

He dropped to his knees and rose his head to the blackened sky scorched with red, not able to remember why he had come to this planet for conquest and why he had involved Halfar. *Ah, yes.* The council wanted a foothold in an uncategorized solar system. It was a random judg- ment and was now costing them everything.

Rass had not made his move just yet when a vortex opened behind him, and from above, a body shot out and struck Kur where he knelt on the ground. Blood gurgled up and a strangled sound came from his lips as he heard Rass screaming. It took him a moment to realize what it was.

"NO!"

The manbeast, Modas, stood towering over him, removing his claws out of Kur's flesh to turn a puzzled look towards Rass. The distraught general came at him, knocking him out of the way. Kur's vision faded just as he felt Rass' arms wrap around him.

Halfar came out of the vortex and saw the tragic scene. He had a suspicion that Rass could not do it. Just as he regretted the destruction of Lassa and almost losing Chardon, he knew Rass was not capable of killing the one he loved. It made it all the worse when he saw Rass snap his head around to face him and scream.

"Why?" He had Kur's body hanging like a ragdoll in his arms.

"I'm sorry."

Halfar motioned his army to regroup with a signal of his hand and they commenced to destroying all of Kur's modified enforcers. It was like hell on Earth tenfold. The sounds, scents and black blood everywhere would make even the most fanatic of gore cringe.

"Can you get him to your healers?" He asked Modas, gesturing to Kur.

"What for?" Modas was not amused. His talons flexed.

Chardon stepped onto the battlefield taking in the horrors of the scene. This was too much to bear.

"Take him to Ganna!" Modas frowned at him. "Now!"

Modas complied by plucking Kur's body from Rass' arms and jumping into the vortex. Chardon went over to Rass and literally dragged him through the vortex, Halfar in tow.

"Was that really necessary?" Chardon referred to the massacre going on behind them.

"Believe me, it is. Those things were never meant to be. Whoever authorized it will have me to deal with shortly."

"The Armada?"

"I left orders to depart as soon as the modified enforcers' numbers reach zero."

"Very thorough." Chardon closed the vortex. Modas would have to go through three more to arrive back on their world. "What about Rass?" They both looked down at the catatonic general. His limbs dangled like rubber from his body, eyes in a blank stare.

"He can recuperate on New Lassa before I send him back to our world as the leader for my armada."

"New Lassa? Did I say we were staying on that world?"

"I said I would fix it."

"Hmmm." He nodded towards Rass. "What makes you think he will obey you this time?"

"I have my reasons. He will be just fine. Plus," He smiled wickedly, "this will give him a chance to nurse Kur back to health."

Charon shook his head in disbelief.

Mara heard the cheering and cries of relief as she led her small group out of the vicinity littered with pieces of modified enforcers. They had successfully rid the area of them without getting noticed by the Earth forces who were engaged in the battle. She made sure that her group blended in somehow so no one was the wiser. Thinking of the clean up almost made her gag. She did not envy the humans for that task. Finding an inauspicious corner off the battlefield, she opened a vortex that led back to their world. Her mission was done.

The same was true of the other sites as humans celebrated their triumph over the alien enemy unaware that it was an internal fight between two alien factions and had nothing to do with them. Chardon returned to the Northern region to speak with the commanding Earth forces officer, reminding him and his men not to tell a soul about how they were helped by another alien race. It would just complicate things. He watched the humans, too tired to celebrate, start to pack up their gear and move out. Whether they kept the promise or not was of no concern since the gate would be sealed for eternity.

Halfar returned to the mother ship and assessed the data on all modified enforcers. When the counter reached zero, he ordered the remaining troops back to the ship and prepare for the trip back to their home world. He had some government tasks to deal with before going back to New Lassa. His scientists needed to assemble a planet bomb to inject life into the planet and another one for its weak sun. Seeing Farin was at top of that list but that would have to wait.

Explanations

Kur could hardly move as he forced his body to obey him. Although healed, he could still feel his wounds. He watched Ganna for a moment, immediately registering her as a threat. Ganna hummed to herself softly while examining the cultures she had collected from him before closing his wounds and reviving him.

Getting her hands on other races biological system made her juices flow. He was sure it had been a long time since she had access to such specimens. The last being when Sestis still lived.

So fascinated and engrossed in her studies, she did not hear Kur stirring on the operating table. She had not ordered his body moved to the recovery chamber because, as he heard her explain, she planned on reopening him for more tests before Chardon came back.

Sitting further up until upright, he tried to extend a talon. The pain was excruciating, forcing him to hiss loudly which made Ganna jump out of her seat in fear. He saw her reach over to her right grasping for the weapon that lay near her fingers.

Chardon entered the chamber in female form. Kur could tell she had a feeling that Ganna was going to try something unsavory with him.

"And that will be enough. I believe your work is done. Why is he not in the recovery chamber?"

"I was waiting until he was stable." Ganna moved her hand back, answering sweetly.

"That was not her intent!" Kur held his torso trying to breathe through pain. "Where am I?"

"A world we acquired after the destruction of our home world."

Kur made the connection from hazy memory.

"I always wondered why he kept your cores when he was the one responsible for your race's demise."

He swung his legs over the table and rested his head against the wall. He felt disoriented.

"There is someone who will be glad to see you are awake. I'll lead you to them."

"I can barely walk," he snapped, pushing himself off the wall to set his feet on the cold floor.

He became aware that he was wearing his battle pants and nothing else as his body shivered. Chardon threw a long-sleeved robe at him along with some leather boots.

"You could use these, yes?"

As he dressed, he kept an eye on Ganna who stared at him with an unnatural lust. Not mating. What she wanted his body for made him dress quicker. Standing up, his vision blurred, and he barely caught himself with one hand bracing the wall. It finally cleared, letting him stand to his full height of seven feet.

Ganna pressed back into her desk. His slender frame must have deceived her into thinking he was smaller than Modas when in fact he was taller and menacing. It satisfied him a little to know she was afraid now.

"Come with me."

Chardon swept an arm towards the door at the same time giving Ganna a look of poison. If they did not need that woman, it would be so easy to rid themselves of her.

Mixed emotions swam around inside Kur's head when Chardon led him to a small living chamber with the bare minimum of furnishings. On the bed curled up in the fetal position was Rass looking small and vulnerable, unlike his usual self. His breathing seemed ragged and certain parts of his body twitched.

"What's wrong with him?" He whirled on Chardon, not sure why he was so angry.

"He's in a state of shock. Last time he saw you, you were presumed dead."

"I don't understand, he was ordered to kill me. Why would…?"

"Do you really think it would be easy for him to murder someone he holds dear even if they do not feel the same?" Chardon interrupted him. Kur's mouth clamped shut. "I will leave you alone. Surely, there is much to clarify." She exited the chamber.

Kur moved slowly to the bed and eased as painlessly as he could next to Rass. Memories of how badly he treated him when they were still intimate so long ago filled his head. Hands shaking, he reached down and caressed his hair. Rass did not stir. Kur's chest began to hurt, and he lay across Rass' body to ease the pain. It should not have turned out this way.

∗∗☼∗∗

Battle scars were a cherished form of storytelling and it gave Mota a sigh of relief to see the wounds he received from the last battle disrupt the smooth new skin he had when revived. They made him feel whole again while he boasted about them to his young siblings. Und was not impressed and just stared disinterested at them. Trinon was inspecting each one with intensity and listening to every detail.

In the doorway stood Jakar watching the scene with the same look as Und. Bragging was a young manbeast's thing. After so many scars and battles it was just natural to forget about all that. With a sigh, he reached over and grabbed Mota by the mane, pulling him out of the commons onto the walk path with him.

"I was just getting to the best part!"

"Hmm."

"You don't even have any! Your body is still pristine after getting your core back."

"I know how to not get hurt in a battle."

Mota was insulted, he could tell. His younger brother was just as good at fighting and he in no way was suggesting incompetence on the battle field.

"Maybe I don't avoid hand combat like some others." Jakar stopped walking, letting Mota know he had gone too far. "I don't mean that." He whispered.

"I should not have said that either."

Jakar resumed walking. They were already late for the debriefing with the council.

Chardon was already in talks with one of the agricultural engineers regarding the planet bomb meant to jump start the planet's growth. Halfar was coming through the gate as they spoke. The success of the mission was debatable. On the one hand, they were able to close the gate leading to Earth and on the other, Kur was not quite dealt with along with a handful of Halfar's advisors who managed to flee.

While Modas escorted Halfar, the two warriors conversed. The talk was strained, there being no amicable relation between them, though in their best interest considering their mates were related. As they neared the commons, Halfar slowed down.

"I want to see Farin."

"There's no time." Modas kept his stride towards the council chamber. "We're late."

"Of course," Halfar let out a heavy breath of air. "Are your little ones well?"

"As could be."

"I heard one your sons had an accident during training."

"His claws were broken off."

It was said so nonchalantly that it did not register with Halfar at first. He halted.

"That is horrifying." It made him shudder.

"He heals fast." They had reached the outer door of the council chamber. "After you."

During the meeting, there were many opinions on what a good target for the planet bomb would be, from agriculture to natural resources. When it came down to the main factor, the sun and its lack of light and warmth, their focus on the matter took priority. This was much to the chagrin of the scientists, engineers and Ganna. Halfar turned the meeting over to his chief science officer who he brought with him from his home world, then signaled Chardon to leave with him.

Outside, they both walked up the short hill and through the fields to the commons where all the little ones congregated. Farin was now crawling a bit on his own. He never found out how far he could go because the older children often picked him up by his middle like a baby manbeast to play. Jaron had left the meeting early, so she was the culprit that grabbed him this time. As she raised him up she caught a glimpse of Chardon from the corner of her eye.

"Is the meeting over?"

"No. The scientists are going over strategy to do something about the sun."

"Oh." She turned her attention back to Farin. "Not interested."

"Can I have my child for a moment?" Halfar held out his arms. Jaron squinted at him then gave the little one up. "Thank you." He pulled Farin to him and smelled his skin.

"He's worse than a nursing maid." Jaron quipped, and Chardon whacked her in the back of her neck. "That was uncalled for!"

"I need to speak with Kur soon." Halfar said, his full attention still on Farin.

"I can take you to him. He may be a bit hostile."

"He's awake?" This was unexpected so soon.

"Ganna was going to take him back down and dissect him. Of course, she was going to reassemble and revive him."

"I'm sure she would have." His sarcasm did not go unnoticed to Jaron who snorted.

Kur nor Rass had moved from their positions on the bed that barely held them. It was a strange sight for Halfar and he wasn't sure if disturbing them was a good idea. The way they were entangled together like two exhausted lovers made him regret asking Rass to rid them of Kur.

As much as he hated to do it, he went to the bed and jostled Kur awake. On reflex, Kur shot out an arm and grabbed Halfar by the wrist ready to toss him across the room. He found his prey would not budge from the weak pressure he had applied. Opening his eyes, he saw Halfar staring down at him with pursed lips. Bearing the pain in his body, he let go and eased up into a sitting position.

"My lord," He bowed his head glancing over at Rass.

"Don't wake him." A closer inspection made him notice Rass had not stirred, he turned to Chardon. "What's wrong with him?"

"This is your doing." Kur sneered then averted his gaze.

"Is it? I am not the only one at fault."

"No, it isn't." Kur hung his head further down in defeat.

"Tell me why? What could you have accomplished with this plan?"

"I was reassured by your advisors I would be given free reign over the armada and there were some hostile worlds needing to be conquered to expand our reach in the galaxy. I know now that Earth was picked at random because they were no real threat to us. It was to get rid of you all along. I was just a pawn to do the deed."

"Why get rid of me, the ruler of our world?"

"They told me that you planned to cede our home world to Razznians and they would control your armada."

"That's outrageous!" Halfar could not believe what he was hearing. "Where did such a lie come from?"

"With the invasion of Lassa, a deal was made to enslave the remaining population on Razzna in exchange for rulership over the Grata system which has seven planets."

"Who would be ruling that solar system?" Halfar was confused. Chardon had a sickening expression as she held her abdomen.

"That female Lassian, Sestis. The deal went south of course when the planet was not only scorched but destroyed with her on it. It was said that you brokered the deal with her since there were rumors you wanted her mate, Lassa's leader." He turned to Chardon making eye contact. "I figured they were right after seeing his obsessive behavior regarding your core."

"I would never…" Halfar was shaking with rage.

Sestis had set in motion more devastation than anyone thought. Chardon stood pale next to him.

"This is not over." Kur finally stood. "The Razznians will not be happy that her end of the deal was not fulfilled. With news that her race has survived and now on a new world, they will come after you."

"How long do we have?"

"Maybe ten years before they find this world and launch an assault."

Modas had entered the chamber more silently than ever.

"We will be ready."

"I wish to redeem myself," Kur slid off the bed and knelt painfully down to one knee, "if it is your will."

"Stand up!" Halfar snapped. "We have something more serious than your redemption to consider!" He strolled up to Modas. "How many manbeasts are there, truly?"

"Enough. In ten years there will be nearly ten thousand."

Chardon tapped her lower lip and her eyes narrowed.

"Sestis." Everything stemmed from her devious actions to gain power at the cost of her race. "Well, I guess we have to fight for our survival after all."

"This time, you will have my armada."

The news traveled quickly around the planet and soon everyone was preparing for a new battle. Months went by gathering knowledge for new technology and how to ration supplies. Halfar sent Kur and Rass to their home world to rectify the bizarre events that his former advisors had created.

A Rising

Trinon stood, now five feet ten inches tall, in front of the giant stone monolith looking up at the top of it. In silent admiration of its size, he unwrapped his hands letting the bandages fall on the ground. Without taking his eyes from the summit, he extended his talons, thicker and sharper than before from aging, and leapt high in the air.

He landed halfway up the stone wall and using his claws reached the top at an unimaginable speed neither out of breath or stamina. Satisfied, he did a back flip off the summit and sailed into the air laying back into the free fall with his eyes closed. The air concaved around him and his body's resistance felt good.

Mota, Jakar, Mara, and Und watched him from their position on a hill across form the monolith as he landed on the ground below in a kneeling position, his fist deep in the dirt. The impact caused a crater ten feet in diameter, and a few inches deep around him. He stood up straight, looking up at the summit again.

"I think he may be ready in five or ten years." Mota announced proudly.

"Or less," Modas added. Jakar nodded in agreement.

"I'll go spar with him." Und volunteered in a defeated tone.

"Oh, you won't get away that easy," Mota quipped. "You are just as ready."

Und smiled knowingly, his droopy lidded eyes holding a glimmer of excitement. He couldn't wait to get into a real fight alongside his siblings.

PART TWO:
SEEDS OF CONVICTION

ONE:

A Spy on Earth

The last alien warships ascended high above the charred remains of cities worldwide, into Earth's atmosphere. The battle between planet Azrom's rebel faction and Earth had come to a screeching halt with only a select few from each respective party knowing why. It was fierce and bloody with casualties disproportionate on the human's side. Somehow, every mutant Azrom enforcer had been wiped out. A mixture of relief and sorrow swept through the inhabitants of Earth.

The Razznian spy, dressed in a hooded track suit to hide the brown scaly skin covering his entire body, watched with curiosity as the humans struggled to comprehend the mass destruction left behind from a battle they had no idea how or why it started. His lidless red eyes scanned the area and his mouth opened to reveal two rows of razor sharp teeth, his equivalent of a smile. Observing, though not interacting with, the battle proved to be a good idea.

He had watched Azrom's armada supporting another alien group on the ground and upon getting a closer look, the Razznian realized they were Lassian; the race supposedly extinct by Halfar's own hands.

How could they be here, and in such large numbers?

He made his way back to the rendezvous point where a portal sat open for his departure back to Razzna. He had a lot to report on.

Home Coming

The sky churned viciously as Azrom's Armada mother ship descended from space at an angle through the stratosphere. All six thrusters rotated maneuvering beneath its underbelly in preparation for landing. The gunmetal hull covered with large spikes forced the air to concave around it as it emerged from the clouds. Correcting its position so it was perpendicular to the ground below, created winds with enough force to bend nearby trees nearly in half and rattle the palace's foundation.

Halfar watched, from the command center of the ship, as his palace guards rushed forward onto the roof to await his arrival. In full battle gear, he stood arms folded with his legs wide apart while the crew around him focused on controlling the ship. Being back on his home world sent a shiver through him. There was a lot of work to accomplish in order to rectify the damage done by his advisors, now deceased. He had dispatched them as a ruler was obligated to do.

The invasion and conquering of Earth, instigated by his advisors with General Kur as a scapegoat, turned into rescuing the human race from his own Armada. Assistance came from warriors of planet Lassa via their leader, Chardon. After the battle ended, the gate to Earth had been severed. Humankind was not ready for interaction with techno- logically advanced alien races.

More damage had been done to his soul and that of his men than anything else. The loss and regret spread wide over the Lassians, who he had nearly made extinct, and his own race. It was a mess he alone had to correct over the next few decades. Right now, he needed a plan for rebuilding his council and the trust of his generals.

With a roar and crushing winds, the ship settled into a hover over the palace platform. A small square of light opened at the underbelly and shot down a few hundred feet from the waiting entourage. The light rescinded and, in its place, stood Halfar with his two Generals, Rass and Kur, flanking him on each side followed by a handful of enforcers. Everyone's hair whipped into their faces as the ship moved laterally across the sky towards the docking bay located ten miles to the east.

The guards dropped down in unison to one knee, bowing their heads. Their left arm lay across the thigh while the other hand lay flat on the ground in front of them. Halfar grimaced at the display. It had been a long time since he witnessed the perfect triangular formation of his guards in full regalia. He glanced at Kur and saw the twinkle of delight in his eyes. Rass seemed unimpressed, for he didn't acknowledge the greeting. After a few moments, the guards stood back up and the leader came forward to address Halfar directly.

"My lord, it is good to see you again. It has been too long." He bowed his head again.

"Yes, a shame it has to be on these circumstances."

"Indeed." The leader's face scrunched up as if he had smelled something rotten. Halfar motioned towards the door leading into the palace and the guards about faced, parting like the red sea to allow passage. "How long will you be staying this time, my lord?" He had to try and keep his lord's fast pace while conversing.

"At the least, until I elect a new council and assure the progress of rebuilding."

As the entourage passed the guards at the palace entry, Halfar saw slight movement out of the corner of his eye and witnessed Rass attempt to stop himself from stumbling by reaching out to place his hand on a wall nearby. His injuries were minor but the mental anguish he suffered had manifested as physical pain. Kur caught him by the elbow on impulse. It occurred in mere seconds and no one else noticed. He worried about both his young Generals.

The doors to the throne room were opened by two guards to reveal a massive hall built like a large cave made of golden Amber rock. Torches along the walls gave it a coppery glow. Giant columns the color of sandstone spaced twenty feet apart from each other stood majestic connecting to the ceiling. Entering the throne room, Halfar motioned for servants with his hand and twenty of them appeared lining up in two rows on either side of the hall. He proceeded to his rightful seat, taking the stone steps two at a time, and turned to face the entrance before plop- ping down in a heap. Rass and Kur came up to take their place on either side of him. A servant advanced and Halfar waved him closer, whispering instructions in his ear. The servant stepped back, bowed low, and left the hall taking four other servants with him.

"My Lord, is there anything you require of your royal guards at this moment?" The captain of the guard stood at attention in the entryway.

"No, keep watch of the gateway portal and wait for another arrival."

"My Lord?" The Captain raised one eyebrow.

"I have," Halfar hesitated for a moment. This was a delicate matter. "Acquired a mate."

There was a palpable silence as the news took hold. Halfar had never taken a mate before or had any interest in procreating for that matter. A mate now seemed a bit too sudden for them.

"She should be arriving two moons from now with a small group and," Halfar sighed heavily knowing this would be yet another shock, "my son." He heard the gasps.

"Congratulations, My Lord!" They all shouted in unison.

"A royal heir is to be celebrated." The Captain announced.

"Yes, yes. When they arrive, we will discuss the details." Halfar waved them away.

As the guards exited the throne room, the doors thundering shut, Kur turned to him and tsked. He was rewarded with a look of disgust complete with narrowed eyes.

"My Lord, divulging such matters on the first day is irresponsible of you. You could have at least waited a moon cycle to spring it."

"It would not have mattered either way."

The male servant from earlier returned with the other four carrying various trays of food and refreshments. Each tray was laid at the edge of the throne's platform. He carried two large cushions on top of his head for the two generals. It was not a moment too soon. Rass eased himself down onto the cushion set beside him and went into a near fetal position. Kur sat down cross legged on his and glanced over with a worried expression.

"Leave us," Halfar ordered. The other servants along the walls hesitated. He knew why. Their ruler should never be left unattended but at the moment he had no patience for it. "Now!" He watched them all flee through the inner chamber doors on the far side of the hall.

Making sure the last one was far gone, Halfar pushed himself off his throne and crawled over to Rass. He checked his breathing by laying a hand on his chest to feel the rise and fall of it. Rass did not stir from the touch. Halfar saw Kur's shadow fall over them. Stealthy as ever. He brushed some of Rass' hair away from his face and stood up next to Kur. They both looked at each other; Halfar contemplating, Kur accusatory.

Knowing their past history as lovers, Halfar giving Rass orders to eliminate Kur seemed especially cruel given Kur's situation. Rass mentally broke in the act and Halfar knew he was to blame. The following months afterwards on the planet New Lassa found Kur trying to repair their damaged relationship.

"He is in no shape to deal with the reforming of the regiments." Kur stated the obvious.

"Then you have to deal with it along with inspection of the battle ships."

"That leaves you to do what, exactly?"

"Deal with the remaining council members who weren't stupid enough to go against me."

"Ahh, well I bid you success."

"First, we rest a bit." Halfar went back to his throne. "You will stay with him for a while after I leave?" Kur's face scrunched up as he turned to him. "Should I not have bothered to ask?" He eased back and began to contemplate how to rectify the damage done.

Chardon surveyed the landscape of New Lassa for the best options to make it more habitable since their original home had been destroyed, scorched black. An event regretted by all involved. Scientists from both races collaborated to find a remedy for the planet's weak sun and now in the works. A brighter sun meant more heat and better vegetation. So far, the highest temperature during the warm season reached a mere twenty one degrees Celsius. The eyes of everyone on the planet over the past few decades started changing to accommodate its light.

Loud screeching from across the fields made Chardon's head snap up and turn towards the sound. It meant one thing; her son was being teased by one of the older manbeasts. She smiled at that. If not by Mota, then possibly Trinon. Soon, they would travel to Azrom to stay with Halfar for a little while.

The visit was more like a war council than a family reunion. Chardon's previous mate, Sestis, had set into motion a string of events that threatened both Lassa and Azrom. Planning should only take a decade at most. The only way to battle their new joint enemy, Razzna, was to combine their forces and hope for victory. Razznians fought with no sense of honor simply because they were not as strong as they appeared.

Off in the distance, a tall male figure advanced towards her. As he got closer she immediately knew who it was. His brown sandy colored mane hung down to the back of his knees, swaying in the light breeze. What started as a tiny smile grew, spreading across his angelic face as he caught sight of Chardon, steely blue eyes reflecting the sunlight. He was wearing a full body suit with the undone robe flapping around his six-foot five-inch muscled frame.

"Trinon," Chardon started to ask his question.

"Hmm?" Even at a distance, a manbeasts' hearing was impeccable.

"Was that you torturing my son earlier?"

Trinon's smile turned into a big wide grin.

"No, not at all."

He stopped a few feet from Chardon and his eyes averted away. All he had to do next was stick his tongue out and Chardon would have smacked him. It was something Trinon became fond of doing lately to appear innocent and cheeky.

"Really?" Chardon's brow lifted.

"Well," Trinon turned back to look down at her, "Mota began the prodding, and, well."

"Explain yourselves."

"We wanted to see if he could climb the monolith." Trinon's tongue slipped out between his lips and Chardon reached up to grab it with the intention of harm. Trinon was faster bobbing sideways to the right.

"He's not a man beast." Chardon chided him.

"Close enough," a new voice replied from behind Trinon.

Mota came up to them with Chardon's son, Farin, in tow. He was only an inch or two taller than Trinon even though he was much older. They were resembling their father more as the years went on. Mota set Farin down and brushed some loose dirt off the sides of his robes before letting him go to his mother.

Farin was tragically beautiful, which was one of the reasons why Chardon felt others wanted to pick on him. He had stark black hair with slight golden colored waves in it and murky green eyes. Instead of finger-nails, he had shiny black talons sharper than any cutting weapon. His full pink mouth that he inherited from Chardon completed the exotic features.

"They dared me to climb the big stone!" Farin's small voice attempted yelling. "My claws just slid on it and couldn't grip!" Chardon saw his disappointed.

"Yes, well, next time they tease you, slice a piece of it off."

Trinon and Mota's posture went erect at such a suggestion. Mota raised a hand in protest.

"Let's not get all out of sorts over a little fun and games."

Chardon sighed. "We are leaving soon and I don't want any incidents."

"Trinon is going to accompany him, so you need not worry." Mota turned back towards the way he came. "I'll see you off when the time comes. I have to tend to the other little ones." He walked away, and Chardon wondered how he got his personality. Neither of his parents were what one might call cheerful.

****☼****

Chardon watched Modas wait in silence as she tended to a dirty Farin in the basin embedded in the chamber's floor. He didn't move an inch for the duration of the event but there was an expression on his face that Chardon did not like. How Modas felt towards Halfar was no secret. In her opinion that should not transfer to her child.

"Could you hand me a drying cloth?"

"As you wish." Modas stepped further into the chamber, removed a cloth from its rack and handed it to Chardon. He never came any closer than required.

"Am I not worthy of your loyalty and protection any longer?"

"You will always have both."

"That's not why I asked, Modas." Chardon spat through gritted teeth.

"What is it you want from me?"

"Stop treating us like pariahs!"

"Understood"

Chardon slapped the wet cloth on the floor, startling both Farin and Modas, and turned to stare at Modas. Her eyes filled with tears.

"Does Modas not like Farin?" Farin asked softly, his eyes opened to their full extent.

Modas' in turn grew wide with shock and obvious shame.

"I do like Farin, very much."

Farin, stark naked and not yet fully dry, smiled sweetly.

"I'll go prepare for the trip to Azrom," he said to Chardon as he left.

In the hallway, Modas strode hurriedly towards the exit. At the end of the corridor he stopped, took a deep shaky breath and smashed his fist against the wall. His head hung down in despair. This was not how he envisioned Chardon's life. As her bodyguard, he should have prevented all that transpired from happening.

Raising his head, he looked up at the weak sun mocking him from above. If it were not for Halfar and his childish tantrum they would still be on their home world. And Chardon would be safe. He would have gotten rid of Sestis easy enough in the beginning, before she had a foothold within the council.

Tiny laughter caught his ear and he cringed with pain. His little ones were playing in the fields further out and adjusting his vision saw Jaron playing with them. He loved her, he did. But, he wondered if things could have been different if he was not forbidden from who he wanted initially. Would it have made me happy?

Modas straightened his posture and continued towards the council room for briefing regarding their Azrom departure. The selection of people the council chose to accompany Chardon was not to his liking.

Trinon, was acceptable but Talas and Kelin he could do without. He had to deal with it because when it came to strategy Talas had no equal and he didn't go anywhere without Kelin. Even more amazing was Jaron and Talas combining their talents lately. Modas sighed heavily. He had hoped to at least minimize Chardon's interactions with Halfar, mate or not.

Halfar stood arms crossed with a look of anxiety and excitement all rolled into one. The gate was opening, signaling the arrival of Chardon's entourage from New Lassa. He would be able to hold his son, Farin, again. Of course, the boy would be a few years older now. He didn't care. A tight embrace was in Farin's near future. This new-found emotion of fatherhood disturbed and amazed him. If he had known how he would feel beforehand he would have had more offspring. He was sure Chardon would be willing to bear more for him.

Flanked on each side of him were his two generals, Rass and Kur. Halfar's cape, the color of human blood, sailed backwards revealing the black body armor underneath. Rass and Kur's were the color of azure sky. Behind them stood rows of royal guards in golden armor and red capes while the servants lined along the bridge wore thin robes. Fabrics in shades of bright reds, blues and gold swirled around in the wind created by the gate. The smell of freshly cleaned and oiled armor whiffed in the air.

The first to set foot on Azromian soil was Modas. He stood still at the threshold looking menacing with his six feet eight-inch frame and both he and Halfar locked eyes. An unspoken resentment exchanged between them and Halfar knew instantly what the man beast's intentions were. He had anticipated that, and a plan was in place to thwart his every move if necessary. Halfar could feel malicious intent coming from his right and snuck a glance at Rass whose expression was far from welcoming. Modas switched his gaze to Rass and made a short nod.

Chardon came forth with Farin and Trinon. She was beautiful as always. Her white and gold robes flowed to the ground and as the sun caught her hair, it turned a deep golden color with streaks of dark red. An after effect of their combined DNA and Halfar approved of the change. His son's features surprised him.

How did I spawn such a beautiful creature? He thought to himself as he opened his arms wide for Farin, who ran joyously towards him.

"Well, I guess I will have to wait my turn then," Chardon sighed.

"I'm sure he has something else in store for you besides an embrace," Talas laughed softly from behind her. His dirty blond hair fell in waves down the middle of his back resting on the reddish-brown leather hide jacket. The color suited him so well, Chardon wanted to ruin it.

Realizing he had yet to formally introduce anyone, Halfar shifted his son to the side and held out a hand to Chardon. As she came near, he grasped her hand and turned to the bridge, the guards parting in the center to allow entry. Hand in hand, they walked to the end and from the balcony, an entire race of people could be seen assembled below. A sea of caped battle armor with a few civilians mixed in waited patiently for their supreme ruler to speak. He had not released any information and knew it would be a shock.

"Victorious!" Halfar's voiced boomed in the air.

"Til death!" Was the resounding reply from the masses and the guards behind him.

Chardon and the rest of her people appeared to be taken aback by the vocal assault. None of them had ever heard something so grand and blood thirsty carry in the air. She finally knew why Halfar was called the Supreme Ruler.

"Though my absence has caused great unrest, I have returned with a new perspective," Halfar paused for a moment to make sure he had the right wording, "and a mate." There was a loud gasp followed by silence. "I present Chardon, the leader of Lassa," he paused again while ushering Chardon forward, "and the mother of my son, Farin." He turned the small boy around for all to see. The silence was deafening, as Halfar waited for a response. Then, an uproar of cheers.

General Kur stepped closer to him and whispered, "I believe you have just assured the security of our race, my lord." With that, Kur returned to his position next to General Rass.

"Let the festival commence!" The captain of the royal guard's command sent the entire mob into a frenzy.

Halfar set Farin down and walked back towards the palace entrance with Chardon beside him. The royal guards closed ranks behind him and the Lassian entourage once the servants entered ahead to prepare service. He suddenly felt free of stress, for once, after decades of tension. Looking down, he saw Farin smiling brightly at him. His chest tightened with pride and affection.

✳✳☼✳✳

Chardon made a mental map of the palace as she followed Halfar down the long hallway to his quarters. Farin clung to his father in silence having no interest in the scenery. The sound of their boots striking the hard floor echoed around them. In the distance, celebratory cheers continued to ring out. The palace walls were sleek and shiny in a cream-colored stone with dark markings swirled throughout it. Each panel was pristine and even the matching floors were devoid of residue one would see from foot traffic. Chardon wondered if they had been cleaned recently due their visit. Halfar must have wanted to make an impression.

As they passed personal chambers, Chardon realized there were no doors and no indication there ever had been. Each entrance was structure like a great hall or foyer. It unnerved her a bit since privacy had always been a standard. Halfar never mentioned the layout of the palace.

"Tell me," Chardon broke the eerie silence. "Why are there no doors?"

Halfar slowed his pace and looked upwards in thought.

"It was never an issue to bring up. We hide nothing." He glanced at her. "Are you concerned?"

"A little apprehensive, yes."

"Hmm." Halfar leaned close to her. "I think, you will find it a non- issue as well. Think of it as," he squinted, "that Earth word."

"Voyeurism?" Chardon's eyebrow arched upwards as she said it.

"Exactly."

"Were you always this perverse?"

Halfar stopped walking and a sheepish smile crossed his face. "Perhaps."

Azrom's idea of festivities were grander than what Lassians were used to. The grand hall was filled to the brim with royalty, guards and food. Talas seemed to be at ease, telling battle stories while Trinon grazed through the food along with Jaron. Chardon watched everyone in the room to get a feel for what was appropriate. She also did it to see who could be trusted.

Halfar clearly had no real affection for his royal bloodline. Many of the royal family were arrogant, slovenly and had delusions of entitlement. They didn't seem to understand that Halfar could take it all away from them at any moment if he so chooses. A quick glance in Kelin's direction found him assessing the same thing.

"If I could do such a thing, I would have a long time ago." Halfar whispered in her ear. He seemed able to read her mind lately.

"Why can't you?" Chardon whispered back.

"My conscience won't let me do it. They are my blood relatives, and," he paused long enough to eat a small fruit, "not all of them are this bad." Chardon gave him a dirty look and resumed her scan of the hall.

One of the royal men caught her gaze. He smiled with malice and lust. His features were similar to Halfar's except his hair was shorter and dark blonde. Something about him made her feel uneasy. He suddenly blanched and turned away leaving Chardon confused until she turned to see Halfar's face.

"Still feel the same way?" Chardon chided him. Halfar's eyes darkened to a deep forest green. "Relax, my love," Chardon laughed. "I am not so easily swayed."

Halfar let out a loud sigh and did as instructed, relaxing onto the large cushion he was sitting on. Chardon reached over and stroked his hair. She stopped, realizing the hall had gone silent and everyone was staring at them. Looking down at Halfar, she saw his eyes were closed, enjoying the caress. In an instant she knew they had seen a weakness in their ruler and her body stiffened. Her people could feel it as well and they stood still waiting to strike if necessary.

A hand clamped onto her wrist, snapping her out of it. Halfar sat up and placed her hand in his. He had a look of acknowledgement and content. As his gaze fell on the occupants of the hall, an intense glow of red engulfed his pupils, making it known there was no opening for exploiting his affection towards Chardon. It even made Jaron turn pale. Chardon was reminded just how ruthless Halfar could be. He was, after all, the cause of Lassa's destruction.

From space, Planet Razzna appeared to be a ball of churning molten lava in shades of deep orange, red, brown and black. Its surface, dark and sinister, added to the aesthetic with black rock covering the land as seas of red frothed along sandy, deep russet brown, beaches. Two moons glowed silver on the north side of the sky like eyes surveying the world for intruders.

Shores of black rock east of the red ocean shimmied, revealing them to be giant ships sleek in structure yet somehow crude. Tiny red dots of light sprung to life along the sides of their hulls making them resemble an insect swarm. A slight humming resonated through the air sending vibrations along the surface. Small creatures camouflaged themselves with the environment as they scurried for cover.

On a craggy mountain sat large silver monuments that shimmered like scales. The tops were daggers shooting upwards ending in spikes. Sleek beetle ships hovered above while others rounded the perimeter in slow circulation. Light from the two moons made the structure glow unnaturally bright, almost blinding. A majestic thing of beauty on Planet Razzna.

A group of twenty Razznians draped in dark hooded robes marched up the paved roadway towards the entrance of the shimmering compound. Included within their ranks was the spy returning from Earth. They all trekked in silence, tired from their journey. As low ranked warriors, they did not get to land their ship close to the base and it had been an hour hike. Only higher ranked officers could use the trans- ports. The trek was a lesson in humility. One thought crossed their leader's mind on the way up; maybe we will be promoted for this information.

At the entrance, the entourage halted in front of fifty-foot-high double doors and waited for the guards on either side to usher them through. A second set of guards on the opposite side pulled the doors open halfway then stepped aside. The two guards waved the group in and as the last one entered the great hall, the doors were pushed shut creating a loud echo.

Everyone in the group removed their hoods out of respect for being in the same vicinity as their ruler. Eyes ranging from gold to blood red looked around before focusing their attention on the corridor nearly a mile long leading to a lift at the end.

Heavy sighs were exhaled as they resigned themselves to the last leg of their journey. On the lift they continued in silence as it went up, then sideways for quite a while and back to ascending until it slowed to a halt. The doors opened to another great hall except this time not five hundred feet from them sat their ruler on his throne. Floor coverings the color of old blood lay from the lift to the throne in contrast with the shiny black marbled interior. Advisors roamed around in black robes, the hoods red on the inside signifying their status. Servants were dressed similarly but the insides of their hoods were the same russet brown as the sands on the ocean beaches and their heads hung low in submission. The shuffling stopped as everyone's eyes landed on the entourage.

"We have come with a report you may find interesting, my lord," the spy announced as his group bowed their heads to their ruler.

Lord Kraznan blinked his blood red eyes and stopped fanning himself with the crude animal hide fabric rigid from chemical treatment. His black and golden colored scaled skin glinted from the hovering bulbs. He set down the fan and adjusted his black robe.

"Proceed." His guttural voice hissed across the hall.

"I have just come from a planet called Earth where Halfar was engaged in a battle with factions of his own enforcers. He seemed to be aiding the Earthlings."

"Intriguing. Continue."

"Halfar's armada and the Earthlings were being assisted by manbeasts and energy wielders."

This made Lord Kraznan sit up straight.

"From where?" he demanded.

"It seems, not all of the Lassians were destroyed. Halfar kept some of them and others who survived have relocated."

Lord Kraznan's eyes grew wide. The deal between himself and the Lassian female leader bequeathed the Lassian race to the Razznians for slavery and a foothold inside planet Azrom's political engine to ultimately bring it down. Sestis would have been made ambassador to several planets Razzna held under their thumb. It was all contingent on Planet Lassa being conquered and in league with Azrom. With the destruction of Lassa and Halfar's unexpected flight from Azrom, the deal was not enforced. But now, knowing there were survivors, he could still enslave them. Their abilities were perfect for manual labor.

"This is most excellent. Your Nest will be promoted." He saw the gleam in their eyes. "For your next mission, you will find out where the Lassians are. You may have to infiltrate Azrom to do so. Are you prepared?"

"Of course, your grace," the group's leader bowed. "We will depart immediately."

"Good. You may move your ship and dock at the main hub to replenish supplies."

As the group left, Lord Kraznan leaned further back into his throne and sat in reverie. Across the five solar systems in their universe, Razznians were considered one of the most feared. It wasn't because of their might but more so their level of ruthlessness. Some have said they even rivaled Azrom during certain time periods.

It may turn out to be a great new era for his species yet. Manual labor was causing undue hardship on the lower ranks since the collapse of their automated drones decades ago. Especially because the manufacturers refused to honor the warranties after fighting broke out between the two races. Having strong manbeasts would alleviate the burden until a new resolution was developed. That female Lassian creature Sestis' proposal would have been a gift.

Sestis

Air condensed and began to swirl, forming a spiral that grew darker until turning a deep purplish black. Pulsing like a pool of liquid it col- lapsed into itself revealing a tunnel of stars. Light shot forth and as it diminished, a small entourage of five were left in its place at the portal entrance on Planet Razzna.

Sestis took one look at the terrain and grimaced. Her impression of the Razznians was low already and this did not help any. The four body guards accompanying her were already on alert in case Lord Kraznan's sudden invitation was a trap. His interest in her agendas struck a suspicion within her but at the same time, intrigue. This may be a great opportunity in her favor.

Squinting to adjust her eyesight, she spotted a figure in a long-hooded robe standing at the control panel. Upon her vision clearing, she took note of the scaly skin and glint of red eyes focused on the console. Behind him stood a small horde of Razznians, all hooded, waiting in silence. As Sestis and her entourage approached, the horde surrounded them. Their move- ments served to guide the visitors towards the only thing on the planet that could be seen even from space; the royal palace.

At the entrance to the palace, Sestis smirked at the gigantic doors. How ridiculous. They were reptilian, not giant beasts. The inner transport system made her laugh as well. Her escorts frown in unison at the sound. Once the doors opened to the throne room, Sestis had to muster all her sanity not to burst into a guffaw. She could feel her guards stiffen behind her.

The throne room was a humid dimly lit hall swarming with lazy Razznians in silken robes being serviced by hooded subordinates. Sestis caught a whiff of something that reminded her of spoiled vegetation. She instinctively raised the back of one hand and discreetly covered her nose. Behind the hanging sleeves, she spoke.

"Lord Kraznan, greetings from Lassa."

She bowed her head slightly. The barrel-chested ruler sat fully in the throne, legs spread wide eagled. His thick tail lay directly in between, the tip hitting the floor. The visual was disgusting and she assumed to know why he did it.

You wish you had genitalia so supreme.

She snickered to herself despite her surroundings. His eyes laid on her and he sat up with what must have been some form of a smile. She couldn't tell because his mouth was two thin lines. Her assumption proved correct when a row of sharp teeth was revealed.

"Lady Sestis, how good of you to accept my invitation."

"It was quite a surprise, thank you."

"To have something so lovely grace our presence," Lord Kraznan sat upright, "Is an honor."

Sestis removed her hand from her mouth and smiled sweetly.

"The pleasure is all mine, I hope."

Her insides tensed, and she felt the meal she consumed beforehand curdle at the thought of him touching her the way most of the other male delegates did when alone with her. She only allowed it to gain rapport with them, and some sense of trust. It was not enjoyed.

"Please, come." He motioned to a doorway off in the back corner to her left. "We can discuss ideas privately." His eyes roamed her entourage. "Unless you do not feel comfortable."

"I think privately would be best." She glanced back at her guards. "Remain here."

Sestis followed the ruler into the secondary room making sure not to accidently step on his dragging tail. It was tempting to do so even knowing how cruel that would be. His crimson robes with gold overlay made him appear more majestic as they flowed around him. She had never really been this close to the ruler and now saw how tall he was   in comparison to his subjects. He also stood above her though not by much.

At nearly 184cm tall, Sestis was by no means someone to underestimate. She was the same height as Chardon, interpreting that as being on equal footing. Even her guards were intimidated by her. She was sure it might have to do with more than just her size. She reached behind her neck and pulled her golden auburn hair forward from the constraints of her high collared cape. The thick waves fell passed her shoulders and covered the front of her dress, hiding her cleavage. Lord Kraznan had peeked over and seemed disappointed. She kept the small smile on her face.

"So, Lord Kraznan, to what do I owe this unexpected gesture?"

Sestis sat down on an oversized plush in the middle of the room. The ruler wasted no time in joining her, his breath brushing her neck making the hairs stood on end.

"It has come to my attention that you have a rather," he paused for the right word, "anathema for the manbeasts of your race." His split tongue slipped out and ran across his lips before going back through the slits of his mouth. Sestis shuddered inwardly.

"They are great warriors, I will admit that, but nothing so special as to rely on them for our protection. We have our own powers just as deadly." She smiled as she said it to emphasize not to test her. That did not deter him in the least for his tongue ran across her cheek, his eyes fluttering in ecstasy.

"Yesss…you are very capable of handling yourself."

Sestis playfully pushed him away with a sly smile on her face, hiding her nausea. It seemed every male species she encountered wanted to touch or taste her flesh regardless of permission despite her imperative to keep them focused on her agenda.

Plan of Action

A general assembly of military power along with the Lassians created a war council to plan battle strategies against the Razznians. After a few years, they were still not in agreement on how to proceed. Battle was another five years away which irritated Halfar. Between his Generals' ideas and that of the Lassians, plans were at opposite ends of the spectrum: Defend or deploy. He liked neither option. The last thing he wanted to do was go into Razznian territory. On the other hand, he didn't want to sit and wait for them to attack Azrom. He wanted no civilian casualties after the last long war that left his people nearly devastated.

Sars stood at the helm of his newly equipped battle cruiser with new-found determination. No longer just a low level Razznian spy, he relished in the chance to prove his worth. A small band of loyal soldiers he chose were part of his crew and he felt the same loyalty to them. The last mission found them on that dreadful planet called Earth and it left much to be desired. Now they headed for planet Azrom, home to Halfar and his deadly Armada. Right into the lion's mouth. Sneaking onto its surface was not for the faint of heart but Sars had a plan, of course.

Getting caught was not an option. The thought of General Rass, or Kur, capturing his men made his scales tingle in fear. A small ting sounded to signal the ship was in proximity of Azrom's orbit. He turned to his navigator seated below him.

"Once we are in position behind the second moon, cloak the ship and stand by." He was answered with a nod. To his second in command standing next to him, he announced, "Prepare the pod suits. We will descend from the far side."

"Of course, sir. The drop will be taxing in the free fall, but it will be quick."

"That is the idea."

"Make sure the thrusters are reversed at least one kilometer before impact."

"Understood."

"Sir, if I may say, this is an audacious plan."

"Exactly. They would never suspect such a bold move."

"Good hunting, sir."

His second in command bowed slightly as Sars left the bridge.

A smile crept on Sars' face as he strode down the corridor. Success without risk was not his idea of a great mission. He was the only one who volunteered for the previous and reaped the reward, apparently having a skillset for infiltration. Slowing to a stop in front of the lift, he waved one hand across the panel to open it. After allowing him in, the lift doors closed automatically and shot downwards to the equipment hold on the lower level. He reached his destination in less than three seconds.

The doors opened and Sars stepped into a din of activity as eleven Razznians slithered about checking their weapons and body suits for any defects. This group of soldiers he trusted above all others. They had been with him from inception into the militia not long after being hatched from different nests but on the same day. Each was like a sibling to him; his own throng.

One of them halted his own preparations to hand Sars his gear before resuming protocol. Sars began his inspection of the pack making sure to go over his equipment twice. When everyone had donned on all the necessary wares, he hit the indicator on the side of the door to open the first airlock. They all filed into the secondary chamber and he could feel their anticipation.

Along the walls were twelve pod suits ready for pilots. They had been specifically designed for this mission and tested only twice before being handed over to Sars. He made his request for their creation as a necessity for the success of the mission. Absentmindedly caressing one nearest to him he was shocked and delighted they were approved.

The podsuits were like personalized drop ships in the form of reinforced body armor able to withstand atmospheric entry. Each unit was fully enclosed, protecting its pilot from the intense heat and possible hard landings. Although, if it went crashing down too fast, the body in- side would liquefy on impact. Hence, the timing of the thrusters per his second in command's instructions.

"Approaching drop point."

The feminine voice boomed from the internal communicators throughout the ship.

Sars, along with his group, strapped themselves into the pod suits and sealed them with the touch of a button located on the left shoulder. Inside the suits, holoscreens lit up displaying the control module for navigation. Tiny connectors spread out along each soldier's body, tapping into their muscles to allow maneuverability. The pod suits were piloted based on the occupant's body movements.

The airlock hissed as all the air was removed and the chamber rotated to lock onto the outer door. A loud click signaled they were in position and the chamber tilted so that their heads pointed out towards the door. On the other side, space waited for their arrival.

"Opening outer lift." The voice announced.

As the door eased open, sucking the air out of the chamber, Sars braced himself even though he knew it would do him no good. He saw the edge of the second moon and just beyond it, planet Azrom seeming so close he felt he could touch them.

"Releasing pods."

One by one, each pod was disconnected from the chamber and projected into the darkness of space at speeds the soldiers had never experienced. The free fall intensified and Sars' watched the distance meter inside his helmet for the correct timing.

"Close your helmet shutters!" He commanded, his voice shaky from the descent. When he saw all the face plates on the pods go black, he did the same. "Activate thrusters!" His teeth clenched down hard as the pod suits barreled mercilessly into Azrom's stratosphere.

****☼****

"Ahh!" Farin yelled with excitement as he climbed onto the balcony's ledge and pointed up to the sky, eyes wide. "Shooting stars!"

Trinon was on the ground resting with his back against the railings and had to turn his head to see what Farin was going on about. Manbeasts had superior sight and his eyes zeroed in on the glowing objects. Even with the afterburn blazing around them he could tell they were not what Farin claimed.

Shooting stars my eye.

He stood up and grabbed Farin under the arms from behind, lifting him off the ledge.

No longer small and demure, Farin was heavier forcing Trinon to put more muscle into lifting him. At five feet eight inches tall, the half Azromian half Lassian was even more stunningly beautiful. His shiny black talons were longer and deadlier. Trinon made sure to keep clear of them.

"Time to go in."

"But, I want to see the rest of the stars." Farin whined as Trinon set him down onto the platform.

"I know, but we'll be late for evening meal."

"Okay!" Farin smiled up at him.

Trinon glanced back once more as the last object headed for the planet's surface. He frowned. *Has it already begun?* A firm battle plan was not even in effect yet.

Soft light, emitted from the large holoscreen set in the center of room on a raised platform, spread across the observation chamber, casting an eerie glow on the faces surrounding it. General Rass, Kur, Modas and Trinon stood in a semicircle watching, in silence, the transmitted images of the tiny fireballs falling out of the sky then crashing to the sur- face. As it progressed, Kur arched an eyebrow in amusement while Rass' eyes went wide in disbelief.

"How bold." Kur broke the mood.

"We need to know who they are." Rass leaned further down, attempting to identify the objects.

"Can you not tell from the characteristics of the ships?" Trinon asked as he too leaned down, setting his forearms flat on the console.

"I have never seen anything like them." Rass responded.

Two royal guards entered the chamber and bowed to the Generals. The first to stand back upright spoke.

"Generals, we have pinpointed the sector of impact. Shall we inform our ruler and send out the scouts?"

Both Rass and Kur slid their eyes towards him and the looks left him feeling cold inside, and afraid. The other guard took a small step back creating the right amount of distance between them just in case.

"No," Rass answered, turning his attention back to the holoscreen. "There is no need for Halfar to know of this at this junction. We are his Generals. It would be a disgrace if we could not handle something as trivial as infiltration."

"No need to worry. Whoever they are, they will not make it off this planet alive," Kur interjected as he focused on the looped transmission.

"Or intact," Rass included.

"How clever." Kur tapped the screen and the image froze. "Now, what shall we do about this, hmm?" Everyone in the room stared at it in confusion until they all saw it. "They have split into three groups."

"Yes, one group is on the outer rim of the city and the other two are on the far side." Rass tapped on the objects near the outer rim. "There is only one reason to land so far into the wastelands outside the perimeter."

"All roads lead to the palace. They are going to have to find a way to hide amongst the merchants of the market square in the town that sits on the outskirts."

"Send out four scout units. We will surround and observe them for the moment." Rass instructed the two guards.

Kur fixed his gaze on Modas and Trinon.

"Let's not cause any ripples, shall we?" Modas nodded in response. "I do not have to ask that Farin be protected now more than ever."

"Done!" Trinon slapped his hands on the console, causing the image to shake wildly before it corrected itself.

Rass and Kur glanced at each other as the two guards, along with Modas and Trinon, exited the chamber. The same thought ran in their minds.

This was going to be thrilling.

Sars surveyed the area his team had landed in while they activated the camouflage on the pod suits. The sky was devoid of clouds making the sun too bright for his reptilian eyes. Powdery beige colored dirt covered the ground forming whirlwinds of dust every time his feet moved along it. Some of the scarce trees appeared dead or dying. There was nothing for as far as the eye could see except for a small community off in the distance. Farther away stood the palace, looming majestic and menacing. So, this is

Azrom. He expected a better environment but then he remembered Halfar was a tyrant who ruled over his race with an iron fist.

"Let's get going. It will take about four days to get to that village. Once there we can plan how to get to the palace." His crew nodded in unison.

"This place…this planet," one of his men began. "It's desolate."

"Mmm hmm. I know." Sars responded.

They all donned long hooded robes and began their march through the Azrom desert towards the royal palace. Sars knew their entry would be obvious by now and had mentally prepared his team and himself for the inevitable fight that might occur. He hoped the other two teams had landed safely and were also headed towards the palace. His orders were complete radio silence until they reached their destination.

****☼****

Trinon found Talas lounging on the ledge of a balcony with a tiny smirk on his face. His arms supported his weight as he leaned back, one leg hanging over and the other propped under him. A small breeze ruffled his blonde tresses, now nearly twice as long as before. He sighed, tilting his head towards Trinon and opened his eyes.

"Sneaking up on me?"

"That's kind of impossible," Trinon replied as he stood next to him and leaned on the ledge. He took in the view of the land before him and frowned.

"Halfar does not treat his people very well, does he? They may be of one race, but I see poverty, discrimination and food depletion."

"How are you so observant? I can see for miles and didn't know all of that."

"It's not about what you see, but how you perceive what you see." Talas looked up at the sky. "I think he means well. He just doesn't know how to rule."

"This from the person who got duped by Sestis and opened the gate for a planet bomb?"

"Ouch!" Talas feigned injury. "Was that really necessary?"

Trinon glanced at him, quickly changing the subject.

"Did you hear about the shooting stars?"

"Oh, yes. The enemy is bringing the battle here and for obvious reasons."

Trinon straightened his posture and stared at Talas in awe.

"You know why?"

"Trinon, I am a strategist above all else and even those two Generals would have figured it out as well." He swung his legs over the ledge and set himself down on the balcony. "Why have you sought me out this time?"

"Can we have a practice session?" Trinon's eyes filled with anticipation.

"You know your father does not approve of you learning new fighting skills from anyone who is not a manbeast."

"He's too full of pride to learn new things, but I am a new generation of manbeast."

"That you are." Talas stretched his body, inhaling, then let out a deep breath. "Fine. Find a good spot then."

"I already did," Trinon smiled mischievously.

The great hall was filled to capacity with Azrom advisors, both military and political, along with the Lassians. Tension ran high as each member sized up the other in intimidation. Lassa was seen as an inferior power on the scale of interstellar battle not an enemy. Chardon knew going in from when he visited the other worlds as a representative. It was the equivalent of being spit on. He could feel Halfar on edge by his side and not just for this reason. Chardon had chosen to attend the meeting as a male to show his strength and authority. Halfar thought it unnecessary, even antagonizing.

Chardon took note of the clash in attire from each race. The Azromians were identical with the only variation being the colors to define ranks and status. His people were a mish mash of different styles, none defining them as the powerful fighters they were, nor what planet they hailed from. Chardon forced himself not to frown. That being known, he felt no need to militarize his race to such an extent. Individuality is what made them Lassian.

Halfar repositioned himself on the gold colored throne with one foot set on its edge so he could rest an elbow on his knee. He was the only one in the room sitting. To his right stood Kur and Rass in full regalia looking bored. To Chardon's left was Modas, Talas and Jaron. The hall seemed to be split down the middle with both races apart from each other on either side like a great river.

"Status!" Halfar yelled, startling everyone out of their staring contests.

Azrom and Lassa's head councilman took a quick glare at each other and the Azromian stepped forward, his head held high in defiance.

"It has been confirmed, my Lord. The Razznians have gathered a battle fleet and are on the move. It seems they have mapped an unusual route to get to our system. A smaller fleet is lying in wait facing the opposite direction."

He smiled as he turned to the Lassian councilman.

"This also confirms our previous assessment." The Lassian began. "The second fleet is waiting for Azrom to open the pathway to Lassa. It was always their agenda to take over and enslave our race per Sestis' deal with them. They obviously underestimate us." He too smiled wide glancing over at the Azrom councilman.

"I find it strange," another Azrom advisor interjected. "Why would their fleet advance on our system? No race has dared outright attack us since the Utalizar war. Being the Razznians are normally not aggressors, would they be so bold as to come here?"

Kur and Rass quickly glanced at each other with a knowing look then reverted their eyes back to the attention of the councilmen. Chardon narrowed his eyes, not able to stop the feeling of dread and betrayal in his gut. Halfar hadn't noticed his two Generals' interaction. Chardon wondered if he already knew something or was totally indifferent to what his military was up to.

"If I may," Chardon spoke. The hall went deathly quiet. Halfar, Rass and Kur slowly turned to stare at him in disbelief. "Since the Razznians have grown so bold as to target both planets, maybe we could cross train our fighters to maximize our success."

Only the sound of a light breeze flowing through the hall could be heard. A dense atmosphere churned about and the faces of the people on the floor below changed into something sinister.

"Train?" Azrom's head military councilman barked. "What could we possibly learn from these...?" He stopped short.

"And why should we let them know our battle techniques? They may try to use them against us in the near future." Another councilman added.

"As if that would work. We will always be superior," said another Azromian.

A loud din filled the room and weapons were drawn when the sound of claws echoed throughout from the Lassian manbeasts preparing for a fight. Chardon pursed his lips in frustration. This was stupidity on both sides.

"Enough!" Halfar commanded.

Weapons were sheathed, and claws detracted. Everyone's attention went to the supreme ruler sitting upright, his knuckles white on the arms of the throne. His eyes had turned a brilliant green and burned with disgust. Chardon looked away, also afraid of that stare.

"Is victory not our goal?" He asked sharply.

"Why, yes, my Lord." The Azrom councilman replied in a shaky tone.

"Then what is the problem?" He turned his head towards the manbeasts lined up on the left side of the hall. "When you underestimate an entire race, what happens?"

"Defeat," the councilman answered softly.

"What happens?" Halfar yelled.

"Defeat!" The councilman cried out.

"These manbeasts are just as strong as us. Learning new fighting techniques benefits all."

"It is quite an audacious proposal," the Lassian councilman announced. "Though our manbeasts are a little leery about teaching out- side their race and vice versa."

Chardon saw a look of defiance on Modas face and knew it was going to be an uphill battle. Trinon, on the other hand looked excited and glanced over at Talas with some sort of anticipation. It must have been on their minds as well. Chardon thought to himself.

"As for battle plans," Halfar continued. "We need to know their trajectories in full to either deter or annihilate successfully. Get to it."

Halfar addressed the last to Kur and Rass as he rose from his throne, stepping down onto the blood red carpet that made a trail across the room all the way to the doors. He held out a hand and Chardon took it.

They exited the great hall together in silence until they reached the end of the balcony where Halfar stopped. He turned to face him then grabbed Chardon by the shoulders and squeezed.

"That was dangerous!" He hissed softly, peeking around the corner to make sure his guards were not in earshot.

"But it is necessary to ensure the survival of both planets."

"I know that, you know that. It's not about the right thing to do, it's about pride!"

"That's…!" Chardon started to yell.

"Stupid," Halfar said softly, letting his arms drop. "My race. We've been through a lot and are very possessive of certain things."

"That's obvious. Now, how do we get both our races to cooperate?"

General Kur strolled down the walkway that ran along the quarters outside. The tip of his long saber nearly touched the ground as it hung low from his side. He stared at the white stone under his feet as he walked in a haze of confusion. Something stirred in him and he was frustrated due to not being able to identify it. A tress of his dark forest green hair fell across one shoulder and he glanced at it as if it were an intruder. It made him realize just how irritated he had become over the tiniest things since coming home.

At the entrance of a personal chamber he stopped mid stride. His back foot sat arched upward on its tip. Not knowing where he was, he raised his head and turned, curious as to what lay inside. The late day sun made it hard to see in the dark room so he waited for his eyes to adjust. As they did, he saw the sleeping figure on the bed stir and raise up.

Rass used one hand to push himself up from under the coverings and the other to shield his eyes from the sunlight. His dark hair had grown down to his waist and wrapped around him like tendrils. Kur pivoted to stand facing him from the entryway. A burning sensation filled his eyes as he advanced into the chamber, shedding saber and clothes as he got closer to the bed. Rass did not seem surprised, not moving even when Kur threw off the coverings revealing that Rass was sleeping naked in female form as he climbed on.

"I'm tired." Rass said in a defeated tone.

"I know." Kur reached around her waist and turned her over. His body covered hers and grabbing the edge of a tossed cover flung it over them. "I need you."

Rass placed her hands on his cheeks and they stared into each other's eyes. They didn't break contact as Kur entered her roughly. It had been too long, and he knew he could not be gentle even if he tried. No, Rass would have to endure his animalistic love making. He could hear no sounds as he watched her mouth forming in cries with her eyes closed tight. Why had he tuned everything out? He asked himself. Shaking his head to clear the fuzziness, he repositioned his body and put some of his weight on his arms as he placed them above on the wall.

Sound returned and the scream filling his ears let him know he was in fact hurting her. He abruptly stopped, looking down at Rass' sweat drenched body, his own sweat dripping onto hers. A sense of dread came over him. The sun was setting. *How long have I been here?* Rass' breathing slowed but he could feel the pulse of her body still going quite fast. Kur removed one hand from the wall and stroked her lips before kissing them.

Relieved that he had not caused any damage, he resumed his thrusts, this time a little less aggressively. He could hear her cries of pleasure and pain which heightened his lust. As he released his seed into her, he finally understood what had been eating away at him; desire. Euphoria swept over him as he buried his head in the crook of Rass' neck.

"Better?" Rass whispered softly in a hoarse voice.

Kur kissed her and rolled over, taking her with him so that she lay on top of him. He watched her fall into a deep sleep within moments, and he followed not long after. The last time he had ever been satisfied was with Rass, and that was nearly half a century ago.

Halfar stood leaning against the rails directly across from Rass' chamber watching his two Generals reconnect after so many decades. He had also been walking along in thought when he noticed Kur's mindless stroll. Curious, he had followed. With his elbows resting on the ledge, hands dangling, he cocked his head to one side and observed Kur's animal descent into brutal sex. *How childish.* A twinge of jealously crept in and Halfar knew where it came from. Seeing them made him wonder if they were still capable of leading his Armada.

We shall see.

Pushing off the ledge, Halfar stood up and walked back down the walkway to the main palace sector. It was getting dark and his advisors were waiting.

TWO:

One thing Modas did not tolerate was others meddling in the affairs of Manbeasts. He felt that his kind had survived all this time due to their strict policy of only handing down their fighting techniques to their own. The Azromians seemed to concur because there was a perpetual stalemate in the battle arena located near the main palace. It wasn't just them. Modas had no intention of teaching his fellow Lassians either and that put a great deal of tension on everyone in the area.

He could see Talas leering at him and knew what the sword wielder was thinking. Even Chardon had suggested that his way was outdated. An invisible line had been drawn in the white sand of the arena floor and no one budged. Both races stood in a single file line across from each other, unhappy with the turn of events.

"How about a short demonstration of fighting skills to clear the air?" General Kur suggested sweetly. "Relieve some tension, maybe?" He sat in the royal pit high above the field in full battle armor looking down on them with contempt.

Modas asked himself for the hundredth time why that creature was allowed to live. The whole plan centered on the General's demise, yet Chardon demanded he be saved. Kur's suggestion was not warranted because Modas had that in mind anyway. He had gone head to head with the mutated enforcers Kur had created but never a true Azrom warrior.

"Agreed." He replied and heard a snort come from Talas at the other end of the line.

"It seems Talas does not approve?" Kur inquired.

"I suppose, my weak and inferior warriors should go sit in the stands and watch the real fighters go at." Talas nodded towards the seating areas and the Lassian warriors broke rank to follow him across the field, leaving just the Manbeasts.

The Azrom Commander turned red. "Are you mocking us?" He yelled, stepping forward with his one arm already forming a giant claw.

Modas stiffened, not expecting a backlash from Talas' judgment to let him handle the demonstration. Without looking back, he could feel Talas' entourage halt at the accusation. There was no need to have the Lassian warriors fight since his race of manbeasts were the better fighters. He didn't understand what the issue was.

MAQUEL A. JACOB | 168

"On the contrary, Commander," Talas replied turning his head slightly. "I just think we should wait our turn. Can't have two races against one, isn't that right General?"

Kur's lips curved into something that wasn't a smile.

"Funny. That is exactly what occurred on Earth, if I remember correctly." Talas shrugged, raising his hands up. "Very well, the Manbeasts will go up against the elite enforcers commanded by Yokun." The Azrom Commander bowed. "And the Lassian warriors will go up against one of the main battalion squads."

"Why would you do that?" Modas demanded.

"Beast against beast, man against man. That's only fair, correct?"

Kur leaned back from the balcony and sat down in the white stone seat behind him.

The squadron of soldiers left the field towards the opposite side of Talas' group and once both sides were seated, Modas surveyed the field. Twelve elites were in front of his seven manbeasts. He liked the odds and to acknowledge so, his claws grew out signaling his warriors to do the same.

"Let the demonstration begin!" Kur cried out with joy as Halfar and Chardon arrived to see the first clash.

One by one, Azrom's elite shifted into their monstrous forms. Grappling claws, scorpion like tails and hard-shelled bodies stood ready for a fight against the flesh and bone of Manbeasts. Each side emitted battle cries of ear piercing decibels and the sounds of their bodies colliding was that of a slaughter house. Blood flowed instantly.

Modas was matched with the commander and was surprised to find himself barely keeping up. The commander had claws that of an Earth lobster, like Halfar. With deadly swipes coming at him full speed, Modas was only able to dodge two or three. He dropped low and swung one leg to topple the commander but a split second before it connected, the creature shot upwards.

Before Modas could move, the commander was inches from him, claws open ready to snap shut around his neck. Calling upon every muscle in his body, he was able to avoid a beheading but not a fairly deep cut along his clavicle. The speed of his movement sent him across the arena, still in a crouched position, raising a tidal wave of white sand on each side of him. He stopped at three quarters the length of arena.

Out of the corner of his eye he saw Talas raise an eyebrow, a tiny smile on his face. Talas then tilted his head towards the middle of the field. As Modas turned he saw a flash of color coming at him and immediately jumped to his right. To his amazement, the blur corrected its advance making a beeline to him. With nowhere else to go, Modas made a bold decision and laid flat on the ground just as the commander got within a few meters. The commander, with no time to correct his direction, went crashing into the wall behind him.

Thinking it was safe to stand up, Modas began to push himself off the ground until he noticed movement in the cloud of debris near the wall.

He was knocked backward and before he could slide any further from the commander, claws grabbed hold of his robes and yanked him back to rest under the commander's other claw ready to strike. As it came down, the commander disappeared, replaced by two leather clad legs standing above him. The gust of wind that had accompanied them died and a long split-back cloak fell over the legs. Between them, Modas saw the commander out cold against another section of the wall, the impact leaving a large chunk of it falling to the ground.

"Losing your touch, old man?" Trinon turned his head back to look down on him.

Modas noticed that there was not a cut or scrape on his son meaning the blood splatter on his cloak and tunic was not his. The cocky smile made him a little angry, mostly proud. Heavy silence caught his ears and he looked around to see the fighting had halted. Everyone seemed to be in awe of Trinon and his Manbeasts seemed confused. Trinon stepped to one side and held out his hand. Modas clasped it and let himself be pulled up. In the seating area, Talas looked proud, and nervous at the same time.

"What's going on? Why have we stopped?"

From above Halfar leaned over the balcony ledge.

"I believe that is enough for today. Please have your wounds tended to and freshen up. There are still a few hours before evening meal, so rest."

With that, he left the royal pit along with Chardon and Kur.

"What just happened, Trinon?" Modas stared at him. "What did you do?" His eyes narrowed as his son's eyes rolled upward and the tip of his tongue peeked out from the corner of his lips.

"I saved your honor?" Trinon replied.

"That's not…!" Modas began.

"Come now." Talas jumped down from the seating area onto the field. "Gladly take your lumps and thank your son." He said playfully.

Modas took another glance around the arena and saw the white sand stained with different shades of blood. He had been too confident in the strength of his Manbeasts and this was the result. In all the decades of touring for the council, Lassian and Azromian warriors had never fought each other, but they did see the other's battles from afar.

We must be stronger.

Everyone exited the arena not talking or looking at each other. It was better that way. Of all the warriors who fought, Trinon was the only one who strode out with his hands clasped behind his head and a stupid grin.

What did I miss? Modas was irritated.

On the platform in the middle of Halfar's meeting chamber Chardon plopped down onto a giant cushion set. Shallow bowls of Azrom flowers in various colors were in each corner. Four more cushions arranged strategically around him awaited their patrons. He leaned back and stared up at the ceiling as he replayed the battle 'demonstration' in his mind. Seeing Modas struggle was a surprise but he knew it was based on the Manbeast's own miscalculations. And then there was Trinon who ended it all.

Loud clanking boots striking the floor broke Chardon's thoughts. Halfar entered the chamber followed by Kur and Talas. As they stepped up onto the platform, also settling down in a giant cushion, servants flowed out of the corners with carafes of cool drink and platters of local fruit. They set them in the center of the platform and left just as stealthily as they came out.

Talas sat legs apart resting his arms on his knees. His head hung low between them, his hair brushing the floor. Kur filled a clear flute from one of the carafes and took a sip before leaning back. Halfar stretched out and crossed his legs and arms while staring upwards. No one spoke for what seemed like minutes.

"Chardon?" Halfar began and turned his head to meet his gaze. "What was that? I have seen manbeasts fight on several occasions but nothing like how young Trinon moved."

"I have an idea," Chardon replied.

"I know for a fact you nor Jaron fight like that either."

Kur raised an eyebrow and took another sip of his drink.

"I believe we have never seen an actually Lassian warrior fight, isn't that so, Chardon?"

"That would be correct."

"You were always surrounded by manbeasts or energy users when you traveled, but never a warrior. We assumed they were inferior and knowing the fighting technique of manbeasts up close, I say Trinon has learned something new from one of them." He glanced over at Talas along with Chardon and Halfar. "It seems we wholly underestimated the Lassian race, my lord."

"Talas." Chardon called to him. When there was no reply, he tried again. "Talas!"

Talas' head shot up and he came into the gaze of all three who sat in his line of sight. His dirty blonde hair went flying backwards in disarray framing his face. A look of shock and confusion greeted them.

"You always told me that you could never compete with a manbeast and all of Lassa believes this."

"Yes."

"Talas." Chardon said his name through gritted teeth.

"I lied." Talas managed a tiny smile and it immediately disappeared.

"What exactly is his title, Chardon?" Halfar inquired.

"He is the leader of our warriors. We don't really have titles."

"So," Kur leaned forward. "The backstabbing, incompetent Talas is actually a true Lassian warrior. Tell me, Talas, is all the lacking a ruse?"

"Pretty much." Talas nodded.

"He is also our strategist along with Jaron, as you know." Chardon added.

"In that case, tell us how to get our races to cooperate." Halfar said.

Talas shook his head and reached into the platter for a small fruit the size of a lemon. He tossed it up in the air a couple of times and then took a bite. After chewing it all and swallowing he replied.

"If I only knew how." Talas took another bite. "Modas won't like this."

"Indeed." Kur leaned back from him as he responded.

⁎⁎☼⁎⁎

The bathing chamber reserved for the manbeasts was larger than any they had ever encountered. Seven of the ten wide basins set deep in the floor and were filled with lightly scented frothing liquid. Glow orbs hovered over them giving some ambience. An attendant sat on the edge of each one waiting for their charge.

Modas and his manbeasts stood at the entryway in hesitation, not ready or willing to strip down and let a stranger scrub them down. All except Trinon, whose lips formed a wide grin before he stripped naked and hurried towards the fourth basin down. He slid into it slowly and made a loud sigh. As he spread his arms across the edge of the tub, leaning his head back, the attendant grabbed a scrubbing sponge from the tray and stepped in with him.

"Better hurry, Father. The water doesn't stay hot forever."

Manbeasts glanced nervously around at each other and then Modas.

Cautiously, they moved towards the open basins and began to remove their blood-stained gear. Modas was the last to step forward and stopped at the empty basin with a male attendant sitting patiently for him. Without looking at anyone, he slowly removed his robes and boots, letting them drop onto the floor. He entered the water and sat on the bench along the inside. Perfectly still, he waited for the attendant who came in sponge in hand to scrub him.

"Oh, Father!" Trinon burst out laughing. "See reason."

Modas glanced over at his son and remained unmoving as the attendant raised his arm and began cleaning. A feeling of humiliation came over even as he knew there was nothing to be done about the bathing or the battle as well. The sponge went past his line of sight and was now on his chest. Jaron was the only other being who had ever touched him while naked. He resisted his urge to slap the man's hand away knowing it would be an insult.

A female attendant came around to the other side of his basin and poured a light-colored powder into the water. As she left, Modas felt the tension in his body start to unwind. She went to all the others, doing the same. Before his eyes closed, his body slumped against the ledge, he could hear Trinon laughing in delight.

"How was your bath? It was refreshing, I hope." Halfar's head advisor asked as the manbeasts crossed the threshold of the same banquet chamber where Halfar's feast for Chardon took place.

"Intriguing." Modas replied.

"Invigorating!" Trinon added.

"Excellent."

The advisor turned from them and went to sit at the table along the far wall closest to the one reserved for Halfar and his group. He gestured to a table opposite his where the Azrom commander and his elite were seated.

"Commander," Modas nodded to him.

"Lassian," The commander spat.

"I will not tolerate any of that!" Halfar burst into the room from the far left, followed by his generals and Chardon.

Every Azrom soldier stood up and bowed, yelling, "My Lord!" Seeing that none of the Lassians did the same, looks of disdain fell upon them.

Halfar was about to make another outburst but was stopped by Chardon, who was in female form per his earlier request. She pointed to Talas sitting at the other table with the Lassian warriors.

"He is neither our lord nor master, thus, we do not bow to him in submission. We will however bow to his allegiance." Talas stood and all the Lassians, including manbeasts, followed suit. They made a bow and returned to sitting. The Azromians did the same.

From the right entrance Trinon came out with Farin and led him to Chardon before going to sit with the rest of the manbeasts. The Azromians sat admiring the little one as he climbed on Halfar's lap when he sat down. His smile was enchanting.

"Father, did you see the shooting stars last moon?"

A great heavy silence filled the room and Trinon covered his face with one hand while Kur turned slowly towards the child in disbelief. Halfar's lips twitched until curving into a smile.

"No, my son, I did not. What kind of shooting stars?"

"They were different colors and it was daylight."

"Well, then. I hate to have missed that." He quickly glanced over the room and saw Trinon then Kur, who showed fear in his eyes as he met his gaze. "Come, Farin. Go sit in your own seat by your mother."

"Okay." Farin left his father's lap and did as he was told.

"Let's feast, shall we?" Halfar announced. He turned to his generals and said softly, "We will discuss shooting stars later, hmm?"

Coming Clean

"Did you not tell Farin that shooting stars in broad daylight should be kept secret?" Rass exclaimed, his outrage directed at Trinon.

"I did, but he was so fascinated with it that he probably felt telling his father was okay." Trinon shrugged in apology. "It's not like we could keep this from Halfar forever."

"No," Rass replied. "But we could at least have a chance to put a plan in motion!"

"I thought the plan was to let them get closer to the palace before grabbing them."

Kur stood leaning against the wall deep in thought. Back in full battle gear, he was planning to participate in the second round of battle demonstrations. At the moment, he seemed frustrated with his arms clasped tight across his chest making Rass uneasy.

"Yes, that is part of the plan. If Halfar decides to squash that, we will have a bigger problem on our hands."

Trinon's expression became serious, shocking Rass at its ferociousness, as he stood to his full height with legs apart, arms folded. Always playful and never taking anything too much at heart, that is how everyone saw the young manbeast. This stance and facial expression was that of a seasoned warrior.

"Maybe not. He does trust you, right?" Trinon finally spoke after a moment.

"Right now? I wouldn't put any stake in that."

"Trust must be earned and when secrets are kept it puts a strain on that trust!" Halfar walked through the entrance, the doors sliding shut behind him. Chardon was by his side along with Modas. "You will tell me what's going on!" He demanded.

Kur looked up from his state of reflection and made eye contact with Halfar.

"We do not know who they are. The ships are not like anything we have ever seen."

"How many?"

"Twelve. A group of four went to three different quadrants of the planet."

"But," Rass interjected. "They are within a certain parameter of the palace. They seem to be moving in a semicircle."

"To surround the palace," Halfar concluded.

"Correct." Kur agreed.

"And your plan is to what, wait for them to show up on our doorstep?" Halfar snapped in disgust.

"In a manner of speaking. We want to get them in range for identification and then we capture." Kur explained.

"Who has the audacity to infiltrate Azrom?"

"Maybe it's the Razznians?" Trinon suggested.

"But as far as we know, they have no such technology to do so," Rass said.

"If it is, then we may need to reassess their fighting ability," Chardon added.

"Not really," Kur pushed himself off the wall. "They are being sneaky, as usual. They have no more fighting skills than they did before. This would be quite bold for them though."

"I will trust you to handle this," Halfar announced. "But mark my words. If it comes down to our planet being in jeopardy, I will not stand for it."

"Agreed."

"Now, you will tell me your strategy in detail."

✳✳☼✳✳

Gloomy sunlight cast faint shadows along the fields near Ganna's lab on New Lassa. She glanced away shaking her head in sorrow. It would take another five years for the sun to adjust itself after receiving a jumpstart years before. The efforts of both Lassian and Azromian scientists was bound to pay off. There were so many other projects on the list that she wasn't sure if all of them could be done.

On their original home world, she had created many weapons from the rich resources of Lassa. This planet did not have the same resilience and she found it more cumbersome than impossible to mold them to her liking. For now, Ganna concentrated on the issue involving the gateway and how to get a long-range weapon to work within it.

✳✳☼✳✳

Sars held up a hand signaling his men to stop. They were at the border of the small village. It had taken them nearly eight days to travel across the barren waste land and they had to do it cloaked. That was the drawback of landing on Azrom practically blind. The quick scan of the surface was not sufficient. Their suits had enough reserve left to infiltrate the village but afterwards it would take at least a day to recharge. He tapped the side of his suit at the collarbone and decloaked, his men doing the same.

From the view through his telescopic goggles he scanned the village. Run down fabricated shacks littered the sector with market stands set in two rows down the middle. A covered outdoor communal dining area was located near the entrance. Five hundred feet of tracks were visible on the ground, the rest disappearing into a shaft leading underground. The robes and tunics worn by the villagers were tattered, worn out and old. Only the ones in military uniform looked halfway decent. Even those were dingy, and battle worn.

"Why is it so much different than the palace?" One of his men inquired. "Even though we are lower soldiers, our ruler still treats us with decency."

"As I said before, Halfar is not a great ruler. Not every race can have one like ours." Sars replied. "I almost feel sorry for them."

"The royals remain prosperous while their people go without. Disgusting."

"Let's continue."

Sars reactivated his cloaking and his men followed suit.

They advanced into the village careful to steer away from the inhabitants. Being invisible did not mean things could pass through them. Food was cooking in various homes and small children came out of them with steaming vessels, heading towards the dining arena. Footsteps made swirls of dust as people made their way down the dirt paved streets. A strange smell lingered with the food and Sars concluded that it was decay.

Further into the village, he had his men spread out and find some discarded robes to don before their suits ran out of energy. He felt bad taking that much from the poor villagers. Azrom was not the mighty and glamorous planet the galaxy was meant to believe. Now he knew why their race did not taste very well during a fight. Poor diet.

****☼****

Some days General Kur felt he was surrounded by incompetence and this was one of them. He had sent trackers out to keep tabs on their uninvited guests. A scout from the first group arrived in the battle chamber giving a lackluster report on the four intruders heading directly towards the palace. Kur could feel a tingling in his fingers, taunting him to unsheathe his long sword and decapitate the soldier.

"Where are they?" He asked restraining his frustration.

"We believe they may have infiltrated a village." The scout answered.

"You believe?"

"We sort of lost sight of them in the middle of the desert."

The scout had a split second to rear back as Kur's long sword flashed in front of him, nicking the side of his neck. A thin line of black blood formed, and he slapped his hand over it on instinct.

Kur held the blade's end position straight out to his side, not a drop of blood on it from the speed of his strike. He returned it to its sheath and smiled. His subordinates backed away from him.

"How could you lose four aliens in the barren wastelands of our desert?"

"We can't explain it, sir."

"I can," General Rass interrupted as he entered the battle chamber.

A quick glance at the scout still holding his neck then at Kur made him raise a questioning eyebrow.

"Please, enlighten us, General." Kur made a mocking bow.

"Tsk!" Rass walked up to the platform sitting in the center of the chamber. He tapped the edge and it became a vidscreen. "I took the liberty of going through their footage during his less than informative report and found this." They all watched as the four aliens trekking across the desert stopped then disappeared. "They have a cloaking application within their suits."

"That does not make me happy." Kur crossed his arms.

"Nor I," Rass replied. "But, we do know one thing."

"And that is?"

"They are coming towards the palace."

"That's obvious! I thought you were going to shed some new insight on the situation, you being a strategist." Kur snapped with sarcasm. The others in the room took another step further away from the Generals.

"Are you mocking me?" Rass spat as his hand grabbed the hilt of his blade.

Both Generals almost got their blades out before a hand stopped them. The grip was so strong neither could move an inch and they both looked up to see who dared interfere. A smiling Trinon stood towering between them. His eyes were closed in what appeared to be exasperation which was unbecoming of the young manbeast.

"Let's play nice, okay?" Trinon spoke loudly.

He let their hands go and they pushed their swords back down. Out of the corner of his eye, Rass saw Modas standing a few feet behind the young one. That cold unflinching stare fixed on his face. Trinon moved away from them and let his father take over his position between the two.

"This is not the time." Modas said.

"Agreed," Kur added.

"If they are cloaked it does makes it harder to track them. Not knowing their destination means we must prepare to defend the palace."

"The palace is always protected by the royal guard."

"Against who?" Modas asked. Rass and Kur stared at each other. "These are not disgruntled villagers, they are an enemy not from this world. If they are indeed Razznian then you will have flesh eating enemies to deal with."

"Eww!" Trinon exclaimed.

Rass turned to the scout and saw the soldier was much farther away than before. He sighed heavily and said, "You're dismissed! Make sure you concentrate on reestablishing a visual. Their cloaks cannot stay up forever."

"Yes, General." The scout bowed low and quickly exited the chamber. To Modas, he asked, "How are you going to position your manbeasts around the palace?"

"There will be two at each end and three at the center entrance of the palace consisting of Trinon, Barbon and myself."

"Barbon?"

"He likes to not be seen or heard but felt in battle. He's quite introverted."

"Aren't all manbeasts?" Kur rolled his eyes as he said it.

"I'm not!" Trinon replied.

"Yes, well." And Kur left it at that.

"What about the Lassian warriors?" Rass asked.

"They are not needed for this."

Both Generals made a face and saw Trinon doing the same. there was obviously no love loss between the two factions of Lassian fighters.

"They can defend the inner wings of the palace, IF the enemy manages to get past us."

"Just to be safe," Rass began, "I would like two or three to accompany the manbeasts you assign. Better safe than sorry, as they say on Earth."

"Filthy planet." Kur literally spat on the floor in disgust.

"How vulgar. So not aesthetically pleasing," Rass sneered.

Kur's eyes narrowed. Everyone in the room knew it was not like him to do such a thing. He uncrossed his arms and strode out of the chamber without another word.

I'm angry!

It made his chest tighten as he let the thought sink in. Being infiltrated was a clear sign Azrom was losing its reputation as a mighty race.

****☼****

A loud rumbling filled the air as the ground shook beneath the village. on the far end, hiding in a rundown shed, Sars and his men squeezed themselves closer together into the wall. He covered his ears as the rumbling became a long screeching. Adjusting his goggles, he saw the cause.

Coming out of the dark hole in the ground was a large mechanical vehicle running on the tracks. It stopped shy of the where the tracks ended and made a hissing sound as if settling down. Royal guards climbed out of the sliding doors and the ones inside began to hand down crates. The villagers had gathered around and took turns picking them up the crates being set on the ground.

Sars zeroed in on one of the crates and could see food rations and other supplies jumbled inside. In under an hour the delivery was over, and the guards boarded the machine. It made a loud boom and its engines whirred into action. Black mist rose from the top before the giant thing rolled backwards into the underground tunnel from which it came.

"What kind of treachery is this?" His second asked, horrified.

"It seems that is how Azrom keeps their people from starving or rebelling."

"We should be taking over this planet, not Lassa," his second continued.

"You may be right. When we report back, it will be a recommendation." Sars relaxed a little and moved away from his men. "It is indeed an eye-opening revelation."

He rose and motioned for them to follow.

"Come. We must find some wildlife to feast on."

"We're not going to snatch an Azromian?" His third asked.

"You know what they taste like. Do you really want that for late meal?" Sars countered.

His men looked at each other as they made scrunched up faces, then shook their heads in disgust. Knowing what they did now, it would be like mercy killings to put the villagers out of their misery. The other factor was that Azromian flesh really wasn't something to be desired. Reactivating their invisible cloaks, they headed out to the outskirts for food.

The horizon became a haze of red the color of fire as the sun set on Azrom, casting dark shadows along the landscape. Halfar stood with his legs apart and arms crossed watching the transformation in silence. A strong breeze swept his hair straight back and he closed his eyes, letting the sensation sink in. Home. Opening his eyes, they landed on the villages off in the distance. A heaviness crept into his chest. Azrom was no stranger to wars but the last one, which he commanded, had left his people in devastation.

"Would you like a report on our honored guests, my Lord?"

Halfar turned his head slightly and found Rass coming up behind him. His general was in casual wear like he had been on Earth. Something about it disturbed him and he wondered where Rass was coming from.

"That would be best, General."

He glanced over and saw a frown crease Rass' face.

"It has become apparent that the infiltrators are using cloaking devices."

"Is that so?" Halfar said sucking in air through his teeth. "They can creep onto the palace grounds undetected then?"

"It seems so but the manbeasts are certain they can combat that."

"Manbeasts do have optimal vision but not even they can't see what is not there."

"Modas is confident."

"Maybe too much." Halfar countered.

"I did request that Lassian warriors also be put in standby."

"Why standby?" Halfar turned to stare at him.

"Manbeasts and Lassian warriors do not seem to get along very well."

Halfar let out a heavy sigh. This was getting tedious. The battle could not be won on a divided front. Modas was making it harder than need be.

"Make sure Talas is near the main gates." Rass cocked his head to one side in confusion. "Just to be certain."

"As you wish, my Lord." Rass bowed low and retreated down the corridor.

"What are you thinking, manbeast?" Halfar asked himself.

Turning back to the horizon he saw that the sun had settled far down into the valley and only a hint of light could be seen, signaling the time for evening meal. He uncrossed his arms and headed the same way as Rass. As he rounded the curve, four of his royal guards step in line with him.

Jaron eyed Talas intensely, filled with concern for him as Modas relayed the plan the Azrom Generals and he had discussed. There was no flicker of emotion in the warrior's expression yet Jaron knew. Talas was seething on the inside. She knew this because she felt the same. For Modas to treat them like inferior beings was unforgivable. As his mate, it made the announcement sting deeper. Neither replied to his words and he seemed to expect none for when he finished, Modas exited the chamber.

"Mother," Trinon started. He had stayed behind fearing the silence that filled the room.

Jaron held up a hand, halting his conversation. She kept her eyes on Talas, waiting. Even Trinon stared down at him worried. Talas began to tap a finger against his thigh, the rhythm slow and calculated. His gaze seemed far off into nothingness, yet a storm raged in it. His lower lip went inward, and he chewed on it for a while.

Jaron was about to yell at him to snap out of it when the chamber doors slid open and Rass appeared. He strode into the room and stopped dead in his tracks as he felt the atmosphere.

"What just happened here?" He demanded.

"Father brought them up to speed on the plan." Trinon replied.

"More like his own agenda," Jaron snapped. "I will not be treated like some second-rate warrior, mate or not!"

"I concur," Rass said making his way further into the room. "I have a message from Halfar for you, Talas."

Talas raised his head up and met the General's gaze. Jaron reared back from it a bit. She had never seen such a look in Talas' eyes before. Rass on the other hand was admiring it.

"Good, you're angry, as you should be. Halfar wants you at the main gates. He feels Modas is a bit too confident about going against something he can't see coming."

"That's just how Father is," Trinon tried soothing the situation in his father's defense.

"That's no excuse!" Jaron yelled.

"I'll leave you to figure out how you want to handle this." Rass left the chamber.

Trinon sat down on the floor crossing his legs and rested both arms on his knees. Jaron smiled a little. Her son had gone from being so dogmatic about everything to now taking things in stride. She couldn't put a finger on what caused such a drastic change but there was a nagging suspicion that Talas had something to do with it.

"Snap out of it!" She whacked Talas in the shoulder blade. He grabbed her wrist as she made contact and turned to stare at her in battle mode. "Talas!" She pulled away from his grasp and she saw his expression clear.

"Sorry, I wasn't paying attention."

"Obviously!" She stood up. "Modas is not in charge. This is not our planet. You need to get it together!"

"Suggestions?" Talas asked comically.

"You're the strategist!"

"So are you, love." Talas pointed at her.

"Stop calling me that," Jaron replied gritting her teeth.

Talas threw his head back and laughed loudly. Trinon clapped his hands, a wide smile spreading ear to ear. Jaron felt her face get hot.

Am I overreacting?

Sitting back down, she put on her game face and started thinking about their options.

"Since Modas does not want you anywhere near him, how about positioning yourself a safe distance?"

Trinon nodded in agreement.

"Maybe in the alcove below so you can be close but not seen?"

Talas tapped his lips and then smiled.

"No." Jaron and Trinon sat up straighter. "Above."

"Above?" They replied in unison.

"I can see far into the distance and still not be in the same vicinity as Modas. The veranda two stories above the main gates would suffice."

"Sneaky," Trinon laughed.

Jaron was impressed at how fast Talas bounced back from the brink of rage. She was starting to respect him a bit more these past few years. Focusing back on the task at hand Jaron added another suggestion.

"You'll need back up. How about two warriors on opposite sides in addition to the ones Modas allowed in the area?"

"Hmm." Talas tilted his head.

"If all the infiltrators converge on the palace at once, that would put a strain on even the manbeasts, the enemy being cloaked."

"Father is not invincible, after all," Trinon interjected.

"Indeed," Talas replied. "I think we may have a plan, love."

Jaron bristled.

"How come you never call me that?" Trinon pouted.

"Ah sweet Trinon," Talas laughed.

"I'm not sweet," Trinon said flatly.

Jaron swiveled towards her son at the tone in his voice. Something cold crept up inside her as both men locked on each other in a knowing stare.

"Don't frighten your mother."

"Oh," Trinon snapped out of it and began laughing. "Sorry!" He ran his fingers through his mane, smiling again.

"What was that?" She demanded.

"Nothing." Trinon, still smiling, stood up and hugged her. "I must go. Father's waiting for me to relieve him. I have to take care of Farin."

He left then.

Jaron turned to Talas and demanded again, "What is going on?"

Talas also stood and stretched his entire body before sending a sideways glance at her. "Nothing you need to worry about..." he stopped before saying 'love.' "He's not a child anymore, true enough. But, he still has a sweet heart."

"That is not what I asked, Talas!"

"Leave it be," Talas snapped. "We have more pressing worries. I will not be killed on this wretched planet."

As they both walked out of the chamber into the corridor, Jaron's own heart felt a stabbing pain. She did not like being left in the dark, especially regarding her own children.

Malfeasance

Thick fog hung over the fields just after dawn on New Lassa forcing the workers to delay their daily tasks. While they waited for it to lift, many of them went to prepare morning meal a bit early. Four male field workers opted to sit outside by the communal building unaware they were being watched, one of them in particular.

A mischievous grin formed on Mara's lips as she eyed the tallest of the men sitting against the wall, one leg outstretched with the other bent. She had been observing him for some time since the end of the Earth battle. There was something about him that she found quite charming, sexy even. His light bronze skin and dark hair were in complete contrast to her. Plans to increase population had been brought up in early debates so she figured it would behoove her to find an ideal mate. Of course, that was a means to an end since it was also because she felt sexually frustrated. Tiny stings assaulted her eyes as her stare lingered a bit too long, straining them.

Oh, he is beautiful! She licked her lips.

Her mother had no idea the kinds of perverse thoughts that ran around in her head and would probably be appalled. Mara kept most of her life private, before her death and now. She had never had a mate, per se, though she did a lot of mating on the sly. This time, she decided, she wanted true love with a permanent mate and found him.

Stepping out from behind the corner of the building, she approached the men slowly. The three standing turned to see her and backed away a little. At least they recognized her as the daughter of a manbeast even if she wasn't one herself. Her prey did not move from his position on the ground but did look puzzled at her presence.

"Good morning," she purred.

"Good morning," the three replied together, their eyes nearly bulging out of their sockets. One of them clutched the front of his shirt.

"Good morning, Mara," the worker still sitting said softly without looking at her.

Mara restrained herself from squealing with glee. This was the first time he had spoken to her and his voice sent shivers all through her body, making her skin tingle. He was definitely the one for her. She leaned forward over him and waited for him to look up. When he did, she saw his beautiful gold eyes with chocolate brown flecks in them.

"Would you accompany me for a stroll before meal this morning…" she smiled and waited for him to say his name.

"Dellus," he said.

"…Dellus?"

"Why me?" His friends scoot around and left him alone with her.

"Because I want to know more about you, Dellus." She replied sweetly.

"I don't think a warrior of your caliber should be associating with a lowly field worker, Mara."

There, he said her name again and she nearly swooned.

"Do not speak such things in my presence," she said sternly.

"But, it's true."

"I do not think that way!" She straightened her posture. "Are you refusing me?"

He hung his head and sighed heavily but rose from the ground to stand before her. They were the exact same height so their eyes met. Neither wavered.

"I am not refusing you. I just don't want to be mauled by any of your siblings for being near you."

"They can be very protective, yes, but I will not let them harm you. Come," She extended her hand to him. "Let's go."

His gaze went to her hand and he shook his head.

"You're trying to get me killed."

Mara grabbed his hand and led them out onto the pathway nearby.

He didn't resist.

On the hilltop above the communal building, Ganna sat watching the interaction between Mara and Dellus. She frowned in disgust and then laughed softly. She knew Mara thought her mating rendezvous were a well-kept secret but Ganna had seen her in action many times. The Whore has found a new toy, she scoffed to herself. It was no secret how much she loathed manbeasts and their offspring was not off limits. She found it fascinating that the ones who were not manbeasts acted like animals in certain situations, like mating.

A thought crept into her mind and she smiled. She could try out the new weapon prototype and take that nasty half manbeast woman down a peg. Ganna assumed that she would be in the clear since Chardon nor Jaron were planet side and not scheduled for a long while. Sestis agenda was still in play, even if she was no longer be with them, with Ganna at the helm.

Working out the details in her head as she got up and walked back to her lab, Ganna eyed the two strolling hand in hand down the pathway. Stupid boy. She could never understand what men saw in the statuesque half breed. Dellus was going to learn a valuable lesson soon enough. Ganna grinned, her expression sinister.

☼

Sars adjusted the zoom on his goggles and the gateway console came into view. Four royal guards held vigilance along with the operator. His group had managed to get close to the palace border and they now sat hidden in the dense trees surrounding the great wall. An entranceway sat below. Too obvious. That was not how they planned to enter royal territory.

Off to the left he spotted movement and focused on it. His communications team was getting into position to set up the coordinates detector. With the battalions in place outside the solar system, it would only be a matter of time before the gateway opened between Azrom and New Lassa. When that happened, they would be able to trace it and attack the planet directly before any help arrived.

"Be ready, my soldiers. The time is near for a frontal assault on Azrom's royal palace."

"Sir!" they all replied.

"This will be a glorious event."

Cloaking themselves, Sars and his group scaled up the rest of the wall and then down on the opposite side onto royal soil. Without knowing, they ran across a pressure sensor planted beneath them.

The battle chamber doors slid open and a royal guard hurried in, barely bowing properly before addressing the two Generals. His boots clapped loudly as he advanced.

"Generals!" he began out of breath. "There has been a perimeter breach on the far side of the wall! I have the coordinates!"

Rass clenched his fists. Kur unfolded his arms and placed his hands flat on the platform. Both regained their demeanor and stood straight. They made brief eye contact.

So it has begun, Rass thought.

He gestured to the soldier and the small chip with the coordinates was placed on the platform. An image of the landscape inside the wall flickered to life and small icons representing the pressure points in the ground glowed red except for one that glowed blue.

"They are headed straight for the main palace entrance." Rass spoke.

"As predicted. How did they scale the wall?" Kur wondered out loud.

"It was no easy task, that is certain," Rass replied. "Contact Modas and have him get his teams in position." He commanded the soldier.

Once the young royal guard left, Kur growled and slammed his fist down on the vidscreen platform, making the image shake. He looked up at Rass and saw the same frustrated expression on his face.

"They are bold." Rass walked around to stand by Kur's side. "If it is indeed the Razznians then we have an even more troubling issue."

"How they got here." Kur nodded as he concurred. "They have acquired a new technology. That, alone, is frightening."

"Well, let's greet them in Azrom fashion, shall we?" Rass said in a honeyed voice.

"Let there be bloodletting," Kur replied as they exited the chamber.

New Lassa

Six workers set the prototype weapon in place on the hilltop across from the gateway console. After nearly two hours, they were able to point the cannon in direct line of the gateway's center below. Ganna was precise in her guidance. Dismissing the workers with a wave of her hand, she admired her new toy, patting it softly. The scientists who would operate the weapon were on their way.

"Now, to get the bait."

Ganna strolled happily along the hill then down onto the pathway leading into the fields. She could see Mara off in the distance stalking her new prey yet again. Dellus was toiling away, oblivious to her hungry stares. Ganna grimaced but continued her approach.

"Mara, dear!" She called out sweetly. The half beast turned at the sound of her name and smiled. "Here! I need you!"

When Mara was only a few feet from her, Ganna changed her expression to one of seriousness. The halfbreed stopped short looking concerned.

"What is it, Ganna?"

"I received word that the Razznians are heading towards Azrom but I found another fleet further away. It would not be on their report." Mara's hands went to cover her mouth and her eyes went wide. "I need you to get word to Chardon and Modas quickly. Can you do that?"

"Of course! When do you need me to go?"

"It will take a bit to open the gateway to Azrom so be ready early afternoon."

"Okay."

"Thank you, dear. See you soon."

Ganna left in a state of elation. Stupid animal. She waited at the edge of the village for Mara to head home before going after Dellus. He wasn't a warrior by any means therefore unlikely to question her request. This was turning out better than she had planned.

With Mara at the gateway's entry and Ganna keeping watch, the console operator initiated the sequence to open a pathway to Azrom. As she entered the black pool swirling before her, Ganna went over to Dellus who was not far away in the adjacent fields.

"I would greatly appreciate it if you stood guard and waited for her to come back through."

"Is she not staying on Azrom for a bit?" Dellus asked confused.

Ganna pursed her lips.

"No, she must deliver it and come right back. We can't have the enemy finding out where New Lassa is."

Dellus went pale.

"Then you can't let her go!"

"It's the only way to warn our comrades," Ganna said smiling, though on the inside she was close to slapping the impudent worker for talking back. "Now go! Hurry!" She watched him head towards the gate.

On Azrom, the console operator saw it light up and the gateway activate. In a panic, he tried to shut it down, his finger flying across the controls. One of the guards sped off to alert his superiors. A direct order was in place since the detection of the Razznian fleets to not open the gate for fear of New Lassa's coordinates being leaked. With horror, the operator could see that the signal was coming from New Lassa.

"Success!" The leader of Sars' communications team exclaimed as he witnessed the gateway activation.

He whirled a finger in the air and his group decoded the coordinates coming through. Complete, the information was sent to the fleet on the outer rim for the jump to New Lassa's location. In his goggles view he saw a flurry of activity around the console. He grinned, saying again, silently.

Success.

Chardon was faster than Halfar as they both ran towards the gate. His chest felt like it was about to implode, and a weakness spread into his legs. He had made it clear that no one on New Lassa was to open the gate, ever, unless he was there to supervise it.

"Shut it down!" Halfar commanded.

"I am, my Lord! It takes a moment!" The console operator cried out. As the gateway powered down, Chardon grabbed his head and bent down to his knees. He let out a small whimper, Halfar resting a hand on his shoulder.

"It was too long," Chardon whispered. "It was traced. I know it, I feel it."

"What is going on, Chardon?" Halfar demanded. "Who on New Lassa can activate the gate?"

"Ganna," Chardon replied.

Halfway into the vortex Mara could see it start to unravel and knew the gate on the other side was shutting down. Keeping her breathing steady to avoid panic, she turned back to the entryway and went into a crouched position. It would take a massive force of energy to catapult herself at top speed before it too closed. Exhaling all the air from her lungs, she launched, becoming a bullet of light.

Even at her high-speed retreat, she could feel something behind her. She had been on Azrom before and this was not familiar air. The moment her body burst through the vortex back onto New Lassa soil, she turned and caught a glimpse of a large ship cruising at a fast pace in the darkness of space towards the still open vortex.

Before she could stand up, a blast of heat whizzed past her, scorching the back of her robe. Out of the corner of her eye she saw it going past Dellus, blackening his right arm as he tried to dodge it. The blue beam sped down into the vortex, making contact with the approaching ship. It exploded into a burst of debris as the vortex snapped shut.

Looking up she could see Ganna on the verge of rejoice when claws took hold of her head and dragged her down the hill. Und had the scientist in a death grip. Mara calculated what just happened and felt a twinge of hatred for the deceitful woman. The scientists who had operated the cannon ran off in fear, not getting far since Lassian warriors blocked their path.

Mara jumped up, wincing from the pain on her back, and hurried over to Dellus. He lay in a daze trying to control his breathing. His right arm was beginning to ooze heated blood that sizzled on its way out. She leaned over him and his gaze averted from the horizon to her.

"Are you alright?" she asked.

"I'll live. You?"

Mara let out a small laugh and then kissed him hungrily. He didn't seem surprised.

"I'm not going to leave you alone," Mara declared.

"I had a feeling," Dellus sighed heavily.

"Don't move." Mara commanded.

Und stopped a few feet from his sister. Ganna had been screaming 'let me go' the whole journey. He released his claws and let her drop on the ground with a thud. Medical workers came in swarms to tend to those injured from the scorching blast.

"What have you done?" Mara screamed at her.

"Did you not see? We destroyed an enemy threat before it could even get here!"

"What you have done, you egotistical creature, is give the enemy our location." Jakar came from the shadows of the setting sun and stood over her. "Do you not think they won't come back with an even larger force?"

"They can bring all they want!" Ganna spat. "We have a weapon now to defeat them. I am going to have more built!"

Jakar hit her in the head with lightning speed, knocking her out. He nodded to a medical worker to get her. Turning to address everyone in the vicinity he yelled out.

"We are now in battle mode! All warriors and technical assistants prepare posts for enemy engagement!" The stunned looks on all their faces spoke volumes. They were not ready. "Thank Ganna for putting us in harm's way."

Jakar walked off heading to the war counsel chamber where the head council members would be shortly.

Standing in the shadows down the corridor away from everyone else running towards the Azrom gate, Talas leaned against the wall with arms crossed. He let his head rest on it while he watched panic ensue. Something told him long ago that Ganna had her own agenda and could not be trusted. When Chardon had given her the order not to open the gate, Talas could see it in her eyes, the defiance. He was surprised how soon she had done it.

He felt a presence closing in on him from behind and caressed the hilt of his long sword with a finger. The scent of spice mixed with mild sweat let him know who it was and he moved his finger away. An arm rested on the wall above his head and he felt body heat.

"I take it, the conniving witch made her move?" Kelin whispered in his ear.

"Oh yes, and ahead of schedule, no less," Talas whispered back.

"Who do you think is more angry right now?"

"Hmm. It's hard to say." Talas tilted his head back. "Are you ready on your end?"

Kelin lifted an eyebrow.

"There is no sign of the enemy approaching the palace."

"Oh, they are. This was a signal to start their assault and since they are already inside the walls, I say it will be within the hour."

"Your deductions frighten me sometimes. They're always dead on." Kelin grabbed Talas by the hair and, pulling his head back further, kissed him hard. "See you after the fight."

"Be careful, my love. And stay clear of the manbeasts for now."

Turning, he watched Kelin disappear around the bend of the corridor. After a moment, he too went down to get into position. Having made himself accustomed to Azrom, he noticed the air had changed. Sometimes, being right was a curse.

With reptilian speed, Sars and his men advanced right up the center pathway of the palace's main entrance. They did not waver in formation or resolve. The closer they got, the more soldiers were visible along the walls. From the looks of it, they had not detected his group's movement. Cloaked from the time they climbed the great wall, his men felt confident in infiltrating the palace right under the guards' noses. At five hundred meters from the palace doors, Sars smiled at his victory.

Modas stood guard with Trinon and Barbon at the main entrance checking the horizon for any sign of the enemy. The royal guards were ready for battle in a six-man formation ahead of his team. His agitation let him know that contact was imminent so waited until he knew the enemy's location before acting. A tense silence had spread in the area.

One level higher above Modas, overlooking the main palace entrance, was Talas and his team. He made sure the Manbeast did not notice his presence as he also waited, but not looking for the same thing. Since the enemy was undoubtedly cloaked, there would be a different precursor to their arrival. Setting one foot on the ledge of the balcony he leaned forward.

The air directly in front of the palace made a strange movement and then shimmied left to right. In that instant, Talas saw the faint glassy outline of a cloaked figure before it disappeared.

Damn it! Without a moment's hesitation, Talas moved.

From above his head Modas heard a noise. Less than a hundred feet in front of him, an Azrom guard's throat was cut. He extended his claws and took a step to defend when he saw movement out of the corner of his eye from up high. Talas catapult from the balcony with one arm and flip over into a feet first dive. Both feet struck solid air, jarring the cloaking mechanism to reveal an enemy. In the same timing, Talas swung one leg up and hit another then using the enemy's shoulder as a launching pad before hitting the ground, he sailed through the air backwards. He pivoted his body midair and landed a punch on an invisible form below him. A loud crunch was heard. As he slid to a halt, his body turned sideways and grabbing hold of something in the air next to him threw it forward. With a thud, the now solidified enemy hit the ground, static surrounding him from the broken suit.

At a full stop, Talas stood breathing hard, coated in sweat. He wiped his mouth with the back of his forearm and looked up. The silence was deafening as everyone stood shocked in mid battle stances. Modas' face showed hostility building at the revelation his actions created.

"So," Kur purred from above. "That's where young Trinon learned that technique."

"Seize the enemy!" Rass commanded. "Get the wounded guards to medical!"

Soldiers went into a flurry around the palace entrance as Modas remained rooted in his position, fist clenched tight. His moment of glory had been stripped from him and felt his manbeasts now looked incompetent. He was waiting for the enemy to get a little closer, so his team could tear them apart and leave one intact for questioning. Seeing the guard with his throat slashed he felt a pang of guilt but was glad to see it was not life threatening. Modas was not happy. He had only seen two of the shimmers that were further away and assumed it was the start of the enemy's formation when in fact it was the end. How did Talas see that? Manbeasts are known for their superior vision and sensory perception but he had never heard of a Lassian who could do the same. But then again, he never bothered to evaluate them as equal beings.

We made a mistake.

He turned to face his son and saw a look of dread on the young manbeast's face. After a while, Modas broke his gaze and followed the rest of the soldiers into the palace. It was a trek of despair for the defeated in his mind.

"Did you see it?" An Azrom guard asked his squadron in a low voice. "That Lassian moved almost better than those Manbeasts."

"Our bodies are too bulk heavy to move like that," a soldier answered.

"Now wait. We do have that one village that has a species able to move that fast."

"But they are not built like us and their shells are much lighter because they have more muscle."

"Still, I think if we can learn a few tricks from them," the squad leader began.

"Have you no pride in our race?" a soldier hissed angrily.

"Pride will not win this battle," the leader snapped. "Do you not know they feel the same as we do?" A hushed silence filled the room. It was no secret how each race felt about the other. "But, now, we have to because our races are forever bound. Have you all forgotten Farin?"

"Lassian and Azrom blood runs through that child's veins."

"And the Razznians have come to our planet."

"Dastardly and stupid."

"It is a bold move, no doubt." The leader stood up. "We need to convince the Lassians that we want to cooperate and let the Manbeasts feel appreciated."

"As long as they do us the same courtesy," the angry soldier spat.

"Of course." The leader added, "I am going to appeal to our Commander."

Once he was gone from the room, the other soldiers remained to nurse their drinks. The moves of Talas replayed in their heads and a slight twinge of jealousy crept in.

Four space podsuits were laid across the floor in the battle chamber along with the cloaking mechanisms. The pods had been retrieved after going over the terrain where they landed with keen observation. Rass stood staring at them in fascination. Such technology coming from a nasty reptilian race baffled him. His thoughts were broken by the movements in the room.

All the Lassians along with Kur, Halfar and his royal guards were also in the chamber admiring the Razznian gear. No one said a word for a long time as everyone took turns touching and inspecting them. There was no mistake in Rass' mind that the work had been contracted out by another more advanced race.

"Who, in their right mind, would sanction a negotiation of technology with Razznians?" Rass asked himself out loud.

"For it to be done so fast, means it was established long ago." Kur answered.

"So, a favor had been called," Halfar smirked.

Chardon looked ill and Rass frowned.

"What is it?" He demanded of the Lassian leader, incurring a warning look from Halfar.

"Sestis," was Chardon's reply.

Dreridian Council

Sestis felt empowered for setting up her first council meeting without Chardon. The gown one of her admirers had made especially for her flowed over her body and across the floor, making her appear regal. Good impressions at these meetings were a must. This time, she only had two loyal Lassian warriors to guard her instead of the usual four. Her disgust for Manbeasts prevented her from trusting any of them with her life.

Today she would set another piece of her agenda in motion to rid Lassa of the manbeasts and Chardon as leader. Just remembering how that Azromian ruler salivated over her mate and the manbeast servant who pined for Chardon in secret nearly made her retch. Using a hand- woven fan, she cooled herself down and continued to the conference room. All she had to do was sit and listen for any snippets of information to help her along so when the afternoon banquet was over, she could negotiate one on one.

The Dreridian ruler left the banquet shortly after it ended and Sestis followed him to his personal library, making sure no one saw her do so. At the entrance of the library she stopped and smoothed her hair along the sides of her face before advancing.

"Lord Pondur, abandoning your guests so soon?" Sestis cooed.

He turned his head towards her and smiled. The cragged ridges of his brow and chin made the bubbled skin seem to expand. He kept his hands behind his back and she assessed the short thick talons. She could take him if he tried to harm her.

"Lady Sestis, how crude of you to sneak around my palace unescorted."

"My apologies, but how else was I to get you alone?"

"Such ambition." He faced her full on. "What do you want, Lassian?"

"We both have a wish to end the Azrom regime. They are not what this galaxy needs anymore."

"True, but they are one of the great military powers." He tilted his head. "You have something sinister in that inferior mind of yours."

"Of course," Sestis replied blushing.

"I'm intrigued. Continue."

"I have made a little agreement with their sworn enemy, the Razznians.

As you know, they do not have the technology currently to combat Azrom at full force. They will have a plan soon. An audacious one."

"And how do you know that?"

"Let's just say I planted a small seed."

"And my race comes in how?"

"Well," Sestis began but Pondur held up a hand.

"Before you continue," he went to a console in the corner of the room and pushed a button. Within seconds, a bulbous creature with craggier bubbled skin than his entered the room. "This is my chief scientist, Lord Greggor." The scientist attempted to bow, his girth in the way. "Please, continue Lady Sestis."

She stopped herself from placing a hand over her face in disgust as the scientist's tongue slipped out and licked his lips. It resembled his face; boils and crags of various size encrusted atop thick meat. Regaining her posture, she went on.

"The Razznians will need a way to infiltrate Azrom and I believe you can provide the necessary route."

"That's insanity!" Lord Pondur exclaimed.

"I did say it was audacious."

"Madness! Are you trying to get us all killed?"

"Wait," Greggor interrupted. "It is bold, yes, but something Azrom would never expect."

"Of course, because no one would ever actively invade the planet of the mightiest warriors in five galaxies," Lord Pondur retorted.

"Exactly," Greggor smiled and saw it dawn on his Lord's face. He turned to Sestis. "How beastly of you to come up with such a thing."

"What is it you want in return?" Lord Pondur asked, his expression serious.

"There is a small solar system in need of leadership and none has been appointed yet."

"Are you not already the leader of your own race?"

"Yes, but, that will end soon with the Razznian take over and Chardon on Azrom."

"You would destroy your own race?" Pondur said incredulously.

"Destroy? Oh no, I want to make it more profitable. There is a difference." Sestis again gave her winning smile. "Of course, I know this will come at a price as well. What is it you wish?"

Lord Pondur snorted and replied while looking at his head scientist.

"It is not I who will need compensation, Lady Sestis."

As he walked towards the door, Sestis grew pale. Her stomach lurched from the banquet food preparing to exit her body by any means necessary.

"Please, use my study to negotiate." Lord Pondur left the room.

Alone with Lord Greggor, she cleared her throat and stepped to the bay windows. She could feel his eyes burning through her back as she fanned herself.

"So, Lord Greggor, what are your terms for this venture?"

"I have a fascination with off world cuisine and it would be such a delight to know the flavor of my meat before preparations."

Sestis whirled around wide eyed.

"You mean to eat me?"

"Oh, no," Lord Greggor laughed. "I want to taste you," he licked his lips again. "From the inside," he added.

"This is your stipulation?" Sestis asked softly, feeling faint. "And just how to you plan to do such a thing?"

"I have been researching your species and found that your body has multiple orifices. One in particular runs the length of your torso."

Sestis instinctively placed her hands on her backside and clasped them together.

"Is that so?"

"If you please," Lord Greggor gestured to the table sitting beside her.

He motioned with one craggy finger for her to turn around and face the window.

Her two guards and two Dreridian advisors had entered the room and Greggor made them shut the door. Sestis thought for a moment if she could get out of this and what other options may appear down the road. Seeing none, she inwardly shrugged. It was just an exploration of her insides with a hideous tongue and it would be over in moments. Well worth the greater plan of moving her agenda forward.

Climbing onto the table on her knees, she lifted her dress and gathered it around her hips. In her calculations, seducing Lord Pondur was the goal so had removed her undergarments beforehand. It now served a new purpose.

"This will seal the deal?" She asked, sensing Greggor directly behind her. Through the window she saw the reflection of him.

"Yes, indeed," he replied.

She watched his tongue come out and the tip ran along the outer rim of her orifice.

Mustering all her strength to not jerk away from the slimy ragged feel of it, she asked.

"And I will have dominion of the system?"

"Absolutely."

Through the reflection in the window she watched his tongue enter her and she felt it slithering around, touching every part. He removed it and licked his lips.

"Delicious. Extraordinary."

With horror, she saw his tongue go back inside her for another taste. Sestis braced herself with one hand on the window and fought the urge to tense up. In the reflection, further back, she saw Lord Pondur smiling with pleasure.

You monster! She screamed at him internally.

The tongue slipped out.

"No tensing up, Lady Sestis. It ruins the experience."

He resumed his 'tasting' of Lassian fare.

After what seemed like eternity, Greggor was done and looking quite satisfied. Sestis climbed down off the table and let the hem of her gown fall to the floor. Shaken but not giving them the satisfaction of showing it, she brushed the front of her hair back down.

"Was that to your liking, Lord Greggor?"

"Indeed. You must send some fresh Lassian sometime. I think it would be such a treat."

Sestis stepped closer to him and whispered in his ear, "That could easily be arranged."

"I look forward to it," he replied softly in hers.

Lord Pondur came forward and addressed her.

"Have you and my head scientist made an agreement?"

"Yes," Sestis said sweetly.

"I will make sure to let the Razznians know of our deal." Pondur made a small wave of his arm to the door.

"Thank you, for your time, Lord Greggor," Sestis curtsied.

"No, no, thank you, Lady Sestis. It was quite enjoyable."

"Lord Pondur," Sestis addressed him as she stopped at the entrance to curtsy for him as well. He kept that horrid smile on his face the whole time and she vowed to make him pay for his actions.

The looks of horror on her guards' faces were nothing compared to the smirks of disdain on the Dreridians. She knew they would tell no one out of loyalty to their Lords. It was now clear that they felt a bargaining chip had come into play. This planet was no longer safe for her to be on alone.

"Come," she motioned to her guards. "Our transport is waiting."

Walking to the hangar, Sestis began to smile. When it was all said and done, her plan was coming into fruition. Just a few more ties to connect and her new title would be Empress.

THREE

Keep Your Enemy Close

Dawn came with thick fog rolling over the hillside, a new phenomenon since the land had been reconfigured. The field workers made their way to continue repairing the damage done nearly a month ago by Ganna's new toy. Parts of the fields located by the gate were scorched bald and vegetation refused to grow there. A process used to regenerate the nutrients of the soil had to be administered every day for a full moon cycle.

Dellus unconsciously rubbed his right arm with the back of his left hand. The stinging pain stopped him, and he had forgotten his instructions not to irritate it. The wound itched as it healed. His three friends who always worked the fields with him came up to his side. One of them slapped him on the good shoulder and grinned.

"Looks like you got yourself a mate," he laughed. "Guess so," Dellus replied.

"I tell you what," another friend began. "If we didn't need a chief scientist with her knowledge and expertise, I would have slit that woman's throat."

"You're not the only one." Dellus started walking into the field. He didn't want to talk about Ganna or the day of the incident any more.

Halfway through his work, he heard someone beckoning him and knew his plan was blown. Off in the distance he could see a council woman waving her hands to make sure he saw her. Setting his tool to the side, out of the way, he went to her. A few meters behind her stood Jakar, his massive frame giving Dellus pause even this far away.

"What can I do for you?" Dellus asked the council woman.

She fidgeted for a moment and glanced at Jakar, then eyed Dellus' arm. "If you would please go to the medical lab for treatment to repair your injury. Jakar will escort you and be on hand to observe."

"Ganna's lab?"

"Umm, correct," she answered nervously.

"Come," Jakar's voice boomed.

Dellus obeyed and followed the manbeast across the hill to Ganna's medical lab. Once there, he felt bile trying to escape and forced it back down. The scientist was sitting at her terminal working merrily along as if she had done nothing wrong. When she turned around to face them, she smiled sweetly.

"Dellus! So good of you to come. We really need to get that burn repaired. You should not have waited so long."

"I didn't want you to touch me," Dellus said with a hint of anger.

"Oh? Why, that's ridiculous. I'm a medical healer before anything else."

Dellus clenched his fists and his lips pressed tight together. The strain on his right arm forced him to loosen his fists. Jakar stepped for- ward and leaned over Ganna.

"Enough with the sugar coating, you disgusting monster. Fix him."

Ganna's facial expressions were struggling between indignation and sincerity. Both battles were lost and it became one of defeat. She picked up a tray prefilled with the necessary treatment for Dellus' burns and set it on the holder of the examination table.

"Please, lie down." She gestured with her hand.

"I am watching you," Jakar said as he went to stand near the entrance.

The look she gave him made it clear they would never be friends. Dellus had a thought as Ganna healed his wounds.

What have I gotten in the middle of?

Until that day, he had been just an ordinary worker who just happened to catch the eye of a female warrior. He had no intention of being a fighter in whatever battle was coming. Glancing over at Ganna he saw something nasty glinting in her eyes while she went through the motions of his treat- ment. Letting her touch him confirmed his initial reason for not wanting her near him. She made his skin crawl.

Azrom

There were no doors or closures for the cells located in the lower bowels of the palace and Chardon wondered how the prisoners were pre- vented from escaping. In truth, it unnerved her wondering about the lack of doors everywhere. Back in female form, she was exhausted from the night before. Halfar thought mating would keep her mind preoccupied from the gate incident and he was insatiable.

Her group came to a halt at a large rectangular cell with four Razznians secured against the walls. Two royal guards stood at each corner outside the cell. Halfar waved them away and he entered along with Chardon, Talas and the two generals. None of the prisoners looked up at their guests.

"Which one is the leader?" Halfar asked Rass.

"Hmm, I would say this one," Rass pointed to Sars. "He is the most stubborn of the twelve. Has not spoken one syllable."

"Is that so?" Halfar went towards him but Chardon stopped him.
"Wait."
She nodded to Talas who nodded back and knelt in front of Sars.

He inspected the Razznian and then spoke to him.

"How could you have come up with such a plan? Not that your race is not ferocious but this is beyond your scope." Sars smiled in response. "Sestis' plan was contingent on Lassa's takeover before focusing on Azrom. If you are attacking Azrom then that means, you knew our race had survived." Talas stood up and looked down on Sars. "How could you know that?"

Sars cackled, making him cough, sending fecks of bloody spittle into the air.

"Earth."

Chardon's insides churned. She saw the realization spread on Talas' face as well. Razznians should have no knowledge of Earth because it was too far from their solar system.

"Spy," Chardon blurted.

"So, the Razznian Empire was spying on the movements of Azrom's ruler." Kur rubbed his lower lip with one finger. "For what purpose?"

"Broken deal," Sars smiled.

Talas held up a hand to signal his need to jump in.

"You haven't spoken in all this time and now you give cryptic responses. I'm curious."

"Whether you know or not, our plan, you cannot stop it. We now know where your race is hiding."

"It won't be that easy, Razznian!" Halfar snapped.

Chardon walked over to stand next to Talas. She waited for Sars to make eye contact and then leaned down so they were inches apart. There was no fear in the Razznian leader and made her uneasy.

"You said Earth. Were you there?" Sars nodded. "How did you leave?"

"Alternate gateway," Sars answered.

"We closed the pathway."

"Yours, not ours. Tapped into Azrom coordinates and created our own."

Rass' head snapped up in surprise along with Kur's while Chardon and Talas went pale. Halfar flexed his fingers trying not to ball them into fists. Chardon knew that the one thing they wanted to avoid was putting Earth in harm's way again which was the reason for closing the pathway.

"Why?" Chardon asked softy.

"It seemed to me, you have affinity for the humans. Maybe human race should be part of battle as well? Will you save them? Sacrifice your advantage to defeat us?"

"We need to find out the pathway they used," Chardon spun around to address Rass.

"It could be a trap to force us to open the gate to Earth," Talas warned.

Sars laughed and choked again.

"No trap. We can go whenever we want."

"Well, this has turned into a three planet battlefield," Kur announced with disdain.

"There is no way Earth has recovered from the last battle," Chardon added.

Sars swallowed hard and leaned his head back on the wall. His restraints adjusted with him as he raised a finger and pointed at Kur.

"Your enforcers made big mess."

"New plan," Talas said and walked out of the cell.

Chardon was the last one out of the cell but before leaving, she turned to look at Sars. There was something else he had on his mind and wasn't telling. The Razznian just stared back at her with pity.

"Let's leave here," Halfar touched her arm and guided her down the corridor.

✳

Manbeasts gathered in an empty stone chamber waiting for their leader to show. Hurt feelings and resentment festered after the Razznian attack on the palace left them standing confused and useless. Seeing their Lassian counterpart take down all four enemies in mere moments took a giant chunk out of their warrior pride. What made matters worse was that Trinon obviously had learned his new fighting technique from Talas.

Modas walked in and everyone hushed. He understood his race and how they felt these past few weeks but now was not the time to draw a line in the sand. As much strife that existed between Manbeasts and Lassian warriors, they would have to put them aside for the good of all, even Azrom.

"It's no surprise that we are now faced with a great dilemma," he started. "This war has become more complicated involving four planets, two against one with an innocent race caught in the middle. To win, we will have to disclose some of our fighting skills," a loud din of outrage interrupted him. "But not all!" Modas bellowed over them. They stopped bickering and turned to acknowledge him. "Make no mistake, Azrom is a liability and the Lassians are still our rivals. We will only offer them a taste of what we can do."

Modas spread his legs shoulder width apart and folded his arms before continuing. He noticed the missing presence of his son, Trinon, who did not agree with his agenda.

So be it.

"We have foolishly underestimated the Lassian warriors and need to heed caution accordingly. I know some of us have mates who are warriors but, do not let that deter you from our main goal."

Movement from outside the entryway made the manbeasts turn their eyes on the cause. The Azrom commander and his elite soldiers waited to be let into the chamber. Modas motioned for his manbeasts to part and the group mingled in with them. Tension was high.

"Because we can no longer win without cooperation, we will be doing a joint training session with the Azrom forces and our Lassian race." He decided to not differentiate in the presence of the Azromians even though a slight rivalry could be seen. "Commander, please accept our teachings as we shall accept yours." The Azrom commander nodded in agreement but Modas saw mistrust in his stare.

Good. We're on the same page.

✳

Repairs to the battle arena were near completion and Kur was in a cheerful mood. He loved the sight of combat and bloodshed. The joint training would commence during the next moon phase which was only ten days away. Beside him, Rass strolled along quietly.

"Are you not excited, General Rass?" Kur asked loudly.

Rass stopped, causing Kur to worry as he too halted. He looked up at the sky then out into the horizon. His left hand began to shake.

"I will not be participating in such a trivial event," Rass responded.

"That's not very convincing." Kur grabbed his left hand and squeezed. "Why?"

"It's…" Rass snatched his hand out of Kur's and continued walking.

Kur immediately knew the answer. Losing control was something all warriors strived to prevent in a battle and Rass had a rage within him that would lead him down that path. Neither had dealt with what happened during and after the Earth battle. Halfar refused to address it. Seeing Rass' hand shake infuriated Kur and his loathing towards Halfar intensified. There was nothing he could do to Azrom's supreme ruler, not yet.

"Then I agree. You shouldn't. The goal is to train not murder."

"I don't like feeling this way!" Rass slammed a fist against the corridor's edge and big chunks crumbled to the ground.

"Just remember, I will always be on your side."

Rass lowered his eyes and adjusted his longsword.

"This is not General like behavior."

Kur let out a loud laugh. "No, but we both know how deadly you are, so it shouldn't matter how you feel at this moment." He tugged on Rass' cloak. "Let's go check on my preparations for the events. It's quite invigorating."

"You mean aesthetically pleasing?"

"Of course! Blood shed does not need to be messy. There is a finesse to it."

Rass rolled his eyes upwards to the side in exasperation.

As they rounded the curve, they nearly ran into Trinon who was toting young Farin. Kur's eyes narrowed at the sight of the child. Instead of roaming around being pampered, the boy should be in combat training like all the other royal Azrom children. Farin confirmed his thoughts.

"Look! I have new claws!" His hands morphed into shiny black grappling claws and hit the ground.

They all watched as he tried in frustration to lift them up. His red face had beads of sweat forming and his lips pouted. With utter defeat he let them hang before retracting them back into hands sporting black lacquer talons.

"Well, at least you know how to control the morphing," Trinon assured.

Rass and Kur looked at each other. Kur decided to recommend to Halfar that Farin be inserted in training. Claws as deadly as those should be used for the glory of Azrom.

"Very good, Farin," Rass cooed and ruffled the boy's hair.

"Trinon says he'll teach me some stuff to defend myself."

"Is that so?" Kur sneered.

Trinon smiled at him. Kur did not see the childlike prankster he usually saw in that smile. This one sent a hint of fear up his spine.

"Let's go, Farin," Trinon commanded cheerfully and bowed his head slightly as they walked past the two Generals.

"Something drastic has changed in that young manbeast, don't you think?" Kur asked his counterpart.

"Frighteningly so," Rass replied. "I think we should keep a better watch on him."

"Agreed."

Kur tapped a finger on his thigh as they walked contemplating on what could have made the young manbeast turn one hundred and eighty degrees in a little over a decade. Lassians were beginning to be more complex than he originally thought. He took a quick look back and was startled to see Trinon meet his gaze before refocusing on Farin.

Pacing from one end of the chamber to the other was not helping Chardon calm his nerves while he contemplated a strategy for Earth. When both forces pulled out, there was an unspoken promise that they would not return anytime soon. Reopening the pathway meant opening old wounds. He found himself chewing on his lower lip and winced when his teeth sunk in hard, drawing blood.

"Don't do that," Halfar's voice chided as he stepped in front of Chardon and licked the smeared blood from his lip. "I'm the only one allowed to hurt you like that."

"Stop," Chardon pushed him away. "I'm being serious."

"So am I," Halfar replied.

"We can't let Earth get sucked into this battle."

"Agreed. But, if our enemy thinks it can tilt the scales they will use it against us."

"There has to be a better alternative," Chardon started chewing his lip again then stopped when Halfar gave him a warning look.

"If there was a way to turn our prisoner into an ally," Halfar thought out loud, stroking his chin.

"You can't be serious?"

"Remember that saying humans had? Keep your friends close."

"And your enemies closer," Chardon finished the line.

"My race has fought the Razznians on several occasions, but nothing too serious. Trade wars mostly. For their ruler to believe we can be taken down so easily tells me how masterful Sestis' manipulations were."

Chardon felt a tinge of pity for the enemy in that moment. They did not deserve to be wiped out. On the other hand, he was not going to let his race be conquered. His pacing ceased, and he made a decision.

"I will interrogate the leader and see how far I get."

"Very well. Just remember," Halfar caressed Chardon's cheek with a taloned finger, "he is the enemy and will do anything for his race, even if it means death."

Strong wind whipped the ends of Modas' cloak around his legs as he stood atop the spiked pillar of a building adjacent to the palace. From high above he had a clear view of a chamber located on the opposite side where no one except royalty and their guards were allowed to venture. Larger than any other personal chamber he had seen and for good reason.

I can see it.

Four guards stood two on each side of the entrance. Two men of the royal family strode towards them and all parties gave a nod of acknowledgement. Inside the chamber, the two royals went separate ways. Multicolored sheer fabrics were draped all over the place and beneath them sat beds and large cushions. Naked bodies lay on them and some were being violated in ways that made Modas ill.

So, this is what Azromians are really like.

Modas fell backwards and descended to the lower level. As he landed kneeling with one hand on the ground for leverage, he caught a glimpse of a figure nearby. He swung around and extended a leg. His foot was caught in midair with one hand.

"That's no way to treat your own race," Talas tsked.

Modas wrenched his foot out of his hand and stood up to his full height. The Lassian warrior, never intimidated, infuriated him. He felt Talas mocked his pride as a Manbeast.

"Why are you hiding in the shadows?" Modas demanded.

"You saw it," Talas said.

"Yes." Modas stepped back from him. That Talas knew about this before he did left a bad taste in his mouth. "What are your thoughts?"

"It's a distraction tactic."

"How so?"

"It's designed to keep the royals and soldiers satiated to quell rebellion."

"It's disgusting, and barbaric," Modas spat.

"Indeed," Talas replied, pushing himself off the wall. "This is how Halfar rules."

"Anyone who treats their race with such disregard is no ally of mine."

"Careful. Our races are already intertwined." Talas walked past him and headed back into the palace.

Modas stood in silence trying to get his head around what he had just seen. After a few minutes of deliberation, he came back to his initial conclusion. Halfar was an enemy who needed to atone for his actions. Chardon may have forgiven the ruler, but not him. This new revelation solidified his feelings towards Azrom.

The dungeon was in direct contrast compared to the rest of the palace and Chardon felt a bit disturbed by it. As a prison it should hold no comfort. Here it bordered on uncivilized. He walked the black stone corridor with care, keeping his cream-colored robe from brushing against anything. In his hand he clutched a small container with a lid by its handle. The contents swished around softly.

At the cell which held Sars and his small group, Chardon turned to stand facing into it. He saw the muscles in the prisoners' arms shaking from distress and fatigue. Nodding to the guards, the barrier was disabled, and Chardon stepped in. The first thing he did was lower the restraints to let their arms rest. Sars looked up at him warily.

"You know why I am here," Chardon began. Sars managed a tiny smile. "I am not going to hurt you if you cooperate. Now, why am I here?"

"Information." Sars laughed.

"Correct. It must have occurred to you that my previous mate did not have your race's welfare in mind when she brokered the deal."

"That being so, we would have strong miners and less burden on our own species."

Chardon sighed. Not only were they lacking in battle skills against Azrom, they were lazy as well? He shook his head in amazement. Looking up he saw the other reptiles eyeing the container he had carried in.

"I take it you're hungry?"

"And what is the price?" Sars asked.

Chardon smiled.

"No price."

He set the container between them and stood back. With their restraints lowered, they were able to easily reach it.

The lid came flying off into the air and the bucket was passed around to each prisoner, their hands digging in to pull out a serving. Bloody entrails and miscellaneous parts slid through their fingers as they shoved it into their greedy mouths. Some fell onto the dirty cell floor. That didn't faze them. They picked them up and continued eating, the sounds wet and crunchy.

Chardon stood looking down on them, lips pursed into a thin line and his eyes wide, fascination mixed with disgust. He forced his fingers not to clench into fists as he watched them. Their diet included other species and Chardon got a glimpse of a horrible death being eaten by a Razznian. At least the creatures butchered for them in the container were killed first.

Razzna

Reptilian tails swished and collided against each other as the Razznian royal advisors bustled around the throne room in a panic after hearing the news about their fallen battle ship at the hands of the Lassians. The report came quickly and now needed to be carefully relayed to their ruler. Military heads roamed throughout the area waiting to give their best strategies for a counterattack.

The doors were opened, allowing the first set of royal guards to march in followed by Lord Kraznan and the rear guards. He saw his throne room full of agitated creatures and knew something was amiss. When they all stopped what they were doing and froze with dreaded stares aimed at him, he got a better idea of what was wrong. Seeing his high commanders also present sent alarms in his head.

"What is this?"

He demanded in an almost chipper tone with a hard edge.

One of his chief advisors managed to regain movement and straightened his hunched over form. Clearing his throat, he slithered towards him, hands clutched tight together. Everyone else watched in silence, waiting for the outcome before moving themselves.

"Yes," he began. "About the strike against the Lassians."

"We were able to find them?" Lord Kraznan was impressed.

"Of course, my Lord." The advisor wrung his hands. "The coordinates were relayed straight from Azrom as Commander Sars had planned."

"Excellent!" Lord Kraznan waved his guards out of the way and stood in the middle of his throne room, scanning all the faces. "So why is there tension in my hall?"

"Well, the vortex opened to the Lassian's new planet and our fleet advanced." The advisor looked around for support and found none so continued. "The first ship was on the threshold of the vortex when it was," he paused and sought help again, "destroyed."

Lord Kraznan frowned.

Surely, I didn't hear that?

He looked around the room as well and saw stunned expressions along with fear. He would not have any of that. Turning to the clearly frightened advisor his gaze bore into him.

"What do you mean, destroyed? By what?"

"Some kind of long range firing weapon. It tore the ship apart in one shot." The advisor lowered his stare. "We lost many, but half of the crew was salvaged." The silence deepened.

"Why are you all shivering in your skins?" Lord Kraznan yelled in a booming voice they had not heard in decades. His anger was palpable. Not so much at having lost soldiers in what was to be a sneak attack, but the actions of his royal council in the face of uncertainty. "This is not our first battle and it will not be our last!"

"My apologies."

The advisor bowed, shivering from the shock of his voice.

All the other members snapped out of their stupor, regaining some form of dignity. Lord Kraznan hissed, his forked tongue vibrating from the act as it slipped out of his mouth. He did not expect this kind of news after a long relaxing mud bath. Sitting down on his throne he arranged his robes to flow on the sides then waved a hand at his military advisors. The six lead commanders stepped up to form a straight line in front of him.

"I believe we have underestimated the Lassians, My Lord," his first commander stated.

"So it seems."

"This was a surprise attack but after reading the report and analyzing the data, it is clear that the Lassians were not warned of our presence from anyone on Azrom."

"Then how did they know to shoot at the first sign of our ships?"

"I can answer that, My Lord," the third commander replied. "We were waiting for a Lassian on Azrom to contact their planet after finding out about our infiltration. That did not occur. Instead, the signal was initiated 'from' the Lassian's planet."

"In short," the first followed, "we were lured by the Lassians."

Lord Kraznan's lidless eyes opened as wide as possible and he was disturbed yet intrigued simultaneously. That the Lassians were so devious by nature never occurred to him. He leaned his large head on the hand he raised as his elbow rested on the throne.

"From the short relay the communications team sent it appears the Azromians along with the Lassian leader were just as surprised when the gate was activated," the sixth commander added.

"How curious," Lord Kraznan said lifting his head up.

"My conclusion is that there is a separate faction within the Lassian race that does not abide by Chardon's rules," his first stated.

"That weapon is a problem," the fourth interjected. Lord Kraznan tilted his head. "It can travel through a vortex and accurately pinpoint a target."

"I know of only one race with that kind of technology and a scientist callous enough to lure us in that manner." Lord Kraznan smiled with his knowledge. "That Lassian whore's companion, Ganna."

He could never forget how Sestis had sent a message to him apologizing for the slain soldier he had accompany her to a meeting in the nearest system. It was soon found out that the soldier had been sent to Lassa for Ganna to dissect as research. The sole purpose was to seek some weakness in the Razznian race. Unfulfilled rage boiled within him for a moment until he came back to the current issue at hand.

"So, we must wait for a better opportunity to strike," he concluded.

"Maybe we can lure them by going with the secondary plan involving Earth?" Number two asked.

The fifth commander looked over and nodded in agreement at the suggestion.

"How is the fare?" The second inquired. "If we must go into battle it would be nice to have a supply for replenishment."

"According to Sars, humans are quite tasty and full of nutrients. He put a few of the ones dying on the battlefield out of their misery."

"There is no way Chardon will let us get to Earth and start a feast," number four shook his head. "That plan is flawed."

"But," his first commander starts, "that is what we want him and Halfar to think. All we have to do is send small teams of twenty or so soldiers through the pathway we created and let them track it."

"From there, we can get to the Lassian planet directly when their reinforcements arrive," the sixth commander hissed.

Lord Kraznan liked the idea but was still a bit skeptical. Something about Earth made his stomach hurt. Good eating or not, it was a planet far behind their technology and really not worth the effort. He couldn't figure out why the Lassian leader was so compelled to protect such a species.

"What about our fleets lying in wait on the outer rim of Azrom's solar system?" Number three asked number six. "Should we move in?"

Before number six answered, Lord Kraznan raised a thick taloned finger to speak. He had also been thinking about this and decided on a new strategy.

"Leave them there on standby. It's too obvious that we would attack so close to this gate incident. Let's play with them a bit and see how Sars' team does wreaking havoc on Azrom."

His councilmen exchanged glances and finally number five spoke up.

"But there has been no communication since then. They all may have been captured by now."

"Of course, they have," Lord Kraznan replied sweetly. "That was also built into the plan."

Azrom

"The Razznian fleet has not moved, General," a lower officer reported.

General Kur was leaning over the digital display that mapped their solar system. He stood uncloaked in a full body tunic, his forest green hair cascading down one shoulder. A look of disdain covered his face and it intensified as he heard the update. Spreading his arms wide on the ledge, he pushed himself up straight. A swirled glint of white light flashed in his eyes and the lower soldier physically flinched from his stare.

The entry doors slid open and Talas entered the room to see the interaction between the two Azromians. He almost smiled but stopped midway and advanced towards Kur. Standing side by side, there was very little contrast. They were similar in stature, Kur the taller, with equal length of hair. Their bodies were made purely of lean muscle and both carried longswords at their hip.

Talas set one hand on the console's ledge and leaned on it a bit.

"I see from your expression that you have come up with the same conclusion I have."

Kur snapped his head towards him, visibly angry.

"They're toying with us," he hissed.

"Yes. Something unprecedented must have happened after the gate opened from New Lassa's side."

"Otherwise, that would have been the signal to advance." Kur finished for him.

He stepped away from the console and let it blink off while he stared into nothing deep in thought. Talas waited patiently for the General to say something. Instead, Kur just turned to him and locked eyes. There was an unspoken decision flowing between them.

After what seemed like an eternity, the two averted their gaze and Talas went to the door to leave the battle chamber. At the entrance, he turned and asked, "By the way, why the battle suit and no royal cloak and what not?"

Kur's lips curved upward.

"I wouldn't want your kind to think I'm not serious during the training battles."

"Oh?" Talas raised an eyebrow. "We never thought that at all."

With that, Talas left.

Strolling down the corridor leading to Chardon's quarters, Talas caught a glimpse of the Azrom sky. At midday the sun's brightness was at full force. He shaded his eyes with one hand and squinted. Before long, he arrived at the doorless entry of Chardon's temporary chamber. His eyes had to adjust to the artificial light inside.

"What brings you here unannounced?" Chardon asked without looking up from the vanity next to the bed.

"It's midday, surely Halfar can contain his urges and wait for sunset."

Chardon finally turned a disapproving face his way, which made him laugh. Even in female form, the Lassian leader did not intimidate him much. Talas strode in and flopped down on the foot of the bed.

"What do you want Talas?" Chardon sounded irritated.

"I need you to allow a team to investigate the gate incident."

"You want me to open the gate to New Lassa?"

"Correct."

"That's very irresponsible of you. I'm disappointed."

"They already have the coordinates, Chardon. Let's not be naïve," Talas said mustering the strength to not snap at his leader.

This was one of the reasons many were willing to betray Chardon in the first place.

"What did you say to me?" Chardon's anger flared along with blue light from her hands.

Talas' narrowed his eyes and he propped up on his hands. He hated when Chardon became indignant and unwilling to listen. His body flattened further into the bed ready to spring off and dodged whatever Chardon threw at him.

"The Razznians are not attacking, Chardon!" That startled her. "Do you want to know why?" He yelled at her. Chardon stared wild eyed at him. "Because something happened on New Lassa that was not part of their plans!"

Chardon's hands dimmed, and the blue light disappeared. She backed away at his outburst and hit the vanity with the side of her hip, making her wince in pain on impact. Talas repositioned his body back upwards and glared at her.

"You can't treat me like some Lassian dog! I am the leader of our race!" Chardon yelled back.

"Then act like it!"

Chardon stood there for a while in a state of confusion and indecision. Talas was annoyed but waited for his leader's reply. She eventually let out a heavy sigh.

"Fine. Take a team and go. But come back and report to me," she warned.

"Of course," Talas replied as he slid off the bed and walked to the entryway. "I'll take Kelin and two manbeasts with me."

Chardon waved him away, traces of anger still present on her face.

He smirked and made his way down the outer corridor.

His fists clenched and unclenched while he walked. Memories of the council meeting on Lassa where Chardon decided to humiliate him in front of other planet dignitaries flooded through his mind. He shook his head to clear away the creeping rage he had felt then trying to return. In his state, he did not realize he had reached the chamber he shared with Kelin.

With two hands, Kelin grabbed hold of him, forcing him to stop walking. They were standing at the foot of the bed and looking up, Talas saw a worried look on his lover's face. Embarrassed, he leaned his head forward and rested it on Kelin's shoulder.

"What is going on?" Kelin asked stroking Talas' lower back.

"Our leader brings out the worst in me sometimes."

"Chardon has always been a spoiled brat," Kelin chuckled. "What more do you want from him?"

"Leadership," Talas snapped and raised his head.

"Oh," Kelin stepped back a bit. "That's a tall order, don't you think?"

"We have to go."

Talas turned away from him and sat in the only chair in the room.

"Where?"

"Home."

Kelin was silent for a moment then nodded. "Your theory."

"General Kur agrees."

"Just us?"

"We're going to take two manbeasts."

"Have you told Modas that yet?" Kelin snorted, shaking his head.

"It's not up to him. Come, the quicker the better."

Kelin kept his distance from his mate as they headed out of the chamber and down to the housing occupied by the manbeasts. Talas felt a little bad about keeping Kelin at bay but there was no time to remedy it right now. He knew Ganna had done something idiotic, and until he had exact information, he had to hold his judgment.

At the communal housing, Talas stood at the entrance, not daring to enter a den of manbeasts with only a longsword and Kelin. The manbeasts were lounging, having drinks and conversing. It all stopped when one, then all, caught a glimpse of them. Modas glared at him as usual.

"Sorry to interrupt your festivities, but we need two manbeasts to accompany us back to New Lassa."

"And I am supposed to just say yes?" Modas snapped.

"It has been approved by Chardon. Are you disobeying our leader's orders?" Talas put on his most winning smile knowing he had already won.

"What for?"

"Just a theory," Talas replied tilting his head to one side.

Modas nodded to the two manbeasts nearest the door and they stood up slowly with no intention of acknowledging Talas as their leader for the mission. He saw Kelin roll his eyes in contempt at the lackluster agreement.

"Don't worry, we won't be gone long."

The team of four complete, they headed to the palace's main gate console Talas could feel his muscle tighten as they got closer.

What have you done, you ignorant woman?

His fingers twitched around the hilt of his longsword.

Added Tension

Deep purple liquid warped inward then spat out towards the gate operator at the console on New Lassa, swirling counter clockwise before it went flat to form a gaping black hole. Light crept in from the middle, growing until it turned the vortex into a white glowing orb with four dark figures taking shape. As they approached, the guardians recognized them and nodded to Jakar who stood nearby just in case there was conflict.

He had a feeling someone would come from Azrom eventually. Seeing Talas and Kelin along with two manbeasts meant Chardon was being cautious. The four stepped over the gate's threshold, onto Lassian soil, and the system was shut down.

"Jakar," Talas greeted the massive manbeast.

"We have much to discuss," Jakar replied as he turned and started walking to the commune.

A stiffness could be felt coming from the four home comers and Jakar knew what it was. There was a new kind of feeling in the air on the planet since the incident. All the people were on edge and didn't know who to trust anymore. With Talas back, he can get a gauge on what really happened.

"Why does it feel like we're about to attend a funeral?" Kelin blurted.

The two manbeasts kept looking around in quick succession with confused looks. Talas kept walking while he glanced at everything around him, seeing telltale signs of scorched soil and empty patches within the fields. Jakar watched him out of the corner of his eye and had more respect for the warrior than before.

"Not quite, but if I had my way," Jakar started then left it at that.

"Ganna," Kelin said and nodded to concur. He stopped in his tracks along with the manbeasts and stared up at the hill across from the gate console. "What in the name of Lassa is that?" He exclaimed.

"Ganna's new toy," Jakar replied without stopping. "Let's continue. The council is waiting."

It wasn't just the spiritual council or the scientific council. All the councils, military and political were included. Ganna was nowhere to be seen. Talas' insides felt like they were in a vice as he entered the chamber and sat down at the end beside Jakar. Kelin and the two manbeasts stood guard at the door.

"So," Talas said trying to sound cheerful. "What could possibly have been so dire that the gate was activated? Chardon's quite puzzled, as am I."

The one designated to speak was from the military council. She wiped a strand of hair from her face and licked her lips before speaking. Talas could tell it was to settle herself. She was clearly angry.

"A new weapon was commissioned by Ganna for the scientific council to create without the approval of the military council." There were hard intakes of breath from the science council. "It is that monstrosity you see on the hilltop. In order to test its power and range, she," the council woman paused. "Ganna suggested that an urgent message needed to be relayed to Chardon and requested Mara to deliver it."

"That stupid…," Kelin began.

Talas' mood sunk, and he could piece it together from there without the narrative. He let the council woman finish.

"The objective was to open the gate to lure the enemy in range at the vortex entrance. Needless to say, the blast was so wide and destruction, it scorched the nearby fields along with many of the workers. It did destroy a Razznian ship on its way into the gate."

"How dare you accuse us of such treachery?" One of the science council men yelled. "We had no idea of her plans!"

"You should have asked," the military council woman spat.

"Ask what? And, even if we did, do you think she would have been honest?" He retorted, his face filling with heat.

"We did not authorize such a weapon and we surely would not have tested it here!"

"Enough!" Talas yelled.

The room went silent. His whole body shook inside, his head hung down almost in his lap. He was so angry he felt nauseous. Jakar set a hand on his thigh and forced his leg to stop moving, making Talas look up at him in surprise.

"You cannot tell my mother," he whispered.

"I can't not tell her." Talas seethed.

He found Kelin staring blankly across the room from his station at the door and regained his focus on the issue at hand. This was a travesty and the last thing he wanted to do was tell Modas or Jaron that Ganna had almost murdered their daughter. A daughter who had already died once from a planet bomb.

"Well," Talas shook his dirty blond locks out of his face. "The enemy was waiting for that. A small team of spies infiltrated Azrom and had a device ready to capture our planet's coordinates once the gate was opened from there." He saw everyone's face in the room grow pale. "What Ganna did initiated their plans. It's great the ship was not able to get through the vortex, but now they know we have a weapon far more advanced in technology than our own. The question will be where we obtained it from."

"That is what we would like to know as well," the military council woman added.

Escorted by four manbeasts, Ganna hummed softly to herself as they guided her to the council chamber. She had no misgivings whatsoever about the cannon's test success. From her lab she had seen the gate open and knew whoever it was came from Azrom. Her humming slowed when she considered Jaron being one of the arrivals. That would not be good for her. Even less appealing was Chardon. Ganna pursed her lips. There was always some obstacle in the way of her and Sestis' agenda.

At the council room door, she could hear the heated tones coming from within and smiled. It was going as planned.

So Azrom was infiltrated.

Her admiration for the deceased female leader grew to new heights. One of her escorts knocked on the door twice and it swung open.

Ganna saw all the council jammed into the chamber and was taken aback. Her gaze landed on Talas and Jakar sitting at the end of the table with equal expressions of disgust directed at her. A hand yanked her arm and she looked over to see Kelin not bothering to address her as he flung her onto the vacant seat cushion near the door.

"Such dour faces, really," Ganna spoke with a small laugh.

Everyone turned to stare at her and she flinched.

Okay, they would take some warming up, she thought to herself.

Talas seemed disappointed in her and that was disturbing. Did he expect more from her in executing the test or was he angry at her actions against the council? He was usually not that hard to gauge.

"Explain this to me, Ganna."

Talas did not avert his stare. Some of the council members were about to speak when he raised one hand and silenced them.

"I thought you of all people would appreciate my tactics." She found him unmoving and continued. "During Sestis' travels to other worlds it became clear that our race was far stronger than most yet underestimated due to our lack of presence. So, she came up with a twofold scheme to rise Lassa to the top of the warrior chain."

The sound of air being sucked through teeth filled the room and Ganna smirked at their discontent. All but Jakar and Talas. Both made no motion of disdain or consent.

"Endangering Azrom and Lassa was part of the plan." Talas said.

"I wouldn't go so far as endanger," Ganna quipped. Seeing the corners of his eyes crease, she changed her demeanor. "It's no secret Sestis nor I have any love for manbeasts and if they were defeated in the invasion of Razzna, then so be it. They could spend the rest of their days slaving in the Razznian mines."

Talons emerged from the manbeasts in the room and she could see hands glowing with energy spring up around the table. Jakar made a motion with his head and the talons were retracted. Talas shook his head slowly and the council members who were ready to blast her powered down.

"That was not the initial plan," Ganna continued, annoyed. "We set in motion a battle that would span three solar systems for a reason. Once the first Razznian forces came to Lassa, we would defeat them. At the same time, the others would ravage Azrom and take them down as a super-power."

"And Chardon?" Talas asked.

"He would be done away with by being given to Halfar and Sestis would be the sole leader of Lassa. We would have a wide stretch across the galaxy and no longer looked over. We would be a new feared super power." Ganna said this with pride.

Stunned silence was the response to her explanation and for a moment she felt vindicated. No one looked at each other, or her, and it went on for quite a long time, which made Ganna realize this was not a good outcome.

"I recommend we kill her, now," the military council woman declared.

"I concur," one of the manbeasts near the door added as his talons reemerged.

Ganna went pale and whipped her head around frantically looking for a way to shield herself. Her plans were falling apart in her head.

"Stop!" Talas placed a hand on his face and exhaled loudly. "That will do no one any good." He let his hand swipe down to his neck where it rested before dropping into his lap.

"No, but it would make us all feel better," Kelin retorted.

"The technology. Where did it come from?"

Talas resumed his questioning.

"What?" Ganna answered still flustered.

"The technology!"

"Oh," Ganna stopped moving, ending in a backwards leaning position. "It was something Sestis acquired through negotiations with the Dreridian race."

She watched Talas nod twice and then rise to his feet. All eyes were on him as he slowly walked across the chamber and came to stand over her. With one hand he clasped his fingers around her neck and lifted her a good ten inches off the floor. She struggled for air, her legs swinging. In his eyes, she saw something she had never seen before in him; Malice. There was no charm or aggravation, just deep searing harmful intent.

"You will come to Azrom with me," he sneered softly.

He let go, dropping her hard back onto the floor and exited the chamber. Kelin followed with a concerned expression. Ganna had never been so afraid of anything in her lifetime until now. She made up her mind then that Talas was more dangerous than any manbeasts.

Sunset brought a cool breeze carrying the earthy smells of the fields across the air. Talas stood on a craggy hilltop, arms crossed with eyes closed, breathing slowly. He needed the fresh air and time alone. Kelin was not far behind but did not disturb him and he was thankful for that. If he had spent one more moment in the same room with that woman, he would have snapped her neck.

When he accessed all the information and saw the look of pride on Ganna's face as she entered the room, he knew it was all a part of Sestis' agenda. She was quite a manipulator, he gave her that and he agreed their race was being underestimated. But, her methods were toxic, and it had caused more harm than good for the Lassians. Their home world being destroyed was one casualty too much.

Running his hands through his hair, he squatted down and looked over the valley. This was New Lassa in all its diminished glory. A planet not quite fit for their race but the scientific council was making progress. He let his arms rest on his knees and his hands dangle.

"You can come closer, my love," he shouted. "I am not so far gone as to attack you."

Kelin stepped out from behind a small hill and came to stand next to him. He stretched his whole body upwards resulting in a few cricks and cracks. The black leather jacket rose above his hip line exposing the definition of his abdomen beneath the thin black tunic. Looking up he found Kelin staring down at him in bemusement.

"See something you like?"

"Hmm," Talas replied as he leaned backward and rested on his elbows, legs outstretched. "Maybe."

"You know I love you."

"Mmm hmm."

"I still think you should have offed her."

Talas closed his eyes, took a deep breath and exhaled through his nose. He let his head flop back and opened his eyes to watch the clouds drift in the sky. A tingling in his hands let him know how much he felt the same way.

"We need her expertise on Azrom. As capable as their scientists are, she has more information than they do."

"All because of Sestis."

"All because of Sestis," Talas repeated sadly.

"Silver lining?"

"Not so much." Talas jumped up from the ground and dusted off his leather leggings. "Let's get back to Azrom and report to our illustrious leader."

"Oh, Chardon won't like this."

"No."

"And Modas."

"I'm more worried about Jaron," Talas added. Kelin snorted. "We'll just have to try and restrain her the best we can.

"Or not," Kelin suggested.

****☼****

A large entourage of Lassian and Azromian soldiers awaited at the gate console for the small group's return. The anticipation of an explanation was high, and Chardon felt a huge ball of tension forming in his gut. Halfar had warned him not to expect a good outcome but there was no need for that advice. Chardon had already decided that whatever Ganna did was never in good taste.

Which is why he was surprised when the scientist showed up along with the group. She looked pale and somewhat frightened as she walked in stride between the four men. The two manbeasts behind her seemed ready to cut her down at the slightest movement. Chardon tried to undo the knots in the pit of his stomach. The news was not good.

"Talas, it's good to see your safe return."

"Thank you." Talas' tone was deadpan.

"Ganna," Chardon tilted his head. "What brings you here?"

"She will explain it all to you herself, won't you dear?"

Talas turned to her.

Something about his voice sent chills through Chardon.

What happened on New Lassa?

He scanned the five faces, and none gave any indication of what it was. Even Kelin was extremely silent as if he were biting his tongue.

"Well, let's proceed to the battle chamber. Our teams await an update."

They all followed the royal guards down the outer corridor and into the palace headed for their destination. Just outside the chamber door the group halted and waited for it to slide open. Halfar, his generals, the Azrom Elite and all the Lassians were present as they entered without speaking.

After everyone was settled in their respective seats, Talas turned to Ganna and his expression scared her into speaking. She relayed her explanation more slowly and with less pride than before and when she was done, waited fearfully to be reprimanded by Chardon. It was not Chardon who reacted first, but a multitude of people.

Talons and longswords were brandished simultaneously but none were as fast as Jaron who flew past everyone and landed a blow that echoed throughout the chamber, causing all to halt. Her right fist glowed electric blue as did her eyes as she stood over Ganna's motionless body. The floor below her had cracked and crumbled a few inches downward forming a crater.

Before Jaron could deliver another blow, Modas grabbed her up- raised hand and pulled her back away from Ganna. Chardon unclenched his fists and let the energy dissipate also feeling Halfar's grip holding him at bay. Talas had not moved.

"Get her to medical," Halfar ordered in an even tone.

Two soldiers gently lifted Ganna out of the crater and carried her out of the chamber.

"Talas," Chardon started but the look he gave made him stop.

"Do I condone her actions? No. But, do I agree with her assessment of our race? I do." Chardon's eyes went wide. What was Talas implying? Sestis was poison. "I'm sure Modas would agree as well."

Chardon looked over at Modas and saw affirmation in the manbeast's expression. Of all the measures taken as their leader, Chardon felt a sense of failure. Had he alone diminished his race's potential? The thought burned a hole in his mind.

"Well, it seems your former mate was a nasty piece of work," Rass said, breaking the silence.

"She already won, didn't she?" Chardon asked softly.

"No," Halfar snapped. "Not by any means. She was ambitious, no doubt about that," Halfar said. "I knew it the first time I met her." He turned to Chardon. "She was going to be your downfall."

The memory of his first encounter of Chardon and, the now infamous, Sestis flowed in his mind.

****☼****

The interstellar council was beginning right before sunset and all the delegates arrived in their full regalia. Halfar, ruler of Azrom, marched forward flanked by a large entourage of royal guards. Servants of the palace hosting the meet made a wide berth. Azromians terrified them. There were rumors that his entire race always smelled of faint traces of blood and wet soil. Even the Razznians, who were reptilian in appearance with shark like teeth, did not exude such murderous intent.

As he passed the foyer, he caught a glimpse of the delegates inside and his eyes locked onto a newcomer dressed in simple robes, standing amid conversation, towering over most. His hair was a golden brown falling across his shoulders in slight waves and his skin had a muted glow. Beside him stood a female with similar features but something about her seemed false and sinister. No, his interest was in the male. All of this he observed in the blink of an eye as he continued his march towards the meeting place.

Sunset signaled for all delegates to be ushered into the conference room, filling it to capacity. The seating was arranged around a large oval table covered with delicacies from each representative's home world. Translator devices were placed at section. Shields covering the floor to ceiling windows wrapped around the room rose up to reveal the city horizon as the sun settled behind its skyline. Glow globes floating strategically along the walls flickered on, illuminating the interior.

"Welcome delegates." The host, Emperor Calabra of planet Jiez, greeted his guests. He waited for the nods of acknowledgement and looks of disdain circle the room before continuing. "This meeting is to determine the resources and needs of territories within our galaxy. I do believe we can accomplish trade negotiations to benefit us all." He glanced around the room and saw the newcomers. "Oh, we do have delegates from the planet Lassa. Please, introduce yourselves."

Halfar turned his gaze towards them and his eyes locked with those of the golden haired male. An unspoken vow transpired between the two in that instant.

"I am Chardon, the leader of my race, and this is my mate, Sestis." Sestis bowed her head. "Our planet is advancing in medical research and alternative agriculture. Because of this, we are also in need of resources."

"Freeloaders looking for handouts," the lord of planet Yaos snorted.

He leaned his gangly blue frame back into his seat and looked to his allies for agreement. A few nods occurred.

"That is not so, I assure you."

Chardon obviously seemed more than a little offended judging by his facial expression. Halfar felt a twinge of pity for him.

"No need to worry, you would not be without company." Halfar interjected as he eyed the Yaosan. "Everyone at this table is out looking for something."

"Except for you, Lord Halfar! You just conquer and take what you want."

"Yes," Halfar hissed, "and yours will be next, hmm?"

"Let's keep things cordial, shall we?" Emperor Calabra raised his hands in a sign of defeat. "Thank you, Lord Chardon. Please, be seated."

Halfar noticed how Sestis beamed at the title of Lord for her mate and could see her disturbing assumption of having the title of Lady.

She will be cause his demise.

Chardon appeared not to be fond of it as he frowned when addressed. He would ask the young leader about that later.

Each delegate took turns stating their case for trade of goods and services as sunset turned into night. Arguments ensued with accusations of deceit and food was thrown out of spite by a handful of delegates. Planetary authority did not equate to civilized behavior. A long bang resounded, and everyone stopped to see where it came from. They saw Halfar's fist planted firmly on the table in front of him. A look of utter disgust on his face.

"I think we should discuss the trade options individually before the night's feast." Emperor Calabra suggested nervously. Everyone, included him, reared backwards as Halfar rose from his seat. "I will go make sure preparations are underway." The emperor fled the room.

Other delegates followed suit, leaving Halfar and his royal guards alone with the Lassians. Sestis came over to properly greet herself and apparently caught whiff of his natural, after battle scent. Old blood mingled with something foul floated into her nostrils. Her eyes narrowed even as she bowed her head graciously, making a loud sniff.

"Lord Halfar, it is a pleasure to make your acquaintance."

"Your intentions are not pure." Halfar whispered in her ear as he leaned forward. "I am not to be toyed with, female." He stood back up and stared across the room at Chardon. "Tread carefully. Negotiations can be treacherous."

"Of course. I appreciate the warning."

She regained her posture and stood straight. Her sweet demeanor would not work on him. There were other delegates who may deem more willing to work with her and it made him angry.

****☼****

Azrom's head of science and medical technology entered the medical bay and walked over to the slab that Ganna lay on. He frowned down at her as he replayed her words in his head. This woman knew nothing of Azrom yet looked down on his race. At first, he had refused to treat her then decided she was valuable to some degree. He stroked his short-trimmed beard then positioned his hand at the side of her face.

Smack!

His hand tingled from the impact and he stepped back as Ganna shot up into a sitting position, eyes wide open in terror. She blinked a few times and focused on him. He smiled showing a full set of white teeth.

"Good, you're awake," he waited for her to slide off the slab and set foot on the floor.

"Where am I?" Ganna asked scratching her head to evenly arrange her silver curls. "And who are you?" She eyed him questioningly.

"I am Lieutenant Treshur, head of the science and medical division. I believe we are," he paused to find the correct term, "like constituents. Of the same fellowship." Just thinking of her as an equal made him queasy.

"Ahh," Ganna's eyes glinted with excitement. "So, what are we going to be working on together?"

Treshur grimaced and turned away from her.

"We have some Razznian gear that is just fascinating. Come, I will show you."

He headed out of the facility making sure she followed him closely. They went down the corridor for a long stretch before stopping at one of the many sliding white doors. It opened and Ganna made a weird sound. Treshur raised his brow. Advancing further in to the chamber, he went to pull out one of the Razznian podsuits.

"Definitely Dreridian!" Ganna exclaimed as she ran a hand over the material. "They did a great job with the specifications in such a short timeline."

How she said it with childlike awe had his fingers caressing the hilt of his longsword. To decapitate the woman was so tempting.

"You know of this design?"

"Not really, but it has all their markings of expertise."

"Yes, I find it fascinating that they had dealings with the Razznians. Your Sestis was a venomous woman." He watched her face scrunch in offense at his words. "We want to duplicate the specifications."

"Oh?" Ganna said as she glanced at him from the corner of her eye. "That would prove time consuming. We can, however, create something like it in less time."

Treshur let his lips curve into a huge smile.

"Exactly what I was thinking."

She had performed just as he had imagined. His task was to get out of her the name of the race responsible for the podsuits and it turned out to be easier than he thought. How proudly the female scientist boasted of her disgusting agenda and experimental findings.

Dreridians, hmm?

Those cunning aristocrats were indeed highly intelligent.

"I will leave you to it, then."

Treshur waved a hand as he went to the door.

"You're letting me do the discovery myself?"

"Oh, there will be others soon to help." He left the chamber and went to report to the generals. Rass, he knew, would especially be pleased.

General Rass slammed his fists down on the vid console and tried to control his breathing. Halfar stood only a few feet away from him, tapping a talon against his bottom lip. A frown creased both of their brows. Kur found it amusing.

"Why so distraught?" Kur asked. "We all know how devious the Dreridians are, let alone a foul indulgent species."

"Partnering with Razzna? That's not just an all-time low, but a slap in the face to the warrior clans in the galaxy!" Rass yelled back in response.

Halfar turned away and sat down in the command chair at the end of the console. Dark thoughts swirled in that tyrant brain of his. Kur cocked his head to one side and waited for his Lord's brilliant idea, or insane theory.

"They are playing a dangerous game." Halfar finally spoke. "Sestis is no longer a factor so their main goal from the beginning was to take down Azrom from within."

Not so insane.

Kur was actually impressed that Halfar came up with it before Rass who also looked over in surprise. Which didn't prepare him for what came next.

"Let the Razznians escape."

Kur blinked a few times to alleviate the shock coursing through his system. Even Rass shot up straight incredulous at their ruler's suggestion. And within seconds Rass had a new kind of expression on his face, something sinister. He liked it, feeling a tightness in his groin.

"Ahh," Rass exclaimed. "Yes, they would immediately rendezvous with their fleet sitting on standby outside our solar system."

"Tsk, tsk," Kur wagged a finger. "They would be aware of us following them."

"Yes, but not before retrieving the podsuits hidden somewhere in the desert."

"What are you getting at?" Kur was confused.

"I have a way of taking over the main fleet's weapons system."

"And all you need is a podsuit we have not tampered with yet," Halfar added.

"Why would you want to…?"

Kur stopped and decided to ask no further. It seemed they were on a wavelength he had no knowledge of.

"I believe Chardon would be our best bet," Halfar suggested.

Kur rolled his eyes in exasperation. One day, Chardon was never going to forgive Halfar for the horrible situations he planted him in. Done with the whole insanity of the plan, he walked out of the battle chamber. He needed to prepare his enforcers for a Razznian escape.

Since the initial set up had been disrupted, Sars waited to move forward with plan B. His group was supposed to be the only one captured while the others planted the seeds of destruction around Azrom, especially in the palace.

Now he had to get at least one of the other teams out of the holding cell. As the leader, he would stay inside. All he needed was a window of opportunity. Hearing the familiar footsteps of his regular visitor, he grinned.

Chardon came into the holding cell and scrutinized the Razznians. He held another bucket in his hand and for a moment, Sars craved it. He eyed his comrades and they got the signal to stay. Caving in to hunger was not the first step in escaping.

"I see we are going into a defiant mode," Chardon stated and it made Sars think the Lassian was reading his mind.

"Just making a stance against our captors."

"I am not your captor," Chardon replied. "You were stupid enough to infiltrate Azrom. They are your captors."

"Do you even know about this planet? Your mate?" Sars shook his head sadly at Chardon. "How blind you are."

"My vision is clear, I assure you."

"You know nothing!" Sars snapped.

Chardon dropped the bucket onto the floor and his hands glowed red. Sars backed further against the wall.

"This planet has secrets you have not seen," Sars smiled.

At that Chardon hesitated and Sars stared at him as the Lassian glanced upwards in contemplation. From his view on the floor he realized with awe that the guards had not activated the shield, again, because Chardon was there. Sars cursed himself inwardly as he ran each visit in his head and saw the same scenario. He could have executed his plan B long ago.

No. This was good. Because Chardon fed them, his men had more strength to fight. Sars made guttural clicking sounds that communicated his idea. It also broke Chardon's reverie and he looked down on them knowing instantly what was about to happen.

His hands glowed a bright orange and the team of Razznians on the left of him snapped the restraints. They tackled forward, sending Chardon flying into the wall opposite the cell. He was back up faster than they thought. Sars watched in dismay as a hole was blasted into one of his men and a chunk of another's abdomen disappeared. Blood sizzled, dripping hot on the floor. Two more Razznians got loose advancing forward, grabbing the bucket to toss at Sars.

Outnumbered, Chardon moved further down the corridor even as Azromian soldiers bustled in to assist. Sars remained still as he saw six of his men get past the guards and Chardon. He could hear screaming in the distance and the familiar sound of blood gurgling out of a wound. Nodding in satisfaction, he opened the bucket and motioned for the remaining three to join him for dinner.

This is not how it was supposed to happen!

Kur walked briskly to the east side of the palace to see what he could salvage of Rass and Halfar's insane plan. There were casualties from Razznians taking the liberty to chew on his soldiers in defense. He drew his longsword hearing cries of battle and agony ahead of him.

Rounding the curve of the outer corridor he came face to face with a Razznian baring razor-sharp teeth coated with Azromian blood. Kur swung and was surprised that he missed when the Razznian flipped backwards to avoid the cut. He increased his speed and the Razznian did the same to keep up with him. Tiny lines of blood appeared on both their bodies as they switched off getting some hits in but nothing fatal.

Kur lunged at him in frustration and watched the Razznian jump off the ledge and land on all fours down on the planet floor. Looking over, he could see four of his soldiers go down, their necks spewing blood from the gaping holes left by the Razznians' bites. A cruiser from the hangar was hijacked and off the enemy went speeding towards the desert on the other side wall. He gripped the ledge hard.

Turning back the way he came, Kur headed for the palace command center where he knew Rass and Halfar would be waiting.

The escaped Razznians made haste to the first rendezvous point where four of the podsuits had been hidden. Once donned, they split up into pairs while the remaining two took the cruiser and headed to their hiding place. Time was of the essence. They could see the Azromian forces cutting across the desert in a storm of dry dirt whirling towards them like a tidal wave. With only moments to spare, the two made it to their suits and activated the cloaking.

Running at a fast pace, in teams of two, each pair found the drop sites and dug up the containers that were previously buried. It took two to lift and open them. Inside were weapon launchers, bomb cartridges included. The collapsible targeting tripods were erected to stabilize the launchers when firing.

Team one consisted of the last two communications officers and their job was to give the signal after contacting the main fleet. They set the array and waited for a reply from command.

"This is madness!" Kur yelled.

He had stormed into the command center and found Halfar and Rass dumbstruck by the turn of events. A large unit was dispatched after the escapees but lost them just as they were closing in. From the reports flooding in it was apparent that the group went separate ways.

"Those damn cloaking devices," Rass exclaimed.

"I don't care about that," Kur said drawing out every syllable. "I have dead soldiers!"

Halfar whirled on him and stood face to face.

"I know!" he seethed.

A royal guard came into the room and bowed low. His face was grim.

"What is it?" Halfar demanded, yelling.

"Incoming, my Lord."

"What?" Halfar reared back in surprise.

Rass grabbed the guard by the front of his tunic.

"Heat signatures from three directions heading towards the palace."

Rass pushed the guard away and fled from the room, grabbing a commlink amplifier. He connected it to the side of his cheek and gave an order.

"All defense forces take position at the impact points and form a barrier! The palace must be protected at all costs!"

Kur followed him out but went the opposite way. Further down the corridor he ran into the Lassian energy users, led by Jaron. He didn't need to ask her anything, she just nodded.

"I will have my team position themselves between the gaps in the impact points and see if we can deflect some of the damage."

"I owe you my gratitude," Kur bowed low to her.

"Stop that! This is no time for that drivel."

Jaron left with her entourage in tow.

Looking up at the horizon he sucked in air as he witnessed the large beams of heat carrying destruction streak across it from all three sides towards the palace. There was no time for training sessions now. It had begun. Knowing what was coming next, he headed for the hangar. A Razznian battle fleet was on its way and he was going to make sure to greet them properly.

Three groups of eight soldiers stood behind barriers at each corner of the palace while they watched the beams come full force at them. As they struck, the soldiers lost their footing causing a breach in the barriers integrity. The blast blinded them and sent their bodies backwards. Thin fissures began to form along the barrier's edges. Not anticipating how wide the beam was, they watched in horror as it overtook the shielded areas and slammed into the exposed parts of the palace.

Jaron and her team were able to deflect some of the blast but where the stray beams landed was a problem. The wall separating the palace from the rest of the planet was decimated in large spots along its perimeter. Even the hangar was hit, most of the cruisers destroyed.

Kur did not flinch from the blasts of cruisers exploding around him as he made his way to the elevator on the far end of the hangar. His stride was slow and purposeful. At the elevator he waited for it to open then stepped in. It slid shut and descended into the bowels of Azrom. Reaching its destination, the doors slid open.

Azrom's mighty Armada was spread farther than the eye could see at ten thousand ships strong. Soldiers were already preparing for battle making way to their assigned ships. From the other side of the cavernous underground hangar, the other elevator opened and Rass came charging out. He stopped for a moment to stare at Kur then resumed his advance.

The two generals met in the middle at the front of the Armada and stood side by side watching one hundred of the ships power up.

"This may be overkill, you know," Rass quipped.

"Nonsense," Kur replied. "A show of force is necessary."

"Oh?" Rass' brow curved upward. "What about aesthetics?"

"That can wait for another time."

"I wonder," Rass continued. "How surprised would they be when our ships launch from underground?”

“They should have known better when they didn’t see a single Armada ship anywhere on the planet surface,” Kur snorted.

“I guess the battle is at hand.”

Halfar’s voice boomed through the cavern.

“Victorious!”

“Til death!” Every soldier including the generals roared back.

Rass and Kur went to their command ships, their thirst for battle increasing.

Anger fueled Chardon’s running speed out of the lower region of the palace and into the blinding aftermath of a Razznian weapon’s impact. The wall beside him crumbled, causing the floor beneath to sway. Dismissing the wreckage, he kept on until he came in contact with a wounded royal guard.

“Where is Halfar?” Chardon demanded.

“Command Center,” the royal guard replied breathlessly as he slid down to the ground.

Chardon looked around at his surroundings and catching his bearings went straight to where Halfar was. He made it, without being scathed further, to find Halfar in a foul mood and his soldiers in a panic.

“Your incompetent guards left me unprotected with the shield down!”

Halfar didn’t turn to face him but answered, “I know.”

“You know?” Chardon shrieked, incredulous.

“That was part of the plan, but as you can see,” Halfar waved an outstretched arm across the console in front of him. “I miscalculated and didn’t expect this.” He finally looked at Chardon and noticed the blood. By the scent he knew some of it was Chardon’s though mostly Razznian. “Are you hurt?”

A ball of golden light expanded around Chardon and electricity shot out haphazardly, zapping equipment and soldiers. The smell of charred flesh filled the air and Chardon yelled in a fit of rage, the heat intensifying. Halfar’s eyes went wide with fear.

The ball of light pulsed inward and before it could expand back out, Chardon went limp, crumbling to the floor. Standing behind him was Modas, calm as ever.

“This is your doing?” Modas asked, glancing back at the doorway.

Halfar held one arm up with the other laid across his chest. He stared at the manbeast trying to gauge what the next move would be.

“I made a mistake.”

“War has begun then.”

“Correct.”

Modas lifted Chardon off the floor and threw him over his shoulder like a sack. He left the room as silently as he came in, stopping in the entrance for a second before turning left.

Research equipment shook violently then slid across the lab slamming into scientists with nowhere to go except against the walls. Ganna crouched down low onto the floor and braced herself by holding tight to an examination table. Hairline fractures snaked up the walls and she felt a sense of panic. Her plans did not entail dying on Azrom. From the deafening booms she knew the Razznians had attacked which meant they were on their way to New Lassa.

Ganna gripped harder, her hands balled into fists. It finally dawned on her that luring the enemy was not the best choice. Would they have found New Lassa eventually? Of course, but her actions led them right to it.

What have I done?

The doors slid open and three Lassian manbeasts bore down on her, wrenching her from the table. More Azrom soldiers entered behind them to rescue their own people. Swiftly, everyone was carried out of the crumbling research lab. She didn't like the way the manbeasts were handling her so roughly but dared not complain.

"What's happening? Where are we going?" She cried out.

"Be silent, monster!" The manbeast to her right barked out at her.

"Let go of me! I can flee on my own two feet!"

She tried to get out of their grip but they held on even tighter to the point of hurting her.

After maneuvering through dangerous routes filled with falling walls and debris, they reached the one platform that was still intact: the gateway. Chardon lay in a heap on the ground while Jaron and Modas checked to make sure all parties were present.

"Open the gate!" Jaron demanded.

The guardian made haste with the coordinates on the console and the pathway to New Lassa burst open.

"You," she pointed to a Lassian warrior and Azromian royal guard. "Take Farin and escort him through. Modas, grab Chardon." Jaron turned to the portal. "Let's go!"

"Why are we leaving?" Ganna asked.

"Because the enemy is going to jam our coordinates in the next hour and we will not be able to help our people defend New Lassa," Jaron snapped. "If you hadn't interfered, we would have at least two more years to prepare. So," Jaron glanced back at her. "We thank you, Ganna." The sarcasm dripped with venom.

Before Ganna could respond, she was pushed forward through the gaping vortex.

FOUR:

Let the Battle Begin

Soon after returning to New Lassa all warriors were given instructions on where to be positioned and what tasks to complete. As leader, Chardon took charge of evacuating the civilians while Jaron held meetings with the military council. Eyeing the giant cannon resting on the hilltop opposite the gateway console he wasn't sure whether to embrace or hate it.

Securing the last latch on the underground bunker, Chardon headed back up to the surface and breathed a sigh of relief that most of his people would now be safe. Atop the hill was a group of scientists led by Ganna fiddling with the cannon, preparing it for action. His left eye twitched and he tasted bile at the back of his throat. Her existence now made him physically ill. He went up to observe.

"Chardon," the four scientists greeted him in unison, bowing their heads slightly.

"Is it almost ready?"

Ganna looked over at him with a forced smile.

"Shortly. I'm not sure it will take them by surprise this time, though."

"No," Chardon narrowed his eyes and looked away from her. "But we can at least shoot down a few ships as they come through."

"Chardon," Ganna started but he turned and walked away.

"Don't," was all he could muster.

There was silence as everyone waited for the gateway to activate and spew out enemy ships. Hours went by but they all stayed vigilant, watching the sky above the console. Right before dawn, it happened.

The sky ripped open on the horizon and a vortex as wide as a mountain appeared. Slow and steady, a large fleet of Razznian ships invaded New Lassa. When the cannon took out two at once on the formation's edge, fighters spilled out of the larger ships like a swarm of insects and spread out across the terrain.

Jaron created a giant ball of energy and flung it towards the swarm in front of her. Some exploded in midair while others crashed down on the planet floor and their occupants sprung out. Manbeasts were ready in a flash to greet them with hand to hand combat. More Razznians came raining down from the ships as they passed over towns, flooding the area with foot soldiers to wipe out anyone who was still standing from the bombardments.

Teeth and talons clashed, creating portraits of blood splatter. Und led a small group of manbeasts into a deserted town now crawling with blood thirsty carnivores and immediately found himself deep in a bloody haze. He tore into the thick reptilian skin of an enemy and got a taste of Razznian blood on his lips. Spitting it out, Und grew angry. He didn't even feel the teeth biting into his shoulder, only that an enemy was on him. Reaching over he punched his talons into the Razznian's head and yanked him off, sending him flying into the waiting claws of another manbeast.

Blood dripped from his wound, yet he didn't stop. There were so many enemy soldiers. A burning heat piercing his shoulder followed by sizzling made him growl out in pain, his body arched backward. The pain subsided, and he turned to find one of his litter sisters backing him up along with a few other energy users.

"Get it together, brother. We have to wipe them off the face of our planet."

Through stinging eyes caused by sweat, he took a deep breath and nodded.

"Let's have some fun then."

She smiled, taking out an enemy with one ball of yellow energy without looking away from him.

"Impressive."

"Oh, you haven't seen anything yet," she winked. "Shall we?"

Three energy users and five manbeasts formed a circle and launched themselves into the fray.

****☼****

From the dark side of Azrom's moon, the Razznian fleet appeared and was met by a defense line of one hundred ships from the Azrom Armada forming a curve four rows deep around the planet. The enemy fleet maneuvered into position in front of them and both sides sat in stillness among the stars.

They simultaneously opened fire on each other, creating a bright criss cross light display. Ten of the Razznian ships broke formation and advanced towards the lower barricade of Armada ships. After four of the Azrom vessels were shot down, careening to the planet surface, the remaining seven of the enemy ships gave pursuit.

General Kur watched the interaction and realized the enemy's strategy too late. He stepped away from his command post and began to shout out orders.

"Tighten the formation and don't let another enemy ship past our defenses! I want fighters deployed now!" He walked to the doorway and paused. "I'm going out!"

There was a heavy silence. No one dared speak up.

Good.

Kur took another step forward and the sliding doors opened. It had been a long time since he battled in a fighter, so he knew what his crew was thinking. He was more of a hand to hand combat type of soldier. Right now, the situation called for his second expertise no matter how rusty he may be. At the ships hangar, he found a technician finishing up the diagnostics run on his fighter and waved him off. He threw off his cloak, tossed his longsword in the side compartment and donned the battle flight suit handed to him. Pulling it on, he leaped into the cockpit and let the system mold around him, securing his body. A vidscreen helmet settled over his head and it activated so he could see through the lens of the fighter.

"There will be six fighters accompanying you, sir. Is that enough?" The technician inquired.

"That's fine." The fighter closed, and the internal systems engaged. He opened an outside channel. "If this ship falls, I will kill every last one of you. Ready for launch!"

Kur's fighter shot out of the hangar with six others following in a 'V' configuration. He could see eight other teams of fighters converging on the enemy and twisting sideways veered towards the main ship. His men kept in line directly behind him.

"What in all of Azrom are you doing?"

Rass' voice spilled out into the cockpit.

"Fighting," Kur replied nonchalant. "No need to yell."

"When was the last time you actually fought in that thing?"

"It doesn't matter," Kur replied as he opened fire, sending a rain of explosive charges at a small group of Razznian fighters. They lit up in a ball of light. "I'm enjoying myself immensely."

"Get back to your ship!"

Kur didn't need to hear anything more. He could tell what Rass really wanted to say. Feeling just a tad guilty, Kur sighed and replied.

"You're not going to lose me."

Silence. Then.

"Good hunting. See you back planet side."

Kur's unit kept in tight formation as they curved around towards the aft of the Razznian's main ship. They were able to glide low enough to avoid the onslaught of attacks by being out of range. Kur searched for a weak spot in the underbelly and finding it, ordered his unit to fire. As they swooped upwards out to the other side for safe distance, the ship shook, and an explosion spread throughout its length.

Out of the corner of his vision, Kur saw a ship in the middle charge forward, its main weapon gathering energy. It rammed into the damaged main ship, pushing it to the side out of the way then corrected its own position.

"No, no, no!" Kur cursed.

Too late, he realized his unit was heading straight into its line of fire with no time to adjust their coordinates or speed. He watched the ship's main weapon fire and his fighter was clipped on the side, the two fighters on his two and six obliterated. He called up every maneuver from memory to keep his fighter from exploding as it fell through Azrom's stratosphere.

Getting closer to the surface he could see ground combat in full swing and he was going to crash right in the middle of it. Off in the distance the blast from the Razznian ship hit the palace directly in the middle at its top. Energy users were bent down almost to their knees, arms upraised as they blocked the attack. It only lessened the damage. The beam was wider than their coverage and the area outside the blast caved in. Knowing there was nothing to be done, he braced for impact. The fighter hit hard forcing it to slide only so far before making a dead stop. Disengaging the system and opening the hatch, he grabbed his longsword and jumped down onto the planet surface.

Within seconds, two Razznians came at him, baring sharp teeth and thick claws. Kur smiled. This was his forte. No hesitation, he ran to meet them halfway. His sword sliced through the air, missing the one closest to him. He morphed the other arm into a claw and snapped the Razznian in half midair. The other enemy charged him in a fit of rage, making Kur laugh.

"Come! Join your comrade in arms in death!"

He brought his word down to cut the Razznian in half and it reversed its advance in barely enough time to only get a deep cut across its chest. At the same time, Kur felt multiple presence behind him and turned to face them, quickly dodging from a strike mere inches from him. More Razznians were behind him. He was surrounded.

A blade went through the one before him and the enemy was yanked backwards as the one next to him peeled apart at an angle from the left shoulder to the right hip. Standing on the opposite side was Talas, gleaming with joy, flecks of blood splatter in his dirty blond hair.

"That was quite a landing, General," Talas laughed as they assumed a defense stance back to back.

"I like to make a grand entrance."

"A little rough up there?"

"Nothing we cannot handle."

"Good to know." Talas raised his longsword. "Shall we?"

"Let there be blood."

"Indeed."

Walls crumbled in large chunks exposing the innards of the palace. Halfar pushed himself up off the scorched, debris filled floor of the command center and stood. For a moment he was baffled by what had happened then rage took over. Azrom had not been attacked in such fashion in four, maybe, five hundred years. An attack that prompted the start of a long war with an enemy far more formidable than Razznians.

He surveyed his surroundings and headed out into the open air. All the soldiers in the command center were down, half of them dead. The survivors would have to hold on and wait until after the battle had died down or was over. Halfar found the stairwell leading down into the lower parts of the palace which were still intact and made his way to the bunker below.

At the entrance, two royal guards bowed deep and opened the doors. The brightly lit room spanned for what seemed like a mile with consoles lit up and their operators in constant motion. They all stopped for a brief second to bow low at their ruler then continued their work.

"I want the cannons online." He spoke in a normal tone.

"Yes, my Lord!" the first row of operators replied.

"Target?" The head operator asked.

"The gate."

There was a pause in the room. "My Lord?"

"Open the gate to Razzna's system."

"Calculating the coordinates now."

"My Lord!" The second operator cried out. "The gate has been disabled. It's locked for some reason!"

Halfar smiled. He knew that would happen. Walking over to the commlink, he selected a sequence code. It was audio only.

"Rass, I need you to open the alternate gateway to the Razznian system."

"Of course, my Lord. Sending the location to the operations center."

"Good."

"Are you angry?" Halfar didn't reply. "Excellent. They did not anticipate this."

Halfar sat in the command seat overseeing the bunker. He watched from the vidscreen as two of the cannons ascended to the surface, the hangar doors sliding open to accommodate them. The giant orbs rotated towards the alternate gateway forming in the horizon. As it expanded, the gaping hole of swirling black and purple cleared to reveal the Razznian solar system beyond.

"Ready cannons for firing."

The operators went into a flurry, their fingers flying across consoles. The giant orbs began to glow bright blue and the lenses inside adjusted once more for accuracy. A gauge on the right side of the vidscreen showed the increase levels of the cannons' energy. When it hit full power, Halfar sat back in his seat.

"Fire." He didn't need to yell.

The terrain shook as the recoil from the cannons vibrated down into the surface. Many of the combatants on the ground were thrown off their footing, away from their opponents. Some of the Razznians looked up and saw the vortex in the sky, the blast of the cannons heading straight for their home world in the distance.

Kur took a gander at Talas and the Lassian's lips pursed as he nodded.

"Not bad. This will tilt the advantage in our favor." Talas nodded towards the enemy standing stunned for a few seconds before going into a frenzy. "They definitely want to kill us all now."

"So be it," Kur spat. "Azrom will be victorious!"

"You do know, we are fighting on New Lassa as well?"

"I have no concerns over that. Your race proved to be a hard one to kill off."

Four long talons went through the side of a Razznian advancing towards them and the body was tossed away. Modas strode up to them, calm and collected, while slashing down Razznians. Opposite him, a group of enemy combatants went flying outward, blood misting above Trinon in the center.

"Good of you to join us, manbeast," Kur said with an edge of malice.

He had not forgiven the warrior for his near untimely demise back on Earth.

"The enemy in the East has been dealt with," was all Modas reported.

"Well, there are three other quadrants to clean up then," Talas quipped. "But, first," he nodded at the nearly one hundred Razznians still on the ground surrounding them.

"Let's make this quick." Modas tilted his head forward in agreement. Kur wiped the blood from his longsword on the leg of his battle suit. The Razznians looked hungry.

✻✻✿✻✻

Chardon couldn't believe how many ships had come through the gateway. Though it had only been seven, he expected one or two. He didn't understand why the Razznians would send more than that for a nearly wiped out race on a barely sustainable planet. His robes were covered in blood, very little of it his own. The ground was partly scorched, yet again, and the cannon had been damaged from a direct hit by the ships weapons.

A Razznian leapt into the air and came at him. Tired yet no less focused, Chardon shot an orb of red light at him. Burned to cinders, the enemy crumbled, the wind carrying the ash remains away. He was keeping his full power at bay because it would devastate the planet more than it had already suffered.

"We can't go on much longer," Jaron spoke to him out of breath. Her hair was matted and sweaty.

"I know, but we have to protect this planet to the very end. It is the only home we have, and we just got it."

"As powerful and capable as we are, this is beyond our expertise." Jaron formed a barrier around them. "We are a ground combat warrior race. We don't have a battle fleet of ships. You have to destroy them all at once."

"I will not harm this planet!" Chardon yelled.

Jaron whirled on him and got so close they shared breath.

"There will not be a planet if you don't!"

"I can't wield it knowing how many will get caught up in it!" Razznians converged on the barrier desperate to get at their prey. "The planet can be fixed! And so can our bodies! What the hell is wrong with you? Stop being spineless and be our leader!"

Chardon's face darkened, his hand went to strike her. She blocked his blow and grabbed it. Her expression was one of rage and disappointment. Outside the barrier Jakar was killing off the last of the enemy who had been clamoring to get through.

"Now I see," Jaron continued. "This is what made Sestis and Talas so frustrated."

Chardon wrenched his hand out of her grip in anger. He was sick of hearing what in his mind was not true. He understood there were times when he wavered and the outcome not ideal. Looking up at the ships spewing out more fighters, he decided.

"Release the barrier." Jaron did and Jakar stood next to her. "Try to get as many to an underground shelter and make sure Ganna is with them." They both frowned. "You think I want her to live? I want to rip her apart. But for now, she is the chief medical officer."

"Will do," Jaron replied. To her son, she said, "Let's go." She stopped and turned. "Oh, the group ahead will make sure no enemy gets near you."

"But, that means…" Chardon blanched.

"Yes, some of them may be destroyed completely. They know that, Chardon." Jaron snapped.

He watched them leave and Lassian warriors took their place to keep the Razznians at bay. In the sky above, the remaining ships kept advancing further into the planet, firing rounds down on the surface. Shaking his hands to loosen them up, he took a deep breath then exhaled slowly. Tears stung his eyes. To save his race, he had to sacrifice many.

A large knot tightened in his stomach, forcing him onto the ground. He wailed in agony holding his midsection tight as his head fell back. Leaning forward, his hands planted on the ground, he stared at the enemy. His body glowed in an array of colors, swirling, building up around him and expanding out. As it spread miles wide in diameter, the air hissing in complaint, it pulsed once, retracting back to him in a nanosecond.

The blast shimmered like multicolored jewels engulfing the entire planet's surface and sky. Everything in its wake was slowly eaten away, disintegrating into nothingness. Screams from Lassian and enemy were short lived. The only safe place was the eye of the storm that was Chardon, hunched over full of despair as he unleashed his power. Inside, there was silence.

✳✳☼✳✳

Surrounded by chaos, Sars sat patiently as he felt the palace walls around him tremble then crumble. His men kept guard in case anyone came back down into the dungeon. Hours went by and finally, he heard the click clat signal echo through. All six hurried into the now broken cell and helped their comrades.

"Bad news to report, sir," The first said.

Sars brushed his hands on the legs of his tunic and frowned.

"Tell me."

"A vortex was opened to our solar system and Azrom sent two cannon blasts through it."

"Our planet will be destroyed?" Sars' lieutenant cried.

"Not destroyed, but," the Razznian lowered his head. "It will be bad."

"So we can't go back home."

"We locked the gateway."

"Then we must unlock it." Sars commanded.

"And go where?"

Sars smiled or what appeared to be the closest thing to one.

"Earth." His men gasped in disgust. "It would be quite easy to lay low for a few years until we can contact our own people. Have you forgotten? We are spies before combat soldiers."

His men perked up at another mission only this time long term. Plus, humans were quite tasty unlike Azromians.

"Hurry, we have to get off this planet before we're caught again."

They crept along the rubble in a tight formation up towards the platform where the gateway console would be, hoping it was still intact. When they arrived, jubilation swept over them to see that it was. The communications officer quickly went to work unjamming the console and setting their alternate coordinates for Earth.

From below came the sound of boots hitting the corridor and they knew it was now or never. Making sure they were ready, the group watched the vortex open in front of them. As they stepped in, ten Azrom soldiers came charging across the platform. Leading them was Talas with one arm outstretched as if trying to grab hold of them from that distance.

"No!" Talas yelled.

Sars turned to him, baring a row of sharp pointy teeth and hissed before being swallowed by the vortex. It closed shut after the last Razznian crossed over the threshold, seconds before Talas could get there.

Azrom's soil lay soaked with Razznian blood. Those who survived were being hauled into a large vehicle to be taken deep into the mines. Some of the Razznians got away from the fighting and a search was underway. The air was still full of heat from the cannons blasts and it intensified the smell of blood.

General Kur walked the battlefield checking bodies to see if there were any Azrom soldiers still breathing. His own body was covered in Razznian blood and he hated the feel of it. This was not aesthetically pleasing by any means. He did say let there be blood, just not on him.

A figure off in the distance steadily advanced towards him and when he could make out who it was, he saw Rass, also covered in blood with a smile across his face. The fight was his ideal arena; vicious and messy. His right arm was still morphed into a giant claw, the tips dragging on the ground.

"Did you have fun, General?" Kur called out.

"Oh, I did." Rass retracted his claw, becoming an arm once again and wiped his mouth with a bloody hand. Kur cringed. "I take it this wasn't to your liking?"

"Obviously. How fairs our supreme ruler?"

"Incensed," Rass replied stopping a few feet from Kur. "His palace has been scarred."

"Along with his pride. That plan he executed just now was brilliant."

"I wonder about that," Rass tapped his lip with a finger. Kur wanted to smack his hand dripping with blood away.

"Regardless, we still have some of those creatures on the loose."

"We'll find them."

Razzna

The moment a vortex appeared in Razzna's system, Lord Kraznan was alerted. At first, he was in a state of disbelief, then he realized what it meant. He didn't need to see the beam traveling through it to know where the situation was headed. This miscalculation on his part would now be the ruin of his race if he didn't figure something out quickly.

"Launch all of the remaining ships and make sure they hold as many of our people as possible." There was a long pause that followed as he watched his councilmen stare in shock. "WE are not abandoning Razzna!"

A sigh of relief filled the room. He knew what they were thinking and rightly so.

"That blast will devastate our world, make no mistake about it. But, we will leave for now and wait for the aftermath to settle down."

"Will we take vengeance on our enemy?"

"Vengeance? I believe we attacked them based on that Lassian whore's suggestion."

"It did seem sound at the time, my Lord."

"Umm, yes it did. We have lost too much in this battle. Time to reassess our agenda. How long before it hits?"

"At its current speed, ten days. This way, your majesty. Your flagship awaits."

Lord Kraznan stood up from his throne and slid proudly down the middle of the room to the entryway. He would save the rest of his race, making the vow even as he reached the hangar.

On board the flagship, every soldier scrambled to complete their checklists and get the engines running. A bright light could be seen in the middle of the vortex and contact was imminent. Lord Kraznan watched thousands of ships leave the planet surface and take to the dark- ness of space. They barely had enough time to get out of range so traveled at top speed to create a small cushion of safety. The flagship lifted off to join them.

The population of Razzna stood silent on each ship when they stopped near the second planet from their own. With deep sadness and horror, they witnessed the beam shoot out of the vortex and head straight for Razzna. A bright ball of fire spread across an entire region, altering the face of the planet. The vortex collapsed inward and snapped shut.

A soldier had come running into the cannon operations chamber nearly sputtering. Halfar had to backhand the man to calm him down. When he relayed his report of Talas going to the gateway in pursuit of Razznians, he couldn't believe it. Now he stood on the platform with the rest of all parties involved staring at the Lassian warrior.

"How did you know?" Halfar asked Talas in a state of confusion.

"It dawned on me that the imprisoned Razznians could have broken out with the others except he kept his team with him in the holding cell. Which means, he was planning to be rescued and return home. Since you fired on Razzna, communication would be impossible and the gateway had been locked down. The only other way out would be to send themselves to Earth. They already had an alternate route, remember?"

Modas frowned at him then. Halfar wondered what made the manbeast hate the Lassian warrior so much even when it benefitted their race. Rass came up from behind the royal guards and stood in front of Talas.

"I too realized it around the same time as you, but I was not close enough."

"Apparently neither was I," Talas sighed heavily. "I missed them by seconds."

"At least we know where they went. Can we get the coordinates from the console?" Halfar asked the guardian.

"I can, and I will." The guardian went down on one knee and bowed his head low. "I am deeply ashamed to have left my post to defend my fellow soldiers."

"Get up!" Halfar snapped. "We were in the midst of battle! There is no way you could have known this would happen!"

"Since the gateway is unlocked, we can open a pathway to New Lassa and see how they are faring." Talas suggested. "It seems you have Azrom under control."

"This battle was far too short and uninspiring. I expected more from them." Halfar stated as he nodded to the guardian to complete the task. "Well, maybe the battle on New Lassa will be more exciting for you," Kur said his tone dripping with sarcasm.

Halfar knew he was angry by the number of casualties and felt the same. This was not the time.

"Open it," Halfar commanded.

He wanted to make sure Chardon and his son were safe. If the planet was overrun with Razznians he would make sure to kill every last one. The gate opened, and the group walked through.

As they set foot on New Lassa, they all gasped at the devastation causing them to choke on the sizzling air. Modas stood still, a multitude of emotions conveying on his face. Talas slumped down to the ground on the back of his legs. Halfar's pupils burned red and his hands balled into fists. Kur and Rass scanned the vicinity for signs of life. The planet surface was in ruins.

Talas got a taste of the dust in the crackling air and his eyes went wide. He clambered up on his feet and stumbled towards a dark patch on the ground. Using his finger, he ran it across and it came up slightly sticky. The smell confirmed that it was Razznian remains. Another dark patch a few feet away made him weep for it was Lassian blood he smelled.

"Gone," he whispered.

Modas went over to him and grabbed the front of his jacket.

"What do you mean, gone?" His anger was palpable.

"Disintegrated." Talas held up his fingers smudged with both remains.

Modas got a whiff and pushed him away.

There was no sound. It was as if the planet had ceased all activity.

"What did this?" Halfar demanded. He too had crouched down at a dark patch and tested its contents.

Modas gritted his teeth and clinched his fists.

"Chardon."

They all looked at him incredulous, except Talas. Halfar went paler than usual and Kur feared he might falter.

"How?" He asked.

Talas stood up. "Chardon is our leader because he has more power than any of us put together. You could say he is a walking planet bomb." He covered his face with his hands and quietly sobbed.

The Azromians turned their heads to let him grieve in peace.

Modas looked off into the distance and saw a mound directly in the center of the aftermath. His vision focused on it and without warning, he sped towards it. Talas removed his hands sensing the manbeast's motion and followed the direction he was heading. At once, the entire group followed.

Sliding to a halt, Modas held himself like a statue as he peered down at the hunched over body. With shaky hands he reached out to feel for any sign of life. There was a faint pulse felt against his fingers from touching the back of the neck. He bent down and went to raise the head.

"Stop!" Talas made it to his side and clamped a hand on Modas wrist. The manbeast smacked his hand away and growled. "You can't move him! Look!"

Against his better judgment, Modas finally saw Chardon's limbs fused together along with his head to his knees. Halfar crawled to Chardon, his hand shaking a mere inch from his hair, not daring to touch him. Talas ran his fingers through his own hair and grabbed hold, tight.

Dark dust swirling around like a storm came barreling towards them, a medical cruiser in its center. At its helm was Ganna with four medics onboard, all wearing protective cloaks and face covering. She came to a screeching halt and they climbed out of the vehicle.

"Step away!" She yelled breathlessly.

"You're alive," Talas spoke, releasing his tresses.

"Of course, I am," Ganna snapped. "We all evacuated into the underground bunkers."

"What underground bunkers?" Talas yelled back.

"The ones I decided to have installed when this battle was brought up. Chardon approved it and made it clear to only use them if necessary." Ganna knelt in front of Chardon and pursed her lips. She motioned for her assistants. "We have to lift him up like this without jarring the body. Come." She placed a hand on Halfar's shoulder. "You need to step away."

Halfar only nodded and inched backwards a few feet. They watched the medics gently carry Chardon and place him in a pod secured in the hatch at the back of the cruiser. Ganna reclaimed her seat at the control and sped off.

"Can you follow her?" Kur asked Modas. Modas snapped out of his despair and turned angry eyes at the Azrom General. "Lead the way."

Ahead of them, the ground opened like a lid being removed from a box. A ramp led down and Ganna's cruiser disappeared inside. Fearing the entrance would close, the group ran towards it, making it in time before it did. The ramp was long, taking them on a nearly one-hour trek to reach the bottom. Double doors slid open and revealed hundreds of Lassians inside.

"How many bunkers are there?" Talas asked no one.

His amazement clear.

"Over a hundred," a familiar voice answered.

Talas looked over to see Kelin, battered and bruised but alive, walking to him. A sheepish grin was fixated on his face.

"You're here."

"You didn't think I died, did you? I'm stronger than that," Kelin wrapped his arms around him and squeezed tight. "I'm glad to see you too," he whispered in Talas' ear.

"I…" Talas begin.

"Shh. There's no need." Kelin released him and straightened his posture. "This bunker has most of the council and those who were closest to the gateway. The ones with enhanced speed tried to save as many as possible before Chardon went all nuclear."

Halfar pushed his way forward and demanded, "Where has Ganna taken Chardon?"

"The medical lab. She had one built in each bunker but this one is fully equipped."

Halfar turned and charged into the direction he thought the lab might be and ran into Jakar who blocked his path. The manbeast stared blankly down at him.

"Move away, manbeast!"

Jakar's eyes darkened, making Halfar step back. "You will not interfere with Chardon's recovery. There is nothing you can do."

"Father!" Farin's high pitched voice rang across the bunker. Halfar turned around and was hit in the midsection by Farin ramming into him. He knelt to his son's level and stroked his head. "Mother is hurt. I can feel it," Farin cried, his voice muffled by Halfar's body.

Lifting Farin's head up, he found a haggard child with dark circles under his eyes and a paler complexion than normal. One of the female workers came over and took the boy's hand, guiding him away.

"Come, young one. You need to rest."

She gave Halfar a nod as she walked away.

"Where is your mother?" Modas asked Jakar. The edge in his tone made his son blink.

"At the far end."

"Is she hurt?"

"Yes," Jakar said.

Modas made his way down the aisle, going further into the bunker.

Making sure no one else was in ear shot, Kelin motioned for the rest of the group to join him to the side. A few Lassians glanced over but did not continue their scrutiny.

"Why are you here?" He hissed at them. "What happened? It must have been really bad." Kelin met each one's gaze. They took turns relaying the situation and Kelin's eyes grew wider with each report. When they were finished, he leaned against a wall and slump down. Talas tried to comfort him.

"It seems we are not needed on New Lassa after all," Kur proclaimed. "Our wounded can stay here until they recover. We have work to do on Azrom."

"I'm not leaving," Halfar snapped.

"No one suggested you should," Rass added, "My Lord."

"Is there anyone who can open the gateway?" Kur inquired of the occupants in the bunker.

A lone male stood up and headed towards them. "I am one of the guardians." He lowered his head. "I am the last guardian. The other three are gone."

"That is unfortunate," Rass shook his head. "Let's get going."

"It would be faster with a cruiser," the Lassian suggested.

"Can one hold all of us?"

Rass gestured to the royal guards who accompanied them.

"Of course."

Once the entourage was on the opposite side of the bunker's entrance, Talas sat down next to Kelin and rested his head on his shoulder. They sat quietly for a long time, Jakar watching them, curious. Realizing there was an audience, Talas sat up and faced Kelin.

"This is bad, my love."

Kelin nodded in agreement. He glanced sideways at him and managed a smile.

"It could have been a whole lot worse." Kelin sighed. "But, we won."

"Did we?" Talas pondered.

Jakar moved, startling the two lovers. His large frame loomed over them like a giant wall of flesh.

"You need to see my mother."

"Yes, I guess I better," Talas replied. "As tacticians, we have to assess the outcome."

"This way."

Talas and Kelin followed the manbeast down the same path as Modas to see Jaron.

Lying flat on her back staring at the ceiling, Jaron remained silent as Modas stood scrutinizing every inch of her body. The facial expression said it all. He was not happy. Although the wounds were minimal, Jaron was spent of energy. She had use everything within her to rescue her people, going at speeds she didn't even know she could achieve. Hearing footsteps coming down the aisle she slowly turned her head to see. Even that motion felt like a chore.

She watched her son, Jakar, extend an arm directing Talas to her.

He looks like warmed over wild beast kill.

Jaron wanted to laugh at him but was too weak. Instead, she narrowed her eyes in disgust at him. From the side of her vision she saw Modas do the same.

"Really, love? Not glad to see me alive?" Talas tried to joke. It came out deadpan.

Jaron licked her dry cracked lips and a raspy, almost guttural voice came out in a whisper.

"Of course, I'm glad you're alive, you twit. I was attempting to act natural."

Talas reached over and clasped her hand, squeezing it softly.

"I'm glad to see you too."

Jaron looked over at Modas.

"Can you leave us for a bit?"

Modas did not like that request and remained.

"Modas," she hissed through gritted teeth. "We don't have time for your rivalry nonsense." That stirred him, and he quickly left, angry. Talas nodded to Kelin and his lover walked back to the other side of the bunker. "Now, tell me what the hell happened."

Recuperation

Weeks after the battle both Azrom and New Lassa were still trying to mend their people and their planet. Halfar traveled back to Azrom only once to oversee the palace repairs. He stayed next to Chardon's sleeping form in the medical recovery bay on New Lassa. Ganna was able to get Chardon to shift into female form, it being the stronger gender, and forced the limbs to detach from each other. It had taken nearly ten days for her body to completely lay flat.

A movement out of the corner of his eye jarred Halfar out of his half slumber. The doors had opened and Farin came in by himself. At first, Halfar was concerned that his son was wondering around without supervision then he remembered. His son had claws to defend himself if necessary. The other thing was that no one on New Lassa would harm him, save Ganna.

"Father!" Farin rushed over to him and climbed in this lap. "Mother hasn't woken up yet?" He placed his small hands on the chamber lid.

"Not yet, little one."

"It should be any day now," Ganna hollered out from across the room, startling them both. Halfar had forgotten she was in there with him.

Farin smiled at that. Halfar felt tired. More tired than he had ever felt in his entire life. Is this what love does to you? The emotions alone were almost too much for him to bear. He questioned whether it was worth all this.

"Come," he lifted Farin off his lap and down onto the floor. "Let's go outside."

The air no longer had that static sizzling effect, making it okay to wander the surface like normal for longer periods of time. Most of the fields were gone along with the wild life but even many of those were saved by the scientific council members before the battle began. A haze lurked all around, minimizing the warmth and appearance of the sun. Workers were out tilling the ground to prepare for replanting, the dark splotches of remains no longer visible.

As father and son walked leisurely, Halfar caught a glimpse of something in the sky above and his gaze fell on the giant monolith somehow untouched, standing majestic as high as the mountains. Planted on top was a manbeast with hands on hips staring out at the horizon, his back towards them so Halfar couldn't see his face. There was no need. He knew it was Trinon, carefree as ever.

Farin pouted. "I wanna' climb it too."

Halfar raised an eyebrow and looked down on Farin's shiny black nails then the monolith. "Maybe there's a trick to getting your claws to dig into it." He watched his son's face light up with hope, which he had none for that happening.

For the first time, Halfar explored some of New Lassa and found it lacking by far from the Lassians original home world. Fresh pain crept up inside him knowing he was to blame. Sending a planet bomb out of spite from being rejected was childish and there was no way for him to fix it. Half the population had been wiped out in an instant.

He thought of his own planet, Azrom, with its many troubles and the tiredness came over him again. Farin tugged at his tunic sleeve and he realized he had stopped walking. Smiling, he continued until they reached a cruiser hub. They were going to do a bit more exploring. He felt duty bound to do so.

Multicolored lights flickered on the control panel of the recovery chamber and when they stopped, the hatch release with a loud hiss, sliding down to reveal its occupant. For a moment, Chardon laid still, taking in her surroundings and deduced that she was in Ganna's medical facility. It appeared a bit different though. Anxiety gripped her.

Was New Lassa destroyed? Is this a new temporary place?

Her hands balled up into fists.

"Are you going to lie there all day?" Ganna's voice traveled to her.

Slowly, Chardon lifted herself into a sitting position. Bile rose up in her throat and she projectile vomited across the edge of the healing capsule onto the floor. She slumped forward shaking from the assault and in awe of its strength, sapping hers in return.

"Oh, my!"

Ganna pressed an icon on the wall and within seconds, two medical assistants came rushing in.

"Please tend to that mess over there. It seems our leader is still not feeling well."

While the assistants went to work, Ganna came over with a cloth and wiped the residual from Chardon's mouth. Not a drop had gotten on the rest of her body. Chardon stared at her, leery as to her motives because she was sure the scientist had no remorse whatsoever for all that transpired.

"Let's get you some robes, shall we?" Ganna smiled and went to the cabinet where she kept fresh ones.

"How long?" Chardon asked in a raspy voice.

Talking made her throat hurt more.

"Hmm, about ten weeks." Ganna came back with a robe. "I must say, you recuperated much faster than I could have imagined."

"Is that so?"

"Oh, and Halfar has been by your side most of the time."

Chardon's head snapped up. "Where is he?"

"Out mapping our decrepit planet to see what can be done for it."

"Where are we?" Chardon asked in a panic.

Ganna gave her a funny look.

"Is there something wrong with your long-term recall?"

"We're on New Lassa?" Chardon was shocked.

"Of course, we are! Why would," Ganna trailed off and pursed her lips. "As powerful as you are, Chardon, you cannot destroy an entire planet." Ganna huffed. "Tone your arrogance."

Small tingles erupted in Chardon's fingers and she knew why. Her body instinctively wanted to murder that woman. The sensation ceased just as quickly, her body too weak to conjure up enough deadly energy for the task.

The doors slid open and Halfar came swiftly in, nearly bulldozing Ganna to the ground. He wrapped his arms around Chardon's naked body and breathed in her scent. She couldn't return his affection and it frustrated her. Seeing the robe, he shook it out and managed to get it on her.

"How are you feeling?" He asked her, concern on his face.

"Like I died." She saw him go pale and laughed at him. It was short lived, her body rejecting the act. "I'm so weak," Chardon whispered softly and felt tears sting her eyes.

Halfar gently lifted her out of the capsule and held her to him. Ganna was about to protest when Halfar turned and stared at her. Chardon could only imagine what kind of look the Azromian ruler had given the woman. Ganna backed away and let them pass.

In the hallway outside the medical bay, Chardon got a first glimpse of the bunker. She had known about Ganna's idea to build them but never knew the specifics. As Halfar carried her through the different areas she was struck by the sheer size of it.

"Are we going outside?"

Halfar halted and Chardon was once again uneasy.

"Not today," Halfar replied. "You need to take it slow."

"I've been down for ten weeks."

Chardon tried to sound angry. Her lack of strength prevented it.

"Which is a miracle in itself that you are awake."

"Tell me," Chardon pleaded.

She wanted to know the damage and she could see he knew what she was asking.

"Not today," he said again and walked on until he came to a doorway.

The doors slid open and Chardon grimaced at the sterile white of the room. Breaking up the monotony were red and brown coverings on the bed along with golden plush pillows, no doubt Halfar's aesthetics. He set her down on it, his body going with hers. They lay there, Chardon wrapped in his arms, for a long time.

"You will tell me," Chardon demanded weakly.

"Or what?" Halfar laughed softly.

"I won't let you touch me ever again."

Halfar turned to look at her and his eyes narrowed.

Be angry all you want, Chardon yelled in her head before drifting off into another deep sleep.

Moving Forward

Fields of golden stalks and vegetation covered much of New Lassa as the surface went through reparations. Growing food was the main priority with housing coming in second. The air quality had equalized in important sectors, the rest remained in a static like haze. Policies for population increase were implemented soon after the first harvest when the census showed another devastating toll on the Lassian race.

Each bunker was emptied out in small batches as parts of the planet became livable again. Chardon sat on a hilltop, propped up by her elbows with both legs bent up. Since coming out of her death sleep she was unable to shift back to her male form. According to Ganna, it stemmed from the amount of energy she exerted. Only time would be the remedy. She scanned the horizon and feeling a breeze, let her head flop back as she closed her eyes.

"I don't have to tell you that your mate has gone insane, do I?"

The voice had a condescending lilt to it and Chardon recognized it as Jaron's. She opened her eyes to find Jaron's face leaning over her as she stared. Dark patches were still visible underneath her cousin's eyes and the smile was strained.

"He is just being overprotective," Chardon replied.

"To think you and Farin are safer on Azrom is a special kind of stupidity."

Jaron sat down next to her and assumed a similar position on the hilltop. She too reveled in the soft breeze just as Chardon had.

"He is no more than your mate," Chardon chided. "Modas wants to lock you away and destroy the key."

"Modas needs to get over the fact that I too am a Lassian warrior. I fight when it is necessary just like he does."

"So, my brilliant cousin, what plans did you and Talas come up with?"

"We think a negotiation with Razzna is in order." Chardon turned and stared at her. Jaron continued. "Of course, Halfar does not agree. But, the truth is he has no say since he has ruined yet another planet."

"Why are we negotiating with the enemy?"

"Sestis set in motion an ill crafted, although quite elaborate, scheme that I don't think neither side took the time to question. The Razznians are a reptilian race and does not have the means to mine their resources.

Rumor has it their automated system malfunctioned, so they had to resort to manual labor. Their bodies are not made for it and that is why they have been enslaving other beings to work them."

"Are you suggesting we give them some of our manbeasts? After all this?" Chardon sat straight, a flash of anger across her face.

"No!" Jaron snapped. "I am not saying that! What is wrong with you?" Chardon flinched from the voracity in her voice. "We can get them an audience with some of the worker trade networks."

"Razzna is in no shape for anything right now. We don't even know if their mines are still intact."

"Considering how deep they are, it is safe to assume they are. If we start soon, they will be prepared when the planet surface is cleared enough for them to return."

Chardon felt a twinge of jealousy. She was the leader of her race and yet had not come to such a simple deduction. There were times when her plans turned out being the best. Ninety percent of the time, it was Jaron or Talas who exceled at strategy and logistics.

"She didn't win," Chardon stated, referencing Sestis.

"You must be joking," Jaron scoffed. "SHE won a few rounds." She glanced over at Chardon. "Are you going to inform your mate of your condition?"

Chardon also glanced down at her midsection and sighed. Halfar being stubborn and prone to bouts of childish tantrums, caved in after a few months of her denying his advances. He told her everything and within days had impregnated her.

"That monster is starting to have an affinity for breeding. I will tell him when he comes for another visit," Chardon answered.

"We are on a breeding initiative. You are no exception."

"But you are?" Chardon eyed her with mild contempt.

"I have thirteen offspring, Chardon, how many do you have?"

"Noted." Chardon got up and brushed flecks of yellow grass off her robes. "Anyone else contributing to the cause?"

Jaron smiled up at her. "Oh yes, Mara found a field worker to play with and is with child. And," Jaron paused, her smile widening. Chardon tilted her head to one side. "It seems Kelin has finally done his due diligence."

"Talas?" Chardon asked incredulous. Jaron nodded in acknowledgement. "The drama!"

"Exactly. I am going to steer clear for a while." Jaron also stood. "There is something else you should know." Her face became serious. "The Dreridians want compensation for the podsuits Sestis commissioned for the Razznians. If something cannot be agreed upon," Jaron stopped.

"You're joking?" Now Chardon was angry. Angrier than she had felt in a long time. "We can't sustain another battle with any race, let alone one three times more advanced than we are."

"Lucky for us, we have Azrom as an ally who also has a grudge against them for plotting with Sestis to infiltrate the planet."

"Halfar didn't take that too lightly. And neither do I, for Razznian ships invading our new planet, forcing me to damage it far more than I wanted to."

"We have a lot to do, leader."

Jaron walked back down the hill from whence she came leaving Chardon to contemplate the course their race had taken.

Villages surrounding the royal palace lay in various states of destruction giving the once majestic structure, now in shambles, the appeal of an ancient ruin. Survivors stumbled through the wreckage searching for remnants of their lives. They never had much but what they did have, they cherished. Some were left with no home to return to.

In the palace, the royals were breathing a sigh of relief for being spared any real damage. Only the main structure of the palace had been hit, sparing the rest of the attached buildings that housed the royal family and their staff. Construction from inside was ongoing and nearly complete with concentration on the outside being last on the list.

General Kur was not onboard with this decision. He felt it was all about aesthetics and having their people see a decrepit palace did not fare well for morale. Even from a distance he could tell some of the villagers were looking up, wondering what would become of their race. It still made him shiver with rage whenever he thought of the audacious plan the Razznians carried out.

Standing in the newly built battle chamber adjacent to the completely redone command center, he waited for Halfar and Rass to join him. After speaking with Talas and Jaron regarding the Dreridians via the communication screen, he had relayed the information to Halfar. A deadly silence had ensued afterwards and then he was ordered to wait here. Four altered enforcers stood at each corner of the room, courtesy of the science division that kept all the data on the last batch he had created for the battle on Earth decades ago.

A loud hiss made him look up and Halfar came charging in, face scrunched up, with Rass in tow looking bored. His supreme ruler stopped short of the console sitting in the middle of the chamber and eyed the enforcers.

"Why are those here? Better yet, where did they come from?"

Kur folded his arms across his chest and cocked his head to one side playfully.

"Why, my Lord, have you forgotten about my pets?" Halfar was not amused. "I had them ordered two cycles ago. These four are part of the first batch."

"I destroyed them for a reason!" Halfar snapped. "They are an abomination!"

"Yet very much needed if we have to go up against Dreridians."

Rass flipped his cloak back over his shoulders so that it lay behind him and laid one hand on the hilt of his longsword. Kur knew what he was waiting for and continued.

"If you think for one moment I would let you or your pet general destroy my soldiers, you are mistaken." He saw Halfar's expression turn to disbelief and Rass stared at him in anger at the 'pet general' reference. "You seemed to have lost focus and made emotion-based decisions detrimental to our race. I will not allow it, supreme ruler or not."

Kur bent his upper body backwards, feeling the air of Halfar's dark claws snap shut mere inches from his face. Rass immediately sprung to action and wedged himself between the two. He turned to glare at Kur and the message was clear. This is not the time. Kur exhaled through his nose and resigned his offensive stance. Both were on the same page and he wondered why Rass was delaying the inevitable.

"Let's not, shall we?" Rass chided. "We are here for the greater good of Azrom, correct?" Halfar, still seething, retracted his claws. "I believe we have a more pressing matter to discuss."

"I will not give those monsters salvation or any kind of helping hand. Razzna deserved what I gave it!" Halfar shouted in defiance.

"There is a bigger picture here." Kur sighed. "We also have to deal with Razznians on Earth."

"No need to worry about that. I received information that another alien race has set up shop within the crime industry's reconnaissance and are willing to take in my officers from before."

Kur's eyes went wide. "You have your officers from Earth? Are they not too old for such a task now?"

Halfar snorted and pivoted to stride towards the other side of the console. "I had them put in stasis. They will be just as fresh as they were back then. Like no time had passed."

Kur placed a hand across his eyes and squeezed them shut as he rubbed his temples. It was the Lassian catastrophe all over again, this time with Earthlings. Halfar had a hard time letting go of the things he wants.

"And the Dreridians?" He asked his Lord.

"Oh, I have something in mind for them."

Halfar's voice dripped with venom.

"And that is?"

"I do not have to relay every one of my agendas to you!"

"As the general of the royal guards and the Armada, I need to know anything pertaining to battles that utilize our forces, so yes you do."

"My Lord," Rass cleared his throat as he bowed slightly. Halfar turned on him and they nearly shared the same breath. "Your new council is waiting. It was your destination before this news came about."

Halfar backed away from him and looked over at Kur.

"We must leave. This discussion will be resumed after," Halfar said. "Along with the issue of your insubordination."

Kur followed the two out of the chamber and in the hall exchanged a glance with Rass.

Patience.

The eight houses of Azrom's royal family were assembled in the great hall where they, along with all the councilmen, awaited their supreme ruler's arrival. A tense atmosphere permeated the room, remnants of the Razznian assault that left Azrom in disarray. Anger blended with disappointment filled everyone's minds.

At long last, footsteps echoed outside the entrance and Halfar appeared with his entourage in tow. His fierce expression spoke volumes. He too was quite angry and frustrated. They rounded the corner and stormed down the aisle to his throne. Kur and Rass flanked him as he dropped down on it.

Two councilmen approached the bottom of the throne's platform and bowed. They glanced at each other and when they rose, the one on the left began speaking.

"My Lord, we have gone over the reports and would like to express our concerns regarding the Dreridian issue."

"Is that so? What are your concerns?" He eyed the room and saw many of the councilmen and royals fidgeting.

"We agree that they must be held accountable for their part in assisting the Razznians. But, given their technological expertise, it would throw us into a new war we are not willing to endure."

"Are you suggesting we not avenge our planet and let them slide?" Halfar sneered.

"No one is saying that!" One of the royal princes snapped.

Halfar looked over to see who it was. His cousin, Lord Romnus, stood apart from the rest of the family. Where Halfar was tall and slender, Romnus was taller and well built. His biceps bulged against his tunic even with his arms relaxed. Dark hair not entirely straight cascaded past his shoulders.

"Then what would you have us do, cousin?" Halfar spat.

"Think about the strain this would cause on our race."

The other councilman in front of the throne cleared his throat.

"What we propose is opening negotiations with the Dreridians."

"That is not an option," Halfar replied shutting down the notion.

A heavy silence swept the hall and some of the councilmen were visibly shaken with rage. Halfar didn't care what they thought. He was the supreme ruler and his word was definitive.

"I will not leave my offspring a legacy of cowardice and defeat!"

"Why bring Farin into this?"

"It isn't just Farin," Halfar yelled. "I have another who will be born soon enough. Azrom must show might!"

This time, there was no cheer of congratulations. Instead, a kind of resentment. The royal family rose in defiance and exited the hall, much to Halfar's surprise. He couldn't believe they had done such a thing. Before he could protest, the two councilmen raised their hands up in surrender.

"My Lord, please do not be offended. These have been troubling times for all of us. Forgive them." They bowed low.

The elder councilman moved forward and also bowed low in front of Halfar.

"I think the topic is too heated for the moment. We should revisit it at a later time, if that is to your liking."

Halfar sat back in his throne and gripped the armrests.

Kur leaned over and whispered, "Let it be, for now." He relaxed his body and pushed himself off the throne. Standing above his audience he glared at them.

While the remaining councilmen bowed low, Halfar strode down the aisle with his two generals and four royal guards. No one uttered a word as he passed by them. As his entourage left the hall, turning the corner then down the corridor, so did most of the council.

Three councilmen and five advisors stayed behind in the hall and gathered near the throne. The first to speak was a councilman and he did not mince words.

"That tyrant will get us all killed!"

"Our race is in jeopardy," the second one added.

"And what's this about a new spawn from that Lassian he mated with?"

"The royal bloodline is getting tainted."

One of the advisors rubbed his jaw, contemplating, then said, "We can remedy that easy enough."

With looks of horror, the others stared at him.

"You're not suggesting we murder his offspring?" The fourth advisor exclaimed.

"Keep your voice down," the second hissed.

"Of course not!" The third snapped. "I am merely saying, if we can convince our ruler to create a child of pure Azrom blood that would be ideal."

"And the two half breeds?" The fourth asked.

"They can be married off into one of the lower royal families."

He waved his hand dismissively.

"Well, with that decided, we can now focus on a new war." The third councilman sighed.

"It's not like we can't win. We are Azromian warriors." The first retorted.

The eight walked out of the hall through the side entrance that lead out to the other side of the palace. There was much more planning to do, the direst being reeling their ruler in to bend at their will.

PART THREE:
BONDS OF CONTRITION

ONE:

Planet Azrom 140 Years Before

Five royal guards wearing armored helmets that kept their hair back while the rest flowed down their backs marched down the marbled outside corridor of the palace leading towards the brothel hall. At nearly seven feet tall, in dingy battle armor with dark cloaks swaying behind them, they looked formidable and clearly on a mission. Their stride did not stop as they rounded the corner of the hall into the brothel. Nearing the center, they halted as one and the leader scanned the room. He was looking for a particular type of whore the ruler would find aesthetically pleasing enough not to reject or kill. The last few years showed his dissatisfaction with many of the choices.

Along the walls sat large canopied beds covered with vast arrays of sheer colored fabrics occupied by couplings engaged in various forms of fornication. In the middle of the hall, two feet high cushions were arranged in one large square with much of the same activity. Soldiers and royal court members were allowed to come and go at any time to release their carnal desires. Most of the whores had been well bedded over the decades.

Off to the right, a small dark-haired figure caught the leader's eye. She had unkempt hair, tanned skin, not much endowments and couldn't have been more than six feet tall. This was quite short for their race, but something about her was alluring, even to him. He motioned at one of his men then towards the bed. The soldier who was in the throes of thrusting into her like an animal, was pulled off and tossed out of the way. The guard dragged her upright by the hair.

As the royal guard hauled her out of the hall with the rest of his men in tow, the leader got a closer look and grimaced. That deadpan expression was something he had seen many times before in whores due to years of lying with scum and not knowing true pleasure. They went on to being killed or commit suicide. This may be her last day alive.

At the royal bath house, the guards shoved her into the arms of a washing servant who immediately pushed her away onto the floor. She wiped her hands on the fabric of her robes and glared at the leader.

"How dare you make me touch one of those dirty things?" The servant yelled.

"Just clean her up and have her taken to our Lord!"

He ignored the hissing sound coming from her mouth and turned away. Leaving the room he wondered if he would be back tonight with another one.

The female washing servant bent down to examine the filthy girl. Her skin crawled just looking at her.

"Such filth!" She stood and motioned the other servants to come closer. "Make sure to scrub her down completely, especially," her eyes lowered to the region between the girl's thighs, "inside there."

Each servant bowed low as she left them to do their work while she observed. If the girl had been a royal or a soldier, she would have personally pampered her.

One of the male servants grabbed the girl by her hair and dragged her into the large basin built into the floor. Only one other person had been in it previously and they had no intentions of changing the water for someone like her. A soft, fluffy long rod was steam sanitized then soaked in a bowl filled with scented oil water.

All four servants stepped into the basin with her, each having a hold on her limbs. One male servant was in charge of her unruly hair while the other three scrubbed off layers of sweat built up over time. Done with the first stage of cleaning, the male held her from behind by the neck as two other servants grabbed her legs spreading them wide. The remaining servant lifted the fluffy rod out of the bowl nearby and flicked it twice. She inserted it between the girl's thighs, pushing it deep inside her, using slow circular thrusts to ensure every inch was clean. Satisfied with the completion of her task, she removed the rod and set it on a cloth outside the basin. It would be disposed of later. The girl had not struggled throughout the whole ordeal.

The male servant pulled her by the underarms out of the bath basin and laid her on the floor while the others drained it. He went over to the communication terminal and hit the call icon. Within minutes two guards came marching in to retrieve the, now clean, female for their ruler. She was treated no better as they too hauled her up roughly by her armpits and carried her out between their huge bodies into the corridor.

✳

Halfar, supreme ruler of Planet Azrom, sat upright in his bed, wearing only a sheer black covering robe while he passed the time analyzing old battles on his holoscreen. His bed was set high nearly three feet off the floor and colored fabrics covered much of it. Plush coverings were spread all over the floor to ensure his feet never touched bare earth. Glow lamps hovered high above in each corner giving the room enough light to not annoy him.

His stark black hair hung loose draping around him in soft tendrils bringing out the strange murky green of his eyes in contrast with pale skin. He had been bored the past forty years with the steady conquests of small worlds for the sake of trade and politics. Nothing fascinated him much anymore so he resorted to reminiscing.

Hard boots striking marble from outside broke his reverie and he looked up to see two of his royal guards stop at the doorway of his bed chamber with a small naked female slumped between them, held up only by their grip. Her hair had fallen forward covering her face. One of the guards grabbed her by the chin and lifted it up so Halfar could get a good look.

What he found in her eyes as she stared directly into his intrigued him. It was a look he knew well; Resentment mixed with despair. He had seen it in many enemies right before the killing blow. In her stare, there was no intention of dying anytime soon. A strong resolve to live vibrated from her soul. He wanted to break her. With a motion of his hand, the two guards tossed her into the chamber and left.

She dragged herself up into a kneeling position and again stared at him. It was protocol to avert your gaze when in the presence of the supreme ruler which made her boldness even more outrageous. Halfar cocked his head to one side, then threw off the bed covers.

"Come here."

His voice boomed throughout the chamber. He watched her hesitate for a brief moment before moving forward. Her steps halted a few feet from the bed but still within his reach. Grabbing her by the hair, he yanked her onto the bed.

"I am sure you understood me when I said here."

While she was still stunned from the assault, he pulled her beneath him and pinned her down. As she regained her sense of surroundings, she began to struggle. So much so, that Halfar was amazed at her strength, needing to readjust the pressure he applied as he forced himself into her. He watched her writhe in pain, refusing to give him the satisfaction of hearing her scream by stifling them. It only made Halfar want to hurt her more. He hadn't even bothered to disrobe for the occasion. Eventually, she did scream and he sighed with contentment at the sound.

"Now, isn't it better to let it out?" He switched to one hand to hold her down and used the other to smack the side of her buttocks. "Stop fighting!" His goal was to incite the opposite and it worked. He pried one of her legs wider and held it up from underneath the knee. She was going to learn how to endure his ferocity because he decided at that moment to keep her.

Shaking uncontrollably, drenched in sweat, the female was hauled off the bed by the same two guards who brought her. Halfar was back sitting up perusing his holoscreen as if nothing had occurred. He snuck a quick glance at her as she was dragged away by her arms and their eyes locked. Seething hatred for him burned from inside hers so he let the corners of his mouth raise a little in a smirk.

After only a month of the routine Halfar made it known to his men that the female was not allowed back in the brothel and, he imagined to the dismay of the royal washers, required to be bathed in one of the royal chambers. She was never allowed to wear any coverings per his instructions and her indifference towards it fascinated him. There was no shame in her eyes or demeanor. On a whim he had her DNA analyzed and found it matched one of the warrior clans known for their intimidating size. She was obviously a runt, in the end doing royal service for the palace.

Halfar turned to her one evening while she lay exhausted and angry, pretending to seem unfazed.

"What is your name?"

It seemed appropriate to know after nearly a year since acquiring her. He could see her face muscles working.

"Rass." She didn't turn to face him.

"Hmm. It's no secret that I enjoy torturing you but I want to see something more." He saw her tense up preparing for another fight. He laughed. "If you submit to me, I will let you train with the royal guard." Her fingers clutched the bed covers beneath her. "You must come to my bed chamber whenever I request and in return, if you are able to advance, I will release you of your bond to become a royal guard."

"Why?" This time, she did turn to look at him.

"You're holding back. This halfhearted fighting you engage in with me is tiring. I want to see the full potential of your hatred unleashed." She raised her eyebrows. "All you need is training to hone the craft of battle."

"But, I have to submit to you?"

"I am your ruler," Halfar replied matter of fact.

He slipped his robe back off and forcibly pulled her to him by her legs, spreading them open around his waist. She started to struggle again as he entered her roughly but stopped after the fourth thrust. Being released from her bonds had to sound appealing and becoming a royal guard more so. Halfar saw a new resolve blossom inside her as he released his seed.

It wasn't long before Rass had beaten most of the first-year guards and killed more than a few that Halfar decided it was time to make him an official royal guard candidate. During training hours, Rass was in male form and in the evening, female for his pleasure. Their relationship became one of mutual respect and trust as the years unfolded with many of the battle strategies Halfar implemented coming from Rass. He had no regrets about bringing the young unknown into his fold.

Since the qualification rounds were closed to all except the participants, with the trainer and Himself as judges, only those involved knew how deadly Rass had become. His speed and agility were unmatched although he did have a rival; another young candidate named Kur who stared from the shadows at Rass with disdain and lust most of the time. Halfar found it amusing.

He began to watch Kur more closely and came to the conclusion that the young soldier had a slew of pent up rage manifesting as superiority. There was a sense of making every battle refined as opposed to mindless barbarism. His attention to aesthetics was intriguing, his fighting skills, frightening.

On a battle session day, Halfar pulled one of the trainers aside determined to find out more about the strange, green haired warrior. They both sidestepped an arc of blood splatter that landed near their feet.

"Where does he come from?" Halfar asked the trainer.

"His mother was a worker in the mines. One of the commanders from the lower royal family dragged her off during an inspection for his master. She gave birth in the mines four moons later."

"You need to clarify," Halfar's eyes darkened.

This disturbed him greatly.

"The lower royals found out about the child and negotiated with the council to raise him in the palace until he reached the age for military training."

"His mother?"

"Still in the mines, my lord."

"Lovely." Halfar's sarcasm was not lost on the trainer. "I'll have her moved into the palace as a handmaiden. Tell no one."

"Of course, my lord." The trainer bowed low.

Halfar returned to the arena to continue his observations of Kur. The story behind the young soldier's existent made him seethe with anger.

"Royal blood." His forehead creased.

War came soon after Rass and Kur were inducted into the royal guard. A twenty yearlong battle against another race who were on equal footing when it came to fighting superiority. In the end, most of his top warriors and generals were killed in battle so Halfar made a bold decision appointing the two rivals as his new generals. He also did this in part because their troops were one of the few left standing when the fighting ended.

With the interstellar council coming up, it would show his determination to keep Azrom's forces intact and that even the massive loss incurred hadn't lessened their reputation as one of the most feared races in the galaxy.

**✷✷☼✷✷

New Lassa

"Ten years," Chardon, the leader of New Lassa, sighed.

In female form, Chardon stood leaning over the window sill of her new chamber staring out at the fairly revived landscape. The Razznian battle ships that had invaded her planet left many sectors in ruins. To ensure the planet's survival, Chardon added insult to injury by using her powers to wipe out everything. The blast traveled like a wave across the planet, disintegrating plants, flesh and machine. Most of her race were saved from it by taking refuge in underground bunkers designed to withstand it.

She forced her dark blue eyes to adjust in order to see farther across the land. Off in the distance Jaron was scolding Trinon who had to look down at his mother. He stood with that disarming smile on his face which infuriated everyone, even her.

A loud galloping sound came from the corridor outside her chamber and she hung her head in anticipation. Only one ball of energetic species made that kind of ruckus. The door flew open, banging against the wall.

Standing out of breath, black hair whipped around like snakes, was Farin. He wore his usual black bodysuit with cloak and shiny leather boots. His pale creamy skin and murky green eyes, inherited from his father, were in stark contrast. Nearly the same height as his mother, he was tall and beautiful at the age of twenty.

"Mother!"

"Yes, Farin?"

"I did it!"

Chardon turned around to lean back against the window sill.

"Did what, Farin?"

He grinned. "I climbed the monolith!" Taking a deep breath and exhaling, he said, "And I did it just as fast as Trinon!"

So that's what happened.

Chardon now understood why Jaron was chastising Trinon. Farin was not a manbeast but he did have shiny black talons able to cut through nearly anything. Because of their sleekness, he could never get a grip on the giant slate that stood as high as a mountain. All the manbeasts practiced on it. She could only imagine the damage done to its surface by Farin's exuberance.

"Is that so?" Chardon crossed her arms and waited.

She didn't have to wait long. Modas, came into the room looking none too happy. A quick glance at her followed by a short bow was all she got before he launched into his complaint.

"Your child sliced through most of the monolith trying to climb it," Modas said through gritted teeth.

"So I heard."

"We need someone who can repair it before it starts to shift from the cracks and collapses."

"Aren't you being overdramatic?"

"No," Modas replied. His teeth still clenched together. "I am not."

Farin's excited expression turned to dread and Chardon almost felt bad for her silly son. What made her not pay it any mind was Modas' behavior on the matter. He had been going off the rails lately and everyone made attempts to keep him in check. All nearly seven feet of his frame shook with indignation.

"I will see to it." Chardon pushed herself from the window and walked over to him. "It is a piece of slab, Modas, regardless of how many generations it has served your species."

That snapped him out of his current state and into one that Chardon found even more offensive: Disgust. It was a 'how dare you' look. A high-pitched whimper from the doorway made the manbeast jerk his head towards Farin. Chardon saw the realization in Modas' eyes and was not surprised when he turned away and strode right out the door.

"Don't worry, Farin. You did nothing wrong. Come."

Chardon opened her arms and Farin ran into them. They stood in an embrace for a moment. When they released each other, both laughed.

Further down the corridor, Modas heard their laughter and fumed. He didn't find it amusing by any means. The monolith was one of the few things salvaged from their original home world and transferred to New Lassa. It had been a training tool for manbeasts for probably centuries, maybe even millennia. No one knew where it came from or how it came to be. Even their hated head scientist, Ganna, had no answers.

Up ahead he watched Trinon walk off away from his mother, unfazed by the lecture. His older brother, Mota, met him and slapped the young man-beast on the back in jest. They had no sense of pride for their history. Both only looked forward and cared nothing for the past. Modas eyes narrowed. They would have to face the past soon enough. His agenda was coming to fruition.

An infant appeared mere centimeters from his face and he stared into the pouty lips of his newly born grandchild who his daughter, Mara, held up proudly. The litter she had been born in had three beast and two energy users. She was, of course, not a manbeast so could never under- stand the plight of manbeasts but he loved her just the same. Grabbing the Lassian child from his daughter's hands, Modas lifted him up higher for closer inspection.

General Kur surveyed the palace grounds from his balcony on the fourth level. He swept his forest green hair off his shoulders and smiled at the progress that had been made. Ten years since the Razznians, attacked Azrom and the planet surface was still in near ruins. Rebuilding the inside of the palace was complete with the outer wall being the last thing project for repairs. Off in the distance, he could see the villages beyond the barrier wall that separated them from the palace. It angered him to see the suffering of his people knowing it all stemmed from Supreme Ruler Halfar's reign.

The first to be compensated should have been their people. At the council's behest, Halfar made reparations of the palace in its entirety a priority over everything else. Kur found his judgement lacking in reason. The same happened when he himself was duped by the royal council into launching a coup against Halfar while on Earth. Instead of finding the root cause, Halfar had commanded Rass to dispatch him, without consid- eration for their history together. Despite the cruelty of it and how Rass' decision would sway, Halfar had insisted. In the end, it only brought them closer physically and philosophically. Both were on the same page when their supreme ruler was involved.

Footsteps echoed behind him and he turned to see Rass strolling towards him, head down in deep thought. A tightening in his groin had him trying to restrain his urges. Rass aroused him often these days by simply being near, especially now with his jet black wavy hair, now down to his waist, brushing against his hips as he walked. Those small pink lips pursed in frustration made Kur lick his own. Rass finally looked up and Kur straightened his posture.

"What troubles you, general?" Kur asked playfully.

"Halfar."

"Hmm. Is he opposing some random council agenda?"

"On the contrary, he's adopting one. It is to further restrict the royal families from the main sector of the palace."

"For what reason?" Kur was suspicious.

"No clue. I have a feeling something is coming and it won't be beneficial to our race."

"That is a given." Kur tilted his head. "Bond with me."

Rass's eyes went wide and he stared at him for a long time.

"Why did you ask that?"

"Because I want you."

"Have you gone insane?" Rass seethed.

Kur stepped closer to him. They locked eyes.

"No." He ran his fingers in Rass's hair. "I want you and no one else."

"This is not the time," Rass whispered.

"When will it be?" Kur snapped. He took a breath. "There is no reason to wait."

He watched the conflict on Rass' face then saw clarity. Rass sighed heavily.

"Then I will be yours."

Filled with a sense of relief and jubilation Kur grabbed Rass by the hair and kissed him roughly. He had waited so long to ask that he had feared it would be too late to claim him. Now there were no obstacles. Figuring out what the concept of love encompassed had given him a new understanding of his feelings for Rass.

"You do realize we cannot announce it yet?" Rass said when Kur released him from his grip.

"I know."

All too well.

Halfar would not be happy. In fact, Kur figured there would be a sense of jealousy and that was the last thing he needed; Halfar declaring war on them out of spite. He used a thumb to wipe his moisture from Rass' lips then resumed viewing the palace project.

"What are you thinking?" Rass inquired, leaning over from the side.

"Our people are suffering, yet I am glad the palace is almost complete. That means we can focus on them soon."

"Don't count on that basis, Kur. I heard no intentions in the council meetings to ensure the care of our people outside the wall."

Kur turned to him and saw truth in that statement. The ones supplying the population with rations were the First Royal House and they would be the ones to deal with. This new restriction could be as a result of it. The council's and the royal's agendas did not complement each other.

"I am disappointed. We still have not resolved the issue of the Razznians on Earth either. Halfar says it is under control, but I am not so sure." Kur drummed his fingers on the ledge.

"Halfar could care less about Earth. The humans who worked for us are just keeping tabs and making sure the Razznians don't interfere in his organizations flow of revenue."

"I always hated that concept of currency. It is only one of three planets we know of that have it and those races always end up destroying themselves because of it." Kur grinned. "So, no revenge tactics?"

"He believes we have dealt a big enough blow."

"Has he forgotten the other part of the equation?" Kur asked. Rass raised an eyebrow at him. "The Dreridians. He advised us that a plan was in the works for holding them jointly responsible for the attacks."

"That plan," Rass stood up straight, "is no longer in play."

"The council," Kur snorted.

"They believe we have more important issues to attend to."

"Then, if the Razznians regroup and come back to avenge the devastation of their home world?"

"We would be wholly unprepared," Rass finished.

Razznians On Earth

Small flickers resembling candle light shining in various windows of an old rundown building could be seen from the road. Nestled in thick brush amongst large trees, the place was in a remote part of town just on the outskirts of the city. A perfect hiding place for the illegal operations of some fifty employees housed inside: drug makers, drug runners and bodyguards.

As far as the state was concerned, the building was an abandoned shell with no electricity or active plumbing and Sars wanted to make sure it stayed that way. So far, they had been free and clear for over three years.

In the farthest room towards the back was a dingy little office set up with a metal desk and three chairs. Sars, Razznian commander and spy, sat behind the desk. After his team of eight fled captivity from the Azrom dungeons during the battle they arrived on Earth. He brought more of his race over the years as business boomed. He found illegal trade was the way to go and his only competition was Halfar's organization with its deep ties to the crime world.

Since his crews worked only at night, staying hidden from humans was not hard and now other aliens resided on Earth. The thing about opening gateways was that they could possibly be detected by off-worlders. Unlike the other aliens who could blend with humans more or less, their reptilian appearance, scaly skin and lidless eyes, scared most away whenever they were actually seen.

The ones who were a threat, his crew ate. Humans really were quite tasty but it wasn't about good eating. Razznian code was to eliminate your enemy and eat what you kill. Leave no remains for ceremony.

"Sir," one of his subordinates called to him.

His third officer had been on a handheld communicator with a colleague. They had opted for low tech, voice only ones.

"Hmm?"

"We got cops sniffing around again."

"Where?"

"Our second branch in the city. There's gonna' be a raid of the apartment building tomorrow night."

Sars snorted at the Razznian's speech. Many had adopted the phonetics of the region for good reason but it still sounded odd coming from a reptile. He had done some research on the Earth species similar to theirs and the human reactions to them since alien refuse had contaminated many of the waters on the planet. It made him feel good to know, even though not evolved, his kind were above humans on the food chain.

"Who tipped them?" Sars had a good idea who.

"One of those Shadow observers working with Halfar's organization."

"Still trying to get us off this rock, huh? Make sure it's empty. I don't want any casualties this time."

"Yes sir." He went back out into the hallway with his handheld.

Only twenty or so Razznians had lost their lives on Earth but Sars wasn't comfortable with any. For each soldier's death, another had to replace them. He kept a strict number of teams to ensure stability. Halfar ran his operation on Earth with an iron fist, inducing economic and physical fear. Sars liked to keep under the radar. There were rumors heard throughout the city about a brutal drug gang that even law enforcement feared and Sars smiled at that. No need to go out of your way to instill terror when it spread naturally.

Another subordinate peeked his head around the doorway.

"This week's batch is complete and packaged up."

"Good. Get ready to move out. Rendezvous with the second branch. They are going to have to work on the streets for a while."

"Yes sir."

Sars stood up, as did his two lieutenants. They all wore dark red hoodies, dark pants and red sneaker boots. It was the best attire for working in the cloak of night. He usually didn't go out with the runners but from time to time he liked to keep tabs on how the operation was going.

"Kill the portables," he instructed.

The remote-controlled LED lamps causing the flickers of light were distinguished with the push of a button. Throwing his hood over his head, Sars followed his crew out the door.

The city was alive for a weeknight which Sars translated into decent sales. He had expected a slow turn but was glad for the surprise. His first lieutenant, who had been with him since nearly birth, stood by, a serious look on his face as he scanned the area for threats. After the infiltration of Azrom, his team had a new level of protection for him that, in his book, bordered on possessiveness. At least one or more of them was never father than five hundred feet away.

Transactions were looking good so far. Each dealer was calm and smooth, making sure they kept their heads down so the buyer didn't accidently see their faces.

"Remember the first five years on Earth?" He asked his first lieutenant. The veteran soldier nodded.

"We have come a long way."

"It's good we figured out after a year that we needed to be in a larger populated city. We nearly ate through that one sector."

"I'm surprised the government ruled it as an unknown epidemic and not mass slaughter."

"Mmm." his lieutenant replied. "It may be because the wounds were not from human or animal bites and once infected did appear diseased."

"That may be true. But there are other aliens on this rock."

"Yes, but they don't eat humans."

Sars glanced over at him. "Not that they know of." He decided to switch the conversation. "Any word on Razzna?"

"Yes."

"Why haven't you told me?" Sars exclaimed.

He searched the soldier's face for signs of a good reason.

"The truth?"

"Obviously!"

"I felt it would distract you. We all want to go home but only a third of the planet is habitable at the moment. A sector furthest from the blast is almost ready but so much has to be rebuilt and being on the outs with the Dreridians means we can't negotiate terms."

Sars hissed in defeat. He knew it would come to this and he was still trying to come up with a solution. From the reports he had heard their ruler said as much. Since the deal with the now deceased Lassian, Sestis, went south leaving Razzna still in dire need, doing the bidding of the Dreridians seem optimal.

Sestis hated the manbeast of her race and brokered a deal that should have seen both sides happy. Halfar, on the other hand dealt a major blow by destroying the planet Lassa along with her. Being far more advanced in technology and commerce, the Dreridians agreed to continue her original plan with some minor adjustments. The successful infiltration of Azrom would have been payment for a new automated system for their mines. No need for the enslavement of Lassian manbeasts or any other race for that matter.

"I understand your concern. You're right. I will find a way to negotiate with the Dreridians. A deal that won't see us enslaved ourselves."

"And Azrom?"

"Oh, I'm sure Halfar has all but forgotten about us and the Dreridians. He will be in for a rude awakening. The Dreridians do nothing for free and when they do not get what they want," Sars didn't finished.

****☼****

Azrom

The gateway's dark pool of stars rippled before turning into a black gaping hole. Light glowed from the center of darkness and four figures emerged from the vortex onto the palace platform where Halfar stood waiting to greet them.

Chardon, Farin, Modas and Trinon, stepped onto the roof. Halfar could not believe Farin was the same child. Now twenty years old, still a baby by Azrom measure, he stood at six feet with creamy skin and long black hair, stunningly beautiful as ever. Farin smiled wide and rushed over to him.

"Father!" His voice was still an octave too high for Halfar's liking.

"Farin," Halfar wrapped his arms around him and squeezed.

Chardon walked over to him, the two manbeasts following dutifully behind her. He could see a kind of tiredness in her eyes and knew it was from the stress of the invasion of New Lassa. Even Modas seemed deflated. Azrom was not the only planet the Razznians ravaged. Farin let go and ran off across the platform then down the corridor, Trinon in pursuit.

"He's in good spirits," Chardon quipped.

"Did something happen on Lassa?"

"No. He's just glad to spend time with you. It's not something he can do often."

"I know. We are still trying to fix things."

Halfar turned his attention to Modas still standing in quiet defiance. The manbeast and he had a mutual disdain for each other so they both nodded in acknowledgement. If there was a way to get rid of him without death, Halfar had not found it yet. He caught Chardon's expression and motioned her to him.

"Come, bask in my arms." Chardon leaned into him as he gently folded his arms around her. "Are you well? I worry about you."

"Just tired trying to keep council members from murdering Ganna."

"That is a hard task." Halfar kissed her softly. "Why don't you rest for the remainder of the day?"

"I will."

Halfar saw Modas frown knowing he would not allow him to watch over Chardon in their personal chamber. He decided to give the manbeast a gift this once.

"If you could make sure she is not disturbed, I would be grateful," Halfar said to him.

Modas lifted his brow in disbelief. Halfar almost laughed at him but kept it in.

"Of course," Modas replied.

They left the platform and headed down the corridor to the main palace. Four royal guards fell in step behind them as they rounded the curve.

Reconfiguration

Azrom's colorful flowers were bustling atop high pedestals in every corner of the banquet hall. Halfar felt a wave of nausea hit him as he watched the royal families in full regal attire trying to impress each other, fawning over fabric and design. He scanned the hall and noticed the first royal house not participating in the spectacle. They appeared bored and as their first cousin, he understood their stance of just going through the motions.

At the center of the first house clan sat Romnus. Their fathers were brothers who fought for supremacy for nearly two centuries until Romnus' father's death in battle. Halfar knew that if Romnus had not bowed out of the fight for rulership, he would be Supreme Ruler at this moment and that alone made him wary of the first house's intentions. So far they were silent on the new policies he had proposed regarding segregation amongst the royal families.

Another of his cousins, Lord Chastan, was already drinking. His eyes leered at the lesser royal females. He came from his mother's side which is why his hair was dark blond with deep waves, worn short. Halfar remembered when Chastan had stared at Chardon with the same lust and it made his blood boil. The man had no shame or restraint.

One of his advisors, Dondar, came forward and whispered, "My lord, it is almost time for the appreciation ceremony. Shall I get them lined up?" Halfar nodded and Dondar alerted the guards with his own nod.

"Bow and address our Supreme Ruler!" The captain of his royal guard yelled.

The hall went silent and all in attendance turned to Halfar seated on his throne and bowed low responding with, "My Lord!" They stood waiting for him to acknowledgement their greeting.

"Resume," said Halfar waving his hand at them.

Halfar wished Chardon and Farin were in attendance. His council suggested otherwise. With the appreciation ceremony they advised it would look like he was flaunting the alliance of non Azromians. He found it a little insulting though obliged. There was no need for unnecessary strife during the rebuilding process. He barely heard the shameless drivel of his courts singing his praise as they prostrated before him.

"Well, that was a farce of a banquet," Chastan slurred.

Walking in stride together the First Royal House members made their way back to their palace. There were seven in all with two females; Chastan's sister, Kuhala and Romnus' half-sister, Reita. At the end of the banquet Romnus made sure they were the first to get up and leave by giving the signal with a glance. He kept watch on Chastan as he weaved down the corridor, the only thing stopping him from tilting over was being wedged between two bodies.

"It was quite informative," Romnus said. "I found it very telling how the third house prostrated themselves at Halfar's feet like slaves."

"Bottom feeders," Reita, scoffed. She stood almost the same height as him and was just as deadly in combat. Her dark hair was pulled back into a tight ponytail that hung down her back. "There is not one among them that can challenge us for the throne."

Romnus looked sideways at her and raised an eyebrow. Surely she wasn't implying that a call to overthrow Halfar was in order? If so, he would have to pull her aside and make her understand it is not something she could voice out loud. He too felt the same way but it was not time.

"I could wipe them out for you, cousin," Chastan said in a temporary state of lucidity.

"Of course you can," his sister, Kuhala, snorted.

"Let's just see how those new policies of his pan out," Romnus added.

He couldn't figure out the council's agenda knowing Halfar had not come up with the idea of segregation. Something was missing in the equation and he needed to find out before mayhem ensued.

Why are you not ruling, cousin?

Azrom's future bode ill at this junction.

****☼****

Chardon could not keep her eyes open no matter how much she tried. They felt heavy along with the rest of her body. She had not been able to rest this well in a long time and it was overdue. After a few blinks, she was able to open them narrowly without having to squint. A dark blur in the corner of the room cleared up, as her vision focused, to show Modas leaning silently against the wall. He was watching over her as usual.

"Why are you so far away?" Chardon whispered.

"I was instructed not to disturb you."

"You never have. And since when did you start taking orders from Halfar?"

"It was not an order, it was a request. He is not my leader."

Something about the way he said it sent a chill in her spine. He was not being himself lately. She watched him unmoving, brooding even.

"What is wrong with you? Why are you being so distant?" She snapped.

Modas looked up at her and his face scrunched up.

"You wouldn't understand. It is an issue that only concerns manbeasts."

"Manbeasts are Lassians! So, it does concern me!"

The effort to yell made Chardon light headed and she closed her eyes.

That mentality always infuriated her and she had no idea where it came from. Sensing Modas move closer she felt a little relief. He was her bodyguard from childhood and knew he would always be by her side.

<h1 style="text-align:center">Modas</h1>

Lassa 200 years ago

Trails of flowers were left behind the leader of Lassa and his mate as they walked down the pathway leading to the council chamber. Two field workers on either side of them scattered handfuls from a woven basket hooked over their arms. Up ahead, two council members waited at the arched entrance to greet them.

"They seem nervous, my love," his mate whispered.

"Of course. I like to make my intentions known."

"We do need a new bodyguard, especially for our young son."

"I am sure, the council and the manbeasts will comply."

The two councilmen bowed slightly and held their arms out gesturing towards the corridor ahead. Down further was the door of the council chamber. Once inside, they made themselves comfortable on the floor cushions at the end of the table. Off to their right was the leader of the manbeasts, with two of his subordinates, his large frame taking up two places. On the left were four council members.

"Midday is a great time for negotiations," the leader stated.

"What brings us together this day?"

"I have just come from the combat trials and saw a splendid manbeast take the title. Your son, Modas. Extraordinary."

"I thank you. He has worked hard."

The leader turned to the council.

"I want to have him removed from the battle roster and placed in my entourage. I'm sure you can accept whoever was runner up."

"As can you," Modas' father retorted. "My son is fit for battle, not babysitting."

"I concur, leader," the councilman said. "We need strong warriors like Modas. Putting him on your detail would be a waste of talent."

The leader was taken aback by the display of resistance to his request. "I am not asking for your approval! I am the leader of this race and want my family protected by the best."

"You are not being reasonable," the second councilman started to complain.

"The answer is no."

They all turned to the manbeast as he said it and the leader saw a look of resolve on his face. He would not budge, that was clear. Angry but not ready to give up, the leader stood as did his mate.

"This discussion is far from over. I will get what is to be mine."

"My son is not yours."

As the leader left the council chamber, a wicked plan crept into his head. He smiled, kissing his mate on the forehead. Not yet, but he will be. There was a small faction of Lassians who had no love for the man- beasts and he knew they would assist.

Modas rushed into his family's outdoor chamber and quickly stripped off his robes. He was covered in sweat and soil from combat training. There was very little time for him to freshen up and head for evening meal but he made haste. Still young yet old enough for battle, he was not at his full height. His father assured him many times that he would grow another foot in the coming years. With no time for washing his mane, he pulled pieces of twigs and debris out, using his fingers to comb it.

Evening meal was a din of noise. Eight manbeasts, seven of them his siblings, were seated on cushions around the table as they grabbed helpings of the steaming meat and vegetables off the serving platters. Modas squeezed in between two of his older brothers and did the same. His father turned to him, their eyes locked.

"The leader made a request for you today."

"A mission?"

"No." His father took a bite of meat and chewed loudly. When he was done, he continued. "He wants you to babysit his family."

"And you said no."

"Of course he said no," his oldest brother yelled. "You are a warrior. We need you in times of battle."

"They have been getting less over the past few decades. Nothing extreme," his younger brother interjected. "Maybe he can be on standby."

The rest of his family looked at the young one and Modas nearly laughed. They were not sure if his younger brother was kidding or just naïve. He on the other hand felt both arguments were correct. Escorting the leader's family around was not ideal. There was no adventure in that. But, with not many battles occurring, he could see why their leader made the request. The question was, 'why me?' Modas couldn't help feeling there was an alternative motive.

"I agree, father. I am of more use on the battlefield."

His father nodded in agreement and the conversation was over. It was time to eat.

Tired from a battle, Modas, along with the other manbeasts, went to their chambers to sleep. Their leader had congratulated his father with a small private meal and invited the family. It had been a short stint, lasting only a few days with worthy opponents. Modas nearly faltered as he got closer to his bed. He was satiated, full beyond reason. As his head hit the cushions, his body grow heavy and he fell asleep.

Danger!

He could feel it. His body would not move the way he wanted as he tried to lift himself off the bed. With every fiber of his being, he forced his adrenaline to push aside whatever was coursing through his veins and catapulted out of his room. Screams, along with roars of battle cries rang throughout the chamber. His speed had been cut by half but fast enough to carry him out into the night air.

Blood splattered on him, covering his whole body and he stopped cold. A Lassian warrior pulled his longsword out of the deep diagonal cut it had made across his father's chest and the great manbeast fell backwards dead onto the ground by his feet. On the sides of his family chamber other Lassian warriors held back the manbeasts who had been awakened by the sounds. Modas could see their eyes were not focused and realized they too had been drugged.

With a howl that frightened the Lassians to halt where they stood, their mission complete, Modas attacked with a newfound ferocity. Within seconds he ripped apart every Lassian warrior in his vicinity, not giving them time to prepare themselves. As he cut the last one, ready to move on to the ones holding his fellow manbeasts at bay, four darts flew into his chest. Stunned he looked at them, stopping for a moment, but resumed his advance. Four more struck him in other parts of his body and with a thud, he hit the ground. He could taste the soil as it entered his mouth, his vision blurring as a Lassian warrior knelt down beside him.

"This is an atrocity!" The head of the military council yelled.

The meeting chamber was filled to capacity with angry Lassians. There was no doubt who had facilitated the assault yet there was nothing to be done about it now that their leader was apparently out of control.

"He will be assassinated for certain," one of his colleagues said. "And I won't lift a finger to stop it!"

"How do we remedy this?" The head of the science council asked.

"We don't," he snapped.

Surprising them was the sound of the chamber door swinging open to reveal their leader standing in the doorway, his mate attached to his arm. He smiled as if nothing was amiss which they all understood he surely knew.

"Councilmen! It is such glorious weather this day! Why are you congregating in the meeting room so early?"

A councilman moved towards him and another grabbed his arm to stop him. The two men met each other's gaze and the suppressor shook his head. Sitting back down, he took a deep breath and exhaled slowly. The head of the military council looked up at his leader with disgust but decided to play his game.

"Have you not heard? A manbeast family was attacked and slaughtered."

"Oh?" Their leader raised his brow and feigned sadness. "How disgraceful. Obviously another manbeast clan over some dispute."

"That is the report from the Lassian warriors who went to assist in diffusing the situation."

"Were there any survivors?"

"One. The young warrior, Modas."

"Is that so?" The leader stepped into the chamber and tapped his bottom lip. "Well, as leader of our race, I feel it is my duty to take the young thing in under my wing."

Another councilman's hands began to glow and his neighbor swatted it, also shaking his head. The military head was at a loss for what to do. The last thing he wanted was for Modas to be in the hands of the one person who had his family murdered. He looked around at his colleagues and was surprised to see nods of approval. Then he understood.

"Yes, that may be fair. You are obligated to do so, after all."

"Indeed. He will no doubt be in grief for some time and not fit for battle. I believe he would find solace in being a personal body guard to my family."

Silence engulfed the room.

"If that is all, you should really get out and enjoy the weather."

"We have to appoint a new leader for the manbeast council."

"Oh, yes. Then get on with it. Just don't take too long. The sun can't wait forever."

With that, the leader and his mate left the council chamber.

"For the love of Lassa!" A council member slammed his fist on the table.

"I know!" Another shouted. "I know, but we must remain patient."

"If he dies, his son becomes leader," the head of science spoke.

"That's fine, we can handle him when the time comes," the head of military stated. "He's still just a child and we can mold him."

"Then we let it run its course?"

"As we concluded, someone will assassinate our leader eventually."

"Hopefully sooner than later."

A sea of darkness engulfed Modas as he sat yet could feel movement around him. Tiny sounds filtered through every now and again but he paid no heed. An emptiness had swallowed him and he had no way of filling it. Images of his family's last meal together in their home flickered in fragments. He felt the stinging of tears, unable to wipe them away.

Hands. Small ones, soft and smooth, planted on his cheeks. They didn't go away even when Modas forced his eyes open to see what and who was in front of him. Slowly, his vision came back, the light hurting his eyes and sitting in front of him was the leader's son, Chardon. His creamy slightly tanned skin and auburn hair appeared to shimmer. Blue eyes, dark as the sky at dusk, stared back at him.

"Don't cry anymore. I'll stay with you," Chardon said.

"What?" He asked.

His own voice sounded like the crunching of dry soil and deduced it was because he was indeed parched.

Before he could recover, Chardon threw his arms around his neck and hugged him. When the young teenage boy released him there was a small smile on his face and Modas still didn't understand why.

"Come along, young Chardon," a servant called.

She was by the doorway waiting for him.

Chardon stood up, still smiling, then raced out of the chamber, the servant following not far behind him. Modas was left slumped on the floor with tears drying as they streaked down his face. Another servant came over and set a bowl of food in front of him.

"Please," she said. "I know you are hurting, but you must eat. You need your strength more than anyone." The servant also laid a hand on his cheek. "This was a horrible tragedy but you must endure," she looked around her then back at him, "for now."

Modas eyes went wide as he watched her leave. Alone in the room he let his gaze scan the area. It was not much, just a small chamber with a window, a bed and a chair. The washing area was hidden behind a curtain along the side wall. His stomach growled like an angry beast and he finally took a closer look at the bowl before him. Using his fingers, he dug into it and ate every morsel, wiping the bowl clean.

Rage crept back inside him. This time, he suppressed it. For now. Those words echoed in his mind and the pieces locked together, making him determined about what needed to happen.

I must bide my time. The right moment will come.

His vision blurred and the room tilted sideways. The food had been drugged. He did not fault her for doing so because if she hadn't, he might have gone and ruined everything. He needed to sleep this time, not be catatonic in a void of his own making. As he drifted off into sleep, he saw Chardon's smiling face.

On the grassy section of the leader's property, he stood waiting for the head servant to escort him into the family's main chamber. He wore a blue chi mere over a simple brown sleeved robe fastened at the waist with a black sash. No more need for his battle robes and body tunic. If one did break out, he wasn't sure he could muster the will to fight. He had to attend to Chardon and his cousin, Jaron, on most days, never really trying to know who they were as individuals.

Over the past few years, he had grown fond of them, Chardon more so than the other. There was a strange form of lust that emitted from the leader's son. Modas felt their species too different even though they were all Lassians. Something about that thought jarred him and he remembered the Lassian warriors who slaughtered his family. No, they were not alike in any way. Footsteps from the hallway behind inside the door made him turn.

The night before, he had gone to check on Chardon and found the young man sitting on his darkened chamber's floor stripped naked with a bed covering barely hiding the lower half. When Chardon turned, Modas realized it was not a young man, but a female who sat before him. The initial shock was broken by Chardon's voice, dripping with honey as she asked, "Am a just as pretty?" Her skin was flushed, the hair around her temple wet with sweat and he could only imagine what she had been doing.

Contemplating her question, he remembered the day before when he told Jaron how pretty she was and Chardon was in the vicinity of the conversation. He looked down at Chardon again and felt the stirring of desire within him. This is wrong. He swiped his hands down his face.

"Yes, Chardon, you are very pretty."

Sensing a presence in the doorway he turned to see the leader standing there looking down on his child with such disgust that he flinched. It was like he wasn't in the room, the leader's gaze was so focused.

"Kila!" the leader yelled. Chardon's servant came running and stopped cold. "Get that thing covered and make sure it's back in male form!"

The stare moved to Modas and he saw it as a signal to leave. Hurrying towards the door he found the leader had somehow already left.

Now he stood waiting to be either praised or chastised, the summons not giving any details on which way the conversation would go. The head servant came out and gestured for him to follow. He had been in the family chamber only a few times, the first nearly a moon after the death of his family.

Most Lassian décor was simple with modest furniture and small vases of fresh picked flowers. The leader had a different flare. Too many colors, overly large furniture and flower petals everywhere. One day he had almost slipped on the floors from a cluster of them beneath his feet. Inside the main living area, the leader sat alone on multiple cushions at the low table.

"Sit," the leader commanded.

"I would prefer to stand. I must not be long, having to escort Chardon soon."

The leader turned and stared at him angrily but Modas didn't waver.

He was not intimidated by the man and refused to show otherwise.

"We have a secret in our midst and it needs to remain so."

"I'm not sure I understand."

"Leaders are chosen because they are unchanging, resolved to their will and person."

Modas pursed his lips. Whatever the man was getting at, he felt threatened.

"That said, as much as I love my mate, her bloodline is tainted. It became apparent when Chardon was nearly twelve that he was a shifter."

Modas relaxed his face and inhaled slowly.

That's all? I'm getting a history lesson?

The leader's face conveyed something else.

"No one," the leader yelled, "is to know about this! Not even our scientists!"

The volume of his voice raised flags of danger in Modas, especially when the leader got up and came so close they exchanged breaths, locking eyes with him.

"You think I don't know how you lust after my son and his cousin? A filthy manbeast drooling, wanting to covet the flesh of our elite? You will never," he emphasized the last word, "touch them! You'll never have them. What you will do is protect my child, always, even when he is leader. You swore an oath to my family and it will be honored."

As the leader stepped back and returned to his cushion, Modas' eyes narrowed. "I did make an oath, but not to you." He watched the leader move to get back up. "It was for Chardon alone and I will protect him, always." With that, he turned and left the chamber, tuning out the outbursts coming from the leader.

****☼****

In the dark of night, on a hillside far away from the village, Modas held a meeting of manbeasts. He had set the date for it nearly a moon ago and only invited those he felt would benefit his cause. There were forty in attendance, all dissatisfied with Chardon's leadership and angry about the past transgressions of his father.

"I don't need to tell you that what is said here cannot be spoken outside this circle," he began. They nodded in agreement so he continued. "As some of you know, my family was murdered at the request of our leader's father." Loud murmurs resounded. "The cores of their bloodline and the Lassians who participated are tainted and must be eradicated."

A curtain of dark fell along with the absence of sound and Modas felt uneasy for the first time since setting his agenda in motion. He understood some manbeasts were not comfortable with the plan but it would be for the greater good of Lassa.

"I know some of you have mates who are not manbeasts, as do I, but we must be united as a race to ensure this does not happen ever again."

Lights formed on the trail below the hilltop and a group of workers strode by. Fearing what the unsuspecting Lassians may report, Modas twirled a finger in the air signaling his manbeast to disperse. He would have to set up another meeting soon.

Off in the distance, Talas stood with one leg set atop a large boulder as he stared out at the hilltop covered in manbeasts, Modas at the helm. He knew what the manbeast was up to and didn't need the earlier hint from Trinon. Sestis had told him the story of the massacre and was not surprised when Modas started to act strange. The version she told about manbeasts going on a rampage, killing Lassian warriors, did not add up so he filled in the gaps and came to the truth. Modas' vendetta was pointless and unjustified in his book. To hold something for so long against the dead and take it out on their descendants was something Talas could not fathom.

"Have you gone mad, manbeast?" he asked aloud of Modas to himself.

Below him Trinon and Und were leaning against the rock bed he stood on. They looked up at him in unison then walked off towards their family chamber that sat two miles ahead of them. Talas shook his head in exasperation. Modas was making things more complicated than need be and he wondered what the manbeast hoped to accomplish. The outcome would be a fissure between every class and a distrust like no other. Modas would lose everything; his mate, his children, loyalty.

Talas turned away from the valley and headed down, carefully climbing the cragged surface the same way he had come up. Kelin was waiting for him when he landed on solid ground.

"Did you see what you came for?" He asked.

"Plenty. I fear the worst."

"Come home. There is nothing to be done now. Our little one is asleep although," Kelin smiled. "I'm sure he wouldn't mind being awakened and held for a while."

Talas smiled back. Being a mother and warrior was not something he had gotten used to yet. Then he frowned, thinking of Modas' agenda. He was endangering everyone, including children. This made Talas' indifference turn to anger.

Oreridian Dreams

Being found out was never a big deal for the Razznians on Earth. They could locate and then eat any person who may report their location. The special task forces coming out of the woodworks were making it harder. Of course, they were still no match for Razznians. Sars speculated it was Halfar's organizations doing the pushing since apparently aliens could sniff out others fairly easy.

"How are we doing on funds," Sars asked his first Lieutenant.

His unit met in the back room of a local dive they owned on the outskirts of the city. Humans rarely entered the place because the reviews cited the atmosphere as 'bloodthirsty'. Sars nodded in agreement of the tag while he waited for a reply.

They have no idea how true that is.

"A little over four hundred million."

"Not enough. I believe Halfar controlled nearly a billion at the tail end of his so-called tenure. No, we need to take a larger chunk of the tristate area."

"We do have an in to branch out into the other states across the continent."

"Not yet, too soon. Any new raids?"

"Two. We were able to hold off the task force and," he chuckled, "it is reported that they are too scared to try again. Some of the officers quit and others are traumatized, deemed unfit for duty."

"I guess that is a plus." Sars paced the room for a bit. "How much merchandise can we create in the next two weeks?"

"About twenty kilos?"

"I may be able to negotiate a buyer." Sars smiled. His rows of sharp teeth exposed.

"For that much?"

"Our product is addictive yet does not have the same harmful side effects as human narcotics. Yes, I know a small group who would love to have it."

His crew stared at him in awe and doubt. He understood why. It was a large order and they had four really good distributors who couldn't handle that kind of load. The plan was to get on equal if not greater footing than

Halfar after he learned of what the Azrom ruler was up to on Earth. This new idea of his would put them closer to that goal.

"I believe we can accomplish all our tasks at hand in the coming years."

"How will this help us get Razzna back on track?"

"Alien species like to chemically escape too."

"Ahh!" His crew replied together.

"This will be a sample shipment then?" His second officer asked.

"But will they even negotiate with us?" His first lieutenant also asked.

"Dreridians are always willing to negotiate. As long as they get something in return." Sars saw his crew relax even in the face of the daunting task of making twenty kilos on top of what their distributors had already ordered. It will work itself out.

✶✶☼✶✶

Lord Pondur, ruler of the Dreridian system, set his chalice down on the conference table. He glanced at his treasurer who in turn looked up.

A meeting had been called after a decade of no response from the Razznians and it was brought to his attention that the coup on Azrom was part failure and success. Both planets suffered damage but Azrom sent a devastating blow to Razzna, an overly aggressive one. He was aware of both side's inability to fight fair but this had gone too far. When it disrupted commerce and the flow of goods, it affected his worlds and he would not tolerate it.

"Payment is due, yet we cannot collect," his treasurer announced.

"And why is that?"

"At first, the Razznians seemed to have disappeared, leaving their solar system. There has been some activity on Razzna recently. It looks like they are only shipping in architects and scientists."

"That is not surprising. They need to find a way to sustain their race until Razzna's surface can be fully repaired."

"It has also come to our attention that New Lassa's surface was nearly destroyed as well, by their leader's own power."

Lord Pondur pursed his already thin lips, the crags on his face deepening. "I could never understand Lassians." He found it fascinating that they were able to survive and relocate after Halfar so selfishly sent a planet bomb, killing the world completely. "New Lassa, is it?"

"Who should we contact for barter, my lord?" The treasurer inquired.

"All of them."

"My Lord?"

"The Lassians, Azrom and Razzna."

"But, New Lassa had nothing to do with the original negotiations and Azrom was the target. I am not following the logic, my lord. Please forgive my ignorance in this matter."

"Simple. It started with that Lassian whore, regardless of her death. She did it on behalf of her race. Azrom has essentially stopped mining operations on Razzna, which means their minerals which only come from

Razzna, are now a rare commodity. Of course, Razzna accepted the goods requested by Sestis and used them. So, all of them."

"Very good, my lord. I understand now."

As the treasurer leaned over his screen to do calculations, his head of science, Lord Greggor, entered the room. Lord Pondur saw him eye the hunched over figure at the table, questioning. Lord Greggor's skin was more cragged with deeper valleys in between and thicker yellow curved talons, his girth twice the normal size of their race. Lord Pondur wondered what the scientist was eating until he remembered past experiments involving other species.

No need to continue that train of thought, he chided himself.

"Is the new treasurer doing well?"

"Hmm, he is learning quite fast. He will take some getting used to."

"My Lord," Greggor began, "we really need to send out a search unit for the Razznians. I have come up with a fail proof system."

"Have you? Then by all means, find them."

"And then?"

"Then what?" Lord Pondur watched his head scientist stare at him cruelly. "Ah. Well that poses a problem doesn't it?" He came around the table to stand in front of Greggor. "If we can repair Razzna, then it would be easy to barter a transfer of rulership. Temporary of course."

"One hundred years, maybe?"

"Sounds like ample enough time to get them back on their scaly hides and pay off their debts."

"What about Azrom? They seem to be angry at us for supplying the Razznians with the equipment. They think we had an ulterior motive."

"Which we still do."

"How about we charge them the same as we will the Razznians?" The treasurer asked. His slender frame came up for air from gazing intently at his screen.

"Their ores are of high grade but I would not want to be ambassador on that decrepit rock for any length of time." Lord Pondur waved his hand in defiance.

"Azrom is going through a rough change. It seems there is dissent."

"Halfar will not rule for much longer." Lord Pondur retrieved his chalice and took a sip of his drink. "Didn't I prophecy this two centuries ago?"

"Yes, my lord, you did. Very observant of you."

Lord Pondur raised his glass and tilted it towards Greggor before taking another sip.

"Let Azrom self-destruct first then we go after them for payment."

"May I, my lord?" The treasurer stood up.

"Hmm?"

"I think we should collect payment despite Azrom's troubles. We may not get it in a timely manner. Also," the officer paused, "it would further facilitate their demise making it easier for us to negotiate a rulership pact."

Both Lord Pondur and Greggor raised their brows at each other and made a small nod. Lord Greggor was the first to speak.

"Impressive."

"You may be worth more than I suspected," Lord Pondur addressed the treasurer.

"Thank you, my lord."

"See to it, then."

The treasurer sat back down and resumed his calculations. Lord Pondur smiled and Lord Greggor helped himself to a drink. It was going to be a prosperous century.

TWO: A Coming Storm

Lord Romnus strolled the palace corridors with his entourage which also included his handmaid, Biandra. He wore his cloak draped around his shoulders, a show of defiance against Halfar's new rule for the royal family to always be presentable. As Halfar's first cousin, Romnus had always tried to be respectful of his decisions when he took the throne, but this new rule left something to be desired. He couldn't help feeling at a loss.

Biandra, handed him a small fruit and he took it without looking down at her. He towered over her by nearly a foot and wondered she how appeared, her smaller frame amongst his large group. It had never occurred to him until recently when one of Halfar's guards smacked her down for defending him. Biandra was by no means helpless but seeing the difference in size from that point of view made him angry at himself for not protecting his own people.

Even now, he remained quiet, boiling with rage at the further segregation of the royal family from the main palace. All their movements had been restricted and Romnus had decided to not abide by it, bucking Halfar's new system at every turn. He could feel tension from his entourage.

A high-pitched laugh came from up ahead followed by a streak of cream and black rounding the corner. The stunningly beautiful Farin, in female form, was running at a side angle and not aware of her surroundings. He stopped just in time to see her screech to a halt mere inches from him. Farin quickly bowed, hitting her head on Romnus' chest. He smiled down at the top of the young one's head as he took a bite of the fruit.

"There is no need to bow to me, young Farin. You are royalty as well."

Farin's head whipped back up nearly clipping Romnus in the chin. He watched those strange green eyes go wide with embarrassment and Romnus let out a small laugh.

Oh, cute and beautiful.

He noticed how tall the young royal had grown, standing a little under a foot shy of him.

"Oh, right." Farin grinned.

Not far behind was Trinon looking bored. Romnus could see something had changed in the manbeast, more so than before. A kind of gloom hung around him even though he smiled gleefully. Being Farin's bodyguard had to be tiring, the young one having endless amounts of energy.

"You shouldn't be here. Your father would be upset if you are not in the main palace," Romnus chastised him.

"I'm just exploring," Farin pouted. "Trinon's with me."

Please don't do that.

Romnus felt an aching in the pit of his stomach and took another bite of fruit to distract his desire. Farin in female form was always a pleasure to see but it made him feel not in control of his manners. Filthy thoughts of what he could do to her roamed in his mind.

"None the less, you should hurry back." He gave Trinon a nod.

"Can I come visit later?" Farin asked.

"Welcome back to Azrom, beautiful Farin," Romnus replied, bowing slightly.

He tsked himself for the dirty thoughts as Farin blushed and ran past, barely missing knocking down his entourage. Halfar would probably try to kill him if he knew how much he wanted Farin. Try was all his cousin could do because Romnus had never been defeated in a fight; especially with regards to Halfar.

Trinon followed Farin at a leisurely pace. Romnus had seen the speed of the young manbeast at the mock battle a decade ago and knew it would take little effort to catch up to Farin.

"Shall we continue, my lord?" Biandra asked, staring up at him.

"My apologies, of course."

Romnus advanced forward. Now he really needed release and they happened to be headed towards the brothel.

Tap, tap, tap.

Halfar's taloned fingers struck the throne's armrests in a slow tempo, a frown fixed on his face. He could not fathom how his child had gone off the grid in such a short time. It made him angry that Trinon did not have a tighter leash on Farin. His council had warned him about letting the two roam outside the main palace unescorted. With the new rules he implemented seeming to have only infuriate the royal family more, the council voiced fears that Farin may be targeted for retaliation.

He leaned forward on his throne, straining his ears for the sound of footsteps and within moments, heard the telltale sounds of running feet along with the steady stride of a manbeast. At the entrance appeared Farin, out of breath, with a wide grin on her face.

"Where have you been?" Halfar's voice thundered. He watched the grin turn to shock and fear. "Have I not told you to stay within the main palace walls?"

"I…" Farin began to speak. She looked over at Trinon who smiled back at her. "I'm sorry, Father," she finally sputtered after gaining what looked like a little courage.

Halfar sat back against the throne and let out a loud sigh, finding it tedious to constantly yell at his child's disobedience. Farin was ever moving and curious about everything. The council's suggestion to lock Farin in a secluded wing sounded tempting but he knew Chardon would never forgive him.

"Trinon, escort Farin to her chamber and make sure she does not leave until evening meal." He saw a darkness form on the manbeast's face as he obeyed. Something about it disturbed him. He noticed the change after the Razznian battle.

Three of his royal advisors came forward, bowing low to him and he averted his gaze to see what they wanted. The first, Mesrod, raised his head and cleared his throat.

"My Lord, as fascinating as Farin can be, you must keep that child at bay. At least until she is of mating age."

"It would be a shame for something to happen to her on the palace grounds," the second, Prevcan, added.

"What do you mean?" Halfar was getting agitated by their tone.

"She is quite beautiful and it is no secret what the soldiers have in mind," Dondar, the third member said.

"No one touches my child unless they want death."

"Yes, I agree, my lord, but that doesn't stop them from trying. Once she has been tainted there is no undoing of it," Dondar replied.

Halfar gripped the edges of his throne knowing they spoke the truth. When Farin turned fifteen, he was able to shift forms and be- come female like his mother. He could feel anxiety creep into him as he watched the first transformation. Farin was indeed too beautiful even for an Azromian.

"I am trying, if you haven't noticed."

"Of course." Mesrod looked over at Dondar and nodded.

"Regarding the royal bloodline," Dondar began, "I believe we should expand your house as much as possible to keep rebellion at bay."

"And you suggest what exactly?"

"Kur is a loyal servant and General of the Armada. He should be brought into the fold to claim his rightful place in the royal house," Prevcan explained.

"Isn't it too soon?" Halfar felt uneasy about telling Kur his origins. It was not a pretty story and Kur just might resent him more than he already did. "He may not be pleased."

"It will be hard at first, but I believe he will come to terms quickly." "He has great ambition. This will be one step further towards his goal," Mesrod added.

Halfar grimaced, letting the thought stew for a moment in his mind, his eyes on the advisors to see what lay beneath their proposal. They we right about Kur's ambition. He had witnessed the lengths his general would go to firsthand. Another loyal servant in the royal house would be beneficial. His mind made up, he nodded slowly.

"Bring him here quietly. No one else is to be present except the five of us."

"The guards?" Dondar asked.

"Only two shall stay in the hall."

"As you command, my lord." They chanted in sync.

Prevcan, turned and left the hall with two royal guards in tow while Dondar, brought his attention back to Halfar. Something else was obviously on his mind and Halfar had a feeling he won't like it.

"My lord. If I may be so bold. Since you are in the mood for procreating, have you ever considered mating with our own to have a full-blooded heir?"

He fought back a blooming rage as he sat on his throne listening to the advisors' words. No, he didn't like it at all. Sitting upright, Halfar leaned forward.

"Are you suggesting a child of my loins is not of royal blood?"

"I am not implying such a thing at all. But, my lord to be honest, Farin and her young sibling are not full blooded Azromians. They are halfbreeds."

Halfar's arms turned black and sleek, growing in length as his hands morphed into shiny black pincers. The other two remaining advisors stepped away.

"As I said, my lord, I mean no offense. It is just something we as advisors must think about in regards to the royal bloodline."

"Please, my lord," Mesrod said calmly, "royal protocol is different than normal Azrom rules. With the state of our people, surely you understand the concerns."

The claws stopped in midair and Halfar paused his rise off the throne. What they said made sense although it made him feel ill. His father had been adamant about the bloodline during his rule but he, himself, had never paid much attention to the old warrior's rants. Now here he was, the Supreme Ruler, having to deal with all the nastiness it entailed. Retracting his claws, he sat back in the throne.

"I do understand. I just don't want to think about that right now. Let's get through Kur's dilemma first."

He heard sighs of relief escape their lips but he wasn't sure if it was because they skirted death or something else entirely.

"Your presence is requested by Supreme Ruler, Halfar, immediately."

That is what the preening shiny faced royal advisor Prevcan spurted out of his mouth as he walked into Kur's chamber unannounced, disrupting his mating with Rass. With his back still to the entryway, he sat up and turned his head to stare at the man. Every kind of venom he could conjure up in in his mind translated to the look on his face. It worked. The advisor stepped so far away from the entrance that he bumped into the veranda, nearly falling over backwards into Azromian air. The drop would have surely kill him. Kur smiled at that.

"What could our lord want at this hour before evening meal?" "It is urgent, General."

"Should we don our full regalia?" Rass asked, sitting up.

"No. Just you are requested, General Kur."

That sent alarms off in Kur's mind and he looked down to see the same apprehension in Rass. Whatever Halfar wanted with him could not end well, he thought. He reached over the side of the bed and pulled his white tunic back on before stepping onto the floor and retrieving his leggings. Putting them on along with his boots he grabbed his longsword and stood.

"You will not be needing your weapon, general."

"I do not venture anywhere without it."

A nervousness about the advisor made him angry and he became suspicious. For Halfar to summon him and to be told no weapon was unheard of. He turned to Rass who nodded shifting back to male form and reach for his robes.

"It is just a talk and," Prevcan paused, "a precaution."

"Very well," Kur snapped as he tossed his longsword onto the bed. "Proceed."

He gestured the royal guards to march and followed the advisor to Halfar's throne room. Two royal guards with twitchy hands on the hilts of their weapons fell in behind him.

The immediate clearing of the room except for three advisors, two guards and Halfar surprised Kur as he entered, making his way to the foot of the throne ready to bow. Halfar raised a hand when Kur was mid bended knee, signaling Kur to rise back up.

"What urgent matter requires I leave my longsword and not be in uniform?" Kur demanded.

"It is a delicate matter."

Kur frowned. "There is nothing delicate on Azrom. Even flowers have might here."

"True but I want to tell you something I should have a long time ago."

"And that is?"

"Your origin."

Kur's eyes went wide, his feet rooted to the floor with a storm of emotions going around in his head. Halfar knows my origin? Sadness, anger, curiosity, and pain rushed in all at once. He lifted his head up to see if Halfar was joking and saw no such thing.

"Your mother worked in the mines."

Halfar looked at him, anticipating some violent reaction but Kur refused to let him see that. Instead he stood perfectly still and let him resume.

"The mines are inspected on rotation by a delegate of the royal family. Each house makes sure it runs smoothly. One such time, the delegate decided to alleviate his sexual pleasures with a female worker. It was brutal and unbecoming of the royal house. The incident was concealed."

"By who?" Kur asked softly.

"The delegate's royal house. When it became known she was pregnant, a deal was made under the condition that you would be raised in the palace for military training. After I found out, her duties were changed to a position in the royal courts."

"I am a royal," Kur said. "Of your bloodline."

"That is so."

"What house?"

"The third. But your mother serves the first. So, as the son of a hand-maiden for the first royal house courts, that is where you belong."

Kur's distant stare changed and his eyes narrowed. A new kind of anger rose up in him as he remembered all the trials and harm Halfar had administered, solidifying his plan to defy him.

"We are cousins," he said through gritted teeth.

"Yes," Halfar sighed heavily. "Your father is the brother of an uncle. An uncle through bonding."

Kur understood why he was not allowed to bring his longsword. They knew he would try to cut them down like the fleas they were. Even Halfar deserved to be skewered for keeping this secret all this time. Not willing to give them what they wanted, Kur turned away from Halfar and strode out into the hall.

He could hear the horrified advisors yelling at his backside.

"You have not shown respect for your lord!"

"You have not been dismissed from the Supreme Ruler's presence!"

"Guards! Seize him at once!"

"Do not obey that order!" Halfar roared.

Kur stopped at the entryway. "Where is she?"

"In the first royal house courtyard. She tends to the children there," Halfar answered.

He left then, heading to his chamber and ran into Rass halfway. His counterpart was in battle armor carrying his longsword in one hand and his own in the other. Rass stepped away from him in dread.

"What? Why are you backing away from me?"

"Do you not know?" Rass breathed. He raised his hands to the sides of Kur's face and let them hover there. "You are shedding tears."

"That is impossible!" Kur snapped.

He felt the wetness course down his face and he tried to fight them back. Rass placed his hands on his cheeks and drew his head to him. They stood foreheads pressed together.

"What has happened, my love?" Rass whispered.

"It is more than I can bare," was Kur's answer.

Together they trekked to the other side of the palace where the royal houses were adjacent to the main. None of the royal guards stopped them so Kur assumed they were ordered to stand down for him. The first royal house sat in the middle of the cluster, bigger than all the other palaces. It was an hour before evening meal yet they could hear children playing in the courtyard. Sand colored structures were decorated on each end by three foot flower beds bursting with Azrom flowers of every color. At the archway leading into the palace, the children were being ushered in by the consorts. One in particular stood out among them.

Her hair was a flowing river of dark forest green down her back, swishing across the shiny green sleeveless dressing robe that was fastened at the waist by a gold metal rope. Her smile was wide and familiar, just like his own. She caught sight of him and Rass out of the corner of her vision and stood straight, motionless.

Kur tilted his head to one side intrigued by her calmness and elegant stance. She was definitely of the royal court. He advanced into the courtyard until he was only a few feet from her.

"So here you are," he spoke.

"Yes, here I am." Her voice had a creaminess that soothed him.

"You are quite beautiful. If you were not my mother," he didn't finish.

"As are you." She ran her fingers through her hair. "They told you."

"Yes."

"They took you from me when you were only a few months old. You were the only child I was not allowed to take care of."

Kur felt his hands ball into fists and seeing this, she reached over and pried them loose. Her strength stunned him.

"General, that is not becoming behavior for a royal."

"Neither what was done to you," Kur yelled.

Spittle flew from his mouth. Embarrassed, he wiped it off with the sleeve of his robe.

"General Rass, are you here for support?"

"Something of that nature," Rass whispered.

"I heard rumors. Are you mated to him?"

Kur became afraid and felt tension coming from Rass. To stop the line of questions, he answered for Rass.

"WE cannot tell anyone of this!" Kur whispered in fear.

"Why is that?"

"Because that would make Halfar angry," a voice called out from the outside corridor.

Kur turned along with his mother and Rass to see Lord Romnus strolling along with his handmaid.

"Isn't that correct, Generals?" He stopped near them and sized up mother and son. "So, you really are of royal blood. I thought it odd that one of our court maidens looked identical to you." Biandra handed him a small fruit. "The question is," he bit into it and chewed, "why did he tell you this now?"

"I am suspicious as well. It was obviously a decision made by his advisors. They even made me forgo my longsword."

"That was probably the smartest decision they had ever made." Romnus shoved the rest of the fruit in his mouth and when he was done consuming it, said, "Come. Let's give you a proper introduction." He nodded to Kur's mother. "You should get going and catch up before your lord comes searching."

Her mouth formed a devious smile that filled Kur with pride at inheriting such a thing. She caressed the side of his face then turned around, entering the palace. Beside him, Rass stared at her in a state of awe.

The communal hall where the first house royals lounged before evening meal reminded Kur of those rustic styled living room images he had seen on Earth. A large Gruloc beast's head hung mounted high above the hearth and the table was made from a fallen tree, the notches still showing in the wood. Dim lighting made the great hall seem smaller, more personal. All seven of the first royal children were present with Kur now making it eight.

He sat down across from Chastan who glared at him for no reason. Kur took his longsword from his waist and clanked it down on the table in front of him. Chastan flinched and his sister let out a mighty laugh that scared even Kur.

"Oh!" She said after finally catching her breath. "Please, you must do that always. It keeps my brother in his place."

"Chastan," Romnus said, "have you forgotten that he is the general of our great Armada?"

Rass snorted. Kur felt the same amusement but decided not to show it. Instead he surveyed his surroundings. He knew all of them, just never had any reason to converse with them. Now seeing the royals up close in their environment, it dawned on him how isolated they already were before Halfar's new decree. That alone made it more disturbing, the timing of this new revelation. He had intended to seek them out regarding the rations for the villages and this was his chance to finally do so.

As if reading his mind, Romnus sat up from his laid-back position at the head of the table, leaned forward and said, "Your loyalty to his reign is needed."

"He doesn't have it," Kur replied.

"Oh, I know. And what do you think, General Rass?"

Rass clutched the front of his cloak.

"Nor mine. Too much has happened and there is no remedy except…" He left it at that.

Kuhala, also dressed in battle gear, finished it for him.

"Removing him from the throne. You can say it. This is a safe place. His royal guards do not dare tread into our palace unless they want a fight."

"It may come to that in time," Romnus added. "Halfar is losing grip on his reign. I fear his advisors have once again taken control."

Kur's chest tightened as he recalled the previous advisors devious plan that manipulated him into doing their dirty work. They had the right idea but the wrong agenda. Halfar does need to go but not at the expense of throwing their race into chaos.

"Enough of this depressing talk." Romnus laid back into his cushion. "Let us feast."

Servants arrived with evening meal and Kur thought they must be having a banquet given the amount of food and drink. He saw Chastan grab a drink before it was barely set on the table. Feeling it rude, he removed his longsword and set it underneath so there would be more room in front of him.

"Let's get to know each other better." Romnus smiled.

Kur kept silent for the duration of the meal but when the platters were cleared, he spoke his mind.

"I am aware that this house is distributing the rations for our people outside the great wall."

"That is correct. You do act fast, don't you, general?" Romnus replied.

"It seems the council does not see the caring of our people as a priority, and I need to find a way to circumvent this without putting a target on your house."

"Our house," Keita corrected him. "You are now part of it as well. As for being a target, it is too late for that."

"We are doing the best that we can," Romnus added. "There has been a restriction on the use of transport vehicles. Some of the tracks were blocked in one sector."

"That's…" Rass gripped the edge of the table. "I had not heard of this."

"Nor would you. It is not something the council speaks of freely."

"Does Halfar know of this as well?" Kur asked but wasn't sure he wanted the answer.

"Probably not," Keita answered.

"So it really is like before. The new council and advisors are just as bad as the previous."

"I think they may be worse. The fact being how sneaky they are," she said.

Kur looked around the table at everyone and realized as a member of royal blood he was obligated to keep the reputation of the royal house intact. He had power, even if it was limited. They still had to abide by protocols, the outcome of not doing so detrimental to their plans.

"I will see what I can do on my end," he announced.

"While in the bowels of a rotting beasts?" Romnus asked.

"Absolutely. I have no choice."

"You're curious."

"I want to see just how short a leash they intend to put on me for the success of their agenda. How far will our Supreme Ruler go to gain my unwavering loyalty?"

Rass slammed a fist on the table.

"No! I can't let you do this. It's too dangerous. He could slide off into a new kind of madness."

"Unfortunately, that is a chance we have to take," Romnus said.

Boots stomping against pavement thundered towards the hall and all their eyes widened collective in disbelief at what they were hearing. To confirm the sounds, a group of six royal guards from the main palace came to a halt at the entrance of the hall with obvious harmful intent in their demeanor.

"Generals! Our lord has demanded you return to the main palace, immediately!"

"And if we refuse?" Kur inquired as he grabbed his longsword from under the table.

"You will come as directed if you wish to not cause conflict within the first royal house."

"Have you forgotten who we are?" Rass stood, his arms already formed into claws. "Have you lost all of your senses that you dare demand from your generals?"

"Our orders are from the Supreme Ruler! His word takes precedence over your rank."

"Then you have also forgotten something else," Romnus added. Every royal at the table stood ready for battle. "To come into my house means you are under my reign. If you wish to deny my authority, so be it."

Kur watched as Chastan morphed along with two others, the two sisters drew blades and Romnus came from the head of the table. The royal guards' leader frowned and nodded his head to the side. The other guards drew weapons and a split second later they were all sprawled backwards on the corridor floor. In front of them stood Romnus, nearly eight feet tall with shiny black pincers the length of a man. His praying mantis like legs were thin yet surrounded by lean muscle.

The leader, still standing at the side, raised his longsword to strike and Romnus caught the blade in a pincer without even looking, snapping it in half. More guards came rushing towards the entrance but were stopped by the house's own royal guards.

The ones who got through were met by the royal family. Romnus grabbed the leader with a claw that engulf the guard's entire body. Blood dripped from where it punctured skin. With a slight movement, he tossed the royal guard out of the hall and over the veranda into the evening Azrom sky.

Kur sat motionless at the table. Everything had moved faster than anticipated. He heard that if Romnus had been in the succession battles, Halfar would not be ruler but didn't know why; until now. He turned to Rass, who also stood rooted to his spot by the side of the table with eyes wide and met his gaze. Looking back towards the entrance, he saw Romnus regain his original form and shake the blood from his right hand, spraying it across the floor.

"Tell our Supreme Ruler that if he or any of his royal guards disrespect our palace in any way ever again, it will be a declaration of war."

Romnus said it calmly with no hint of malice, only a statement of fact. The royal guards backed away and left the area of the palace, returning to their posts on the dividing line of the main palace. Only the five on the ground were left and they stood up cautiously. Kur sheathed his longsword and motioned for Rass to follow.

"No need," he said. "I will personally deliver the message myself." Kur stared at the five royal guards and they eventually understood.

Two turned and headed forward as he and Rass exited the hall. The other three fell in line behind them. He took a quick glance at Romnus who smiled ever so slightly. Kur saw what was really in those bright green eyes; rage.

Halfar was not pleased when his generals came into the throne room after evening meal relaying Romnus' message. He turned to his advisors questioning and saw them fidget. This is not what he had planned.

"I requested that my generals be present for a late evening council session with the military advisors and somehow," he paused for effect, "a royal guard is on the brink of death and the First Royal House is ready to engage in battle against their ruler!"

"My lord, I am not sure why the royal guards went into the palace in such a manner," Mesrod said. "That goes against protocol."

"They said the order came from you personally," Kur interjected.

"To bring you back by force if necessary? I would not do that! For them to treat their own generals this way is," Halfar couldn't find the words. It was just too outrageous. He didn't know what was happening. Signals were getting crossed.

"Please send a request to Lord Romnus for an audience tomorrow. A request," he stressed. "I need to apologize for this and try to fix it."

"Of course, my lord," Prevcan bowed.

"Not any of you!" he snapped. Halfar turned to Kur. "Lord Kur, would you please do this as a member of the First Royal House, and a favor to me?"

He saw Kur struggling with an answer and realized he didn't blame him for being wary. To his relief Kur nodded.

"I will relay your request in the morning, my lord." Kur bowed low.

"Thank you. I will be in the battle conference chamber shortly."

As his generals left, he got up from his throne with lightning speed and wrapped one hand around Prevcan's throat. He lifted the Azromian off the floor and looked deep into his eyes.

"If I find that you were behind this, I will snap you in half and feed you to the mongrels outside the wall." He dropped the advisor and headed out of the throne room, four of his royal guards flanking him.

****☼****

Rumors spread across New Lassa about an uprising. Chardon paid it no mind for she was certain that Modas would not launch some hellish assault on his own people. It had been going on for a little over two years and now she was starting to see tiny fractures in the Lassians' trust of one another. Small incidents of aggression between the man- beasts and the sword wielders became numerous. This was not how Lassians behaved.

We have become our own worst enemy.

Chardon walked down the hill to Jaron and Modas' family chamber. Time to get some answers.

Her cousin, Jaron, looked up from her gardening with a scrunched up face that relaxed when she saw Chardon. She always tried to appear angry or disgusted about everything and it just made her laugh, which infuriated Jaron.

"What brings you down this way?"

"I was searching for you mate."

Jaron made another strange face.

"He is not with you. That is odd."

"Yes, it is. The rumors are spreading. Do you know what this is about?"

"Hmm. Not really, but I did get a hint of it being about something that happened in the past. My guess is the murder of his family."

"But that was by a rival manbeast clan. What does that have to do with all of us?"

"If the system were more stable, maybe it would not have happened."

"Again, that was in the past under my father's leadership, not mine."

"Manbeasts hold grudges."

"All of them are rebelling?" Chardon shouted.

"No!" Jaron snapped back. "They do not all share the same sentiment. Trinon and Und are actually appalled by some of the manbeasts behavior the past few years. I think maybe most of my litter feels that way."

"What do I do, cousin? Why is this happening after everything we have been through?" Chardon plopped down in the dirt next to her.

"Honestly?" Jaron sat back and stared at her.

"Yes."

"Your leadership skills are lacking."

Chardon felt like she had been punched in her midsection. Her cousin was always quite blunt but this was a bit much even for her.

"In the past hundred years and more, you have let others sway your decisions. The ones you do execute are based on emotion, not logic. If you want to fix this, you need to show true leadership. Do not back down."

"I get it!" Chardon grabbed a handful of soil and squeezed it in her fist.

"Do you? I hope so." Jaron stood up and held out a hand to help her up. "About this so-called uprising that may or may not happen in a few years yet, you can't do anything."

"What? Why?"

"It has to run its course and then after the debris settles you can fix it. Because if it does happen, there will be a lot of despair."

"Don't they know this?"

"I don't think it is part of the equation. I think they don't care. But they will when it happens and they will have great regret."

"I need to stop this!"

Chardon pleaded with her but Jaron shook her head.

"And that is why I never trusted manbeasts."

The voice interrupting was all too familiar.

Chardon and Jaron turned to see Ganna walking towards them carrying a large potted plant. She thumped it down on the ground and wiped her brow with the back of her sleeve. The last person she wanted to see was their head scientist. If their race didn't need her, she would have slit the woman's throat a long time ago.

"You do not need to comment on this or anything else," Jaron seethed.

"Yes, yes, you wish to kill me." Ganna waved a hand in the air. "Join the ranks and wait your turn. In the meantime, I created a plant that will spread like fire. It should bring a harvest within months and will span a wide girth in meters."

Ganna turned to walk away then stopped. She gave them a winning smile and added, "If you need me to create something to eradicate the manbeasts, you know where to find me."

As she walked away, Chardon and Jaron held each other at bay.

When she was no longer in sight they let go of each other.

Meetings were in the dark of night for a reason and Modas prohibited any light be brought to them, the moon giving off a sufficient amount. He had to call an emergency gathering because of the increased incidents. Some of his manbeasts were sabotaging the agenda early and he needed to rein them in. They had to exercise patience for a few more years which meant squashing the rumors quickly. Having that kind of mistrust now would be like losing Lassa all over again.

"What are you doing? Have I not explained the reason for this cause?"

A few mumbles could be heard and that infuriated him. He too had been slipping over the years and needed to regain Chardon's trust. Telling them to do what he hasn't would sound like preaching.

"We must be calculated and in sync with our efforts. Yes, we should be angry but this is to establish a new order to ensure this does not happen ever again."

"Will Chardon be our final sacrifice?" A manbeast asked.

Others laughed.

Modas felt his eyes burn and he roared. When everyone was silent, stunned out of their thoughts, he made it clear.

"No one harms our leader! Has your core gone dim?"

"I thought we were recreating the actions of the father. Chardon must die."

Four manbeasts nodded in agreement then saw the looks from others in the group. Modas could see them become aware how wrong they were. He had never said anything about recreating the past. That would be disastrous.

"Why would you think that? We are not murderers." Modas snapped.

"We want to be heard. For them to feel our pain. To instill fear of the manbeasts once again so we are not underestimated," Barbon stated. Modas was thankful for him trying to steer them towards the true cause. "Calm yourselves and make this right. Make the rumors go away. If they know we are coming there is no element of surprise." He watched some hang their heads in shame. "That is all for now. Go home and be kind until it is time."

Modas watched them disperse and a nagging feeling tugged at his gut. A few of his manbeast looked dissatisfied with the notion of killing Chardon being off the agenda. *They won't listen.* He immediately got nauseous and dry heaved over the hilltops edge. This kind of sickness had never happened to him before.

Is this a bad omen?

Standing to his full height, he jumped down from the edge.

Fateful Encounters

Another visit to Azrom without her mother or younger brother made Farin elated because she could roam the palace, under Trinon's watchful eye of course. But lately he was letting her go off on her own. She felt better being in female form and relished it. A quick overview of her body finally filled out in all the right places made her wish for better attire to accentuate her assets.

She ran around the corner of a veranda on the palace's far side, where she had never been and noticed the sun was blocked. Up ahead she saw royal guards at the entrance of a chamber and smiled.

I wonder whose it is.

Curiosity piqued, she headed straight for it.

As she neared the entrance, the two guards turned their heads towards her with eyes bulging out of their sockets at the sight of her. They both gripped their weapons, ready to bar the entrance when Lord Chastan came out.

He was straightening his top robe over one shoulder and looked over at the guards. They removed their hands from their weapons and resumed watch. Farin grinned as she caught a glimpse of the inside before Chastan blocked her view, an obvious move to stop her from seeing.

So it's true.

Feigning ignorance, she stepped back from the entrance a bit and exclaimed, "Lord Chastan! What are you doing? Were you visiting?" Lord Chastan let out a small laugh and hooked his arm in hers, steering her from the chamber.

"My beautiful Farin, this is no place for you to be."

They walked back down the outer corridor.

"Why?"

"Because there are those who would gladly desecrate you with no regard for their lives. And if you are harmed within our palace, Halfar would kill us all."

"Oh. So you would protect me?"

Lord Chastan smiled. "Of course. You shouldn't be here with me."

"Everyone says that."

"Your father will be searching for you."

"Where are you going now?"

His pace slowed and a sinister look came on his face. She could tell he was thinking something unclean.

"Would you take a bath with me? Being scrubbed by an attendant is so impersonal."

"Really? Like in the communal basins I heard about?"

"Not quite, this one is for royals only."

"I haven't had one since I got back on Azrom."

"Then let's get clean together."

They walked arm in arm to a bath chamber further in the palace than she had ever been and admired the large basin set deep into the floor. Lord Chastan nodded to the attendant who hurriedly ran the water and added the solvents. The washing cloths and sponges were set on the edge and the attendant fled the chamber.

Turning around to walk backwards into the chamber, Lord Chastan took her hand and guided her to the changing station to the right of the entrance. He reached over to push her hair from her shoulder then gently pulled her robe down until it fell on its own to the floor. He knelt down and did the same with her leggings and boots.

Farin giggled, startling him to stand back up.

"Your turn."

She pulled off his robes, tearing at them, each layer flying into the air haphazardly. She adored the look on his face at her boldness.

The attendant returned to fold their clothing in a neat square pile and left again. Farin got the impression that Lord Chastan was not very nice to the attendants and probably harassed them brutally; sexually. It didn't matter if they were male or female.

He held her hand as she stepped down into the basin and settled on the ledge. Expecting a drunken splash, she was surprised by how gracefully he slid into the water. With smooth precision, he gently pulled her by the hips to him, not disturbing the water. His hands came up dripping wet, soaking her hair as he brushed his fingers in it.

"You are quite beautiful," he whispered in her ear.

His breath was hot and she could feel him getting aroused. She smiled, tilting her head back and pushed away from him.

"Lord Chastan, that's dirty."

"Well, we are here to bathe." He reached behind him and removed the sponge from the ledge. "May I?"

Farin turned around and let him move her hair to one side so he could wash her back. His touch was very soft and again she wondered how he could be so crude in public. Even when his hands roamed to the front of her and ran the sponge down her breasts, one side at a time. She turned back around to face him.

"My turn?" He asked.

She grinned then used both her arms to scoop up water and splash him. At first, he was stunned but recovered quickly and did the same to her. They laughed like children as they wrestled with each other, not caring about their nakedness. Farin was having fun.

Out of breath, they went back to washing each other, Farin making sure to wash every part of him she deemed unclean. She watched his eyes close in ecstasy as she ran the cloth around his genitals, scrubbing gently. He's so easy. When she was done, he grabbed her by the waist and set her on the inside ledge. He spread her legs wide and let them rest on his shoulders while he used one hand to wash between her thighs.

"Ahh, that tickles!" Farin laughed, throwing her head back. It didn't tickle, it felt heavenly. He stopped and pulled her legs down around his waist. "Why did you stop?" Farin asked searching for an explanation on his face.

"Because," he replied, tangling his fingers in her hair, "if your father found out, my demise would be imminent."

"But I'll never tell."

"No," he sighed, "you wouldn't"

He kissed her then, hard, blocking off her air supply. She stared at him as he disengaged and saw fear in his eyes. Smiling to change his mood, she wrapped her arms around his neck and blew warm air in his face.

"What are you doing?" He laughed.

"Making you feel better."

"You already have."

"With just a kiss?"

"Ummm, maybe more than that." He swatted the side of her buttocks and pushed away from her. "We need to go."

"Why?" Before he could answer, she said, "My father."

"Correct."

He got out of the basin and pulled her by the underarms onto the ledge. The attendant appeared with large drying towels but Chastan only took one and dried them both off with it. They laughed the entire time while the attendant took care of the basin, as they dressed.

"Come on, if I'm going to get caught at least it won't be in a bathing chamber."

She let him lead her by the hand to another part of the royal palace and was taken aback by the golden colored inner corridors. Handmaids traveled along with purpose, moving out of their way and bowing low at the same time. Lord Chastan stopped at the entrance of a personal chamber and found it to be his.

Entering his chamber, he went to a shelf and removed a large tablet. She came closer and he set it on the bed. A virtual board game appeared on the display.

"Let's play."

"I've never played this game. What is it called?"

"It's called Konterra and it's a game of strategy."

"So, you'll let me win?"

"No." Farin pouted and he laughed at her. "You can't learn if I do that."

"Fine." She crawled on the bed across from him and he set it up. "What do I get if I win?"

"What do you want?"

Farin blushed, her pale skin turning the lightest shade of pink.

"I want to have more fun in the palace. Will you show me?"

"I would do anything for the beautiful Farin," Chastan replied.

Of course, you would.

Farin giggled again and settled further onto the bed.

Boots striking hard on the lacquered halls of the First Royal house caused panicked handmaids to usher their masters into random available rooms out of harm's way. A small group of Halfar's royal guard was marching with purpose, faces scrunched up as if something smelled rotten. They formed a perfect diamond, one in the front and rear with two of them in the middle side by side. Chastan's handmaid, Ponnae, paled and hurried ahead of them towards her master's chamber. She knew who they had come for. Gathering the edges of her robes, she broke into a near run.

As the sound of the guards' advance began to disappear she rounded the corner at the end of the corridor and deeper into the palace. Directly in her path, Lord Romnus and his entourage were headed towards her. His face frowned as he looked at her. She had no choice now, she had to tell him.

"Lord Romnus," she greeted him.

She bowed deep and tried to catch her breath.

"Why are you in such a hurry?" He seemed angry.

"I must warn my Lord to send off Lady Farin."

"Oh?" Lord Romnus replied playfully.

"Halfar's royal guards are in the family palace."

Something dark and unholy spread across his expression and she could tell he was going to address it. That was not ideal but he was royalty and could probably get away with doing so. To her surprise, they all turned around and Romnus gestured her forward.

"Come, let's get Lady Farin safely away."

Grateful for the back up in case the royal guard did catch up, she obeyed and continued her fast-paced stride to Lord Chastan. Not two corridors away she heard the boots get louder. She broke into a full run ahead of Lord Romnus' group and made it to the chamber entrance.

Lord Chastan and Lady Farin were playing a board game on the bed, laughing and tagging each other. She exhaled and blurted out, "My Lord!" They both turned to her, smiling. "Lady Farin must be escorted out, now."

Her master gave her a warning look. She knew her tone bordered on insubordination but there was no time. He could punish her later. In her defense, Lord Romnus came up behind her.

"It really is imperative that you go, Lady Farin," Lord Romnus commanded lightly.

Lady Farin began to pout.

"But I just learned how to play! I'm having fun."

"Yes, well your father has sent his royal guards into our palace looking for you."

Lord Chastan's eyes went wider. She saw fear on her master's face. It was a rare thing to see since he feared almost nothing. He started shutting down the game.

"Fine, I'll go," Lady Farin huffed. She leaned over to Lord Chastan, her face dangerously close to his. "But I can come back, right? You'll play with me again?"

"As much as we love having you come to visit us, we are trying to not be slaughtered because of it," Lord Romnus answered for her master.

Lady Farin stood up with her hands balled into fists.

"I know."

Lord Chastan nodded to her and she held out a hand to Lady Farin who took it.

"Make sure you find Trinon, Lady Farin. This could become messy," Lord Romnus said to her.

With a nod, Lady Farin followed her out of the chamber and down a private corridor hidden in the walls. She kept a good grip on the Lady's hand, not in the mood to fall for her childish games of running off on her own. This was a serious matter and her first priority was the safety of her master.

Lord Romnus waited patiently for the royal guards as they came around the corner of the corridor breeding intent to harm if the situation necessitated it-again. He forced his mouth into a smile as they marched up to him at Lord Chastan's chamber entryway.

"Where is she?" The leader roared. "We know she was sighted in this palace with Lord Chastan!"

"Lord Chastan has had many females in his presence. You have to clarify…" he was not allowed to finished.

"Do not kolbrec me, royal!"

Royals watching from their doorways gasped at the term only uttered by mothers to unruly children.

Lord Romnus held out an arm to his side, stopping what he knew was his own guards grabbing the hilts of their longswords. His eyes narrowed and locked on the leader's, who flinched slightly, looking sideways without moving his head to make sure no one saw it. Romnus didn't let his stare waver as he spoke.

"You have entered the palace of the First Royal house without my consent. Here, I am Supreme Ruler and you will tell Halfar this is not acceptable." He did not raise his voice and knew there was no need.

"You may rule here but Halfar is the Supreme Ruler of our race. You would do well to remind this palace of that. We will find that halfbreed in due time," the leader spat as he spun a finger in the air. The royal guards made their way back from which they came.

"Halfbreed?" Romnus asked no one. "Now, that is telling."

"I think I have a fear for her," Lord Chastan said.

"I think you should." Romnus eyed him. "What, exactly, were you doing with the beautiful Farin?"

"You saw, we were playing a game." Lord Chastan smiled sweetly.

"And before that?"

"What are you implying?"

"They said you were sighted with her, Chastan."

"We bathed together. That is all."

Romnus was well aware of Chastan's ideas regarding baths. His stomach cringed. Then he thought about it logically and came to the conclusion that the beautiful Farin would not have allowed such debauchery be administered on her. She was feral and ripe for mating but not reckless.

"I hope so, for your sake," Lord Romnus turned away, "and ours."

He and his entourage left to resume their walk to his original destination. His rage against Halfar combined with the image of Chastan touching Farin made him force back a sudden surge of bile that filled his throat. The latter should be of no concern. Farin ending up with another after Chastan before he got her was fine. That way she would be well seasoned in mating.

It was the first that infuriated him more. Since the forced segregation, it was explicit that no royal house would be invaded in such a manner. Halfar was breaking his own rules for his own agenda. Halfbreed? For Halfar to allow his inner circle to define his first born as such meant the council was pushing harder.

He decided to let Chastan and Farin's relationship flourish a bit. It would put her under the protection of the First Royal house. If even her father tried to harm her, he could retaliate on her behalf. Plucking the round fruit from Biandra's upstretched hand, he took a bite, engulfing half of it. The juice dripped down his neck and he wipe his face with the back of his robe's sleeve, he felt his eyes burning. The end of Halfar's reign was near.

It didn't take long for Trinon to reattach himself to Farin. Even though he let her roam, she was always in his sights. He was testing the waters to see how bad Azrom was becoming for the young royal. Halfar was putting a shorter leash on his child as each year passed. The encounter he just witnessed with Lord Romnus and Halfar's royal guard confirmed his fears. Farin was in danger from her own father. That one term he heard the leader spit out is what gave him cause for alarm.

Seeing Lord Chastan's handmaid lead Farin down the stone paved ramp that ended back on the side of the main palace, Trinon jumped off the steeple above and landed soundlessly behind them. He smiled at how well it went and decided he had now perfected it.

"Trinon, are you upset with me?" Farin asked.

That startled the handmaid who nearly stumbled backwards as she turned and saw him so close behind them. Her look of terror was almost comical. He set a hand on Farin's head and shook it.

"How? Where did you…?" The handmaid stuttered.

"It's okay now. You can go back to Lord Chastan. I'm sure you're worried about leaving him with my father's royal guards," Farin said. Her smile faltered a bit.

"I am, thank you."

With a low bow, the handmaid ran back up the ramp. He felt bad for her. It was obvious to him that she would end up in the middle of all this and not come out unscathed. His hand still on Farin's head, he gripped harder, forcing her to turn around and face him.

"I cannot protect you if you do reckless things."

He made sure his voice was low enough for only her to hear. Royal guards were everywhere in the main palace. Her mouth trembled and he folded her tight in his arms. He had been with Farin since infancy and if he was of mating age when she was born he could be her father. Years of watching, training, protecting. He was not going to let her own father destroy her, let alone anyone else.

"I'm sorry." His robes muffled her whimper.

"You're not stupid and you're not weak. Acting like it is one thing, being is another."

Farin pulled away from him and smiled for real this time.

"Manbeast!" A royal guard yelled at him. "You are lacking in your duties!"

He turned to the four royal guards from earlier and the disrespect they exuded rubbed him the wrong way. With a grin, he instantly grew claws from his left hand and swiped across all four at chest level. Their breast plates split in two, the lower halves falling to the ground in loud clanks. Other royal guards looked over and Trinon saw them itching for a fight, but hesitating.

"Let's play nice, shall we? I have been watching Farin all day, as usual," he laughed.

"You lie! She was seen with Lord Chastan!"

"She is never alone," Trinon replied.

This time he didn't smile, letting his voice drop an octave lower along with his stare. He watched it strike fear in the royal guards around him. At nearly seven feet tall like most of his family, he towered over the guards. Out of the corner of his vision he saw two royal advisors and their guards come towards them in what may become a brawl if the royal guards decided to strike back. The other three were still in awe of their breast plates on the ground. Retracting his claws and resuming his goofy demeanor, he waited for the reprimand.

"What is going on?" Mesrod, Halfar's first advisor, demanded. He noticed the half-cut uniforms and stared at him in anger. "Did you do this?"

"Yep!" He replied in Earth slang he learned from Kelin. His understanding the improper dialect conveyed a kind of disrespect. "I sure did!"

"Why would you do such a thing?" Prevcan, the second advisor, asked.

"Simple. They weren't being nice," Trinon said. He reached back and ruffled the back of his mane. "I don't like that."

Mesrod pursed his lips and his brow furrowed.

"Return to your posts," he commanded the royal guards, including the four in front of him.

They picked up the other half of their breast plates and marched off back into the main palace. Prevcan tsked at him.

"Halfar will not be pleased with your idea of watching, manbeast."

Trinon cocked his head to one side at the last word the advisor uttered and waited. He saw the realization enter the man.

"My apologies, Trinon," the advisor cooed.

"Can I rip your throat out?" Trinon asked playfully.

"What?" The two advisors asked, horrified.

"Kidding," Trinon laughed.

"Please see that Lady Farin," he said it with obvious disdain, "is confined to her chamber for now."

"Of course."

Trinon watched them wait for his bow and he gave them no indication that he would. After a few moments he guessed they realized it as well and walked off in a state of anger. He did like that.

Talas stretched the fingerless leather glove over one hand, pulling it tight. In female form she was not much different with the exception of the barely there breasts and slight curve of her hips. Her body was all lean muscle so it didn't surprise anyone that she wasn't more endowed. The deep rust colored leather jacket strained slightly across the chest making it impossible to close all the way. Even her leather leggings hugged a bit too much, but not enough to restrict her movements.

She felt moody. Raising one hand to inspect the glove's fit, it occurred to her that this feeling was due to her female form. It caused a shift in her psyche. Movement from behind made her turn and she saw Kelin setting up the weapons table for training. She let out a soft sigh watching him be meticulous with the arrangement.

A finger was poking at her breasts and she heard a giggle. On instinct, she slapped the finger away and turned her attention to the culprit; Trinon.

"Cushy," he laughed.

His nearly seven-foot frame was bent towards her but she still had to look up at him.

"Don't do that!"

"It's fun sparring when you're in female form. You get all ferocious."

"Is that so?" Talas frowned at him. He smiled that big goofy grin.

"Can I join in?"

"As long as your father doesn't intervene, again."

This time Trinon made a sour face. The childlike grin gone. A serious look surfaced.

"My father is stuck in the past." His natural tenor emerged and Talas thought about how shocking it would be for anyone else to hear. Only three people knew what he truly sounded like.

"And you're not?"

"Not in the same way."

Trinon, along with Talas, watched Kelin approaching and his childlike demeanor returned. He placed one hand high above his mane, rubbing the back of his head and let out a loud laugh. His eyes squeezed shut and mouth went wide open.

Don't overdo it. Talas silently chided him.

Seeing his transitions, and knowing why he had to do it, hurt her. For years she watched the young manbeast struggle all by himself. Having his litter brother, Und, to confide in didn't give him much solace. She wanted to embrace him like a small child but that was his mother's duty.

"Feel better?" Trinon exclaimed.

"What?" Talas snapped out of her reverie.

"You were being all moody."

Trinon walked away backwards and turned as he neared the combat training arena.

"Observant little," Talas started to curse but was stopped by laughter behind her.

Kelin rested an arm on her shoulder and kissed the side of her head. Blonde strands stuck to his face and formed a web before falling back in place as he disengaged.

"I swear the two of you are like twin stars on opposite axis. It's kind of cute, how he teases you."

Talas eyed her mate and felt a sense of guilt. She didn't like hiding things from him after all the chaos they had been through but it was not her tale to tell. Now she knew why she was moody. It wasn't just her female hormones, it was the date. What a terrible anniversary. She grabbed the hilt of her longsword and headed for the arena. At least she would get to release some of her frustrations for a while.

✱✱☼✱✱

Rass stood perfectly still as Halfar marched into the conference chamber, his stride full of purpose. For the Supreme Ruler to roam the palace unguarded meant nothing good would come from this visit. He also knew that Halfar was the only one aware of his location at this hour of the day. Taking a quick scan of his face, he tried to decipher his ruler's mood. When Halfar did look up to meet his gaze, something like icy liquid ran through his body.

"Are we alone?" Halfar asked. His tone was brisk.

Rass blinked then noted his surroundings. "Yes, my lord."

"Good. I have decided that the council is correct in their assessment of a pure-blooded heir."

"Have you spoken with Chardon about this?"

"Chardon has nothing to do with this matter! She is not of Azrom."

Rass reared back as fear began to form in him. The way Halfar spoke bordered on madness.

"That being so," Rass tried to quash the heat, "she is your mate."

"She won't be the only one. I can have as many as needed." Halfar stepped closer. "After having offspring, I felt like I had wasted so many decades by not solidifying my bloodline. The first to bear my seed should have been you."

Alarms went off in his head and the rest of the color drained from his already pale complexion as he tried to step away. Halfar grabbed hold of his forearms, stopping him.

"I am already mated to Kur, my lord."

"He can have you," Halfar's grip tightened, "when I'm done."

"I cannot…"

Halfar's eyes burned with an intensity he had only witnessed during battle.

"You belong to me," he seethed. Rass felt his own eyes start to widen and fought the urge. He knew Halfar could already smell his fear. "If I had not dragged you out of the brothel and wanted you, this junction in your life would not be possible. You will submit to me!" He leaned in and sniffed at his hair, inhaling deep. Rass stiffened.

In that moment, he knew how far his ruler had come unhinged. Halfar let him go and walked backwards to the doors, his eyes never leaving Rass'. At the entrance he turned and exited the chamber.

The doors slid shut, a loud swishing sound he had never noticed before emitted from the sealing mechanism, and his legs buckled. He reached out to the viewing platform and used it to keep himself from falling. It had been a long time since he had felt so defenseless. Not since his early years in the brothel. It reminded him how much he feared Halfar and chided himself for forgetting that fact. He had grown arrogant over the past century and was now paying the price.

Afraid Halfar might return, Rass quickly came to his senses and fled the chamber. The only place he could think to go was the First Royal House palace, where Kur was.

Rass finally made it to the communal hall by using every tactic he could think of to sneak out of the main palace. Kur sat at the table end closest to the entrance. He halted for a moment at the archway and watched Kur sip his drink while listening to Romnus speak. There was no sound. Rass felt panic.

When his eyes refocused, he saw everyone getting up from the table staring at him with great concern. Kur was right in front of him, yelling. When did he get there?

"What's happened?" Kur yelled again.

"Halfar," Rass managed to whisper. Then he noticed the room. "Not here, please." Rass took hold of Kur's tunic.

Kur turned to the royals. "I must go."

They found an empty chamber along the outer corridor and stepped inside. Kur placed his hands around Rass' neck. So warm. Rass leaned forward until his forehead touched Kur's.

"What is it?" Kur demanded. "What madness has he spouted now?"

"He wants pure blooded offspring."

"Yes, the council has poisoned his mind with that."

Rass began to shake and used Kur to hold himself steady.

"He is going to force me to bear his seed." He felt Kur's hands tighten as they slid away, his fingers digging into flesh.

"You are mine," Kur said through gritted teeth.

"He does not care. His claim to rights is that he owned me first."

Kur pushed himself away and began to leave the chamber. Rass knew that look on his face and hurried after him, pulling him back.

"No!"

"He's gone too far!"

"I won't let him have me!" Rass snapped back.

"And how are you going to stop him?"

Now there was fear in Kur's eyes and Rass began to understand their predicament.

"I don't know," Rass replied softly.

Kur wrapped his arms around him. They remained that way for a while.

Servants bustled around the communal hall replenishing empty platters and drinks. Romnus clapped loudly, once, getting them to stop moving, then waved them away. Once they were gone he brought his attention to the other royals. Although they tried to hide it, all of them were shaken by the young general's appearance earlier. Invoking that one name sent them into a frenzy as of late. He, on the other hand, kept his composure. In truth, it didn't surprise him that his cousin had done something bordering on insanity. The royal houses were in a state of heightened security these past few years.

"What should we do about this, Romnus?" Reita asked.

He leaned back against the wall and contemplated for a moment.

"First, we need to know what he's done."

"Does it matter? He needs to be stopped!" Chastan yelled.

Romnus looked around at his family members' faces and saw tension on the verge of snapping. "I understand your concerns, I do. But you know we cannot move against Halfar unless we have a solid plan in place." Kuhala began playing with her short blade, swirling it between her nimble fingers. "And no, we cannot kill him." She stopped the motion of her blade and laid it flat on the table. "Kur has an idea, I just don't want to do it." They all stared at him, their anger evident. "You know how I feel about being next in succession."

"How you feel is of no concern to us, brother. This is for the glory of Azrom," his sister chided him.

"What glory we have left," Chastan snorted.

"Enough!"

Romnus was tired but more than anything, he was disgusted. This was not how he envisioned Azrom under Halfar's rule. If he had known, seen some hint of this, he would never had withdrawn from the succession battle.

Farin clung tight against the wall as a group of royal guards marched across the platform a mere five hundred feet from her. She took a peek around the corner as they disappeared down the adjacent stairway. The first royal house palace side was less than a third of a kilometer away. If her speed was constant like Trinon had taught her, it would be a cinch to get there in under two seconds. Crunching down into a launch position, she exhaled slowly then pushed off.

Her ability to stop was lacking so she ended up slamming into the wall of the courtyard to the dismay of the three consorts and the children. In an attempt to not damage her face, she had turned away from the wall. She pushed herself off and stepped back holding the left side of her face. When she turned around, Kur's mother, Emalli, stood in front of her.

"Hurry before they see you." Her tone was firm.

"I know."

Farin ran through the archway and into the corridor of the palace. She found the golden hallways and ran into Chastan's handmaid. The woman gasped loudly at seeing her and something like fear passed over her face.

"Please?" Farin said.

The handmaid sighed and turned around to escort her to Chastan's chamber. Of course, he was there lounging on his bed playing that game of strategy like he always did in the mid afternoon. He looked up from it and she smiled at him.

"The beautiful Farin," he exclaimed. He patted the top of the bed.

"Lord Chastan," Farin answered with a giggle as she hopped up beside him.

"You play a dangerous game," he said.

Farin didn't like talking about this again. It was always brought up every time she showed up. She knew what was going on and refused to live in a cage. As everyone kept pointing out, she was a royal too.

"I want to play! This time, I know I can beat you."

"Is that so?"

Chastan swiped a hand across the virtual board and reset it.

"Mmm hmm."

"And, what do you get if you win?"

"Whatever I want."

"And, if I win?"

"Whatever I want."

"Isn't that wrong?"

Farin smiled. "Do you not want the same thing?"

She saw him understand what she was implying.

"You're trying to get me killed."

"No, just trying to have fun." She felt her mood darken for a second. As if noticing it, he caressed her cheek.

"Let's have some fun then." Midway through the game, when she figured it was a called game, she tackled him down on the bed and kissed him. At first, he seemed surprised then his body relaxed and he let her do what she wanted. Straddling him, she sat up and stared down at him. He

was very pretty and did have a sweet side to him, although she wasn't sure
if it was a ruse or not, just to get her.

He reached up with one hand and ran it down from her neck to her
breasts. She pulled her robes off from the shoulders and let him tug them
the rest of the way down. He undid the sash and tossed the robes on the
floor. She removed his tunic and pulled his leggings off in one motion, his
expression full of amazement.

"Why are you always so impatient?" he asked.

Farin leaned over and planted her hands on both sides of his chest
and slid them under his armpits. She brushed her lips against his, teasing
him before kissing him full on. His hands grabbed hold of her hips and he
slid her down until she could feel the hardness of him force its way into
her roughly. It hurts! Why couldn't he learn to be gentle?

His hips thrust upwards into her with powerful force, the pace faster
than she liked and she kept her hands under him, gripping the bed covers
beneath. She could hear herself crying out. He liked the sound of it and
wouldn't cease his rhythm. Her back arched sending her hair around her
like a spider's web.

She could feel the sweat coming off her, making contact with his and
their bodies slid across each other as if oiled. She became lightheaded, the
muscles in her womb contracting and her arms started to shake.

Chastan grabbed her by the hair with one hand and he let out a loud
grunt that turned into a growl and she felt his seed spew into her as they
let out a final cry. Pain, ecstasy and euphoria claimed her all at once and she
fell atop him with a resounding smack.

Covered in each other's juices, they lay like that for what seemed hours
though only moments had past. Shaky, she lifted her head and kissed him.
It stopped his heavy breathing for a second and he just looked at her.
Then, she burst out laughing.

"Oh, you are so very dangerous," Chastan said. He cupped her buttocks and slid her off his now soft member. "Really, Farin. You will get us
all killed."

"Don't say that!" Farin swatted his head and climbed off him.

She found her robes on the floor and redressed. Chastan sat up and
did the same. The game was still counting down when they both looked at
it and she laughed again.

"Shall I deliver the finishing blow?"

"You haven't won yet."

"Oh?"

Farin laid on her stomach and observed the last moves of the game
while Chastan sat propped up on one elbow with his head resting on it. He
was just being arrogant and a sore loser, she thought to herself.

She vowed to come back whenever she wanted and did so for weeks
on end knowing her luck was bound to run out eventually.

Just not the way it did.

✳✴☼✴✳

Halfar couldn't believe where his child had gone yet again. He had repeatedly confined her to the main palace but somehow, she managed to sneak out and end up back in the First Royal House palace. This time, he decided to fetch her himself along with four of his royal guards. Romnus brought this down on himself. He had asked his cousin numerous times to restrict Farin from entering his palace.

Deep into the first royal house palace he turned down the inner corridors, passing through the golden halls, watching royals and their servants scurry away in fear. It was probably the look on his face, he thought, for he was indeed incensed.

Within minutes he saw Romnus coming down the corridor from the opposite side and between them, a female servant standing in the entryway of a chamber glancing back at him in terror as she talked to whoever was inside. Then she ran in.

"Lord Chastan!" Ponnae came to the entrance of her lord's chamber out of breath and scared to death. Alarmed, she saw Lady Farin naked on top of her master and knew they had just finished mating. Lady Farin had her back to the entrance so had to turn to look at her.

"Lady Farin! You must go, now!"

Lord Chastan's face went ashen and he quickly lifted Lady Farin off him so he could get dressed. Lady Farin halfheartedly moved to find her robes and Ponnae snapped. She rushed into the chamber and hurriedly helped Lady Farin into her robes, stepping back towards the entrance as the two readjusted themselves on the bed, now fully clothed. Ponnae turned around cautiously, feeling a presence behind her and breathed a sigh of relief when she found Lord Romnus standing there. His gaze fell on Lady Farin and Chastan.

Not a second passed before Lord Halfar also appeared next to him, royal guards in tow. Her master sat frozen on the bed, not sure what to do and she couldn't think either. Lady Farin just looked up with a smile on her face.

"I hope you are having fun," Halfar yelled.

"I was," Farin laughed. "Lord Chastan was teaching me how to play this strategy game." The game was indeed still counting down on the edge of the bed.

"Did he now? Get up!" He commanded.

Lady Farin flinched and slid off the bed.

"I just wanted a companion, father."

"You can't blame her for that. She has no one to engage with in the palace," Romnus added.

"Don't!" Lord Halfar warned him.

"It was just a game, cousin."

The moment Farin got to the entrance, two of the royal guards snatched her roughly and headed down the corridor. Lord Halfar stared at her master briefly then said.

"I will publicly execute you if I find you near her again."

Lord Halfar turned to leave but to her shock and amazement, Lord

Romnus blocked him. She had never seen them side by side and noticed Lord Romnus was taller and bulkier.

"You will not threaten my family in my palace, cousin."

Lord Halfar's and Lord Romnus' guards unsheathed their longswords. She raised her hands to her mouth then her master grabbed her by the shoulders and into the furthest part of the room. Lord Halfar took a quick glance at her then back to Lord Romnus. That look scared her more than anything. After what seemed like an eternity, the stalemate was broken by Lord Halfar. He made a gesture and his royal guards sheathed their weapons. Lord Romnus stepped to the side to let him through, his guards still battle ready.

Her legs buckled and she slid to the ground in her master's arms. She had forfeited her life to protect Lady Farin and her master's relationship. And she knew, Halfar knew it.

Two days!

Farin stared at the walls of her chamber and tried to think of something to do by herself. She was not allowed outside, her meals brought to her and four guards escorted her to the bath. Trinon was always near, hidden from them. He said it was to make them feel more comfortable but she knew it was to see if they would harm her or not. The guards would 'accidentally' come into the bath thinking she was done to find her still in the water, naked. One of them would unconsciously fondle his crotch while he stared at her hungrily. He was the most dangerous.

She winced at the pain in her abdomen and did a few breathing techniques. They came off and on since the start of the new moon and she wasn't sure if it was anxiety or she was being poisoned. She put nothing past her father's advisors. This time it blossomed like fire and it lifted her off the bed as she cried out. Tears sprung from her eyes and she couldn't shake it.

Trinon emerged and held her down until it passed. He looked at her then placed a hand on her belly. At first her mind went blank, confused by his action, then she understood. Clasping her hands over her mouth she cried and screamed. When her hands weren't enough to muffle the sound, Trinon brought her to his broad chest and stifled it.

"We have to go. Right now," Trinon said. She nodded.

He lifted her up and walked out onto the veranda. With one leap he landed on the gate platform on the other side of the palace. The guardian stared at them in puzzlement. Trinon set her down and knocked him out before he could question their reason for being there. Then he opened the gateway to New Lassa. Right before it closed shut royal guards came running down the corridor towards the gate.

Safe.

Safe Advantage

Sunlight started to wane, casting shadows along the hilltop where Farin sat with her legs extended out. The breeze made her close her eyes and smile. Beside her, wrapped in soft cloths, was her newly born son gurgling happily. Her sudden unauthorized flight back to Lassa after realizing she was with child had her father angry, demanding she return soon. Something blocked the breeze so she opened her eyes and saw her mother towering over her.

"You need to get inside and rest."

"I'm fine."

She saw the look her mother gave and decided not to have a verbal fight. There was a sadness in her mother and she could guess where it stemmed from. Rolling over on her side, she picked up her baby then sat up to a kneeling position. A wave of weakness came over her and her mother was right there to steady her.

"It takes a lot out of you. Come," her mother said.

"I'm sorry," she whispered.

Her mother frowned.

"What for? You did nothing wrong."

"He has to stay hidden here on New Lassa and you'll end up having to care for him while I'm away."

"If it keeps him safe, I'd gladly do it. I just need you to be more careful. Your father has…changed."

Farin laughed. It was much more than that. Her father was being manipulated like a puppet and had gone insane with power. She couldn't tell her mother, who still loved him. There was a chance he might see reason and stop his madness. She looked down at her tiny son of three days. He looked more like her than Chastan but there was a hint of him in those tiny features. Such a beautiful lifeform who could not know his father until it was deemed safe.

"I'm so sorry." This she said for Chastan.

Farin held him close to her bosom as she slowly rose from the ground with the help of her mother.

"When does your father want you back on Azrom?"

"Four moons."

"And how long does he expect you to stay?"

"About the same. Mother," she met her gaze, "I'm afraid."

Her mother enclosed her and the baby in her arms. Farin relaxed her body and breathed in the scent of her mother's hair. When she let go, there was a wet stain on her mother's robe.

"Thank you, I needed that."

"I know," her mother replied. "Now stop stalling."

On the way down, Farin caught a glimpse of Trinon watching from a higher hill. She felt guilty for putting him in such a position. It was too late for that now.

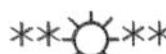

Romnus knew he wasn't being delusional when he saw Farin strolling along the outer corridor of the First Royal House's palace. He just couldn't fathom how no one else noticed. He watched her breasts nearly strain against her robes as they heaved up and down with every step she made. The slight color in her usually pale skin also gave it away. He decided to feign ignorance.

Her stride slowed as she spotted him and he gave her a broad smile as he opened his arms, waiting for her. It was something he always did lately whenever he saw her. Any excuse to lay his hands on her was a good tactic in his book. She slammed into him giggling, her hair covering his face and he inhaled deep. She smelled of open air after a rainfall. He dug his fingers into her hair to hold her closer to him and let the other hand trail down her spine to rest just above the curve of her buttocks. Her body relaxed and he could feel how soft she had become.

"Did you miss me?" she asked, looking up at him.

"Tremendously." Romnus reluctantly let her go and stepped back a bit. "I see you're defying your father's demands yet again."

Her face scrunched up and her stance stiffened.

"I am not a prisoner. He can't keep me locked away like that!"

"He shouldn't, but he will and can. Be careful, beautiful Farin." He brushed her cheek with the back of his hand and her head tilted into it.

"I will."

"Promise me." He gave her a serious look.

"I swear it." Farin smiled up at him again.

"Good. I believe Chastan will be glad to see you."

"Really?" She cocked her head.

He laughed, forgetting how observant she was assuming that Chastan took to the brothel more than most.

"Walk with me, Farin. Chastan can wait."

Her smile sent a shiver right down to his groin, forcing it to tighten.

Fortunately, patience was a trait he had an abundance of.

Even on the holoscreen hovering above in the newly constructed war room, the Dreridians' appeared made of rough rocks bond together, forming crags. Halfar stood glaring at Lord Pondur's smiling image. It had taken days for the connection to be established because he felt there was no rush to speak with them. As far as he was concerned, the Dreridians were also the enemy.

His two generals did not agree which infuriated him. The entire race should embrace his agenda and mirror his views. Something about the way Lord Pondur grinned made him wonder if the greedy trade merchant sensed it. Kur and Rass stood silent by his side.

"Lord Halfar, good to see you are well." Pondur bowed forward ever so slightly.

"Despite your part in the attempt to cripple my planet and my people, I am always victorious." He purposely left out addressing the Dreridian ruler.

"Til death!" every soldier in the room resounded.

A craggy brow lifted on Lord Pondur's face and he seemed amused by the outburst.

"Oh, Lord Halfar. We have no intention of letting you meet your demise. We simply helped out a desperate race who continued on a flawed plan."

"You gave those reptiles an advantage over us!"

"Did we?" Lord Pondur raised a delicate chalice to his stone cracked lips and took a small sip from it. "I am baffled by this. Did you not raze Razzna's surface, leaving them no choice but to flee?"

Halfar clenched his fists at his sides. He had no response to that so gritted his teeth to remain silent for a moment. The minute infiltration team that consisted of twelve Razznians was just a slight hiccup and he had to confess that yes, he overreacted to a small fleet entering Azrom space that his generals could, and did, handle.

"What do you want?" he finally asked.

"A meeting of course." Pondur took another small sip and set his chalice down beside him. In the background Halfar could see a lean figure bent over a handheld holoscreen, oblivious to the conversation.

"For what purpose?"

"Payment." Pondur leaned back and folded his hands in his lap.

Halfar could feel the rage building up inside him as he watched the Dreridian sit patiently waiting for his reply. Before he could, Pondur continued.

"Of course, we shall meet here on our home world. I fear my envoy would be in jeopardy if I were to arrive at Azrom."

"You would be correct," Halfar seethed.

"The Lassians must be in attendance as well."

"What?" Halfar jerked his head up to meet Pondur's gaze.

"This entire plan originated from the Lassians."

"Chardon had nothing to do with that plan!"

"Is Chardon not the leader of Lassa and responsible for any decisions made on behalf of his race, regardless of who made it? Sestis was his mate and also leader. Do the same rules not apply to Azrom?"

"When?"

"Let's say in three moons. I am sure you can prepare within that timeframe."

"And what of the Razznians?"

"Oh, they will be there as well." Pondur smiled again.

"How? You said they left Razzna."

"We were able to establish communication." Pondur waved a hand at the screen. "That is of no concern right now. You should bring any delegates necessary for the negotiations." Pondur tilted his head forward, not even attempting a bow. The holoscreen went black.

"That…" Halfar found he couldn't utter a single profanity. Too many phrases could be used and his mind didn't know which one to pick. He had a sour taste in his mouth.

Turning to his generals, he was about to ask their opinion when three of his royal advisors spoke ahead of him. They were here as observers only and Halfar was taken aback by their audacity.

"I believe this would be a great platform to reeducate them on Azrom ideals, my lord," Mesrod stated.

"Take Lord Romnus with you as a show of force," Prevcan suggested. "His brute demeanor would put them on edge."

Halfar saw Kur and Rass' jaws clinch tight and they remained silent.

Seeming to pick up on this, Dondar, his third advisor interjected.

"As revered as they are in battle, my lord, your generals are not schooled in the ways of commerce and politics."

In his mind, that made sense. He knew how devoted to Azrom his generals were but it was also true that they had little dealings with this side of rulership. Having his cousin there would show that he was not the only one with Azrom's future in mind.

"So be it," he announced. He returned his gaze back to Kur and Rass. "Make the preparations for a hostile encounter, just in case."

"As you wish, my lord," they replied in unison, bowing low.

Leaving the war room, he tried to figure out how much strength he could muster while in the same room as Razznians. He would not initiate a fight but would engage if they did. Now Lassa was to come to the table as well. He went to his chamber to talk with Chardon on his private commwave.

Chardon did a final check on his list of talking points as he headed towards the gate to meet up with Halfar on Azrom. From there, they would both journey to the Dreridian solar system. It was no mystery what they wanted and Chardon found Halfar's stubbornness to negotiate frustrating. He was starting to see a big change in his lover's demeanor and he didn't like it. He also noticed Halfar's harsher treatment of Farin and their youngest child, Chafar. At one point, Chardon heard rumors of royal guards mistreating Farin and hoped, for Halfar's sake, that it was just that; rumors.

Behind him, Modas trudged along silently. There was some unspoken agreement to not speak for the duration of the journey. Tension drifted off the manbeast. Farin was already on Azrom from the time before and,

Halfar assured him, under careful watch. Trinon was there so he didn't worry too much. The decision to go in male form was his own much to Halfar's dislike. Chardon had taken to hearing his own councils' suggestions and it was unanimous. Going as Halfar's mate would make it seem they had conceded New Lassa to Azrom. He didn't dare tell him that, knowing the ruler's tendency to lash out in anger, more so these past few years.

"Modas!" Chardon turned around and halted. The manbeast, startled out of his brooding, stopped in his tracks and looked up at him. "If conflict breaks out."

"We are prepared for that," said Modas with a raised a hand.

"Good. Let's get this over with."

Chardon eyed the entourage he had picked for the meeting. Talas, Modas, Mara and Ganna, the latter only as a necessity. He couldn't stand being in the same vicinity as the chief scientist yet he agreed with his choices; a Lassian warrior, a manbeast, an energy user and a mad scientist.

Let's see how they perform for the Dreridians.

Two vortices opened up side by side, their gaping mouths ready to eject what they had swallowed previously. From the first came a gleaming white monstrosity nearly a mile in its diameter, its massive body decelerating as it cleared the vortex. Halfar's Armada ship was the only one of its kind. The other vortex brought forth a ship blood red, nearly black in color, its red lights giving it the appearance of a giant insect. Though half the size of Azrom's, it appeared deadlier. The Razznians had arrived.

On what seemed like a timed maneuver, both ships sent out carriers towards the surface of the solar system's conquering planet. A guidance system locked on and brought them to the main docking hub of the commonwealth. The two ships weren't the only ones landing and the hub was bustling with activity.

An urge to vomit came over Chardon as the Azrom carrier settled into the designated slot before being clamped down. He had forgotten how much he hated traveling to other worlds for that reason. Out of the corner of his vision, he saw Lord Romnus raise an eyebrow at him with a grin on his face. In the face of possible humiliation, Chardon held back the nausea and rose from his seat.

He could see the Razznian ship docked catty corner from theirs on the right and rage came creeping in. *Not now!* Chardon forced it down. Halfar turned to him and a knowing look transpired between them. In the corridor leading out of the carrier, he noticed the size of their combined entourage. There were seven royal guards, four of them Halfar's, the two generals, his group and Lord Romnus'. They appeared to be coming for a fight indeed.

When he was visiting other worlds with Sestis, they had come to meet Lord Pondur once at an interstellar meeting in the Huun system. His mate at the time was quite comfortable making conversation with the diplomats but he stayed focused and only asked what was needed. He felt disappointment and guilt for not ceasing her downward spiral sooner.

On the platform below a Dreridian convoy waited for both ships' passengers to disembark. Chardon took a good look at the craggy skinned species in tailored wardrobes made of the finest textiles. They stood in a pyramid formation, a tall, portly male at the front. He wondered how different a diet this one had than the others.

To the right of their group came the Razznians and Chardon got his first look at their ruler. It was shocking to see the massive reptile lumber down his ship's ramp onto the platform, Commander Sars following close behind with his own men and six Razznian soldiers. Sars made eye contact with him and again that look of pity was on his face. It angered Chardon because he had no idea why the Razznian would feel that way towards him.

"Honored guests, I am Lord Greggor. Such a pleasure to welcome you to our fair home world." He made a slight bow with one arm across his chest, hand laid flat.

"Lord Greggor. To finally meet the creator of such fine machines is our honor." The Razznian ruler stopped his advance.

"The pleasure was mine, Lord Kraznan."

"Are we done with the stroking of ego?" Halfar spat.

"You are on their home world, Lord Halfar," Lord Kraznan retorted. "You should show respect. Or do you not require it of your own guests on Azrom?"

Halfar looked as if he had been physically assaulted into silence and Chardon feared there would be bloodshed. A hand brushed his shoulder and he saw Lord Romnus approach the Dreridians.

"My apologies, Lord Greggor. I am Lord Romnus of the First Royal House of Azrom." He bowed deep, as did his entourage, then turned to the Razznians and did the same. "Greetings, Lord Kraznan." Romnus stepped back behind Halfar's group.

Not knowing what to make of the situation as Halfar stood dumbfounded, Chardon made a bold decision and introduced himself as well.

"I am Chardon, the leader of New Lassa. We are grateful for your welcome, Lord Greggor. Greetings to you, Lord Kraznan." He tilted his head slightly. Deep enough to show some respect but just enough to show his place in all this.

Halfar was clenching and unclenching his fists several times until finally he too made a sweeping gesture, bowing nearly to his knees while keeping his eyes on the Razznians and Dreridians.

"Apologies. Lord Greggor, Lord Kraznan."

As he stood back up his overdramatic greeting cemented his obvious disdain.

Kur and Rass stayed back, glancing at each other. Chardon's skin crawled and he felt tiny raised bumps form as if the temperature had dropped. This meeting was not going to go well in his mind. He remembered his first interstellar campaign, where he met Halfar, and the lack of obedience amongst the different leaders.

"Come, this way," Lord Greggor commanded.

The conference chamber was larger than Chardon had expected and also unexpected was the other world leaders already present around the table. He recognized a few from his previous visits on their planets. The Yaos leader grimaced at him and he gave him an equal look back. All the guards were required to either stand against the walls or along the corridor outside. Chardon was glad to have just four people so they were able to sit at the table together. Halfar sat across from him along with his generals and only Lord Kraznan and Sars were seated near the edge.

A few minutes later, Lord Pondur entered the chamber and sat at the head of the table with Lord Greggor and a thin male not quite of the same height seating themselves on either side of him. Servants came carrying trays of beverages made to each representative's tastes. Chardon wondered how they would know and Lord Greggor answered his unspoken question.

"Please enjoy. I have done extensive research on your species and I'm sure you will find them quite accurate.

Ganna snorted as she stared at the chalice set in front of the Lassians.

"Extensive research, hmm? So how many of these species did you consume, Lord Greggor?"

Silence fell over the room and some halted their chalices inches from their lips. Lord Greggor laughed.

"I assure you, this comes strictly from chemistry."

The smile on his face told Chardon otherwise but he knew it would be rude to not partake. He watched the faces of the other diplomats come to the same conclusion and they all took a tiny sip. From his view above the chalice as he tilted it up, he saw Lord Greggor and Ganna engaged in a staring contest, a mutual understanding passing between them that made Chardon shudder.

Across from him, Halfar had the chalice in his hand, slowly swishing the liquid around. His gaze was on Lord Pondur who sat straight in his seat, legs crossed, and sipping his drink. Chardon turned to Mara who shook her head.

Lord Pondur set his chalice down and placed both hands on the table.

"Let's begin, shall we?" He scanned the room, making sure he had everyone's attention. Chardon found it unnecessary. They were all here to pay heed. "As you know, a small outbreak occurred between Azrom, Razzna and New Lassa. This tantrum was brought about by the Lassian female leader, Sestis who commissioned the Razznians to go up against Azrom."

"Such stupidity!" The Yaos leader exclaimed.

He sought approval from the other world leaders and received nods.

"Yes, I would agree. Because of all this, Azrom thought it necessary to send a hyper dimensional beam to Razzna, thus destroying much of the surface and collapsing the mines. Some of you at this table rely on Razznian ore for its many attributes and now it has become a rare commodity, driving the amount of barter to new levels. So now we have a dilemma."

"Who pays for the disruption in commerce and damage to trade?"

Lord Greggor piped in before taking a sip of his drink.

Chardon sat upright in his seat. New Lassa had nothing to offer in exchange for such a barter. Halfar seemed unfazed by this and the Razznians looked like they were prepared for it. Modas was frowning next to him with arms crossed over his chest.

"You look frightened Lord Chardon," Lord Pondur said.

All eyes fell on him. He wanted to leave the room but held fast. He was the leader of an entire race and would not show any more weakness.

"Frightened? No. I am just surprised you would involve us when you know we are just starting to adjust to a new planet."

"Yes, also because of Azrom's ill balanced judgement."

"What are the terms?" Halfar asked impatiently.

"My treasurer will explain." Lord Pondur gestured to the lanky Dreridian hovered over his handheld holoscreen.

The treasurer stood and cleared his throat.

"For exchange of natural resources to alleviate the debt, a rulership pact will be negotiated for each planet. Razzna will share joint ruling for one half century and we will install a new automated mining system. After the duration is complete, the system will have made up for the demand."

Lord Kraznan's lidless eyes narrowed into slits. He obviously didn't like the idea and Chardon didn't blame him, then he realized this may be New Lassa's fate as well. Anger welled back up.

"Since New Lassa is not on our trade client roster, we will have to establish what can be produced from the planet that is of value. An ambassador will be assigned to oversee production for one century."

"On Lassa's head you will not!" Ganna yelled as her fist slammed on the table.

Halfar turned sideways in his seat and leaned towards the Dreridians.

"This plan, it does not pertain to Azrom. I am supreme ruler, no one else." His eyes had that burning glow Chardon had witnessed only once and it signaled combat.

"Azrom will ramp up production of their mines with an ambassador for fifty years due to its level of stability in contrast with Razzna and New Lassa," the treasurer continued, paying Halfar no mind.

"There will be nothing of the kind!" Halfar yelled.

"Your juvenile confrontations have caused strife in our trade networks!" another leader roared. "This will ensure profits!"

"Maybe there is another alternative?" Romnus asked politely.

Lord Pondur cocked his head to one side and smiled.

"Ah, Lord Romnus. The next in line of succession who conceded his position for his younger family members."

Halfar whirled on his cousin.

"What do you think you're doing? WE are not negotiating!" He turned his attention back to Pondur. "If anyone should be compensated, it is Azrom for your poor judgement in assisting Razzna to harm us!"

Arguments broke out all around the table and the yelling formed a cacophony of sound that hurt Chardon's hearing. He tried to block it out, squeezing his eyes shut as he did so. It didn't work. Lord Romnus was sitting at the table calmly eating a fruit Biandra had plucked from her robes. His gaze was locked on Lord Pondur. Chardon watched some strange communication transpire between the two

"You know what I find interesting about your three races?" Lord Pondur spoke, his voice cutting through the sound. Everyone stopped arguing and turned to face him. "You only have an interest in technology when it applies to transport. To this day, you all insist on getting your own hands dirty in battle."

"It's called honor. We like to look our enemy in the eyes when we bring them to death's embrace," Halfar said through gritted teeth. "We don't mow them down behind their backs, unlike your kind."

"Of course we do, it is an element of war. Eliminate your enemy." Lord Pondur picked up his chalice and took another sip of his drink.

"You will not set foot on Azrom and take from us as you wish!"

"If Azrom does not agree to the terms, then all commerce from the Dreridian system will be blocked from Azrom. No new shipments will flow."

"Then so be it!" Halfar stood.

"Tread carefully, Lord Halfar. Your people need resources."

"If any of them cannot show strength for Azrom then they do not deserve my compassion!"

Chardon cringed in his seat as if he had been struck. The look and tone coming from Halfar was not the mate he knew. Catching a glance at Sars, he saw pity and finally realized what it was for. Halfar had always been known as a ruthless, cunning ruler but because he was in love with him didn't see how deep it went. Halfar had just condemned his people to an existence of strife. Lord Romnus had dropped his half-eaten fruit on the table and sat in a state of what could only be shock.

"We are leaving!" Halfar turned to the door and when no one followed him, he turned back around. A crazed wide-eyed stare formed on his face. Kur and Rass jumped up and went to his side. He looked over at Chardon. "Did you hear me?"

Chardon snapped out of his haze and their eyes locked.

"What is right for Azrom is not necessarily right for New Lassa. You can leave, but I am going to stay and negotiate for MY race."

The crazed look worsened.

"Do as you wish," Halfar spat and left the room.

"Good for you, leader!" Ganna exclaimed. "I knew you had it in you."

"I believe we should do separate negotiations from this point forward," Lord Pondur stated. He turned to the end of the table to his right. "Lord Romnus, are you staying on behalf of Azrom?"

Chardon didn't even realize he hadn't gone with Halfar. What was the royal thinking? He hoped it wasn't a tactic to go against his own ruler.

"I am just observing, Lord Pondur. Since Lord Chardon and Lord Halfar are mated I find it my duty to make sure New Lassa is not being raped by your greed." He looked at the other diplomats in the room. "Or theirs."

"And Azrom?"

"As I have asked, is there no alternative?"

"Are you negotiating, Lord Romnus?"

Chardon gave the royal a look that he hoped said 'don't do it'. Lord Romnus seemed to have noticed but there was something else.

"Is that not what you do?" Lord Romnus replied.

Lord Pondur smiled at that and sipped some more of his drink. Chardon felt a large boulder plummet into his gut. Things were not going so well. And throughout the entire session, Talas remained unnaturally silent. That alone frightened him.

A great divide had formed on the Azrom carrier when Chardon returned with Lord Romnus. No one spoke during the ride back to the Armada ship still orbiting the Dreridian home world. It was worse than any funeral march yet no one had died; not yet. Passing through the vortex, Chardon noticed the route was different and before he could ask, the ship came out on the other side into familiar territory. Halfar had brought them to New Lassa.

"Are we going to continue talks with my council?" He asked Halfar.

"I assume you are. I will not be joining." His level tone held contempt.

"So, you are just going to drop us down and go back to Azrom without at least seeing your offspring?"

"I will see them as I see fit. Do you really want me to come now?"

Chardon stood up in anger about to yell at him, finding Halfar's behavior unacceptable, when Talas clamped a hand around his wrist. Looking down at the warrior he saw Talas stare at him for a moment then let go.

"No. I suppose not."

"Escort them to the carrier and New Lassa," Halfar commanded his guards.

On the way to the hangar, Chardon felt uneasy in the presence of the royal guards. It seemed as though they harbored ill will against them. Talas walked in dead silence, keeping his fingers on the hilt of his longsword as they headed out.

The journey down to the surface was no better with communication nonexistent. Once the carrier landed, Halfar's guards remained seated and the hatch was opened remotely for his people. The lack of respect for his title and his race made Chardon wonder if it was by Halfar's decree or of their own doing. Within minutes after the last Lassian stepped onto the planet, the carrier was ascending back up towards the Armada ship.

Talas finally spoke.

"Well, that was eye opening, don't you agree, Ganna?"

"I believe that is an understatement. The audacity."

"They are more advanced than us and the others, for that matter."

"That does not give them the right to dictate those kinds of terms."

"But, you did not back down," Talas remarked. "And neither did you, Chardon. I'm glad."

"Yes, for one particular moment I thought we were going to have to have you removed as leader. Well done keeping our best interests at the forefront."

"Why do I feel like a child being praise for good behaving?" Chardon snapped.

"Don't take it as such," Talas said.

"Look, the council is waiting," Mara exclaimed, pointing ahead.

A large tent had been erected in the middle of a field and all the council leaders were assembled. With it being such a beautiful day out, he couldn't blame them for conducting the meeting outdoors. He turned to Ganna and for the first time, appreciated her presence. If it weren't for her knowledge and quick mind, they might be under Dreridian rule or at war.

"So, what did the Dreridians propose?" Jaron came strolling out from the crowd.

Chardon had that feeling of being chastised again. It never ceased to amaze him how Jaron kept up such a ruse, knowing she was more caring than anyone.

"Let's get it over with," he declared.

Modas stood outside the tent along with three other manbeasts, guarding all four corners. Chardon sat in the middle at the table while field workers came with bowls of produce and carafes of drinks.

"Ganna will explain. I am too exhausted and angry to do so." The council gave Ganna a wary look, an unease filling the room and Chardon sighed. Baby steps. "She was able to negotiate a deal better than any of us," he continued as he waved a finger at Talas, Modas and Mara.

"Well then," Ganna started, "I will tell you their proposal." She made herself more comfortable on her cushion. "They propose we let them research then harvest any valuable resources New Lassa may have for commercial trade under the supervision of a Dreridian ambassador for one half century."

Accusatory glances immediately came Chardon's way and his defenses went up. He could tell what they were thinking; that he caved in the face of the enemy. Ganna came to his rescue.

"Our leader refused their proposal and did not falter." Wide eyed shock was the response which offended Chardon even more. "We came to a compromise. I will offer my services in conjunction with their scientists to build clientele for New Lassa and release ten percent of any valuable resources we find to them as barter payment."

"No ambassadors?" the head of military asked.

"No dictatorship?" the head of agriculture asked.

"None of that," Ganna replied proudly.

"Then what are these services for? What does the Dreridians want?" This time Ganna frowned.

"Weapons."

"For them to use on other races, including ours?" the head of military cried out.

"Make no mistake! Whatever new weapons we jointly create, I will make sure is also in our possession as well. We will not be so far behind in technology as we once were."

"Once again, you have saved us from doom," Chardon said softly.

"It's what I do, leader. My only goal has always been to make Lassa capable of holding her own in the face of conflict."

"And we owe you gratitude for that. Though, we are still quite angry with you, I will concede to that." The nods around the table confirmed it. "Now if you'll excuse me. Ganna can take it from here?"

Chardon rose from the table and left the meeting, heading straight to Farin's personal chamber. Inside she found Farin on the bed playing with her child, making the little one let out an infectious giggle. He went and sat down on the bed next to her and used his fingers to join in tickling the baby's belly.

"How was the meeting?" Farin asked.

"Everything went well."

"And father?"

Chardon stopped tickling the baby for a second.

"It's worse than I could have imagined."

"He didn't come planet side to see me or Chafar." Farin looked over in the corner of the room and Chardon noticed her younger child slumped against the wall sleeping. He was covered in dirt and had a look of content on his face. "Why is father so angry? What happened at the meeting?"

"I stayed to negotiate for New Lassa after he refused to do so for Azrom. I told him what was good for his race did not mean it was for mine."

"Oh!" Farin's beautiful face scrunched up with worry. He hated seeing that. She should be happy but had to live like a prisoner. "His council is probably happy about it."

"I have no doubt. If his manic behavior causes harm to my people, especially you, I will show no mercy."

"Even though you love him?"

"More so because I do." He turned back to Chafar. "Why is he covered in dirt asleep on your floor?"

Farin giggled. "He's been training with the warriors."

"But he's an energy user."

"That doesn't mean he can't learn to fight in combat like a warrior, mother." The way Farin said it made Chardon feel like he had been restricting not only his children, but his race. "That's what's wrong with our people right now. No one is willing to cross share their knowledge."

Chardon sat up straight, her words hitting like a boulder to the chest. Farin was right. He always knew how observant she was but this was a whole new level on par with Talas or Trinon.

"You're correct, my child, and I am going to try and fix that."

****☼****

When the carrier touched down on the roof of Azrom's main palace, Lord Romnus immediately exited the opened hatch. His entourage kept in tight formation behind him and they swiftly made their way to his own palace, disregarding Halfar's royal guards' demanding they halt. The faster he distanced himself from his cousin, the better. His blood felt like it was boiling beneath his skin and he had no idea what would happen if he were to engage them at that moment.

The group nearly ran down the staircase adjacent to the palaces' dividing line then across the courtyard into his own. He steered them towards the communal hall and as he set foot over the threshold, let out a roar that turned into a high-pitched trill, lowering to a deep tone. The servants in the room became visibly shaken and some had covered their ears in vain as they passed out from the frequency.

Seated at the table, the heads of the first royal house family halted what they were doing, now staring at him in fear. He brushed his hair back from his face and stood tall. Biandra brought out a fruit from her robe's sleeve, handing it to him. His family members' stares, still wide with wonder, followed him as he sat at the head of the table and settled into the cushions.

"Halfar," Reita breathed.

"Halfar," he said.

"What happened? What was this meeting for?" Chastan asked.

"Apparently, the Dreridians wanted compensation."

"For what?" Kuhala yelled. "They helped the Razznians attack us!"

"Actually, no, they didn't." He saw the shock on their faces. "This was something set in motion long ago by Chardon's former mate. The Dreridians do not want compensation for anything regarding that."

"Then what?"

"By our retaliation against Razzna, we have essentially destroyed commerce for the ore they mine, which was already a high valued commodity. Azrom is being held responsible for that."

"But we were in the midst of a battle!" Chastan cried out.

"That did not warrant our cannon be fired to raze the surface of Razzna," Romnus shot back.

"I do agree, it was overly aggressive," Kuhala said.

"Halfar refused to negotiate and left the meeting."

"But, that also affects our trade."

"Exactly. A blockade has been placed on Azrom."

Reita leaned forward, terror on her face.

"Our people need many of those outside resources! We have not recovered from the last great war over a century ago!"

"Our people will starve and live in worse conditions than they already are. The battle with Razzna did us no favors," Lord Aloni, who hardly ever spoke, added. He had recovered from the initial shock of Romnus' entry and was now engaged. Romnus felt relief, worried that Aloni would remain quiet.

"I know."

Romnus took a bite of the fruit in his hand and felt the effect of its nectar course through his body. A normal Azromian would be put down like a death blow, the sedative juices being so strong but it only managed to calm him down.

"What do we do?" Chastan asked.

"Nothing."

"What?" Reita and Chastan yelled at once.

"We have to wait and see," Aloni replied. "If it becomes clear Azrom is indeed going to be crippled, we will act. Until then," he tapered off.

"Out!" Halfar roared.

He had made it to the throne room and his two advisors went to brief their colleagues while he settled himself on his throne. For what seemed like an hour, he had sat fuming before deciding he wanted to be alone. The decibel of his command made everyone flinch and they fled from the room. Now alone, he went over the meeting in his mind, unable to forgive Chardon for going against his demand to leave.

His advisors slowly crept back into his throne room some time later and bowed deep at his feet. The mock fear gleaming in their eyes was a joke. They were not afraid of him by any means because their job was to help him rule.

"My lord, I truly understand your anger. That was a blatant defiance on your mate's part." Prevcan began.

"Which is why we are so adamant in finding a true Azromian to be at your side. Only one of our own can relate to Azrom's needs." Mesrod's lips curved up.

"You must also find a way to keep Farin in check when she is here." Dondar added his opinion.

"I propose you have her visit only twice a cycle for no more than four moons until she is mated." Mesrod suggested.

"Her manbeast is not efficient in watching her and should be left on New Lassa. Our royal guards are quite capable of doing the task, maybe even better." Prevcan stated.

Halfar nodded in agreement at the bombardment of ideas. He would not monopolize Farin's time on Azrom but he did see reason to get rid of the manbeast. Countless times he had to send guards out to find her when she snuck out of her chamber. Chardon would be angry. He no longer cared. This was for the sake of his race, not Lassa's as it was told to him.

"Agreed. I will discuss this matter with them on their next visit."

"Very well, my lord," Mesrod said. He bowed deep along with the others and he was alone once again.

The five advisors walked slowly down the outer corridor enjoying the midafternoon air. Royal guards bowed to them as they passed.

"This is coming to fruition better than we had planned," Prevcan remarked.

"Yes, we can get rid of the manbeast, give that halfbreed to some high ranked soldier or lower royal and have the people of Azrom in the palms of our hands," Jabarz piped up.

"There will be dissent," Dondar warned.

"Of course, but it can be easily squelched with the right discipline. Fear is always a great motivation to stay obedient," Mesrod answered.

"What of the first royal house? They are helping the destitute," Calba asked.

"Let them. That is of no concern and they are no threat. We have an entire royal army at our disposal and no matter how strong they are, can- not fight such might." Mesrod waved a hand as if brushing it off.

They all smiled, bowing in greeting to some of the royals visiting by appointment only.

Yes, it's all going well, Mesrod thought to himself.

∗∗☼∗∗

The gate opened and the rooftop of Azrom's main palace came into view. Chardon, back in female form for Halfar's sake, stepped onto the platform with Farin, Chafar and Trinon beside her. Modas had become unbearable and so she commanded him to stay on New Lassa. She could defend herself if need be but had never come into harm's way on Azrom since the battle.

In front of her stood two advisors and four royal guards. Not a good sign. Halfar always greeted them when they visited. She turned to Trinon who also seemed disturbed by this.

What is happening?

"Lady Chardon, Lady Farin and," Mesrod paused, "Young Lord Chafar. How wonderful to see you again. "Our Lord has been so busy lately. I am sure he would appreciate some personal time."

"Is he well?"

"Of course. He's just in the middle of restructuring some logistics. Come, let's get you settled." The way he waited for them to move gave Chardon the impression that it was an order, not a request. "A small banquet for just the family is being prepared." He smiled.

Chardon nodded to his group and they followed with two guards ahead and two positioned behind them like prisoners led to the dungeon. A hand brushed against hers and clasped it. Farin was shaking. Chafar's full lips went thin seeing that. She knew he hated being on Azrom and this situation was only going to make it worse.

They first led Chafar to his chamber, leaving two guards at the entrance, then Farin and Trinon, doing the same. At her own personal chamber, Chardon sighed.

So I am not staying with Halfar.

Two guards were position at her entrance as well.

"We will come to escort you to evening meal later. Please, rest until then."

"I wanted to take a walk in the gardens," Chardon said.

"Oh? I think you should rest for the day. We will discuss a trip to the gardens tomorrow, perhaps?"

"There will be no perhaps. What is going on?"

"Nothing, I assure you. If you insist, I will have the guards escort you."

"They never have before."

"Things are different now, aren't they?" Mesrod gave her a look that said she was to blame for this.

"Fine, bring my children and Trinon so we can go on a family stroll before mealtime."

Chardon watched the advisor's eyes narrow even as he smiled in acknowledgement.

"As you wish."

He left with his partner and the royal guards.

Evening meal was fraught with such tension that Chardon almost couldn't eat. An awkward silence set heavy above them like a veil of smoke. Having had enough, she slammed her fist down on the table, the bowls jumping up off the surface and landing with a melody of clanks. Halfar looked up from his platter and stared at her with such contempt that she reared back away from him. Trinon's claws came out as he stood in the vicinity behind her.

An advisor came over to Halfar and whispered in his ear. His face changed and he sighed heavily.

"What is it, my love? Is the food not to your liking?"

"No! You will not be cordial to me because your advisors think you should! If we are not welcome here then we leave!"

Chardon stood up and gestured for her children to do the same. A mortified look fell on Halfar's face.

"Wait!" He stood and held a hand out in front of him. "Don't go. I'm sorry. It has been a stressful time and not my intention to take it out on all of you."

His advisors seemed displeased with his outburst and Chardon claimed victory.

"Is that so?" she asked.

"Yes. Chafar, come. I am sorry to have neglected you lately."

Chafar slowly got up from his seat and went to his father. Where Halfar's embraces was tight, Chafar's was lackluster. When he let go, he gestured for Farin who also reluctantly went to him. They sat back down and Trinon retracted his claws.

"Please, let's finish our meal," Halfar suggested.

Conversation was light and Chardon could hear nothing. Her mind had turned the volume down to nearly white noise as she continued to eat while watching everyone else's mouths move. It should not be this way.

"Shall we retire to bed? It is later than we thought." Halfar's voice cut through the deafening static.

"I have not finished arranging my chamber so I will be up regardless."

"What do you mean? My chamber is always prepared."

She saw his advisors squirm.

So it's not Halfar's doing.

He looked around the table and then at his advisors before returning her gaze.

"I am in a personal chamber of your advisor's choosing."

"What?" Halfar's soft tone peppered with malice sent shivers down her spine.

"You have been so busy, my lord. I felt some rest alone would do you good until tomorrow, at least." Prevcan stumbled over his words.

"You made a decision FOR me?"

"My apologies, my lord," he said, bowing deep.

"I am sorry," Halfar said to her. "We do have things to discuss, but that can come later." He stood up from the table and came around to her with his hand held out. "Please, come with me."

Chardon glanced over at her children who nodded. She took his hand and let him lead her out of the banquet hall. He had that familiar mischievous grin she loved on his face and for a second, she forgot that he was on the verge of losing his mind.

It didn't take long for her to be reminded when they reached his chamber. He literally tossed her onto the bed then climbed on top of her, tearing at her robes. She heard the fabric rip as he grabbed hold of them at the collar and pulled. They splayed open all the down, the sash torn in half, and he laid the tattered edges at her side.

Hunger. Rage. Those were what she saw in his eyes.

He stripped naked and wrapped his hands around her knees, pulling her to him violently. She tried to get loose from him even as he plunged into her like some wild beast. When she was able to get leverage and attempted to turn from underneath him, he surprised her by partially morphing one arm and bringing the pincer a hair from her neck. They opened and embedded themselves into the pillows beneath her head, holding her neck down. She didn't dare move as the tiny teeth of the pincer made contact with her skin.

Each thrust was more painful than the one before and she thought right before passing out that he was going to kill her.

The pain came back fiercely along with a garbled sound. She forced her eyes open and found Halfar looming over her in a state of panic. His hands were gripping the sides of her face and he seemed to be yelling. A look of relief came over him and his hands slid down to her shoulders.

"I'm sorry," he cried in a weak voice.

That brought her out of the blurry space she was in. She had never seen Halfar cry. The tears were big and dripped down onto her breasts like rain. Then everything changed. He looked up at her and the tears stopped. Sitting up, he wiped his face and climbed off her. That expression was the same as that advisor's; this was her fault.

Halfar dressed quickly and headed out the chamber. Before he disappeared around the corner she heard the orders he gave the guards.

"See that she is escorted to her own chamber before I return at sunrise."

By morning, Chardon had recovered and rounded up her children with the help of Trinon to make way towards the gate. She would not stay on Azrom any longer nor her children. Halfar had changed into a being she didn't know. Their psychic bond so strong before was nowhere to be found, the severed link between them painful. In her plan to escape, she and Trinon had to knock out their guards in order to buy time and they had made it to the gate.

Halfar and his royal guards were not a minute behind them. There he stood ever the supreme ruler. Two of his advisors were with him as well and Chardon cast an evil stare at them. They just smiled.

"Where are you going?" Halfar demanded.

"Home."

"I never asked you to leave," he yelled.

"You didn't have to," Chardon snapped.

Halfar made a nod and four guards came at Farin, grabbing her by the arms. Trinon drew claws and Chardon let energy grow in her hands. As they both prepared to strike the guards, Halfar stood between them and his guards.

"Stop!"

"Let go of my child!" Chardon yelled back.

"Farin stays here with me." He looked over at Trinon as he signaled ten more guards to cover him. "Without the manbeast. We have no need for him. We can protect her on our own."

"Why would she need protection?" Chafar asked loudly.

Halfar was taken aback by his son's question and Chardon felt ill.

Yes, why?

She watched the rough way the guards handled her child and unleashed a ball of energy on them. Farin got herself out of the way in time.

"What are you doing?" Halfar roared. "She will be back in four moons!"

"If I ever see or hear of you or any of your so called royal guards treat my child this way again I will never forgive you. And I will come back and kill every last one."

The gate was activated, forming the vortex that would send her back to New Lassa. In that moment, as she turned away from Halfar, she vowed to keep that promise.

Halfar turned away from the gate and looked down on the two half dead guards on the ground. Farin was unharmed but shaken. This is not what he wanted. It was only to keep Farin safe while on Azrom, nothing more. The way Chardon looked at him as she left felt like he had been run through with a longsword. Realizing he had an audience, Halfar regained his demeanor and started giving orders.

"Take these guards to the medical bay. I want a meeting with the councils before evening meal. Bring my child to the throne room." He looked down on her then and the endless disobedience filled his mind.

Two other guards picked her up after Halfar walked away. He didn't look back because he might witness them manhandling her again. As long as he didn't see it, he could feign ignorance. A pain stabbed him at the thought yet he decided to dismiss it.

In the throne room, he sat letting his gaze bear down on Farin as he took a good look at her. She was indeed beautiful and well-rounded for mating. He could see the four guards he had assigned to her leer in the corridor. A certainty that they would never touch her for he would surely kill them was his reassurance.

"You are to stay in your chamber unless otherwise requested," he spoke to her sharply. "You will only stay four moons and only twice a cycle. That is until I find an appropriate mate for you. Do you understand me?"

Farin just stood there unmoving with her head down.

"Do you understand?" He yelled.

She looked up then, tears in her eyes. "Yes."

"Yes, what?"

"Yes, father."

"Yes," Halfar rose up from his throne, "what?"

"Yes, my lord," she cried out softly between sobs.

"Good." Halfar sat back down. "Take her to her chamber," he ordered the guards.

He turned his head away as they came and dragged her out of the throne room. Even with his eyes averted he could still see the way they held her. It's for her own good. Halfar felt that pain again and forced it away. He had no time for pity.

The bonding ceremony for Kur and Rass was getting closer by the hour. Servants ran to and fro setting up the banquet hall and arranging flowers. In their chamber were six tailors doing last moment alterations of the ceremonial robes. Kur glanced over at the one he was to wear and frowned. It looked heavy and gaudy. The fabric was pearl with gold and silver accents, the inside a light shimmering green. White leggings and a gold tunic were picked for his undergarment.

"Such beautiful work, isn't it?" The master tailor beamed.

"Of course it is," Kur replied.

Rass had been sent off to a stylist for her hair. He was angry about that. Rass' hair was just fine the way it was. The idea of them doing unnatural things to it gave him pause. Lord Romnus came into the chamber, took one look at his wardrobe and raised an eyebrow.

"Not my choosing," Kur explained.

"No."

Kur peeked around. "No entourage this afternoon?"

"They are further down the corridor making sure no one disturbs us."

Kur clapped his hands and gestured towards the entrance. Everyone set down their work and left the chamber. He turned to Romnus.

"What has happened now?"

"I want you to get Lady Farin out of her chamber."

"She is to attend the ceremony. Her guards have escorted her to the bath already is what I was told."

"Then I will fetch her from there."

"Romnus, this is a dangerous plan. Halfar keeps her on a short tether."

"All the more reason to snatch her, even for a day and make him relent."

"Don't ruin my bonding ceremony, Romnus," Kur warned.

"I would do no such thing. Oh," he said as he went to the corridor, "don't worry about Rass. Your mother is quite capable."

"My mother?"

"She has many talents. One of them just happens to be a stylist. Congratulations, General."

Romnus led his entourage down the bathing corridor in a near run. He had a sinking feeling in the pit of his stomach and couldn't squelch it. As they neared the royal sector, he held up a hand for his entourage to hold while he continued on. He found the bath chamber she was in by the two guards at the entrance in relax formation looking in laughing. From his distance he could also see inside and the blood drained from his face.

One of the guards had walked in just as she was reaching for the towel held by the attendant to dry herself. The attendant was pushed away and the guard slammed Farin into the wall, the side of her face planted firmly against it. He grabbed her wrists and held them up above her head with one hand while he inserted the other between her buttocks and squeezed her flesh before gliding it up her back.

"You should really dry yourself off, Lady Farin before you become prone to illness," he sneered in her ear. Letting go, he smacked her ass and threw the towel at her. The attendant moved to leave the room but the other guard stopped him.

"Do your job properly next time or our lord will hear about it."

All four guards positioned themselves at the entrance, proud of their little stint. Romnus approached them then and they looked up at him with contempt. He smiled and morphed both his arms into giant pincers. The guards went pale and moved out of his way.

"Thank you." Romnus returned his arms back to normal and entered the bath.

The attendant was shaking from fright so he placed a hand on the man's shoulder and nodded for him to step away. Farin too was shaking but a look of defiance set on her fair facial features. He knelt and carefully wrapped his arms around her from behind. Her body went limp and fell into him.

"I will save you from this, my beautiful Farin. I promise. Just hold on a little while longer."

"Okay," she whispered.

Romnus turned his head back to the entrance. The guard who had assaulted Farin stared at them then smirked. Recalling the guard's name; Batis, he gripped Farin tighter. A hopelessness engulfed him.

The main palace hall was nearly bursting at the seams close to over capacity. Representatives from all four royal houses were in attendance for the bonding ceremony of their newfound royal brethren who just happened to also be one of the Armada Generals. That he was bonding with the other General made the occasion even more significant. Halfar didn't find it all that joyous and he was put off by the number of royals in his main palace.

His advisors told him this was a necessity, a show of good faith. They also insisted that Farin be let out for the festivities as well. After much thought, he agreed. Not having Farin attend would stir up questions he had no intention of answering. He had even granted Romnus' request to have her stay in the first house palace for a few days after the ceremony.

Being a guest in his own domain infuriated him but he knew he had to endure. The supreme ruler did officiate bonding ceremonies, yet he felt the council should have made an exception considering the strife Azrom was currently in. Of course, if he had been asked to do it, he would have denied the request for union. It was so much better when his generals hated each other. He remembered the hesitation in Rass to kill Kur on Earth.

Was there ever really hate?

The head of the council for domestic affairs entered the hall from the left entrance and walked up to stand on the platform overlooking the guests. Two of his councilmen came to stand on either side of him and a hush fell over the hall. Halfar turned his head to watch. His table was near the platform where the newly bonded couple would sit after the ceremony. As supreme ruler he demanded that they not sit side by side. He would be between them, his advisors noting that he must always be the center of attention even in events such as this one.

"Greetings, my lord," the official said, bowing low, "and honored guests. Let us rejoice in the bonding of our two finest warriors, Kur, General and Lord and General Rass."

Ethereal music combined with the tinging of chimes echoed through the hall and at the entrance appeared Kur and Rass. Halfar had never seen them in royal attire, and was awestruck by the sheer sparkling of their dress but mostly how enticing Rass looked in female form draped in royal fabric.

Her hair had been manipulated and styled into large bouncing coils that shined as if lacquered. The gown was the same shiny green color as the inside of Kur's robe and it complemented her skin. Each stitch of embroidery matched the other's attire. Jealousy and lust consumed him and it took every fiber of his being not to jump up and cancel the ceremony.

Kur and Rass made their slow secession down the aisle created by the masses who preened and whispered well wishes as they passed. Kur assisted Rass up the narrow stairs to the platform and there they halted side by side in front of the official.

"Do you swear devotion to each other even in death?"

"I swear this," they both said together.

"You will demonstrate your proof." He nodded to the councilman on his right.

A knife was produced, and the couple held out their wrists. With one swift cut, the councilman sliced both at the same time without blood splatter. The thin cuts stayed fused for a moment then opened, spilling blood that dripped down into chalices placed directly beneath each arm.

When the chalices were half full, the second councilman came with fabric folded in his arms. He unraveled it and bringing the two wrists together, bound them with it, stopping the blood flow.

The councilmen each picked up a chalice and handed Kur's to Rass and Rass' to Kur. Halfar had seen a few bonding ceremonies and it always fascinated him when the couples stared at the chalice of each other's blood for a moment before tentatively drinking it, taking forever. To his shock, that didn't happen. Kur and Rass stared at each other without averting their eyes as they downed the contents of the chalices in one gulp then handing them back.

Small cheers and sounds of astonishment went softly around the hall. The official nodded in approval and placed his hand on the wad of fabric covering their wrists.

"By Azrom's decree, you are now Lord and Lady of the first royal house. Present yourselves."

He removed his hand and let them turn to the guests. They bowed deeply and the thunderous clapping began mixed with more cheers. The fabric was removed, the councilmen checking to make sure the wounds were sealed, then replaced it with shiny green ribbon on each.

"The bonding is complete!"

"Not until their mating after evening meal," Halfar heard Chastan chuckle.

He looked over at the table next to his where his first cousins sat. Chastan had been drinking already. He assumed it was before the ceremony. His servants wouldn't dare sneak the young lord a drink in his presence.

The bonded couple was escorted down the platform and to their seats at Halfar's table. Kur was to his right and Rass to his left. A strained kind of atmosphere occurred and he smiled. To separate the newly bonded was in bad taste.

"Let the festivities commence!" Halfar shouted gleefully.

At his command, the food and drink began to flow.

On Rass' left sat Farin in a royal blue gown and he saw the two clasp hands under the table. He wondered what that was for. Farin did not smile and picked at her meal when it was placed in front of her. It angered him. So much so that he leaned close to Rass' ear and whispered.

"Tell my child to enjoy your special occasion or I will rescind my blessing."

Rass' eyes went wide and she turned to him. He smiled back at her and she in turn did what she was told. Farin struggled with her facial expression until the corners of her mouth peaked upwards into a small smile, yet her eyes were dull. He felt eyes on him and looked to his right. Kur and the rest of the first royal house were assessing him like he was some kind of pariah. Smirking, he went back to his meal.

One by one, the royal house representatives came to the table to greet Halfar and congratulate the bonded couple. Romnus sat back in his seat and observed his cousin relishing in the fact that he was wedged between the two. In the far corner he could see the advisors delighted with the outcome. A clanking sound from his side made him avert his stare to see Chastan had knocked over a chalice.

"If you cannot keep Farin safe this night or any other these next few days, I will gladly find someone else who can," he whispered to Chastan. Startled, Chastan's head popped up and he looked around his table, then at Farin on the far end of Halfar's. He glanced down at his spilled chalice and frowned. A servant came to right it and was about to refill it when he clamped his hand over the mouth. The servant bowed and walked away.

"You are letting Chastan be responsible for Farin?" Kuhala laughed softly. "Please, let me handle this. He is of no use."

Chastan slammed his fist on the table.

"I won't let anyone harm her! Ever!"

Romnus grimaced. It was safe to say that Chastan will have sobered up by the end of the banquet and there would be no issue. For added assurance, he had Farin drink a concoction earlier that, unbeknownst to her, destroyed the male seed should it find itself in her womb. He was certain of her fertility and the last thing they needed was her impregnated, again.

****☼****

The opening vortex added strength to the wind on the platform atop the main palace. Chardon hesitantly stepped onto its surface and felt the gate close behind her. Standing next to her was Und in place of Trinon. She didn't want to be here but had to make sure Farin was okay before taking her home to New Lassa for a while until the next visit per Halfar's insistence. Hearing about Kur and Rass' ceremony and not being invited made her fume.

Ahead of her were four royal guards and Dondar. He had a grin on his face so she conjured a ball of energy for him. His grin faded, replaced with a look of fear.

"That is not necessary, Lady Chardon!"

"Is it not? I am under the impression that I was to fight my way to my child by any means."

"I assure you, Lady Farin is well," he glanced at the guards who refused to engage him. "I will take you to her first."

"That is what I want, thank you."

She turned to Und. He took a quick look back at her. This was hostile territory. The quicker they grabbed Farin and left the better they would both feel.

At the entrance to Farin's chamber, Chardon saw the four royal guards stationed there and the rage returned. There was no reason for Halfar to set that many on his child for the sole purpose of confinement. The leader of the guards, Batis, caught sight of her and frowned. She wanted nothing more than to have Und slice him apart. His look let her know he underestimated her. Big mistake.

Chardon went up to him and holding back her full might, backhanded him across the face, sending him flat on the ground. Blood trickled from his mouth and his comrades went to unsheathing their weapons while Und grew claws. The advisor clasped his hands together.

"Do not engage!" he ordered the guards. "Lady Chardon, I am not sure why you insist on," he was not allowed to finish.

"You think I don't know how my child has been treated here? As her mother, I want to remind them that she is not just Halfar's and I will not tolerate it in my presence. I thought I made myself clear before. I will administer punishment every time I am here until treatment of my child is resolved." She looked down at Batis as he moved to get up.

Chardon went into the chamber and climbed on the bed. Farin was in a deep sleep, one filled with struggle as she watched her child tremor, small sounds of terror emitting from her lips. She stroked Farin's forehead damp with sweat.

"Und," she called. The manbeast came further into the chamber and stood by the bed's side. "Wet me a cloth." As he did so, she turned to the advisor and the now six guards at the entrance. "You can leave."

"Lady Chardon, these guards are assigned," again she did not let him finish.

"They are not needed here. My kind can protect her at this juncture," she sneered throwing Halfar's words back at the advisor.

"Very well. I will have you escorted to the throne room when it is time for departure. I am sure our lord would want to see you off.

"Good, I will relish in the three days of peace."

She watched them leave, Batis giving her a look of vengeance. He was of no concern to her and the last person she wanted to see was Halfar. As much as she still loved him, she knew there was no reasoning with him. It may be his death that stops his madness this time.

****☼****

The corridor was mostly empty during early afternoon and Halfar took advantage of this by roaming it without guards to his destination. He did request they position themselves moments after reaching his goal to ensure no one disrupted him. The sun was at its brightest making the outer corridor gleam like white pearl. His palace was such a beautiful structure, he laughed inwardly.

He stopped at the entrance of the chamber he wanted and stood looking inside it. The room was much bigger than the previous chamber the residents had occupied and allowed more light in. Cream walls, light colored floor coverings and sheer green and white fabric covered the tops of the bed. The bedding was the same cream as the walls with green undercovers peeking out.

On the bed lay Rass sleeping on her side in a white robe, her hair in disarray. It had been two moons since the bonding ceremony and both his generals were present less and less in the war room. No matter. He could easily strip them of their positions if he wanted, although his advisors warned him against such a move. Right now, all he wanted was to impregnate Rass for the glory of Azrom and his own ego.

He walked further in to stand at the foot of the bed and waited for Rass to feel his presence. It didn't take long. Rass slowly raised her head from the pillow and wiped sleep from her eyes. They stared at each other and Halfar saw the panic in her even though she tried to remain calm. He could tell from the way she was sleeping that she had been mating with Kur only this morning. So, she's weak from exhaustion.

"Stay away from me," she said.

"You dare order your lord?" Halfar yelled. He climbed onto the bed and yanked the covers from her body.

"Don't do this!"

"You will submit to me." He growled in her ear as he leaned down onto her.

"I will fight you," she cried out.

"That won't stop me. I don't need you conscious to accomplish my goal."

Rass's eyes widened and he knew what she saw in him. Deep seeded lust. His guards were already at the entrance to wave away anyone who neared the chamber. To his surprise, Rass morphed an arm and moved to strike. He dodged it and landed a blow to her side but that only angered her and she was able to counter with a direct hit to the back of his shoulder blade. He moved forward to lessen the impact, knowing it could have easily cracked the bone.

Grabbing hold of her ankle, he was able to pull her fully off the bed and into the air, smacking her against the headboard. It cracked into pieces as she landed back on the bed. Upset from the time being wasted, he ripped the robe off her and held her down by a pincer, removing his leggings while she still lay disoriented.

Kur hurried along the corridor to his chamber with Aloni and Kuhala. Romnus had suggested at his bonding ceremony that he invest in a private intel to watch his chamber from the satellite castle across the way. He thought it would be useful and so he was stricken with fear when the report came in that Halfar and two of his royal guards were at his chamber. Rass had been sleeping when he left this morning. Supreme Ruler or not, he would strike him down if Rass was desecrated in any- way. He knew Rass would fight and there would be blood, but if Halfar somehow got his seed in her, the next round of bloodshed would be his.

He wasted no time and struck down the first guard as he came up to his chamber entrance. Kuhala took down the other and they all advanced into the room. Halfar was straddling a naked, half-conscious Rass. Kur noticed the torn beddings, the destroyed headboard and blood splatter. Halfar stopped his penetration and sat still. Then he turned and met eyes with him.

Three against one. Kur made his decision. Halfar was stronger than him but if the other two backed him up, there could be a chance. He was about to strike when Aloni stopped him and nodded to the entrance. Royal guards, six of them, were blocking it and he felt his heart sink. Halfar's face scrunched into a frown and Kur was confused until he looked back again and saw behind them, Romnus' royal guards.

"You will leave this quadrant of the first royal house, my lord," the captain of Romnus' royal guard demanded.

"What did you say?" Halfar replied. His eyes went red.

The unsheathing of longswords was like a hurricane ripping out trees. Kur lifted his own and went into a battle stance.

"Get off my beloved," he said calmly.

Halfar disengaged himself from Rass and pulled his leggings back up. He slowly slid off the bed and stood in front of Kur. They didn't move for a long time. Halfar stepped around him and went to his royal guards.

"Sheath your swords. We're leaving." He turned back to Kur. "I get what I want."

Kur didn't drop his sword.

"No, you won't. She belongs to me."

As they left, leaving Romnus' guards in the corridor, Kur dropped his sword with a loud clank and crawled onto the bed, gathering Rass in his arms. Her eyes were glazed over and blood seeped from the back of her head. A high pitched raspy cry came out of him in short succession and he couldn't stop it.

Halfar sat on his throne seething, his urges not satiated. He couldn't figure out how Kur knew to come and interrupt his fun. For a few brief moments he felt the familiar warmth of being inside his former slave despite her being only half conscious. That Kur was going to fight him head on was laughable.

An echo of boots forced him out of his reverie and three advisors came into the room. They bowed deep at the bottom of the throne.

"My lord, it is time for Lady Farin to depart with her mother to New Lassa. I informed her that you would like to see them off."

"What? Chardon is here?"

Halfar brought up the date in his mind and realized it was indeed time for Farin to leave.

On cue, Farin's four royal guards came escorting her along with Chardon and Und. He reared back in his throne. Chardon did not look up at him. Her expression was that of disinterest.

"Chardon, my love," he said sweetly, "I was not informed of your arrival. When did you?"

"Three days ago, my lord," his advisor answered for her.

She won't speak to me.

Halfar felt that pain creep in and this time it lingered. He realized that no matter how good Rass felt, it was nothing compared to Chardon. But, this was all her fault. If she had just been loyal to him, he wouldn't have to hurt her, alienate her. She was not of Azrom, as his advisors constantly pointed out. He came down from his throne and went to stand before them.

"I should have been informed of your arrival. Come, we can talk on our way to the platform."

He was leading them to the side exit by the throne when a loud ruckus traveled down the corridor and into the room.

"Dear cousin, I have warned you on so many occasions and I feel we are not communicating well."

Lord Romnus stood in his throne room with a full battle-ready unit of royal guards behind him as well as Kur and three other royals. He had a smile that conveyed disappointment, and malice.

"Lord Romnus, what brings you unannounced into my throne room?" Halfar motioned with his head and twenty royal guards surrounded them. He glanced at Chardon who halted and turned to see what was going on.

"When your advisors suggested you find a vessel for your pure-blooded offspring, I was amused by it. But the fact that you went after the mate of a lord in the first royal house, namely Lord Kur's mate, I find it disrespectful and unbecoming of a supreme ruler."

"Halfar," Chardon whispered, "tried to impregnate General Rass? For a pure blood?"

"Oh yes, in the most violent way. Lucky for you, cousin, she recovers quickly." Romnus moved closer. "Make no mistake that any other incident such as this will be a declaration of war."

"Let's not move too hastily," Prevan cried out. "I am sure there has been some misunderstanding, as you've stated.

"I was not mistaken when I decided to strike him down if he did not climb off of my beloved," Kur replied.

Silence. Halfar felt panic.

Chardon glanced at him then Kur, her eyes hooded.

"I am so sorry, you had to endure such a thing," she said to Kur. "Please tell Rass I offer the love of Lassa up to her." She placed a hand on Farin's back. "Let's go home."

Romnus turned away, his entire entourage following. Kur gave him one last look before leaving the throne room. Halfar clenched his fists and went after Chardon. She was already ahead of him at the elevator that ascended to the gate's platform. He made it just as the pod activated to go up. They all rode up without saying word. The pain inside him was almost unbearable.

The gate was already in flux when they arrived on the platform, a vortex forming as they reached the threshold.

"Chardon," he called to her. She stopped but didn't turn around. "It was for the sake of Azrom," he snapped. "You would do the same for your race!"

Farin held a hand to her mouth, tears streaking down her cheeks. Und glared at him from a sideways glanced.

"Goodbye Halfar. Farin will be back as promised."

The trio walked off into the vortex and disappeared. Halfar found himself alone with the exception of the gate operator. Hate filled him. He just wasn't sure if it was towards her or himself.

An atmosphere of tension and heat engulfed the entourage of the first royal house stemming from Romnus but mostly General Kur. It put Biandra on edge and she deliberated with herself on whether to hand her master the small fruit that would calm him down or give it to General Kur. She had waited in the corridor as instructed to ensure safe distance in case a battle erupted in the throne room. Deep within her soul she knew there would be a declaration of war between the royal houses and the supreme ruler in short time. From what she witnessed, Lord Halfar was not in control of the palace or himself.

Despite her misgiving, she reached into her robe and pulled out one of the small fruits. She barely got it held up to his shoulder when he smacked her hand away. The intake of air from his soldiers made him halt. Her skin became clammy and she braced herself for whatever verbal onslaught he was about to unleash.

Nothing.

She peeked up and saw Lord Romnus staring at them all with a wildness only seen in beasts. Then it softened replaced with shame. He inhaled, holding it in, then exhaled slowly before holding his hand out to her. She set the fruit in his hand and quickly hid her own. There was a bruise forming and he didn't need to see that. Lord Romnus prided himself on never hurting his own.

Lord Kur had also stopped, seemingly puzzled by the display and she couldn't help but smile from embarrassment.

"Are you as angry as I?" Lord Kur asked her master.

"More than you know," Lord Romnus replied.

He took half the fruit in one bite.

"I remember saying he had gone too far once."

"And?"

"It is much more than that. He just made an enemy of his two generals. What is he thinking?"

"He's not," Lord Romnus answered.

Lord Kur eyed her for a moment then pointed at the fruit in her master's hand.

"What is that you are always feeding him?"

She looked up at her master and their eyes met. A mischievous smile spread across his face and he nodded. Dismayed, she tried to dissuade him with her own look but he just smiled wider. Going into her inner pouch, she pulled out a fruit and handing it to Lord Kur, tried to stop her hand from shaking.

"It's quite sweet," her master said. "It calms the soul."

That awful smile remained.

"Hmm?"

Lord Kur twisted the fruit in his hand, getting a better look at it.

He began to walk and took a bite as he went. The entourage was moving again. A few minutes later, Lord Kur faltered, his eyes wide with terror. She watched him try to force his body to stand and then he went face forward down on the cold pavement of the outer corridor. His eyes rolled around in their sockets as the eyelids fluttered shut.

"Pick him up," Lord Romnus ordered. "That solves my dilemma on how to get him back to reason."

"My Lord," she whispered, "That was," she stopped.

"Cruel? Irresponsible?" She nodded. "My apologies. I should not have put you in that position."

He laid a hand on the top of her head briefly then continued on towards his palace. Lord Kur was draped across the shoulder of a royal guard ahead of them. Things were going to get worse, she could feel it. Handmaids like her were going to get caught in the middle. She was frightened.

**⚹

Modas watched the sunset from atop a hill while waiting for the other manbeasts to show up. After the meeting with the Dreridians, he came upon the decision to set his plan in motion ahead of schedule. The negotiations left him feeling sour and he didn't trust anyone in that conference room. New Lassa needed a stronger leader and warriors more fitting to the task of defending her. He would get vengeance and create a new order in one movement.

Tonight, he had to make sure every manbeast participating knew their roles to play and reiterate to the ones veering off course to stay on point. He didn't want any deaths on his hands. Just because the previous leader was a monster didn't mean they had to be.

The last spark of sunlight disappeared in the horizon and he felt the presence of a large number of manbeasts signaling it was time to finish what he had started over a century ago.

Jaron was waiting for him when he returned home and he could tell by her expression that she was not happy to see him so late. He figured she suspected what he was up to but this time he wouldn't deny it.

"How did your vengeance meeting go?"

"That's not what it is!" He calmed himself. "I am trying to fix things. You weren't in that meeting. We are in danger and we cannot defend this world as we are now."

"As we are now is because YOU have divided us."

"This is not my doing! Don't you dare," he stopped.

"You are going to let manbeasts tear this planet apart over something that happened when you were a young manbeast and possibly get our leader killed in the process. Who will lead us then?" she snapped.

"I would never let anything happened to Chardon!" he yelled back.

Jaron's eyes narrowed. "No, of course not. Because Chardon was who you wanted in the first place. I just happened to be in the same line of vision."

Modas backed away from her. The tone of her voice dripped with malice. It may have been true in the beginning but he loved her more than he ever did Chardon. Hurt he made her feel that way all this time, he turned away and left.

"This will end badly for you and all of Lassa!" she called out to him.

He never glanced back. The crack in her voice told him she was crying.

"We must set up a defense, NOW!" Jaron yelled as she burst into Chardon's chamber.

She ran as fast as she could, knowing there wasn't much time. On her way over outbreaks of battles were already being reported.

Modas worked fast.

Chardon just stood there staring at her with a look of surprise.

"He couldn't. He told me he was not going to do this," Chardon said.

"He was lying! How could you believe him?" Jaron grabbed Chardon by the front of his robe. "What are you going to do, leader?"

A dark look fell over Chardon's face.

"If he really wants war, then so be it. Dispatch groups to each quadrant."

"Understood."

"And make sure no one is killed."

Jaron stopped mid step and turned to him.

"Really?"

Chardon stared down at her.

"Yes. I will not have murdering my own race on my hands!" He sighed, slumping his shoulders. "Thank Lassa Farin is on Azrom."

THREE: Alliances

Simple Plans

Homes were burning. Screams of terror and rage mingled in the night air. It took him back in time to the day his entire family was slaughtered. From his vantage point atop a cliff Modas scanned the surface below. For nearly a century he wanted the non manbeast Lassians to know how it felt but something was wrong. He didn't feel avenged, this didn't satisfy him. Instead he felt fear; dread. With it, a sense of guilt.

The manbeasts who helped him initiate his cause assured him there would be no deaths. Too much had transpired and although he held animosity towards the Lassian warriors, they were still his people. The race's population had suffered enough. But, there would be bloodshed. Ganna's medical team was going to be busy.

Again. That sense of knowing his agenda was now being tainted; unjustified and dismantled. Adjusting his vision he focused on the village Chardon and his own family lived. At first he was satisfied with the fights erupting and already in full swing.

He could see Talas and Kelin barely holding off four manbeasts as they made their way back to their home, one side caved in exposing its innards. They seemed overly desperate and he almost smiled until Modas' gaze shifted and he saw why they ran so franticly. With shock, he watched his daughter, Una, raise her claws. Below her on the broken floor were Talas and Kelin's children. The two infants were in striking range and the oldest was already on the ground bleeding. He could hear the infants' cries and his legs moved on their own as he leapt off the cliff. Even pushing his body to tremendous speeds, he knew he wouldn't make it. He too became desperate and kept going. Still focused on his destination, he saw Talas and Kelin stop cold, a scream emitting from Talas worse than anything he had ever heard as Una's claws entered the first infant. Ribbons of blood flew upwards with her claws as she pulled them out in one quick motion.

Modas could feel the stinging of tears in his eyes, blurring his vision but he strained them, forcing his eyes to readjust.

This is not what I wanted!

He was almost 500 feet away when a flash of fabric came from the opposite side in front of him, halting his advance. Und, flew into Una and punched her into the ground, forming a small crater beneath her. The look on his face spoke volumes. Modas didn't dare speak as he turned to see

Talas in despair on his knees moving forward, shakily, towards his home. A wildness in his eyes.

Not bearing to watch, he averted his gaze and it landed on the four manbeasts behind Kelin. They too had halted at the sight of Una striking the infant, their claws retracted. Modas' vision seemed to waver as if he were tilting and his eyes locked with Kelin's.

Murderous intent. That is what he found staring back at him and seeing it in Kelin terrified him. Never had he, or anyone else, seen such malice in the warrior. Even in battles, Kelin was passionate and driven, not overtly aggressive. He feared Kelin may not even know what was happening to him, having been pushed to the edge.

Ganna herself came running to the scene with three medical assistants behind her. She scooped up the bloody infant while her aides retrieved and took care of the other two children. Modas stood rooted to the ground where he stood. In an attempt to remove himself from Kelin's stare, he caught Ganna's pause in her stride as she cast a glare at him. In her eyes he saw something else. There was no surprise in what had just occurred. It was like she expected as much, saying 'I knew it'. And that is when he realized; this attack confirmed for her and the late Sestis what they had concluded all along. Manbeasts were just genetically made monsters with no sense of gratitude or belonging.

Und stood towering over his sister's unconscious body also staring at him. He could see the rage boiling in his son. Modas mindlessly pivoted to his right and went towards Talas who had stopped mid crawl. In his mind he had to get Talas away from here but as he got within a few feet of the fallen warrior he heard crackling and the air buzzed. Dark blue light cascaded on the ground.

"Get away from him!"

Kelin had formed large energy orbs in each hand, ready to unleash them. Modas halted. The manbeasts behind Kelin shook their heads in unison at him. A stalemate ensued for what seemed like eternity until Kelin rescinded the orbs and went over to Talas' side. He gently lifted his mate off the ground and carried him away.

"Are you satisfied, father?" Und spat.

Modas turned back to his son. Und grabbed his sister by an arm and dragged her out of the dilapidated home, then disappeared into the night.

One of the manbeasts came over to him and rested a hand on his shoulder.

"We knew there were discontent factions within our ranks. We can try all we want but we can't control everyone."

"Not this," Modas spoke softly.

"Yes, it has all gone terribly wrong."

A sudden thought crossed Modas' mind and his eyes widened. He remembered the meeting a few years ago where a small group was intent on eliminating their leader.

"Chardon!"

"It would take more than a few manbeasts to take our leader down."

"No, only one, if their lucky." Modas knew all too well.

"Then we must hurry."

Modas nodded and they headed towards the communal building where he was sure Chardon would be in full battle mode.

What have I done?

Chardon didn't want to harm the misguided manbeasts surrounding him in anger. He searched their faces for some sense of hesitation or regret, finding neither. Six in all, they bared teeth and claws already caked with the dried blood of their fellow Lassians.

It really has come to this.

Standing beside him was Mara, breathing heavy from the fight. They were both determined to shield Jaron who lay behind them on the ground bleeding from four deep punctures in her left shoulder that ran down to her abdomen. Claws had gone right through her front to back. Seeing her struggle to stay conscious through excruciating pain gave Chardon more resolve to stop them.

"Don't force my hand," he pleaded with the manbeasts. "If I must…I will use it…again."

This made them hesitate in their advance, giving him and Mara a window of opportunity. But, they weren't able to take it. From out of the dark came a blur of motion and the six manbeasts were knocked back a few hundred feet flying in the air like leaves in the wind before crashing down with loud thuds. In their place was Modas accompanied by three manbeasts. Chardon flinched when he turned a wild eyed stare at him, mouth twitching. Modas was in a sea of sadness, regret and madness. It was as if the great manbeast had come unhinged and it worsened as his gaze fell on Jaron.

Chardon knew why Modas had come so quickly; to save his leader. But Jaron was his mate and for the first time, Chardon felt relief that he had finally realized who was more important.

"You don't touch her!"

Mara rushed over to her mother and cradled her in her arms. Her stare burned into Modas, causing him to back away. Jaron had finally given in to her injuries and was unconscious.

****☼****

The royal advisors stood around in a huddle off to the side of the throne while Halfar sat watching them. Everything in him said they were corrupt yet their words resonated with him. He had given Farin some leeway in visiting the first royal house palace to alleviate conflict because he was tired of having to keep tabs on her every waking hour each day.

Sometime earlier in the new season he noticed how developed she had become and how her guards often leered at her. His advisors suggested many times to find a lower royal to mate with her and now he understood. He wasn't ready to mate her to anyone but he knew it was only a matter of time before someone snatched her. If they did manage to somehow take her, he would tear them apart, publicly.

Tapping a finger on the armrest of his throne, he asked, "Are you done plotting so we can commence our meeting?"

All five turned to- wards him and bowed.

"Our apologies, my lord," Mesrod replied. "We tend to congregate so often that it is part of our making."

"Yes, well the council is waiting. We need to put an end to these incidents of rebellion."

"Our people are upset about the blockade the Dreridians have placed on us," Prevcan stated.

"We have endured worse than this."

Halfar stepped down from his platform and walked towards the corridor to the left of him.

"What of Lady Farin?" Dondar inquired. "It would be wise to have her confined when you are away for these meetings."

"She is residing in the first royal house palace for the next moon phase." He saw the frown appear on three of his advisors' faces. "I do not have time for such constant supervision!"

"Of course, my lord."

Four royal guards followed Halfar into the corridor. He felt bothered by his advisors' reaction to Farin not being in the main palace and couldn't figure out what the issue was aside from her safety.

Dark grey sky hung over the region of the palace due to the cold weather making its way across Azrom. Most of the red flowers had closed their buds turning a pale violet to give a hint of life in the gloom. The landscape mirrored Farin's disposition as of late these past few weeks, wishing she could immerse herself in its dark embrace. Romnus had advised her to keep up the gleeful façade, a task she found harder to complete each day.

She leaned over the veranda just outside the first royal palace's banquet hall and looked down. Far below she could see Batis lounging around the palace's boundary line along with his men while they waited for her to return. From her view they were tiny monsters. Batis turned around to look up, meeting her gaze, then smiled. She flinched, backing away and returned to the hall where the rest of the royal members waited.

"Come sit with us out of the cold, beautiful Farin!" Chastan sang, holding a hand out to her.

"The air felt nice." Farin sat down beside him

"Yes, the season is changing." He took hold of her sleeve and tugged. "Time for heavier wear."

Romnus glanced over at her.

"It's getting late, we should disperse for the evening."

"What about my guards?"

"Batis will be fine where he is."

She could hear and see the darkness fill him. From the moment he had come to get her for General Kur's bonding ceremony only to find

Batis abusing her, he despised the soldier.

"No need for them," Chastan waved a hand, "I will escort you to your chamber."

He had volunteered as she knew he would. They had been spending more time together since her father started to allow visits. Their mating used to be fun but now as she tried to keep him focused on her she began to realize he could not be tamed. Romnus had warned her about his attention span waning after a while and of course, she knew soon after giving birth to their son on Lassa that he was not what she thought.

Their son, a child he still could not know about.

"One last drink before we go?" Romnus gestured to a servant who turned and picked up a tray that had already been prepared. The servant carried it over and waited. "The elegant azure colored chalice is for you, beautiful Farin."

"How fitting," Reita cooed.

Farin reached over and carefully lifted the chalice off the tray. She inspected the delicate curves of its structure, marveling at how it sparkled like a gem.

"You had this made for me?" She almost couldn't contain her joy. He always knew how to make her smile, unlike Chastan.

"Of course. Anything for you."

Lord Aloni and Reita made a stern face and she wondered for the thousandth times how they really felt about her. Romnus raised his drink once the servant had finished serving everyone.

"To blood that binds."

They all raised their chalices and quickly downed the contents. Farin was never good at that so it took longer to consume her own. When she set her empty chalice on the table, Chastan stood, grabbing her hand to pull her up.

"Shall we, Lady Farin?"

Farin made a small bow to the royal family members. "May you rest well." She turned and left side by side with Chastan.

In her chamber, Farin crawled on the bed and laid flat on her back to stare at the ceiling. Immediately after, Chastan blocked her view with his flushed angelic face. He let one hand caress her breasts as he smiled down on her.

"You really are quite beautiful," he whispered.

She found no comfort in that since he frequented the brothel every chance he could. It was apparent to her that she was never going to be enough for him. Lowering onto her, his lips brushed hers. Farin felt exhausted from the stress her father had created and her body would not respond the way she wanted.

"Will you just hold me?"

"Only if you're unrobed," he laughed as he proceeded to undress her then himself.

He was groping her with fervor but it began to lessen until she saw his eyes flutter. In moments he was asleep, his nude body wrapped around her like a reptile. She was surprisingly relieved. Sleep took her as well as she pulled him closer into her arms.

Dondar stood stunned at the entrance of Farin's chamber along with Batis. He had donned on leather footings as suggested by Batis to eliminate the sound of their advance. The guard had told him of the recent rendezvous' between Lady Farin and Lord Chastan. He had not expected this. She was tainted, he was sure of it. And, as Batis reported on his observations, possibly by Lord Romnus as well. It solidified his advice to keep her confined. Now she was going through the palaces spreading her thighs for anyone who would want it.

It dawned on him that his lord would never believe him. He turned to Batis.

"Leave them be, until morning before they wake. Do you have a reconnaissance device?" Batis nodded. "Record this. I will tell our ruler there is a problem in this palace that needs his direct attention and then show him. Be ready to escort that half breed to the throne room when he requests her."

The smile on Batis face made the advisor cringe. He never liked the soldier and his men. Their methods for just about everything in life were barbaric. Pushing that aside from his mind, he focused on his new task. He had to report this to his colleagues. They would be just as thrilled as he was right then. Together, he and Batis crept slowly away back to the main palace border.

Halfar did not like being tested so early in the morning even if he had not slept during the night. His advisors had sour expressions and he almost feared what they were up to now. Sitting on his throne in casual attire, he threw one leg over the side of the armrest out of habit and leaned an elbow on the other.

"What is it?"

His first advisor moved cautiously forward and bowed deeper than usual. "My lord, there has been a development in the first royal house that needs to be addressed."

"And?" Halfar was getting irritated.

They had a flare for the dramatic sometimes and it tried his patience.

"We will show you."

He waved Dondar up and a recon device was produced.

Halfar watched it flicker to life and then the image cleared to perfect resolution. He felt his blood turn to ice water in his veins and a stabbing pain erupt in his chest as he stared at the image of his child wrapped in the arms of Lord Chastan. Of all the royal members of the first house, he was the worst. Halfar was well versed in Chastan's perversions and knowing his child was one of his conquests made bile rise up in his throat. He found that his body was now sitting upright and his hands were gripping the armrests so hard, the stone began to fracture.

"We are sorry, my lord. We did try to warn you. She is not fit to be in your presence and now tainted beyond finding a suitable mate. Putting her in the brothel would have been better than this."

Halfar wasn't listening anymore after that. He could see the advisor was still speaking but there was no sound. A flash of memory came to him and he remembered Chastan's scared handmaid as he marched down the corridor to her master's chamber. If she knew then so did Romnus who appeared at the right moment that time.

"Bring me Chastan's handmaid and Romnus' pet."

It took all he had not to yell.

His advisors looked confused then two of them left with a set of royal guards accompanying each. He sat back in his throne and waited patiently. They would be gathering essentials for their masters and un- guarded. He was going to teach them a lesson in true reign.

Within an hour, he heard the crying and yelling of Chastan's hand- maid, Ponnae. He knew it was her because Romnus' personal servant, Biandra, would never show fear in the face of his guards. The two females were dragged roughly into the throne room and thrown at his feet.

"Show them," he commanded Dondar.

Ponnae's eyes grew wide with terror while Biandra just stared unmoved while they watched. It told him his hunch was right. They both knew what was going on in their masters' palace. He felt stupid for lifting the ban and allowing her to visit.

"You were accomplices to this. For that, you will be punished," he seethed.

The indignation on Biandra's face angered him further.

"Since you like to observe, maybe it's time you participated," he said to Ponnae. "Take her to the lower guards. Let them determine her fate."

He liked the fear that oozes from her very being.

For Biandra he stepped down and backhanded her with the claw he had morphed his hand into. She went into the air and skidded across the floor as she landed.

"Bring the Gruloc tamer."

His advisors pursed their lips simultaneously as they watched his royal guards oblige. He was amused by their reaction, so sure it was what they expected of him. Smiling, Halfar stood in the middle of his throne room listening to the handmaids cries fade as she was carried off.

Two of his royal guards came into the room carrying what he had requested. The Gruloc tamer was a giant whip, the fattest part nearly four inches in diameter and the end coming to a needle point. It stretched fifteen feet, weighing approximately forty kilos. Grulocs were large beasts that stood eight feet in height and could push an entire structure down with its solid muscle giving the massive frame extraordinary weight to accomplish the task. Many of their kind had been made to submit using the taming whip.

He went over to Biandra and using his claw, ripped her robes open to expose her flesh. Two columns were moved to stand side by side and tethers were secured on them. With a finger, he gestured to her then the columns. Guards dragged her to her feet and tied her wrists together before attaching the tether. From the opposite sides, they pulled the ends until her body dangled three feet off the floor.

Standing twenty feet away from her he let his eyes linger on her for a moment. Everyone in the throne room stepped far away, not wanting to get accidentally hit by the tamer. Halfar wound it up into the air several times then let it go. The sound when it made contact to her skin was that of bones crushing but Azromians were tougher than that.

He wanted to break her. Her face contorted but she didn't scream. No. She was not going to give him that satisfaction. No matter. She was going to suffer for as long as he deemed it. He wound it up again unleashing another blow. By the fifth time, there was blood dripping on his throne room floor but she still refused to scream for him. He expected nothing less from one of Romnus' pets.

There were six of them surrounding Ponnae as she lay face down on the chamber floor being beaten. She bit her tongue to stop herself from screaming and they seemed to like that. When she was sure they might have had enough since they ceased the beatings, she let her tongue go, tasting her own blood. She was mistaken. Two of them held her down while one from behind used his sword to slice open her robe. Out of fear, she screamed and they laughed.

They took their time having a turn, always two holding her in position for whoever was next, another slamming her head into the floor after each time. When all six had finished, they left her there, bloody, in pain. She felt like dying then. A separate set of guards came in and lifted her off the floor. She saw the ceiling move as they carried her off down stone stairs and into a dark chamber she knew well; the dungeon.

Tired, yet still angry, Halfar dropped the tamer and ordered it away. He stared at the mess in his throne room then his clothes. Even at a distance, the blood splatter reached him.

"Clean this up! I have to change."

He left the throne room and marched to his chamber alone. His guard knew better than to follow him when he was in this state. He whipped off his once white tunic and brown leggings, now stained with blood. Naked, he examined the lean muscle taunt with unfulfilled rage in the mirror. Grabbing a towel from the wet basin he meticulously wiped away every drop of blood from his flesh.

Halfar returned to his throne room wearing clean garments, the rage slightly subsided but his blood still boiled within him. The throne room was spotless as if nothing had ever happened and he decided to reward the cleaning servants later. His advisors kept their distance as he slowly sat down.

"Bring her to me."

He knew he didn't have to specify who. Batis and his men bowed low then rushed off down the corridor. Halfar thought he saw the soldier smile and was certain Farin would be brought in non-too gently. It was her own fault. Morning was in full swing meaning Chastan would have fled her chamber by now and Romnus would notice he was missing a member of his entourage.

The sound of claws scraping against stone screeched into his ears. From around the corner of the entrance came Farin fighting against her four guards, mainly Batis who finally gripped her wrist and flung her into the throne room. She landed halfway inside, bruised and bloody, in front of him. He held on to the armrests and leaned forward.

"Did you sleep well, my child? Was Chastan's flesh keeping you warm?"

Her face drained of color, her eyes widened and tears formed. She was in a dressing robe so he assumed Batis had dragged her out of bed naked and put it on her. There was silence in the room. His advisors had looks of approval.

"You have made a mockery of my kindness and disrespected my will on every occasion. Was that amusing for you?" She still did not answer him.

"My lord," Mesrod interrupted. The five had turned from their deliberations and stood side by side to face the throne. "It is a shame that she is no longer fit to be formally mated."

"Then what am I to do with this filthy thing?" Halfar asked. His voice was close to yelling but he had restrained himself. "She no longer has value in my court."

"That is true, my lord. No one in the royal houses would want her now, save for maybe Lord Chastan. And he would tire of her soon enough."

"See what you have done?" He finally yelled at her. She was crying softly still sitting with her legs sprawled awkwardly apart. "Even with royal blood coursing through your veins, you are nothing but trash!"

Batis advanced further into the throne room and bowed. There was a grin on his face. One even Halfar could see held nothing nice.

"If she is no longer fit for royalty, I would gladly take her. She could still at least be of use mated to a royal guard. That would keep her in the palace under your watch. She is of royal blood, as you've said."

"Yes," Prevcan said. "Half breed she is but of your seed. We can't have the people or the royal houses against us. She is beloved by them." Halfar sat back in his throne and thought for a moment. It did make sense to keep her in his circle. This time he would make sure to have a tighter rein on her. He met Batis' stare.

"Take her, if you want her." He waved her away.

"Thank you, my lord." Batis made another deep bow. "If you don't mind, I would like to seal the bond, with your permission."

"She's yours now. You can do as you please with her."

Farin screamed as Batis grabbed her by hair and forcibly removed her from the middle of the throne room with his three subordinates behind him. Halfar cringed at the sound, but endured it. They were just outside the entrance and he could see what was about to occur.

Farin fought with everything in her being even though she knew Batis was much stronger. She was barely past twenty and he was a seasoned war soldier of a hundred and forty years, maybe more. When they arrived just outside the threshold, she was at the point of defeat. Her body was too damaged for any longer of a fight along with blood loss. She could see it streaked across the throne room floor behind her. Batis threw her down on the floor, keeping hold of her dressing gown which tore partially from her body. Ringing filled her head as it landed hard on the surface bouncing slightly.

"Do not fret, lovely Farin," Batis laughed, removing his breast plate and cloak. They fell beside him in a clank. He bent over and grabbed one of her ankles, pulling her to him. "I will make sure my men get to taste royal flesh as well when I'm done. You will be thoroughly satiated before long."

A longsword with a hint of green in the blade went through the guard to Batis' right. It ran down in a diagonal path from shoulder to abdomen before disappearing back out from where it entered. The guards opposite Batis on the left protecting the advisors were collective cut down in the same moment. Halfar sat up in his throne, eyes bulging. From behind the advisors came Romnus. He went to Batis and yanked the soldier by his hair into the air and threw him into the throne room. Halfar counted twenty or more royal guards loyal only to Romnus invade his throne room. General Kur appeared from the right, having dispatched the other two of Batis' unit. Blood was everywhere, even on his attire and he seemed to not care. There was nothing aesthetically pleasing about the bloodshed he just caused.

"I have warned you cousin," Romnus stated.

His left arm now a pincer was driven down into Batis who lay flat on his back. Romnus stood up and kicked his body further in but to the side away from him.

Halfar, still angry, stood up as well. He walked down the steps of his throne and onto the floor.

"You dare come to my palace after the deceit you perpetuated? Passing my child along your royal court? Was she to your liking, cousin?" he spat.

"I have never mated with Farin. If that is what your advisors have reported, they are mistaken. You do not listen to reason. I warned you that harming anyone of my royal house would be a declaration of war."

"Farin is not of your house! She is my child to do with as I see fit!"

"She is mated to Chastan and the mother of his child," Romnus replied calmly, "therefore part of MY royal house."

Loud gasps echoed through the room and Halfar sat stunned. He looked over to Farin lying half naked in a bloody heap, then to his advisors who were suddenly frightened. Romnus glanced in the same direction.

"Once again, you have been manipulated by a corrupt council instead of ruling on your own. How much lack of judgement do you now possess to do this?"

"I am the supreme ruler of Azrom! How dare you judge me?"

Halfar morphed his entire body, rising to nearly seven feet tall. A hint of dark red glinted along the armored shell of his body and the pincers opened. Romnus tilted his head slightly then morphed as well. It had been a long time since Halfar had seen his cousin's full form and forgot how enormous and truly menacing Romnus was, easily over eight feet in height. His black lacquered body and pincers dwarfed his own. For the first time, Halfar was caught off guard and it cost him.

As large as Romnus was, his speed defied reason. Before Halfar could think of moving, his cousin was in the same breathing space and a pincer made contact with his chest. His body was slammed into the stairs at the base of his throne. All the air left through his mouth as he tasted his own blood and knew the damage was bad. With one blow, Romnus had taken him down.

His cousin turned and walked away, morphing back to normal as he did so. Kur, Aloni and Kuhala stood waiting for him in the middle of the room. He turned to face Halfar again and sighed.

"You have brought this upon both our houses. I want mine and Chastan's handmaid returned. I know that in your madness, you have done something foul to them but let me make it clear. If they are near death or harmed in such a way that it is deemed worse than death, your reign ends."

The royal entourage exited the throne room. He watched Romnus carefully lift Farin off the ground and cradle her in his arms. She seemed so small against his broadness. Batis lay broken covered in blood near a column and his advisors were visibly shaken. Two of them had slumped to the floor in fear. Azrom might apparently had its limits, Halfar thought silently.

A medical servant came rushing in and injected healing gel directly into his chest while he remained unmoved on the steps. He didn't dare try to rise, the pain excruciating, and not sure if Romnus would return to deliver a killing blow.

It all began to sink is as his wound sealed. Farin had already found a mate and birthed a child? Have I been so blinded by my advisors that I did not see? Another revelation popped in his head. Chardon knew. There was no way Farin would have a child and her mother not know. More importantly, it was obvious that the child was not born on Azrom, leaving New Lassa. He took one look at the advisors again and immediately felt nauseous.

What have I done?

Feeling the tissue fuse back together in his chest, was not a moment too soon as his body pitched forward from the power of bile coming up to vacate. A second wave sent him to his hands and knees, the ends of his hair dragging in the pool of vomit. *What have I done?* The tears stinging his eyes felt like hot embers being pressed into them. He could feel the tension in the air. His royal court had just witnessed the downfall of their supreme ruler and he had no idea how to transition from this.

Romnus went straight to his chamber and laid Farin down on the bed. Within moments, his personal medical team swarmed into the room and he stepped back to let them perform their work. He wanted to go back and dismantle Batis piece by piece then move on to the advisors. Halfar would be last to deal with. Behind him, General Kur stood silent. A new dilemma must have been brewing in his head.

Aloni went to retrieve Chastan from the royal bath. That he didn't bother to inquire his handmaid's whereabouts when he went back to his own chamber this morning was testament to his lack of leadership. It was why Romnus never gave him any real assignments for the royal house. Chastan's priorities were not in line with his or the other family members.

"This will end badly, won't it?" Kur asked.

"That depends on what Halfar will do after this. If he does not submit, there will be war between two royal houses. If he accepts his newfound situation, then I will be lenient."

"The royal advisors?"

"The same. If they defy me, they die."

Kur snorted. "That is not the same, Lord Romnus."

"She will need to rest for a while. Let's leave her be." Romnus walked out of the chamber.

"You love her," Kur said.

Romnus stopped at the veranda and wrapped his hands around the stone railing. He looked out into the horizon and let the morning breeze sweep over him then turned back to Kur.

"Yes, I do."

"Yet, you're willing to let Chastan have her?"

"He doesn't have her. But, for now, we can let Halfar and the rest of Azrom think he does."

"She's so young!" Kur exclaimed, slamming a fist into his own thigh. "One usually doesn't mate until the age of fifty."

Romnus smiled. "Farin never saw it that way. She likes to define her own destiny, even when it turns out to be wrong." Darkness filled him as he was about to call on his entourage. "You will search for our handmaids?"

"No need to search. He would have thrown them in the dungeon to rot. I'll go get them. Medical treatment should be ready and waiting."

"I will bring them with me."

Kur stared at him incredulous.

"You can't be serious? Why would you want to come?"

"To bear witness to Halfar's madness. I want to know just how far he has gone."

"What if it's worse than death, as you stated?"

"Then there will be nothing for Halfar to redeem."

Romnus contemplated the real possibility that Halfar had indeed gone to a darkness so foul he may have to put both handmaids out of their suffering. Losing part of his entourage was like losing part of his family and Chastan's handmaid was loyal to a fault. Pushing his rage to the side, he was glad Biandra had left a fruit by his bedside the night before. Eating it was the first thing he did when he awakened. It was only an hour later that the guards he had posted to watch the main palace came bursting in past his chamber guards to deliver the report. By that time, the effects of the fruit had kicked in so he was able to remain calm. Halfar should thank her for saving his life for without it, he would have easily torn his cousin apart.

The dungeon had been newly enforced after the Razznian attack yet remained cold and barren with stale air. Romnus and the rest of the family leaders were led by Kur down into the deepest part of the palace. Guards watching the corridor did not engage them, instead moving away in fear as they passed. News traveled fast. Romnus saw the tremors in Chastan's hands, knowing what the young lord was thinking. Unlike Biandra, Ponnae was a timid creature.

Kur halted in front of two cells across from each other and went pale. Romnus stepped around him to take a look. In one sat Biandra, slumped against the wall, her body bloody, swollen, tattered, yet her eyes still shone with defiance. She squinted her one good eye and seeing him forced a tight grin.

That's my loyal servant.

He smiled back. A burning rage like nothing he had ever felt rose in him, negating the effects of the fruit. He kept his sanity by sheer will. Then he turned to the other cell.

The strangled cry that came out of Chastan was nothing compared to what Romnus thought he felt. Aloni raise a hand to his mouth, the sleeve covering the lower part of his face. Kur just stood, head reared back in awe. Chastan fell to his knees, hands extended in front of him. This was worse than death.

Even from his distance, he could see the shredded tissue between her thighs. They had literally destroyed her womb. The abrasions and bruising told where the bones had been broken. She lay on her stomach, head turned to one side, her eyes void of everything. A soft puff of dust by her lips meant she was still alive, barely.

"We kill them now!" Kuhala shouted. He knew she was referencing whoever did this, but now was not the time.

"Have patience," he stated. "We will find who did this."

"Patience?" Chastan whispered. He dropped his hands down to the floor. "I want them torn apart." He raised his shaking hands again. "I want to tear them apart."

Romnus motioned to the medical team and they dispersed into two groups. He figured it would take weeks, maybe months, for the healing gels to repair such damage. A tremor went through his body, forcing him to turn back down the corridor and make his way out the dungeon. He couldn't bear another second of the tragic scene. Halfar had lost his mind. That was his final conclusion.

Reaching above ground, his legs faltered and he gripped the stone walls of the dungeon's entrance. His vision blurred until he saw everything in shades of red.

I'm losing control!

He raised a closed fist to hit the wall. It morphed on its own and the giant pincer punched through. His legs formed into lean muscled praying mantis legs and before he lost his senses completely, launched into the fields on the other side of the palace where his beloved fruit grew.

Field workers cried out in terror as he tore through the orchard, flattening the tall stalks, making a path to his prize. Barely of his own mind, he snatched a handful of them, shoving them into his gaping mouth and began to devour. With so much of its juices coursing into him all at once, his body froze from the shock. He immediately came to his own mind but too late as his vision cleared briefly before his entire system shut down. Romnus went face down into the dirt like a dying Gruloc beast, shaking the ground beneath him.

New Lassa was left in a state of anger and chaos in the aftermath of the manbeasts' insurgence. When the wounded count was announced, there was enough shame and blame to go around. Chardon made the decision to remain in male form to show his seriousness. For some reason he felt it was the best course.

As much as he despised Ganna, she had come through on all fronts. Her swift actions were unprecedented because she had expected it.

That angered him more. She and Sestis knew this would happen centuries ago and waited for the event with baited breath. The wide division within Lassa's three species never occurred to him. Manbeasts were created so many millennia ago that he assumed it was a non-issue. They were Lassians, plain and simple, just like the energy users and the warriors and everyone else. Everything had been fine until his father's leadership. He wasn't told all the circumstances but just finding out about them was no excuse for his poor judgement in leading his race.

In a bunker nearby, he sat on a concave bench along the wall of the large healing chamber, watching over the wounded as medical pods re- paired their bodies. The chamber was full to capacity as well as another bunker in the east. He had chosen the bench closest to the little ones section. The tiny pod before him held Talas' infant boy. Thin tendrils of light ran back and forth inside the wounds, slowly closing them while reconnecting any blood vessels.

"You don't have to stay and watch," a female voice chimed up.

Chardon looked up, coming face to face with Ganna. She too was tired, he could see it in her demeanor. The scientist went about checking each pod's data, making adjustments as needed.

"Yes, I do."

"It's not your fault, really."

"How can you say that?" He snapped. "I."

"Are you a terrible leader? Of course. But this was set long before you became one. The reason I dislike manbeasts is because they are generally prideful and overly aggressive."

"That's not true! Modas was not like that and neither are his children." He stopped as he looked at Talas' child who was nearly killed by one of Modas' own.

"There are exceptions to the rule like all races," Ganna continued. "But we were not concerned with them."

"You mean Sestis and yourself?"

Ganna let out a loud sigh.

"As a scientist I am always fascinated with the evolution of species, especially my own. Since we had closed off our access to other worlds there was no reason to keep such a large force of manbeasts. Sestis was just weeding out the bad from the good and finding a remedy that benefitted our race."

"No she wasn't!"

"Ah, yes. Her ambition did get in the way of the original plan and I tried to justify so much of it. Now, I just want to make our race better. Not a super power like she wanted, but as I said before, capable of holding our own against any enemy."

Chardon actually welcomed Ganna's blunt honesty. It dawned on him that it was not loyalty to Sestis or anything else. Ganna was always trying to find a way to make their lives better. Her execution lacked finesse.

"You will help me?"

"No," she replied turning to look at him. "I will help our race, in the name of Lassa."

A loud beep interrupted them and she ran over to the origin of the sound. Chardon stood up and went over to see what was going on. In the pod lay his cousin, Jaron, her skin not quite back to normal color. A few strands of pale red hair were visible, a sign of premature aging. Lassians didn't get those until they were at least four or five hundred years old.

"Oh my," Ganna commented, noticing the strands. "I think it makes her look more distinguished, don't you?"

He stepped away from the pod and leaned on the one behind him. Tears streamed down his cheeks and he tried to fight them back. The second beep sounded as the pod purged the dry liquid from its chamber.

"I better contact her family," Ganna said. She moved to the commlink.

Chardon grabbed her wrist and stopped it midway.

"Don't."

He knew Modas would be there in seconds and he was the last person Jaron needed to see when she woke up. Leader and scientist locked eyes and they silently concurred.

The pod's locking mechanism disengaged with another beep and the hatch receded exposing Jaron's naked body to the bunker's open air. Ganna went to a cabinet and retrieved a robe, tossing it to him. He caught it and waited.

Jaron's eyes fluttered sporadically until finally they slowly opened to slits. The light hit them and she winced in pain. Chardon knew that feeling from when he had just awakened from a healing pod before. Forcing her eyes to open wider, Jaron stared up at the ceiling for a long time. Tears ran down the sides of her face as she covered it with both hands. Gently, he lifted her and arranged the robe around her. She bent over all the way and continued to cry.

Ganna gave him a nod and exited the healing chamber. He couldn't bear it; not understanding the heartache and rage Jaron must be feeling. The doors opened again and he thought Ganna had forgot something until he heard a loud gasp. Mara stood in the entryway with tears forming. She sniffed hard, not letting a drop fall. He envied her strength.

"Mother?"

Jaron removed her hands from her face and looked up. Mara went and wrapped her arms tight around her. Chardon watched her stare at the red strands in her mother's hair, knowing what it meant and squeezed tighter.

"Don't bruise her, Mara. She just woke up."

"I don't care," Mara sobbed.

"I do," Jaron said. "Let go of me, you foolish girl."

They both laughed at her usual disdain for affection. She reciprocated with a look that matched. Chardon tried to help her out of the chamber and was shocked when she smacked his hand away.

"Don't touch me!"

"Mother!"

"Don't! You should have stopped this!"

"You can't blame him for this, mother! It was father who started this!"

"You are the leader of our race!" She ignored her daughter's outcry. "I warned you. Now look what we have." He hung his head and backed away from her. Her eyes softened then and she smiled a little. "I'm sorry," she too hung her head and resumed crying.

"What do we do, leader? Everyone is so angry." Mara asked.

"I don't know, but I have to fix this somehow."

"Where is he?" Jaron suddenly blurted out. She amazingly had stopped crying and now had a look of poison.

"I think," he replied, "we should wait on that."

"Chardon!"

"No!"

"I'm going to have to agree, mother. None of us have spoken to him and he is not around. He may be hiding in a cave meditating."

"That won't help him this time," she snapped.

"No, it won't. But, he needs to stay away for now. He knows that, at least." Chardon held out his hand. "Come on, let's get you out of here."

"Are you going to fill me in on why so many healing pods are in use?"

He exchanged a look with Mara. It was going to have to be done sooner than later and he knew the first person she would want to speak to about strategy was Talas. That was not a viable option and wouldn't be for a little while longer. Right on cue she asked.

"Where is Talas? I would have thought he would come running to see me back."

"This way," Mara spoke softly. She helped her mother out of the pod.

"What's wrong? Why are you both quiet?" Jaron's eyes bulged. "Is he…?"

"Just come," Mara nudged.

He led her to the little ones section on the other side of the healing chamber and stopped at the farthest pod. Jaron's hands went to her mouth as she saw the wounds being repaired on the infant boy. Her look of horror turned to rage.

"Who did this?" She demanded.

Mara didn't turn to her but responded. "Una."

Jaron's' hands clenched tight, all the color drained back out of her skin and her eyes went blank. There was nothing anyone could say to her now.

In the dark chamber. Jaron peered in to decipher a presence as she crept on unsteady legs towards the bed sitting against the far wall. Her eyes adjusted and finally a lump became visible on top of it. Light strands of hair hung over the edge. She went to the side and pulled the nearby chair closer so she could speak softly. On the other side of the bed lay Kelin, in deep slumber. Jaron didn't want to wake him with any talk above a whisper.

She sat on the chair, easing herself down slowly and jolted with fright midway. Talas lay on the bed, eyes opened staring into the abyss. There was no life in them. One arm crooked under her, the hand limp. When Talas didn't register her being there, Jaron continued her descent into the chair. She brushed some of the strands from Talas' face and a whimper followed.

Through the decades, she had never truly despised Talas, although there had been moments of disappointment and even envy, never hatred. Looking back she realized how much energy she had wasted being angry and cruel to the warrior. And not just Talas. When she learned about Modas' feelings for Chardon from long ago it explained her own feelings of distrust towards him. Her unconscious decision to ration out affection spread onto everyone around her.

Now here she was showing affection to the one person who everyone deemed her rival. She snorted softly. Talas had the one thing she envied most of all; conviction.

"Why have you come?"

It was barely a whisper, like it had been breathed out and startled her out of her thoughts. She looked over and saw Talas focused on her. Those words of air came from Talas' lips.

"Shh," Jaron answered. "Don't speak. Just sleep."

Talas balled her hand into a fist and her eyes narrowed.

"Why?" she demanded more forcefully, yet still barely audible. "Did you come for entertainment?" Talas choked a little and coughed. Tears brimmed.

"Of course not," Jaron seethed, trying not to yell. "I would never do such a thing."

"You have no love for my sake," Talas sputtered, "so why?"

Sobbing quietly with eyes squeezed tight, Talas started to curl further into a ball. Jaron had enough. She grabbed the edge of the bed cover and yanked it off just Talas. The room has chilly and she watched the shocked reaction from Talas.

"Get up!" She didn't care anymore if Kelin woke up as well. Seeing them both in such a pitiful state angered her more than Modas' unjust coup. "Your children need you! Get up and go take care of them!"

Talas stared up at her in awe, then rage crossed her face. Jaron smirked.

That's right, get angry at me.

She waited for Talas to get up, ready for a scuffle then remembered she wasn't in any condition to fight any more than Talas was.

Before Talas could plummet to the floor, Kelin reached over and stopped her fall.

"Let me go!" Talas' voice croaked slightly. She took in too much air and had trouble regulating her breathing for a moment.

"You too!" Jaron addressed Kelin. He gave her a look she didn't like but let it slide.

Kelin activated the glow orbs in the corners of the chamber and Talas leapt at her. She stumbled backwards, having no intention of let- ting the grieving warrior land a blow and lost her footing.

Oh, for the love of Lassa, this is going to hurt.

As she got closer to the floor, a hand grabbed her arm, stopping her fall. She used it as leverage to right herself and came in the direct gaze of Talas with a stunned expression. Kelin stood not far behind on the end of the bed with the same look.

Hands shaking, Talas reached over and pulled a few strands of her hair. In the now brightly lit room her red streaks shined like fire. Jaron gently took her hair out of Talas' hand and backed away.

"Good, you're up. Let's go."

"Jaron," Kelin called out.

She was not going to hear what either of them had to say. She knew that tone; pity. "I know I haven't been very nice to you in our life- time together but you need to know this. I have never hated you." She felt the tears well up then stream down her face so she sniffed loudly while wiping her nose with the back of her hand.

"Now come on."

Jaron walked out of the chamber to give them time to get dressed properly. Her body gave out and she slid to the corridor's floor. She felt so weak, drained of everything. There was no time for that. The person she had to face, the one who needed to tell HER why, was still missing.

You can't hide forever, Modas.

****☼****

Shivering from the waterfall, Modas focused on stillness while the pressure rushing down on him was almost too much to bear,. The reason he had sought out the waterfall and stumbled into it was due to insects becoming increasingly attracted to his pungent body scent. His mane had grown tangled from neglect as he wandered the planet surface in a state of despair. He had stripped down to his leggings and was attempting to meditate while being cleansed.

He sat akimbo on a large rock beneath it, hands folded in his lap as he tried to focus on nothingness. It failed. He remembered when Jaron was pregnant with their first litter after returning from Earth and he told her that she meant everything to him. The strength of the water bent him over further and he let out a loud cry that was drowned out by its rushing roar. Modas planted both hands on the wet stone and let the water beat down on him.

There was no more vengeance, no hatred, left inside of him. All that remained was guilt and sadness. Jaron should have been the one person he protected. She would despise him for this, he knew, and it would take a miracle for her to forgive him. Again, he saw his daughter's face full of hate as she ran her claws through a helpless infant. Bile tried to make its way up his throat and he forced it down. No good. It came back up with brute force, sending him to his knees.

Using all the strength he could muster, he pushed himself up off the stone and stepped down into the shallow creek. Drenched, he stood staring up at the horizon and a pain crept in him. This was not their home world, this was not Lassa which made what he had done more heartbreaking.

Apologies were not going to be accepted.

What am I supposed to do?

The person he feared most was Jaron. She had warned him over and over that his agenda was nothing but a petty tantrum. After he had finally convinced Mara to let him take Jaron to the medical chamber she was taken away from him by force. No one wanted him near her let alone in the same room. Stricken with grief he started his trek.

Movement from one of the cliffs above him put him on alert and he quickly spit out the last of his vomit, wiping his mouth with the back of his hand. His claws slowly extended.

"So this is where you came to hide from your sins," his son, Mota, called down. He leapt along the ridges of the cliff until he landed on the ground and walked towards him.

Modas tried to gauge his son's mood and determined it was neutral. He rescinded his claws and turned to him, Mota stopping a few feet away to look him over.

"You look like a dead hoisen beast left out in the hot sun, father."
Modas grimaced at his joke. It was in bad taste even for him. He saw
Mota spot the pool of vomit spreading thin in the water.

"How did you find me?" Modas was surprised how cracked his voice
sounded.

"You sound like one on its last light too."

Modas felt tired. So very tired. Even at the death of his family, he did
not have this feeling of utter defeat. Back then, he was filled with fire.

"You need to come back."

Modas just stared at him. He knew that but wasn't ready. As if reading
his mind, his son sighed.

"Whether you're ready or not, it is imperative that you explain your
actions to the council," he paused, "and my mother."

"I know," Modas whispered.

Mota went to his pile of robes and tossed them at him. Modas caught
them, holding them to his chest. He raised his gaze up at his son and could
feel the tears stinging his eyes.

"I can't," he replied. "I can't explain this. It wasn't supposed to happen
this way."

"What did you think would happen, father?" Mota yelled. "You turned
our clans against our own people and fueled dissent for over a century!"

Modas flinched violently from his son's words as if he had been
physically assaulted. He never knew how just words could hurt so much.
Seeing Mota waiting patiently, he finally let his robes hang long from his
hands before donning them.

"I guess it's going to take a while to get back. You don't look strong
enough to go at any speed other than walking."

"That is true," Modas replied softly.

His son paused mid stride and turned back to look at him. "If you
need to know, the infant is doing well. Talas not so much, but everyone is
getting back on track."

Relief nearly took him back to his knees. If Una had killed the child,
he would not be going back to explain. He would be going back for her
memorial.

Trinon

Madness.

The arguments in the council chamber grew louder and more heated as the session went on. Trinon sat in a corner of the room disgusted and angry, not understanding how it had come to this. When claws and swords were brandished, he had enough. Knocking everyone and everything in his path out of the way, he exited the chamber. Halfway down the corrido he heard footsteps running after him and didn't turn around to see who they belonged to.

In the open air outside the temple, he inhaled deep then let it out. He proceeded up the hill on the opposite side and could still sense his pursuers. At the top, he sat down on the grassy knoll and stretched his legs out a bit, keeping them bent at the knees. His hands were planted flat on the ground and he threw his head back, letting his mane cascade down like a waterfall.

"Trinon!" His mother called to him. He kept his eyes closed. "Answer me!"

He opened his eyes and glanced up at her. She was furious and he saw fear on her face. It was inevitable. Trailing behind her was Talas and Kelin along with Und who looked worried. Infuriated, he frowned, not wanting to be soothed like some baby beast.

"I can hear you."

That stopped her mid stride and he regretted his tone.

"What is wrong with you? You haven't been yourself in years and I don't understand! Why won't you talk to me?"

His hands turned into fists and grabbed chunks of grass, his fingers embedded deep in the soil. A surge of panic gripped him. Talas came over and laid a hand on his shoulder.

"Be still, she has a right to know. I told you that before."

"Know what?" His mother snapped. The fear could be heard in her voice. "Trinon?"

Talas squeezed his shoulder and Trinon just nodded.

"You know that after the battle with the Razznians we reached out to other planets for resources until our planet recovered?"

"Of course I do."

"There was one planet that we visited where the natives were more than happy to assist us."

Trinon fell into a lull and he could see the lush green forests of that planet. The exotic foliage and how the air smelled slightly sweet. There was laughter all around him and even adults played in the trees with the young ones.

"We made negotiations and were sending what we could back through the gate."

"You mean the vegetation?"

"Correct."

"They were amazing. I wished we could have gotten more."

"So do I," Talas said sadly. His mother frowned.

The taste of the fruit fed to him by her small fingertips, the juice running down his chin and her laughing at his lack of manners. He could smell her deep brown hair as it brushed against his forearms.

"There was another race who inhabited a neighboring planet that also traded goods for their vegetation and they did not like sharing. Their leader came, making threats but never raised a battle with them."

"Oh Lassa's love," Jaron whispered.

"They attacked the planet and targeted us." Talas paused for a moment. "The leader of the planet assisting us had a daughter. She took a liking to Trinon and they spent each day together for the three years we were there."

Yes, she thought he was quite funny and beautiful. She told him so many times while they lay on the beach or atop a hill overlooking the forests. Her hair always adorned on one side with a single giant flower of vibrant color in contrast to her bronze skin.

"She was only a few months from giving birth when the attack happened."

Fire raining down on the forests. The smell of burnt timber and flesh. Dark clouds the color of charcoal as they churned from the heat and smoke. Her hand clasped tight in his as they ran for shelter. The enemy fighters descending onto the surface like spores.

"The fight was brutal and unjustified. Many of us were hurt but the planet and its people suffered more."

"They just destroyed the resource they craved so much," Kelin balked.

"Truly disgraceful." Talas looked down on Trinon who didn't acknowledge him. The quicker the story was told and over with, the better. "In their rampage, Trinon's mate was hit by a barrage of laser fire."

Fighting back tears he could see vividly her hands holding her swollen belly as he turned to help over a fallen tree trunk. The look of surprise as stray laser fire from behind tore through her creating three holes that opened up like screams. Her belly torn to shreds, spilling out onto the ground, her shoulder and thigh like chopped raw meat. Him catching her in his arms in a state of shock.

"Trinon became something…else."

The time of darkness he couldn't recall for so long revealed itself to him. He could see enemy fighters being torn apart in a haze of red and realized it was he who was delivering the death rites. At some point he was grabbed from behind and restrained. He remembered howling and screaming to the sky above.

"Containing him took nearly all of us. He went insane. Seeing the carnage caused by his decree, the enemy leader ceased the fighting and helped with the wounded. But it was too late for apologies. They were allowed to stay for repairs. The leader of the planet made a decision to banish them from setting foot on his planet again."

The long trek into their humble gathering space, still wounded he was barely able to walk,. Rows of their people along the aisle letting him pass. Seeing her grief stricken father on his seat at the end staring down on him in pity. His stumble to the floor on his knees as he bowed low in front of him, forehead to the ground, and said, "I am sorry for not protecting your child." No one moving for a long time and then feeling a thin hand set on top his mane. Knowing it was her mother who adored him.

"He was badly wounded and didn't know it. When he went to apologize to her parents and her people, we had to literally drag him up off the floor. Once our group was healed, we returned to the ship with a few gifts from the people despite the devastation of the forests."

He remembered being dragged onto the ship and left slumped against the inner hull of the corridor in a daze. Talas looking down on him full of worry watching his catatonic stare into nothingness. Und picking him up like a grain satchel and tossing him over his shoulder. Carrying him to an empty bunk in the crew quarters.

"We kept his relationship with her a secret so for our group only Und and I knew about it."

They traveled halfway in the ship, deciding to use the gate at the last moment. Trinon felt numb, his vision blurry all the time and his hearing muted. The final leg of the journey, Talas and Und cornered him in the control room. He was sitting on the floor leaning against the wall,   one knee drawn up, when they towered over him.

"Trinon is always smiling," Und said.

"Trinon loves to be playful and take things as they come," Talas added.

"You must return to Lassa as the Trinon we know."

Then it hit him; they were right. How could he explain his current state? Could he pull it off? He didn't have to worry because the moment his feet planted on New Lassa's soil his body reacted on its own. The corners of his mouth twitched upwards until he had a big smile on his face.

He looked out to his family and the other Lassians who came to greet them and exclaimed, "We sure had a lot of fun! You should have been there!" He saw Talas and Und's face take on horrified expressions before they dissolved. Inside, his core felt broken and dimmed.

"It took everything in me to keep this secret, but I told him, he should tell you at least." Talas turned to Kelin. "I'm sorry to have kept this from you."

Trinon swerved his body towards them and in his tenor voice, a bit lower than usual, "You cannot tell father!"

His command startled them.

No regrets for that, he was serious. His mother's eyes filled with tears and her hand covered her mouth, stifling whatever sound would erupt. He could tell she wanted to hug him, knowing not to. She took a chance and threw her arms around him. He surprised himself by not pushing her away but burying his face in her bosom and began crying.

"If father knew, he may understand," Und said after Trinon had stopped sobbing.

He gave his litter brother a look that he hoped would signal his anger. Und just stared back at him in defiance. Their mother, sensing the tension stood and whacked them both in the back of the head.

"Stop that! What is wrong with you?" She wiped her face. "We will not tell your father because I don't think he understands anything right now. What he's done has essentially ruined our race."

"Do you still love him?" Trinon asked.

"I don't know." His mother hung her head.

To his and everyone else's shock, his father's voice rang in the air.

"You're right. I probably wouldn't have understood."

Modas came out from behind the curve of the hill and stepped forward so that he was face to face with Trinon.

"But I do now. You need not have gone through that alone. I've failed you."

"You understand now? Good! Do you see how trivial your vengeance was? How I wanted no part of your madness?"

He felt a new kind of disappointment in his father and litter sister, Una. Nothing could fix this quickly. Wishing he were back on that lush planet full of forests, he stood up and looked out at the horizon.

Jaron walked back down the hill towards the council chamber, leaving Trinon to some alone time. The way he had left the session, it would have caused an uproar. She was sure Modas was confused at his son's outburst but he shouldn't have been. From the beginning, most of their children did not approve of the uprising and now he was full of regret. She and Talas knew it would come to that.

Do you still love him?

Those words haunted her and the answer she gave made it worse. The lies and deceit he had spun for so long were large and deep. How could she forgive him so easily? The answer; she couldn't. It was too much. Nearly a century of hatred and this is what he ends with?

She entered the council chamber to a hushed silence. Everyone had frowns on their faces and knew why. They were ashamed of their own behavior as they should be. Trinon held on longer than expected. She had been on the verge of sending a ball of energy into the middle of the fray herself. A few heads turned to acknowledge her return as she went to take her seat.

Modas went to stand by the window and leaned against it with his arms folded. He seemed less ferocious now. Jaron almost pitied him until the reason they were in the chamber came back to her. He turned to her.

"Will Trinon be alright?"

Her eyes bulged out of their sockets in disbelief, as did a few councilmen.

"No, Modas! He is not well!" His eyes grew wide and he backed away from her with nowhere to go, hitting the wall with a thud. "Do you think anyone in this room is well after the heartache you caused?”

"I..."

"Don't you dare speak!" She roared.

In the midst of the silence she caught a glimpse of Chardon sitting at the table shell shocked. This was going to be a difficult task for her cousin and she hoped the unskilled leader would take the reins and soar.

There was no light. Romnus felt like he was enveloped inside a deep black hole, his body heavy, as if it had been filled with ore then hardened. He tried to lift his hands and nothing happened. Stillness. It had a calming effect and he decided to let his mind sink deeper.

A tiny prick in his neck made Romnus rear up from his position gasping for air, instantly grabbing his chest. His vision returned and he found himself in his own chamber with servants silently milling around. Reita stood at the foot of his bed staring down at him disapprovingly.

"You weigh more than a Gruloc, did you know that? It took an entire unit to remove you from the grove. What were you thinking, eating so many of them?"

At first, he didn't understand what she was talking about, then all the events that transpired before he made the mad dash into the fields came flooding back. Anger rose and was immediately shut down by a massive headache. He applied pressure with the palm of his hands to ease the pain.

"Don't go rolling around too much."

Reita pointed to the area beside him.

Romnus looked over. The beautiful Farin was lying next to him in what he assumed was a heavily drug induced sleep. Most of her wounds had healed. The damage obviously left her drained of energy. He had been wounded in enough battles to deduct that much.

"How long?" His own voice sounded cracked and broken to his ears.

"Only a few days."

"Halfar?"

"In hiding at his palace. It seems he has confined himself to his chamber."

"The royal advisors?"

"Scared." Reita smiled when she said it.

"And," he began.

"Biandra is already lucid and quite angry at you for the recent episode."

"I'm sure she is."

Romnus motioned to a servant.

"My garments."

"Going somewhere?"

"Are you here to stop me?" he asked as he reached over to retrieve the robes from the servant. "I am not going to the main palace. Chastan needs to be told."

His sister frowned.

"He will be shocked, then devastated."

"Then, won't care."

"Yes, this won't be his first offspring and I am sure, not his last."

"It will be the last with her," Romnus replied.

He slid off the bed, the robes falling into place as he stood. Walking to the other side of the bed, he leaned over and lightly kissed Farin on the lips. When he turned to the entrance, Reita had a smirk on her face, staring at his bare feet.

"Come, lover, we have much to discuss." Reita got to the corridor then stopped. "Oh, and Chardon is returning to retrieve Farin."

"That will not be an option now."

"Are you not even going to negotiate with her?"

"I believe once she understands the situation, she will agree with me."

He took another look at Farin before following Reita down the corridor. Even broken and scarred she was just as beautiful.

Chastan sat dumbfounded at the table in the communal hall.

"I have a child, with Farin?"

The rest of the royal house members waited for the information to sink in. None of them had known except Romnus somehow. He glanced over at Kur who shook his head. *Not even he knew about this?* First there was elation of having a child with the beautiful Farin, then a twinge of anger. *She kept it from me!*

As though reading his mind, Romnus spoke.

"She had to hide the child for the obvious reason. She could not gauge how Halfar would react to such news."

"That is no consolation! We would have protected her!"

Chastan made eye contact with each member of his family and saw something in them that he didn't like. It was as if they disagreed or was it disappointment?

I am wrong to assume that?

"Farin is young and headstrong, you are not. It was a dangerous game you played. You should have known better than to engage."

His sister lowered her gaze from his.

"The palaces are in an uproar and this news has added to it," Romnus stated.

"The houses know I have fathered a child with Farin?" Chastan could feel a ball of tension form in his gut. "Then I am mated to Farin?"

"It appears to be so," Kuhala answered.

Mated.

He did not like that term. He adored Farin, but not enough to bond with her for eternity. There were others who had birthed his offspring, none of royal blood of course. If he had to play the part to keep her safe, then so be it. His sister was right. He should have known better. Farin was nearly thirty years too young to be mating yet he let himself indulge.

"When can I meet my child?"

"That we cannot know. It still may not be safe here. Chardon will be arriving shortly and it can be discussed then." Reita stood after that and headed out the hall.

"Halfar is the root cause of this. If he hadn't restricted her, she wouldn't have venture into my arms."

He too stood and left the hall. As he walked out into the corridor the ball of tension tightened. The last thing he wanted to be was responsible for Farin's happiness. Looking up at the sky he determined the time of day and decided the brothel would not be full. He headed in its direction.

The remaining family members took sips of their drinks in silence after Chastan left, knowing where he was headed. Romnus tapped a rolled up scroll he had been reading earlier on the edge of the table. Such childish resolve. For Chastan to blame his inability to restrain himself on Halfar's strict child rearing was an insult to everyone in the room.

"WE must make sure he holds true to the façade for a little longer," Aloni finally spoke. He sipped from his chalice slowly.

"Just like WE would protect Farin, not him?" Kur snapped. He turned on Romnus. "How and when did you know?"

Romnus stopped tapping the scroll. "Did none of you notice?" All eyes went wide. "She was well rounded when she returned from Lassa some years ago. Even her fair skin had gained some color. Really, you did not see it?"

"To be that observant of Farin speaks volumes about your own feelings for her," Aloni pointed at him.

He glanced at the ceiling, contemplating it then nodded. There wasn't much he didn't know about Farin. What he found odd was that Chastan never noticed how much time she spent with him instead of her supposed lover. Refocusing on the issue, he commented.

"Chastan is going to be a problem at some point. The royal structure is about to be reconfigured."

"Then you will take over rulership?" Kuhala exclaimed.

Her excitement was obvious. Aloni turned his head towards him and he saw the gleaming.

"I have made it clear, I do not wish to rule. If I were ruler, I would destroy everything," he paused, "in order to make it better."

That silenced them, taking the excitement out of the air. Kur made a face.

"When you say everything, what do you mean?"

"Exactly that. I would be deemed worse than Halfar and our fathers combined."

"But you would make it better?"

Aloni explained for him. "To create a new order with a clean slate, one must first destroy the previous. Lord Romnus would be assassinated within half a century, or less."

"But, you would make it better?" Kur reiterated.

"Eventually the people will see the truth and yes, Azrom would be reborn."

Kur leaned back and folded his arms in deep thought. Romnus was curious as to what scheme the general had churning in his mind. It would have to wait for now.

"I must go check on our downed females then deal with Chardon when she arrives."

"Oh, I am sure Chardon will not let Halfar live once she finds out," Kur said.

"We have to prevent that from happening, General Kur. If she were to kill him, and on Azrom soil, there would be war between our worlds." Kur seemed to dislike the idea. Romnus got up from the table. As he passed him on the end, he patted the general on the shoulder. "It will be fine. I am sure you will find a way."

His entourage, sans Biandra, waited for him in the corridor. She would be his first visit, then Farin. Ponnae he decided to save for last because if she was unable to survive, he would end her suffering.

The gate atop the main palace burst open revealing a black and purple galaxy swirling around in the vortex before flattening. A single ray of light appeared like a runway and a small group of figures came forward. Chardon was the first to step onto the platform, followed by Chafar, Trinon and Talas. Reita noticed the weariness exuding from their bodies, a sign that great strife had occurred on New Lassa. She sighed. This was not going to make things easier.

"Lady Chardon, it is good to see you."

"Halfar has not come to greet me, yet again?"

"There is an explanation for that. One you won't like."

"I am sure."

"Let us get you some refreshments first and you can tell me what has happened to make all of you so unapproachable."

That jolted the Lassian leader. "You can tell?"

Reita smiled. "Oh, yes. It is deep within you. I can feel it radiating from your core."

They walked in silence until Reita turned to the staircase leading to the first royal house palace. She watched the frown grow on Chardon's face.

"Why are we not staying in the main palace?" she asked. "That is one place you do not want to be in."

Reita led the group across the courtyard where Kur's mother, Emalli, held the audience of the royal children. She glanced at the group and bowed her head.

"Who is that?" Chardon whispered.

Reita laughed at the awe in her eyes.

"That is Emalli, Kur's mother. I'd forgotten that you have never met."

"Beautiful," Chardon replied softly.

That made Emalli laugh.

"Kur said the same thing when he met me for the first time. Such a perverted child. He takes after his father in that."

"Come," Reita chided Chardon. "We have a small meal prepared."

When she returned to the communal hall with her guests, Romnus and Chastan were gone. Only Aloni, Kuhala and Kur remained. A fresh round of food and drink was placed on the table as they all sat down.

"I met your mother, General Kur," Chardon addressed him.

"Hmm. Stunning isn't she? If I weren't mated already, I'd have taken her."

Chardon blanched. "She's your mother."

"A shame about that. We would have remarkable offspring."

"Stop telling such disgraceful things," Reita snapped, staring at him.

He snorted and took a sip of his drink. She turned to Chardon.

"Now tell me what has happened on New Lassa."

That got the other members attention.

"Modas launched an uprising. Manbeasts against us all."

"That's madness!" Kur yelled.

"Yes, well, it turned out badly. He says it was not supposed to happen the way it did."

"What did he expect? Was there to be no blood shed in this uprising?" Kuhala asked.

"Oh, he expected bloodshed, just not the kind that occurred."

"I am not understanding." Aloni frowned.

"Children were also assaulted, as well as his own mate," Talas explained.

"So New Lassa is not a safe haven at this time?" Reita plucked a round of bread from the tray. "That may be to our advantage then."

"What are you talking about?" Chardon looked around the room. "What is going on here that we have to be in this palace and New Lassa's predicament is an advantage?"

"We think it is best if Farin stays on Azrom. And, in a short time that her child be brought here as well."

Chardon and Trinon both looked startled. Chardon set down the fruit she was eating.

"You know about her child? Does Halfar?"

Reita noted the fear in her voice.

"Yes, there was an incident and all was revealed."

"What incident?"

Reita suddenly felt uncomfortable. Delivering such news was not her forte and she didn't want to have the Lassians restrained afterwards. She watched Chafar continue eating and drinking as if none of this concerned him but there was a glint in his eyes. Something foul, like the one his father had on occasion although the boy resembled a Lassian more so than an Azromian. She took a deep breath and prepared to tell them.

"Halfar lost his mind and gave Farin to his royal guards as a gift." Romnus' voice boomed into the hall and stopped her before she began.

His blunt revelation made her angry. This was not going to go well.

"What?"

Chardon shot up from the table and whirled around to face him.

"I was able to get my guards into the main palace before too much damage was done. She is resting for now, her wounds healing properly."

Chafar stopped eating and also stood.

"Where is my sister?"

Reita gave her half-brother a dirty look.

With her stare she asked him 'What now?'

"There is no need to see her now. She is still resting."

That only made Trinon rise from the table and step towards Romnus.

"It is not up to you, Lord Romnus. This may be your palace, but Chardon is her mother and Chafar her brother. If you deny them access, I will have to be their key."

Seeing her brother and the young manbeast face to face, Reita got up to intercede. Trinon had grown, as he would, to nearly as tall as Romnus. Her brother didn't have far to look down at him.

"You expect me to leave my child here, in a hostile environment?"

"No more than New Lassa from what I overheard." Romnus did not avert his eyes from Trinon's. "Very well," He moved from Trinon's view. "My guards will escort you to her."

Chardon went to stand next to Trinon.

"And then you will tell me what is going on in the palace, before I decide whether to kill her father or not!"

"That cannot, and will not, happen," Romnus sighed.

"That is not the answer."

As they left, Reita slapped her brother.

"What are you doing? We were supposed to neutralize the situation! You just aggravated it!"

"There was no reason to sweeten it. You agree, don't you Talas?"

Reita turned around and true enough, the Lassian warrior was still seated at the table sipping his drink. The dark patches around his eyes made him look hollow.

"He'll have to do more than beg for forgiveness this time," Talas replied.

"Halfar? Beg? Those two words are not synonymous," Kuhala snorted.

"His reign may be over," Romnus added.

Talas set down his drink and laid his arms on the table, hands flat.

"As it should. I have long thought his rule was ill structured, lacking and cruel. But there was something I couldn't see. An element that steered it."

"You are quite observant as well, Lassian. You are correct. Halfar has been manipulated and plotted against by the royal advisors for centuries and he has probably just recently realized it due to this incident."

"You want us to take him." Talas turned his head to them.

"He needs time to heal and reassess what he truly wants."

Reita stood confused by their conversation. It was like they were speaking in a language only they knew. She almost envied it.

Watching her child sleep in obvious pain, made Chardon want to storm the main palace and demand Halfar reveal himself. The chamber was dimly lit, casting soft shadows on the bed. Chafar sat down on one side of her and used a finger to arrange her hair away from her forehead. Chardon found the lone seat in the chamber and pulled it up to the other side of the bed. She carefully inspected the faded wounds on Farin's arms and face with shaky hands. Trinon stood at the foot of the bed, his fists clenched tight.

"My beautiful child, what has he done to you?" She glanced at the guards. "Who did this to her?"

They shifted uneasily then one of them replied, "Her guard, Batis and his unit."

She remembered him and that she had warned him about harming her child. "Where is he?"

"Lord Romnus broke most of his bones, so he is in medical being treated."

"He's not dead?" No one answered. She understood why they were leery to give her any more information. In her current state of mind she wouldn't trust herself either.

A medical servant entered the room then stopped when she saw Chardon. "My apologies," she bowed and was about to leave.

"No, stay. I need to know her condition."

The servant resumed her advance into the chamber. "She suffered a lot of damage. She fought hard. Some bones were broken and a few deep wounds which took some time to heal."

"Was she," Chardon couldn't finish the words, let alone the thought.

"Violated? Thankfully, no. Lord Romnus got to her right before it was to occur."

She felt ill and drained. A heaviness came down on her as it echoed in her mind. Right before it was to occur.

"Poor Ponnae was not so lucky. Six royal guards had their way with her. She may not live," the servant continued.

Chardon felt her own eyes widen in disbelief. Even Chafar and Trinon turned to the servant. In the history of Lassa, as far as she knew, there had never been such an incident as that. What had gone wrong on Azrom to allow that kind of behavior?

"Who is Ponnae?" The name rang familiar.

"Lord Chastan's handmaid," the servant replied. "Lord Halfar had her and Romnus' handmaid punished for allowing Lady Farin and Lord Chastan to mate." The servant came over to the bed with an injection gun. "If you please, I must administer more healing gel."

"Of course."

Chardon moved out her way. She looked at Trinon, then her son and made a decision. If Halfar had truly lost his mind, then she would help him regain it. But, if he was just being the cruel dictator the Razznians claim him to be, his natural state, then no Azromian would stop her from ending his life and his reign in one act.

A guard appeared at the entrance to Halfar's chamber, adding to the already small group blocking access from either side of the corridors. Halfar noticed the nervous glance, along with the guard's reluctance to enter the room.

"A message, my lord."

"Speak it."

"Lady Chardon is at the first royal house palace."

Fear gripped him. One deeper than anything he had ever felt.

"Who is accompanied with her?"

"Your son, Chafar, the warrior Talas and the young manbeast, Trinon."

"Is that all?"

"Yes, my lord."

"Dismissed."

The guard nearly ran into a fellow soldier as he spun around quickly to leave.

I wish I could flee as well.

It was only a matter of time before Chardon came looking for him and he had no explanation for his actions. To tell her he let himself be manipulated into harming his own child would be like crawling into his own grave. He had no doubt she'd want to kill him. She was on the list of many who wished for his head. There was chanting from the people demanding a new ruler. Azrom's love for Farin was deeply rooted.

Lost in thought, he did not hear the ruckus outside his chamber until it was too late. He barely had a chance to look up and see the cause. The back of Chardon's hand swept across his face and he saw a blurry haze of starlight in his head before hitting the floor on the side of the bed. His vision tried to correct itself as he attempted to push up onto his hands and knees. The room tilted. She had given him a powerful blow but he was thankful she did not use her power. He remembered what New Lassa looked like after she had unleashed it. If she did that now she would take out not just him, but every Azromian on the surface.

"Get up!" Chardon commanded. "And look at me!"

His guards had unsheathed their weapons, some morphing and he raised a hand, signaling them to stop. Too late. Trinon literally picked them off two and three at a time, tossing them over the veranda. The guards who were left backed away from the chamber's entrance and his reach. Halfar dropped his hand and obeyed Chardon's request. He flinched as their eyes met but she grabbed the sides of his head, refusing to let him look away.

"Why have you done this?"

Halfar squeezed his eyes shut and she shook his head to make him open them. They stayed that way for a long time, him on his knees while she held his head in a firm grip, looking down at him. So much despair filled him and the thought that he might have finally lost her came crashing down.

Feeling weak, and monstrous he took hold of the front of her robe and cried out into her bosom. He found himself doing it again and again, his voice giving way with each one. The room had gone black but he could still hear his own screaming, feel Chardon's hands on his face and smell Lassian earth on her robes.

When he finally stopped, his body slumped down. Chardon moved her hands to the back of his head and stopped him from falling back- wards. She held him close to her and he let himself rest there. He understood that he had been too young to rule, many of the elders against his entrance in the battle for rulership. The ones who insisted were his father's royal advisors. Two of whom were now part of his own. He had killed the others for the assassination attempt they manipulated Kur into delivering on Earth.

Am I worse than my father, and his father before him?

He felt Chardon's fingers run through his hair at the top of his head.

I want to stay here, just like this.

Four royal guards from Romnus' palace charged into the room, ruining his solace. Chardon let him go so he could stand. The soldiers had on their most menacing faces and it almost made Halfar laugh. He could take them all out in seconds.

"Your presence is requested in the throne room," the leader stated.

"I am being summoned to my own throne room? By who?"

"General Kur."

That surprised him. There was nothing dictating the military had jurisdiction over the monarchy.

"I am supreme ruler and no one summons me." Halfar stepped for- ward, pincers raised, and the guards backed away. "But, I will indulge him this time. Leave us," he snarled.

Chardon nodded to Trinon as the guards left and the manbeast blocked the entrance. Halfar turned and came face to face with his son, Chafar. He had not spent much time with the young warrior in training, now nearly equal in height with him. An expression of disappointment was aimed at him. He placed a hand on Chafar's cheek.

"I know. I'm sorry to have neglected you all this time."

"That is an issue, father, but the one I'm worried about is your treat- ment of Farin." He removed Halfar's hand from his face. "I would hear her called halfbreed in your presence, yet you did nothing to deter it."

Halfar winced, his son's words felt like being run through with a longsword.

"Come, let's go see what your General has in mind."

Chardon held out a hand.

"Yes, I am curious as well." Halfar took her hand and they waked out into the corridor.

Romnus' guards led the way with Trinon, Chafar and what was left of his own guards trailing behind.

General Kur marched into the throne room, General Rass at his side, just in time to see Halfar enter from the side along with Chardon and her entourage. From his position in the middle of the room, he could tell there was a difference in Halfar. It took a moment to figure out what it was: defeat. A haggard expression was plastered on his face and his body language suggested fatigue. Kur glanced behind him as the rest of his soldiers arrived. He had brought six enforcers and eight guards just in case Halfar had truly gone mad and wanted to battle.

Halfar stood in front of his throne, an attempt at appearing defiant seemed to be in progress. Kur waited for his ruler to get himself together. He clutched the scroll Romnus had left on the table earlier in his hands. The document was ancient but it detailed the monarchy and how it was to be structured. That is what he was basing his current actions on.

The royals of the first house and representatives from the other four flowed into the room as well. Kur had taken most of the day to convince them to attend his meeting. He looked back to Halfar and he seemed ready.

"What has gone wrong in your mind that you dare to summon me, your supreme ruler?" Halfar yelled.

"It is not me that has had something go wrong mentally," Kur replied then added, "My lord."

The royal advisors were huddled in the far corner with looks of despair on their faces. *You should be afraid.* Kur stepped forward and unfurled the scroll. He held it at his waist as he addressed Halfar.

"For your actions against the royal houses and the people of Azrom, by Monarchy law you have been deemed unfit to rule."

Loud gasps erupted from the now large audience in the throne room. Halfar's face faltered for a moment then a kind of knowing replaced it. Kur inwardly breathed a sigh of relief. There would be no need to restrain him by force. He raised the scroll up and read the relevant passage.

"In the event the ruler is deemed unfit to rule, the head of military will take control and appoint a ruler." Kur rolled the scroll back up. "I, as General of Azrom's militia, with the consent of General Rass, decree your reign is over." A hushed silence followed and all eyes focused on Halfar. "Due to the nature of your crimes, I recommend that you be exiled from Azrom until a firm duration is set."

Again, loud gasps were heard. He glanced over at the royal advisors and the councilmen who conspired with them. Their punishment was due soon enough. Kur looked to Chardon as Halfar backed into the edge of the throne's platform in a state of shock.

"I know you are angry and it is your decision, but are you willing to accept him on New Lassa as your mate?"

Chardon lowered her head for a moment then raised it.

"I will take Halfar to New Lassa."

"I am grateful to you," Kur bowed out of respect for her decision. She could have easily declined, leaving Halfar's fate in his hands. "With this, I appointed Lord Romnus of the first house as Supreme Ruler of Azrom."

He turned around to the royals behind him and saw the pained expression on Lord Romnus' face. Further in, the other royals stood dumbfounded. No one spoke for a long time and Kur wondered what was going to happen next.

"As the law dictates, I must accept your decision or face a battle for rulership," Halfar stated.

Kur turned back to him, surprised that he knew that. Then he chided himself for not realizing it. Halfar was always searching in the old databases to learn everything about Azrom. He waited for his reply. Halfar regained his composure and walked towards the center of the room and stared at Lord Romnus.

"I know that if you had not backed out of the battle so long ago that you would have ruled Azrom instead, and I cannot defeat you in a true battle." Halfar exhaled. "I accept you as Supreme Ruler in my steed and will go into exile."

Then Halfar did what no one thought they would ever see. He went down on one knee and bowed low to Romnus. Kur was stunned immobile and didn't notice Lord Romnus walk past him and lay a hand on Halfar's head.

"I thank you, cousin. Now, rise. I will give you a few days reprieve, but you must leave Azrom when called."

"I understand," Halfar seemed to struggle with something internally, then said, "my lord."

Lord Romnus faced Kur while Halfar stood up and returned to Chardon's side.

"I do not want this. I thought I made clear, my feelings about ruling."

"Yes, you did," Kur answered. "But you said you would make Azrom better and that is my only requirement for your reign."

Lord Romnus wiped his face with one hand and stared down at him.

"What happens next will be on your hands."

"I will support and protect you." Kur went down on one knee and bowed low. "My lord."

In slow succession, everyone in the room did the same, leaving Lord Romnus the only one standing. Even Chardon and her people bowed. Kur took yet another glance at the royal advisors and councilmen. He knew they would sprint out of the throne room at the first chance and convene for a new strategy. As if hearing his thoughts, Lord Romnus whispered down to him.

"Make sure they are under close guard. I'll rip them apart if I feel for one moment they have defied me."

"As you request, my lord. I have already made arrangements for such an event." He saw Rass smile beside him. It was his mate's responsibility to see it through.

When everyone rose back up, Kur noticed some of the lower royals frowning. He recognized them from the fourth house. They had eyed the advisors earlier and Kur assessed there was going to be issues concerning them later. Lord Romnus caught this as well and nodded to him. A change in ruler was a harsh transition, especially when no blood was shed in the transfer. Given the current circumstances, he knew the people of Azrom would understand. As battle hungry their race may be, going into a losing one was an ill decision for a warrior.

Kur motioned for the royal council magistrate. The man stepped out from the crowd and walked up to the platform next to the throne. Lord

Romnus followed, taking the steps up to the throne slowly. At the foot of it, he turned to face the audience.

"I hereby anoint you, Lord Romnus, Supreme Ruler of Azrom," the magistrate announced.

Lord Romnus eased down onto the throne. His body fit perfectly into it, unlike Halfar whose slender frame had been nearly dwarfed by it. All heads bowed low to him and that nagging sense of foreboding came over him. He could see it in some of the royal guards and the council, their hostile intent. The magistrate went out onto the balcony and made a summons to the royal guards below to assemble the people.

After the throne room was cleared of everyone except those necessary to the royal court, Lord Romnus stepped down and approached General Kur. They stood face to face for a long time, randomly glancing at the royal advisors.

"You do realize what you have done?" Romnus asked Kur. "I will tear this planet apart."

"As you have said many times over, but you also promised to make it better. So I will trust in you as I had Halfar until it is deemed necessary to remove you as well."

"Then let us begin." Lord Romnus turned to the advisors. "Now, for all of you."

The royal advisors snapped their attention towards him. Fear and loathing filled their expressions. He waited for them to approach, which they did, slowly. Kur's eyes narrowed and Romnus set a hand on his shoulder to calm him.

"I want a meeting with the Dreridians within the next lunar phase. And, you will only deliver my agenda, nothing more. They will tell me if you try to negotiate otherwise and your lives end there." Some of them frowned. "Do we have an understanding?"

"Yes, my lord," they cried out in unison."

Kur raised an eyebrow at him. Romnus knew the general was curious about what he had discussed with the Dreridians after Halfar had stormed out of the meeting. He smiled at him. All in due time. The royal advisors scurried out of the room and Romnus watched them until they disappeared around the bend.

Mesrod walked at a brisk pace ahead of his constituents as they made their way towards the conference chamber. No one spoke a word until they were inside where he slammed his fists down on the console in the center of the room. Calba and Jabarz flinched.

"This was not supposed to happen! This is a disaster!"

"I never thought Halfar would be overthrown so late in our agenda," Prevcan stated.

"General Kur is more clever than we anticipated," Dondar added. "Where did he find that scroll?" Mesrod asked himself.

"It would have come from the royal library," Dondar replied. "What's done is done. Now we must find a way to get in Lord Romnus' good graces and try to steer our agenda back on course."

"He will be a hard one to turn," Prevcan said.

"But it can be done if we are careful," Dondar concurred.

"And determined," Calba added with Jabarz nodding with him. "Let's get this whole Dreridian affair over with. The quicker we sever our ties with those creatures, the better."

Mesrod straightened his robes as he said it and made his way to the door. He was angry at the outcome but he believed it could be remedied. Azrom's future always relied on the advice and counsel of the royal courts because rulers were so undependable. In his eyes, Lord Romnus was no different. Even so, he felt his skin crawl with anxiety.

Halfar stared at Farin's sleeping form on the bed and his chest felt like it was going to rupture, spilling out his innards. He didn't dare move any further into the chamber for he had no right. The scene of Batis and his men wrestling her to the ground, intent on having their way with her right in the corridor, sent a sharp pain in his head and he struggled back tears. He wanted to reach out and caress her hair. The way Trinon turned to look at him made him rethink it.

In two days, he would have to leave Azrom and make New Lassa his home for as long as his cousin decreed. At first, he was angry then realized it was what he had wanted long ago after the fight on Earth. The current circumstance was not ideal. Still, he needed the break in routine to feel like he could still love. His view landed on Chardon who raised her head and stared back.

"I know I won't be forgiven. All I can do is promise you I would never harm any of you from this day forward."

"You have no idea how right you are," Chardon answered. "When she is well enough, a handmaid will be assigned to escort her son to Azrom."

Halfar felt his blood race. He would get to see Farin's child for a brief while. Then his skin heated up as he thought of the child's father. Chastan was not the type to show endearment for his children and that his fourth cousin did not think to restrain himself with someone so young angered him.

"There will be no retaliation," Chardon chided him.

"I know," he replied.

He smiled, delighted she could read his mind again after fearing their bond had been permanently severed.

"Come, we need to let her rest."

Chafar leaned over and kissed his sister's forehead before easing off the bed to obey his mother. Halfar was the last to exit the chamber and he took one last look back at Farin.

"I'm so sorry, my beautiful child," he whispered.

He turned away and ran into Chardon who stood blocking his path.

She caressed his cheek for a moment then walked ahead of him.

FOUR: New Order

Negotiations

Traveling to the Dreridian system gave Romnus time to settle his nerves and steel his resolve. General Kur and two of the royal advisors had insisted on accompanying him for the meeting. Prevcan and Dondar sat in their seats with sour expressions. Romnus snorted and leaned his head back against the bulkhead. He had decided not to use the giant royal ship for the journey because he wanted to appear humbled in the eyes of the Dreridians. Halfar wanted to convey might when he came, Romnus was going to negotiate.

"Approaching Dreridian outpost," the pilot announced over the commlink.

Romnus opened his eyes and lifted his head up straight. Biandra held a fruit in front of him. She didn't even look to see if he acknowledged it. He took it from her hand and shoved the whole thing in his mouth. The juices squeezing out onto his lips as he chewed it.

"Azrom vessel cleared for descent to hangar B-I-4-4-V. Please make sure to secure your ship once docked," a voice from the outpost satellite instructed.

The landing was not very smooth. His body jerked sideways then pitched forward from the ship maneuvering into the docking clamps. Biandra was gritting her teeth against the pain caused by the rough movements. Her body, though healed of wounds, was still sensitive. The advisors seemed flustered by the jarring and then there was General Kur, sound asleep as if nothing had occurred. Romnus almost had a mind to strangle the pilot.

As they exited the ship and stepped onto the platform, the same group from the previous meeting stood waiting patiently to escort them. Lord Greggor appeared to be in a jovial state and smiled. The craggy mounds of his face made Romnus think the whole face would come apart and crumble to the ground.

"Lord Romnus," Lord Greggor exclaimed while spreading his arms wide open. "Or should I say Supreme Ruler of Azrom?"

"Whatever suits your taste would be efficient," Romnus answered.

"Not quite settled in your new role? Well, you have plenty of time for that. Come, now. We have much to discuss."

Romnus noticed Lord Greggor cast a side glance at the two royal advisors.

Did everyone in the known galaxy harbor distrust for the Azromian advisors? He asked himself.

It was true they had been in the royal court for nearly three centuries, a third of it during the time of Halfar's father. His entourage was strangely quiet and he wondered if it was due to the nature of the meeting. The heavy debt laid on Azrom by the Dreridians would cripple a lesser civilization. Greggor looked back at him as they walked and smiled again. Romnus could tell what the scientist was thinking; it was payday.

"Oh," Lord Greggor piped up. "I forgot to inform you. This will be a joint meeting. We need to clear up a few things with Razzna and New Lassa."

"Is that so?" Romnus frowned and the effects of the fruit kicked in, easing his anxiety.

"No need to worry, your former ruler is not present. I heard you exiled him to New Lassa. Very lenient of you."

"He is first and foremost of my bloodline."

Lord Greggor waved a meaty hand in the air.

"Of course, of course."

They reached the palace and headed up to the conference room. Romnus and company were ushered through the archway into the open layout. The floor to ceiling panoramic window gave them a view of the massive hangars bustling with ships coming and going. Off in the horizon were great cities blinking with multicolored lights. Dusk was upon them.

At the table sat Sars, with three soldiers from his unit, and Chardon with Talas and Mota. The Lassians looked weathered, perhaps even defeated somewhat. He had heard about the uprising led by Modas. Owing a debt was just adding insult to injury. As for the Razznians, Romnus saw optimism in their demeanor. He sat down at the table, General Kur to his right and the advisors to his left. His guards stayed near the entryway accompanied by Biandra.

Lord Pondur was already seated at the head of the table sipping from a fragile chalice while his treasurer sat hunched over a tablet deep in concentration. There was no doubt the lean creature was crunching numbers in favor of the Dreridians. Romnus just hoped the burden would not be too far leaning. A fair transfer of goods was his goal.

"Now that we are all settled, I want to clear up an important matter," Lord Greggor announced. "New Lassa was willing to send a large group of manbeasts to assist with Razzna's situation. That will no longer be necessary."

Relief came over Chardon and Romnus was glad for him. Sars had a confused look on his face and he concluded the Razznian did not know of the Lassian's proposal.

"In exchange for shipments of a new product we will upgrade and bring online a new mining system for Razzna. This way, we can get their resources back on the market faster."

"Product?" Chardon asked.

He turned to Sars. "What product? From where?"

Lord Greggor grinned and answered him.

"Why, something new and exciting that they developed on Earth. I believe they are on the verge of exceeding Halfar's organization."

Chardon went pale and Romnus knew why. The last thing the galaxy needed was another recreational drug for thieves and smugglers to get in on. All the Dreridians saw was revenue, a new commodity driving commerce.

"As for New Lassa, we would still like to insist on an ambassador to oversee," Lord Greggor paused, "to work with your science council on our joint projects."

"And I have stated before and will again that is not up for negotiation. With the current state of our planet, I do not need or want a foreign entity in the mix." Chardon had leaned forward, resting his elbows on the table.

"Our race has been peaceful and thriving for a very long time," Talas added. "This current setback is merely a tiny blemish in our history. We do not need your input." Mota nodded in agreement.

"With that settled," Lord Pondur said, "there is now the issue of Azrom." He set his chalice down and sat even straighter in his seat. "Please," he gestured to his treasurer.

The intense Dreridian cleared his throat and looked up at Romnus.

"In order to satisfy the ramifications of your planet's actions, in conjunction with Razzna's contribution, you will need to produce and ship one billion kaedirons of Azrom resources. This can include plant life, ore and precious metals. Azrom flowers are a well-known product but the ore and metals are what we most need."

Romnus thanked the gods, and Biandra, for the fruit he had ingested earlier because if not, his reaction would bode badly for Azrom. He could feel the urge to strike trying to stir within him but it was in a losing battle. One billion kaedirons would take nearly three decades at their current rate of production. His hands shook violently for a few short seconds then stopped. A headache bloomed open, its petals reaching every corner of his cranium, making him wince.

"That's insane!" General Kur finally exploded. His hands also shook but with rage.

"I agree," Chardon interjected. "That is outrageous at best."

"Really?" Lord Pondur asked, his eyebrow raised. "How much do you think the rebuilding of Razzna's trade should cost then? Even with the new product, it will take at least fifty years for it to return to its normal flow."

"There must be a better alternative," Prevcan exclaimed. "This was a result of a battle. The Razznians infiltrated Azrom. We did not start this."

"Was your planet devastated?" Lord Pondur asked softly.

"Of course not," Prevcan snapped.

"Then you see the reason for my course of action."

Silence engulfed the room. Romnus had to agree, the cannon fire sent to Razzna was overkill. He knew Azrom would not suffer much in the battle. Halfar's decision had cost everyone dearly.

"What is the time line?" He asked.

"Since Azrom has the capabilities for mass shipments, once we lift the embargo it should take two decades."

"And during that time we have no bargaining position for trade?"

"Correct," the treasurer spoke. "After the shipment of one million kaedirons in Azrom product, you will be able to resume normal trade commerce."

"What if we delivered it in less time?"

"Let's not be ambitious, Lord Romnus. Your race can only produce so much in a certain amount of time. Just stick to the timeline," Lord Greggor chided.

"What if we could?" Romnus asked again.

A sliver of irritation moved inside of him. That silence again. He wasn't saying anything unusual. They were here to negotiate and he already had a plan in motion.

"If you did, then a bonus credit would be given and you could start trading within two years of clearing the debt," the treasurer replied.

"Done," Romnus said.

Everyone sat still at the table. Lord Pondur was in the middle of raising his chalice to his lips and halted. His eyes narrowed as the two Lords stared at each other. Romnus forced his mouth to curve into a smile.

"Have you gone mad?" Dondar yelled. "We cannot do such a thing!"

All eyes shifted to him. The color drained from his face as he realized what just happened. Romnus cocked his head to one side and was curious to know if this is how they treated Halfar when he ruled. The fear in the advisor's eyes pleased him.

"I meant to say, it is nearly impossible, my lord," he corrected himself.

"I would have to agree," Lord Pondur said. He set his chalice back down on the table. "How would you do it?"

"That is for me to ponder. You just need to keep your end of the deal."

"My treasurer will compile the necessary documents. They will be transferred within the next seasonal cycle."

Lord Greggor clapped his large hands together, the slapping sound of thick meat echoed through the room. "Well, since the negotiations are now over, let's have a feast to commemorate our joint business venture."

"More like thievery," Mota whispered to Chardon.

Romnus let out a little laugh. It was true. He glanced over at General Kur who sat with his arms crossed while looking down intently at the floor. *I warned you.* Kur had promised to protect him from any assassination attempts for the next fifty years if need be, but what he was about to put in motion would test that loyalty. He guaranteed it. Azrom was going to be thrown into chaos by his own hands.

With the informal festivities over, Romnus' entourage was escorted back to their ship. During lift off, Prevcan leaned closer to him and began to whisper.

"My lord, you can't mean to adhere to such a short time table. Even if we were to match the Razznians in production, it would take decades."

"Advisor Prevcan, are you insinuating that I do not have Azrom's best interest?"

"No," Prevcan replied. His eyes went wide with shock. "I just simply cannot fathom how you would achieve such a feat."

"You shall know soon enough."

Romnus watched the advisor sit back against the bulkhead and exchange a look with his counterpart. The scheming would begin as soon as they landed on Azrom. He contemplated a guess as to what they had in mind. General Kur kept a keen eye on them from where he sat at the end of the row. Leaning his head back, Romnus let out a loud sigh as he closed his eyes. He really didn't want to be Supreme Ruler.

The moment Romnus released them from his care, Prevcan and Dondar headed straight to the meeting room where the other advisors waited. Four council members were also in attendance when they arrived. Mesrod stood from his seat at the head of the table and gestured for them to be seated before returning to his own.

"What news and how do the terms look?" Mesrod asked.

"It is madness," Prevcan answered. "The Dreridians want one billion kaedirons of Azrom production."

"Unacceptable!" The head of the trade council yelled. "That would take…"

"Yes," Prevcan said, "and Romnus has agreed to deliver it in less time than required."

"That's impossible!" Jabarz added.

Mesrod became unusually silent and it caused the others in the room to follow suit as they turned to observe him. He had one hand caressing his chin and the other tucked under the opposite arm. Then he smiled.

"It seems Lord Romnus has no sense of social responsibility." He planted his hands flat on the table's surface. "To do such a thing would require a great strain on our people and resources. It would cause," he paused, "undue hardship. Strife."

"A rebellion would be imminent within the first few years," the head of science and agriculture stated.

"Yes, he would be despised." Mesrod smiled wider.

Dondar perked up and sat straight.

"The assassination attempts alone could send a message."

"We can be rid of this ruler as well until a more suitable one can be put in place." Mesrod stood up and paced the room. "But, we must be patient. This will take some time although his reign will be short lived."

"It will be the shortest reign in the history of Azrom," the trade councilman snorted.

"Let him do what he pleases. It will only benefit our agenda." Mesrod stopped at the window and looked out onto the palace grounds. "Victorious," he said softly.

"Til death," the others murmured.

Darkness filled the chamber but Romnus' vision adjusted quickly and he found his way to the bed. He was exhausted and wanted to sleep. Letting his garments fall to the floor as he took them off, he climbed onto the bed and under the covers. He eased down against the pillows and wrapped one arm around Farin, drawing her close to his body. She didn't stir. His body's internal rhythm slowed, matching hers, lulling him to sleep.

Images flooded his mind. Dissent of the people, betrayal, senseless acts of violence and blood flashed before him in quick succession. His brows furrowed as he tried to force them away but they were relentless. Suddenly, a sense of calm swept through erasing it all and he was left with the beautiful Farin smiling at him. A soft glow surrounded her and in the background behind her was the palace square full of Azromians cheering.

Romnus jolted out of his slumber and for a moment forgot where he was until Farin moved. He looked down at her sleeping face and breathed a sigh of relief that the dream was over.

Or was it a premonition? He asked himself.

Long ago he had visions of being Supreme Ruler if he had gone through with the battle for rulership. That's why he backed out and Halfar became the one victorious. Now he felt his actions had only delayed fate. If that was the case then it meant he had to change Azrom and make it flourish once more.

Beams of light spread across the chamber, landing on the bed. Morning had arrived. His body demanded a few more hours, deeming the sleep he had as insufficient. Soft fingertips brushed his cheek. Farin stared up at him and smiled.

Time to get up, he chided himself.

Although they slept in the same chamber, in the same bed, he refused to touch her in any sexual manner. It was for both their sakes because there would be no turning back. He wanted her more than anything in the galaxy. That would have to wait.

"I see you slept well."

He leaned down and kissed her softly on the lips.

"I don't think you did," Farin whispered. "You were holding me so tight. Was it a night terror?"

"Hmm, not quite."

"How did the negotiations fare?"

"As expected."

Farin frowned and a sadness came over her.

"You will go forward with your plan?"

"I must."

"You have to tell them. Kur, the royal family and maybe some of the council."

"I can't do that. It won't work that way."

"I don't want you to be hurt," Farin whispered in his ear. "The people won't understand and some will try to assassinate you."

"I know, but that is part of the plan."

Farin sat up to sit on her knees.

"Then you have to stay with me. Do whatever I want until this is over."

"Are you going to lord over me for the next decade and a half?"

"Absolutely!"

"I can't play such a dangerous game with you," Romnus said. Farin didn't seem to like that. "Chastan played with you when he shouldn't have and I have more sense than that."

"That's not what I mean."

"Yet true."

"You don't want me?"

"Farin." Romnus sighed. He gazed into her eyes and she grinned. "We must get ready for morning meal."

"Will you announce your first decree today?"

Farin had a serious expression which nearly startled him.

"I haven't decided yet."

"Don't. Wait a little while longer." Farin brushed her lips across his for a brief moment then gave him a quick kiss before jumping off the bed. "Let's go take a bath!"

Kur paced his chamber barefoot so not to wake Rass who was still sound asleep. Ideas about what Romnus had in store for Azrom swirled around in his head and none of them were mild. The planet and its people were going to suffer. There was no way around it. Whatever his new ruler decreed he would not appear shocked, because drastic measures were necessary. Growing up in the training camps, he knew firsthand how bad the social structure was. Whenever he traveled to the different sectors for inspection, it made him cringe to see the poverty.

Yet, no one complained because we were a mighty race. Victorious until our last breath.

Beyond the corridor, sunrise was in full swing. He stood in the archway of the chamber and watched the rays sweep across the surface. A mighty race. Yes, one that deserved better. Halfar became ruler so young and did not think to repair the damage done by his father. Then a new war came and nearly crippled them again.

He thought about the deal with the Dreridians as the sun rose to the same level as the balcony, forcing him to shield his eyes. All of Azrom's secrets were going to see the light of day as well. Kur turned away and found Rass just about to sit up from under the covers. He would tell her about the meeting later. For now, he just wanted to be near his mate; crawl back into bed and wrap his arms around Rass.

Just a little longer, he pleaded, *before the chaos.*

****☼****

There was debate on whether to inform Halfar of Romnus' deal with the Dreridians and Chardon was on the side of not doing so. Back in female form, she waited by the doorway watching him play with Farin's young son. Only a few years old the little one was quite intelligent and never able to keep still, like his mother. Halfar was actually laughing.

His first moon cycle on New Lassa was a lesson in heartache for both of them. Chardon left him alone most of the time for two reasons: she was furious with him and he needed to understand the weight of his actions. In two weeks, the little one would be back with his mother on Azrom which was probably for the better. Her initial feeling was insult, thinking Romnus had no faith in her race keeping mother and child safe. As time passed, it became clear that it was unfair to Chastan. He should have the option of getting to know his son.

"Is he behaving?" Chardon pushed herself off the door frame and entered the room.

Halfar looked up, startled for a moment at her appearance, then his attention went back to his grandchild. The smile on his face faded away and Chardon could feel his sorrow.

"As well as one could hope. He has so much energy."

"And we know where he gets it from," Chardon laughed as she ran her fingers in the little one's hair.

"I don't think he should be on Azrom."

Chardon looked over at him.

"Why do you say that?"

"Chastan is not who you think he is and with the sudden change in rulership, there could be chaos. I know the royal council and the advisors were none too happy with Romnus' appointment. They could decide to assassinate him and everyone around him, including Farin."

"That is a given. But I am sure Romnus will protect her with his life and Kur will protect him."

"You seem so optimistic."

"Why are you not?"

The little one squirmed his way out of Halfar's grip and made a straight away to the door, giggling the whole time. He ran right into Und, who appeared blocking his exit, and went down with a soft "oof ". Und picked him up by the armpits and carried him off down the corridor.

Halfar stood up and came face to face with Chardon. She searched his eyes for something that may resemble happiness and found none. It was still too soon for that. An awkward silence came between them. Not able to tolerate his hesitation any longer, she grabbed him by the sides of his head and brought him to her. Their lips touched lightly and she waited for him to engage. He was tentative at first, then finally kissed her with the hunger she knew he had been keeping inside for so long.

As they disengaged she whispered to him. "Just because I'm angry with you doesn't mean I don't love you."

"I can't act like I didn't cause such grief for you and our children. I feel as if I've lost everything."

"Not yet." Chardon held him. "And, Farin is not helpless. She's more ferocious than you think, or have you forgotten?"

✳✳☼✳✳

Sparks flew as two longswords clashed together, making a loud clank that rang in the air. Farin sat leaning forward on her knees while she watched a group of royal guards spar in the training arena near the courtyard. Her hands gripped her thighs, the fingers digging into the fabric of her robe. She remembered her fight with Batis, knowing she wouldn't win yet determined to not leave him unscathed. As great a fighter as she was, Batis was battle seasoned and twice her size. Like a newborn against a giant. Her teeth clenched together in frustration.

Lady Emalli came out of the archway and settled down beside her. Farin flinched when she felt her fingers slide across her back and rest on her shoulder. Emalli drew her in and Farin relaxed, laying her head on her bosom. She smelled nice, like fresh flowers just blooming.

"Do not chastise yourself so brutally," Lady Emalli said softly. "No one expects a child able to defend themselves against such violence." Farin reached out and circled an arm around her waist. "That being, you holding your own with such a beast like Batis is quite telling. You are a formidable adversary, young Farin."

Farin felt a smile creep on her face. She and her brother had trained with manbeasts and Lassian warriors, becoming well versed in fighting techniques. The proof of her short lived success was that she was still here and not broken. The sounds from the sparring soldiers called her attention back to them. This time, she would learn how Azrom fought.

From the balcony above the courtyard, Romnus watched Farin stare intently at the guards in training. He knew how she felt and agreed with the assessment of her own fighting abilities. It was time for him to set his plan in motion and she would have to defend herself now more than ever. Of course, he would not let anyone get that close to her. Just in case, she needed to do her due diligence.

Thinking of Batis, he had not decided what to do with the soldier still being held in the dungeon after his wounds had healed. Romnus wanted to tear him apart one more time for good measure before debating his fate. A thought occurred and shocked him yet, a very productive one that dealt with both issues simultaneously.

Going over the details in his head, Romnus turned away from the balcony and headed down the corridor towards the dungeon entrance. His entourage fell in place behind him and Biandra held out his favorite fruit. He glanced down at it and pondered if he would need it when facing Batis. Taking the fruit, he bit into it. Better safe than regret killing the soldier.

Seeing Batis dirty and wretched, bound to the wall of his cell made Romnus a tad giddy. The steeled look he gave made it even more priceless. Such hatred should not go to waste. He stood at the cell's entrance, his stare bearing down on Batis. They engaged in a silent contest and Batis was the first to severe eye contact.

"At least you still have some pride intact," Romnus scolded him. "Now, address your Supreme Ruler."

Batis turned his head to him and spat. The glob of saliva landed just inside the cell's threshold.

"My Lord," he said, bowing slightly. His restraints only let him bend so far.

Romnus' guards grabbed the hilts of their longswords, ready to draw. He raised a hand signaling them to stop. He gestured for the dungeon guard to open the cell and Batis stiffened, his eyes wide with trepidation.

"I have a proposal for you," Romnus said as he stepped into the cell to tower over him. Batis cocked his head. "Since you have such an affinity for Farin, you are going to train her in combat."

"Is that so?"

"That is the only way I would ever let you touch her."

"What if I decide to kill her," Batis asked. His eyes narrowed and a sly smile appeared.

"Oh, she's not that easy to kill, you should know better than that. And I will tear you apart."

Batis let out a hoarse laugh that made him cough.

"So she's being given to me after all."

Romnus deactivated the restraints and Batis fell forward in a heap.

"Get up," Romnus ordered.

"What about the rest of my unit?"

"They will have a different task to complete with a new leader." He knelt down by the soldier and whispered, "If you truly want Azrom to be beautiful and glorious once more, you will swear loyalty to me."

"What makes you any better than Halfar?"

Batis still sat with his forehead touching the filthy cell floor, his breath causing dried debris to move around his mouth.

"You shall see." Romnus stood back up and left the cell. His entourage halted halfway down the corridor and waited for Batis to stumble forward and catch up. "This will be quite entertaining."

∗☼∗

Hordes representing every province on Azrom was assembled within the wall surrounding the palace that separated its land from the rest of the sector. Thick tension hung in the air. Romnus scanned the multitude of faces full of curiosity about why they had been summoned. Across the planet, holoscreens hovered above villages displaying his image as he stood on the palace balcony. Behind him were Generals Kur and Rass, Lady Farin, his entourage and Batis.

"People of Azrom," his voice boomed out. "I know you have heard rumors of our debt to the Dreridian conglomerate and I am here to confirm your fears." Loud murmurs rose up. "Due to this debt, I have made a decree that you will abide." From a vid feed farther in the horizon he could see everyone behind him tense. "As of now, all able bodied citizens will work the mines and the fields. Those soldiers not on campaign will also contribute to the work load."

Cries of outrage spanned the crowd and the decibel level was almost too much to bear.

"Tyrant!"

"Monster!"

"You're no better than Halfar!"

"Slaver!"

Romnus took all of it in. He expected as much.

"Those of you who do not comply will be stripped of status and confined to the dungeons." More yells of profane language this time in their native tongue. "Those who rebel," he paused, "will have their entire horde sentenced to torture and confined to the mines until the end of our debt."

A hush flowed like a wave over the people as they stared back in confusion at him. He could see them affirming his resolve by trying to find some solace in his bright green eyes. His were not the murky forest green like Halfar's and they shone like gems in the vid feeds.

Yes, I am serious.

From various sections in the crowd, fighting erupted between the guards keeping peace and outraged citizens. Chaos was imminent and he felt something break inside him as blood flew. With fists clenched so tight he could feel his own blood seeping in his hands, Romnus looked down into the melee.

"Enough!"

The fighting was brought under control and he waited for the rebels to be removed.

"Shifts will be determined through allotments. It will begin at daybreak tomorrow. You are free to disperse."

Romnus turned his back to the crowd and the vid screens. He came face to face with General Kur who just nodded. He unclenched his fists and wiped the blood on his robes as he strode off into the throne room ahead, his entourage following. In the right corner of his vision he saw the royal advisors gloating.

He sat down on the throne and let his head fall back against the top ledge. When he lifted back up at his newly formed entourage, he found worry and despair.

"Now the real strife begins," he laughed. Then regretted it.

"Yes, there will be discontent across the planet," Kur stated.

"You didn't want to rule or live long, did you?" Batis scoffed.

He tensed when a blade settled across his neck.

"You forgot something," Rass whispered in his ear.

"My apologies, my lord," Batis addressed him.

Romnus waved his hand and Rass sheathed his short blade. More than just tension ran high. A sense of doom shone in their eyes. Sighing, he leaned forward until his elbows rested comfortably on his knees then glanced around to make sure the royal advisors were still outside and out of earshot, before speaking.

"This agenda is to better Azrom. I know the timetable seems

impossible but there is a reason for it. I need you to trust that what I am doing is only for the sake of our planet and our people. There will be many attempts on my life as well as the royal family that all of you standing here before me have sworn to protect. I will hold you to that."

"I promised you, so I plan to do so," Kur said.

"What are we committing?" Batis asked. "Ten, twenty, fifty years?"

"I want to clear the debt in fifteen years."

"My lord!" Prevcan exclaimed as he entered the throne room with the other advisors. "That is impossible!"

Romnus sat up straight and eased back into the throne.

What impeccable timing.

He fought the urge to snap all their heads off. Mesrod had a smug expression and the other three exchanged shifty glances.

"It can be done."

"At the expense of citizens dying from over exposure in the mines or toiling endlessly in the fields?"

"Lord Prevcan," General Kur purred. "Are you implying that our Supreme Ruler is using his agenda to murder our people?"

The advisor went pale.

"Of course not," he snapped. "I believe this is undue hardship."

"Forgive me, my lord, but I find it irresponsible," Mesrod added, bowing low.

Romnus could feel the juices from the fruit ebbing away inside him.

No, you find it intriguing, like an open invitation to further your own agenda.

He caught Biandra's eye and she stepped up to the throne, presenting a fruit from inside her robes. Kur, along with his personal guards had their fingertips on the hilt of their longswords. He assumed they felt the same towards the advisors.

"It is a means to an end. I would advise that you put your faith in my plan."

He watched Mesrod's face scrunch up before relaxing and raised his head to meet his gaze.

"I understand, my lord. We are behind you with strength and conviction."

Batis burst out laughing, causing everyone to flinch. He went on for a few seconds then cleared his throat. The advisors gave him looks of disdain.

"Leave me," Romnus commanded.

They all dispersed, leaving him alone in the throne room. General Kur halted at the entrance and turned to give him one last look. Romnus nodded in acknowledgement. Azrom was being broken in preparation for its revival.

Farin's black talons sliced through the column along with the soldier who hid behind it. Blood arced straight out like an asteroid belt right as another soldier came up behind her. She turned, feeling the air being cut inches from her face, and leapt backwards. Her body sailed in an arc, as if weightless before twisting ninety degrees so that her feet could land on the still toppling column. Using it as a launch pad, she dove right for the solider.

He was still in the process of advancing towards her when a fortuitous slip of his foot on a pool of blood increased his momentum, leaving him vulnerable. His eyes went wide with fear as there was no time for him to dodge. Farin morphed her right hand into a giant pincer and snapped them shut, slicing him from his left underarm to his right shoulder. His torso and lower body slid away at an angle, his mouth still open from a battle cry.

Landing in a crouched position, she slid backwards coming to a full stop and hurried to Romnus' side. Without hesitation, she pulled the longsword out of his shoulder and flicked it hard, sending blood splatter across the throne room floor. This was the fourth attempt on Romnus' life in the past twelve years since his decree regarding the debt. The only difference this time was how close the assassins had gotten to harm him. Farin bent down and formed a small ball of energy, using it to cauterize the wound.

"It's not so bad," she quipped.

Romnus smiled and brushed some of her hair away from her face. He seemed defeated somehow, long ago resigning to his fate. It made her angry. Taking a look around, she counted the number of bodies staining the floor. Batis shoved a dead soldier out of his way with one foot and sheathed his longsword.

"They were more determined than I have ever seen," he said while advancing to their side. His hand grazed across her backside. "Nicely done, Lady Farin."

She smacked his hand away with her free hand. The other she pushed harder into Romnus as she felt him try to rise and get to Batis. This was not the time or the place for domestic fighting.

"Stop that! We have a dire situation here!"

"I taught you well."

"It wasn't just you," she snapped.

Learning all the Lassian techniques along with Azrom's was a great benefit. By combining Talas and Trinon's signature moves, she had created her own, becoming deadly. Her mother had always said she was ferocious as an infant and now she could claim that title. At thirty four, which was still considered child years, she felt accomplished for her age. Most talents or powers didn't manifest until the age of fifty. Farin grinned. *I'm just special.* She snapped out of her self-indulgence and focused on Romnus.

"Can you stand?"

"Of course, I can stand. I just need to catch my bearings a moment."

"Good. We are moving, now."

Batis cocked his head to one side and listened for anything that may set off a warning sign. Satisfied there was none, he waited with her for Romnus to get up.

"How many?" Romnus asked.

"Eight," Batis replied.

"All dead?"

"Yes," Farin answered.

"I don't want to kill my own people," Romnus said through gritted teeth.

"I know," she said.

In Romnus' chamber, Farin ripped off the sleeve of his robe, exposing the wound to light for better scrutiny. Batis turned away and walked out of the room, leaving them alone. She got within millimeters of the wound and frowned.

"Damn, it's deep."

"Hmm."

"We need to get the medics in here."

"Where is my entourage?"

"Ambushed in the corridor. They handled the second wave."

"A second wave? It has gotten worse."

"You have a meeting with the Dreridians next moon. It's almost over."

Farin went to move away from him on the bed but he caught her by the wrist and pulled her closer. She felt his nose embed itself in her hair and heard sniffing. He did that often yet still refused to touch her sexually. It frustrated her sometimes, the reason why, but as far as the people of Azrom were concerned, she was mated to Chastan.

"We don't have time for you to sniff me all day." She disengaged from him and went to the entryway. "Where is Kur?"

"Come back to me," Romnus demanded softly.

Farin looked over her shoulder at him.

"After we get your wound treated, I will let you hold me until sunset."

Romnus frowned, resting his head on the cushions. She giggled, surprising herself. She hadn't done that in a long time since there was not much to laugh at over the years. Her mother probably felt the same.

****☼****

New Lassa

Chardon took one look at the itinerary Ganna had laid before her and grimaced. With each year of them finding new ways to clear off their Dreridian debt, Ganna dove deeper into the planets nether regions to find precious morsels to exploit.

"You have no idea what is out there. For all we know the Ginge Ocean could be treacherous."

"That's the beauty of it," Ganna exclaimed. "Have I not produced many new things to the Dreridians' liking?"

"You have, but it is getting a bit dangerous. Plus, we are still in the process of social restructuring for our race."

Chardon placed both hands flat on the console and stared at the itinerary again.

"That is something you can handle on your own. I need to satisfy my scientific agenda."

"Then you will take a large crew?"

"Naturally."

"Then safe journey," Chardon said as she rose up from her position.

As Ganna left the conference chamber, she went to the cushion on the end of the console and plopped down. It contoured to her body and she relaxed into it, closing her eyes. Movement from the entrance caught her attention and she opened them. Modas walked into the chamber and stood just inside the doorway.

He looked haggard, like he had aged too fast or not slept in days. A great rift had formed between the manbeasts who joined the rebellion for change and the ones who only wanted to harm others. Being the leader of his kind was no easy task from the start and his agenda had made it nearly impossible. She almost felt sorry for him. Almost. The past years had been hard on everyone. Halfar was finally settling into a more peaceful life letting Chardon rest easy. She missed Farin and knew her daughter was dealing with her own chaos on Azrom.

"What is it Modas?"

"I would like to have Una moved to a rehabilitation facility closer to our home."

Una.

Chardon propped herself on her elbows and contemplated the request. His daughter had fell into a dark place after realizing what she had done in the throes of her madness, combined with the injury inflicted by her brother Und. The female manbeast was mostly catatonic and rail thin, having to be fed intravenously which provided little nutrition when factoring in how much a manbeast consumed on a daily basis.

"That should be better, I think. I will let the medical staff know to transfer her."

She saw the relief on his face. The mighty manbeast was less of one now in her eyes. every now and again she would see his strength peeking out. He was by no means defeated.

"Thank you, leader." Modas bowed to her and left the room. Chardon frowned, hating the way he said it. With all that had happened, he should be able to speak with her candidly. The withdrawal was painful.

I will fix this.

Ocean skimmers sailed across the Ginge Ocean at leisurely speeds. They were a new addition to New Lassa's transportation agenda, their design pilfered by Ganna from some of the schematics in the Dreridian archives. She had added her own ideas to them and her scientists were more than a little thrilled when the first fleet was built. Ten ships headed towards the eastern side of the planet for a science expedition to find out what their new home was hiding in its corners.

Each vessel was operated by a crew of twenty manbeasts resolved to their fate after the rebellion. Ganna made the proposal to have all manbeasts, regardless of their involvement or lack of, perform labor in conjunction with planet reparations. Chardon did not like the inclusiveness and forced her to revise it. All she wanted to do was make sure none of the manbeasts sat idle. There would be no telling what horrors they'd come up with if left to think.

On this journey, she had Chafar and Und as bodyguards in case something unexpected happened. The younger child of Halfar was too quiet for her taste, his deadpan demeanor making it difficult to gauge what he was thinking.

"How long before we reach landfall?" she asked the manbeast at the helm. Her eyes squinted as she looked out through the panoramic window.

"We should see land before nightfall," he answered.

Ganna nodded in approval and turned to the blinking signal to her left from the communications console. Only one person would be keeping tabs on her. Especially since she was hundreds of miles away with a large group of manbeasts. She reached over and touched the link icon. Jaron's face appeared on the screen.

"And how are things going so far?"

"Really, Jaron? Is that what you wish to know?"

"Of course, because I know you would not be stupid enough to try and take out that many manbeasts. I would personally come for you."

"I have been informed we should reach land by nightfall."

"Are the ships holding up?"

"I created them, so yes. They are superb."

"That's good to hear. I will check back with you in a few days then."

The screen went black and Ganna sighed. This expedition was on the tail end of their debt to the Dreridians. She hoped to find yet another resource suitable for bargaining and get them one step closer to fulfilling the quota. Twelve years was not a long time by any means, but it was still too long to repay a debt. After hearing what Lord Romnus had done to speed up Azrom's timetable, Ganna insisted they do the same. Only a few more years were left and both New Lassa and Azrom would be free of the

Dreridians. She almost felt bad for the Razznians who were locked into a fifty year contract.

Ahead of the fleet she noticed the water swell upwards like a giant bubble. At first she thought it might be an anomaly of the ocean current until she saw it get bigger.

"Full stop!" She cried into the fleet intercom system. All the ships halted, hovering above the waters.

The bubble rose higher and when it towered over the fleet tenfold, the water broke away to reveal a creature of black oily skin with a bulbous head baring six rows of pointy teeth. Large grappling tentacles, four in all slapped the water and send fifty foot tidal waves towards them.

"Eva…!"

The crews were already taking action to get the fleet out of harm's way. Und stood with his arms crossed next to the navigator and Chafar leaned against the bulkhead. She couldn't tell what either of them were thinking and was shocked, no confounded, when Und finally spoke.

"We should take it down and serve it for evening meal."

The navigator nodded as did Chafar. Ganna found herself standing legs wide apart with her mouth gaped open. She felt her eyes straining as they nearly bulged out of their sockets. Even in her sometimes maddened state of research, she knew this was a moment of danger. This was no time for capture and experimentation. She turned her head towards the vessels on her left and witnessed a new form of madness from the manbeasts. They had heard him via the still open intercom and went about attempting to try and do just what Und suggested, by any means necessary.

All the skimmers were equipped with weapons, one being a harpoon for catching large fish. A reinforced net was attached to the ship and could be released when their prey was caught to drag it close for easier lifting onto the deck. The manbeasts were going about making ready these two items.

"Has Lassa's wisdom fled your minds?" she yelled, still wild eyed.

"What? You dissect it, we claim the meat as you go," Und said.

"Isn't this part of your scientific curiosity?" Chafar added.

She chastised herself for being surprised. Manbeasts would take on any opportunity to show off their prowess. The ship rocked and just as she turned to the observation window she saw a giant tentacle slap one of the vessels down into the ocean's surface. The impact caused another wave and this time, they were engulfed by it.

Lucky rodents!

Ganna threw her torn and ragged travel bag onto the sand and looked back at the remaining vessels cruising onto the beach. She had lost three ships but not any of the crew, to her amazement; and disappointment. They had done the deed in a uniformed effort, bringing the giant creature down piece by piece. The main body was being kept refrigerated for her until she could muster the strength to start dissecting it.

Her body ached all over from being tossed around her ship by waves created from the thing thrashing about. Some of the manbeasts had taken one of the tentacles and was in the process of slicing it up. Barbarians. She was surprised they didn't just bite into it, eating it raw like the animals they were.

"Only you would think we are a bunch of senseless animals," Und snapped, jarring her out of her thought.

"I didn't say anything of the sort!"

"No, you were just thinking it. It was so obvious, you may have well said it."

Ganna pursed her lips.

"Fine, but look at what you are doing. None of us are sure it is even edible."

"Oh, I'm sure it is. It never stopped us from eating any of the other creatures we encountered."

"THEY are not that," Ganna pointed to the giant tentacle, "BIG!"

"Look at it this way. We now have enough rations to last for months on end."

Ganna went pale and her stomach felt queasy.

"I will not eat that thing."

Und laughed, backing away from her before turning to go help slice the tentacle.

Seeing the vid feed of the manbeasts' conquest, Jaron slapped a hand across her mouth to subdue her laughter. Ganna's face appeared in the foreground and she didn't look too please. It was more fodder for Jaron so she squeezed her eyes shut for a few seconds and inhaled deep, letting it out between her fingers.

"Does this amuse you? I lost three vessels! And those heathens did not make it any better."

"So, you found a new food source in the process?" Jaron asked, her voice muffled by her hand.

"In a way and much more."

"Oh?" Jaron removed her hand. "Do tell."

"It seems the creature's bodily fluids have another use. I am not one to condone hunting of a species, but we may need to acquire another one for a generous supply."

"Yes, you seem so out of sorts for suggesting it," Jaron deadpanned. "I think the Dreridians will like it as much as we will. And, they are not getting rights to it."

"A battle against the Dreridian treasurer?" Jaron raised an eyebrow.

"This find is ours and they can negotiate trade. I will not just give them every resource we come across."

"Well said. I agree. As I used to say on Earth, they can suck it."

"What?" Ganna reared back somewhat confused.

"It means they can suffer in the flames of Lassa's light."

"Oh. Then yes, indeed."

"Hurry back."

"No rush. My team still has to explore the terrain we landed on."

"Then do it and hurry back. The quicker we get to see your new find and peddle it to the Dreridians, the better."

Jaron touched the icon to deactivate the vidscreen and sat down in the nearby cushion. She used her fingers to wipe away strands of fire red hair from her face and let her head drop back. Almost there. Then she could focus on Modas and how to fix what he had broken. Their relationship was strained but she knew deep down, she still loved him. Getting rid of the obstacle called Dreridian debt was first on the list.

⚹☼⚹

This time, Romnus traveled to the Dreridian home world in his royal ship with a small fleet in tow as guardians. He knew only the main ship would be permitted to land but he wanted to show Azrom's might. They did not need to tip the Dreridians on how torn apart and in shambles the planet was. They had surely heard rumors. He sat in the lounge of the ship surrounded by his entourage. Farin was asleep with her head resting on his shoulder. Next to her was Batis pretending to look bored but Romnus saw his eyes zeroed in on Farin's bosom.

General Kur was seated across from him in a state of silence. He always wondered what the military elite was thinking in those moments. Scanning the lounge he counted twelve and realized his group may be too large. A moot point now.

"We are cleared for landing, my lord," the pilot announced over the commlink. "We will be there shortly."

Romnus did not reply. He had faith in the crew's expertise. Nudging Farin awake, he stood up and made his way to the hangar. His four royal guards fell in formation, two ahead and two behind, with Farin and Biandra on either side of him. Batis stayed in the rear along with Kur to oversee Mesrod and the head of agriculture who basically demanded he attend the meeting.

The hatch opened for the ramp to extend down onto the docking floor. Romnus didn't even feel the ship land. He wanted to reward the crew but could not think of anything off hand. Down below, standing in their usual triangular formation were Lord Greggor and his faithful entourage. The Dreridian looked as if he had gotten bigger in girth. Romnus decided not to dwell on ideas of what the creature was eating. A quick glance to his left found him staring at a ship he had never seen before. Lord Greggor noticed his interest.

"Ah, yes. The Lassians arrived in that beautiful machine. I am quite impressed with Ganna and her team's ingenuity."

Romnus gaped at the giant ship with its sleek oval design and muted tones of color that reminded him of New Lassa's surface. He drew his attention away and silently congratulated them on finally getting ships to travel with instead of relying on the vortex so much. Once his people set foot on the tarmac, Lord Greggor turned away and walked towards the elevators. Without needing to be told, Romnus and his entourage followed.

Inside the conference room, Romnus saw Chardon already seated at the table flanked by Ganna and Talas. Modas stood nearby and his appearance was shocking. The manbeast had seen better days. A deep weariness exuded from him. Moving along the edge of the table, Romnus noticed Sars seated with both elbows up, hands templed in front of him. They made a quick nod of acknowledgement as Romnus sat.

Farin had a huge smile on her face as she nodded to her mother. Chardon smiled back. They would have to reminisce later after the meeting. Everyone waited silently for Lord Pondur and the treasurer to arrive. Romnus felt his fingers tapping the tabletop and stopped. Biandra held out the small fruit and he took it from her slowly. There was no reason to be on edge for this meeting. Then he realized it wasn't the meeting, it was what had to happen afterwards on Azrom.

Lord Pondur strode in posture erect, looking dignified, his treasurer right on his heels carrying the tablet containing every transaction made in the past fifty years. A servant appeared with a chalice and poured liquid from a carafe into it. Lord Pondur waited until the servant slunk away before raising the drink to his craggy lips, taking a delicate sip.

"This is quite unprecedented, all of you demanding a meeting so soon before your quotas' timetable is up." He set his chalice down. "But, I do like to be updated on the flow of commerce."

The treasurer activated his tablet and began going through the uploaded data from all of them. He frowned after some time then nodded in approval. Looking up from his screen, he addressed Lord Pondur.

"It seems, my lord, that Azrom has indeed met their quota ahead of schedule."

Lord Pondur and Lord Greggor both halted their drinks in midair.

"Are you certain?" Lord Pondur glanced at him.

"Very. Would you like to see the data?"

Lord Pondur waved a hand at him. "That is not necessary. The others?"

"Almost for the Lassians, but they do have a proposal. Razzna has also ramped up production and close to the end."

"How prolific all of you are. I never would have guessed the depths of your convictions. Well done."

Lord Greggor set his chalice down on a small stand near the entryway and cleared his throat.

"What is this proposal that you deem with erase the rest of your debt, Lassians?"

Ganna smiled. Romnus reared back from it and noticed everyone else did as well. It was never a good thing when Ganna was this happy. This time it may be warranted.

"Your kind has had some difficulty creating apparatus for research of your acidic oceans. The deep crevices of your bodies are susceptible to irritation and corrosion."

"Yes, but we have wonderful mobile suits that are impervious to the harms of our waters."

"But you still would like to able to touch your findings and know the actually texture of the water."

Lord Greggor stroked the rocky mounds of his chin.

"That would be ideal. Continue."

"We have found a new resource that is capable of attaching and sealing itself to organic subjects and can be easily peeled away. The remnants can be reconstituted for up to four uses before it breaks down."

Lord Greggor's eyes went wide and his hands started to shake.

"Show me! I want to see this new compound."

"Is this something extraordinary or just good?" Lord Pondur asked seemingly unimpressed.

"It is more than extraordinary!" Lord Greggor exclaimed.

Ganna reached down by her side and produced a clear circular casing that housed a black slush. It moved extremely slow inside the bubble, then clung to the edges before receding. Watching it, Romnus thought it looked like Azromian blood, only thicker.

"Come," Lord Greggor huffed, gesturing Ganna to the door.

"You're testing it now?" Lord Pondur frowned.

"Of course. I will bring her back before the evening banquet and give you my decision."

"Very well."

As Lord Greggor left with Ganna and his guards, Lord Pondur turned his attention to Romnus.

"What do you want?"

Romnus heard a sense of resentment in the Dreridian's tone. Having the debt cleared ahead of time meant there would be no interest collected. That was part of his initial plan. He glanced at the councilman and Mesrod. His request had to be cryptic but nonetheless understandable.

"I want access to the outer rim so we can barter for supplies."

"Is that so?" Lord Pondur's eyes narrowed into slits. "What could you possibly want from the outer rim?"

"They have commodities beneficial to Azrom."

"You're not going to divulge the reason then?"

Dreridians were highly intelligent and Romnus knew he couldn't hide his reluctance to tell him his plans. The treasurer was hunched over his tablet again.

"What is your timeframe for bargaining?" The treasurer blurted without looking up.

Romnus tapped his fingers on the table then replied, "Five years."

"That's all?" The treasurer was perplexed.

Lord Pondur gave him a glare making obvious his wariness towards Romnus.

"Yes, that is all I need to acquire what I want."

"Shall I authorize it, my lord?" Lord Pondur nodded, not turning his gaze from him. The treasurer's fingers went flying across the tablet.

"Very well, Lord Romnus. I have cleared Azrom's debt and releasing access for trade."

"I give you my gratitude," Romnus said as he bowed his head to Lord Pondur.

"And you?" Lord Pondur snapped, addressing Sars.

Sars looked towards Romnus as if asking for permission then smiled. Or what passed as one for a reptile.

"Your overseers off our planet within ten years. We will have our debt cleared by then and there would be no reason for your presence on Razzna."

"Bold aren't we, reptile?"

"Now that we can bargain on the outer rim, I can also negotiate goods for Razzna," Romnus spoke.

"Are you not enemies?" Lord Pondur barked. "Did Razzna not invade both New Lassa and Azrom? What am I missing in this scenario?"

"We were made enemies based on lies and someone else's agenda," Talas answered. "We all understand this and have decided to negotiate a truce."

"This stemmed from you suggesting trade in parts of the galaxy not charted." Kur continued where Talas left off. "I had never heard of Earth until the council informed me of it by way of your race."

"We are just three primitive races trying too hard, remember?" Romnus smiled.

"Yes," Lord Pondur grinned. "I will keep watch and see how your kind progresses. Please," he picked up his chalice, "prove me wrong." He took a small sip and glared over the rim at them.

The moment they all filed into the banquet hall, Farin ran to her mother and flung herself into her arms. Chardon steeled herself to take the onslaught. Farin found that amusing, knowing her usual lunge would probably hurt due to her being taller and more filled out.

"I missed you!"

"Yes, I see that," her mother said. "Now let go before we both hit the floor."

Farin did as she was told and for the first time was able to look her mother in the eyes on the same level.

"Are you doing well?" Her mother asked.

"Everything is fine."

"Then why do I get the feeling it's not. What is Romnus planning?"

Farin lowered her gaze. "I can't tell you that."

"Farin," her mother said in a warning tone.

"He's making Azrom better. That's all there is."

"How?"

"Can't we just enjoy being together for this short while? Please?"

From the corner of her eye she saw Talas frown. He had been listening and her heart sank. He was so intuitive that she could tell he was figuring it out. Bringing her attention back to her mother, she threw her arms around her mother's neck.

"I want to tell you about the good things. Like how my little one is no longer so and a pain."

"Because he is just like you."

Farin laughed. "You think so?"

She stole a glance at Romnus who just gave her a forlorn look as she and her mother laughed. Until Azrom was whole again, not even her mother can know of his agenda.

After the banquet, Romnus and his entourage were escorted immediately back to the docking bay and sent off under scrutiny of Lord Greggor's guards. Inside the ship, Romnus hurried to the lounge and took to a floor cushion that barely handled his size. He laid an arm across his face and exhaled.

"And now?" General Kur raised an eyebrow at him.

"We move on to phase two."

"What is this phase two?" The agriculture councilman exclaimed. "You have made many decrees, all sending Azrom spiraling down into the depths of despair! We deserve an explanation!"

"You deserve nothing," Romnus spat. He lifted himself up and stared at him. "Have you forgotten? I am Supreme Ruler. You do as I decree regardless of if it suits you."

Mesrod smiled. "I beg your pardon, my lord, but General Kur can remove you from rulership if he so inclines."

"Which I do not," Kur interjected. "I back his agenda fully. You should do the same."

The smile faded and the councilman seemed unsure of himself. Romnus didn't like them in his circle and especially not on his ship. His trust in them was nil and he had no doubt they were entrenched in their own agenda with him in their way.

"Preparing to enter vortex," the navigator's voice announced.

Romnus got up from the floor and went to his seat to strap in. Once he was back on Azrom, the real pain would begin.

They will forgive me when it's over and I am dead.

He felt truth in that.

There was no fanfare when they arrived back on Azrom. No royal guards in splendid arrays of color to greet the Supreme Ruler. Romnus didn't expect any to begin with. He made his way to the throne room via the staircase that wound down to the main level and curved into the secret corridor. The entire royal court stood in wait for him in the throne room, speech withheld until he was seated.

"The initial start of phase two is going slow but there is progress," Kur began. "There are rumors that some of the royal family members, namely Chastan, have been overly zealous."

"Excuse my ignorance, my lord," Mesrod interrupted. "But, what does phase two entail?"

"We are negotiating with the territories to have them vacate their lands and move into sectors I have prepared for temporary living," Romnus replied.

He saw the rest of the advisors and two other councilmen enter at that moment and what he said registered on their facial expressions.

"That borders on slavery. Why would you remove our people from their homes and imprison them?"

"Because I need to destroy the villages and I cannot do that if the people are still there."

Sharp intakes of air resounded.

"Madness," someone said. People turned to see who had spoken but no one seemed to fess it.

"The only way to ensure the safety and wellbeing of our race is to keep them within close proximity of my reach. Order must be maintained."

"Have you not had enough rebellion?" A councilman cried out. His face was flushed with anger.

"They can rebel if they want. They know the consequences of such actions."

"Destruction will start in the north," Kur continued.

"I want it to commence in two locations at once. The quicker we get the ground levelled, the faster we can get the citizens in the confinement sectors."

"Why?" Prevcan yelled. "Why are you doing such a thing? The people are working the mines and fields nonstop to keep to your timetable."

"Exactly. They are rarely in their villages and so have no need for them."

Many of the royal court went pale as if ill and Romnus fought to keep his composure. He could hear the harshness in his voice. It was necessary to convey his will. They despise me tenfold. Locking eyes with Kur, the general gave him a reassuring look.

"Continue with negotiations. I don't want bloodshed."

"That is inevitable," Mesrod stated.

"No," Romnus roared back, "it is not!" He turned to Batis. "See to it."

"As you wish, my lord," Batis answered, bowing low.

"You all know what needs to be done. You are dismissed."

There was hesitation in the movement of the crowd then a sudden stream of people fled from the throne room. Romnus gripped the sides of the arm rests and Farin placed a hand on top of his. As much as he adored her, it would take more than that to ease his anxiety.

Mesrod removed his gloves as he entered the advisors' meeting room and slapped them down on the center console. He laid his hands flat on it and leaned over with his head hanging down. After a moment, he turned towards his comrades.

"This would not be happening," he started softly, "if he were not still alive!" he shouted.

Calba and Jabarz flinched while Dondar and Prevan sat further back in their seats. He scanned their faces for some explanation even though he was certain there was none.

"Each attempt has failed. Why is that?"

"He's not easy to kill, Lord Mesrod," Calba replied. "We were close this last time. My men were able to wound him."

"Close does not make him dead."

Mesrod slammed his fist on the console.

"No, but getting that close to him means he has let his guard down somewhat," Jabarz said.

"Which he will no longer do since it was so close," Mesrod reminded them. "He is now more wary than before and we have a crisis on our hands."

"But, you said his actions would give us reason to form a coup." Calba seemed perplexed.

"A coup, yes. That is not possible any longer. He is about to enslave the inhabitants of our planet, throwing it into a form of chaos I do not know how to reverse."

"How could he get away with this? How does he get them to comply?" Jabarz questioned.

"It's obvious. Brute force," Dondar quipped.

"Kill him! I do not want to hear about another failure," Mesrod ordered.

"It will take some time. He will be prepared for one so soon."

"You have less than five years. Get it done."

Mesrod took a deep breath and exhaled slowly. He was getting tired of trying to steer insane rulers onto the right path that benefitted Azrom. From Romnus' father to Halfar's father and the two sons put together, he concluded that the royal bloodline must have been tainted somewhere along the way. It was time to cleanse the palace.

⁎⁎☼⁎⁎

Reports from across the planet came in droves, all disheartening yet some sense of accomplishment could be felt. Every second phase of the moon a new shipment arrived on Azrom and the goods stored in a secret location underground not far from the palace.

Romnus walked along the outer corridor by himself and smiled a little. The royal advisors probably thought he would use brute force but instead he had each village gassed before transporting all its citizens to the designated sectors. Bloodshed was not an option. Of course, there was hostility when they awoke in a new environment stripped of most of their belongings.

Movement to the right of him on the ground below caught his eye and he took a quick glance. Batis stopped walking and looked directly up at him, an eyebrow raised up. It was a bold move for him to stroll the palace unguarded but he refused to be deterred by yet another assassination attempt. He nodded to Batis and continued down the corridor. He was the Supreme Ruler. If he couldn't walk safely in his own palace, then who could? Then he grinned. *There is no safety if you're hated.*

A messenger came bearing towards him, skidding to a halt to slow his advance. The young soldier was winded with beads of sweat lining his forehead. He gulped a few times to catch his breath then spewed out his message.

"My lord! You have to stop Lord Chastan. He has gone mad."

"What do you mean, gone mad? Where is he?"

"He went to negotiate with one of the eastern villages. It's one of the last few still holding out but not rebelling." The soldier frowned. "Lord Farregun and his three brothers rule that territory, I believe."

"Yes, they are from the fifth royal house. What is the problem?" The messenger's face went rigid and it gave Romnus a sense of dread.

Hands clenched at his sides, the young soldier blurted, "He has resorted to unprecedented measures of persuasion."

Romnus raised his head up high and looked down at the young soldier as if he had given him something rotten. That description could entail anything. He knew it had to be bad. Maybe worse than he thought. Chastan was a bit rough and ill equipped to handle others. He could not see it being anything of horrors.

"Fine, I will send Aloni and General Rass to see to it."

"Of course, my lord," the young soldier bowed, "but they must hurry."

Turning on his heels, the messenger sprinted off from whence he came, leaving Romnus to ponder what was so dire about Chastan's behavior.

From a distance Aloni could see the village through his surveillance goggles and adjusted the lenses with a side tap to zoom in. He nodded at General Rass to do the same. They were on open land skimmers for their speed and the weather was mild enough. The high velocity created forcible winds that sent their hair straight back as they leaned forward to be more aerodynamic. Six royal guards on their own skimmers were keeping up behind them. The more the distance narrowed, the more they both saw what was occurring and they pushed the skimmers to full power. It was true. Chastan had gone mad.

Chastan's guards held the crowd back and struck down anyone who tried to break into his makeshift arena. On his left was Lord Farregun, nearly cut to ribbons tied to a stake embedded in the ground. Lying belly down with his face turned to one side was his younger brother, barely able to stay conscious. To Chastan's right was the older brother, decapitated. The man had tried to stop him from getting at his daughter so had to be put down. Behind him was the daughter, impaled by two rods in each arm to a board propped up at a forty five degree angle.

Her gown was ripped open down the middle and he had already raped her in front of everyone. Lord Farregun's daughter had been the first and she too was on the board next to her cousin, unconscious.

"Please," Lord Farregun whispered. "Stop this."

"You could have prevented this if you had complied with my demands. All you had to do was leave as instructed and give your daughters to me. They would have been a great addition to my royal court, but now."

Chastan flipped the short dagger he had used to cut open the gown in his hand then turned back to the dead brother's daughter. He ran the blade deep into her womb, the screams coming from not just her but the crowd as well. He smiled at his work.

"No one will have her."

Pain blossomed through his chest and looking down, he found the source. The blade of a longsword was sticking out of him. He tried to cry out but only ended up choking on his own blood, falling to his knees on the ground. The dagger slipped out of his hand.

General Rass came around him and pulled the longsword out of his back. Chastan saw his own blood spray in the air before darkness took him.

"What in all of Azrom has happened here?" Aloni cried out.

He observed the crowd then turned his attention to the royal family members in front of him. General Rass stood at the semicircle of guards. This could be bad. He had no doubt Rass could cut down every last one of Chastan's men. It went against Romnus' decree of no bloodshed.

Blood.

Aloni squeezed his eyes shut and tried not to think too far ahead on what to do in their current situation. The people would blame their Supreme Ruler because he had sent Chastan there.

"You will take your master to the medical wing of the palace and wait there. You do not venture anywhere else or I will cut you down faster than I did him. Do you understand?"

Rass had a demonic look in his eyes and Aloni was convinced of the threat. Apparently so were they, for they immediately dispersed, taking a nearly dead Chastan with them. They loaded him and themselves into the transport ship near Farregun's palace, taking off quickly.

Aloni held his breath for a brief moment watching the crowd, waiting for any kind of hostile reaction. Instead, the servants and handmaids rushed forward and tended to the daughters and the surviving brothers.

"You must know that this was not Lord Romnus' agenda," Aloni spoke. "His decree specifically forbade bloodshed. I do not know what Lord Chastan's reason for this was."

"He came to take our land and enslave us like the rest," a handmaid exclaimed. "Isn't that Lord Romnus' order?"

Aloni sighed and addressed Rass.

"I will tell them, and only them." Rass nodded.

He moved further into the middle of the crowd.

"Lord Romnus is not enslaving you. He's trying to make Azrom better. In order to do so, he must level everything. He asks," Aloni paused.

"We ask that you please be patient with us during this transition. You can hate your Supreme Ruler, even wish him death. In the end you will see he was right."

"So, we are to trust you? After this?" Lord Farregun's advisor pushed through the crowd and came face to face with him.

"Yes, even after this. As I said, this was not part of Lord Romnus' decree."

"Then you have royal family members with their own agendas?"

"I hope this is the worse and last of such things."

General Rass tapped the earbud in his right ear. "Send a medical team and the transport ships."

"Immediately, general," a muffled voice replied.

"Do we really want to show this feed to Lord Romnus?" Aloni asked Rass.

"He must see it!" Farregun's advisor demanded. "He needs to know what his own blood is doing!"

Aloni found himself staring up at the sky to see the small blip that was Chastan's ship disappear into the horizon.

What have you done, cousin?

"Romnus will not like this."

Fury filled Romnus as he watched the simultaneous feed from both Aloni and Rass. The two holoscreens were far enough away from him that he could see every detail on each one. This was far worse than madness. He could never have imagined Chastan capable of such heinous behavior. Seeing what he did to, the now deceased, Lord Than's daughter with the dagger nearly made him retch. Even when repaired, the girl would still know that pain, never able to find a mate she could trust. The feed ended and the throne room was silent.

"Where is he?" Romnus boomed.

"Still being treated in the medical bay. I figured you would not want him dead, although I nearly did kill him." General Rass tapped the hilt of his longsword. "I wanted to kill him."

"What else has he done?"

"I was able to get a good amount of information out of his guards. He has been terrorizing the territories and acquiring what he sees fit to have before sending the gas."

"Acquiring?" Romnus was puzzled at first, then remembered what Chastan said to Lord Farregun. "Women? He was acquiring women? For what..." Romnus held up a hand. "No, wait. I think I know. Sex slaves."

"Yes, his own personal brothel. He had even requisitioned a chamber and I was led to it." Aloni pursed his lips and exhaled. "It is more like a brothel of debauchery. I don't think I have ever seen," he stopped short of explaining and Romnus was grateful for that.

He suddenly felt ill. "Does Farin know?"

"She will soon enough," Rass replied. "She heard he was injured and is rushing to his side."

"Well, she might just kill him for you," Romnus stated.

Running at top speed, Farin careened down the halls of the first royal house palace towards the medical bay. She had no idea what had happened. If Chastan was so hurt he needed emergency attention then it must be bad. When she came to the clearing of the great hall, a royal guard held up a hand signaling her to halt. At first, she was going to plow right through him but something in the way he did it made her comply.

"Why have you stopped me?" She bent over to catch her breath, letting her arms dangle by her sides, the sleeves of her black robe nearly touching the floor. Her eyes went wide. "Has something happened? Has he?"

Her vision blurred and the sound went down to almost mute as he relayed what happened at Lord Farregun's palace. Her body stood frozen in a slump as her mind tried to process it. Chastan had turned into some kind of monster? Half drunk, mating crazed Chastan who backed away from a fight most of the time? It hit her hard, the disgust, forcing her body to come erect.

With everything that Romnus was setting in motion, she was still adored by the people of Azrom. Being Chastan's mate was to keep up appearance but now she had ample reason to sever ties with him. All would understand her decision. She suddenly felt weary, nodding her head when he finished then turned back. She wanted to lie down and not think for a long time.

**⚬

New Lassa

Halfar watched the sun set in the horizon from a hilltop above the compound he lived in with Chardon. Each day was peaceful despite series of tension and small episodes of chaos. He understood their disbelief at the rebellion, not being a race of warriors always fighting like Azrom. They did not know centuries of strife as he did. Off in the distance below, he saw the gate open and Chardon's giant oval ship come through. Ganna had outdone herself with that piece of technology.

Pushing himself up off the ground, he turned away from the harsh glare as the last remnants of sunlight glinted off its hull. He headed down the side of the hill to go welcome his mate back home. Halfar smiled at that sentiment. Not being Supreme Ruler was a gift he planned to cherish for as long as he could. In the first few years, he was resentful, finding Chardon's faith in him condescending. Now, he had a better grasp on why she felt that way.

Meeting Chardon's group on the trail leading to the temple, he searched their faces for a sign of what may have transpired with the Dreridians and the hideous smile from Ganna told him plenty. It must have been a success. He reached for his mate and pulled her into a long embrace. Chardon smelled of burnt air, the result of space travel through the vortex. That didn't deter him from burying his nose in the crook of her neck.

"So it is done?" He asked her softly.

"Yes. They agreed to clear the debt early due to Ganna's new find."

"Greed does have its advantages at some point."

"Well, we are grateful they are very greedy." Chardon moved her hands up his back and squeezed before letting go. "We have to address the council. Want to sit in?"

Halfar disengaged from her and cocked his head. Joining in on council matters was something he rarely did because it reminded him that he was no longer a leader of anyone or any race. Chardon knew this, so for her to ask meant there was something else that needed his specific attention.

"I will, since you have requested it."

"I saw Farin." Chardon spoke it nonchalantly, taking him off guard.

The group continued their advance towards the temple and Halfar kept in stride with them.

"How was she?"

"Taller, more rounded."

"Does she have more offspring?"

"No."

Chardon seemed to find it just as odd as he did by her expression.

"You learned something you didn't like when speaking with her." It wasn't quite a question but he expected an answer.

"More a combination of what Romnus is doing and what she didn't tell me."

"Hmm?"

"Talas has a theory and he's usually right. I want you to hear what he thinks and see if you agree."

"Has he told you this theory?"

"No, he wants to make sure you hear it with us."

A tightening in the pit of his stomach forced him to inhale sharply. Exhaling didn't help ease the tension so he decided to steer the conversation back to Farin.

"So, how tall is she?"

"Taller than the both of us. And," Chardon slowed down her pace, "she seems to be quite strong. Like she is fighting all the time. I could tell how well toned her muscles were by her body movements."

That did disturb him. Although Farin had been trained by Lassian energy users and manbeasts, it was not for her to become a warrior. Only a means to defend herself if necessary. Whatever was happening on Azrom could not be good. They had abided Romnus' wishes all this time to not open the pathway to Azrom, sacrificing their ties to Farin. If Talas' theory proved a dire need, he would break that promise, consequences be damned.

Arriving at the temple's side entrance, the entire group formed a single file line in order to enter the narrow hallway. The walk was quiet, devoid of speaking. Inside the council chamber were all the representatives of Lassian divisions. With Chardon's group adding to the numbers, the chamber was nearly filled to maximum capacity. Halfar barely had time to settle down into a seating cushion when the session began. He only heard half of what they were discussing but he got the gist of it. Hearing Lord Pondur's reaction to the three races putting aside their differences for the time being made him laugh along with a few others.

Most of this side of the galaxy was comprised of bipedal lifeforms with similar biological structures. It was when you ventured out towards the outer rim that it got strange and frightening. Razzna was not quite on the verge and had variations of their species. Halfar had only seen one or two beings from the outer rim and didn't care to see them again or any others. Then he realized they were indeed talking about the outer rim and Romnus' bargaining request. His hands clenched into fists.

The council meeting over, everyone dispersed except Chardon's inner circle. Jaron, Kelin, Talas, Ganna, Trinon, Mara and Und sat sipping the last of their drinks, taking a breather from the constant barrage of questions and answers. Chafar just stood leaning against the wall with arms crossed, mimicking Modas. Halfar sat still, not finishing his drink, lost in thought. He then turned to Talas who caught his eye and halted his cup as it touched his bottom lip.

Talas set it down and made himself comfortable in his seat. The others saw this and did the same.

"Romnus has cleared Azrom's debt in record time," he blurted out. Halfar felt his own eyes widen at the implication. "I have an idea of how that occurred, but I would like to confirm it with you."

Halfar frowned and rested his still clenched fists on the table.

"It would mean mines and fields production at a rate five times the normal output. It would put a tremendous strain on the worker population."

"Unless," Talas stated.

"Unless he made a decree to force the entire population to work on a constant rotation."

"That's insane?" Jaron spurted. "It borders on slavery."

"Which would turn Azrom into a hostile planet, a race against its own self." Halfar tried to control his breathing before continuing. "It's not worth it. Everyone Azromian would try to assassinate him to alleviate the strife."

"That is what I believe is happening. He is moving on to a second phase that involves bargaining with the outer rim. He is restructuring something but I can't put my finger on it."

With that notion, Halfar's mind tumbled backwards into his memories and landed on a conversation he and Romnus had regarding rulership. His cousin had told him and the royal family that if he were to become ruler, he would destroy everything in order to make Azrom thrive. The beings on the outer rim specialized in materials used for building elements of worlds, including structures.

"He can't possibly mean to do this," Halfar said to himself.

"Do what?" Chardon asked.

"Level the surface. Raze the villages and start all over."

Talas flinched. Halfar couldn't blame him. It was an extreme measure.

"Then that means the entire royal family is in constant danger, Farin included."

Halfar nodded.

"We have to find a way to Azrom. He's locked the pathway for the main gates."

Ganna snorted at that. "I have other ways to get to Azrom."

"If what you say is true and assassination attempts on Romnus are high, then with Farin by his side she has no choice but to defend both him and herself," Trinon spoke up. "I don't like that."

"Neither do I." Chardon glanced at Halfar and they silently agreed. "Travel takes time and it has already been over a year on Azrom since your return. If you can get a new pathway opened fairly soon, we can get there before his five year mark." He addressed Ganna specifically.

"It shall be done. Excuse me." Ganna got up and left the chamber.

"Can they hold much longer?" Kelin caressed his chin. "With such an implementation, the attempts will become frequent."

"And more brutal." Jaron added.

"Oh, sweet Farin. She has so much to deal with. At least she has the backing of the royal family," Mara said.

"Not necessarily," Halfar unclenched one hand to wave a finger at her. "There are some from the lower houses who wish to ascend to the throne by unconventional means."

"Are you going to reclaim your throne?" Chafar asked mildly. Halfar looked up with a jolt and found all of them staring at him.

"No. I do not wish to rule any longer. That said, I will not let Azrom be destroyed or ruled by yet another tyrant if that is what I find Romnus to be."

"Then it's settled," Chardon declared as she stood up. "We leave for Azrom as soon as possible."

Halfar let his other hand rest, the stiff numbness slowly subsiding.

Please wait for me.

He hoped his plea would reach Romnus and Farin.

End Game

Dungeon cells overflowing with royal guards and soldiers who rebelled against Romnus' decree made cleanliness next to impossible. The servants did the best they could. Kur was not enjoying the sight of Azrom soldiers trapped in an underground cage because they refused to trust in their supreme ruler's vision. It was almost over and he was sure they would see the outcome as a great thing for Azrom. He couldn't lie to himself and say it was not a challenge to keep the faith. There were times when he questioned even his own judgement in naming Romnus the new ruler.

An imprisoned royal guard rammed himself against the beams of his cell to try and grab a servant bent down a few inches from the bottom with a vacuum tool. The servant was quick on his feet and leaped backwards out of reach. The royal guard let out a frustrated roar, hit a beam and cursed as his skin sizzled where he had made contact. Kur saw them turning into barbarians, regressing to primal instinct. Not wanting to stay longer than needed, he left the observation to his unit leader and went back up to the palace courtyard.

He strolled along deep in his own thoughts and ended up at the first royal house palace's courtyard. His mother, Emalli, was there tending to the royal children. Farin's precocious son was among them, though he was now of teen years. His blond hair was straight like Farin's and hung just past his shoulders. He was a beautiful boy.

"When do I get to hold a child of yours and Rass'?" She asked him, meeting his gaze.

"Your intuition is extraordinary. Very soon. I wanted to wait before announcing the news."

"There may not be anything left when this is over, my son."

"Rass also brought that to my attention."

"You cannot protect him forever, no matter how great a warrior you may be."

"I have been successful so far."

"Mmm, but the advisors are getting desperate. They have the backing of some of the council members too."

"You are assuming they are the ones responsible for the constant attacks."

"General." She only called him that when she was angry. "Even you are not so naïve."

Kur dropped his head. The anger inside of him crept back up and he had to force it away. He was well aware of the advisors attempts to end not just Romnus' life but his, Rass' and Farin's. A thought came to him.

"I need you to do something for me. Something that requires immediate attention."

Emalli raised an eyebrow and smiled. "What do you need?"

"Someone who can protect Rass and the first royal house."

"Oh? There is such a being who is stronger than Rass and yourself?"

"Yes, Rass' father." His mother sat up straighter, a shocked look on her flawless face. "I need you to find him."

"That may take resources you cannot hide."

"I don't wish to hide it. If asked, the reason would be to connect with Rass' bloodline as I have with you."

"Then I will do this for you. For our family line."

His mother stood up to her full height, just shy of his own and placed a hand on his cheek. He leaned his head into it and closed his eyes. Just a little longer.

****☼****

A poisoned dart came sailing across the outer corridor as Lord Romnus walked with his entourage. He reacted before his guards, hearing it cut the air and caught it with his bare hands, thus letting the tip enter flesh. The effect was instant, bringing him to one knee as he clutched his chest. Farin had already pulled the dart from his hand and tossed it over the ledge. Biandra knelt next to him and rammed an injection rod full of antidote in his neck.

They were prepared for almost every scenario lately and he thanked his entourage silently as the pain subsided. Glancing back, he saw Batis lowering a crossbow and followed the guard's gaze to a soldier falling down towards the ground below. Romnus stood up brushing off his robes and took a few deep breaths.

"Are you alright, my lord?"

Biandra concealed the rod back into the folds of her robe.

"For now." He turned to Farin. "Did you touch the tip?"

"I was careful, unlike you," she snapped. "What were you thinking?"

He cowered from her anger. It didn't suit her at all.

"That was quite reckless of you, if I can add to that," Batis said.

"My apologies, it was instinct."

They continued on, heading to his royal chamber in the main palace. At the entrance, Batis and Biandra stood guard while the others split up to patrol the corridor from each direction. Farin went inside with him. He rubbed the injection site on his neck and planted one hand on the wall by their bed for leverage. Looking out at the afternoon sky, his mind felt cloudy and knew it could only be a residual effect of the poison.

Farin stood on the other side a few feet away from him. The thought of not being closer to her stirred something within. A deep desperation that had always been there; pushed away every time. Reaching out with his free hand, he snatched her from where she stood and drew her to him. His lips found hers and he kissed her, deeply, hungrily. Time stood still.

When he finally pulled away, he said, "Rule with me."

Batis' head peeked around the entrance. Romnus paid him no mind and kept his stare locked on Farin's eyes. They were wide with what he could only describe as a stunned look.

"You….I," she stuttered. Her eyes moved to and fro searching his. She wriggled out of his embrace and stepped backwards towards the entrance. "You don't want someone like me," she whispered. "I'm too young."

"I need you. Rule with me."

"I agree," Batis stated. "You are the only choice to be by his side." Biandra nodded.

Farin turned and ran from the chamber. He heard the guards cry out in surprise as she past them. Romnus found himself standing in the middle of the chamber, dejected.

"She needs time to think it through. I wouldn't worry, my lord. She will say yes in time."

Batis' reassurance irritated him because he was probably right. Farin had grown far beyond her years physically and psychologically. Her advice was always relevant and never steered him wrong when he implemented them. Maybe she was still too young. Taking a few steps back, he bumped against the foot of the bed and sat down on it. Time was something he had little of these days.

Royal guards crowded into the first royal house palace courtyard, forming a semicircle around the center. A vortex had suddenly appeared nearly sucking some of the royal children into it. Emalli and her fellow handmaids were able to get them rounded up and safely into the palace. She then returned to see who could be coming through at such a remote location far from a main gate console.

Kur was at the forefront with Romnus and the other members of their royal house behind him. Whoever was coming either had no clue that an alarm had been raised the moment the vortex was detected, or they did know and were prepared to defend themselves. Emalli was not surprised and started laughing as the group stepped out of the vortex.

Chardon, Halfar, Trinon, Talas and Chafar were already in fighting stances, weapons drawn, then hesitated when her laugh caught their ears. Emalli stopped and wiped tears from her eyes. She saw the incredulous look on her son's face and nearly started up again. She restrained herself.

"What are you doing?" Kur demanded, addressing Halfar.

They all straightened their stance and concealed their weapons. Halfar came forward and nodded towards Romnus.

"I came because he has lost his mind just as I had. Did you think we would stand by and wait for Farin to be killed after you put her in such a dangerous situation?"

"You don't even know what the situation is," Romnus hissed.

"Process of deduction," Talas spoke up. "I brainstormed everything you said at the meeting and ran it by Halfar. He came up with the logical answer."

"You are too intelligent for your own good," Kur snapped at Talas. "And you," he stared at Halfar, "are supposed to be exiled. How do you think we are to explain this?"

"Who says I am here?" Halfar cocked his head.

Emalli erupted into laughter again, breaking all their trains of thought. She let herself get it all out of her system then walked up to Halfar.

"This is advantageous for us all. Now, I won't need to drudge up useless information to fulfill your request, my son." Kur eyed her questioningly. "Who would know better where to find Rass' father than the former Supreme Ruler?"

Romnus turned and mirrored Kur's expression. The two warriors had a stare off before Kur spoke.

"Rass is with child. I need someone who can protect her and the first royal house. As competent as you all are, the next attack may be bigger than we anticipate."

Halfar locked eyes with Emalli. "I do know where he would be. It would have taken you a long time to find him and I believe none of you have much of that."

"Excellent! Now," she slowly turned to Kur. "Tell the guards to back away so we can continue this discussion inside."

"Disperse!" Kur ordered. "You tell no one of this event. It stays within this courtyard."

Weapons were sheathed and fists slammed into the left side of breast plates in acknowledgement. The guards bowed to Romnus and emptied out of the courtyard. Emalli grimaced at the display of discipline. She found it insincere.

"Where is Farin? I thought she was part of your entourage?" Chardon asked.

"Hiding from Romnus with her son," Batis answered.

His presence registered for the first time with Halfar and Chardon and they moved towards him.

"Wait!" Romnus held up a hand. "He is now part of my entourage as well."

"What madness is this?" Halfar demanded.

"I made him an offer and he is Farin's combat trainer."

"A very quick learner, the beautiful Farin," Batis added.

"After what he did?" Halfar roared.

"At your behest." Batis smiled wickedly at him.

That silence everyone. Emalli sighed heavily and grabbed Halfar by the sleeve.

"Come, we have much to discuss." She addressed Kur and Romnus as she walked away, her back to them. "I'm sure you can manage entertaining our guests."

Aloni was the first to speak. "We need protection? Really?" He toyed with his longsword.

Kur gave him a sideways glance.

"Yes, you all do. I cannot be in two palaces at once."

"And Rass' father is what?"

"I have no idea, but knowing how powerful Rass is gave me a clue."

The entire group headed into the palace and entered the main banquet hall. Reita summoned servants into action and drinks were brought instantly. As they all sat down at the giant wood table, Chardon looked around at each of them.

"Where is Chastan?"

Drinks halted in midair. Kuhala frowned. An ominous cloud of anger filled the hall.

"My brother is no longer part of the royal house at this time. He has behaved," Kuhala stopped.

"Chastan dove into a higher level of madness that I could not have fathomed," Aloni finished.

"Did it have anything to do with Farin?" Chardon asked.

"No, but their mated status was severed on that day. She will have nothing to do with him and rightly so."

"That's a relief." Chardon set her drink down. "Now, you need to let us help you. This is not something you should have tried to do on your own and in such an isolated manner."

"In hind sight, you are correct," Romnus stated. "At the time I thought it was the best course of action."

"Will you go over it in detail then?"

"Are you giving me a choice?"

"No."

Everyone then took large gulps of their drinks before setting them down on the table. Not even the royal house knew the plan in any detail. This would be the first time they heard it in its entirety. Romnus looked uneasy but settled into the cushion at the end of the table and began explaining his agenda.

"My timing could not have been any better and I feel fate has intervened," Halfar said to Emalli as they sat in her private chamber. A handmaid set drinks down and hurried out of the room.

"How so, my former lord?"

"Halfar is sufficient." He glared at her.

"My apologies, please continue."

She picked up her drink and sipped daintily.

"If my timetable is correct, in two moons a fleet sent on campaign decades ago will be returning. Rass' father is a commander on that ship."

"Oh? Where did you send this campaign?"

"Why is that relevant?"

"What are they bringing back?"

Halfar sat startled for a moment then tried to remember. When it came to him, he smiled.

"Advantageous indeed," he finally replied. "Seeds. To diversify our crops. The harvests have been lacking."

"That is an understatement. With the heavy burden from constant turning of crops, the soil won't yield what it used to."

Halfar rubbed the bottom of his chin.

"Then the soil needs treatment as well before we can plant them."

"I will let the council of agriculture handle that. I have work to do in regards to my mission." Emalli stood up and gestured for Halfar to exit her chamber. "I'm sure they are waiting for you."

The meeting was brief and to the point which suited him fine. He arrived at the banquet hall just as Romnus started to explain his agenda. Instead of interrupting by taking a seat at the table, he held up a finger to the servants to stay where they were and sat on a cushion just inside the archway. He listened to every word.

"Are you going to finally join us, cousin?" Romnus asked him after he finished talking.

"I was trying not to be rude in your palace," he replied. He rose up and made his way to an empty spot at the table. "That is some agenda, cousin."

"You both say cousin as if it's a dirty word," Talas interjected.

"On the contrary, it's a term of endearment," Romnus cooed. "So, Halfar. What exactly is Rass?"

"There is a village on the far North of the planet where the people grow larger than normal. We use them as second wave soldiers because of their mass and," he paused, "their incredible speed despite their size."

"Those monstrosities we clear a path for and do not fight alongside?" Reita cried out.

"Yes, those."

"Rass is nowhere near that size. How do you conclude that?"

"In each species there is always an anomaly. Rass would be considered a runt. He was conceived by a whore in the brothel. His father rarely frequented the chamber so it was pure luck that he impregnated his selection. Since Rass was born in the palace that is where he remained."

"To be made a whore in the brothel like his mother," Kur spat angrily.

"I had no say in that. I didn't even know of Rass until," Halfar stopped himself. No one else needed to know more than that.

"Then, this warrior would be ideal for being in charge of our safety since no assassins would dare come at him," Kuhala said.

"Don't be so sure," Aloni said, raising a hand.

"The advisors are getting bolder. It's only a matter of time."

Batis crossed his arms.

"By the way," Chardon interrupted. "Why is Farin hiding from you?"

Romnus' looked up, surprised that she had remembered what Batis stated earlier. Halfar was not and had decided to wait until later to ask the same thing. He should have known Chardon was not going to let it slide.

This time Batis laughed out loud. "He asked her to rule with him."

Romnus gave him a warning look. The soldier met his gaze and smiled.

"Rule with you?" Chardon asked unsure.

"AS in Queen?" Halfar yelled. His fists slammed down on the table and his brow furrowed.

"Oh?" Chardon slapped a hand across her mouth.

"So what?" Chafar leaned on the table resting his elbows. "If she bonds with a Supreme Ruler, that's what happens, right?"

"There hasn't been a Queen of Azrom in over 500 years," Halfar replied.

"That's preposterous!" Chardon exclaimed.

"No. My father never bonded with my mother," Halfar explained.

"And neither did my father to my mother when he reigned," Romnus continued.

"For that matter, neither did their father, if my history is correct," Aloni added.

"Why would you put such a burden on her?" Chardon yelled at Romnus.

"It's not a burden!" Romnus slapped his hand down on the table, causing it to shake on impact. "I want her and no one else."

There was a silence.

"You finally decided to be honest with yourself," Reita laughed. "Good. Now all you have to do is convince her."

"Because she is of royal blood, it would solidify our bloodline." Aloni turned to Halfar. "You have no objection?"

"For her to be mated to Romnus, no. It's the Queen part I am objecting to. You have no idea how our race would respond to having a Queen after so long."

"She is adored by all of Azrom. I think she will be well accepted," Kuhala said.

"That being if we pull this off without all of us being assassinated," Talas quipped.

Farin sat in her son's chamber deep in her own thoughts. She had let him go to play with the other royal children and leave her to be alone for a while. The kiss Romnus planted on her that day kept repeating itself in her mind. He had never kissed her like that before. Worse, SHE had never been kissed like that before. Chastan's were a bit rough and sloppy, Batis' resembled being assaulted by some starving animal, while Romnus left her warm and lightheaded. Her insides had tensed up, especially between her thighs. She knew then, unequivocally, how much he wanted her.

The sound of boots striking the floor outside in the hallway, caught her attention and she stood up, muscles flexed. She let the short blade concealed in her sleeve slide into the palm of her hand. Only a few people knew where she may be and they were not in the vicinity to her knowledge. The tip of a boot appeared at the entryway and she lunged.

Chafar blocked her strike with his own longsword, pushing her back further into the chamber.

"I heard you were hiding," he said.

Shocked at his presence, she stood in a defensive stance staring at him.

"Are we really going to spar in this tiny space?" He sheathed his weapon and leaned against the entrance's frame. That deadpan look on his face irritated her.

"What are you doing here?" She yelled at him. "How?" He shrugged.

"Chafar!"

"Farin?"

She dropped her guard and slid the short blade back into the hidden sheath in her sleeve. They would get nowhere. Her brother always had that demeanor, never smiling, his minimal words reminding her of Modas.

"What's happening?"

"Talas had an epiphany."

Farin went rigid. She had known he would figure it out in short time.

"And what does that have to do with you being here?"

"Not just me."

"You can't mean?" She shook head, hoping he would follow suit.

"Father has returned as well. It must be kept secret."

"Does Romnus know?" The look on her brother's face told her the answer. "So now what?"

"We are going to help you see this through. To the end."

"I guess there is no other way."

"Mmm. At least you will be Queen after this."

Farin's head shot up and she stared at him. "What did you say?"

"Did he not ask you to rule with him? That would make you Queen."

"I have not given him an answer!"

"Then you should do that. He has a right to know what you're think-

"You're talking a lot, brother."

"Only when it's necessary." Chafar pushed off the frame. "Walk with me, sister."

And she realized it may be the first, last and only time they would be able to talk.

****☼****

Romnus, Kur and Halfar watched the massive command ship settle down onto the hangar dock and the clamps grab hold, securing it to the surface. A handful of royal guards stood behind them, their numbers low to ensure there would be no breach of information. The hatch opened and the ramp came down as one hundred Azrom soldiers came marching down. They made four neat rows, one behind the other, in front of the three leaders. In the middle of each row stood the commanders and the one in the last row was unmistakable, twice the size of the soldiers in his unit.

Kur was barely over seven feet tall. The monster he saw was clearly a foot taller than him. Thick jet black hair spilled across the shoulders and tanned skin from many suns was visible at the face, neck and hands. His uniform was different as well. A black cloak with animal fur lining the lapel and edges was combined with black leggings and boots. His waist held no longsword and Kur understood why. Morphed, the commander would be gigantic, his sheer size instilling fear among enemies.

"You have been gone a long time. We commend you on your campaign's success." Kur addressed them while the crew unloaded the ship's cargo. "In your absence, there has been a change in rulership. Halfar has," Kur looked over at Romnus.

"Abdicated," Halfar offered.

"And Lord Romnus has graciously accepted the title of Supreme Ruler."

The soldiers slammed their fists into their chest plates and bowed down on one knee. Romnus looked down on them in what Kur interpreted as disdain then the ruler smiled.

"Rise, warriors. You need rest and I know you would like to go home to your villages, but." Romnus wiped his face with one hand then sighed.

"In lieu of restructuring the planet, temporary sectors have been established. Everything you need awaits you as does your families. Please, accept my apologies during this transition."

As the soldiers filed out, Kur called out the commander in the back row.

"Commander Abras. A word with you."

The giant stopped so suddenly, he created a small gust of wind.

Impressive.

Kur stayed where he was, not daring to get any closer, feeling dwarfed by the warrior. Commander Abras pivoted gracefully towards him and stood at ease.

"Please accompany us to the royal palace. We have a situation to discuss."

"As you command."

The deep baritone of his voice boomed in the air, sending shivers down Kur's spine. He glanced at Halfar and Romnus. They too seemed to step back from the sound and Kur suddenly felt fear. What if finding out he has a child made him extremely paternal? The soldier would tear him apart if he so much as yelled at Rass during one of their many arguments.

The three of them led the way, walking faster than normal because one step from commander Abras was like three of their own. By the time they reached the conference chamber in the palace, Kur's chest had tightened and he was by no means out of shape. Abras stood just inside the entrance waiting to be instructed as a good soldier should and Kur relaxed at that a little.

"Please, take a seat."

Romnus, who was a hair taller than Kur, barely fit into one of the seats so when the giant commander sat down, the chair bowed, changing shape to a near flat surface. He made the chair look like it was for a small one yet showed no sign of discomfort. Kur nodded to Halfar. The former ruler blinked in confusion. Kur tilted his head towards the commander then Halfar understood, though not happy.

"When you last visited the brothel about two centuries ago, you impregnated your choice. The child was raised in the palace." Commander Abras' eyes shifted to Halfar. He saw nothing registered in those eyes. "I eventually brought him into my care."

Kur's face heated up and his eyes narrowed at Halfar. That was not what he called it but kept that to himself. Rass' father may actually become angry if he knew the real story and the three of them would not be able to handle the monster.

"You would know him now as General Rass." Something glinted in the giant's eyes and Kur wasn't sure if it was good or bad. "Also, General Rass and General Kur are bonded to each other."

"Hmm." The sound vibrated through the room, ringing their ears.

"Lord Romnus has put forth an agenda that is not popular with the people of Azrom. More importantly, some of the heads of government and the royal courts are also against him. I would like you to protect and defend Rass along with the first royal house."

"Why are royal guards insufficient?" Commander Abras asked, making them wince at his voice.

"The assassination attempts are getting bolder and we are not sure who is involved. We try to keep a small number in the know. Also, Rass is with child and cannot fight at full strength."

"Then eliminate the threat."

"That is where you come in. If it comes down to it, the advisors, the councilmen and any guards on their side must be dealt with. They will come for all of us in due time."

"What is their agenda?"

"To remove any within Lord Romnus' circle and find a more 'suitable' ruler they can control."

"Understood."

"You will be escorted to the first royal house palace from here."

Kur gestured for him to follow the guards outside the entrance. When he was gone, Kur slid down in his seat and breathed a sigh of relief.

"Were you frightened, General Kur?"

Romnus had a smirk on his face.

"You would be too if that were Farin's father."

"Noted. You must tread carefully from now on."

Halfar stared at the entrance.

"He is very protective of Rass."

Kur sat up. "How do you know? He made no indication of such."

"During battles, he made sure Rass' unit was protected on all sides. He must have a natural instinct."

Romnus burst out laughing. Kur frowned at him. This was not humorous for him.

Farin could not sit and eat meals in peace due to the royal family pestering her to say yes to Romnus' proposal was getting tiring. And Romnus not saying a word to deter them. She was almost furious at him then realized it was her own fault for not giving an answer. That had been over a year ago and time was running out. Earlier, when she went out to survey the last of the villages to be destroyed she saw Azrom was a wasteland. There was no sign of life. The sectors where most of the population was being held were littered with large white squares easily mistaken for power plants. No windows, just vents at the four corners of the roof and one in the center.

The role of Queen took on so many connotations that her head felt like it was spinning. She thought about it as she walked down the outer corridor of the main palace, not paying attention to her surroundings. Her head butted into something firm and she looked up in surprise, ready to apologize.

Romnus towered over her and his expression made his intent clear. Before she could back away, he pulled her to him.

"Stop running away from me," he whispered in her ear.

His kiss set her body on fire and her hand automatically went to his chest, grabbing a handful of his cloak. The other just hung to her side lifeless. She gasped for air and the kiss went deeper. Lightheaded, she felt her body go limp but he held her firm.

"How barbaric, my lord." Batis' voice cut through the fog. "In broad daylight on the veranda."

Romnus released her and his lips pulled from hers as if sticky. She shuddered.

"Be more careful," Romnus chided her.

He stepped past her and continued down the corridor with Batis and two guards behind him. Batis smiled at her and brushed his hand across her hips.

"You should just say yes," he laughed softly.

****☼****

Time to move.

Mesrod could feel it. His plans were in full swing. He would finally be able to wipe the royal slate clean, getting control of Azrom back into the hands of the government officials along with the royal courts. Each advisor had a group tasked to eliminate their targets. Once that was accomplished, he would signal the soldiers he had turned to his side decades ago to release the people of Azrom. He had noticed strange and elaborate structures being erected where the villages used to be and seeing how beautifully done they were knew who the recipients would be. He had long heard the royal families complain about the lack of territory they controlled and being confined to the palaces.

Mesrod went over the plans in his head. The first act would be to get rid of that halfbreed. Her child was mostly of royal blood so he could be contained and raised properly. Next would be the Generals and their offspring. There was no need for it in the palace. Killing infants was not ideal but he wanted to eliminate any events of retaliation from the child when it reached maturity. Romnus was his responsibility and he had a full arsenal to handle him and his entourage. The very last part would be to infiltrate New Lassa and kill off Halfar and the other half breed. If Chardon got in the way, then she would have to be dealt with as well.

The chamber door opened. Dondar and Prevcan walked over to him with looks of great resolve and he approved. Their agenda would not work if they didn't have murderous intent. A council member had been assigned for each group to bear witness and record the historic events. The hostile overthrow of a Supreme Ruler had not been done in two millennia and needed to be noted for prosperity.

"Are we ready? Is everything in place?" He asked them both.

"All units are heading into position now. We are just going over some last minute adjustments and will wait for your signal." Prevcan gave him a short bow.

"The councilmen are ready and the poison is being loaded into weapons as we speak," Dondar stated.

"Good. There will be no signal. At mid-dawn on the second moon, we strike. There is no turning back, no aborting the agenda. Understood?"

"Yes, Lord Mesrod," they replied together. "Let's see it done."

The two left him alone in the chamber and for the first time in ages, he genuinely smiled.

Biandra set her basket down on the ground and stretched. The field was brimming with fruit and the stalks were high, just shy of her own height. They were denser in the row she had chosen to do her picking. That didn't stop her from hearing the strange whisking sounds coming in her direction. Not a moment too soon, she leapt upwards, keeping her eyes on the space below.

As she arched backwards, a view of the assault was made clear. Tiny needle like shards pierced the fruit stalks in the surrounding area where she had stood, killing them instantly. The stalks withered, crashing to the ground and the fruit decayed to rot, turning into a thick liquid that stained the soil black.

There was no place to hide so while in midair she calculated the distance from her location to the palace courtyard. Lord Romnus was able to clear it in mere seconds. She was not as fast. Some of the poisonous shards would hit her which left little time to administer the antidote. She saw the second wave coming at her as she landed into a launching position.

This will be close.

Using every ounce of muscle, she shot forth towards the palace.

Six guards were taking a break with Chafar and Trinon outside Farin's chamber for a game of virtual cards. Trinon laughed at the looks of frustration whenever he or Chafar won a turn. The sun was barely peeking over the horizon. Trinon waved a hand across the holodeck of cards, erasing them and stood. His eyesight adjusted on the fields beyond the courtyard and landed on the needle like spray following a blur which could only be Biandra. She would be the only one out in the fields around dawn.

Sensing that something was wrong, Chafar and the guards rose up.

"No! Don't!"

Trinon tried to push them all back down as four of the guards were struck by multiple shards. From his view he could see the attack had come from the rooftop of the palace across the way. The four guards convulsed then lay still as tiny shards dissolved into them from their body heat. He had heard about the poison darts but this was a new way to administer the deadly fluid. No need for injection, just high velocity projectiles capable of piercing flesh. Each volley spewed out dozens at a time.

"We're sitting open like easy prey," Chafar noted.

"Shall we jump?" One of the remaining guards glanced over the ledge, gauging the descent.

"You would not survive it intact," Trinon replied.

Another onslaught of poison projectiles came over the veranda, missing them by millimeters. Trinon cautiously lifted his head to spot the culprit and found no need to act. A long rod stuck out of the assailant's neck and he fell head first down to the ground below. Trinon turned to his right. Batis was lowering his crossbow, a look of pure menace on his face.

"They think Farin is asleep in her chamber," he announced.

"So they've come to get her first." Chafar took a glance around. "Where to now?"

"This would be a first step. If for some reason she would not be here, then they would be ready at the second most likely site. With her son."

"That's inside the first royal house palace."

Trinon stood up and pivoted towards that direction.

"Let's go," Batis ordered.

As they rounded the first corner, bodies lay in their wake. A few shards of poison were melting on the platform. From where they stood all the way down to the staircase that led into the courtyard, royal guards were frozen mid death throes. Then a trans-portal opened and an entire unit of soldiers spilled out to surround the group of five. Batis tsked and dropped the crossbow, unsheathing his longsword instead. The other two guards and Chafar followed suit. Trinon extended his claws.

Screams from all sides made commander Abras wince in fury. He knew something was amiss when one of the hallways ahead of him had become silent. Arriving at the foyer, he found dozens of royal family members along with their guards and handmaids dead in various forms of agony. He stepped on something tiny and moving his foot off it found the tiny shard crushed and melting.

Four blades came into his immediate view and he swerved using his speed to dodge and his massive size to pummel the soldiers whose hands were attached to them. They went flying into separate sections of the foyer, hitting the walls with simultaneous crashes. That didn't deter them for they were back on their feet and coming at him again. The one on his left finally got a good look at him and hesitated for a split second. That was all Abras needed.

Snatching the soldier by the legs, Abras used him as a weapon, swinging him like a longsword against his comrades. Blood splattered as flesh and bone met each other in a blur of lightning fast strikes. When the three were down, crumbled in bloody mounds, he dropped the wilted broken body of the first and advanced further into the palace. He could hear swords clashing ahead in the vicinity of Rass and Kur's personal chamber. Instead of using the corridor, he launched himself through the walls, creating a shortcut.

Along with Rass, Aloni and Kuhala fended off intruders. They were struggling from the sheer number of soldiers opposing them. Kuhala seemed dazed and he found melting shards of poison on the chamber floor. In the far corner was Rass' infant bundled up and shielded by the chest plate he should have been wearing. Abras could see Rass was beyond the point of rage. The carnage under his feet was no doubt from him. Limbs were strewn in all directions, ribcages ripped open and heads decapitated. Even Aloni and Kuhala were standing a far distance from him, defending the child from inside. Despite all the destruction, Rass was not unscathed. Abras calculated his son would not last another hour of fighting and Kuhala would drop any moment, the amount of poison in her system overriding the antidote vaccine. He counted twenty three soldiers left to deal with so made a decision. As the soldiers charged forth, he morphed into his full form.

His uniform stretched in vain to accommodate the shift as the legs formed into giant praying mantis limbs full of muscle and the pincers of his arms grew to the size of two men. The torso widened to reveal the definition of the abdomen. Rows of muscle packs bulged against the fabric. Standing at over ten feet tall, he glowered down at them. Some soldiers screamed in terror while others came at him emitting desperate battle cries, too late to halt their advance. Abras approved. They had to commit to death or victory or both. That was the Azrom way.

He brought down his right claw on the soldiers in reach and heard the wet squishing sound of bone and tissue liquefying. His left did the same on the other side, bringing down the total number of soldiers to fifteen. The area was not large enough for him to use his full speed but even at half, he could do damage. Within seconds, he circled the still charging soldiers. His claws opened from behind them and engulfed an equal amount in each. He snapped them shut, cutting all of his prey in half.

He regressed back to his normal size and form only to witness Rass falter. He dashed forward and caught him before his body hit the floor. Rass' longsword slid from his hands as Abras cradled him.

"It is over," Abras spoke. "It is done."

"For now," Aloni said. He grabbed Kuhala by the armpits and dragged her into the far corner on the other side of the chamber. "If they were bold enough to ambush Rass here, then that means the rest of the palace, including the main, is under siege."

"Those," Kuhala managed to breathe, "poison…shards. Problem."

"Yes, they took out most of our guards and anyone else in their path instantly."

Abras had no suggestions on how to combat that. He too would have been taken down if enough of the shards had gotten into him. He pawed the hair from Rass' face and looked over at the sleeping infant. Nearly two years old and already showing no fear in the midst of a battle, made Abras proud.

Biandra purposely overshot her target and ended up past the courtyard into the first foyer of the palace. She crawled to a wall and propped herself up. From her sleeve, she brought out an injection rod and pushed the needle into her thigh, releasing more of the antidote. Footsteps came closer to her position as her vision failed her. Warped colored shadows came into view at the entrance in the corridor. If it was the enemy, she was doomed. Her body gave in and she slumped unconscious.

Everywhere around the palace, chaos had broken out. Chardon used her energy to create a shield whenever those poison projectiles came. Halfar was being cautious, staying out of range of the poisonous spray while cutting down soldiers who came within close proximity. The enemy was smarter than she thought which posed a great hardship on the three. Their guards were long since dead and no sign of reinforcements so far. Romnus had lost all sanity for a brief moment when his royal guards, who had been a part of his entourage for nearly a century, were mowed down like insects. It took everything Chardon had to talk him back down and see reason; they had to move.

On her left was the hall leading to the courtyard and to the right was a banquet hall. Its smaller size seemed ideal for a short break to recalibrate their strategy so she steered their escape towards it. Once inside the hall, Chardon removed her outer robe already torn to shreds then tossed it aside. It was covered in blood and in the way of her fighting.

"Hurry, they will be coming down this way shortly."

When no one answered her, she turned to yell at them again. Romnus was standing still, his gaze on the floor against a wall. Halfar had grabbed his cousin's arm and held it in a death grip. Biandra lay crumbled, her body seemingly devoid of bones by the way it lay limp, but there was a rise and fall of her chest. Something in Romnus' eyes told her that this hall was going to be their last stand. Biandra was the only survivor of his original entourage and she knew he would not leave her to die.

"I will not run any longer. Let them come," Romnus said softly.

"Agreed," Halfar added.

Light spilled into the hall as the sun rose, shining down on the blood soaked soil and white walls of the palace. The sound of metal clashing from the outside could be heard. Over that were boots stomping down the corridor just around the corner. Chardon wiped flecks of blood from her forehead.

"Here they come."

The stomping moved in succession then slowed as they approached the hall's entrance. At the archway appeared Mesrod followed by a councilman and Chardon counted nearly thirty soldiers. He smiled at the three of them and she felt a sickness in her gut.

"Lord Romnus. I came to personally see to it that your reign ends today before sunset. But, I never expected that you would have our former ruler here as well with his off world mate. This is glorious!" Mesrod's eyes narrowed and he looked up at them from a downward stare. "I don't have to infiltrate New Lassa now to get rid of them."

Chardon saw Halfar's arms form into giant pincers and Romnus grew in height and girth. She noticed the councilman was wearing recorder goggles and a wide grin. Channeling her energy into both hands, she formed two orbs of red light that crackled in the air. Mesrod stepped out of the way and the thirty soldiers charged in.

She had never seen Halfar truly fight so it surprised her when instead of going into the soldiers before him, he jumped a foot in the air and spun. The momentum added to the swipe of his claw and cut a large gash across the chest of four soldiers, cutting through the breast plates and flesh. He didn't bother to land, using one of the bodies as a launching pad into the next wave.

Two soldiers were nearly upon her so she broke out of her awe to smash the red orbs of energy into their heads. There was a loud sizzling pop sound as they dropped and Chardon found her hands covered in sticky, cooked blood. Disgusted, she wiped her hands on the sides of her tunic and formed two more orbs, this time blue. They had less power than the red ones yet just as effective. She decided they would be enough for this battle.

"Stay still, you disgusting halfbreed," Dondar screeched.

Farin crouched further onto the floor of the meeting hall. The beautiful multicolored sheers that lined the ceiling were now in tatters and blood smeared the walls and floors. Her bodyguards had been murdered, while surrounded protecting her, with poison shards. One had nicked her in the bicep. The antidote took care of that. She gave the councilman with the recording goggles a dirty look while she kept a view of Dondar.

He had sent ten soldiers to deal with her and he himself, a former royal guard, would join in the fight. *So be it.* She was going to take him down as well and send him to Romnus for a true punishment. Her movements from one end of the hall to another was infuriating him and she liked it. The strategy was to allow time so she could figure out a way to get rid of them with one blow. It was proving difficult due to Dondar's involvement. He was a seasoned murderer and she was out of her league. She then remembered her training with Batis, also a well-seasoned killer, and found the answer.

Since her claws were heavier than the rest of body it would normally be a hindrance. But with the right momentum, she could destroy her prey with one movement. Speed she learned from training with the manbeasts and Dondar could be taken down with an energy orb. Timing it just right and knowing when to morph was key. To do that, she would need one of her arms not morphed. Running it through in her head, she nodded to herself.

"End game," she sneered.

Dondar laughed. "For you, half breed, it is. Kill her!"

He came at her from an angle as the soldiers advanced head on, three on either side ready to split off and surround her. She smiled. That's exactly how she wanted it. Backing up a little, her body tensed, then sprung forward up in the air. Dondar leapt up to match her height but she was already curving down towards the soldiers. Her left hand became a shiny black pincer the same length as her legs as she spin. It hit the soldier from the left and continued on across the line until it reached the last on the right of her. Blood sprayed over her like rain.

As her body came around in rotation to face Dondar, her right hand formed a blue glowing orb. He was coming down fast from his descent, longsword poised to skewer her. The weight of her pincer dragged her down as expected, giving her leverage and she released the energy orb. He veered to dodge it and was still hit, a large chunk taken out from his side. Dondar slammed into the floor, a smoldering piece of meat, not yet dead. Farin landed on both her feet and whirled on the councilman. He inched closer to the wall with nowhere to go. The carnage of soldiers was blocking the entryway. She was on him in one flash step and her fist connected with his head, bouncing it off the wall behind him before he too fell in a heap.

Bloodied, hurt and angry, Farin grabbed him and the bloody mess that was Dondar, by their robe collars, one in each hand. She dragged them out of the hall and headed towards the throne room. A laugh erupted from her and she figured maybe she had finally lost her mind.

She found, upon her arrival, the idea to converge in the throne room was not an original one. Her brother, Batis, Trinon, Aloni and Abras were all there with a half bloodied advisor and their accompanying councilmen. Batis turned to her and looked down at Dondar. He raised an eyebrow and she nodded.

"Very good, my pet. That is impressive. He won't live long, you know?" He walked over to her and stood less than an inch from her.

"I'm hoping he lasts until Romnus gets his hands on him."

"Hmm." Batis grabbed the back of her hair and kissed her ravenously. He let go and she smacked his arm down. "You're such a natural killer. Makes me want you more."

"Stop that! This is not the time for your amusements."

She caught Chafar and Trinon eyeing her in obvious dissent. The two would never understand the explanation for her dynamic with Batis. For the training sessions to work, they had to know each other's strengths and weaknesses, mentally and physically, to put them at equal advantage.

A loud rumble from above made her look up at hairline cracks spreading across the ceiling. She looked to the others, then up again. The fissures grew larger and pieces of the ceiling came crumbling down. At the last second, everyone leapt backwards, dragging their prizes with them, towards the walls as it caved in the center. Along with the giant chunks of debris came bodies.

Clouds of dust swirled in the air dispersing out from the middle and settling on the floor. Farin counted at least eight figures, maybe more. One of them she was certain of. Romnus rose up out of the debris holding his right side with his left hand. Blood blossomed from the wound to match the one across his left shoulder. Her mother sat up from landing on her back, a nasty gash along her temple. Blood dripped from a mangled pincer on her father's morphed arm. Before she could move to their aid, Romnus' body shimmied and the battle resumed in a blur of movements.

Not wasting any more time, Batis hefted his short blade in his hand then drew back and sent it into the fray. The bodies of soldiers came flying outwards and in the center stood Romnus, her mother, and father. Mesrod lay on the floor twitching and screaming with the hilt of Batis' short blade sticking out of his right eye. The royal advisor's hands hovered, not sure whether to leave it or pull it free. Batis eliminated his options by going over and retrieving his blade. Only half the eye came out with it, spilling bloody tissue onto Mesrod's face.

The throne room looked like hell on Earth. She had seen footage of that battle and her mother described it as such. She went to Romnus' side and tried to help him up. He was too heavy and they both slumped down to the floor.

"We brought you presents," Farin quipped. Romnus looked at her in a disappointing way. "See." She pointed to the royal advisors laying on the floor unconscious. Some of the rumble had knocked them out.

"Where's Jabarz?"

Farin looked around at the advisors and realized that yes, Jabarz was missing. Then again, so was General Kur.

Soldiers loyal to the royal advisors kept vigilance over the sectors housing Azrom's people while waiting for the signal to break open the seals and release the occupants. Jabarz was stationed at the main hub closest to the palace that housed the workers of the mines and fields. The councilman assigned to him had already documented the different sectors and was now also waiting to see the outcome of an enraged people crashing into the palace only to see that vengeance had already been done on their behalf.

So engrossed in their glee, that they were taken by surprise then terror as the soldiers around them were snatched up and ripped apart by modified enforcers. Jabarz turned towards the palace and off in the distance stood General Kur with an entire squadron of royal guards behind him. A second set of enforcers bounded across the terrain heading in the direction of the other sectors nearby.

"No!" Jabarz screamed in a rage.

This was not going to happen on his watch. He had not been a front line soldier in sometime but he still knew how to wield a longsword and use his pincers for murder. That is what he had in mind for General Kur as he confiscated a longsword from the severed waist of a dead soldier. Pushing the councilman out of the way, he sprinted headlong to Kur's position. The general did not move an inch, standing with arms crossed at his chest, then his eyes narrowed as he understood Jabarz's intent.

Good! Face me, coward.

Jabarz used his lower body to flip until he was flying feet first.

His boots struck the blade of Kur's longsword and pushed the general back a few feet. He had not seen the general unsheathe and was impressed with such speed. Pushing off the blade, Jabarz jumped back and landed on his feet a few yards from Kur. Even at this distance, the general appeared quite large. Behind him, he heard the crunching sound of bones being snapped.

"You would kill your own kind? Because they do not agree to our insane ruler's ideals?"

"It was your collective agenda that started this," Kur answered. "You started the killing first. If a soldier decides to join in the murder of his own people then they should be prepared to receive the same treatment."

"You're out here alone," Jabarz laughed, "while inside the palace, your precious mate and all of Romnus' people are being slaughtered."

General Kur cocked his head. "Do you really think it would be that easy to take down Lord Romnus, or General Rass for that matter? I assure you, even if you get some of them, the wrath from those who survive will have made you wish for death sooner."

Jabarz didn't wait for him to continue. He lunged at Kur with all his fury. The general dodged. Not to be taken lightly, he went for another attack. Kur blocked with his longsword again and they stood face to face, blade to blade. They pushed away from each other and Jabarz immediately went for a low blow. His blade swung, missing Kur by mere millimeters as the general bend forward while leaping back. Frustrated, he called out to him.

"Why are you dodging me, great general? Are you afraid to shed blood?"

"Sectors are secure, General Kur," a royal guard reported from behind Jabarz.

Startled he moved sideways in case it was an ambush. Kur's blade struck him from behind, piercing the meat below his ribcage. It caught on the bone and Kur was able to lift him up in the air like a barbarian showing off his prize. With a flick of the blade, Kur released him into the air and let his body crash to the ground. On impact a glob of blood bubbled up and exploded out of his mouth. General Kur came to stand above him, looking down in disgust.

"Shallow words," was all he heard Kur say before darkness took him.

The throne room was a nightmare. Servants cleared away the rumble as best they could and medical personnel treated the wounds of everyone in the vicinity, even the traitors. Romnus was being helped by royal guards into his throne, the only thing in the room still fully intact. At the base of the throne lay the other four advisors and the council- men who had conspired with them. Kur gestured to the guards dragging Jabarz by his armpits to set him alongside the others. They dumped him like the trash he was.

"I had a feeling you would all come out victorious," he said.

"Til death!" Royal guards cried out, stopping their tasks to do so.

Halfar cringed at the display. Kur grimaced and made a note in his mind to change that battle cry. It no longer rang sincere, just a slogan to recite whenever the word victorious was uttered.

"Get them on their knees," Romnus demanded. "And bring out the magistrate along with the rest of the council."

A small group of guards forced the culprits to their knees. Another group went to fetch those requested. Time felt like an eternity and Kur was relieved when they returned. Upon entering the throne room, the magistrates drew in sharp breaths and surveyed the damage ahead of them. The other council members did the same as they stepped over the threshold of the room. They all bowed low to Romnus as they neared the throne, not moving any closer to the half dead men kneeling in a row before him.

"My lord, what has happened here?" The head magistrate asked in awe. "You had no knowledge of this?"

"This? What is this? What madness has occurred?"

"The royal advisors and councilmen before you have been staging an agenda for quite some time. It involved my assassination, the murder of Lady Farin and Generals Rass and Kur."

"Preposterous! No one is that daft! What reason could they have?"

Calba, the least injured of the five, spoke up.

"Our reason? The bloodline is tainted! Halfar and Romnus have both dove into madness. Even that drunken man whore Chastan, went insane. We have some unknown half breed with free reign of the palace and our people enslaved in sterile sectors to make way for more royal housing."

Stunned silence followed.

"Yes, I did lose my mind," Halfar began, "but that does not constitute my bloodline to be deemed tainted."

"I'm curious." Kur turned to Calba. "Where did you come up with the idea that we are building housing for the royal families?" He asked in the sweetest tone.

Prevcan answered instead. "We saw those new structures with splendid homes and access to the trade networks. We are not stupid."

"Oh, but you are." Romnus leaned forward, wincing from the pain in his side. "Bear witness, magistrates and councilmen." He nodded to Kur.

Kur went and stood in front of the two rows of traitors, advisors in front, councilmen behind them.

"For the act of treason against Azrom, the death of innocents and the attempted assassination of our Supreme Ruler, it is by Supreme Ruler Romnus' decree that you be executed for your sins."

Mesrod spat on Kur's boots and an onslaught of profanity erupted from the accused men. Kur stepped away and allowed Commander Abras to stand in front of them. He unsheathed his longsword, a ten foot blade forged special for his species' size, and made one slash across the air before them. He sheathed his sword and stepped back.

The curses and yelling abruptly stopped. Some of the accused open their mouths in surprise but nothing came out as the top portion of their bodies slid to the left, tumbling onto the floor. For a millisecond there was no blood, then it flowed like a river forming a pool of red around them.

"The decree has been handed down. Are there any objections?" Kur asked.

The magistrate tapped a button on his wristband and opened his hands. A virtual tablet appeared and he began entering data. When he was done, it disappeared.

"The decree has been noted and there are no objections to this ruling. We should have seen the warning signs, my lord. Please accept our deepest apologies." The magistrate bowed low.

A New Era

Farin had been dodging the royal family for weeks since the attack and could find nowhere to run. Due to this, she was in a state of distress, constantly in tears. Her mother warned her not to run away and face the problem head on. Less, a problem, more a very heavy decision. Even her brother kept asking why she didn't just go to Romnus and say yes. If she had not heard about there not being a Queen in five hundred years, she might have been more open to the idea.

She had been ambushed four times this very day and her heart beat was elevated to the point where it was hard to catch her breath. Her usual black robes felt heavy as she ran down the outer corridor, looking behind her for anyone who may have followed her. It was a mistake. She forgot to look ahead as well. Farin ran right into Batis' arms.

"There you are, beautiful Farin." He clasped his hands behind her back, pinning her to him.

Farin stared up into his eyes, pleading with them. He laughed at her and wiped away the tears forming at the corners of her eyes.

"Please, let me go. I just want to go to my room. I just want to," she looked down, trying to think of something.

He leaned down until their lips were barely touching.

"This will be the last kiss I give to you."

To her surprise, it was not his usual brutal savage kiss, but a passionate one. He kissed her more and it seemed to go on for a long time. When he finally pulled away, there was a look of regret and longing. He unclasped his hands then grabbed hers.

"What are you?" She didn't get to finish her question.

Batis pulled her behind him by one hand all the way to the throne room and as he entered, released her like a ragdoll onto the floor in the middle of the room. She stared up at the base of the throne, not daring to look up.

"Supreme Ruler, Lord Romnus has approved you as a candidate to be his bonded mate. It has been cleared by the magistrate and the royal council. Do you accept?" Batis yelled out.

Romnus had moved to the edge of his seat when Batis showed up with her and he remained there now. She could feel his anxiety drifting down to her. A quick glance and she noticed the magistrates, the royal council, her mother and father, her brother, the royal courts and even Chastan waiting for her reply. She balled her hands into fists and let them rest on her thighs as the tears fell down her face, staining her robes. Taking a breath, she let out a high pitched cry then looked up to find Romnus had come down from his throne to stand over her.

"Yes!" She cried out in defeat and hung her head.

Romnus knelt down, gathering her in his arms and held her while she continued to cry. She didn't even know why she was crying because feeling his arms around her always made her feel better.

"We will have a Queen," the magistrate announced, excitement in his tone.

"It's a perfect day, my lord," the head of social affairs commented. "This is also the day you release the people from the sectors."

Farin raised her head and stared up at Romnus.

"Is that true?"

"It is," he replied, wiping away the rest of her tears.

"Did you plan this?"

"No. I found myself surrounded by everyone and then Batis brought you her." He squeezed her closer. "Are you sure? Do you want me as much as I need you?"

"I'm sure."

"We shall send out the announcement after the people have settled in," the magistrate declared.

The villagers exited the transport in a single file and stepped out onto fertile land. Gone were the dead trees that had marked the entrance of their territory. There were now tall healthy ones, fields bursting with vegetation they had not seen before along with familiar ones and a waterway instead of the giant well. What truly mesmerized them were the homes that sat scattered throughout the village. Beautiful, pristine buildings waiting to be claimed by their new owners.

"They are all identical but can be recolored and the insides customized to your liking. You will no longer need to live impoverished. This is Lord Romnus' gift to the people of Azrom," Lord Aloni announced.

"What is that building at the end?" A man asked.

"That is the marketplace where you can barter your wares with other villages on the planet. It has full interface so you don't have to limit yourself to one territory."

Loud exclamations of "Oohs" and "Ahhs" filled his ears, making lord Aloni happy. That was the reaction of every village so far. And every time, they expressed shame and regret for not trusting the Supreme Ruler. Some did express anger at how the transition was executed and Lord Aloni had to agree with the people of Azrom in that regard.

Twenty years of strife was nothing in their life time. It was more than they should have endured.

****☼****

As word spread of a new Queen, the planet became a plethora full of well wishes and gifts for Farin. She didn't understand what she had done to deserve such adoration, amazed at how beloved she was. The cabinet members of New Lassa had arrived last week and Mara was making a fuss over the bonding ceremony gown with Emalli. Farin fled all of it to find a place of peace and quiet.

The library looked fairly dark so she ducked into it and found the first seat. She didn't bother turning up the glow orbs above so hadn't noticed the seat was already occupied. She let out a yelp as her hands press down on firm thighs then arched her body back up. Large arms wrapped around her, pulling her back down.

"What are you running from this time, my love?" Romnus' voice breathed into her hair.

She relaxed and leaned back into him. "I thought the fuss over Rass and Kur's bonding ceremony was overwhelming. This is madness."

"Hmm. It is tiring. What colors are you leaning towards?"

"You may not like it."

"Whatever it may be, I will love you."

Farin twisted her body so she could face him in the dim light. He had a small tablet in his free hand and was reading. She suddenly felt jilted and annoyed.

"Are you even going to pay attention to me?"

Romnus set the tablet down, grabbed her by the buttocks and drew her to him. He kissed her.

"Is that better?"

"Are you going to finish reading while I'm here?"

"Farin, my love. You dropped onto me in a dark library."

"Don't ignore me," she said softly.

"I am not Chastan. I would never ignore you."

She laid her head on his shoulder listening to the inner workings of his body, each beat strong.

Sunlight flooded the throne room from the entrance and the newly structured ceiling now showing the sky. All the adjacent rooms above had been torn out to accommodate it. The room was close to maximum capacity and from what had been reported, a mass of nearly two hundred thousand people were outside the palace. Romnus couldn't understand why so many had come when they could witness the bonding ceremony on the planetary communication network every village had. For prosperity. He had forgotten about that.

Sitting on a cushion in the far corner by the entryway, he waited for the ceremonial entourage to bring Farin to him. His leggings were a light lavender color like the winter flowers and matched the sash around his waist. The robe was black with blood red trim and he wore the long- sword he owned but never used. His hair had been washed, tugged at and brought to shiny jet black waves; it's natural state. He had no idea his hair was dull and dried out from mistreatment over the past few decades.

"Now you look like royalty," Halfar laughed.

"Really? And how do you keep your hair in good condition?"

"After you've been on Earth a while, you find it is imperative when holding a higher state of authority."

"I am bonding with your child."

"Yes." Halfar folded his arms. "But better Farin than someone from the lower royal family. I think she is too good for you, personally."

"You may be right."

Chimes began ringing and the first group of chaperones entered the throne room, Farin behind, followed by the tail end of them. Romnus sucked in a deep breath and forgot to exhale. The dream he had years ago of Farin wearing that gown waving to the people of Azrom flashed before him. Time stopped and he watched her come closer to his position near the entrance. He exhaled and everything resumed at normal speed.

She wore a lavender gown with a red sash, her hair piled up high at the front the rest spilling down her back. The flowers entwined in it were flowers from spring and winter; red and purple. Romnus stood up and made his way to her. He took her hand in his and together they walked down the aisle. They went slowly up the stairs to the two thrones of equal size and style signifying one was no more important than the other.

The magistrate stood between them and cleared his throat.

A councilman stood in wait.

"Greetings, my lord," he said, bowing low to Romnus, "and honored guests. This day we rejoice in the bonding of our Supreme Ruler, Lord Romnus, and the beautiful Lady Farin."

The aisle created by the masses filled in with the royal families and other guests followed by a hush.

"Do you swear devotion to each other, and to Azrom, even in death?" "We swear this," they both said together.

"You shall now demonstrate proof of your will." He nodded to the councilman on his left.

The councilman produced the ceremonial knife and the couple held out their wrists. He sliced both with a smooth swipe, preventing blood splatter. The blood dripped down into the chalices placed directly beneath each arm. A second councilman came with a bundle of red fabric folded in his arms. Seeing the chalices half full, he unraveled it and bringing the two wrists together, bound them with it to stop the blood flow.

The councilmen each picked up a chalice and handed one to Romnus, the other to Farin. They stared at each other and without breaking eye contact, downed the contents of the chalices then handed them back. The official nodded proudly and placed his hand on the fabric covering their wrists.

"As royal magistrate and by Azrom's decree, I present to you Romnus Supreme Ruler and Farin, Queen of Azrom!"

He removed his hand and let them turn to the guests. They bowed deeply and the thunderous clapping began. The fabric was removed so the councilmen could check to make sure the wounds were sealed, then cut the red fabric in two, wrapping each wrist. They sat down on their thrones with their hands still joined together and smiled at the audience.

"The bonding is complete!"

Loud roars and cheers resounded in the hall.

Music erupted and food on giant trays carried by servants came filing into the room. Drinks were poured in sloppy succession to make sure every cup, mug and chalice was filled. When that was done, Romnus and Farin stepped down from their thrones and walked the length of the throne room to the balcony. Farin let go of Romnus' hand and turned to him. The smile on her face was the same as in the dream.

"I present to you, our new Queen!" The royal announcer's voice boomed over the communication feed.

Below, two hundred thousand Azromians cheered and she burst into laughter. Not the halfhearted one he always heard. No, a real one full of joy. Romnus turned to Halfar and he too recognized its authenticity. As she waved to her people, Chardon stepped up behind him.

"If you harm her, Romnus."

"I know. But you won't need to worry about that."

"The people would kill him first," Halfar said.

"True." Chardon slid an arm around Halfar. "So, my love, would you have ever wanted to bond with me?"

Romnus stifled a laugh as Halfar stiffened and turned to her.

"You want that now? After I am no longer ruler?"

"Because you are no longer ruler."

"Father," Farin called to him without looking back, still waving. "We are both free now." She finally turned around and with a smile more beautiful than anything they had ever seen said, "Find your joy!"

~END~

ABOUT THE AUTHOR

Maquel A. Jacob has had a passion for the written word since the age of seven, reading everything she could get her hands on which included encyclopedias and the thesaurus. At twelve, she had her first encounter with a Stephen King novel and was hooked. She became inspired to write her own brand of fiction, combining multiple genres to keep things interesting.

Always ready to learn new things, her search for knowledge never ceases. She has an AAS in Accounting, an AAS Business Administration, went to Cosmetology school and studied Digital Film and Video for two years.

She is a huge Anime fan, loves a great bottle of wine and rocks out to heavy metal music. Green and lush Oregon is where she works part time in accounting and spends her free time spinning tales of imaginary worlds in her head, daydreaming.